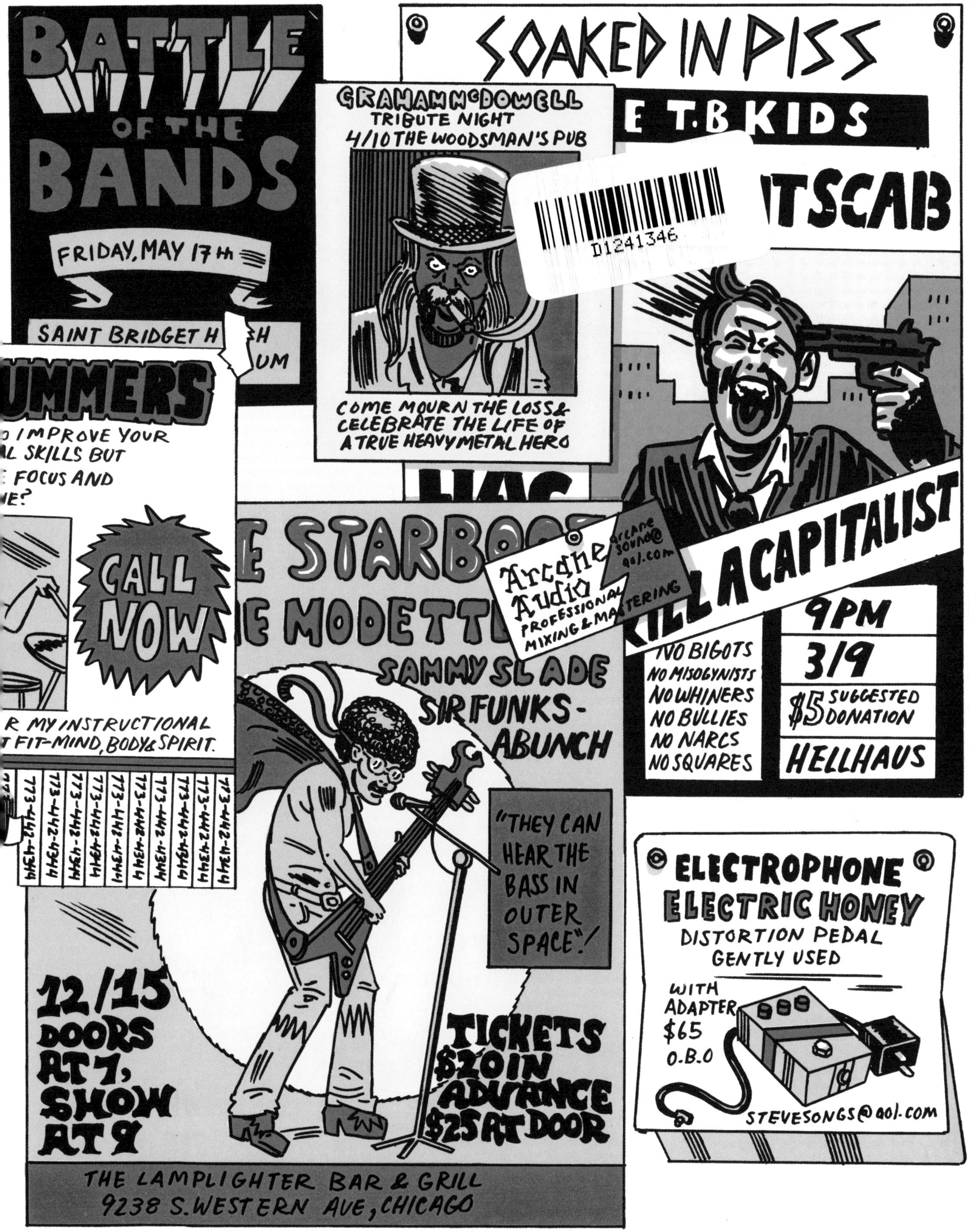

BATTLE OF THE BANDS
FRIDAY, MAY 17th
SAINT BRIDGET H SH UM
SOAKED IN PISS
E T.B KIDS
TSCAB
D1241346
GRAHAM McDOWELL TRIBUTE NIGHT
4/10 THE WOODSMAN'S PUB
COME MOURN THE LOSS & CELEBRATE THE LIFE OF A TRUE HEAVY METAL HERO
UMMERS
O IMPROVE YOUR
AL SKILLS BUT
E FOCUS AND
NE?
CALL NOW
R MY INSTRUCTIONAL
T FIT-MIND, BODY & SPIRIT.
773-442-4344
E STARBO
E MODETT
SAMMY SLADE
SIR FUNKS-ABUNCH
"THEY CAN HEAR THE BASS IN OUTER SPACE"!
12/15
DOORS AT 7, SHOW AT 9
TICKETS $20 IN ADVANCE $25 AT DOOR
THE LAMPLIGHTER BAR & GRILL
9238 S. WESTERN AVE, CHICAGO
Arcane Audio
PROFESSIONAL MIXING & MASTERING
arcane sound@aol.com
KILL A CAPITALIST
NO BIGOTS
NO MISOGYNISTS
NO WHINERS
NO BULLIES
NO NARCS
NO SQUARES
9PM
3/9
$5 SUGGESTED DONATION
HELLHAUS
ELECTROPHONE
ELECTRIC HONEY
DISTORTION PEDAL
GENTLY USED
WITH ADAPTER
$65
O.B.O
STEVESONGS@aol.com

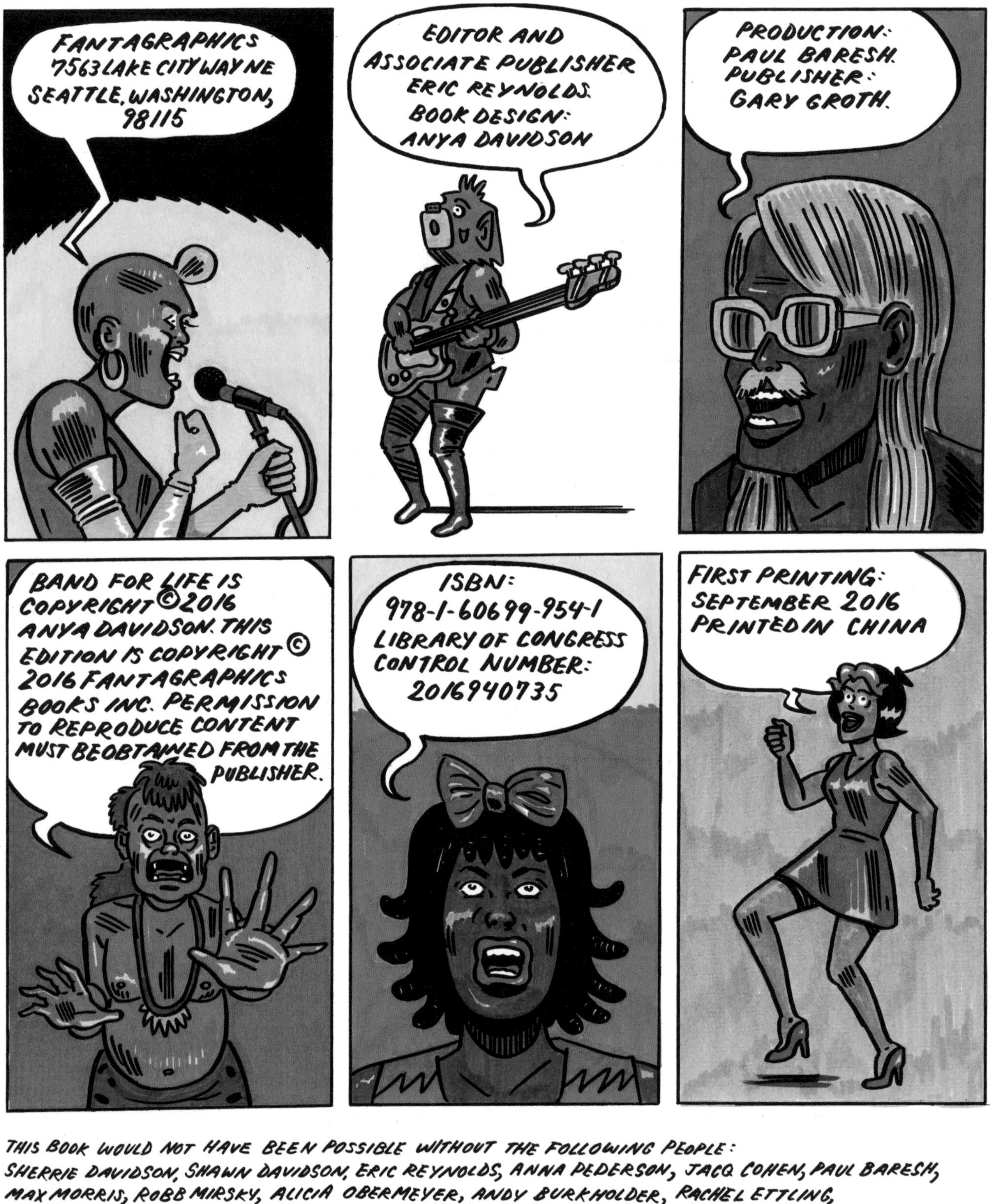
FANTAGRAPHICS 7563 LAKE CITY WAY NE SEATTLE, WASHINGTON, 98115
EDITOR AND ASSOCIATE PUBLISHER ERIC REYNOLDS. BOOK DESIGN: ANYA DAVIDSON
PRODUCTION: PAUL BARESH. PUBLISHER: GARY GROTH.
BAND FOR LIFE IS COPYRIGHT © 2016 ANYA DAVIDSON. THIS EDITION IS COPYRIGHT © 2016 FANTAGRAPHICS BOOKS INC. PERMISSION TO REPRODUCE CONTENT MUST BE OBTAINED FROM THE PUBLISHER.
ISBN: 978-1-60699-954-1 LIBRARY OF CONGRESS CONTROL NUMBER: 2016940735
FIRST PRINTING: SEPTEMBER 2016 PRINTED IN CHINA

THIS BOOK WOULD NOT HAVE BEEN POSSIBLE WITHOUT THE FOLLOWING PEOPLE:
SHERRIE DAVIDSON, SHAWN DAVIDSON, ERIC REYNOLDS, ANNA PEDERSON, JACQ COHEN, PAUL BARESH, MAX MORRIS, ROBB MIRSKY, ALICIA OBERMEYER, ANDY BURKHOLDER, RACHEL ETTLING, CARRIE VINARSKY, KYLE REYNOLDS, ZACK WEIL, JAIL FLANAGAN, SETH SHER, JON ZIEMBA, VANESSA HARRIS, KATE GRONNER, MOLLY O'CONNELL, CHRIS DAY, CONOR STECHSCHULTE, MAIRE O'NEILL, NICK JACKSON AND LALE WESTVIND, TOM TOYE AND LAURA PEREZ-HARRIS, FRANK SANTORO, THE REAL GUNTIT.

FOR LANE, MY FAVORITE CARTOONIST

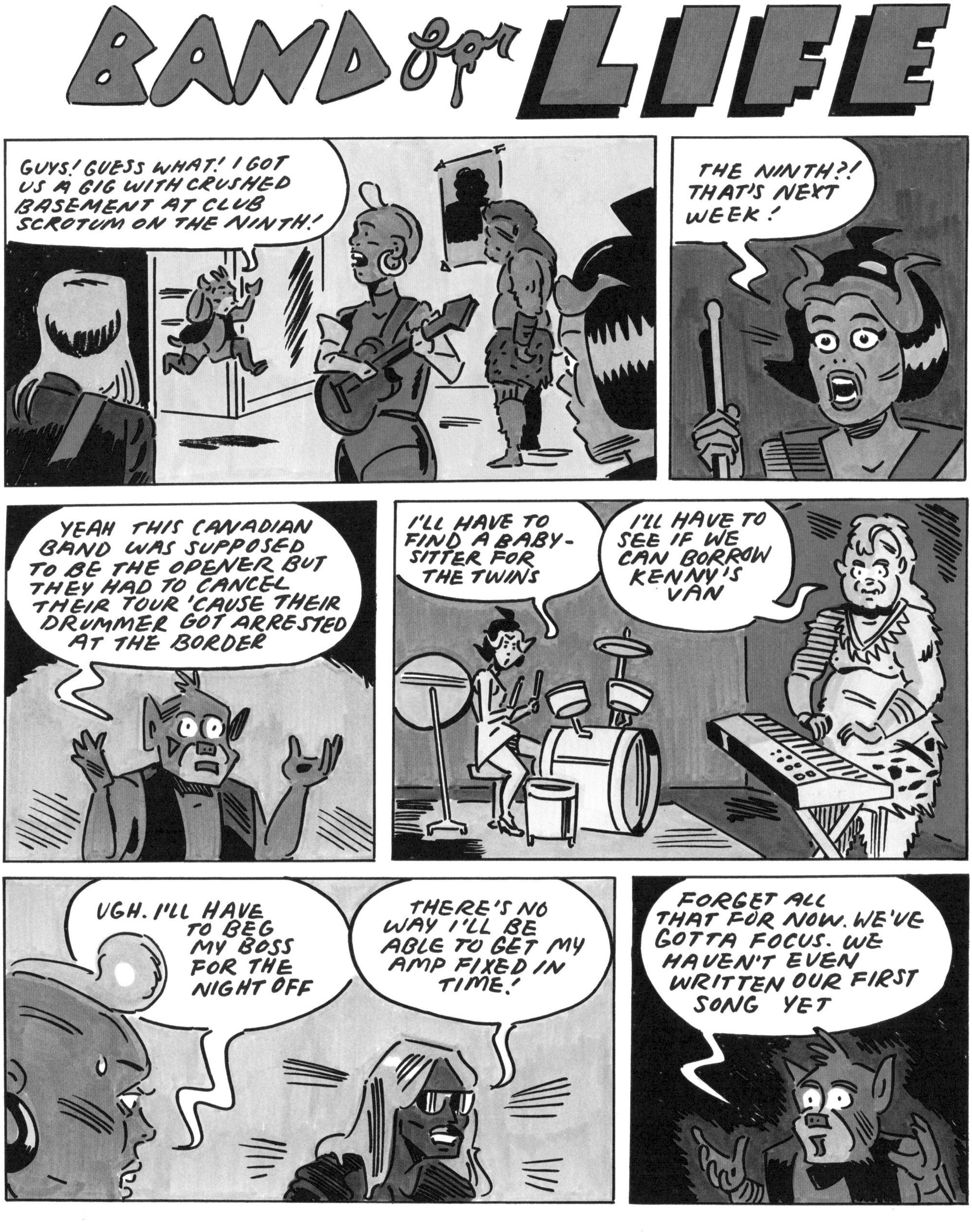
BAND for LIFE
GUYS! GUESS WHAT! I GOT US A GIG WITH CRUSHED BASEMENT AT CLUB SCROTUM ON THE NINTH!
THE NINTH?! THAT'S NEXT WEEK!
YEAH THIS CANADIAN BAND WAS SUPPOSED TO BE THE OPENER BUT THEY HAD TO CANCEL THEIR TOUR 'CAUSE THEIR DRUMMER GOT ARRESTED AT THE BORDER
I'LL HAVE TO FIND A BABY-SITTER FOR THE TWINS
I'LL HAVE TO SEE IF WE CAN BORROW KENNY'S VAN
UGH. I'LL HAVE TO BEG MY BOSS FOR THE NIGHT OFF
THERE'S NO WAY I'LL BE ABLE TO GET MY AMP FIXED IN TIME!
FORGET ALL THAT FOR NOW. WE'VE GOTTA FOCUS. WE HAVEN'T EVEN WRITTEN OUR FIRST SONG YET

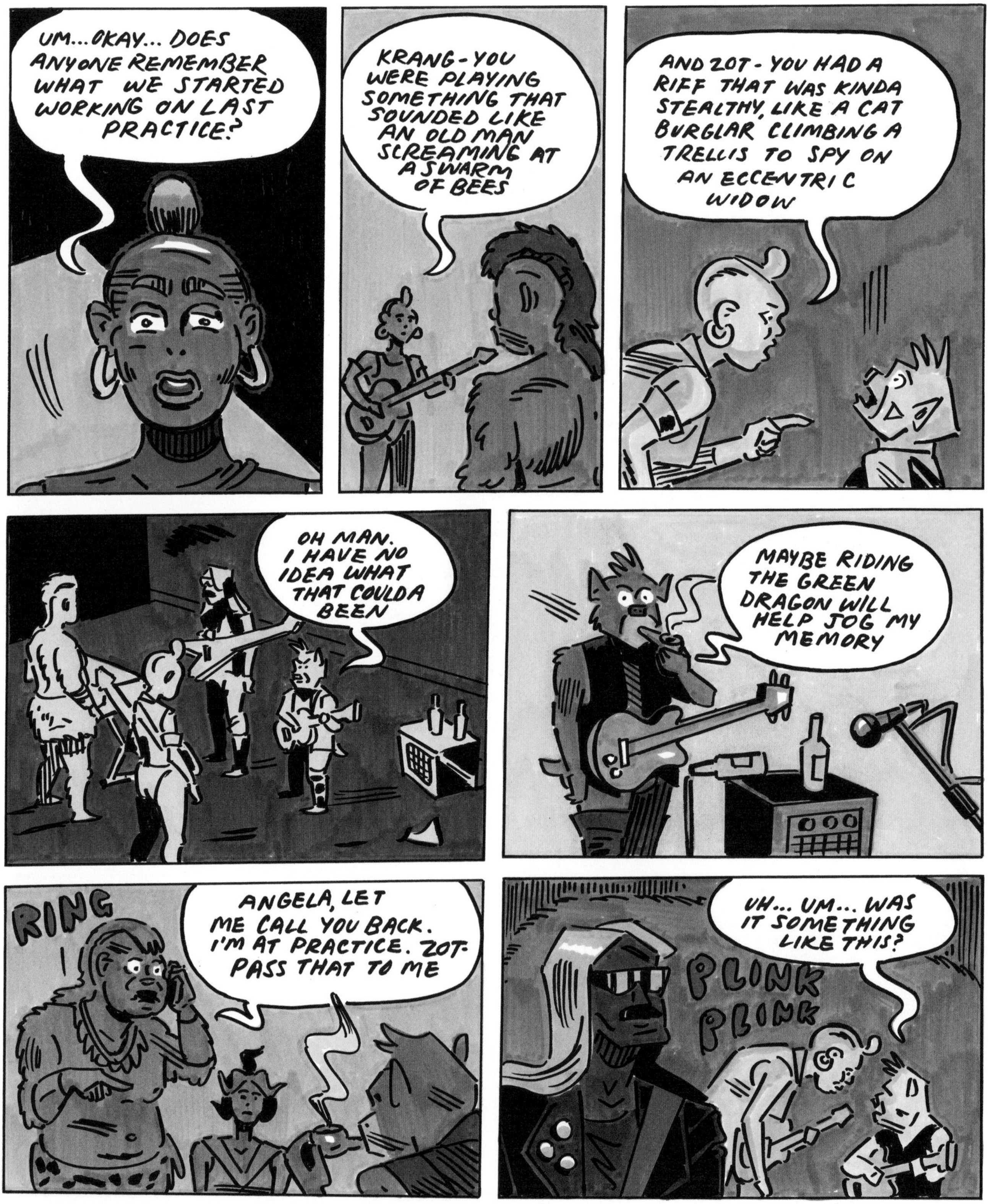
UM...OKAY... DOES ANYONE REMEMBER WHAT WE STARTED WORKING ON LAST PRACTICE?
KRANG - YOU WERE PLAYING SOMETHING THAT SOUNDED LIKE AN OLD MAN SCREAMING AT A SWARM OF BEES
AND ZOT - YOU HAD A RIFF THAT WAS KINDA STEALTHY, LIKE A CAT BURGLAR CLIMBING A TRELLIS TO SPY ON AN ECCENTRIC WIDOW
OH MAN. I HAVE NO IDEA WHAT THAT COULDA BEEN
MAYBE RIDING THE GREEN DRAGON WILL HELP JOG MY MEMORY
RING
ANGELA, LET ME CALL YOU BACK. I'M AT PRACTICE. ZOT - PASS THAT TO ME
UH... UM... WAS IT SOMETHING LIKE THIS?
PLINK
PLINK

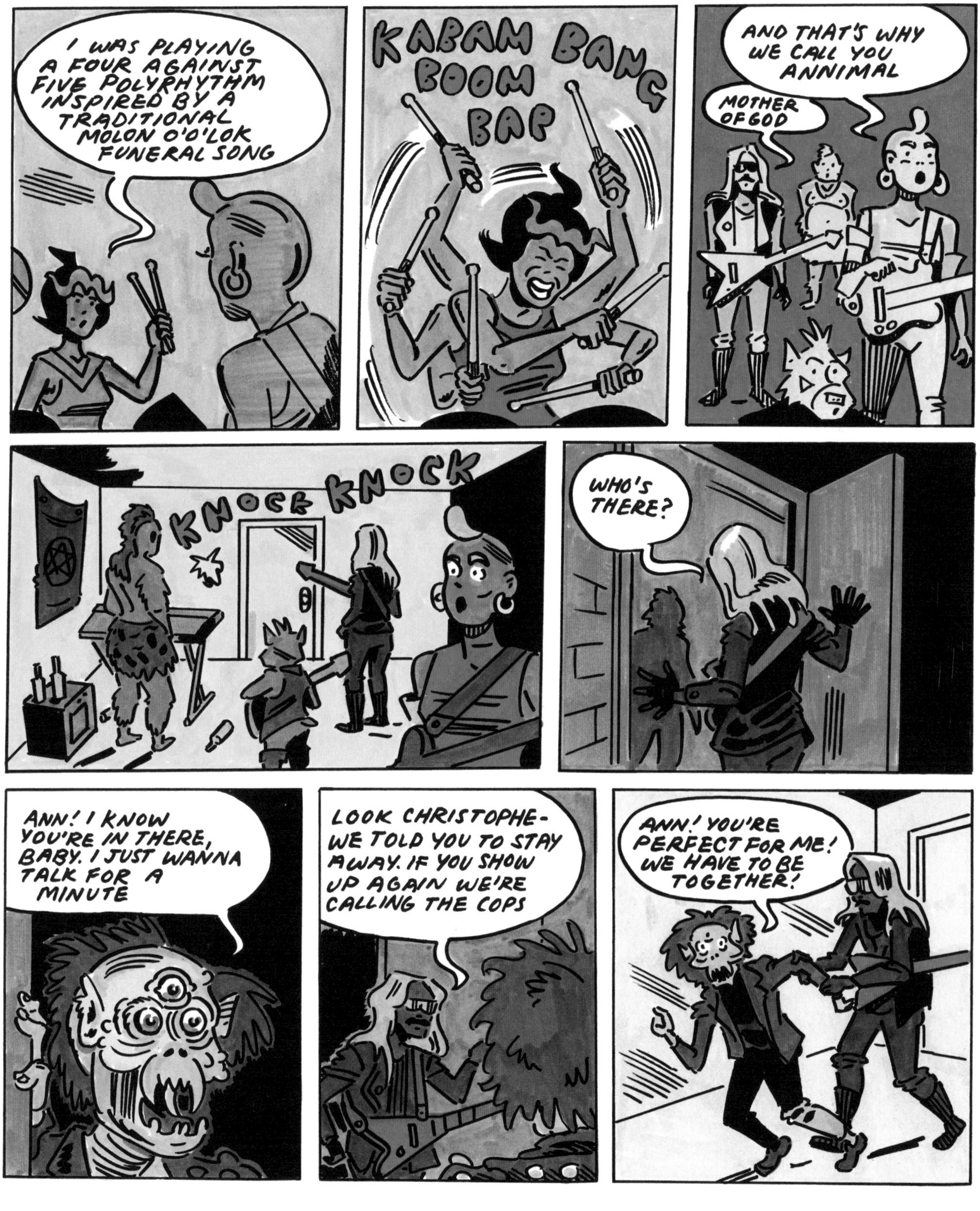
I WAS PLAYING A FOUR AGAINST FIVE POLYRHYTHM INSPIRED BY A TRADITIONAL MOLON O'O'LOK FUNERAL SONG
KABAM BANG BOOM BAP
AND THAT'S WHY WE CALL YOU ANNIMAL
MOTHER OF GOD
KNOCK KNOCK
WHO'S THERE?
ANN! I KNOW YOU'RE IN THERE, BABY. I JUST WANNA TALK FOR A MINUTE
LOOK CHRISTOPHE- WE TOLD YOU TO STAY AWAY. IF YOU SHOW UP AGAIN WE'RE CALLING THE COPS
ANN! YOU'RE PERFECT FOR ME! WE HAVE TO BE TOGETHER!

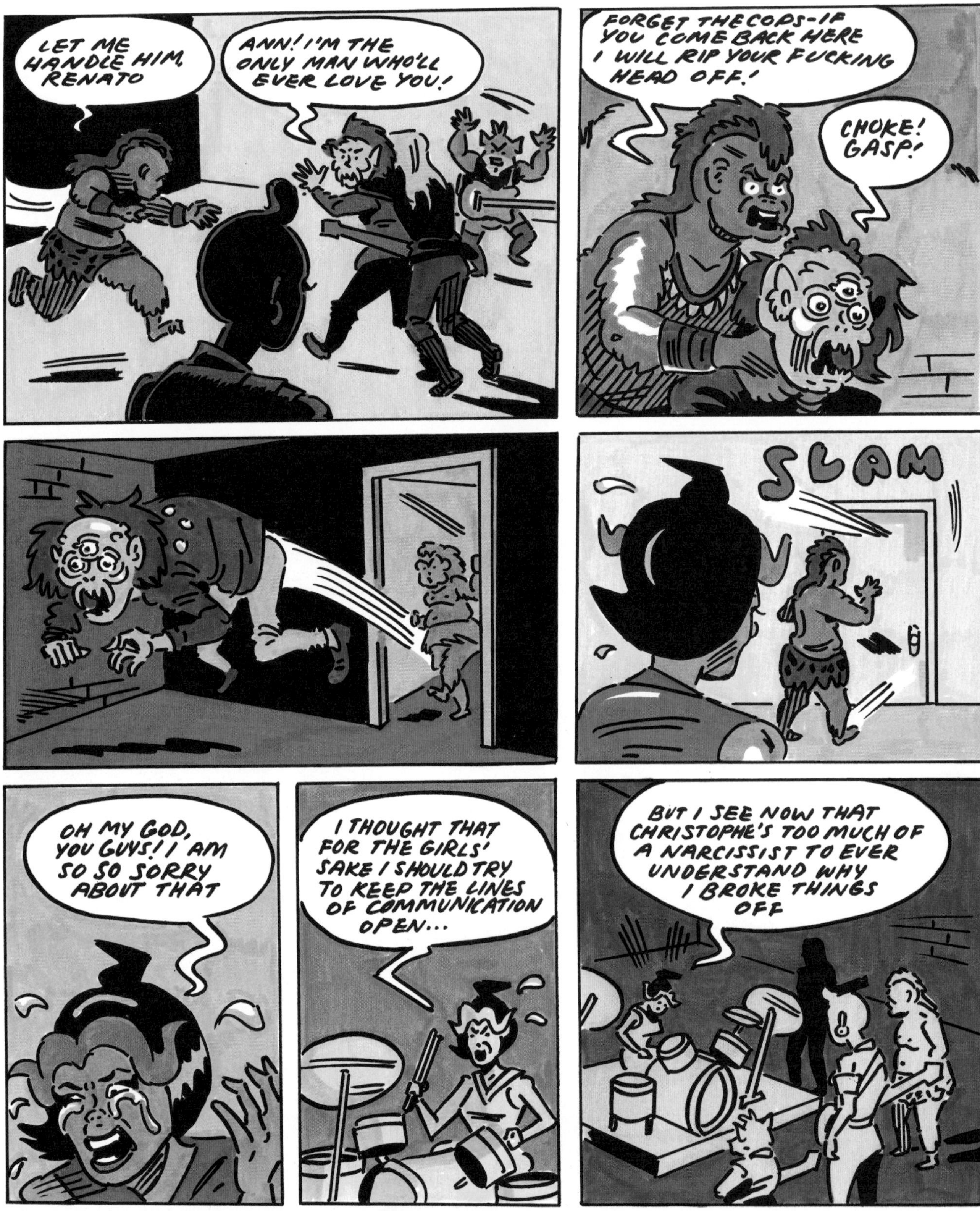
LET ME HANDLE HIM, RENATO
ANN! I'M THE ONLY MAN WHO'LL EVER LOVE YOU!
FORGET THE COPS-IF YOU COME BACK HERE I WILL RIP YOUR FUCKING HEAD OFF!
CHOKE! GASP!
SLAM
OH MY GOD, YOU GUYS! I AM SO SO SORRY ABOUT THAT
I THOUGHT THAT FOR THE GIRLS' SAKE I SHOULD TRY TO KEEP THE LINES OF COMMUNICATION OPEN...
BUT I SEE NOW THAT CHRISTOPHE'S TOO MUCH OF A NARCISSIST TO EVER UNDERSTAND WHY I BROKE THINGS OFF

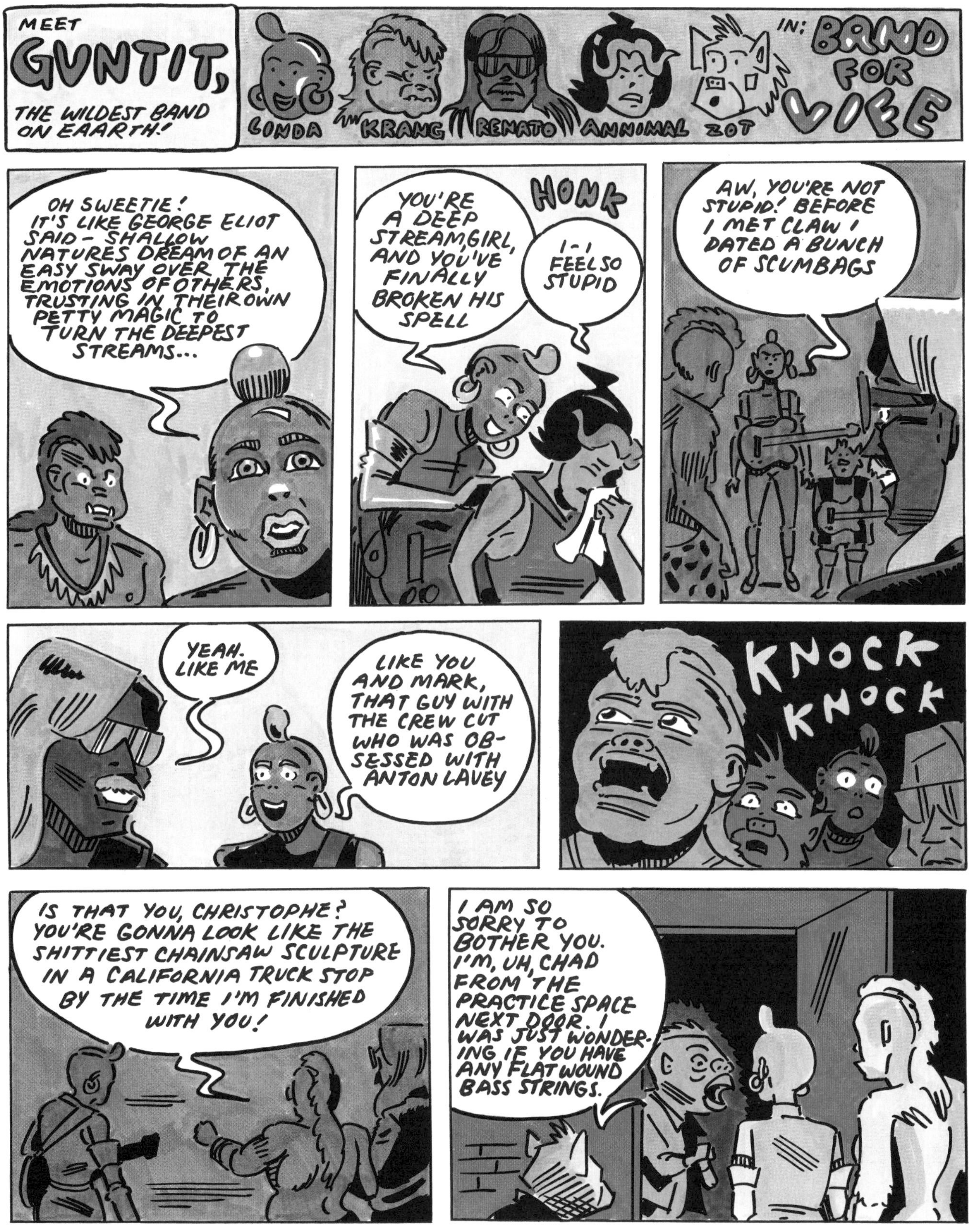
MEET
GUNTIT,
THE WILDEST BAND ON EAARTH!
LINDA
KRANG
RENATO
ANNIMAL
ZOT
IN: BAND FOR LIFE
OH SWEETIE! IT'S LIKE GEORGE ELIOT SAID- SHALLOW NATURES DREAM OF AN EASY SWAY OVER THE EMOTIONS OF OTHERS, TRUSTING IN THEIR OWN PETTY MAGIC TO TURN THE DEEPEST STREAMS...
YOU'RE A DEEP STREAM, GIRL, AND YOU'VE FINALLY BROKEN HIS SPELL
HONK
I-I FEEL SO STUPID
AW, YOU'RE NOT STUPID! BEFORE I MET CLAW I DATED A BUNCH OF SCUMBAGS
YEAH. LIKE ME
LIKE YOU AND MARK, THAT GUY WITH THE CREW CUT WHO WAS OB-SESSED WITH ANTON LAVEY
KNOCK KNOCK
IS THAT YOU, CHRISTOPHE? YOU'RE GONNA LOOK LIKE THE SHITTIEST CHAINSAW SCULPTURE IN A CALIFORNIA TRUCK STOP BY THE TIME I'M FINISHED WITH YOU!
I AM SO SORRY TO BOTHER YOU. I'M, UH, CHAD FROM THE PRACTICE SPACE NEXT DOOR. I WAS JUST WONDER-ING IF YOU HAVE ANY FLATWOUND BASS STRINGS.

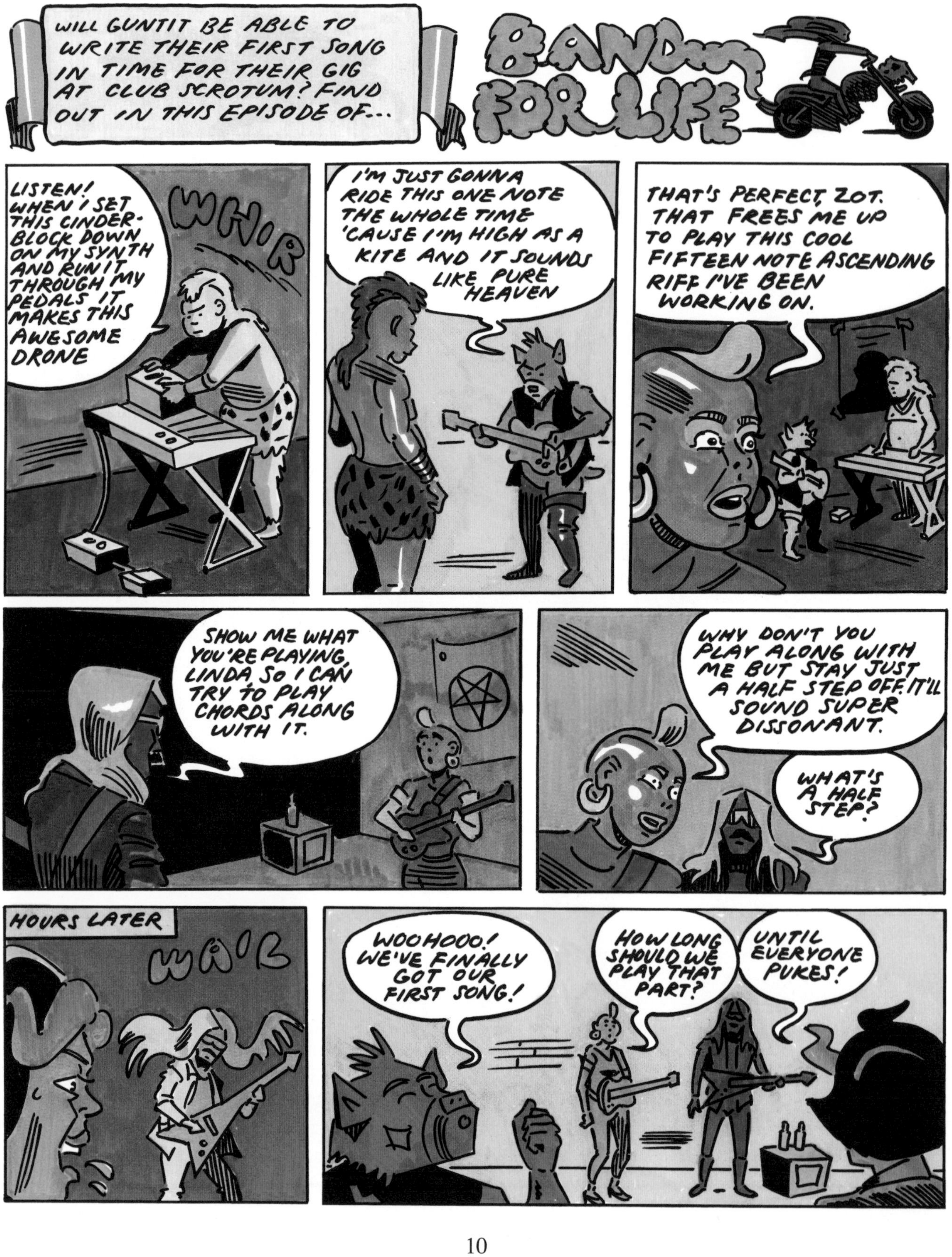
WILL GUNTIT BE ABLE TO WRITE THEIR FIRST SONG IN TIME FOR THEIR GIG AT CLUB SCROTUM? FIND OUT IN THIS EPISODE OF...
BAND FOR LIFE
LISTEN! WHEN I SET THIS CINDER-BLOCK DOWN ON MY SYNTH AND RUN IT THROUGH MY PEDALS IT MAKES THIS AWESOME DRONE
WHIR
I'M JUST GONNA RIDE THIS ONE NOTE THE WHOLE TIME 'CAUSE I'M HIGH AS A KITE AND IT SOUNDS LIKE PURE HEAVEN
THAT'S PERFECT, ZOT. THAT FREES ME UP TO PLAY THIS COOL FIFTEEN NOTE ASCENDING RIFF I'VE BEEN WORKING ON.
SHOW ME WHAT YOU'RE PLAYING, LINDA SO I CAN TRY TO PLAY CHORDS ALONG WITH IT.
WHY DON'T YOU PLAY ALONG WITH ME BUT STAY JUST A HALF STEP OFF. IT'LL SOUND SUPER DISSONANT.
WHAT'S A HALF STEP?
HOURS LATER
WAIL
WOOHOOO! WE'VE FINALLY GOT OUR FIRST SONG!
HOW LONG SHOULD WE PLAY THAT PART?
UNTIL EVERYONE PUKES!

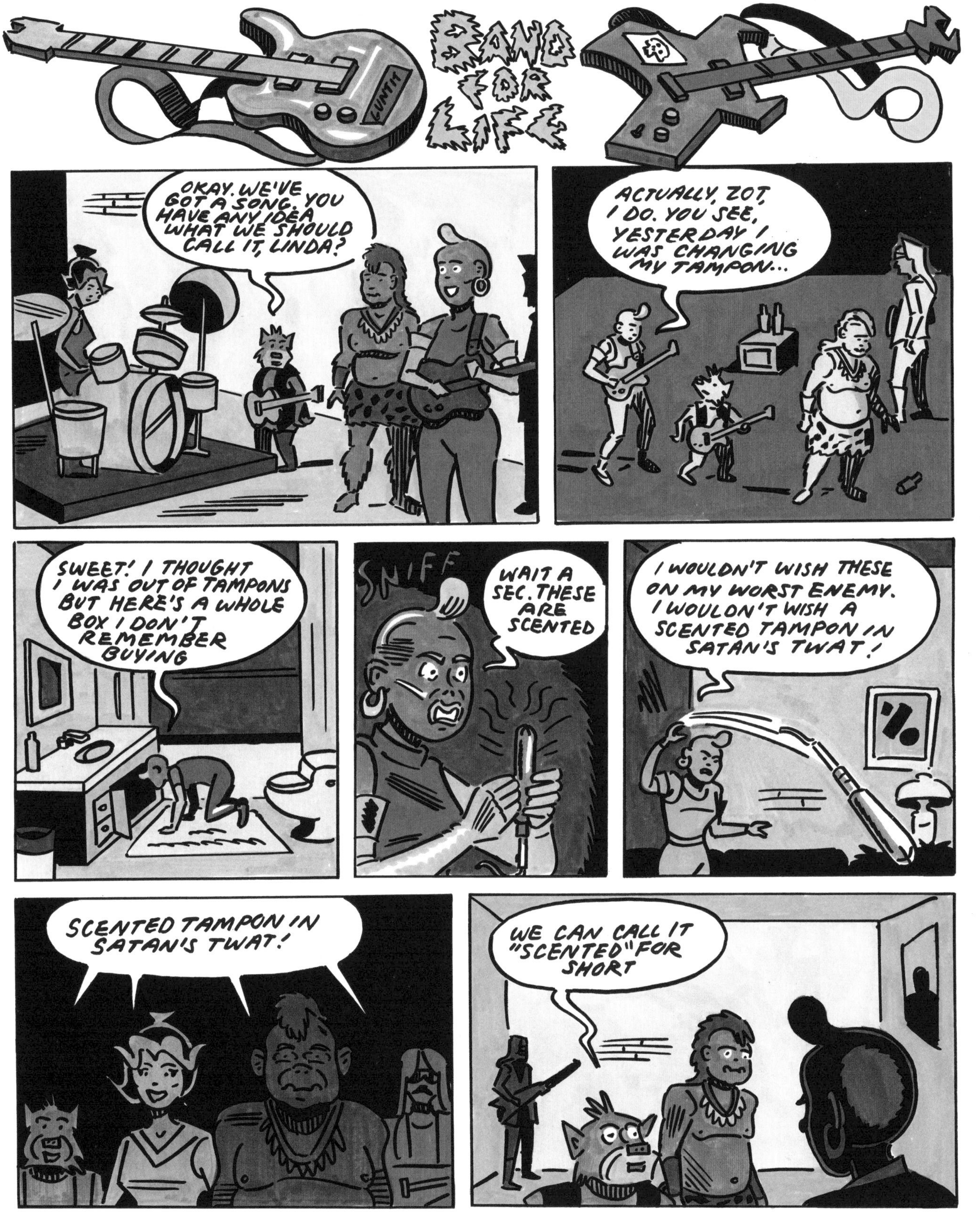

BAND FOR LIFE
LUNTIT
OKAY. WE'VE GOT A SONG. YOU HAVE ANY IDEA WHAT WE SHOULD CALL IT, LINDA?
ACTUALLY, ZOT, I DO. YOU SEE, YESTERDAY I WAS CHANGING MY TAMPON...
SWEET! I THOUGHT I WAS OUT OF TAMPONS BUT HERE'S A WHOLE BOX I DON'T REMEMBER BUYING
SNIFF
WAIT A SEC. THESE ARE SCENTED
I WOULDN'T WISH THESE ON MY WORST ENEMY. I WOULDN'T WISH A SCENTED TAMPON IN SATAN'S TWAT!
SCENTED TAMPON IN SATAN'S TWAT!
WE CAN CALL IT "SCENTED" FOR SHORT

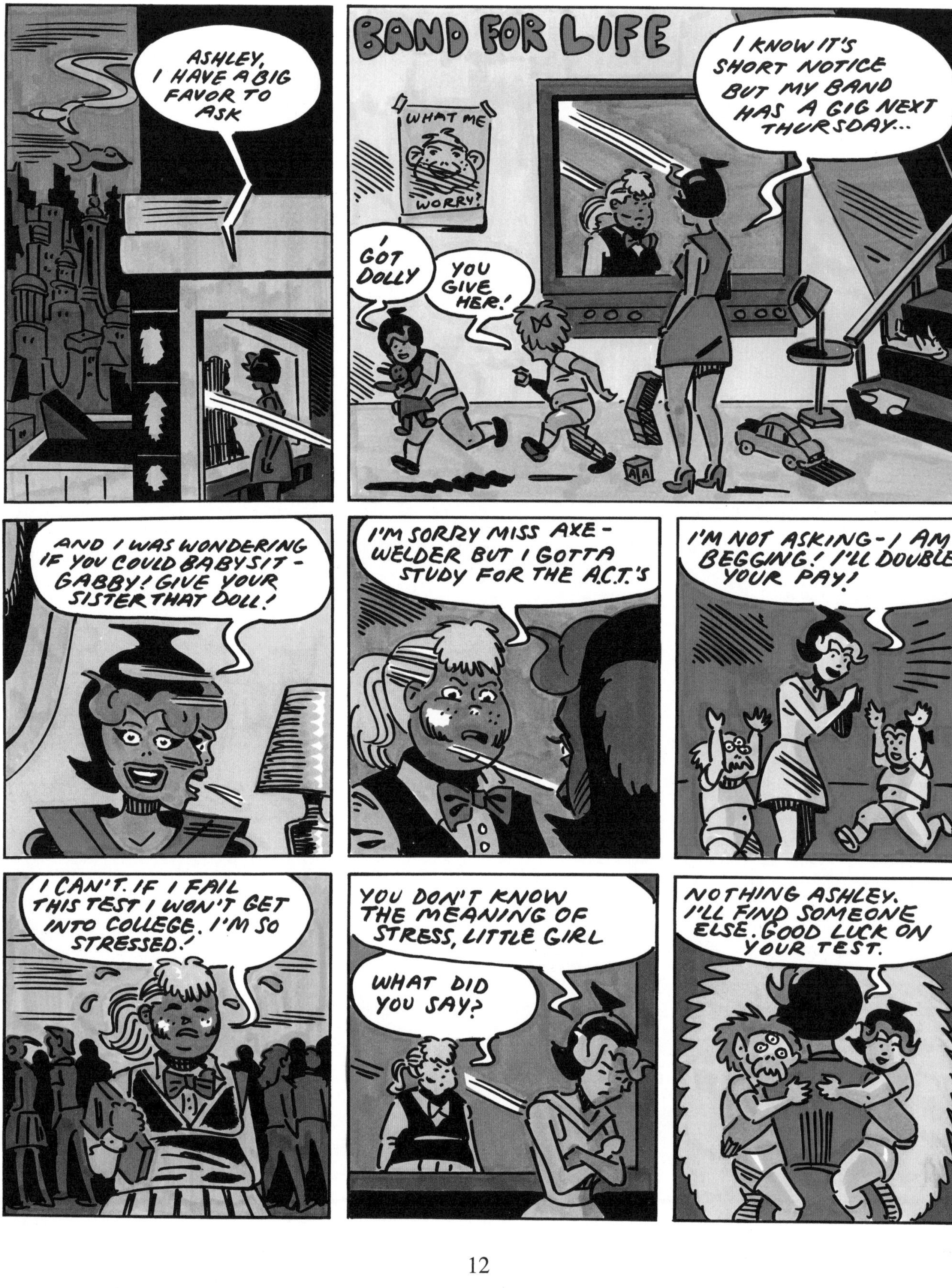
ASHLEY, I HAVE A BIG FAVOR TO ASK
BAND FOR LIFE
I KNOW IT'S SHORT NOTICE BUT MY BAND HAS A GIG NEXT THURSDAY...
WHAT ME WORRY?
I GOT DOLLY
YOU GIVE HER!
AND I WAS WONDERING IF YOU COULD BABYSIT - GABBY! GIVE YOUR SISTER THAT DOLL!
I'M SORRY MISS AXE-WELDER BUT I GOTTA STUDY FOR THE A.C.T.'S
I'M NOT ASKING - I AM BEGGING! I'LL DOUBLE YOUR PAY!
I CAN'T. IF I FAIL THIS TEST I WON'T GET INTO COLLEGE. I'M SO STRESSED!
YOU DON'T KNOW THE MEANING OF STRESS, LITTLE GIRL
WHAT DID YOU SAY?
NOTHING ASHLEY. I'LL FIND SOMEONE ELSE. GOOD LUCK ON YOUR TEST.

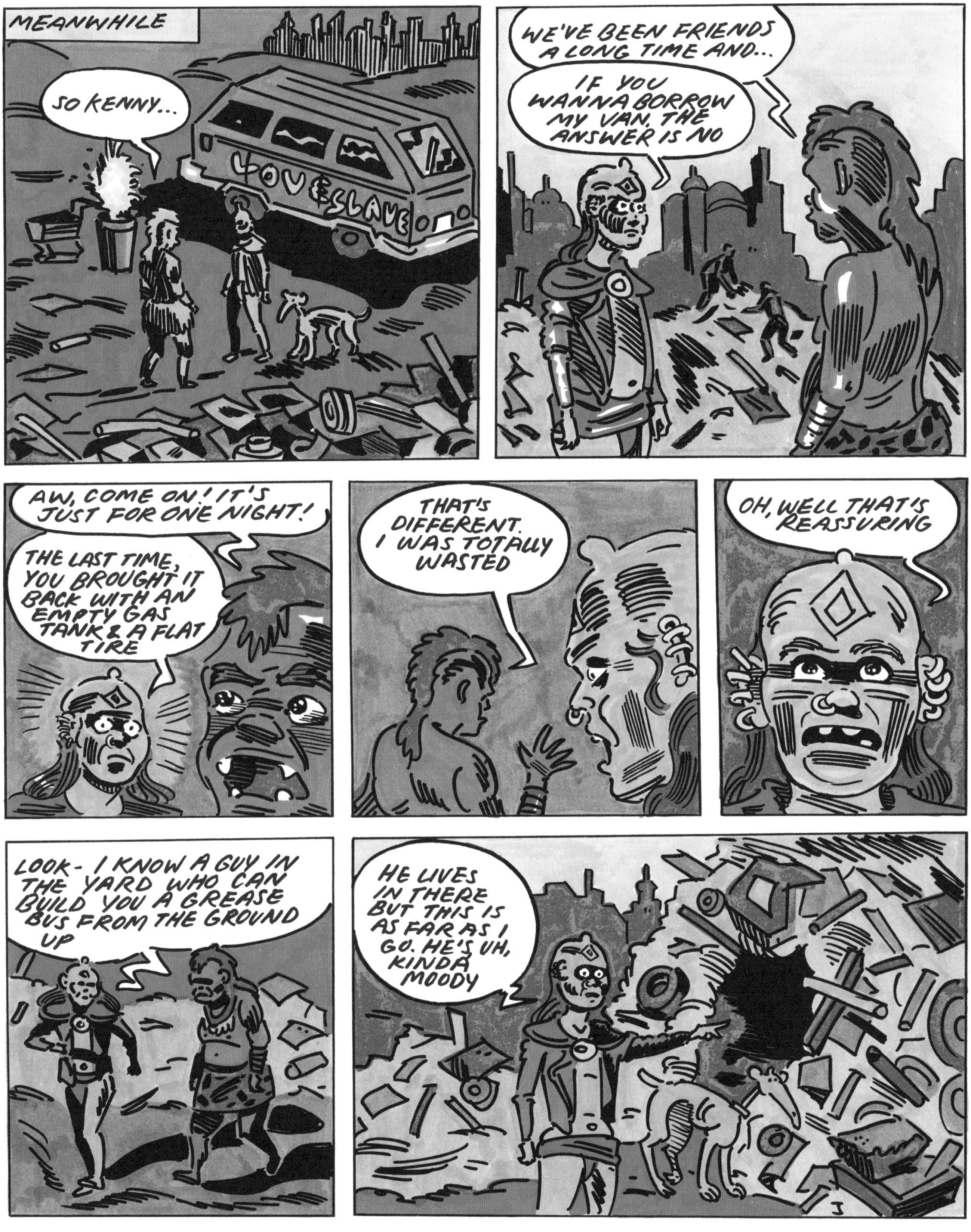
MEANWHILE
SO KENNY...
LOVESLAVE
WE'VE BEEN FRIENDS A LONG TIME AND...
IF YOU WANNA BORROW MY VAN, THE ANSWER IS NO
AW, COME ON! IT'S JUST FOR ONE NIGHT!
THE LAST TIME, YOU BROUGHT IT BACK WITH AN EMPTY GAS TANK & A FLAT TIRE
THAT'S DIFFERENT. I WAS TOTALLY WASTED
OH, WELL THAT'S REASSURING
LOOK- I KNOW A GUY IN THE YARD WHO CAN BUILD YOU A GREASE BUS FROM THE GROUND UP
HE LIVES IN THERE BUT THIS IS AS FAR AS I GO. HE'S UH, KINDA MOODY

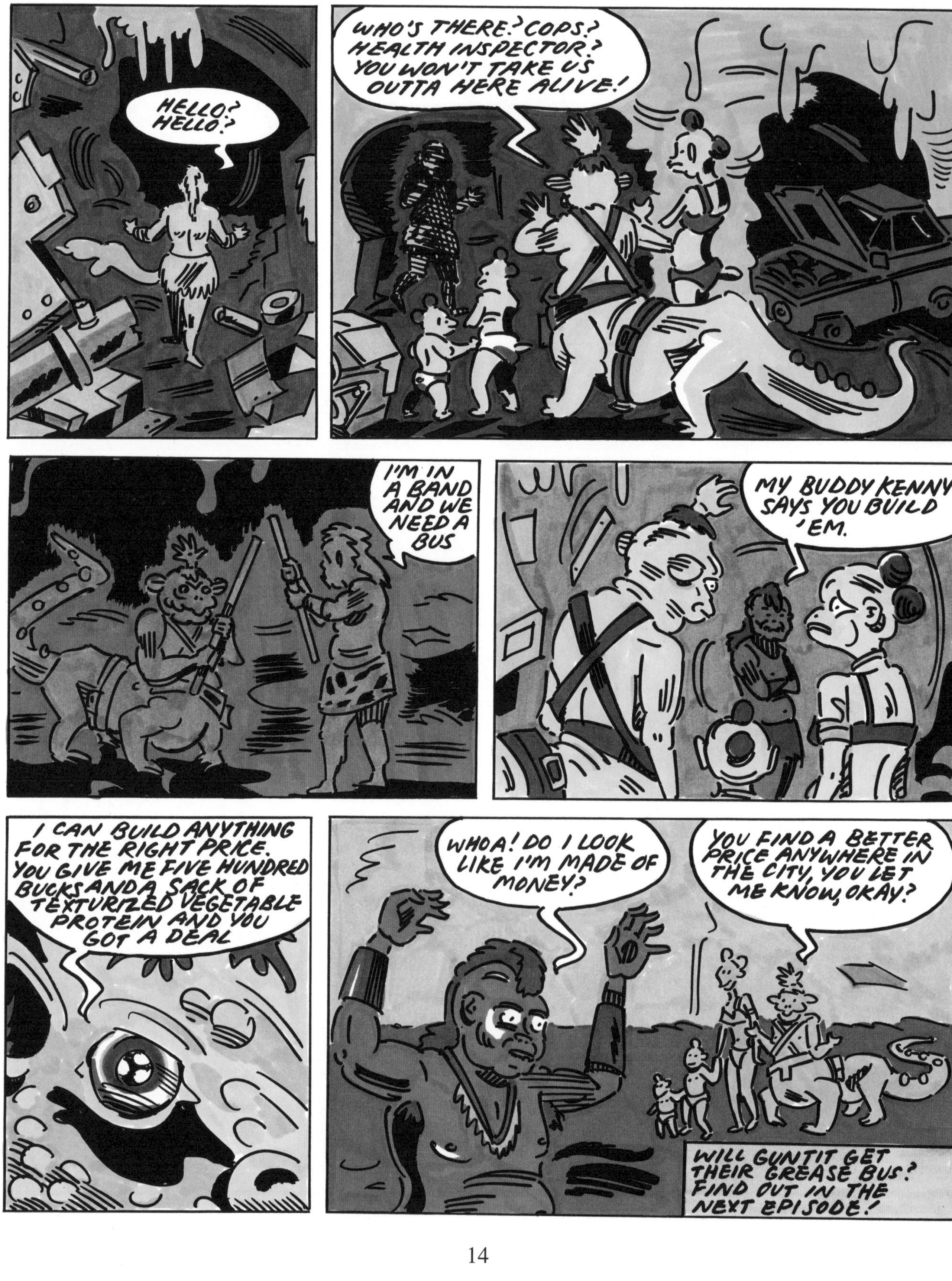
HELLO? HELLO?
WHO'S THERE? COPS? HEALTH INSPECTOR? YOU WON'T TAKE US OUTTA HERE ALIVE!
I'M IN A BAND AND WE NEED A BUS
MY BUDDY KENNY SAYS YOU BUILD 'EM.
I CAN BUILD ANYTHING FOR THE RIGHT PRICE. YOU GIVE ME FIVE HUNDRED BUCKS AND A SACK OF TEXTURIZED VEGETABLE PROTEIN AND YOU GOT A DEAL
WHOA! DO I LOOK LIKE I'M MADE OF MONEY?
YOU FIND A BETTER PRICE ANYWHERE IN THE CITY, YOU LET ME KNOW, OKAY?
WILL GUNTIT GET THEIR GREASE BUS? FIND OUT IN THE NEXT EPISODE!

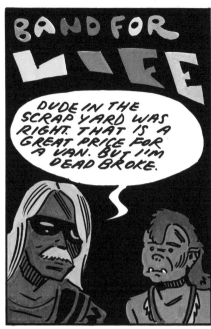

BAND FOR LIFE

DUDE IN THE SCRAP YARD WAS RIGHT. THAT IS A GREAT PRICE FOR A VAN. BUT I'M DEAD BROKE.

THIS TOTAL SCRATCHER OPENED A SHOP DOWN THE STREET FROM MINE AND HE'S CHARGING ROCK-BOTTOM PRICES. I'M LOSING BUSINESS.

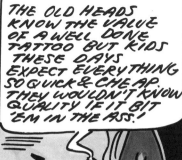

THE OLD HEADS KNOW THE VALUE OF A WELL DONE TATTOO BUT KIDS THESE DAYS EXPECT EVERYTHING SO QUICK & CHEAP. THEY WOULDN'T KNOW QUALITY IF IT BIT 'EM IN THE ASS!

WELL DON'T LOOK AT ME. EVERY SPARE DIME OF MINE IS GOING TO NAPPIES & FORMULA

WAIT! I KNOW—LET'S TAKE THE MONEY WE POOLED FOR THIS MONTH'S PRACTICE SPACE RENT AND GAMBLE IT DOWN AT THE RIVERBOAT CASINO

WHAT!? THAT'S INSANE!

IF WE LOSE THAT MONEY WE'LL BE OUT ON THE STREET WITH OUR GEAR

WHAT ABOUT YOU, ZOT? YOU'VE GOT A STEADY, WELL-PAYING JOB

NOT ANYMORE

OH NO! WHAT HAPPENED?!

I REACHED MY MORON THRESHOLD

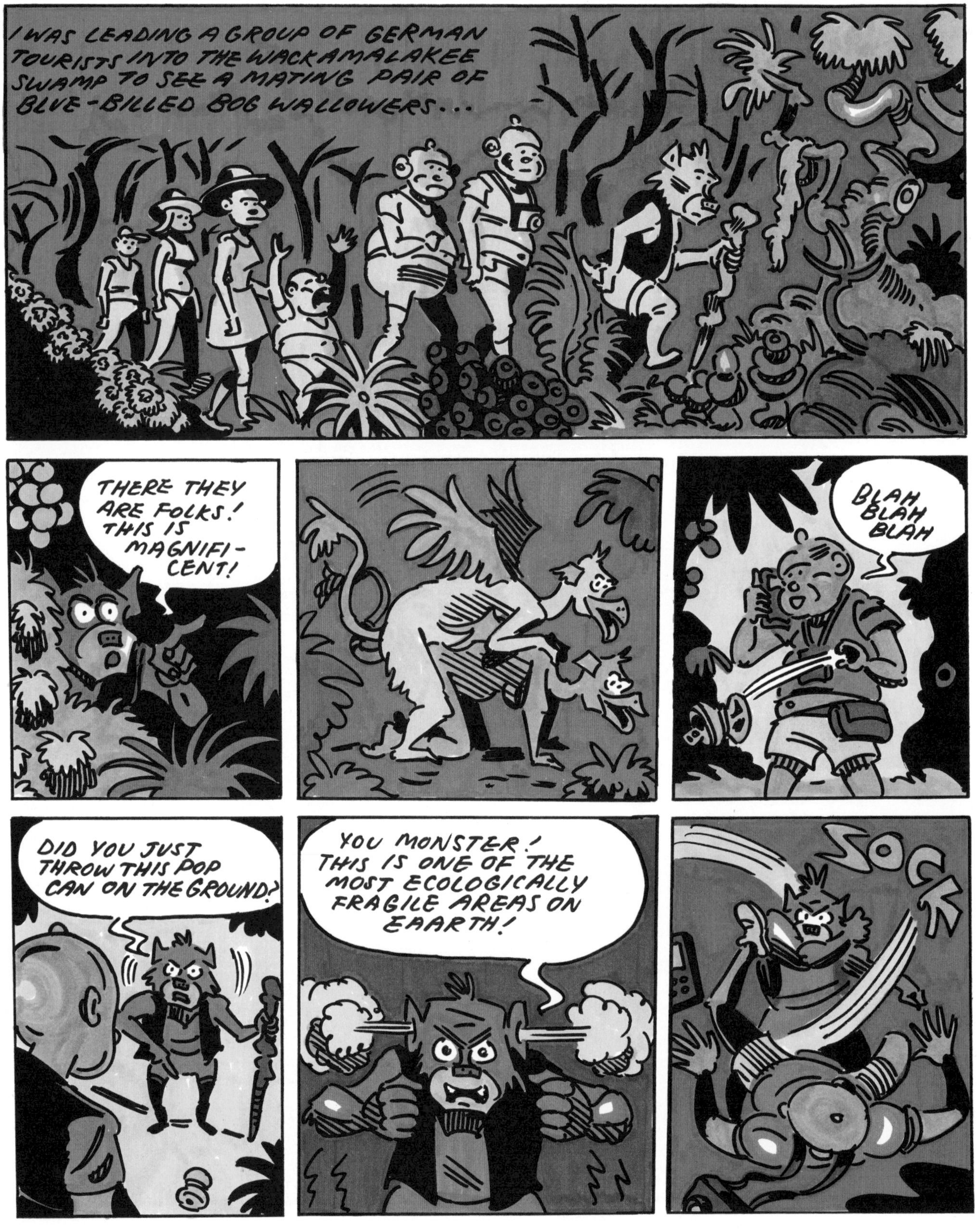
I WAS LEADING A GROUP OF GERMAN TOURISTS INTO THE WACKAMALAKEE SWAMP TO SEE A MATING PAIR OF BLUE-BILLED BOG WALLOWERS...
THERE THEY ARE FOLKS! THIS IS MAGNIFI-CENT!
BLAH BLAH BLAH
DID YOU JUST THROW THIS POP CAN ON THE GROUND?
YOU MONSTER! THIS IS ONE OF THE MOST ECOLOGICALLY FRAGILE AREAS ON EAARTH!
SOCK

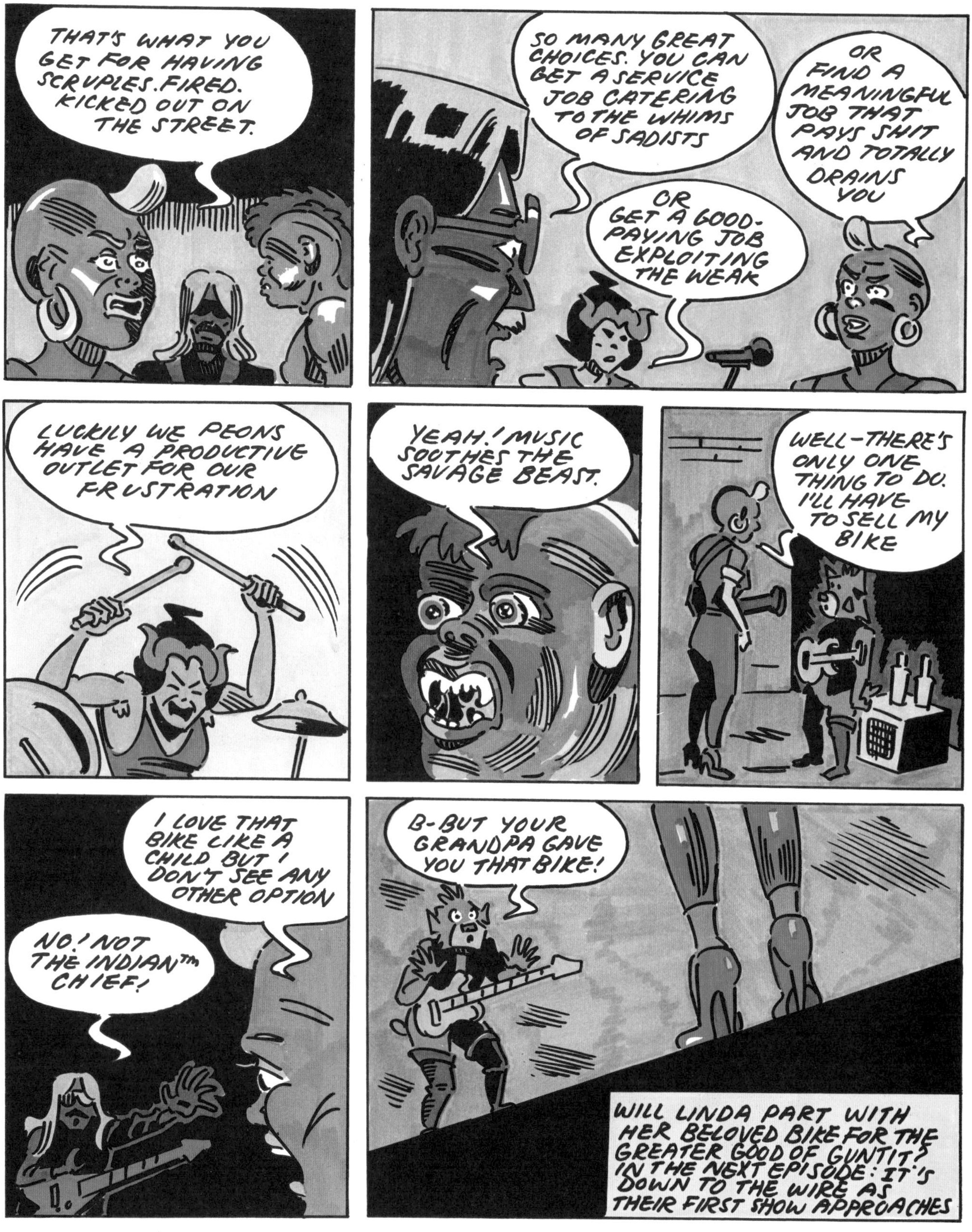

THAT'S WHAT YOU GET FOR HAVING SCRUPLES. FIRED. KICKED OUT ON THE STREET.
SO MANY GREAT CHOICES. YOU CAN GET A SERVICE JOB CATERING TO THE WHIMS OF SADISTS
OR FIND A MEANINGFUL JOB THAT PAYS SHIT AND TOTALLY DRAINS YOU
OR GET A GOOD-PAYING JOB EXPLOITING THE WEAK
LUCKILY WE PEONS HAVE A PRODUCTIVE OUTLET FOR OUR FRUSTRATION
YEAH! MUSIC SOOTHES THE SAVAGE BEAST.
WELL—THERE'S ONLY ONE THING TO DO. I'LL HAVE TO SELL MY BIKE
I LOVE THAT BIKE LIKE A CHILD BUT I DON'T SEE ANY OTHER OPTION
NO! NOT THE INDIAN™ CHIEF!
B-BUT YOUR GRANDPA GAVE YOU THAT BIKE!
WILL LINDA PART WITH HER BELOVED BIKE FOR THE GREATER GOOD OF GUNTIT? IN THE NEXT EPISODE: IT'S DOWN TO THE WIRE AS THEIR FIRST SHOW APPROACHES

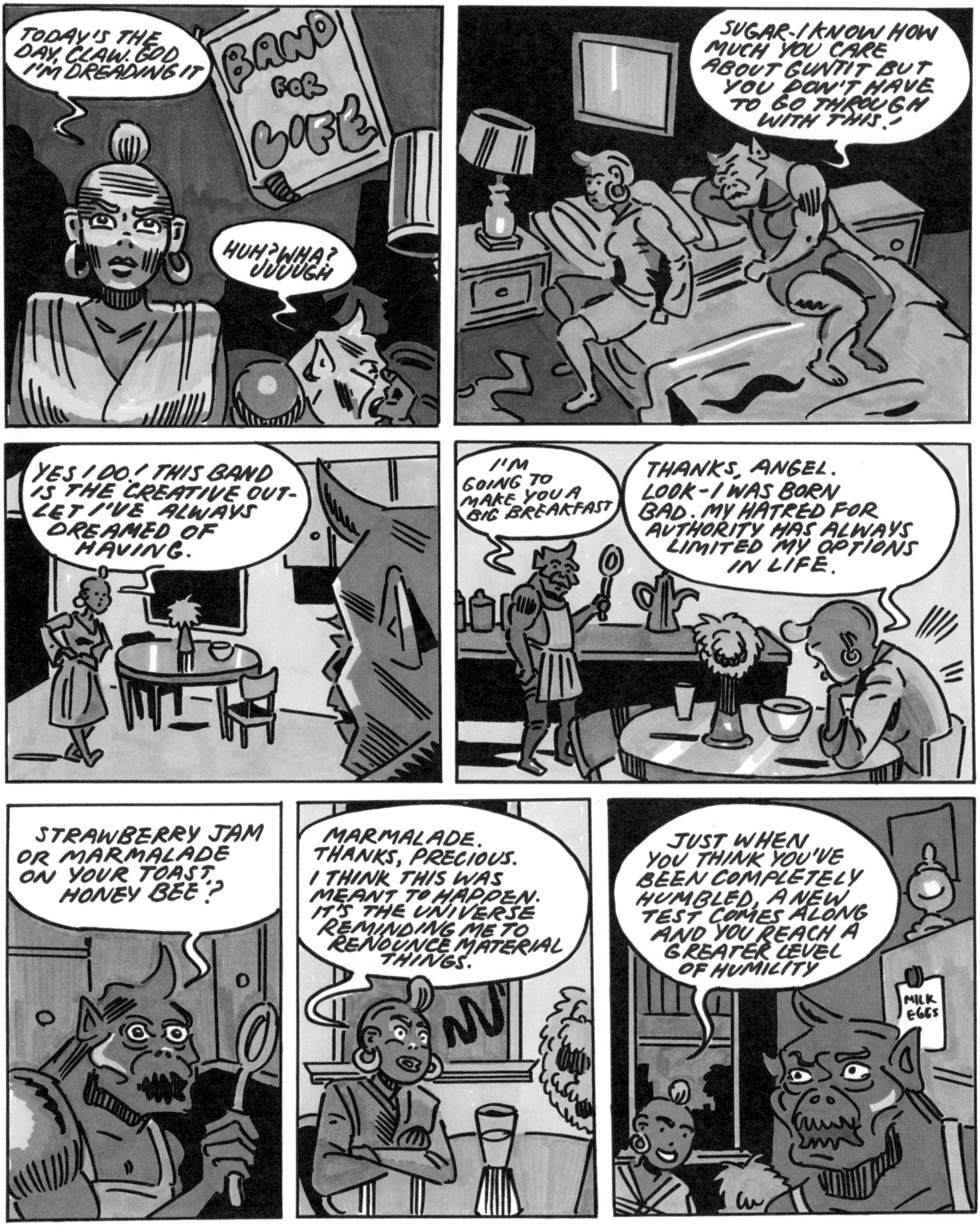
TODAY'S THE DAY, CLAW. GOD I'M DREADING IT
BAND FOR LIFE
HUH? WHA? UUUUGH
SUGAR-I KNOW HOW MUCH YOU CARE ABOUT GUNTIT BUT YOU DON'T HAVE TO GO THROUGH WITH THIS!
YES I DO! THIS BAND IS THE CREATIVE OUTLET I'VE ALWAYS DREAMED OF HAVING.
I'M GOING TO MAKE YOU A BIG BREAKFAST
THANKS, ANGEL. LOOK-I WAS BORN BAD. MY HATRED FOR AUTHORITY HAS ALWAYS LIMITED MY OPTIONS IN LIFE.
STRAWBERRY JAM OR MARMALADE ON YOUR TOAST, HONEY BEE?
MARMALADE. THANKS, PRECIOUS. I THINK THIS WAS MEANT TO HAPPEN. IT'S THE UNIVERSE REMINDING ME TO RENOUNCE MATERIAL THINGS.
JUST WHEN YOU THINK YOU'VE BEEN COMPLETELY HUMBLED, A NEW TEST COMES ALONG AND YOU REACH A GREATER LEVEL OF HUMILITY
MILK EGGS

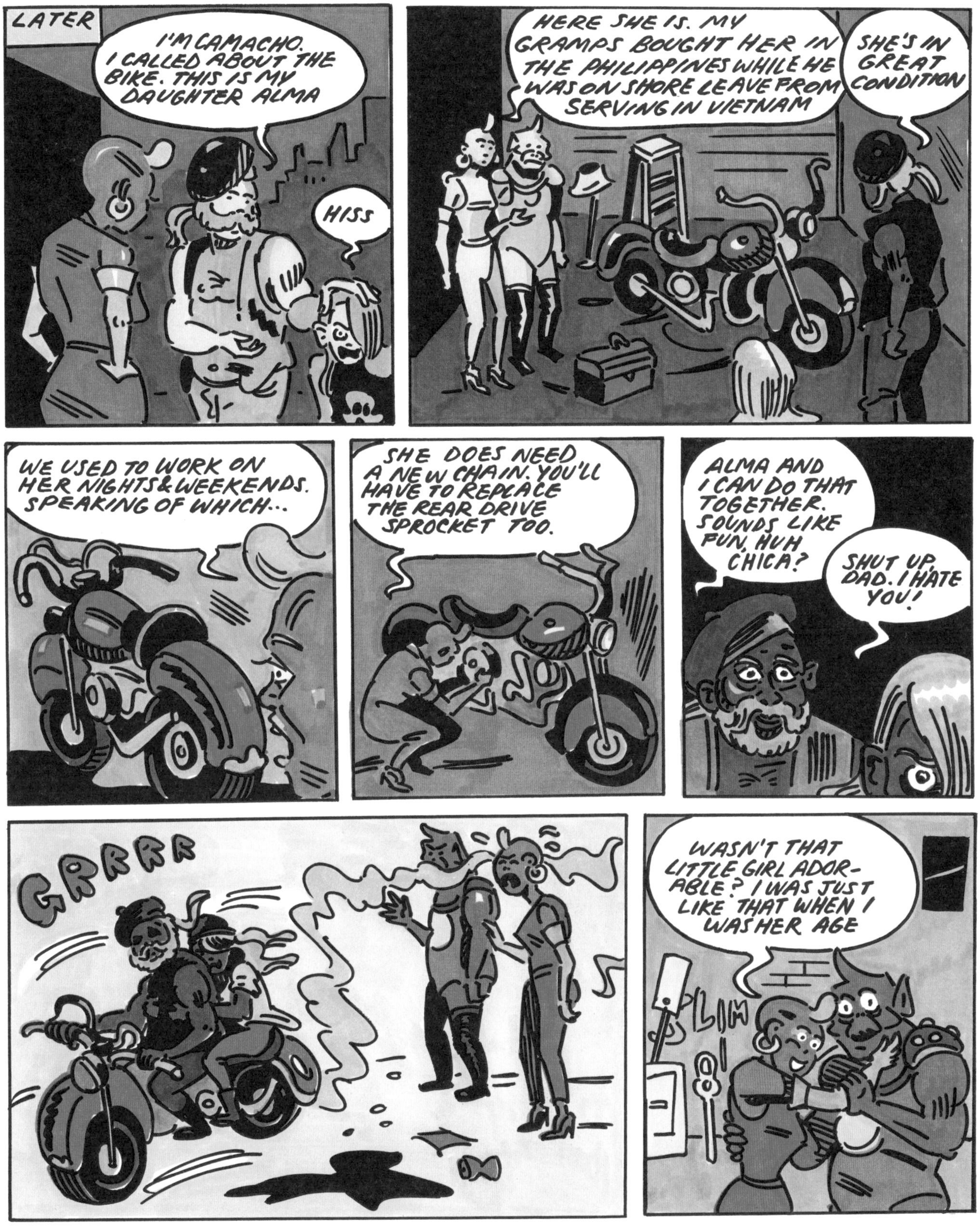

LATER
I'M CAMACHO. I CALLED ABOUT THE BIKE. THIS IS MY DAUGHTER ALMA
HISS
HERE SHE IS. MY GRAMPS BOUGHT HER IN THE PHILIPPINES WHILE HE WAS ON SHORE LEAVE FROM SERVING IN VIETNAM
SHE'S IN GREAT CONDITION
WE USED TO WORK ON HER NIGHTS & WEEKENDS. SPEAKING OF WHICH...
SHE DOES NEED A NEW CHAIN. YOU'LL HAVE TO REPLACE THE REAR DRIVE SPROCKET TOO.
ALMA AND I CAN DO THAT TOGETHER. SOUNDS LIKE FUN, HUH CHICA?
SHUT UP, DAD. I HATE YOU!
GRRRR
WASN'T THAT LITTLE GIRL ADOR-ABLE? I WAS JUST LIKE THAT WHEN I WAS HER AGE

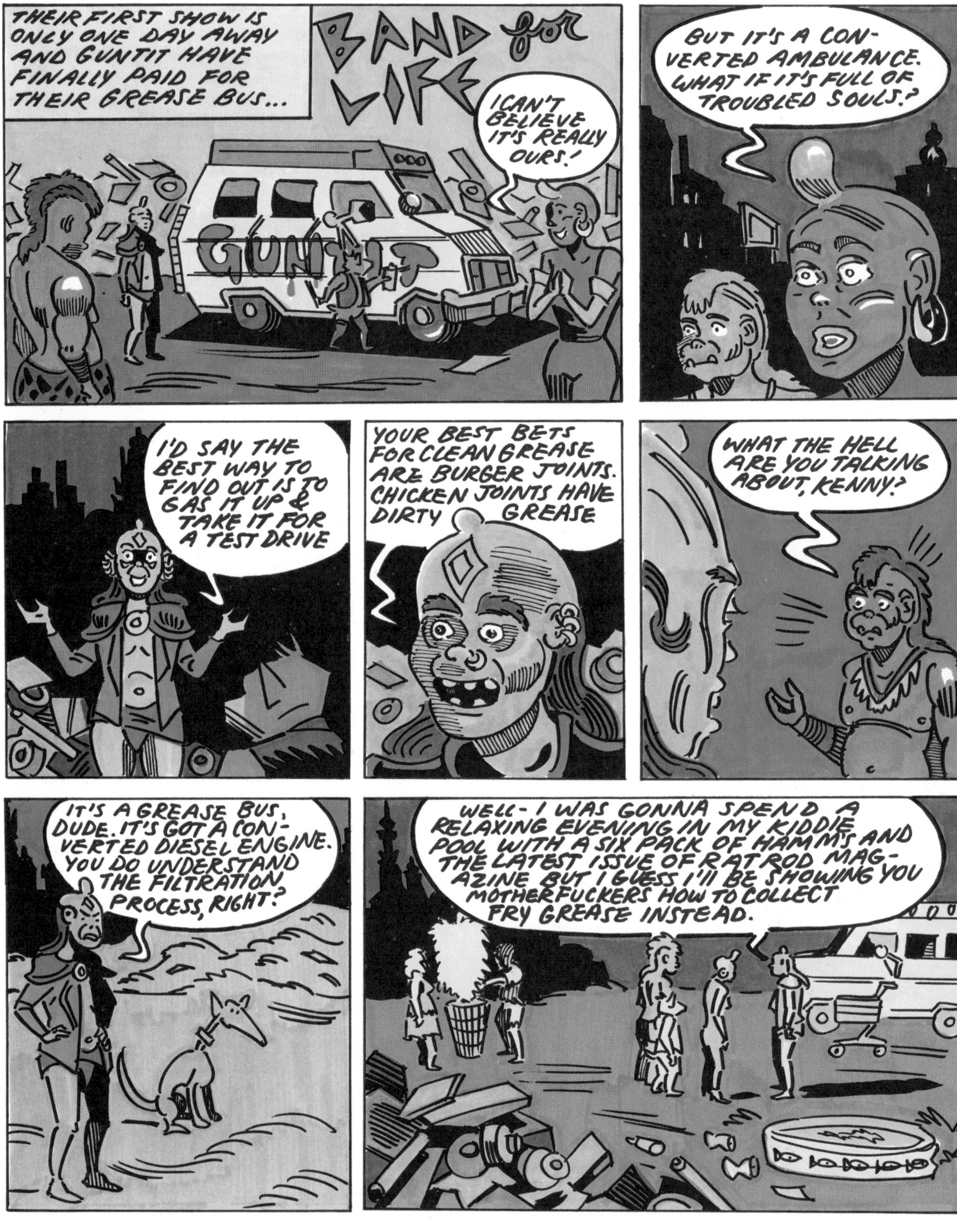

THEIR FIRST SHOW IS ONLY ONE DAY AWAY AND GUNTIT HAVE FINALLY PAID FOR THEIR GREASE BUS...
BAND for LIFE
I CAN'T BELIEVE IT'S REALLY OURS!
GUNTIT
BUT IT'S A CONVERTED AMBULANCE. WHAT IF IT'S FULL OF TROUBLED SOULS?
I'D SAY THE BEST WAY TO FIND OUT IS TO GAS IT UP & TAKE IT FOR A TEST DRIVE
YOUR BEST BETS FOR CLEAN GREASE ARE BURGER JOINTS. CHICKEN JOINTS HAVE DIRTY GREASE
WHAT THE HELL ARE YOU TALKING ABOUT, KENNY?
IT'S A GREASE BUS, DUDE. IT'S GOT A CONVERTED DIESEL ENGINE. YOU DO UNDERSTAND THE FILTRATION PROCESS, RIGHT?
WELL- I WAS GONNA SPEND A RELAXING EVENING IN MY KIDDIE POOL WITH A SIX PACK OF HAMM'S AND THE LATEST ISSUE OF RAT ROD MAGAZINE BUT I GUESS I'LL BE SHOWING YOU MOTHERFUCKERS HOW TO COLLECT FRY GREASE INSTEAD.

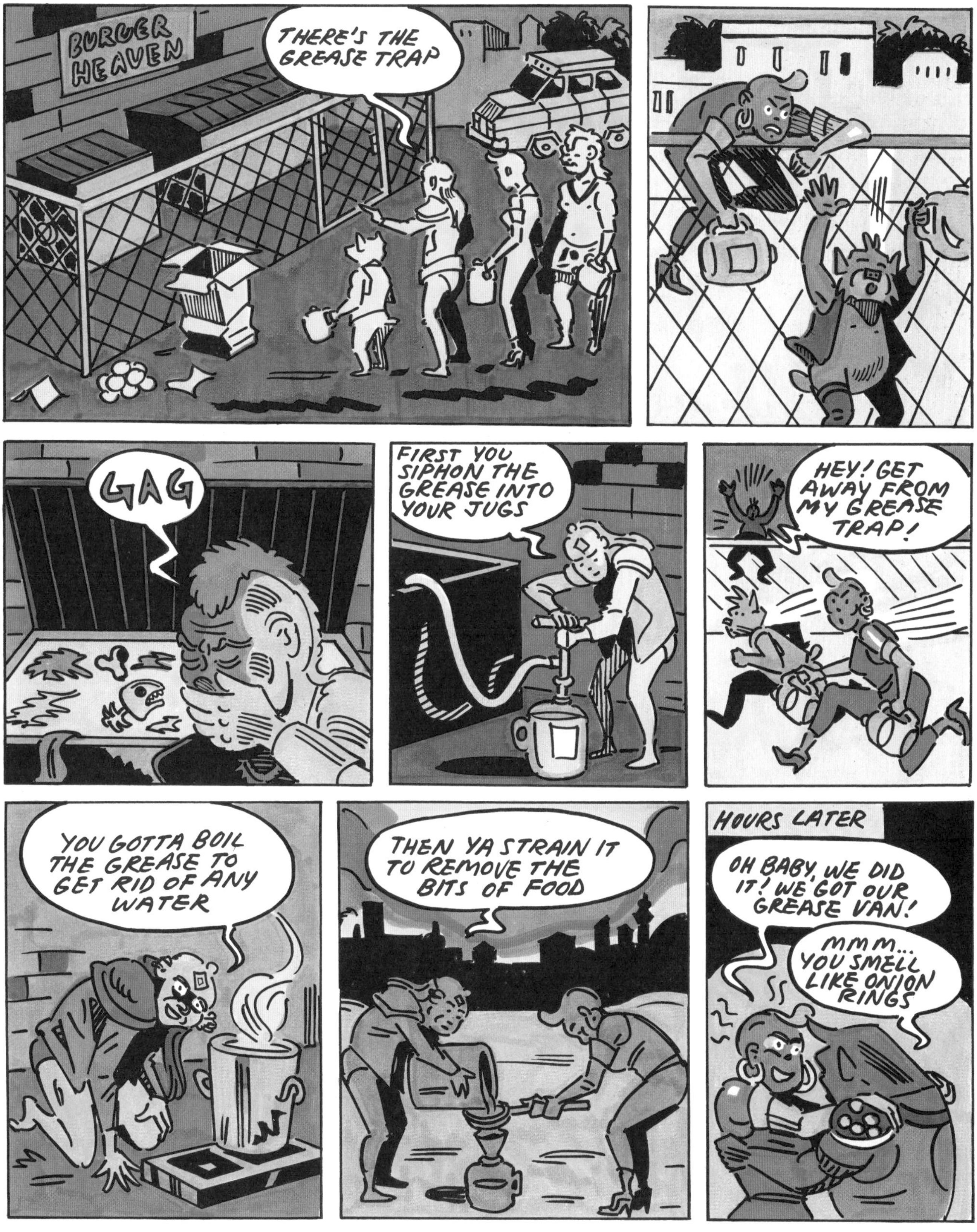
BURGER HEAVEN
THERE'S THE GREASE TRAP
GAG
FIRST YOU SIPHON THE GREASE INTO YOUR JUGS
HEY! GET AWAY FROM MY GREASE TRAP!
YOU GOTTA BOIL THE GREASE TO GET RID OF ANY WATER
THEN YA STRAIN IT TO REMOVE THE BITS OF FOOD
HOURS LATER
OH BABY, WE DID IT! WE GOT OUR GREASE VAN!
MMM... YOU SMELL LIKE ONION RINGS

THE DAY OF GUNTIT'S FIRST SHOW HAS ARRIVED AND AS THE CRITICAL HOUR DRAWS NEAR, ANNIMAL, THE BAND'S DRUMMER, FIGHTS TO KEEP IT TOGETHER

HI MISS KLEINFELTER

WHAT CAN I DO FOR YOU, ANN?

I'VE GOT A SHOW TONIGHT AND I'VE ASKED EVERYONE BUT I CAN'T FIND A BABYSITTER

I WAS AN ONLY CHILD AND I NEVER HAD CHILDREN

I HAVE A DOCTORATE IN COMPARATIVE LITERATURE. I'VE NEVER CHANGED A DIAPER IN MY LIFE

OH-UH

DO YOU THINK THAT BECAUSE I'M OLD, I HAVE NOTHING BETTER TO DO?

I PROMISE IF YOU EVER NEED ANY NEIGHBORLY FAVORS I'LL...

OKAY, OKAY. I ADMIT THE NOVELTY DOES APPEAL TO ME

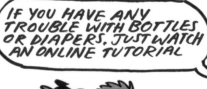

IF YOU HAVE ANY TROUBLE WITH BOTTLES OR DIAPERS, JUST WATCH AN ONLINE TUTORIAL

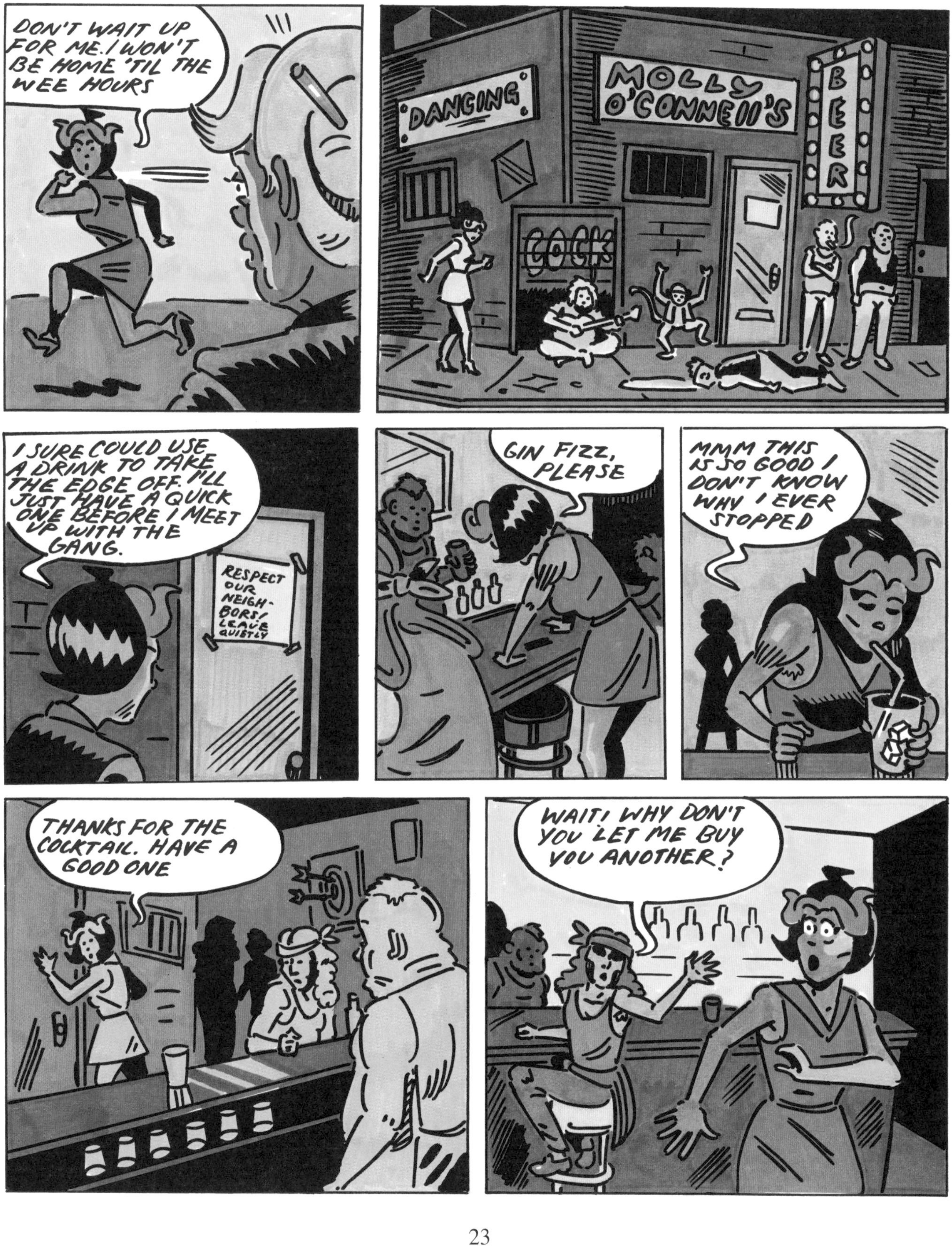
DON'T WAIT UP FOR ME. I WON'T BE HOME 'TIL THE WEE HOURS
DANCING
MOLLY O'CONNELL'S
BEER
COCK
I SURE COULD USE A DRINK TO TAKE THE EDGE OFF. I'LL JUST HAVE A QUICK ONE BEFORE I MEET UP WITH THE GANG.
RESPECT OUR NEIGH-BORS! LEAVE QUIETLY
GIN FIZZ, PLEASE
MMM THIS IS SO GOOD I DON'T KNOW WHY I EVER STOPPED
THANKS FOR THE COCKTAIL. HAVE A GOOD ONE
WAIT! WHY DON'T YOU LET ME BUY YOU ANOTHER?

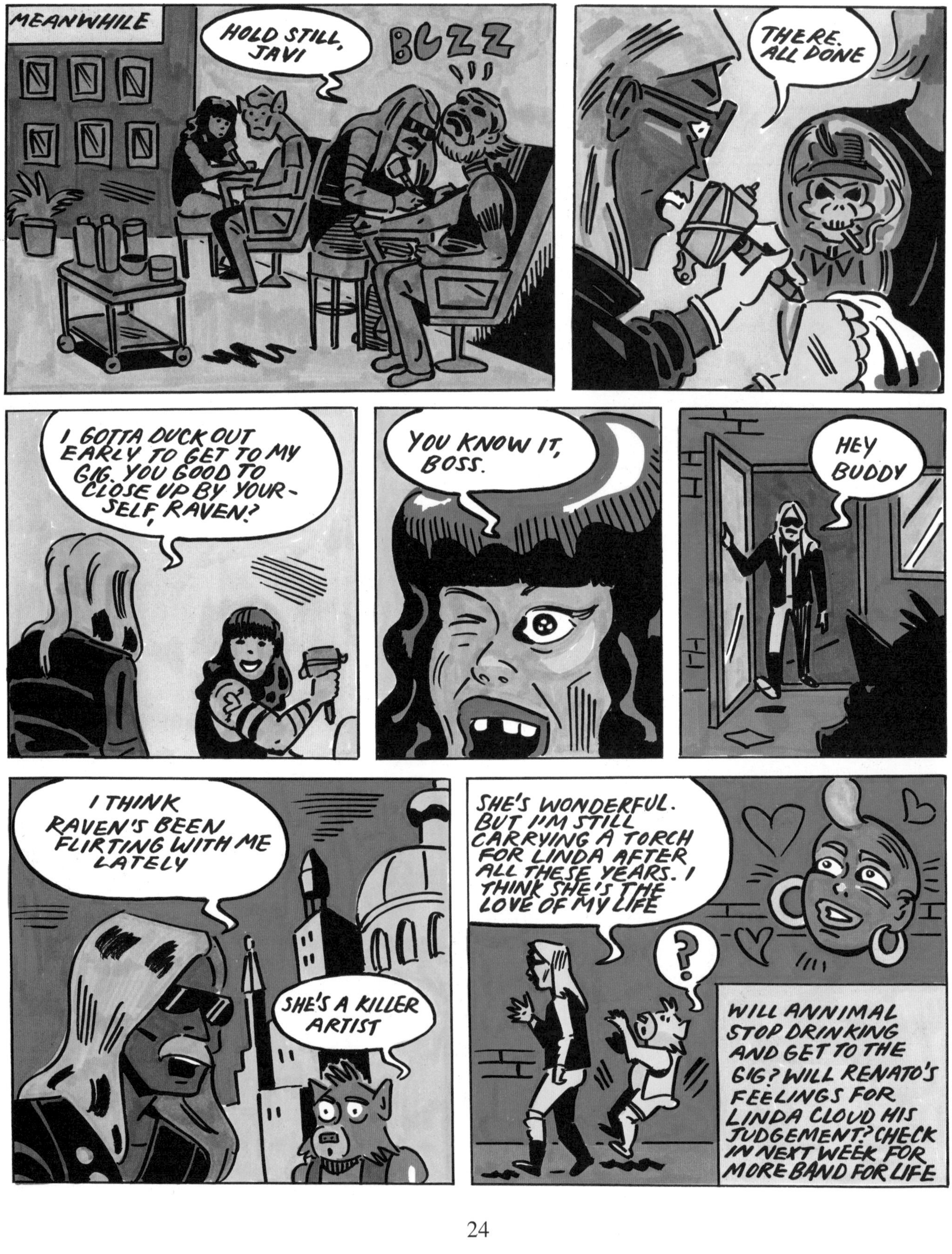
MEANWHILE
HOLD STILL, JAVI
BZZZ
THERE. ALL DONE
I GOTTA DUCK OUT EARLY TO GET TO MY GIG. YOU GOOD TO CLOSE UP BY YOURSELF, RAVEN?
YOU KNOW IT, BOSS.
HEY BUDDY
I THINK RAVEN'S BEEN FLIRTING WITH ME LATELY
SHE'S A KILLER ARTIST
SHE'S WONDERFUL. BUT I'M STILL CARRYING A TORCH FOR LINDA AFTER ALL THESE YEARS. I THINK SHE'S THE LOVE OF MY LIFE
?
WILL ANNIMAL STOP DRINKING AND GET TO THE GIG? WILL RENATO'S FEELINGS FOR LINDA CLOUD HIS JUDGEMENT? CHECK IN NEXT WEEK FOR MORE BAND FOR LIFE

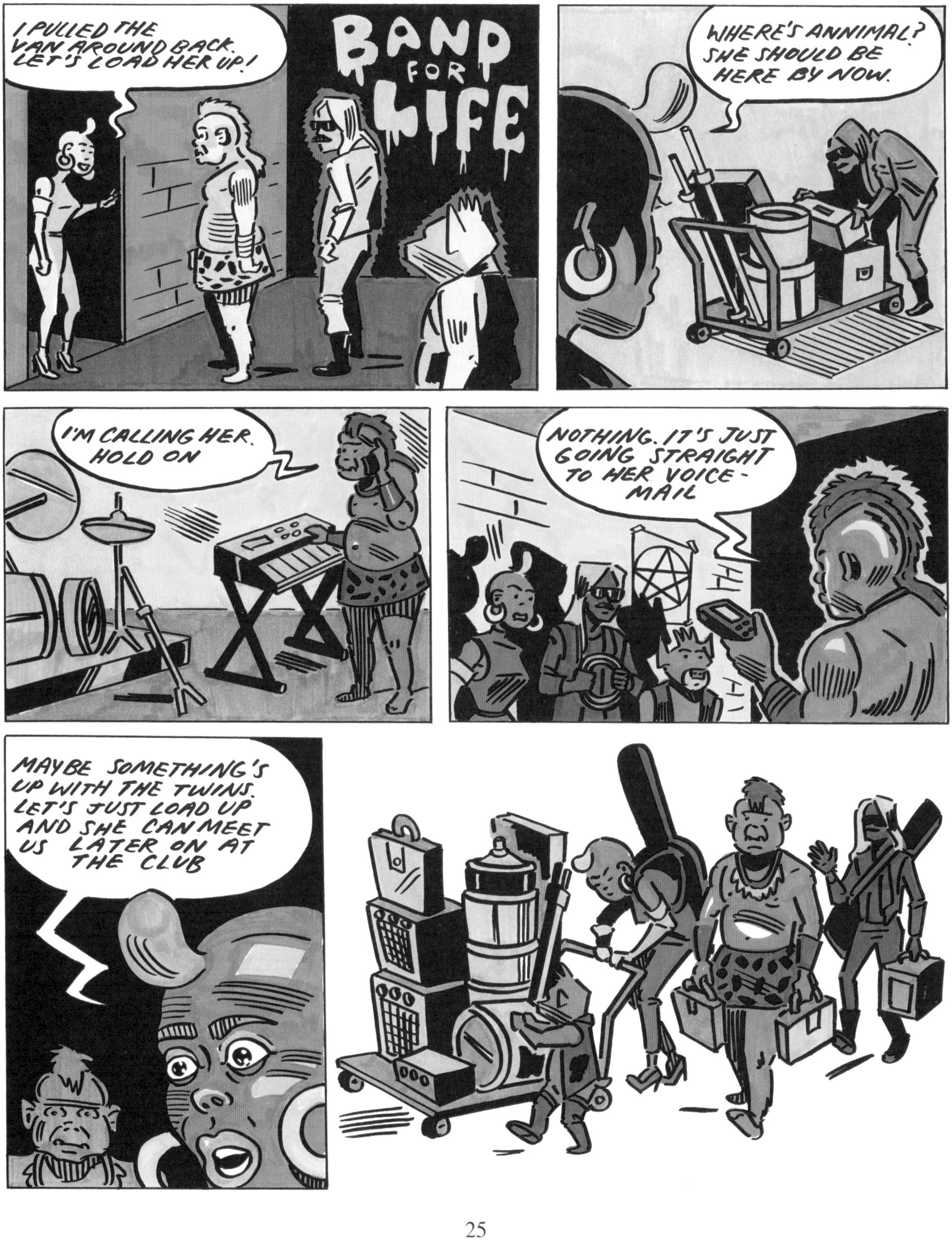
I PULLED THE VAN AROUND BACK. LET'S LOAD HER UP!
BAND FOR LIFE
WHERE'S ANNIMAL? SHE SHOULD BE HERE BY NOW.
I'M CALLING HER. HOLD ON
NOTHING. IT'S JUST GOING STRAIGHT TO HER VOICE-MAIL
MAYBE SOMETHING'S UP WITH THE TWINS. LET'S JUST LOAD UP AND SHE CAN MEET US LATER ON AT THE CLUB

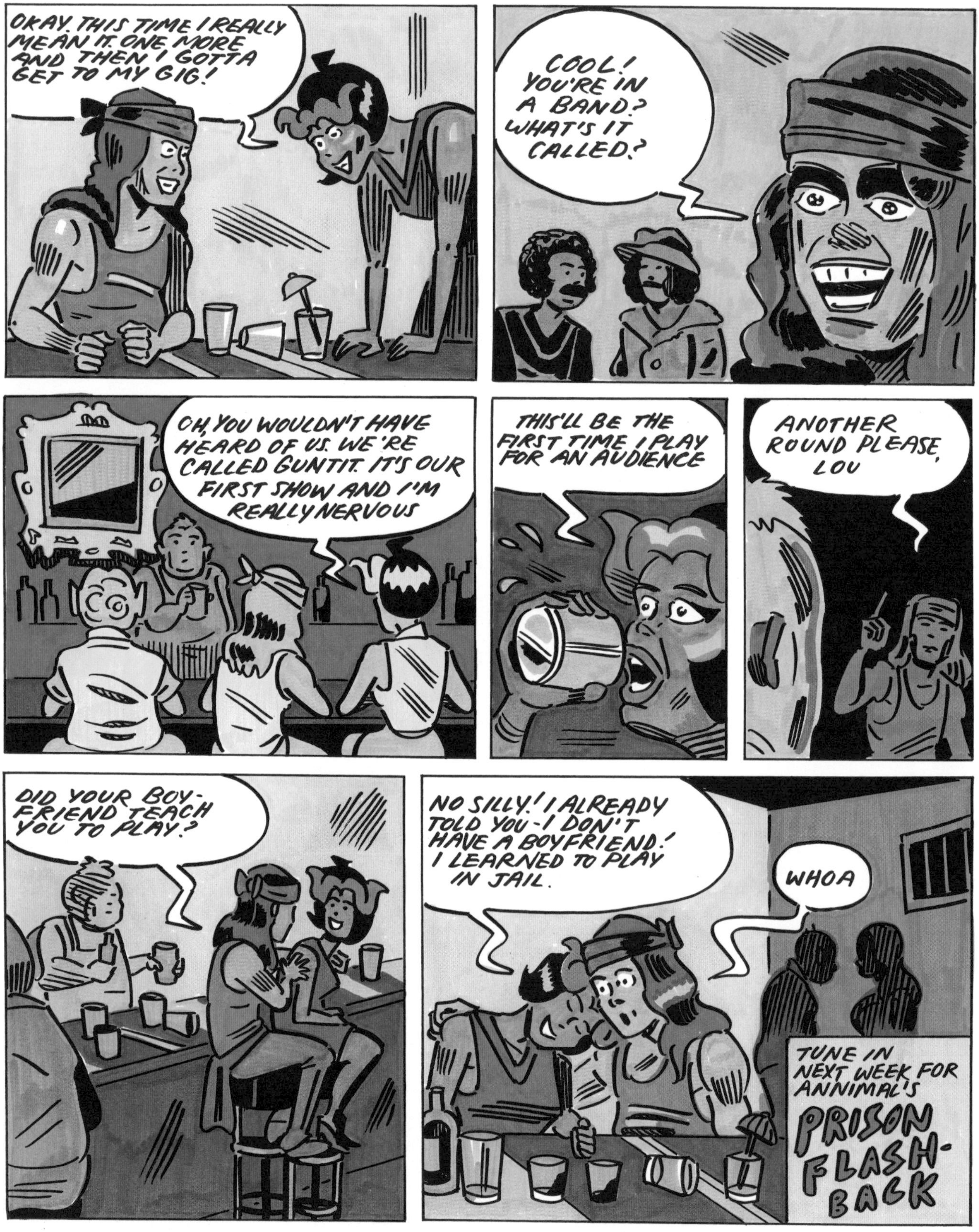
OKAY. THIS TIME I REALLY MEAN IT. ONE MORE AND THEN I GOTTA GET TO MY GIG!
COOL! YOU'RE IN A BAND? WHAT'S IT CALLED?
OH, YOU WOULDN'T HAVE HEARD OF US. WE'RE CALLED GUNTIT. IT'S OUR FIRST SHOW AND I'M REALLY NERVOUS
THIS'LL BE THE FIRST TIME I PLAY FOR AN AUDIENCE
ANOTHER ROUND PLEASE, LOU
DID YOUR BOY-FRIEND TEACH YOU TO PLAY?
NO SILLY! I ALREADY TOLD YOU-I DON'T HAVE A BOYFRIEND! I LEARNED TO PLAY IN JAIL.
WHOA
TUNE IN NEXT WEEK FOR ANNIMAL'S
PRISON FLASH-BACK

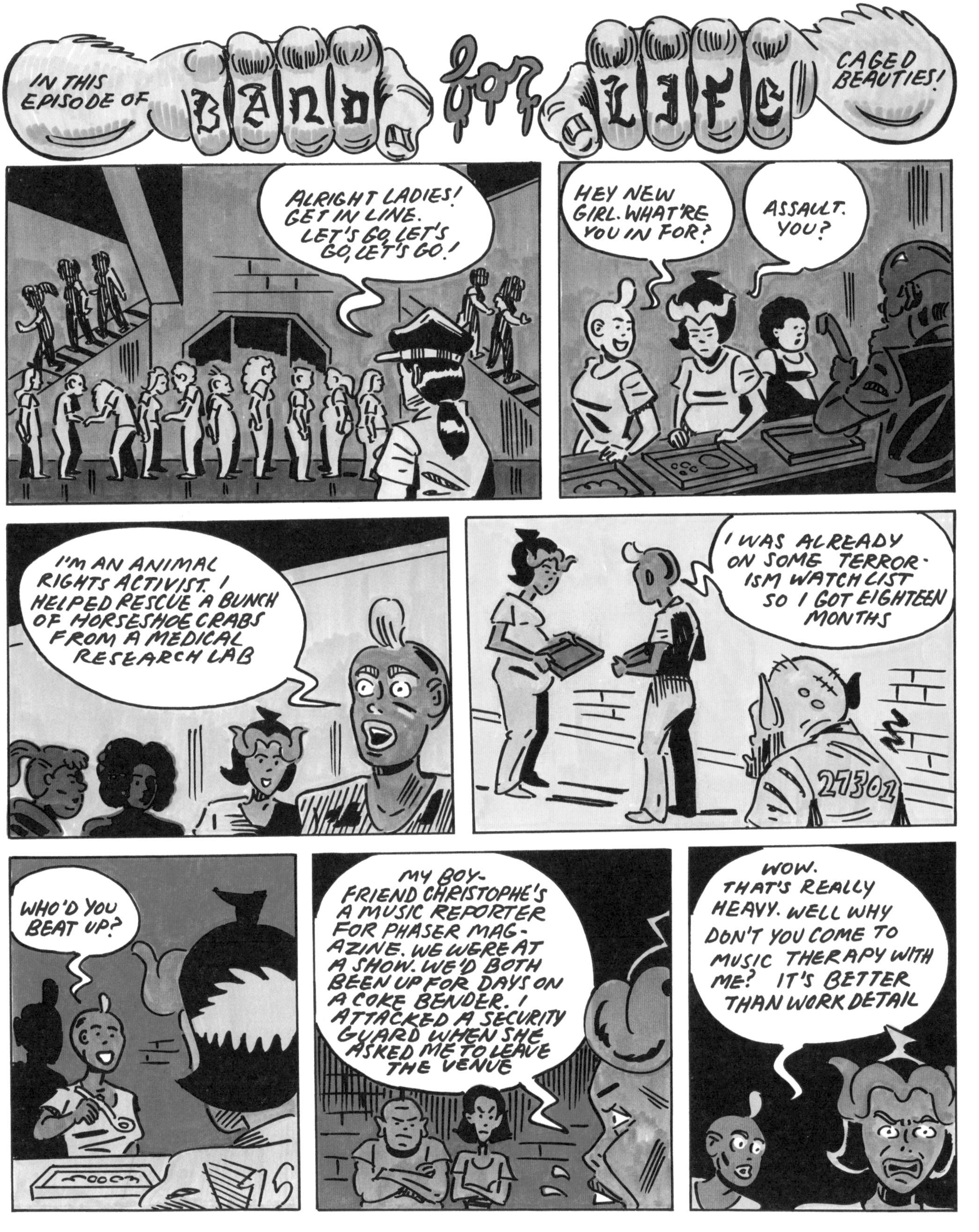
IN THIS EPISODE OF
BAND FOR LIFE
CAGED BEAUTIES!
ALRIGHT LADIES! GET IN LINE. LET'S GO, LET'S GO, LET'S GO!
HEY NEW GIRL. WHAT'RE YOU IN FOR?
ASSAULT. YOU?
I'M AN ANIMAL RIGHTS ACTIVIST. I HELPED RESCUE A BUNCH OF HORSESHOE CRABS FROM A MEDICAL RESEARCH LAB
I WAS ALREADY ON SOME TERROR-ISM WATCH LIST SO I GOT EIGHTEEN MONTHS
27301
WHO'D YOU BEAT UP?
MY BOY-FRIEND CHRISTOPHE'S A MUSIC REPORTER FOR PHASER MAG-AZINE. WE WERE AT A SHOW. WE'D BOTH BEEN UP FOR DAYS ON A COKE BENDER. I ATTACKED A SECURITY GUARD WHEN SHE ASKED ME TO LEAVE THE VENUE
WOW. THAT'S REALLY HEAVY. WELL WHY DON'T YOU COME TO MUSIC THERAPY WITH ME? IT'S BETTER THAN WORK DETAIL

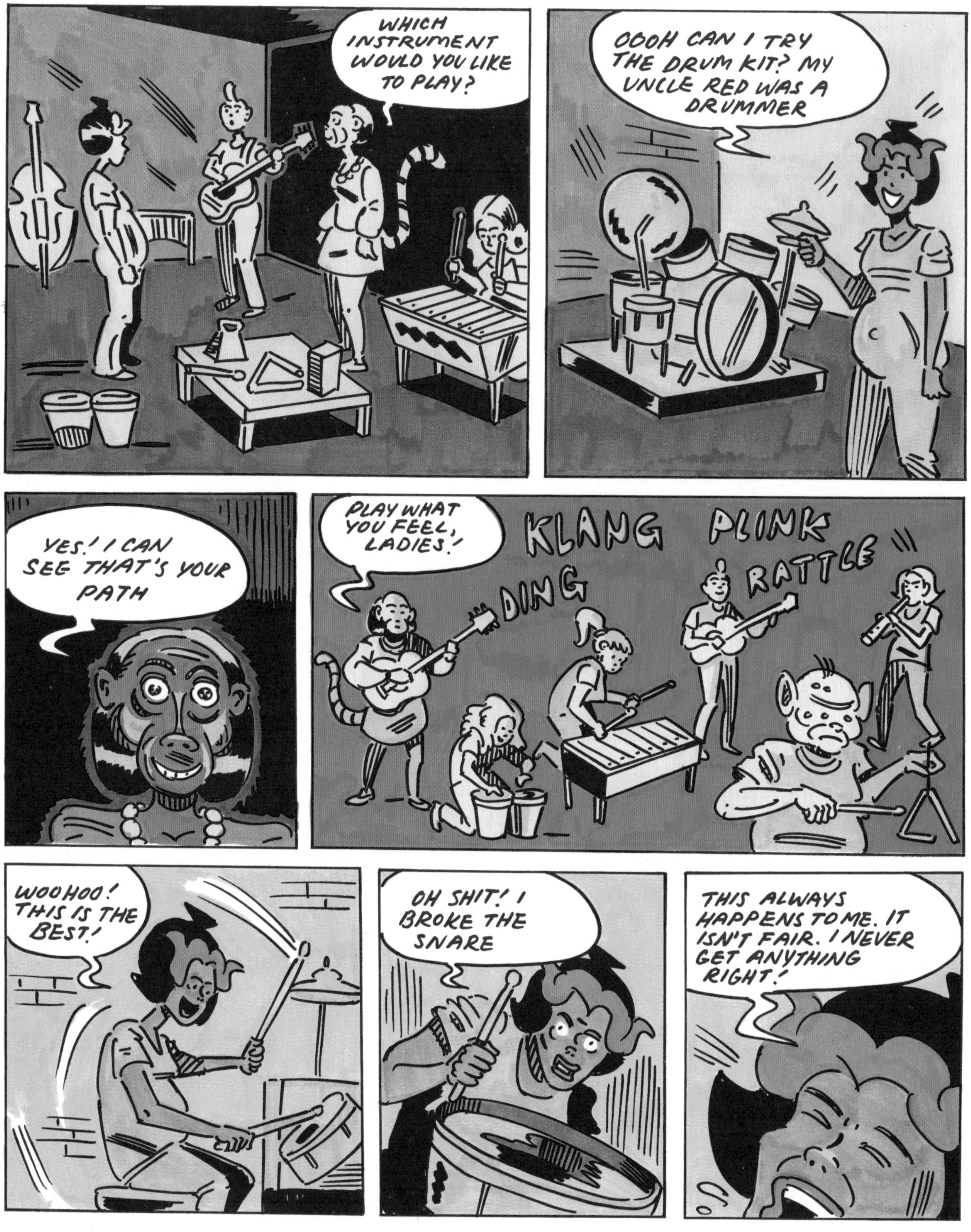
WHICH INSTRUMENT WOULD YOU LIKE TO PLAY?
OOOH CAN I TRY THE DRUM KIT? MY UNCLE RED WAS A DRUMMER
YES! I CAN SEE THAT'S YOUR PATH
PLAY WHAT YOU FEEL, LADIES!
KLANG
PLINK
DING
RATTLE
WOOHOO! THIS IS THE BEST!
OH SHIT! I BROKE THE SNARE
THIS ALWAYS HAPPENS TO ME. IT ISN'T FAIR. I NEVER GET ANYTHING RIGHT!

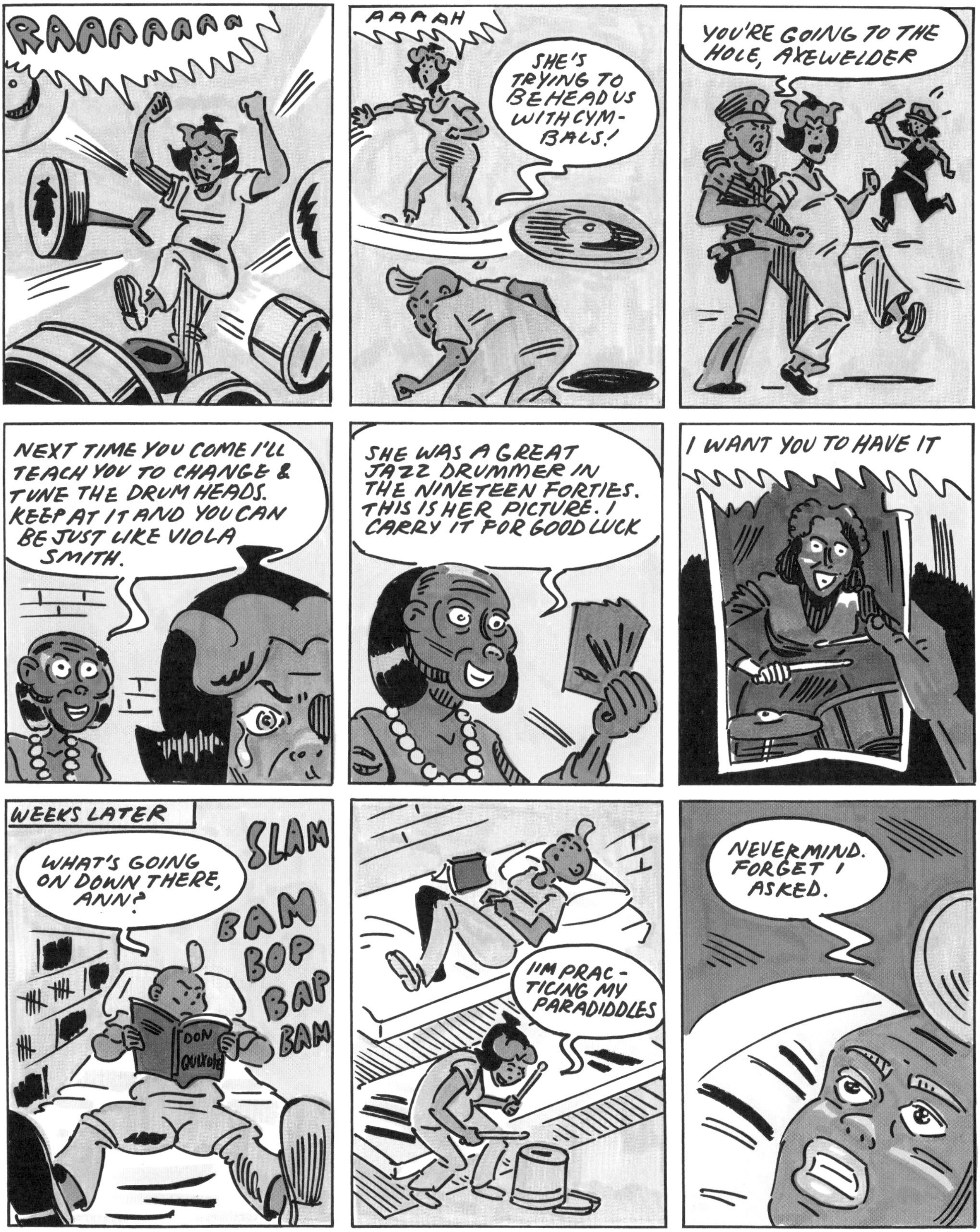

RAAAAAAA
AAAAH
SHE'S TRYING TO BEHEAD US WITH CYMBALS!
YOU'RE GOING TO THE HOLE, AXEWELDER
NEXT TIME YOU COME I'LL TEACH YOU TO CHANGE & TUNE THE DRUM HEADS. KEEP AT IT AND YOU CAN BE JUST LIKE VIOLA SMITH.
SHE WAS A GREAT JAZZ DRUMMER IN THE NINETEEN FORTIES. THIS IS HER PICTURE. I CARRY IT FOR GOOD LUCK
I WANT YOU TO HAVE IT
WEEKS LATER
WHAT'S GOING ON DOWN THERE, ANN?
SLAM
BAM
BOP
BAP
BAM
DON QUIXOTE
I'M PRACTICING MY PARADIDDLES
NEVERMIND. FORGET I ASKED.

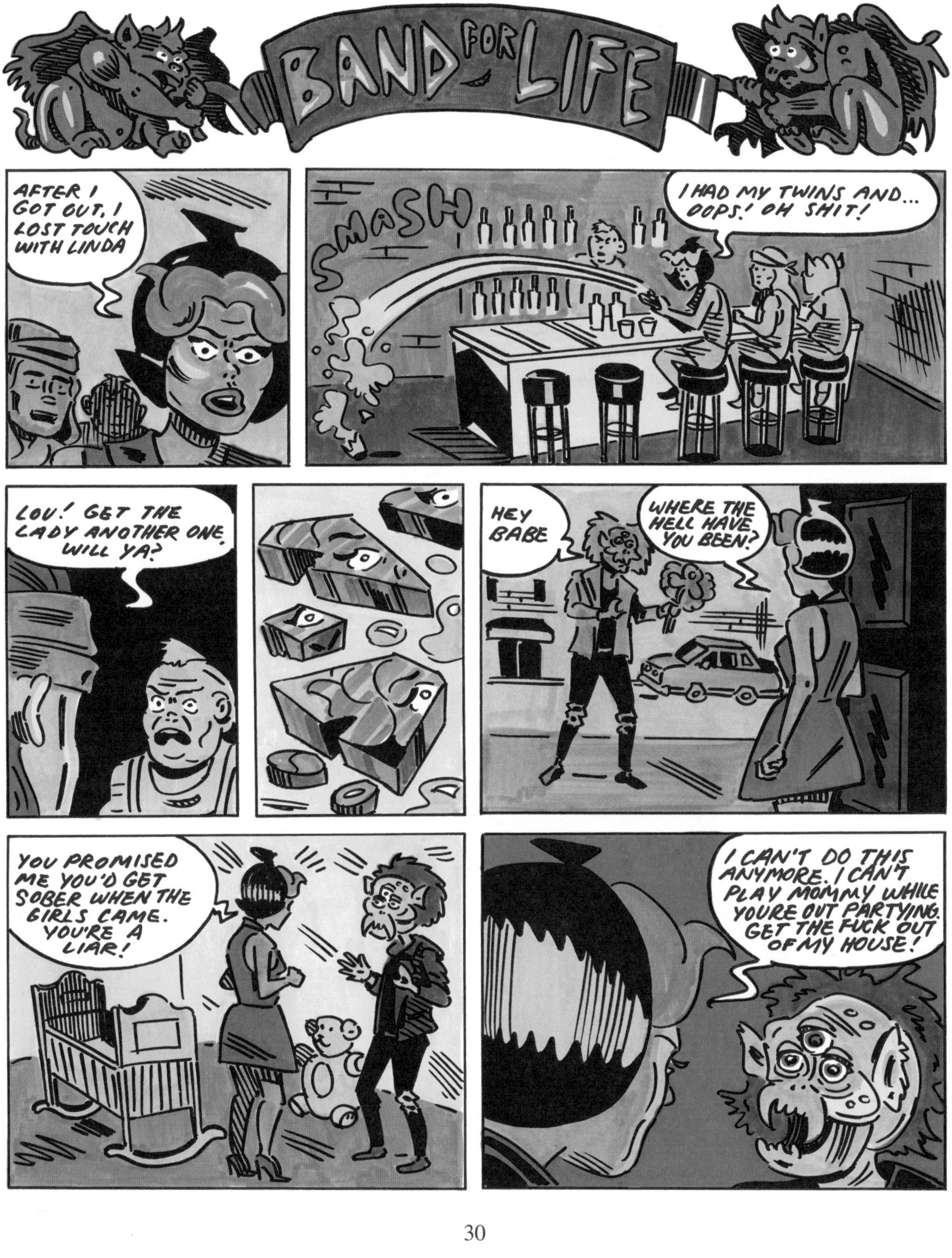
BAND FOR LIFE
AFTER I GOT OUT, I LOST TOUCH WITH LINDA
SMASH
I HAD MY TWINS AND... OOPS! OH SHIT!
LOU! GET THE LADY ANOTHER ONE WILL YA?
HEY BABE
WHERE THE HELL HAVE YOU BEEN?
YOU PROMISED ME YOU'D GET SOBER WHEN THE GIRLS CAME. YOU'RE A LIAR!
I CAN'T DO THIS ANYMORE. I CAN'T PLAY MOMMY WHILE YOURE OUT PARTYING. GET THE FUCK OUT OF MY HOUSE!

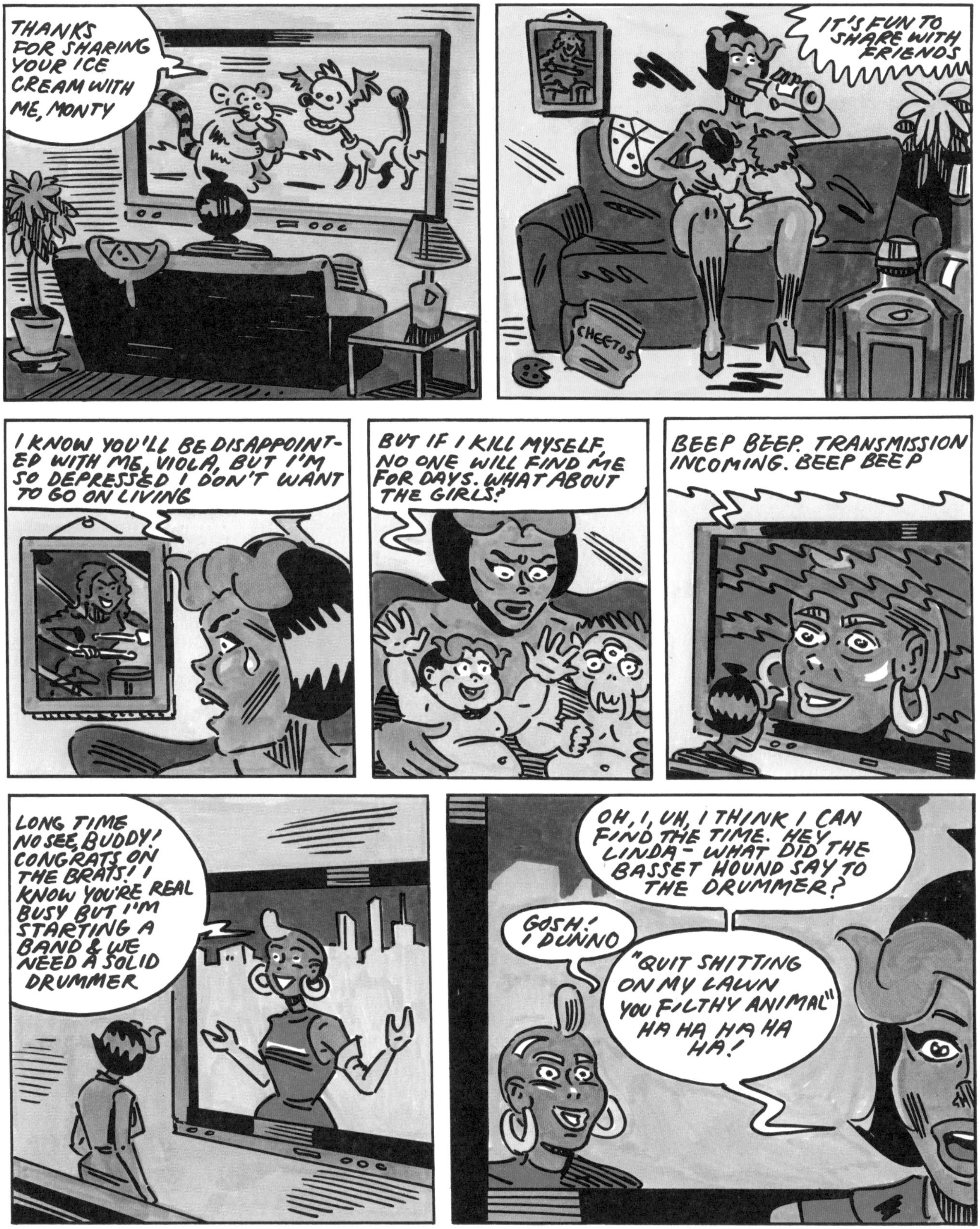
THANKS FOR SHARING YOUR ICE CREAM WITH ME, MONTY
IT'S FUN TO SHARE WITH FRIENDS
CHEETOS
I KNOW YOU'LL BE DISAPPOINTED WITH ME, VIOLA, BUT I'M SO DEPRESSED I DON'T WANT TO GO ON LIVING
BUT IF I KILL MYSELF, NO ONE WILL FIND ME FOR DAYS. WHAT ABOUT THE GIRLS?
BEEP BEEP. TRANSMISSION INCOMING. BEEP BEEP
LONG TIME NO SEE, BUDDY! CONGRATS ON THE BRATS! I KNOW YOU'RE REAL BUSY BUT I'M STARTING A BAND & WE NEED A SOLID DRUMMER
OH, I, UH, I THINK I CAN FIND THE TIME. HEY LINDA- WHAT DID THE BASSET HOUND SAY TO THE DRUMMER?
GOSH! I DUNNO
"QUIT SHITTING ON MY LAWN YOU FILTHY ANIMAL" HA HA HA HA HA!

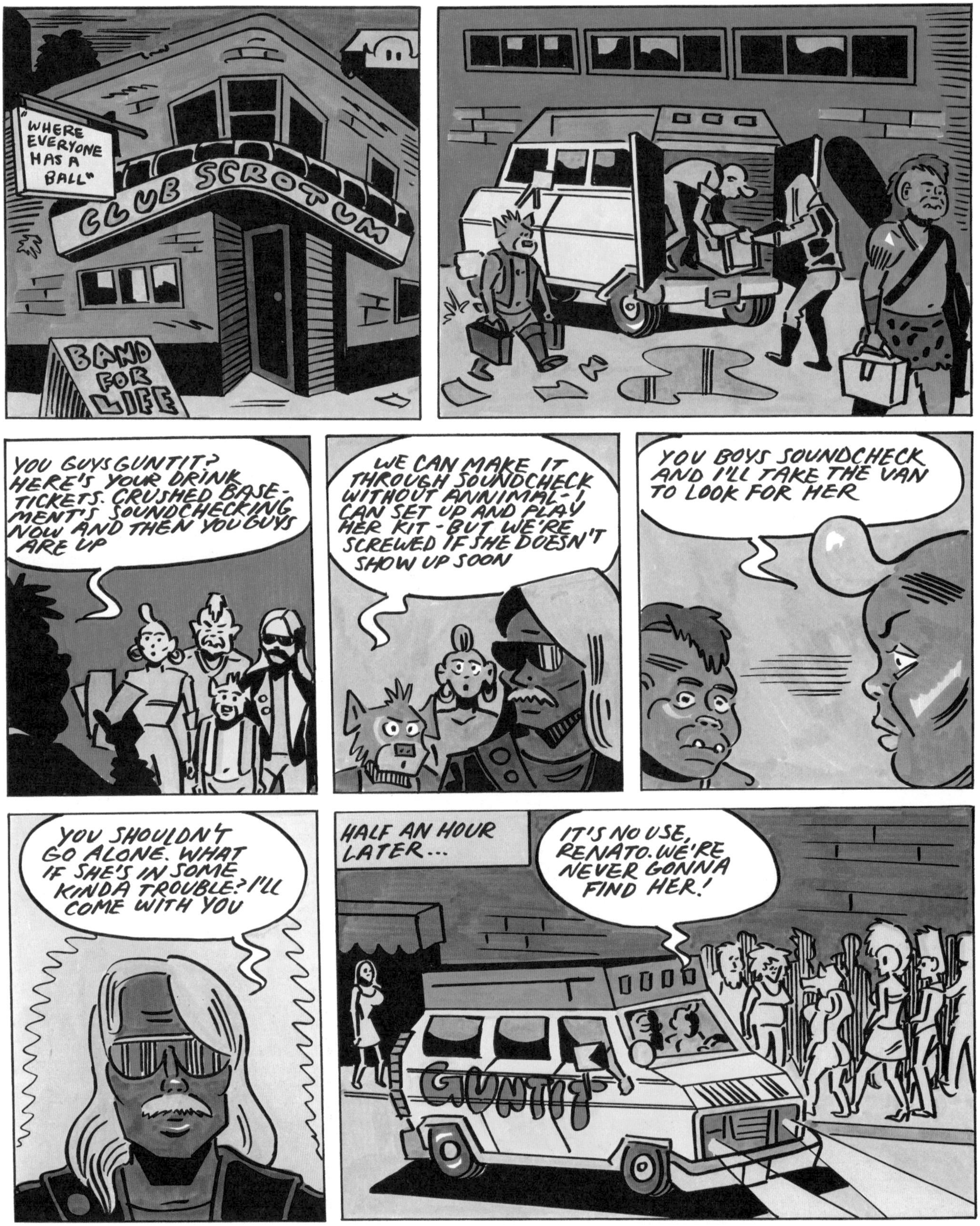
"WHERE EVERYONE HAS A BALL"
CLUB SCROTUM
BAND FOR LIFE
YOU GUYS GUNTIT? HERE'S YOUR DRINK TICKETS. CRUSHED BASEMENT'S SOUNDCHECKING NOW AND THEN YOU GUYS ARE UP
WE CAN MAKE IT THROUGH SOUNDCHECK WITHOUT ANNIMAL- I CAN SET UP AND PLAY HER KIT - BUT WE'RE SCREWED IF SHE DOESN'T SHOW UP SOON
YOU BOYS SOUNDCHECK AND I'LL TAKE THE VAN TO LOOK FOR HER
YOU SHOULDN'T GO ALONE. WHAT IF SHE'S IN SOME KINDA TROUBLE? I'LL COME WITH YOU
HALF AN HOUR LATER...
IT'S NO USE, RENATO. WE'RE NEVER GONNA FIND HER!
GUNTIT

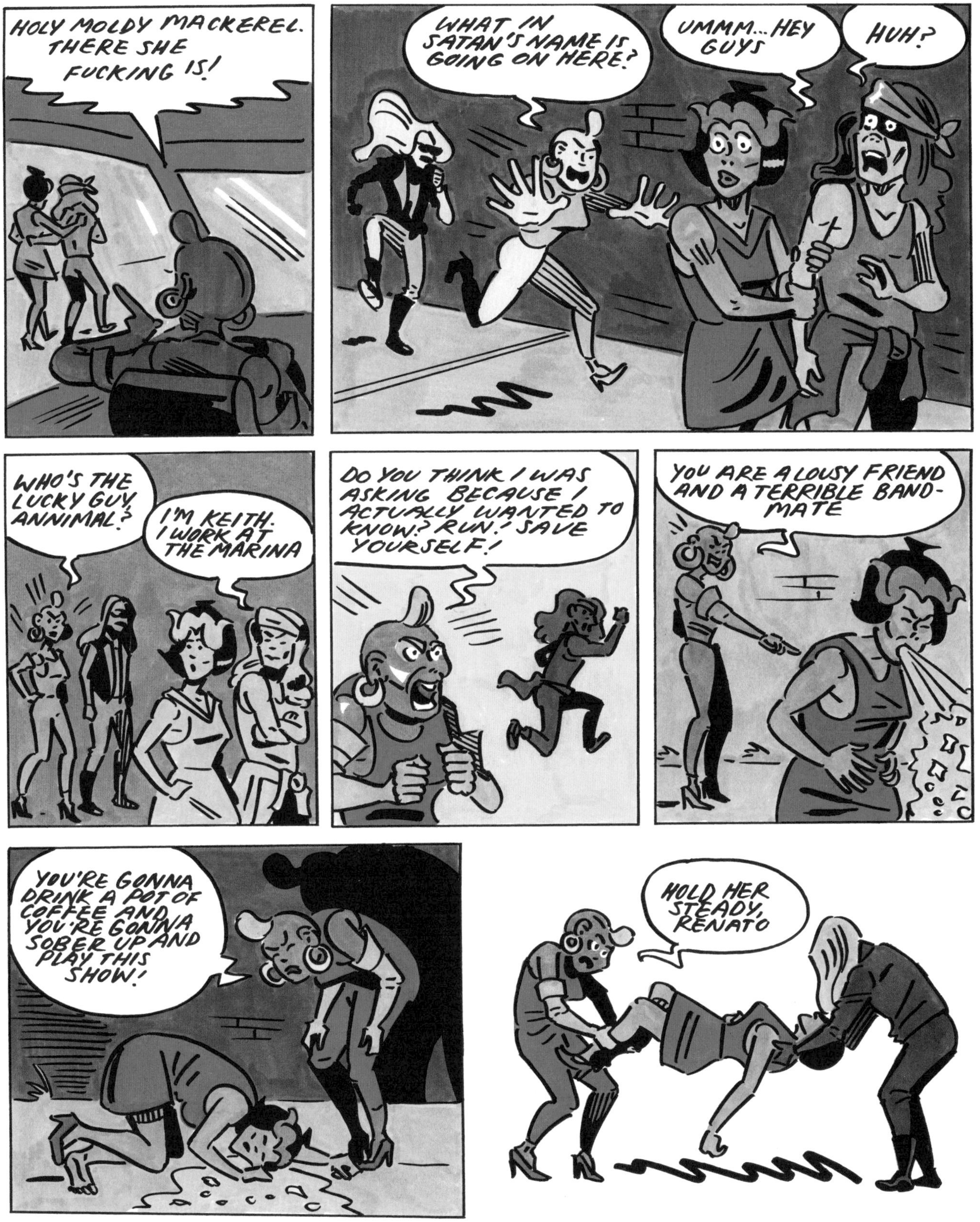
HOLY MOLDY MACKEREL. THERE SHE FUCKING IS!
WHAT IN SATAN'S NAME IS GOING ON HERE?
UMMM... HEY GUYS
HUH?
WHO'S THE LUCKY GUY, ANNIMAL?
I'M KEITH. I WORK AT THE MARINA
DO YOU THINK I WAS ASKING BECAUSE I ACTUALLY WANTED TO KNOW? RUN! SAVE YOURSELF!
YOU ARE A LOUSY FRIEND AND A TERRIBLE BAND-MATE
YOU'RE GONNA DRINK A POT OF COFFEE AND YOU'RE GONNA SOBER UP AND PLAY THIS SHOW!
HOLD HER STEADY, RENATO

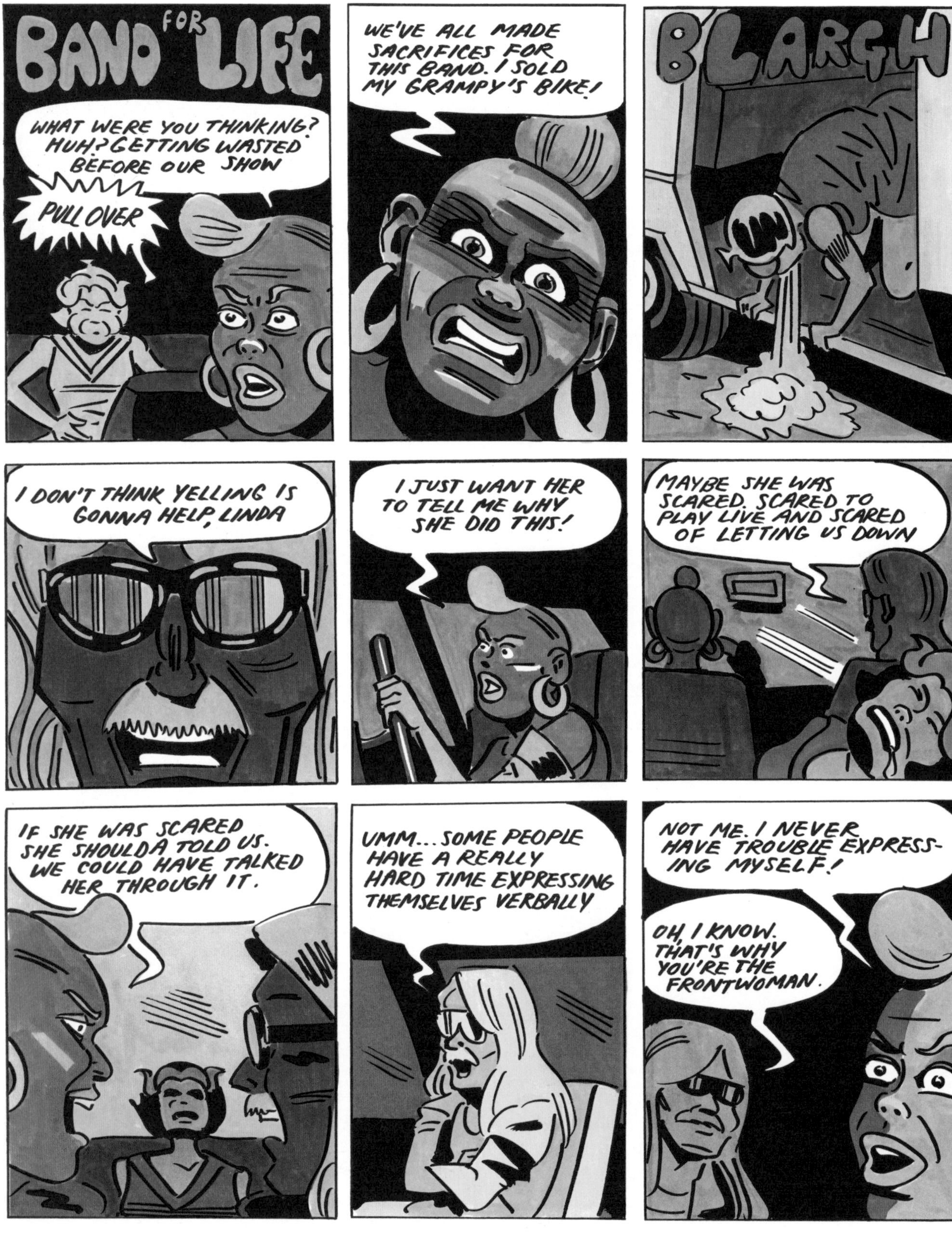
BAND FOR LIFE
WHAT WERE YOU THINKING? HUH? GETTING WASTED BEFORE OUR SHOW
PULL OVER
WE'VE ALL MADE SACRIFICES FOR THIS BAND. I SOLD MY GRAMPY'S BIKE!
BLARGH
I DON'T THINK YELLING IS GONNA HELP, LINDA
I JUST WANT HER TO TELL ME WHY SHE DID THIS!
MAYBE SHE WAS SCARED. SCARED TO PLAY LIVE AND SCARED OF LETTING US DOWN
IF SHE WAS SCARED SHE SHOULDA TOLD US. WE COULD HAVE TALKED HER THROUGH IT.
UMM... SOME PEOPLE HAVE A REALLY HARD TIME EXPRESSING THEMSELVES VERBALLY
NOT ME. I NEVER HAVE TROUBLE EXPRESS-ING MYSELF!
OH, I KNOW. THAT'S WHY YOU'RE THE FRONTWOMAN.

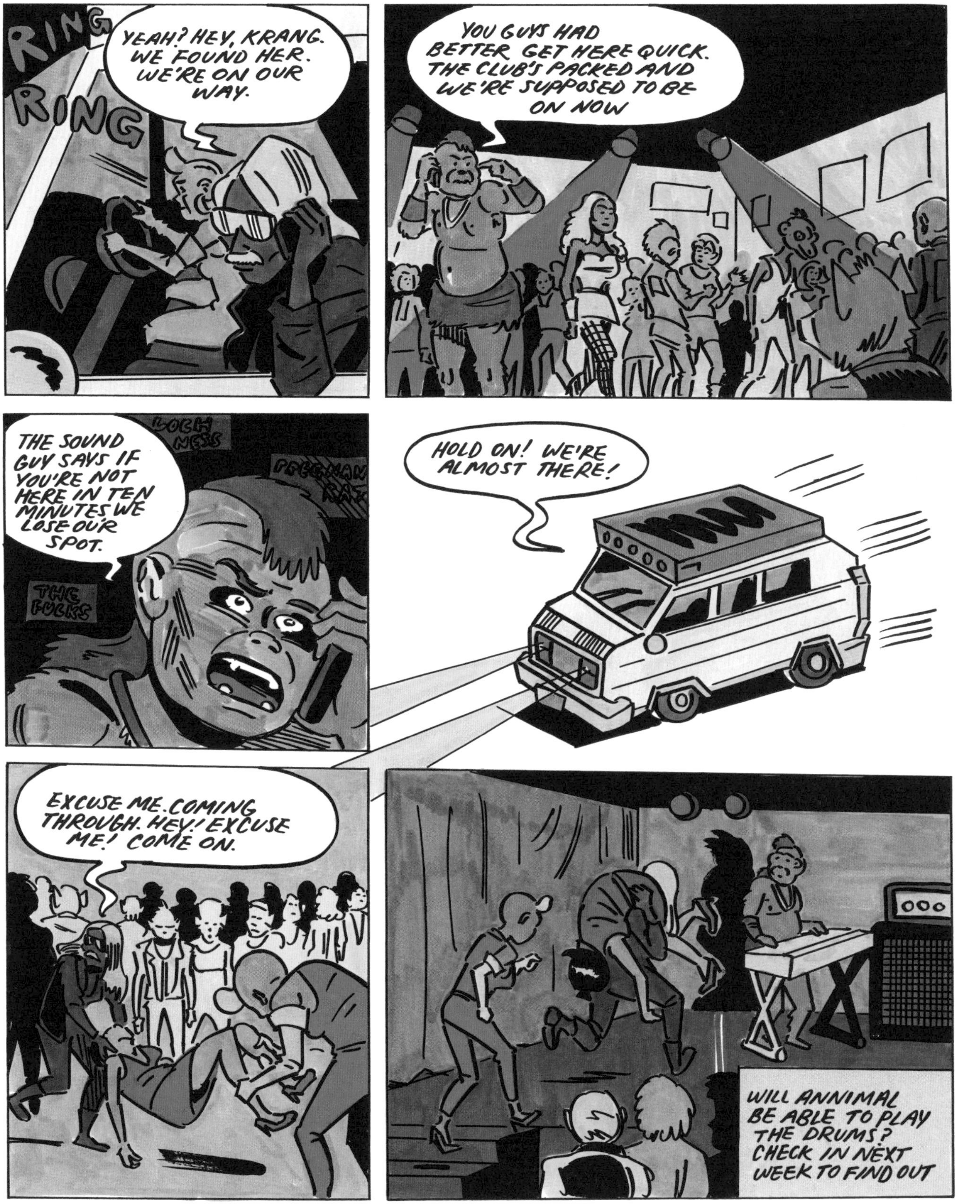
RING
RING
YEAH? HEY, KRANG. WE FOUND HER. WE'RE ON OUR WAY.
YOU GUYS HAD BETTER GET HERE QUICK. THE CLUB'S PACKED AND WE'RE SUPPOSED TO BE ON NOW
LOCH NESS
THE FUCKS
THE SOUND GUY SAYS IF YOU'RE NOT HERE IN TEN MINUTES WE LOSE OUR SPOT.
HOLD ON! WE'RE ALMOST THERE!
EXCUSE ME. COMING THROUGH. HEY! EXCUSE ME! COME ON.
WILL ANNIMAL BE ABLE TO PLAY THE DRUMS? CHECK IN NEXT WEEK TO FIND OUT

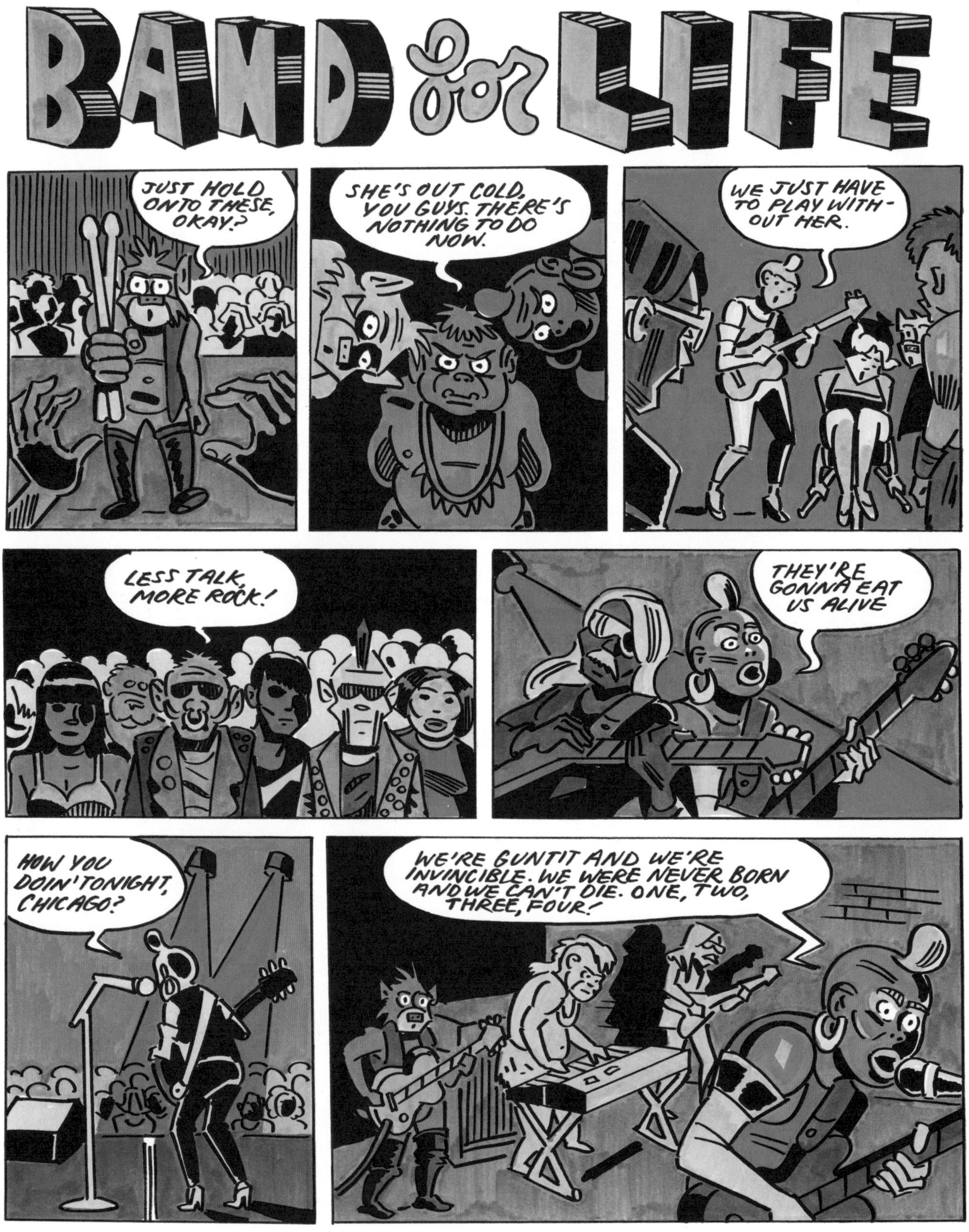
BAND for LIFE
JUST HOLD ONTO THESE, OKAY?
SHE'S OUT COLD, YOU GUYS. THERE'S NOTHING TO DO NOW.
WE JUST HAVE TO PLAY WITH-OUT HER.
LESS TALK, MORE ROCK!
THEY'RE GONNA EAT US ALIVE
HOW YOU DOIN' TONIGHT, CHICAGO?
WE'RE GUNTIT AND WE'RE INVINCIBLE. WE WERE NEVER BORN AND WE CAN'T DIE. ONE, TWO, THREE, FOUR!

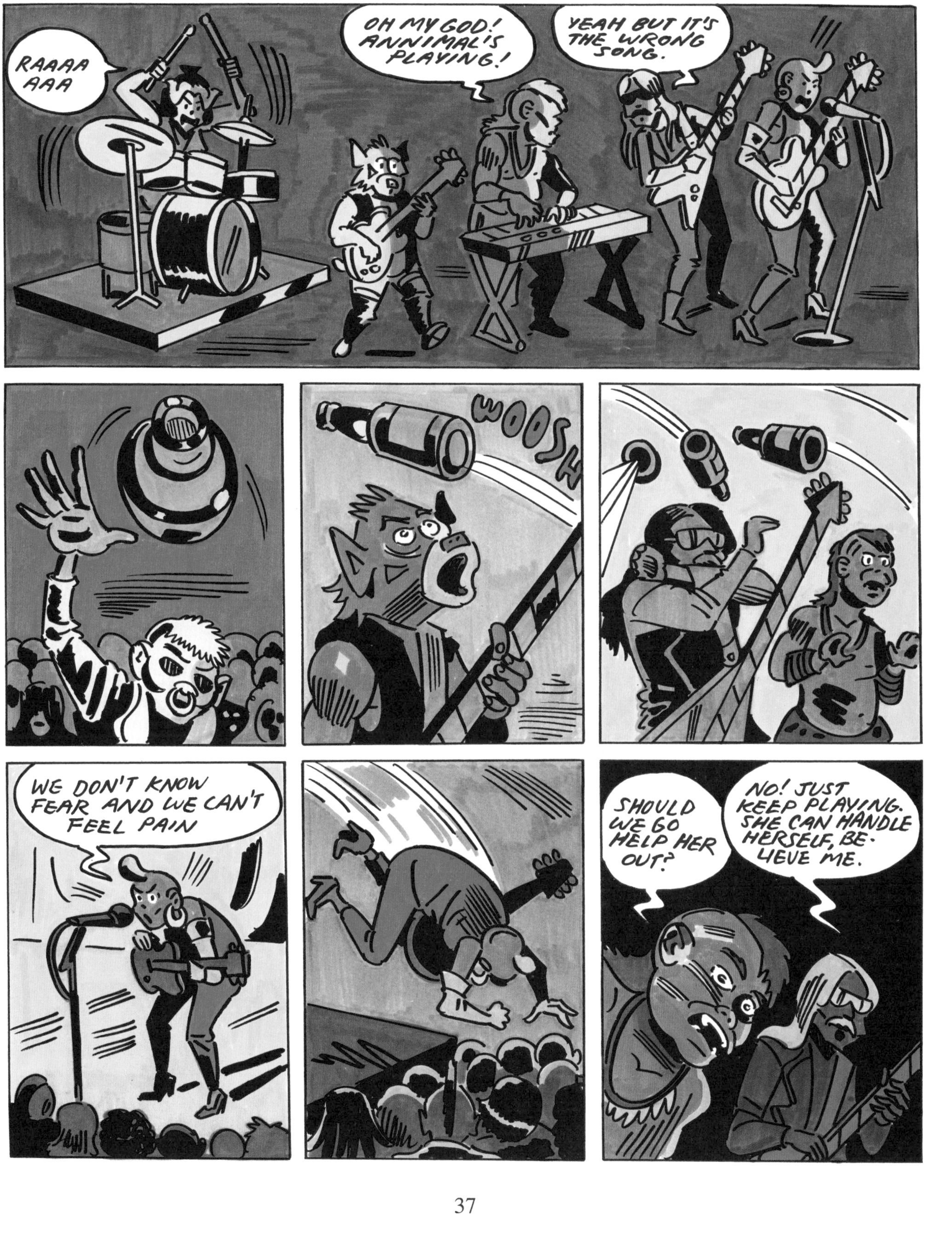
RAAAA AAA
OH MY GOD! ANNIMAL'S PLAYING!
YEAH BUT IT'S THE WRONG SONG.
WOOSH
WE DON'T KNOW FEAR AND WE CAN'T FEEL PAIN
SHOULD WE GO HELP HER OUT?
NO! JUST KEEP PLAYING. SHE CAN HANDLE HERSELF, BE-LIEVE ME.

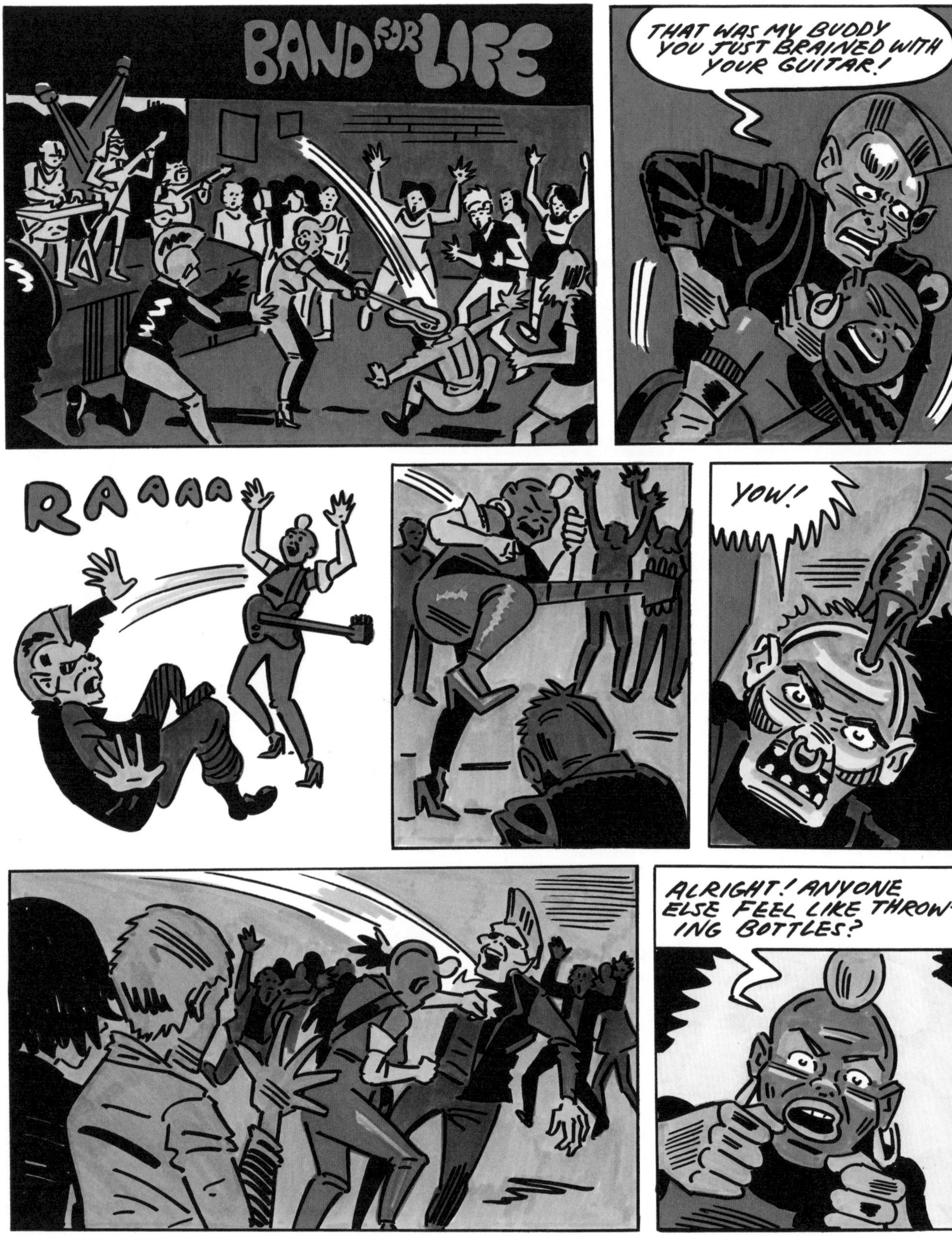

BAND FOR LIFE
THAT WAS MY BUDDY YOU JUST BRAINED WITH YOUR GUITAR!
RAAAA
YOW!
ALRIGHT! ANYONE ELSE FEEL LIKE THROWING BOTTLES?

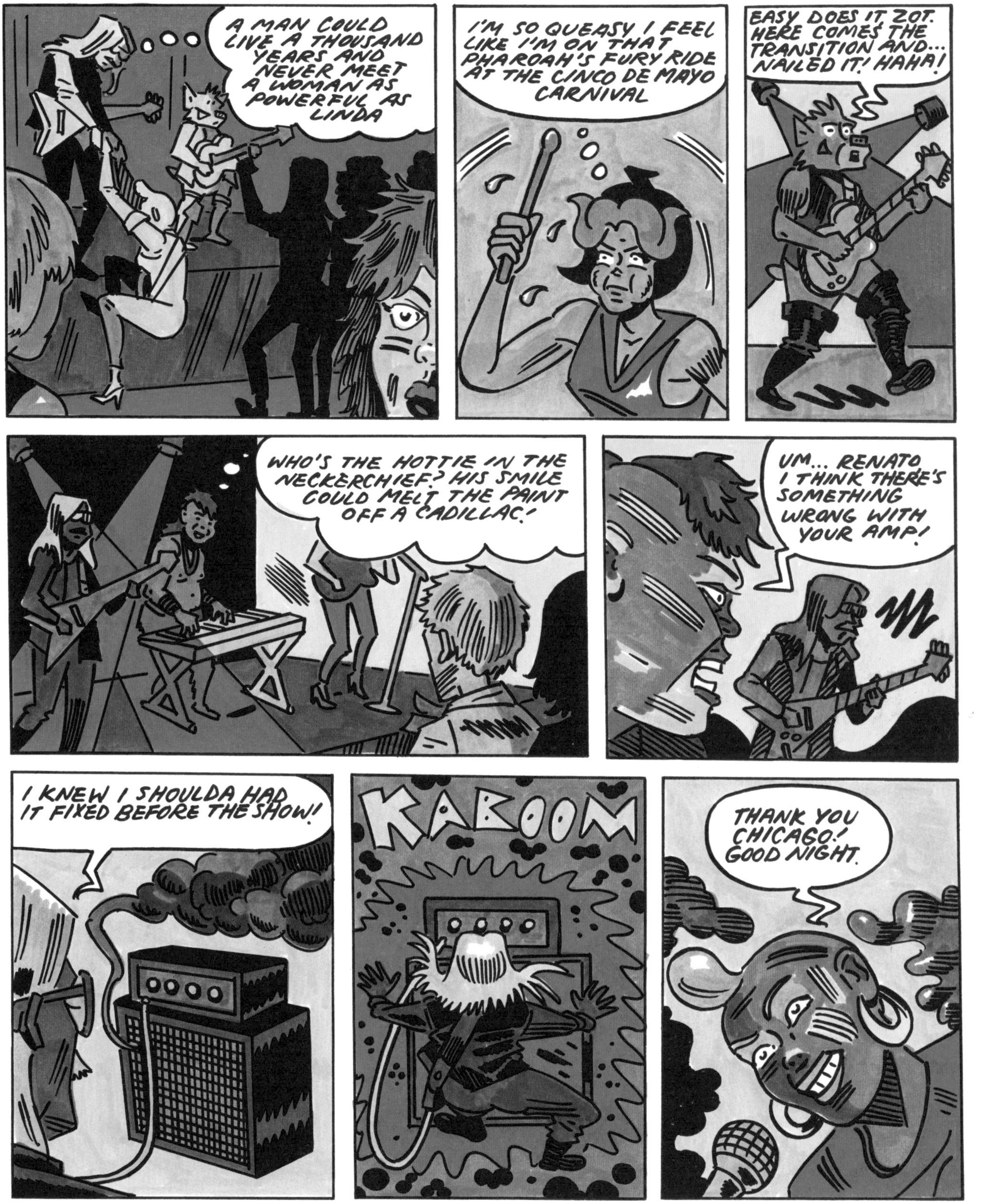
A MAN COULD LIVE A THOUSAND YEARS AND NEVER MEET A WOMAN AS POWERFUL AS LINDA
I'M SO QUEASY I FEEL LIKE I'M ON THAT PHAROAH'S FURY RIDE AT THE CINCO DE MAYO CARNIVAL
EASY DOES IT, ZOT. HERE COMES THE TRANSITION AND... NAILED IT! HAHA!
WHO'S THE HOTTIE IN THE NECKERCHIEF? HIS SMILE COULD MELT THE PAINT OFF A CADILLAC!
UM... RENATO I THINK THERE'S SOMETHING WRONG WITH YOUR AMP!
I KNEW I SHOULDA HAD IT FIXED BEFORE THE SHOW!
KABOOM
THANK YOU CHICAGO! GOOD NIGHT.

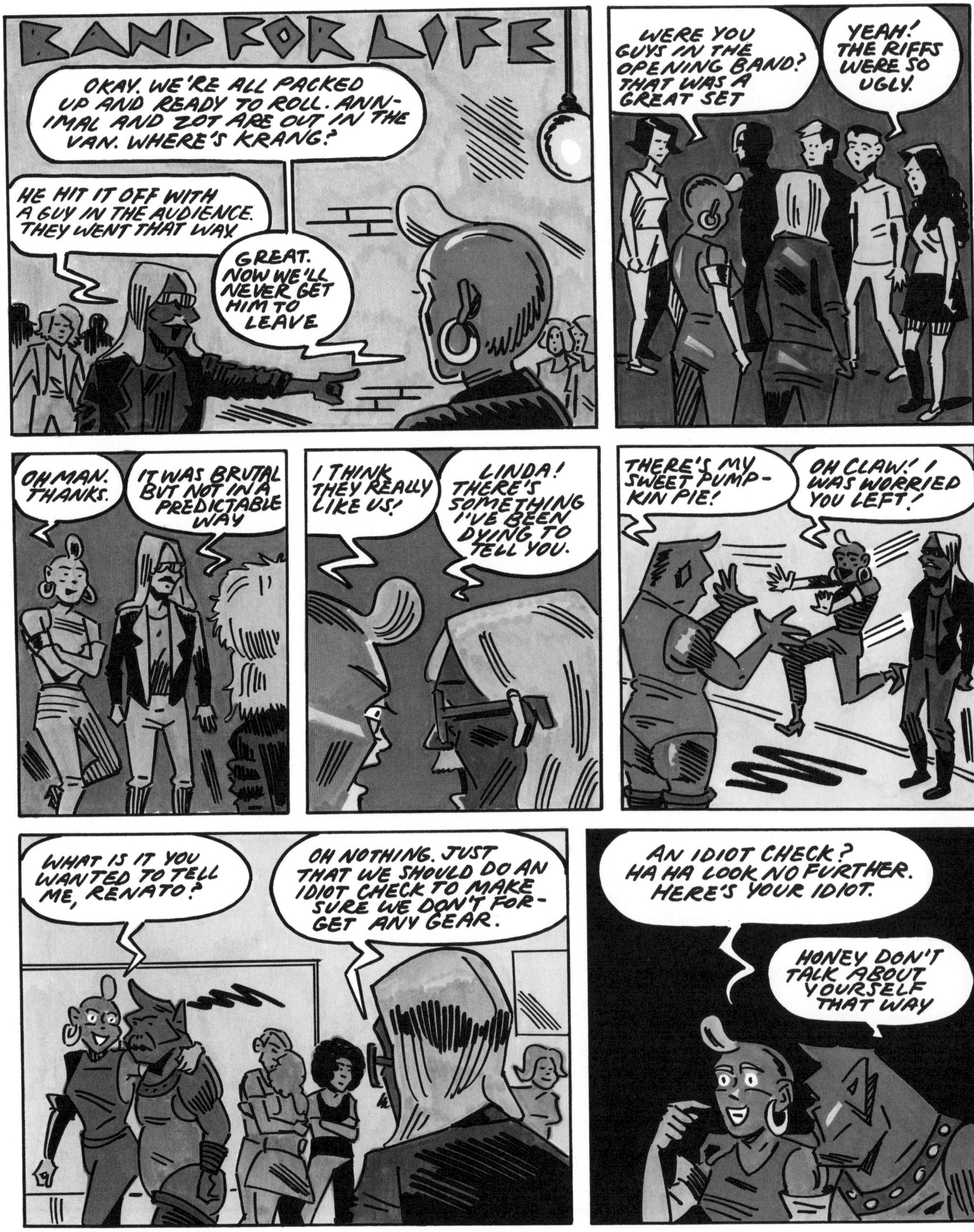
BAND FOR LIFE
OKAY. WE'RE ALL PACKED UP AND READY TO ROLL. ANNIMAL AND ZOT ARE OUT IN THE VAN. WHERE'S KRANG?
HE HIT IT OFF WITH A GUY IN THE AUDIENCE. THEY WENT THAT WAY.
GREAT. NOW WE'LL NEVER GET HIM TO LEAVE
WERE YOU GUYS IN THE OPENING BAND? THAT WAS A GREAT SET
YEAH! THE RIFFS WERE SO UGLY.
OH MAN. THANKS.
IT WAS BRUTAL BUT NOT IN A PREDICTABLE WAY
I THINK THEY REALLY LIKE US!
LINDA! THERE'S SOMETHING I'VE BEEN DYING TO TELL YOU.
THERE'S MY SWEET PUMPKIN PIE!
OH CLAW! I WAS WORRIED YOU LEFT!
WHAT IS IT YOU WANTED TO TELL ME, RENATO?
OH NOTHING. JUST THAT WE SHOULD DO AN IDIOT CHECK TO MAKE SURE WE DON'T FORGET ANY GEAR.
AN IDIOT CHECK? HA HA LOOK NO FURTHER. HERE'S YOUR IDIOT.
HONEY DON'T TALK ABOUT YOURSELF THAT WAY

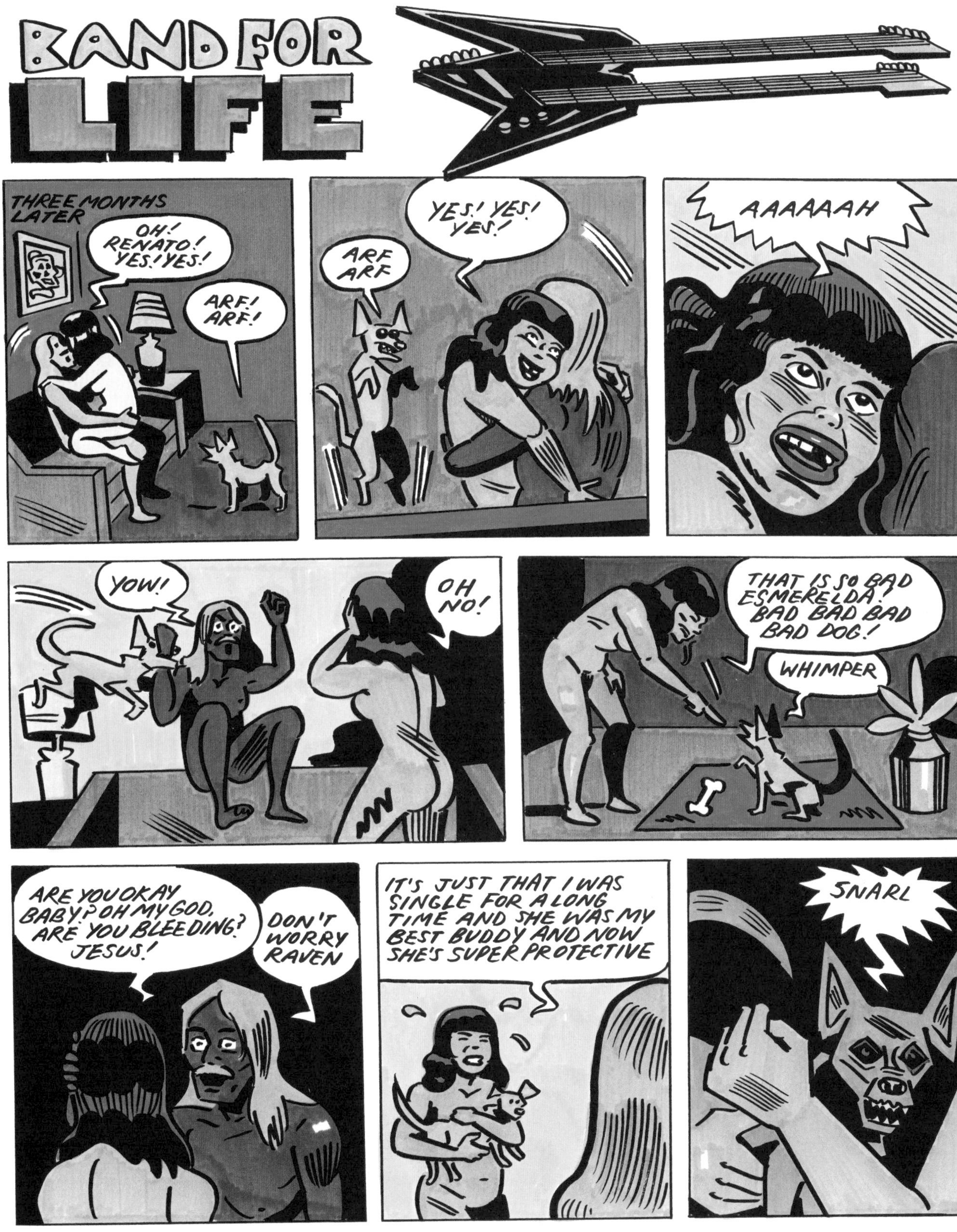
BAND FOR LIFE
THREE MONTHS LATER
OH! RENATO! YES! YES!
ARF! ARF!
ARF ARF
YES! YES! YES!
AAAAAAH
YOW!
OH NO!
THAT IS SO BAD ESMERELDA! BAD BAD BAD BAD DOG!
WHIMPER
ARE YOU OKAY BABY? OH MY GOD, ARE YOU BLEEDING? JESUS!
DON'T WORRY RAVEN
IT'S JUST THAT I WAS SINGLE FOR A LONG TIME AND SHE WAS MY BEST BUDDY AND NOW SHE'S SUPER PROTECTIVE
SNARL

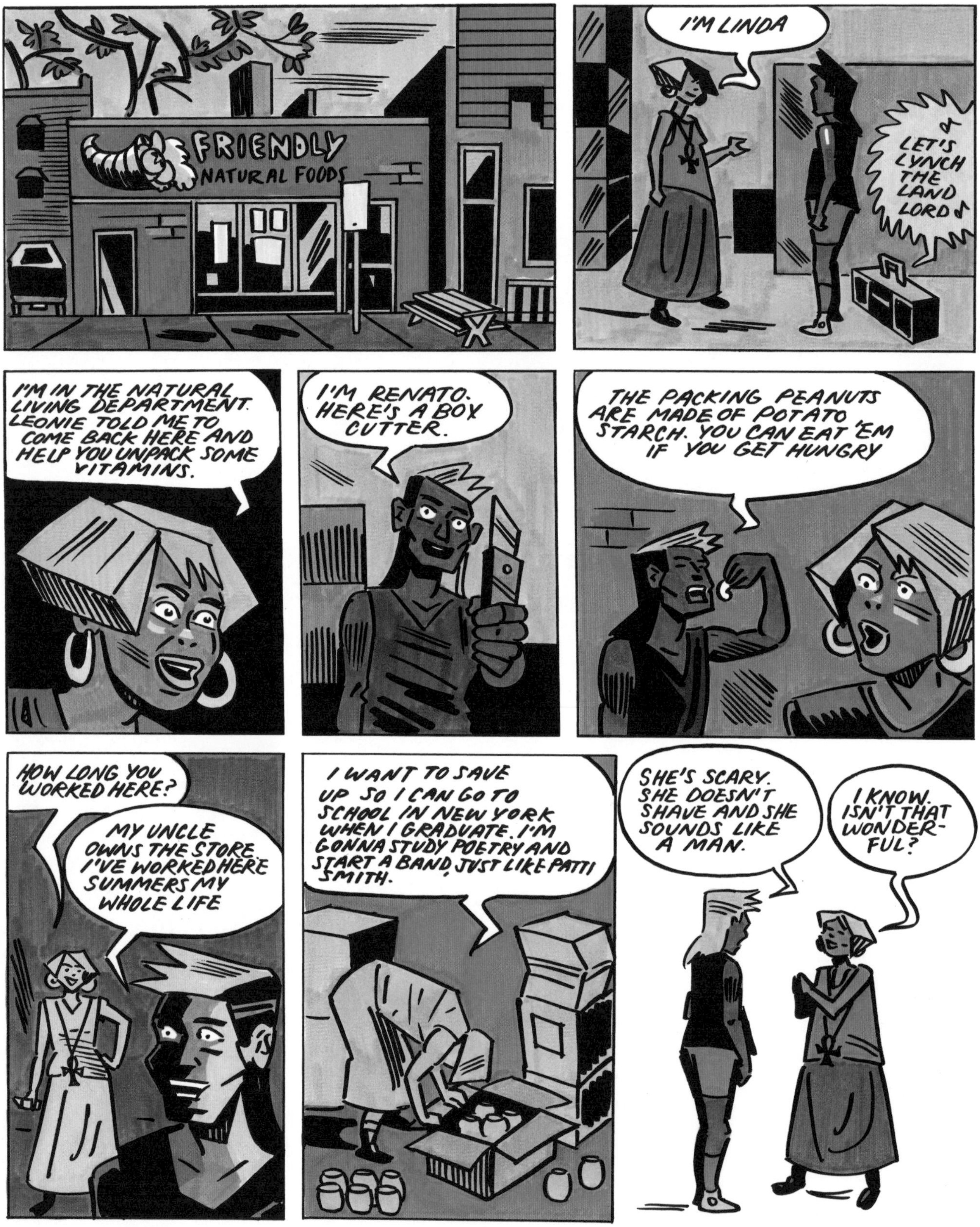
FRIENDLY NATURAL FOODS
I'M LINDA
& LET'S LYNCH THE LAND LORD ♪
I'M IN THE NATURAL LIVING DEPARTMENT. LEONIE TOLD ME TO COME BACK HERE AND HELP YOU UNPACK SOME VITAMINS.
I'M RENATO. HERE'S A BOX CUTTER.
THE PACKING PEANUTS ARE MADE OF POTATO STARCH. YOU CAN EAT 'EM IF YOU GET HUNGRY
HOW LONG YOU WORKED HERE?
MY UNCLE OWNS THE STORE. I'VE WORKED HERE SUMMERS MY WHOLE LIFE
I WANT TO SAVE UP SO I CAN GO TO SCHOOL IN NEW YORK WHEN I GRADUATE. I'M GONNA STUDY POETRY AND START A BAND, JUST LIKE PATTI SMITH.
SHE'S SCARY. SHE DOESN'T SHAVE AND SHE SOUNDS LIKE A MAN.
I KNOW. ISN'T THAT WONDER-FUL?

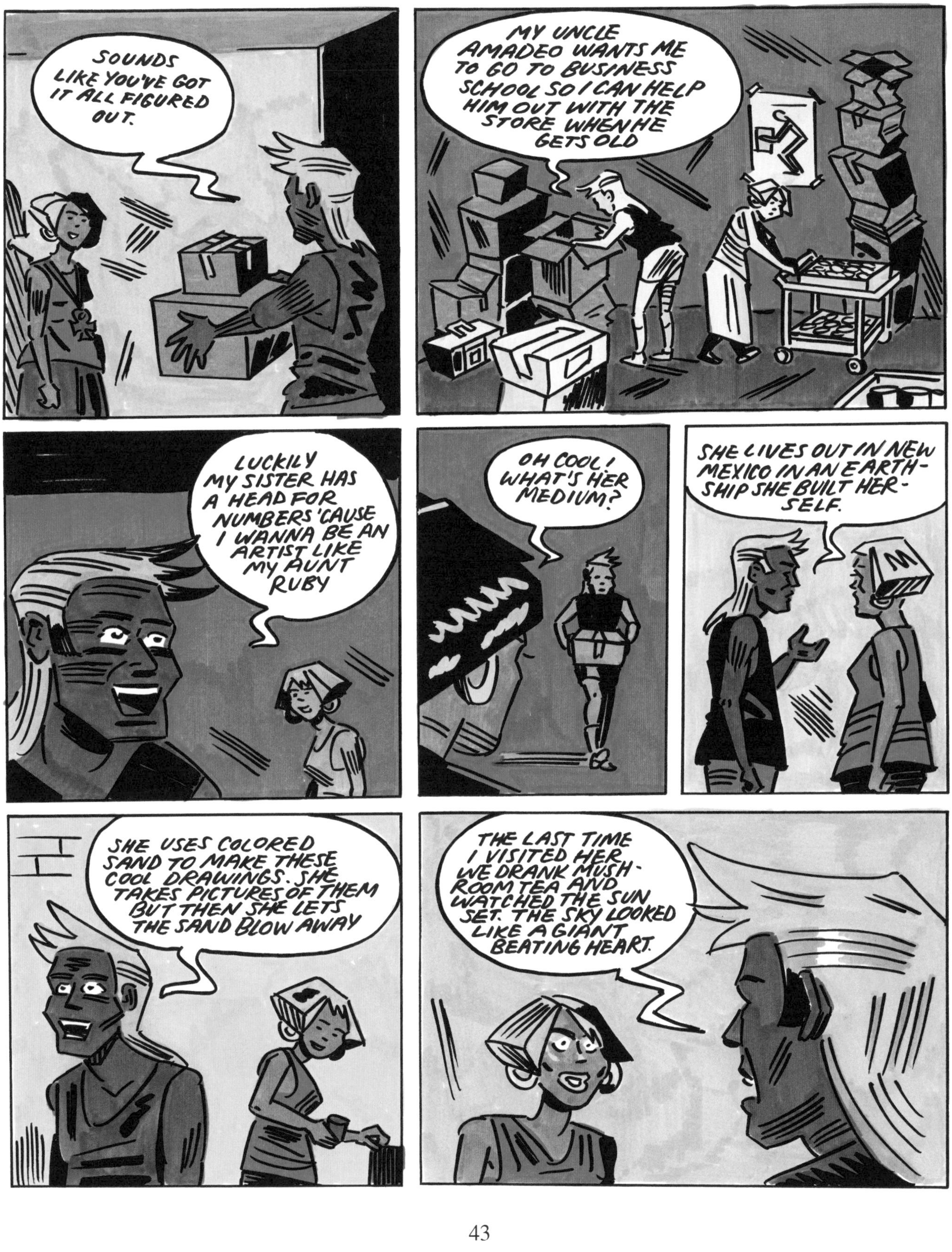
SOUNDS LIKE YOU'VE GOT IT ALL FIGURED OUT.
MY UNCLE AMADEO WANTS ME TO GO TO BUSINESS SCHOOL SO I CAN HELP HIM OUT WITH THE STORE WHEN HE GETS OLD
LUCKILY MY SISTER HAS A HEAD FOR NUMBERS 'CAUSE I WANNA BE AN ARTIST LIKE MY AUNT RUBY
OH COOL! WHAT'S HER MEDIUM?
SHE LIVES OUT IN NEW MEXICO IN AN EARTH-SHIP SHE BUILT HER-SELF.
SHE USES COLORED SAND TO MAKE THESE COOL DRAWINGS. SHE TAKES PICTURES OF THEM BUT THEN SHE LETS THE SAND BLOW AWAY
THE LAST TIME I VISITED HER WE DRANK MUSH-ROOM TEA AND WATCHED THE SUN SET. THE SKY LOOKED LIKE A GIANT BEATING HEART.

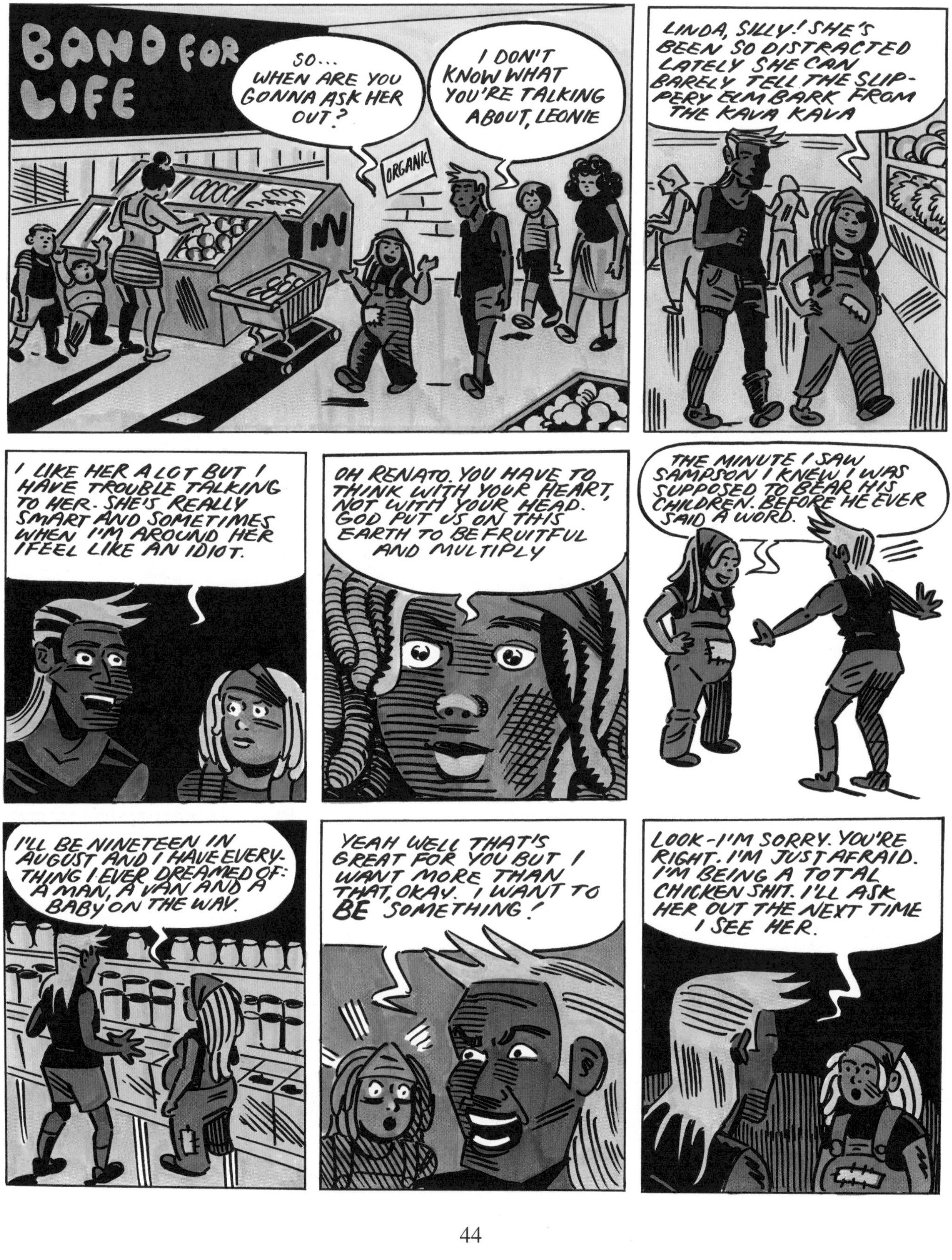
BAND FOR LIFE
SO... WHEN ARE YOU GONNA ASK HER OUT?
ORGANIC
I DON'T KNOW WHAT YOU'RE TALKING ABOUT, LEONIE
LINDA, SILLY! SHE'S BEEN SO DISTRACTED LATELY SHE CAN BARELY TELL THE SLIPPERY ELM BARK FROM THE KAVA KAVA
I LIKE HER A LOT BUT I HAVE TROUBLE TALKING TO HER. SHE'S REALLY SMART AND SOMETIMES WHEN I'M AROUND HER I FEEL LIKE AN IDIOT.
OH RENATO. YOU HAVE TO THINK WITH YOUR HEART, NOT WITH YOUR HEAD. GOD PUT US ON THIS EARTH TO BE FRUITFUL AND MULTIPLY
THE MINUTE I SAW SAMPSON I KNEW I WAS SUPPOSED TO BEAR HIS CHILDREN. BEFORE HE EVER SAID A WORD.
I'LL BE NINETEEN IN AUGUST AND I HAVE EVERYTHING I EVER DREAMED OF: A MAN, A VAN AND A BABY ON THE WAY.
YEAH WELL THAT'S GREAT FOR YOU BUT I WANT MORE THAN THAT, OKAY. I WANT TO BE SOMETHING!
LOOK - I'M SORRY. YOU'RE RIGHT. I'M JUST AFRAID. I'M BEING A TOTAL CHICKEN SHIT. I'LL ASK HER OUT THE NEXT TIME I SEE HER.

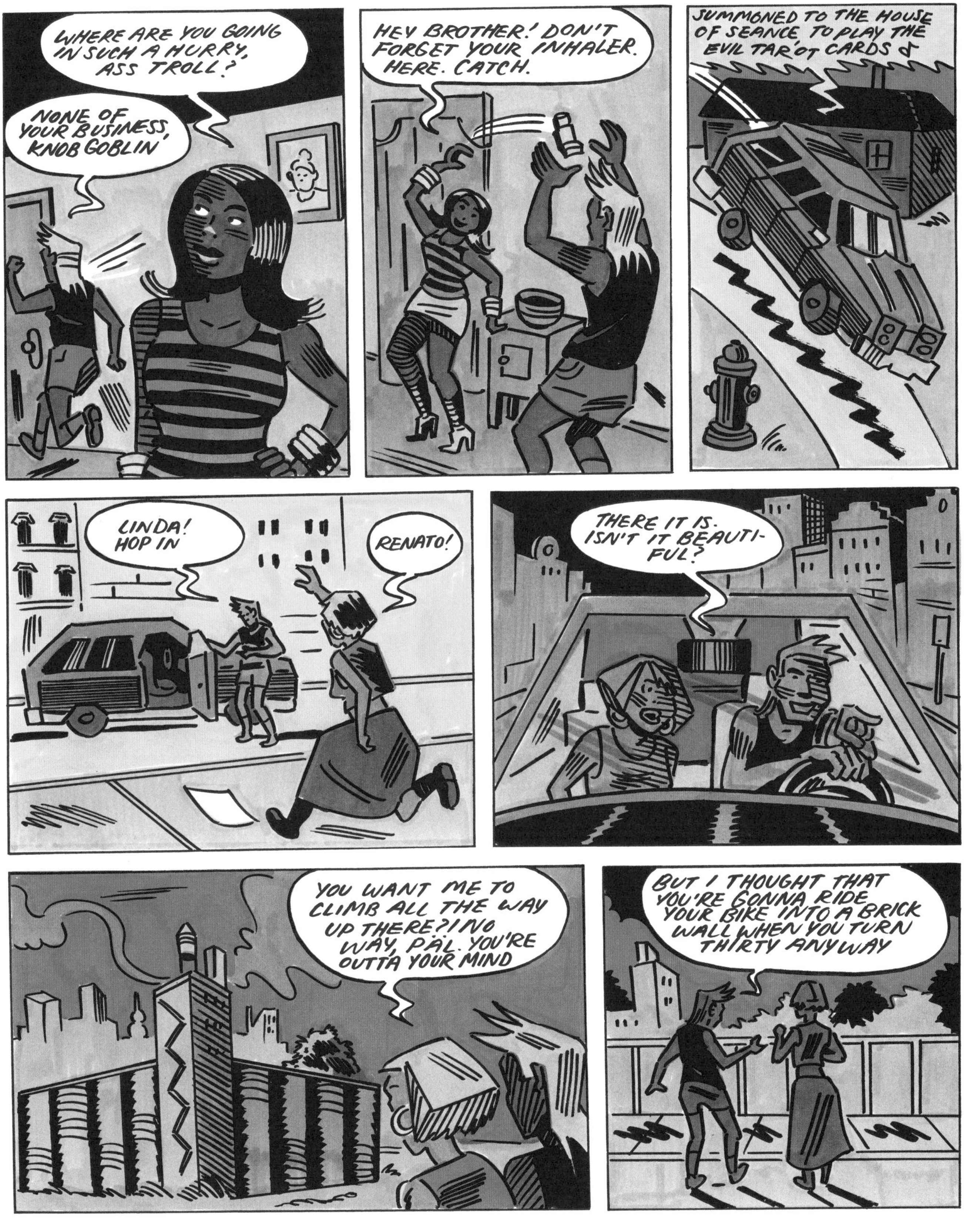

WHERE ARE YOU GOING IN SUCH A HURRY, ASS TROLL?
NONE OF YOUR BUSINESS, KNOB GOBLIN
HEY BROTHER! DON'T FORGET YOUR INHALER. HERE. CATCH.
SUMMONED TO THE HOUSE OF SEANCE TO PLAY THE EVIL TAROT CARDS ♪
LINDA! HOP IN
RENATO!
THERE IT IS. ISN'T IT BEAUTI-FUL?
YOU WANT ME TO CLIMB ALL THE WAY UP THERE?! NO WAY, PAL. YOU'RE OUTTA YOUR MIND
BUT I THOUGHT THAT YOU'RE GONNA RIDE YOUR BIKE INTO A BRICK WALL WHEN YOU TURN THIRTY ANYWAY

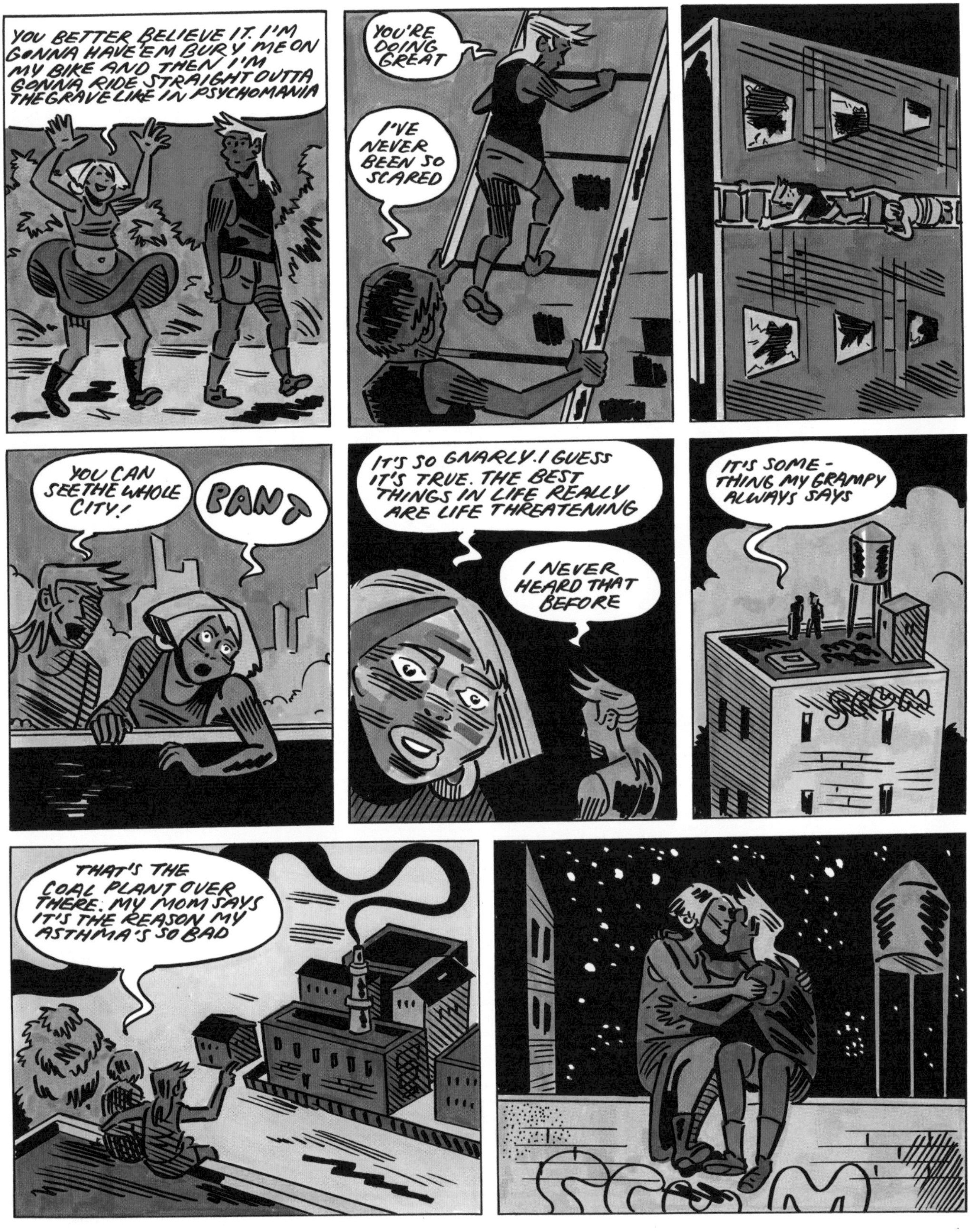
YOU BETTER BELIEVE IT. I'M GONNA HAVE 'EM BURY ME ON MY BIKE AND THEN I'M GONNA RIDE STRAIGHT OUTTA THE GRAVE LIKE IN PSYCHOMANIA
YOU'RE DOING GREAT
I'VE NEVER BEEN SO SCARED
YOU CAN SEE THE WHOLE CITY!
PANT
IT'S SO GNARLY. I GUESS IT'S TRUE. THE BEST THINGS IN LIFE REALLY ARE LIFE THREATENING
I NEVER HEARD THAT BEFORE
IT'S SOME-THING MY GRAMPY ALWAYS SAYS
THAT'S THE COAL PLANT OVER THERE. MY MOM SAYS IT'S THE REASON MY ASTHMA'S SO BAD

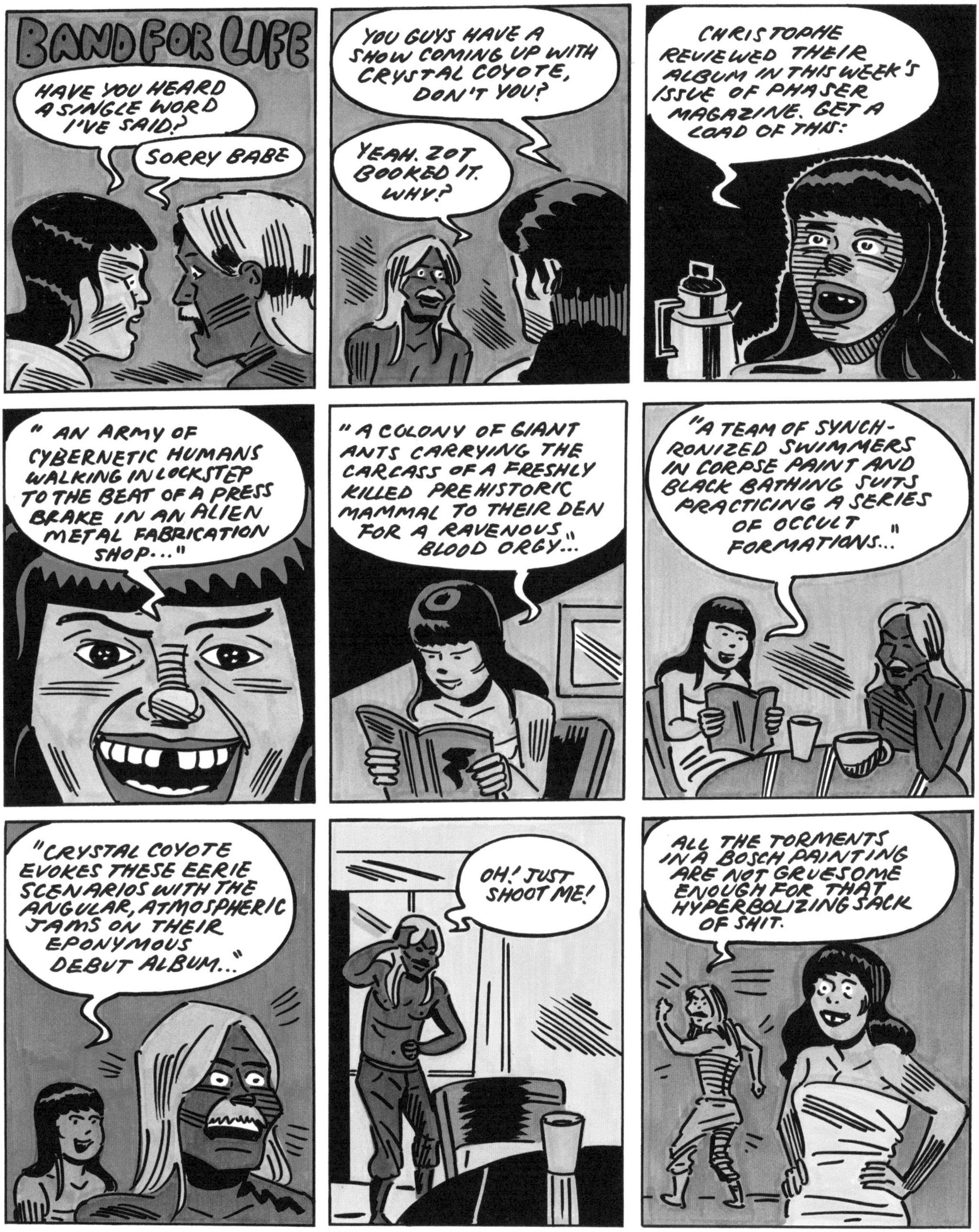
BAND FOR LIFE
HAVE YOU HEARD A SINGLE WORD I'VE SAID?
SORRY BABE
YOU GUYS HAVE A SHOW COMING UP WITH CRYSTAL COYOTE, DON'T YOU?
YEAH. ZOT BOOKED IT. WHY?
CHRISTOPHE REVIEWED THEIR ALBUM IN THIS WEEK'S ISSUE OF PHASER MAGAZINE. GET A LOAD OF THIS:
"AN ARMY OF CYBERNETIC HUMANS WALKING IN LOCKSTEP TO THE BEAT OF A PRESS BRAKE IN AN ALIEN METAL FABRICATION SHOP..."
"A COLONY OF GIANT ANTS CARRYING THE CARCASS OF A FRESHLY KILLED PREHISTORIC MAMMAL TO THEIR DEN FOR A RAVENOUS BLOOD ORGY..."
"A TEAM OF SYNCHRONIZED SWIMMERS IN CORPSE PAINT AND BLACK BATHING SUITS PRACTICING A SERIES OF OCCULT FORMATIONS..."
"CRYSTAL COYOTE EVOKES THESE EERIE SCENARIOS WITH THE ANGULAR, ATMOSPHERIC JAMS ON THEIR EPONYMOUS DEBUT ALBUM..."
OH! JUST SHOOT ME!
ALL THE TORMENTS IN A BOSCH PAINTING ARE NOT GRUESOME ENOUGH FOR THAT HYPERBOLIZING SACK OF SHIT.

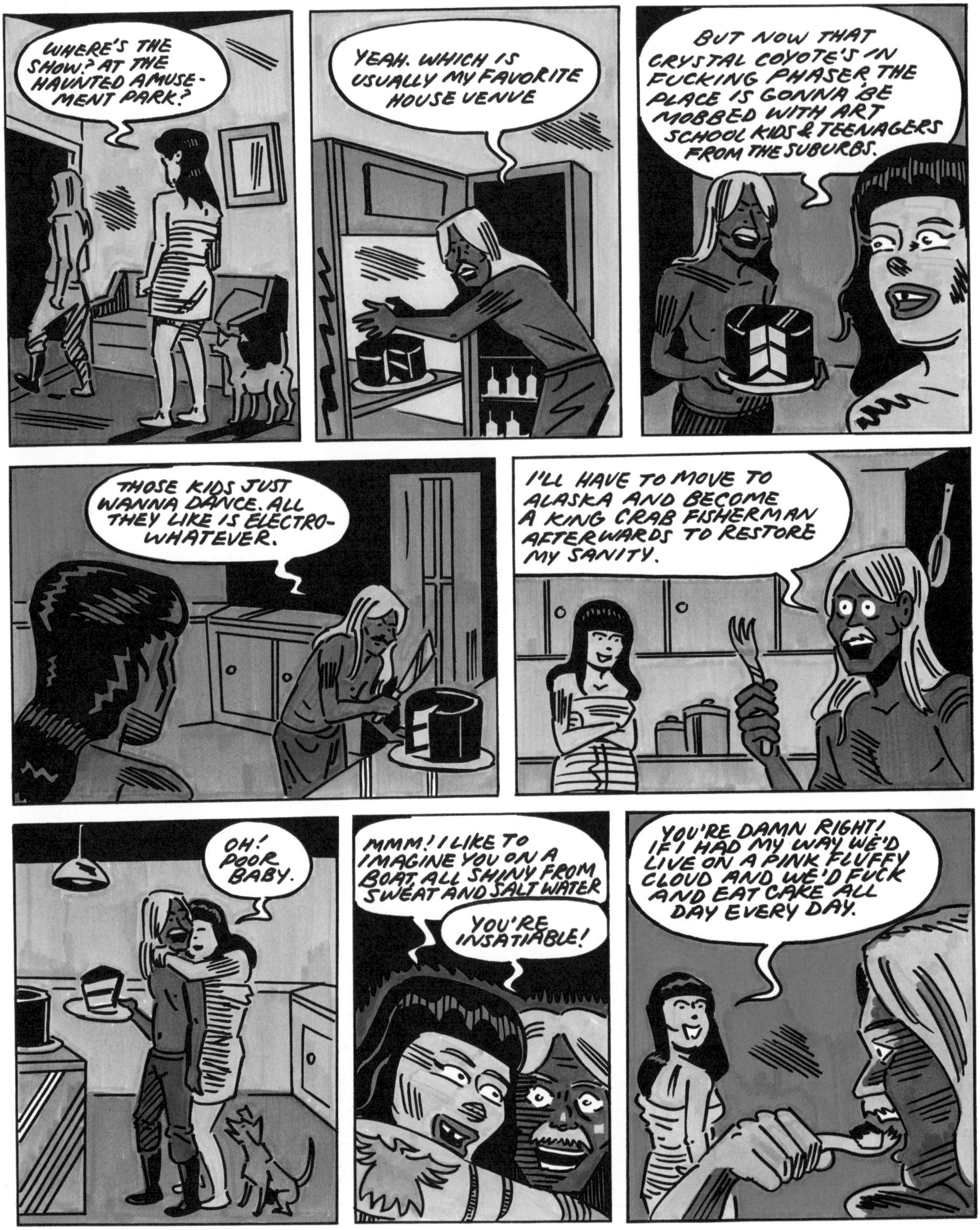
WHERE'S THE SHOW? AT THE HAUNTED AMUSEMENT PARK?
YEAH. WHICH IS USUALLY MY FAVORITE HOUSE VENUE
BUT NOW THAT CRYSTAL COYOTE'S IN FUCKING PHASER, THE PLACE IS GONNA BE MOBBED WITH ART SCHOOL KIDS & TEENAGERS FROM THE SUBURBS.
THOSE KIDS JUST WANNA DANCE. ALL THEY LIKE IS ELECTRO-WHATEVER.
I'LL HAVE TO MOVE TO ALASKA AND BECOME A KING CRAB FISHERMAN AFTERWARDS TO RESTORE MY SANITY.
OH! POOR BABY.
MMM! I LIKE TO IMAGINE YOU ON A BOAT, ALL SHINY FROM SWEAT AND SALT WATER
YOU'RE INSATIABLE!
YOU'RE DAMN RIGHT! IF I HAD MY WAY WE'D LIVE ON A PINK FLUFFY CLOUD AND WE'D FUCK AND EAT CAKE ALL DAY EVERY DAY.

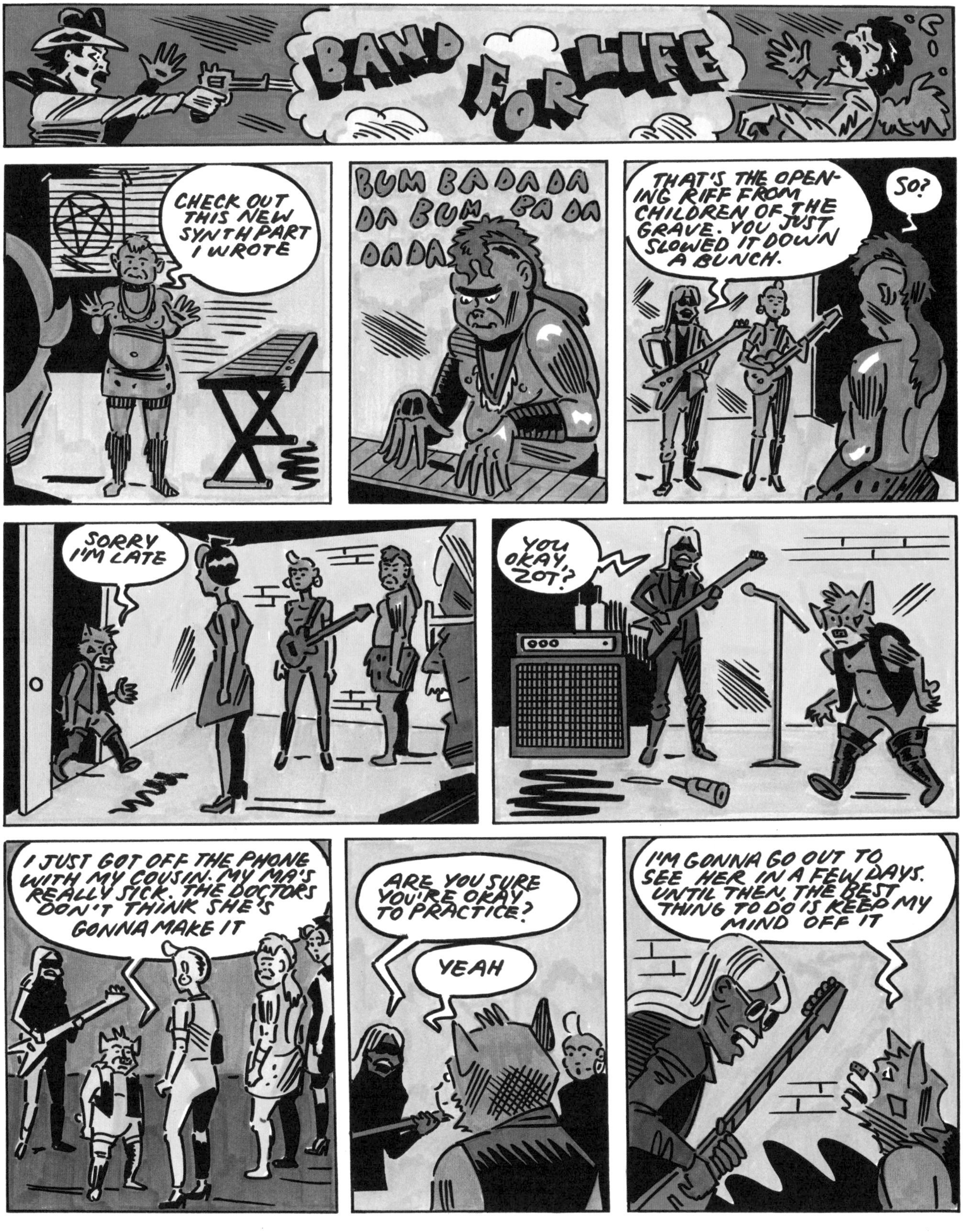
BAND FOR LIFE
CHECK OUT THIS NEW SYNTH PART I WROTE
BUM BA DA DA DA BUM BA DA DA DA
THAT'S THE OPENING RIFF FROM CHILDREN OF THE GRAVE. YOU JUST SLOWED IT DOWN A BUNCH.
SO?
SORRY I'M LATE
YOU OKAY, ZOT?
I JUST GOT OFF THE PHONE WITH MY COUSIN. MY MA'S REALLY SICK. THE DOCTORS DON'T THINK SHE'S GONNA MAKE IT
ARE YOU SURE YOU'RE OKAY TO PRACTICE?
YEAH
I'M GONNA GO OUT TO SEE HER IN A FEW DAYS. UNTIL THEN, THE BEST THING TO DO IS KEEP MY MIND OFF IT

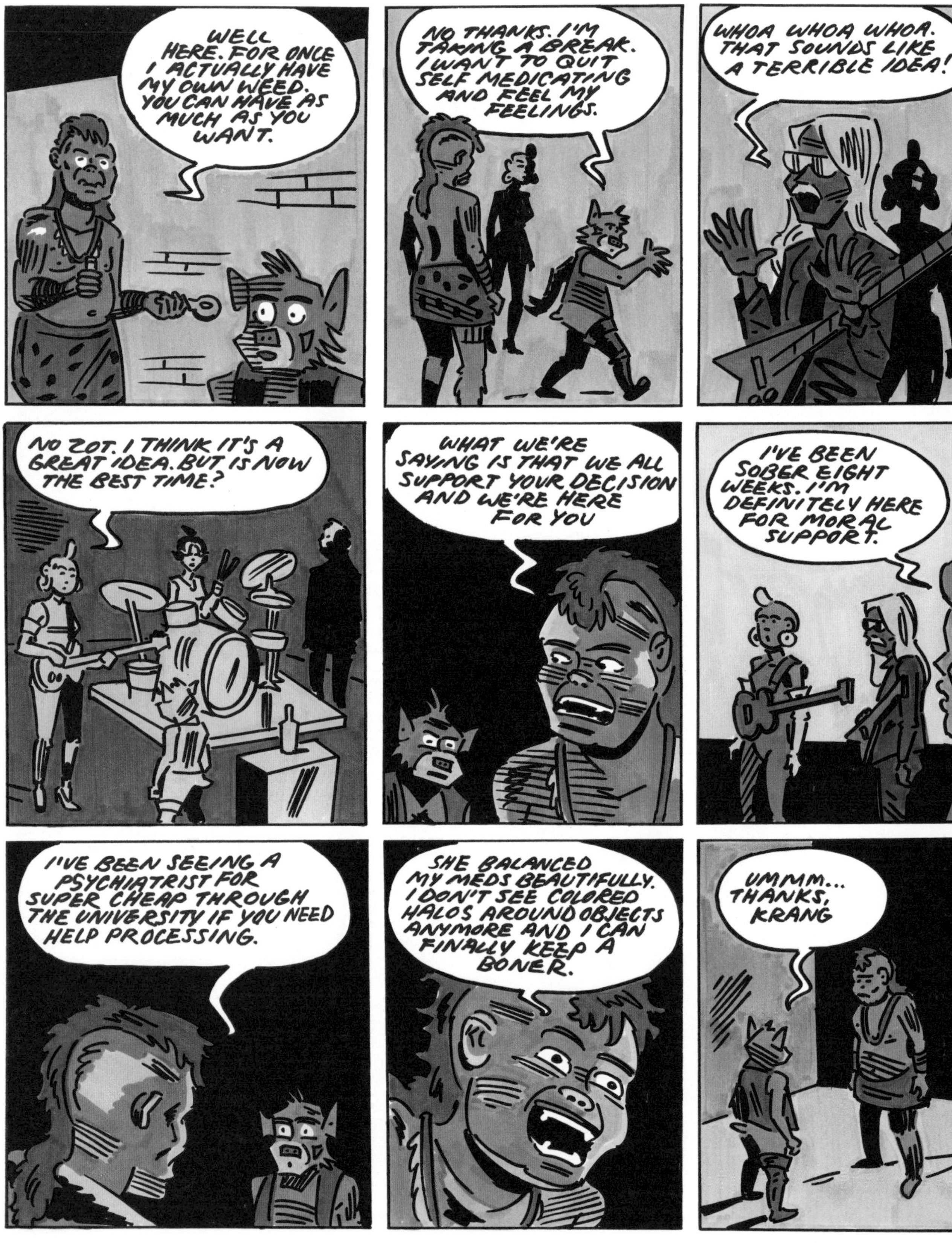
WELL HERE. FOR ONCE I ACTUALLY HAVE MY OWN WEED. YOU CAN HAVE AS MUCH AS YOU WANT.
NO THANKS. I'M TAKING A BREAK. I WANT TO QUIT SELF MEDICATING AND FEEL MY FEELINGS.
WHOA WHOA WHOA. THAT SOUNDS LIKE A TERRIBLE IDEA!
NO ZOT. I THINK IT'S A GREAT IDEA. BUT IS NOW THE BEST TIME?
WHAT WE'RE SAYING IS THAT WE ALL SUPPORT YOUR DECISION AND WE'RE HERE FOR YOU
I'VE BEEN SOBER EIGHT WEEKS. I'M DEFINITELY HERE FOR MORAL SUPPORT.
I'VE BEEN SEEING A PSYCHIATRIST FOR SUPER CHEAP THROUGH THE UNIVERSITY IF YOU NEED HELP PROCESSING.
SHE BALANCED MY MEDS BEAUTIFULLY. I DON'T SEE COLORED HALOS AROUND OBJECTS ANYMORE AND I CAN FINALLY KEEP A BONER.
UMMM... THANKS, KRANG

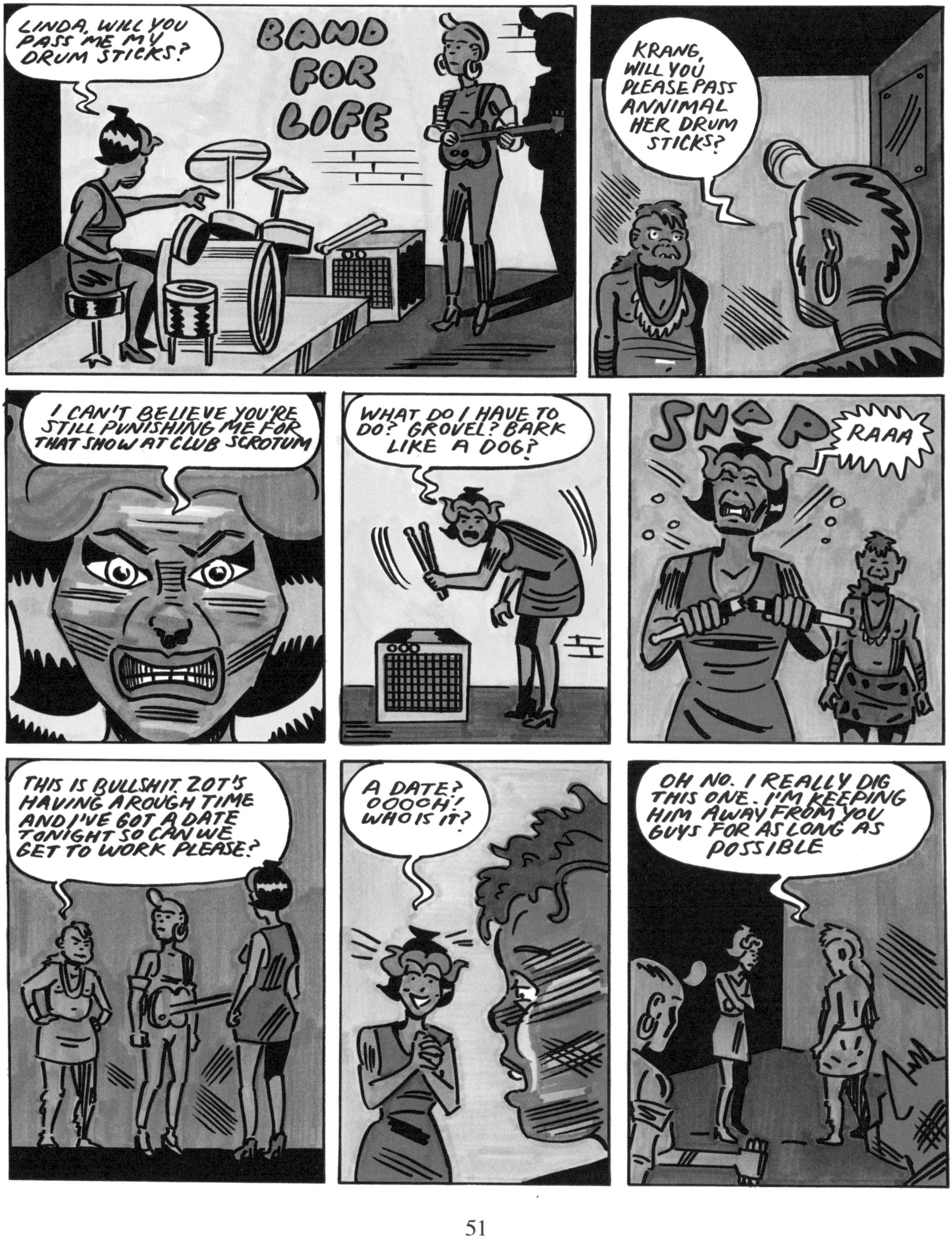
LINDA, WILL YOU PASS ME MY DRUM STICKS?
BAND FOR LIFE
KRANG, WILL YOU PLEASE PASS ANNIMAL HER DRUM STICKS?
I CAN'T BELIEVE YOU'RE STILL PUNISHING ME FOR THAT SHOW AT CLUB SCROTUM
WHAT DO I HAVE TO DO? GROVEL? BARK LIKE A DOG?
SNAP
RAAA
THIS IS BULLSHIT. ZOT'S HAVING A ROUGH TIME AND I'VE GOT A DATE TONIGHT SO CAN WE GET TO WORK PLEASE?
A DATE? OOOCH! WHO IS IT?
OH NO. I REALLY DIG THIS ONE. I'M KEEPING HIM AWAY FROM YOU GUYS FOR AS LONG AS POSSIBLE

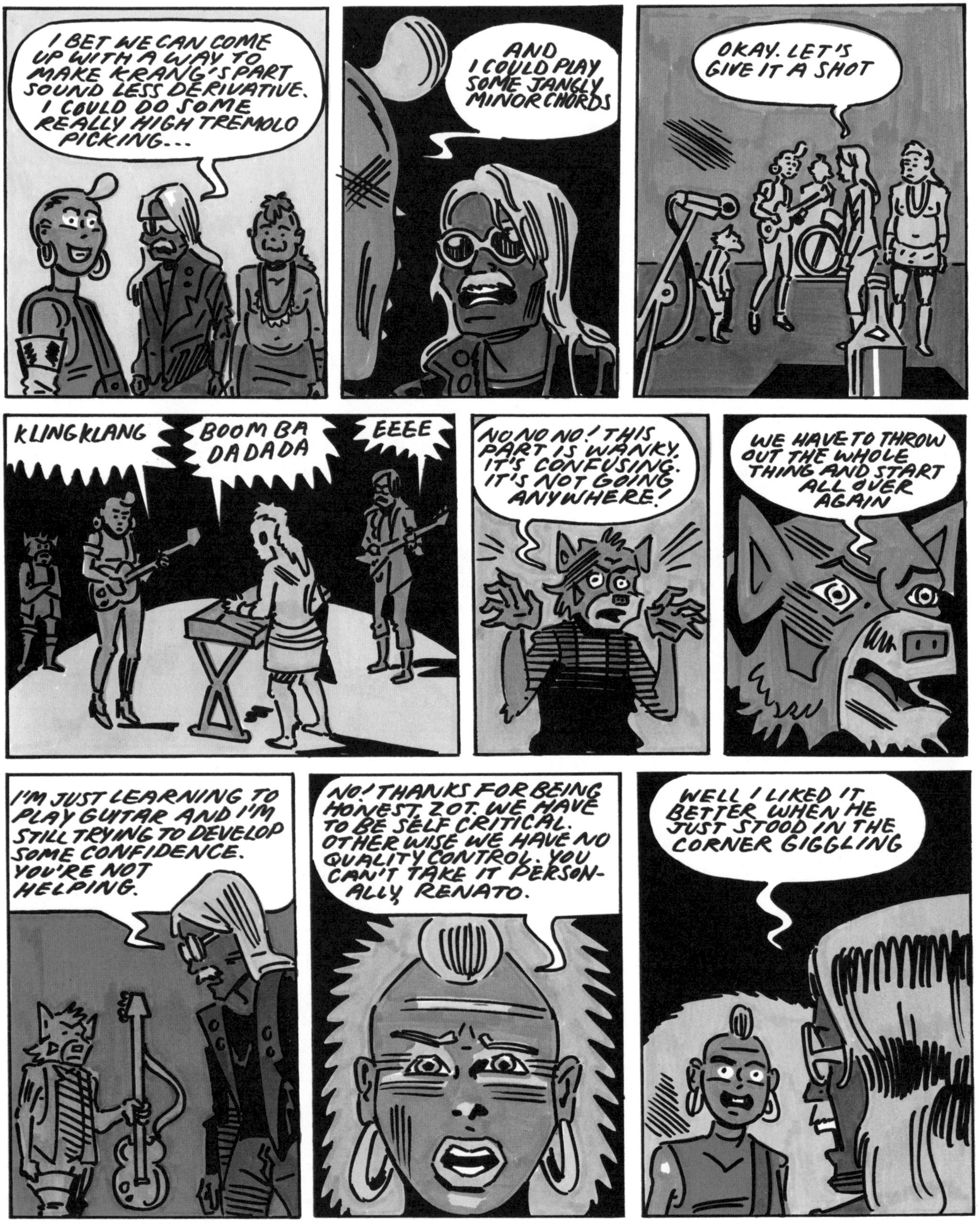
I BET WE CAN COME UP WITH A WAY TO MAKE KRANG'S PART SOUND LESS DERIVATIVE. I COULD DO SOME REALLY HIGH TREMOLO PICKING...
AND I COULD PLAY SOME JANGLY MINOR CHORDS
OKAY. LET'S GIVE IT A SHOT
KLINGKLANG
BOOM BA DADADA
EEEE
NO NO NO! THIS PART IS WANKY. IT'S CONFUSING. IT'S NOT GOING ANYWHERE!
WE HAVE TO THROW OUT THE WHOLE THING AND START ALL OVER AGAIN
I'M JUST LEARNING TO PLAY GUITAR AND I'M STILL TRYING TO DEVELOP SOME CONFIDENCE. YOU'RE NOT HELPING.
NO! THANKS FOR BEING HONEST, ZOT. WE HAVE TO BE SELF CRITICAL. OTHER WISE WE HAVE NO QUALITY CONTROL. YOU CAN'T TAKE IT PERSON-ALLY, RENATO.
WELL I LIKED IT BETTER WHEN HE JUST STOOD IN THE CORNER GIGGLING

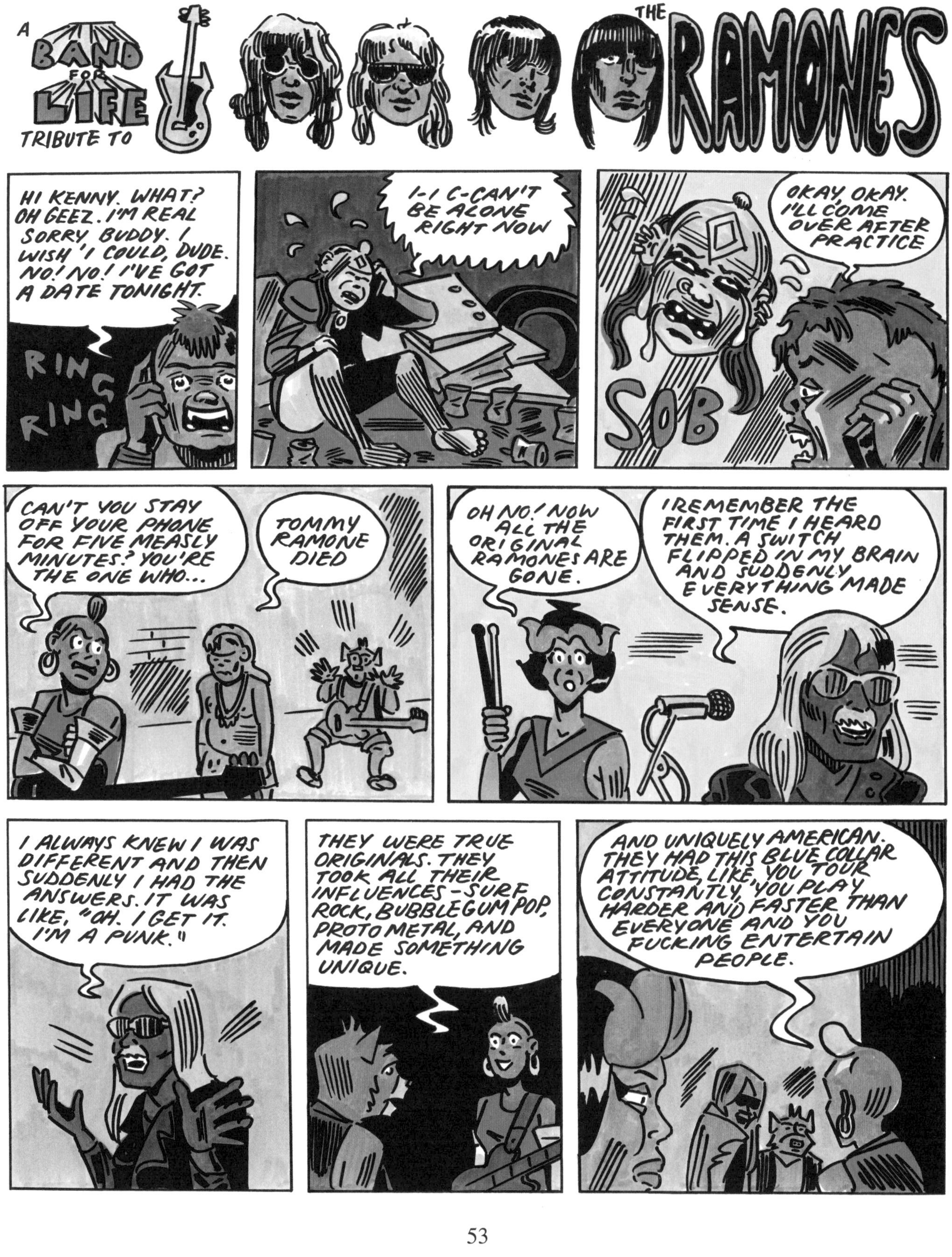
A BAND FOR LIFE TRIBUTE TO THE RAMONES
HI KENNY. WHAT? OH GEEZ. I'M REAL SORRY, BUDDY. I WISH I COULD, DUDE. NO! NO! I'VE GOT A DATE TONIGHT.
RING RING
I-I C-CAN'T BE ALONE RIGHT NOW
OKAY, OKAY. I'LL COME OVER AFTER PRACTICE
SOB
CAN'T YOU STAY OFF YOUR PHONE FOR FIVE MEASLY MINUTES? YOU'RE THE ONE WHO...
TOMMY RAMONE DIED
OH NO! NOW ALL THE ORIGINAL RAMONES ARE GONE.
I REMEMBER THE FIRST TIME I HEARD THEM. A SWITCH FLIPPED IN MY BRAIN AND SUDDENLY EVERYTHING MADE SENSE.
I ALWAYS KNEW I WAS DIFFERENT AND THEN SUDDENLY I HAD THE ANSWERS. IT WAS LIKE, "OH. I GET IT. I'M A PUNK."
THEY WERE TRUE ORIGINALS. THEY TOOK ALL THEIR INFLUENCES - SURF ROCK, BUBBLEGUM POP, PROTO METAL, AND MADE SOMETHING UNIQUE.
AND UNIQUELY AMERICAN. THEY HAD THIS BLUE COLLAR ATTITUDE, LIKE, YOU TOUR CONSTANTLY, YOU PLAY HARDER AND FASTER THAN EVERYONE AND YOU FUCKING ENTERTAIN PEOPLE.

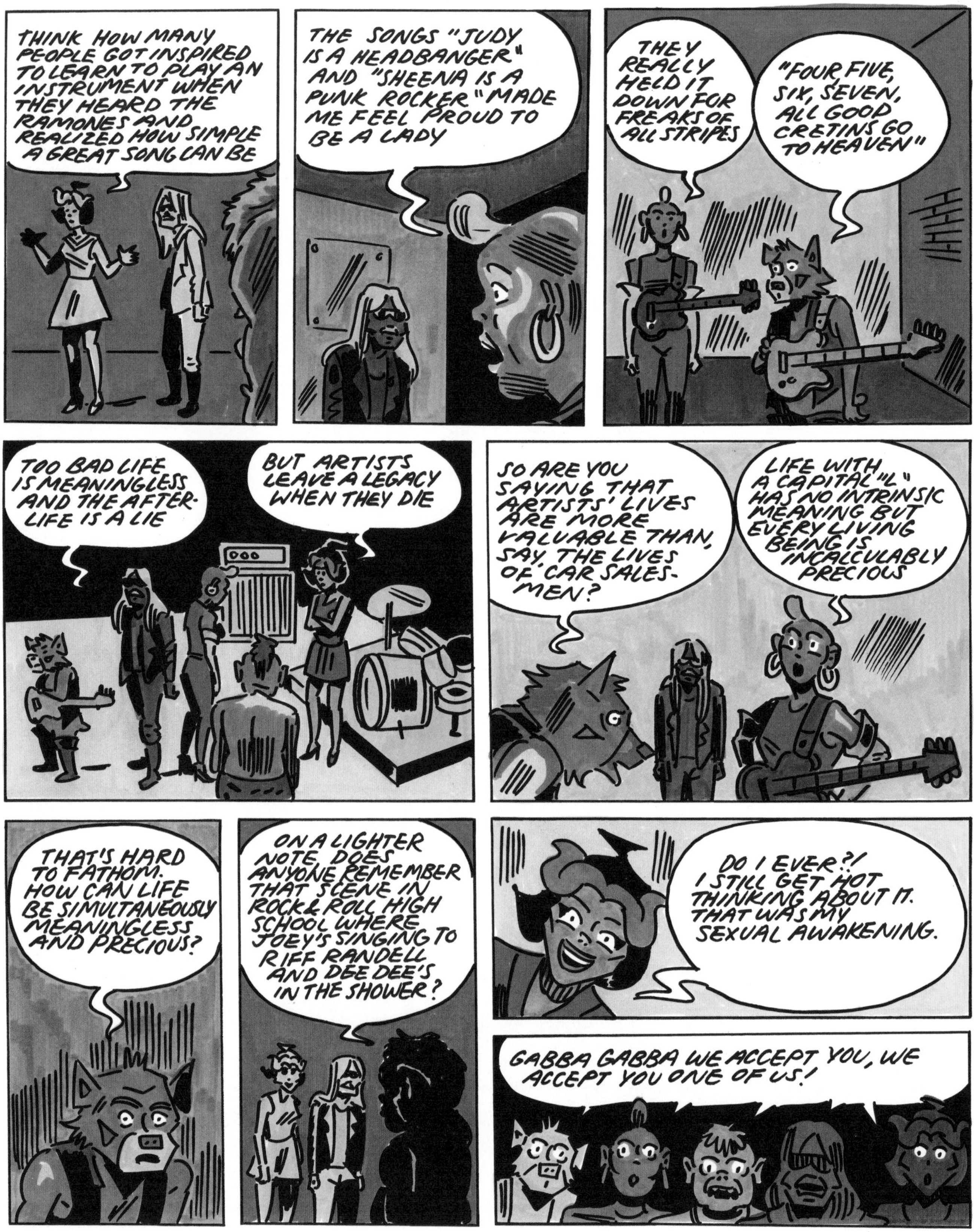
THINK HOW MANY PEOPLE GOT INSPIRED TO LEARN TO PLAY AN INSTRUMENT WHEN THEY HEARD THE RAMONES AND REALIZED HOW SIMPLE A GREAT SONG CAN BE
THE SONGS "JUDY IS A HEADBANGER" AND "SHEENA IS A PUNK ROCKER" MADE ME FEEL PROUD TO BE A LADY
THEY REALLY HELD IT DOWN FOR FREAKS OF ALL STRIPES
"FOUR, FIVE, SIX, SEVEN, ALL GOOD CRETINS GO TO HEAVEN"
TOO BAD LIFE IS MEANINGLESS AND THE AFTER-LIFE IS A LIE
BUT ARTISTS LEAVE A LEGACY WHEN THEY DIE
SO ARE YOU SAYING THAT ARTISTS' LIVES ARE MORE VALUABLE THAN, SAY, THE LIVES OF CAR SALES-MEN?
LIFE WITH A CAPITAL "L" HAS NO INTRINSIC MEANING BUT EVERY LIVING BEING IS INCALCULABLY PRECIOUS
THAT'S HARD TO FATHOM. HOW CAN LIFE BE SIMULTANEOUSLY MEANINGLESS AND PRECIOUS?
ON A LIGHTER NOTE, DOES ANYONE REMEMBER THAT SCENE IN ROCK & ROLL HIGH SCHOOL WHERE JOEY'S SINGING TO RIFF RANDELL AND DEE DEE'S IN THE SHOWER?
DO I EVER?! I STILL GET HOT THINKING ABOUT IT. THAT WAS MY SEXUAL AWAKENING.
GABBA GABBA WE ACCEPT YOU, WE ACCEPT YOU ONE OF US!

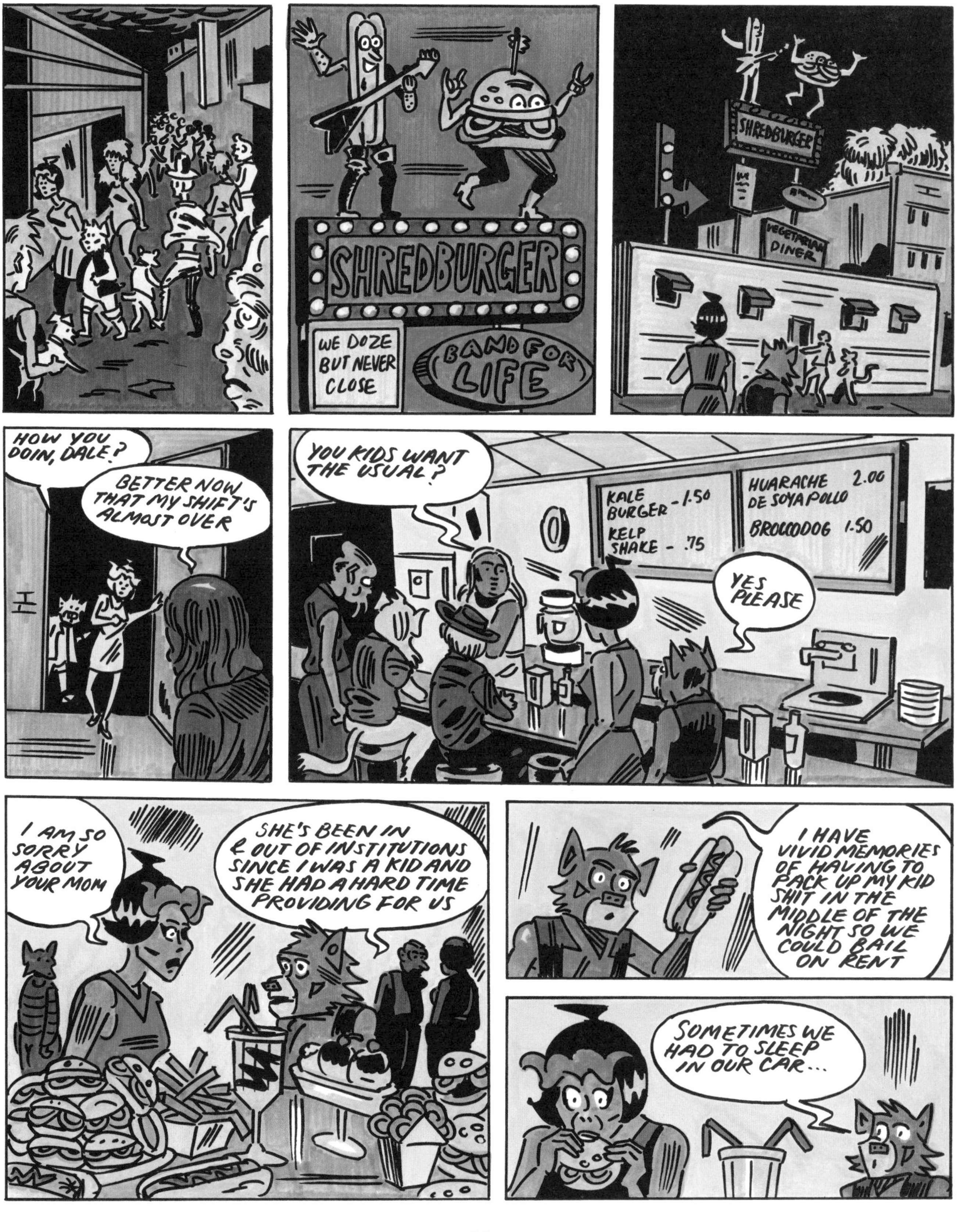
SHREDBURGER
WE DOZE BUT NEVER CLOSE
BAND FOR LIFE
SHREDBURGER
VEGETARIAN DINER
HOW YOU DOIN, DALE?
BETTER NOW THAT MY SHIFT'S ALMOST OVER
YOU KIDS WANT THE USUAL?
KALE BURGER - 1.50
KELP SHAKE - .75
HUARACHE DE SOYA POLLO 2.00
BROCCODOG 1.50
YES PLEASE
I AM SO SORRY ABOUT YOUR MOM
SHE'S BEEN IN & OUT OF INSTITUTIONS SINCE I WAS A KID AND SHE HAD A HARD TIME PROVIDING FOR US
I HAVE VIVID MEMORIES OF HAVING TO PACK UP MY KID SHIT IN THE MIDDLE OF THE NIGHT SO WE COULD BAIL ON RENT
SOMETIMES WE HAD TO SLEEP IN OUR CAR...

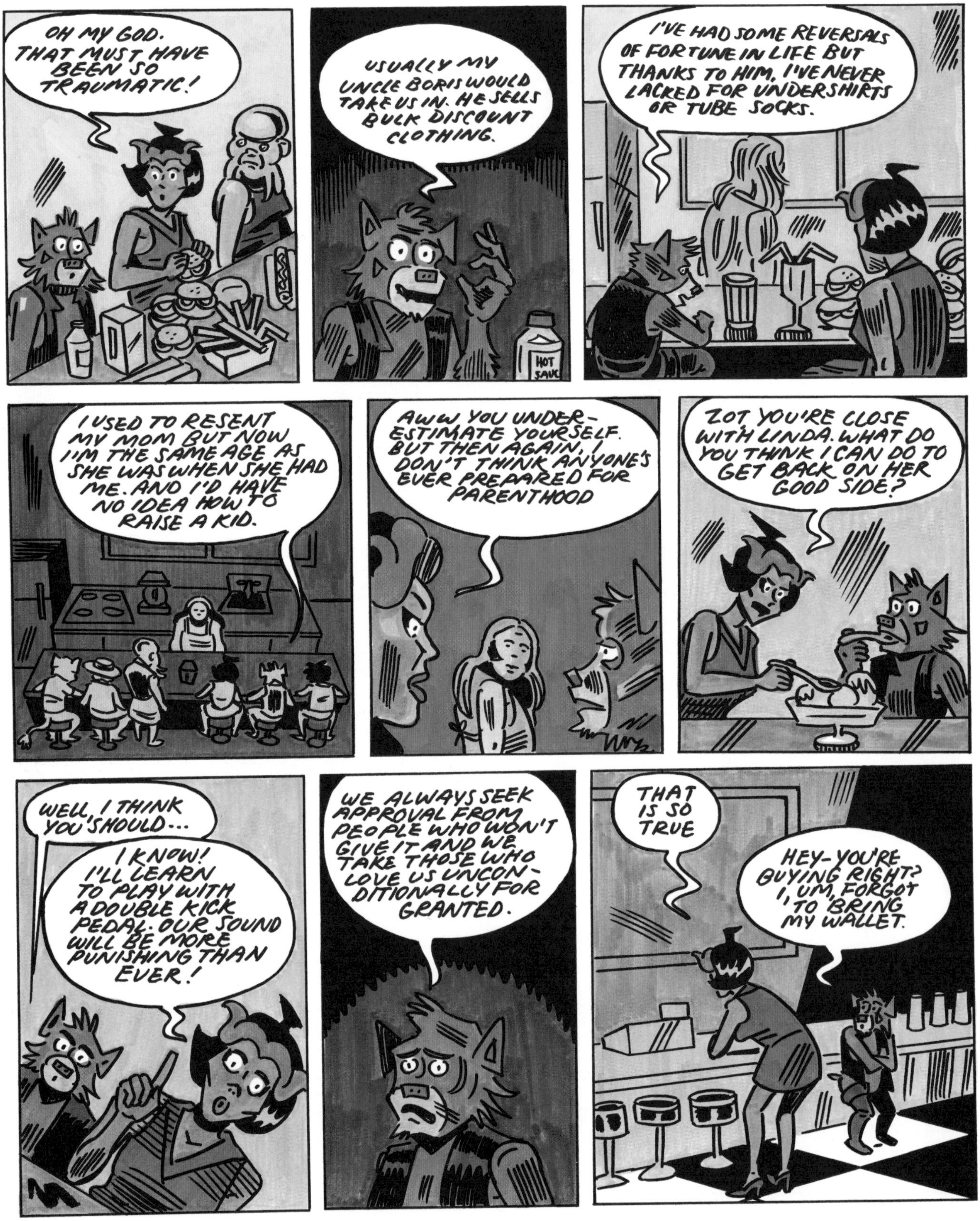
OH MY GOD. THAT MUST HAVE BEEN SO TRAUMATIC!
USUALLY MY UNCLE BORIS WOULD TAKE US IN. HE SELLS BULK DISCOUNT CLOTHING.
HOT SAUC
I'VE HAD SOME REVERSALS OF FORTUNE IN LIFE BUT THANKS TO HIM, I'VE NEVER LACKED FOR UNDERSHIRTS OR TUBE SOCKS.
I USED TO RESENT MY MOM BUT NOW I'M THE SAME AGE AS SHE WAS WHEN SHE HAD ME. AND I'D HAVE NO IDEA HOW TO RAISE A KID.
AWW YOU UNDER-ESTIMATE YOURSELF. BUT THEN AGAIN, I DON'T THINK ANYONE'S EVER PREPARED FOR PARENTHOOD
ZOT, YOU'RE CLOSE WITH LINDA. WHAT DO YOU THINK I CAN DO TO GET BACK ON HER GOOD SIDE?
WELL, I THINK YOU SHOULD...
I KNOW! I'LL LEARN TO PLAY WITH A DOUBLE KICK PEDAL. OUR SOUND WILL BE MORE PUNISHING THAN EVER!
WE ALWAYS SEEK APPROVAL FROM PEOPLE WHO WON'T GIVE IT AND WE TAKE THOSE WHO LOVE US UNCON-DITIONALLY FOR GRANTED.
THAT IS SO TRUE
HEY- YOU'RE BUYING RIGHT? I, UM, FORGOT TO BRING MY WALLET.

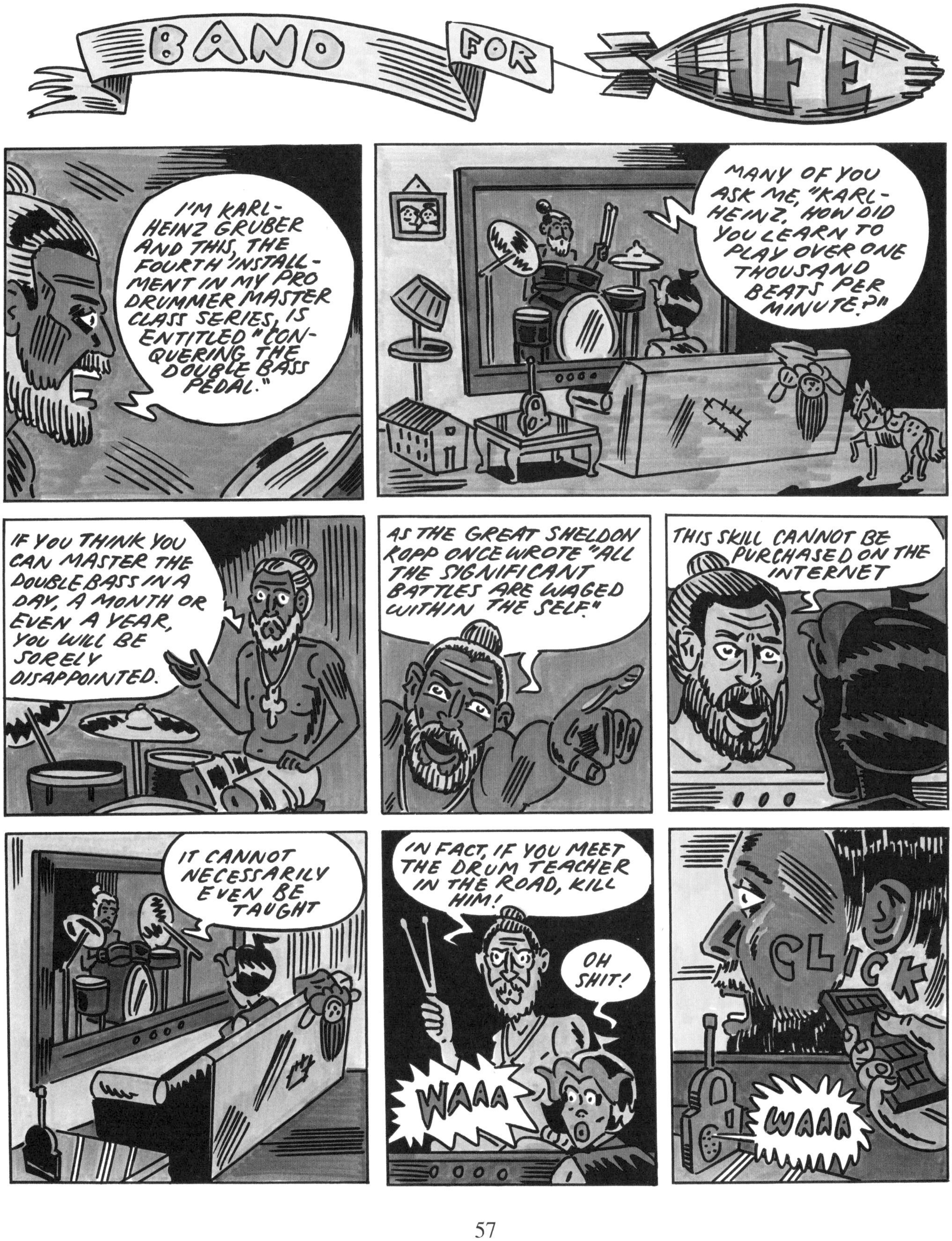
BAND FOR LIFE
I'M KARL-HEINZ GRUBER AND THIS, THE FOURTH INSTALLMENT IN MY PRO DRUMMER MASTER CLASS SERIES, IS ENTITLED "CONQUERING THE DOUBLE BASS PEDAL."
MANY OF YOU ASK ME, "KARL-HEINZ, HOW DID YOU LEARN TO PLAY OVER ONE THOUSAND BEATS PER MINUTE?"
IF YOU THINK YOU CAN MASTER THE DOUBLE BASS IN A DAY, A MONTH OR EVEN A YEAR, YOU WILL BE SORELY DISAPPOINTED.
AS THE GREAT SHELDON KOPP ONCE WROTE "ALL THE SIGNIFICANT BATTLES ARE WAGED WITHIN THE SELF."
THIS SKILL CANNOT BE PURCHASED ON THE INTERNET
IT CANNOT NECESSARILY EVEN BE TAUGHT
IN FACT, IF YOU MEET THE DRUM TEACHER IN THE ROAD, KILL HIM!
OH SHIT!
WAAA
CLICK
WAAA

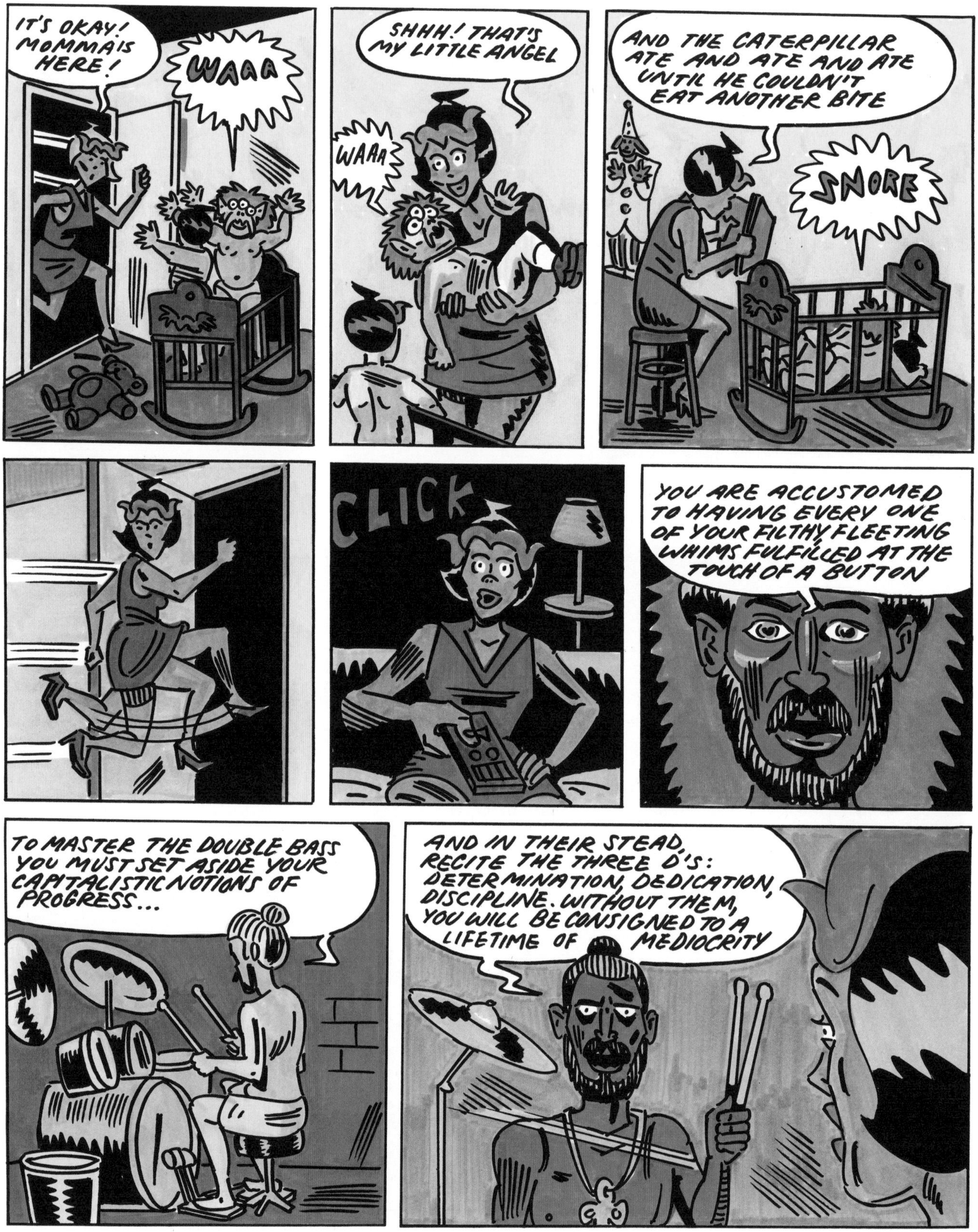
IT'S OKAY! MOMMA IS HERE!
WAAA
SHHH! THAT'S MY LITTLE ANGEL
WAAA
AND THE CATERPILLAR ATE AND ATE AND ATE UNTIL HE COULDN'T EAT ANOTHER BITE
SNORE
CLICK
YOU ARE ACCUSTOMED TO HAVING EVERY ONE OF YOUR FILTHY, FLEETING WHIMS FULFILLED AT THE TOUCH OF A BUTTON
TO MASTER THE DOUBLE BASS YOU MUST SET ASIDE YOUR CAPITALISTIC NOTIONS OF PROGRESS...
AND IN THEIR STEAD, RECITE THE THREE D'S: DETERMINATION, DEDICATION, DISCIPLINE. WITHOUT THEM, YOU WILL BE CONSIGNED TO A LIFETIME OF MEDIOCRITY

BAND FOR LIFE

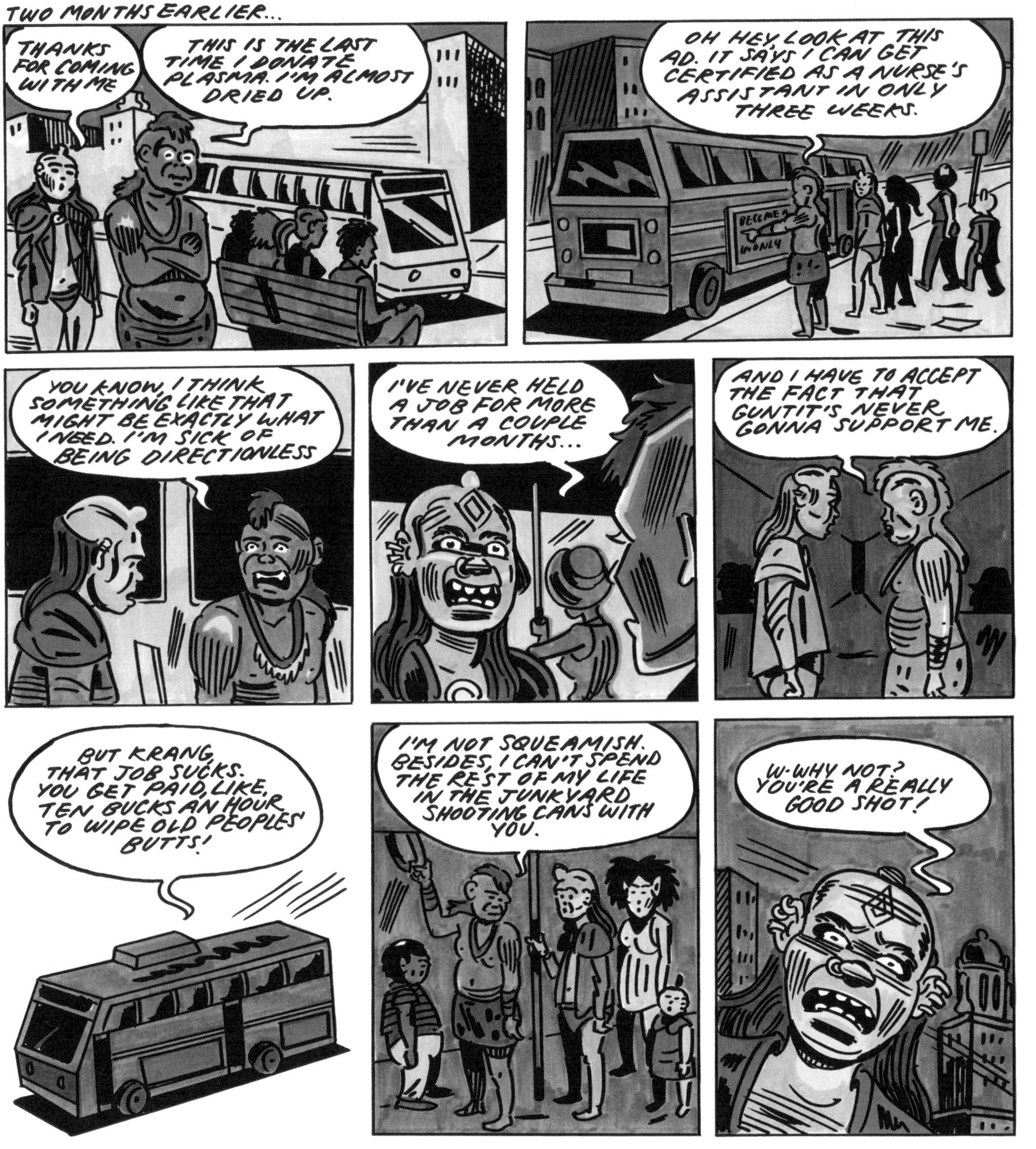
TWO MONTHS EARLIER...
THANKS FOR COMING WITH ME
THIS IS THE LAST TIME I DONATE PLASMA. I'M ALMOST DRIED UP.
OH HEY, LOOK AT THIS AD. IT SAYS I CAN GET CERTIFIED AS A NURSE'S ASSISTANT IN ONLY THREE WEEKS.
YOU KNOW, I THINK SOMETHING LIKE THAT MIGHT BE EXACTLY WHAT I NEED. I'M SICK OF BEING DIRECTIONLESS
I'VE NEVER HELD A JOB FOR MORE THAN A COUPLE MONTHS...
AND I HAVE TO ACCEPT THE FACT THAT GUNTIT'S NEVER GONNA SUPPORT ME.
BUT KRANG, THAT JOB SUCKS. YOU GET PAID, LIKE, TEN BUCKS AN HOUR TO WIPE OLD PEOPLES' BUTTS!
I'M NOT SQUEAMISH. BESIDES, I CAN'T SPEND THE REST OF MY LIFE IN THE JUNKYARD SHOOTING CANS WITH YOU.
W-WHY NOT? YOU'RE A REALLY GOOD SHOT!

PRESENT DAY

COUNTY HOSPITAL

BAND FOR LIFE

HELLO MISTER DETWEILER. I'M ELLIOT, I'M A NURSE HERE, AND THIS IS MY ASSISTANT KRANG

I CAN'T GET OVER THE FACT THAT WE'RE CO-WORKERS BUT WE ENDED UP GETTING TOGETHER ONLINE.

BODY TEMPERATURE NINETY-SEVEN POINT EIGHT

YOU STOOD OUT LIKE A DIAMOND IN A COAL MINE. THE OTHER GUYS I MET WERE NON-ENTITIES.

I MEAN, GET REAL! DRINKING CRAFT BEER IS GREAT AFTER A LONG DAY BUT IT DOESN'T COUNT AS A HOBBY!

NOW I'M GOING TO TAKE YOUR PULSE.

YOU'RE INQUISITIVE, FUNNY PASSIONATE ABOUT NURSING...

AND YOU'RE CUTE, CARING AND CREATIVE. PULSE IS A LITTLE HIGH. ONE-TWENTY-ONE.

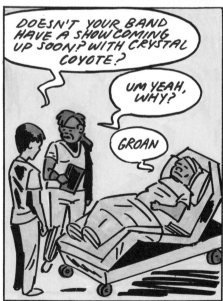

DOESN'T YOUR BAND HAVE A SHOW COMING UP SOON? WITH CRYSTAL COYOTE?

UM YEAH, WHY?

GROAN

60

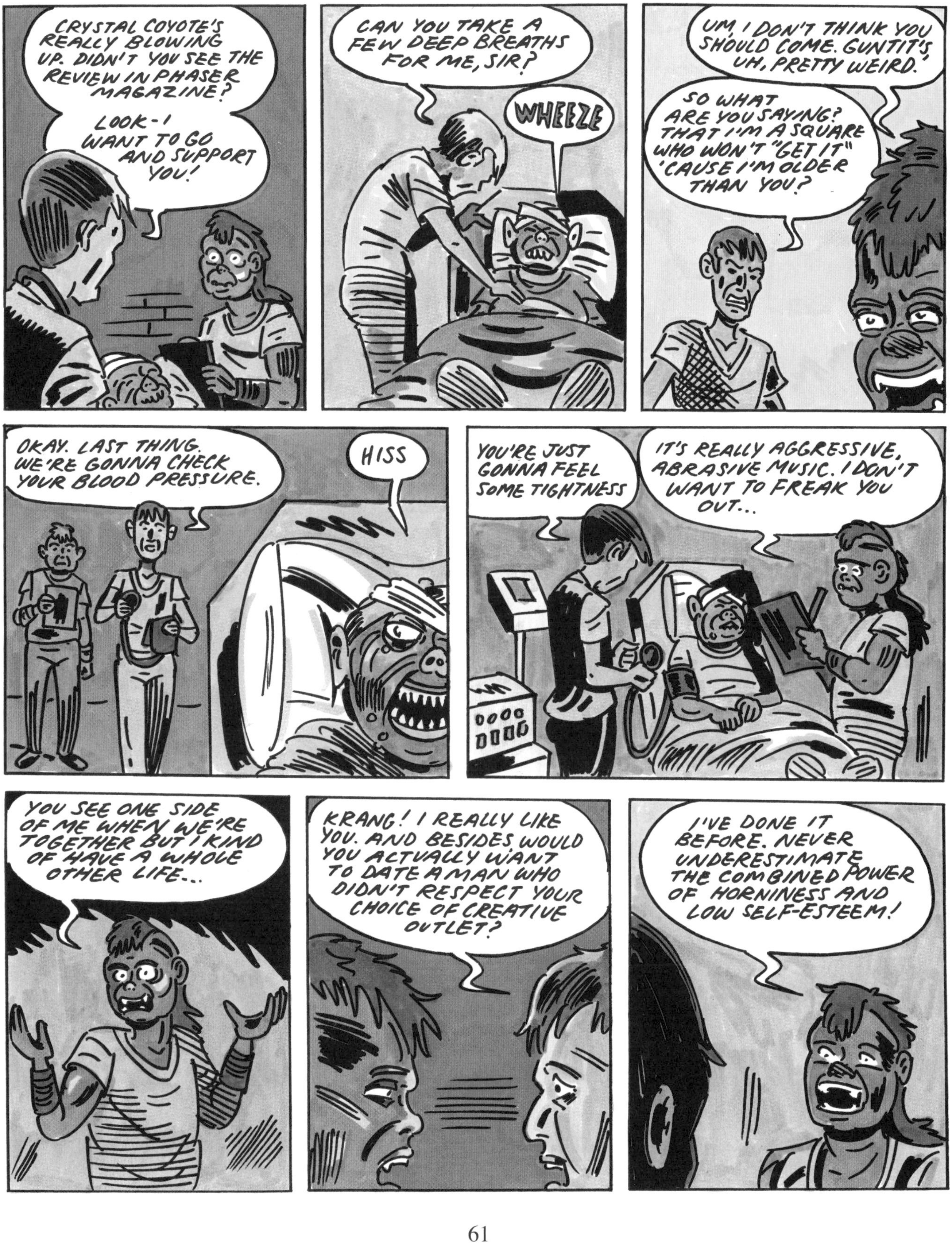
CRYSTAL COYOTE'S REALLY BLOWING UP. DIDN'T YOU SEE THE REVIEW IN PHASER MAGAZINE?
LOOK-I WANT TO GO AND SUPPORT YOU!
CAN YOU TAKE A FEW DEEP BREATHS FOR ME, SIR?
WHEEZE
UM, I DON'T THINK YOU SHOULD COME. GUNTIT'S, UH, PRETTY WEIRD.
SO WHAT ARE YOU SAYING? THAT I'M A SQUARE WHO WON'T "GET IT" 'CAUSE I'M OLDER THAN YOU?
OKAY. LAST THING. WE'RE GONNA CHECK YOUR BLOOD PRESSURE.
HISS
YOU'RE JUST GONNA FEEL SOME TIGHTNESS
IT'S REALLY AGGRESSIVE, ABRASIVE MUSIC. I DON'T WANT TO FREAK YOU OUT...
YOU SEE ONE SIDE OF ME WHEN WE'RE TOGETHER BUT I KIND OF HAVE A WHOLE OTHER LIFE...
KRANG! I REALLY LIKE YOU. AND BESIDES WOULD YOU ACTUALLY WANT TO DATE A MAN WHO DIDN'T RESPECT YOUR CHOICE OF CREATIVE OUTLET?
I'VE DONE IT BEFORE. NEVER UNDERESTIMATE THE COMBINED POWER OF HORNINESS AND LOW SELF-ESTEEM!

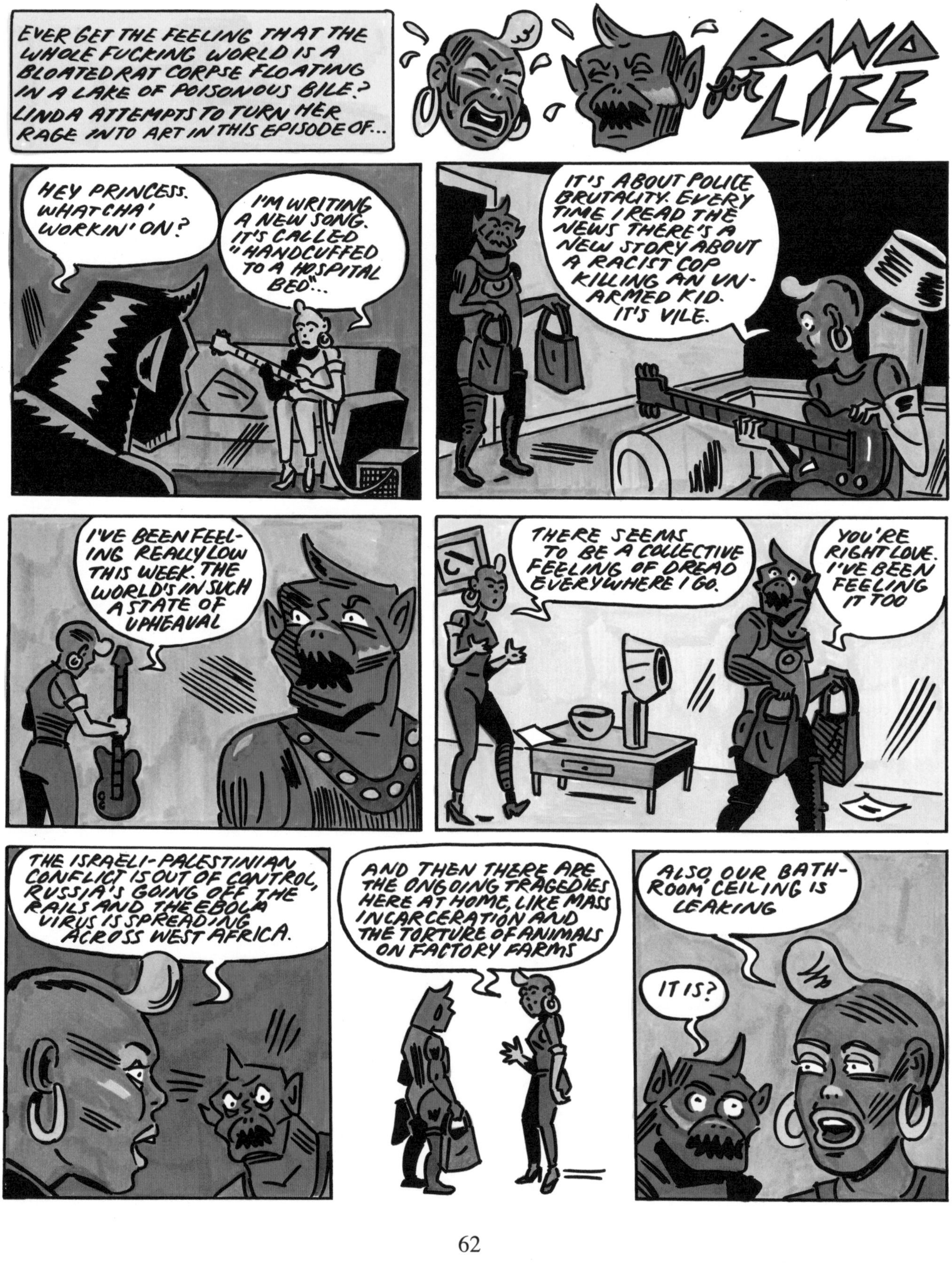
EVER GET THE FEELING THAT THE WHOLE FUCKING WORLD IS A BLOATED RAT CORPSE FLOATING IN A LAKE OF POISONOUS BILE? LINDA ATTEMPTS TO TURN HER RAGE INTO ART IN THIS EPISODE OF...
BAND for LIFE
HEY PRINCESS. WHATCHA' WORKIN' ON?
I'M WRITING A NEW SONG. IT'S CALLED "HANDCUFFED TO A HOSPITAL BED"...
IT'S ABOUT POLICE BRUTALITY. EVERY TIME I READ THE NEWS THERE'S A NEW STORY ABOUT A RACIST COP KILLING AN UN-ARMED KID. IT'S VILE.
I'VE BEEN FEEL-ING REALLY LOW THIS WEEK. THE WORLD'S IN SUCH A STATE OF UPHEAVAL
THERE SEEMS TO BE A COLLECTIVE FEELING OF DREAD EVERYWHERE I GO.
YOU'RE RIGHT LOVE. I'VE BEEN FEELING IT TOO
THE ISRAELI-PALESTINIAN CONFLICT IS OUT OF CONTROL, RUSSIA'S GOING OFF THE RAILS AND THE EBOLA VIRUS IS SPREADING ACROSS WEST AFRICA.
AND THEN THERE ARE THE ONGOING TRAGEDIES HERE AT HOME, LIKE MASS INCARCERATION AND THE TORTURE OF ANIMALS ON FACTORY FARMS
ALSO, OUR BATH-ROOM CEILING IS LEAKING
IT IS?

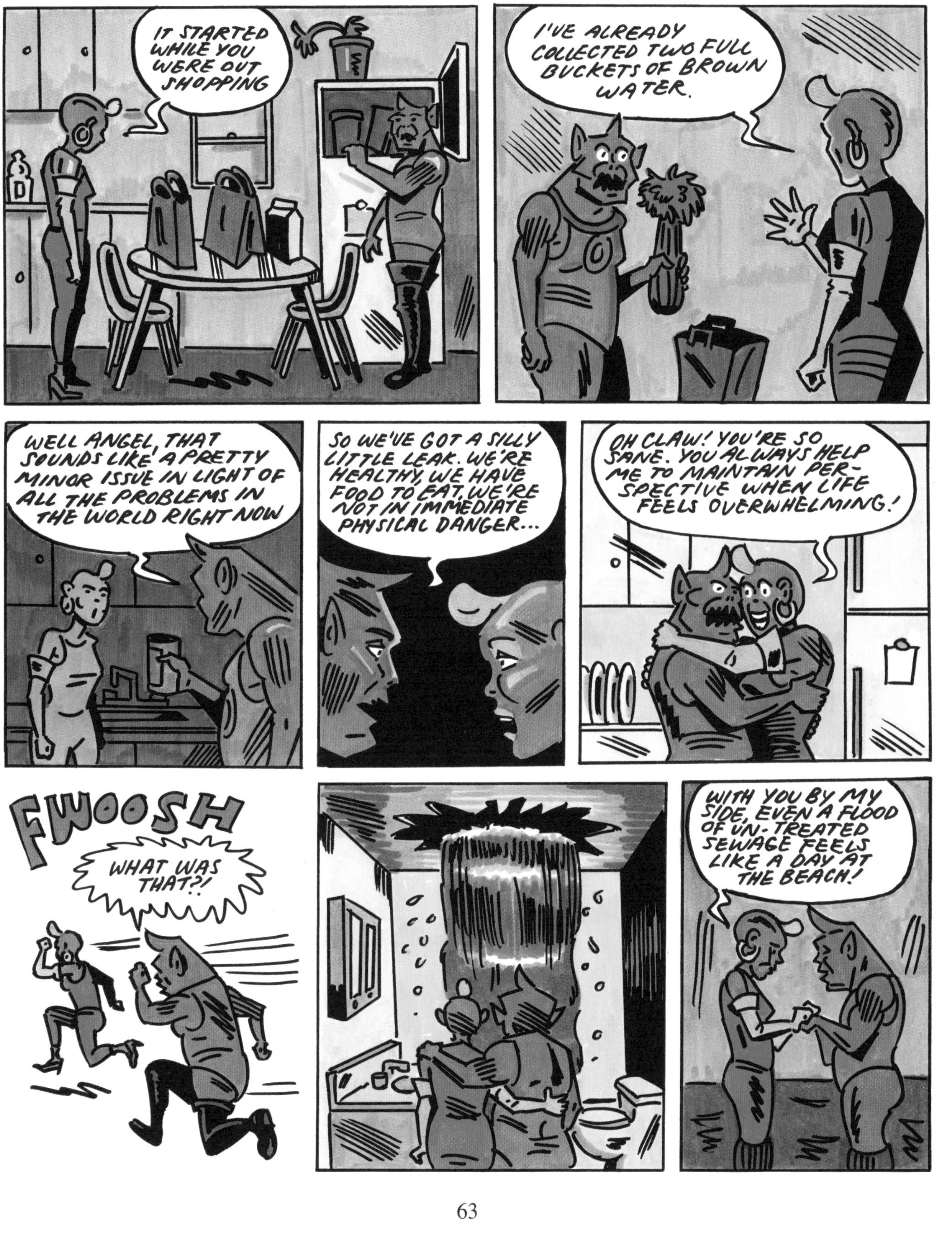
IT STARTED WHILE YOU WERE OUT SHOPPING
I'VE ALREADY COLLECTED TWO FULL BUCKETS OF BROWN WATER.
WELL ANGEL, THAT SOUNDS LIKE A PRETTY MINOR ISSUE IN LIGHT OF ALL THE PROBLEMS IN THE WORLD RIGHT NOW
SO WE'VE GOT A SILLY LITTLE LEAK. WE'RE HEALTHY, WE HAVE FOOD TO EAT, WE'RE NOT IN IMMEDIATE PHYSICAL DANGER...
OH CLAW! YOU'RE SO SANE. YOU ALWAYS HELP ME TO MAINTAIN PER-SPECTIVE WHEN LIFE FEELS OVERWHELMING!
FWOOSH
WHAT WAS THAT?!
WITH YOU BY MY SIDE, EVEN A FLOOD OF UN-TREATED SEWAGE FEELS LIKE A DAY AT THE BEACH!

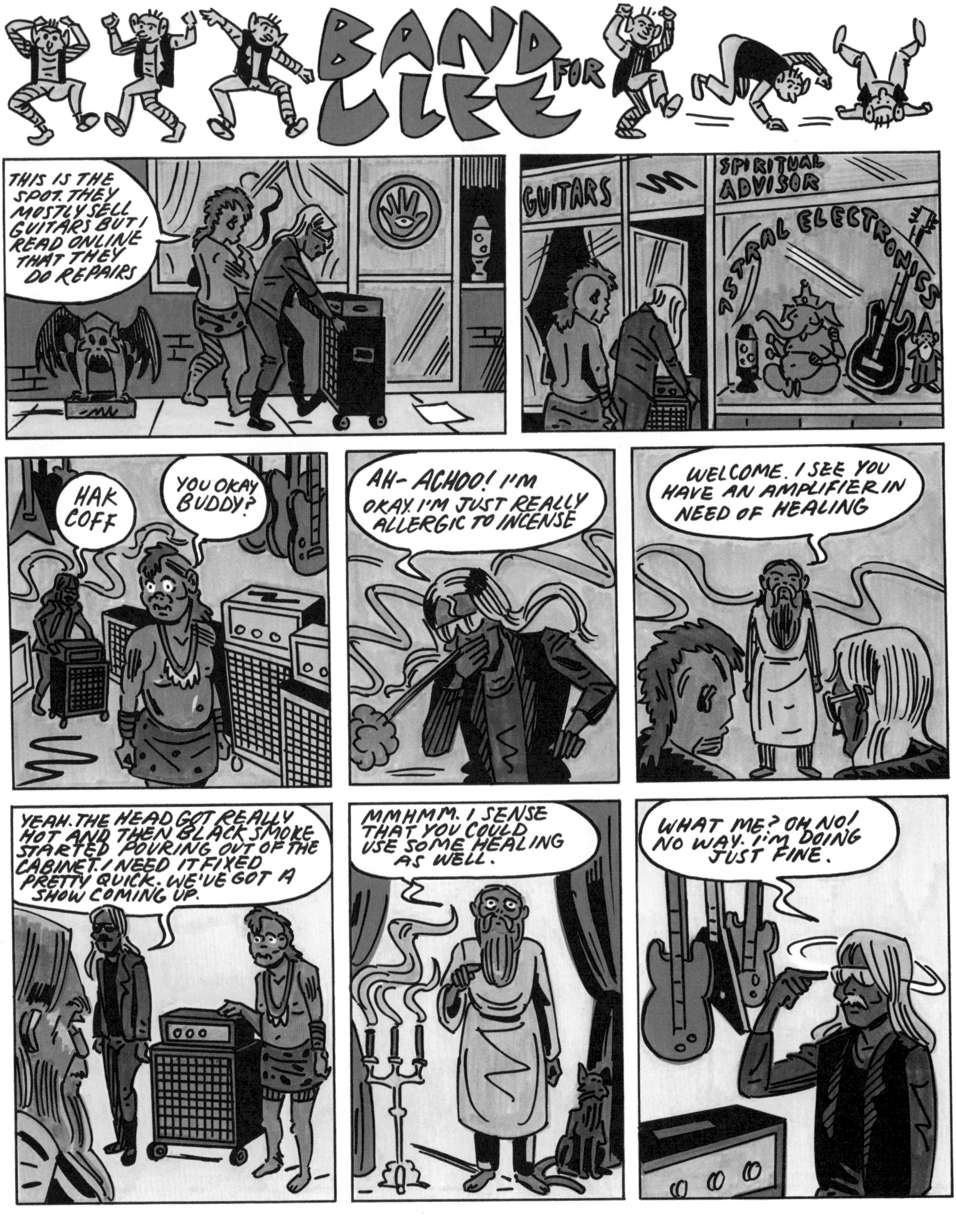
BAND FOR LIFE
THIS IS THE SPOT. THEY MOSTLY SELL GUITARS BUT I READ ONLINE THAT THEY DO REPAIRS
GUITARS
SPIRITUAL ADVISOR
ASTRAL ELECTRONICS
HAK COFF
YOU OKAY BUDDY?
AH- ACHOO! I'M OKAY. I'M JUST REALLY ALLERGIC TO INCENSE
WELCOME. I SEE YOU HAVE AN AMPLIFIER IN NEED OF HEALING
YEAH. THE HEAD GOT REALLY HOT AND THEN BLACK SMOKE STARTED POURING OUT OF THE CABINET. I NEED IT FIXED PRETTY QUICK. WE'VE GOT A SHOW COMING UP.
MMHMM. I SENSE THAT YOU COULD USE SOME HEALING AS WELL.
WHAT ME? OH NO! NO WAY. I'M DOING JUST FINE.

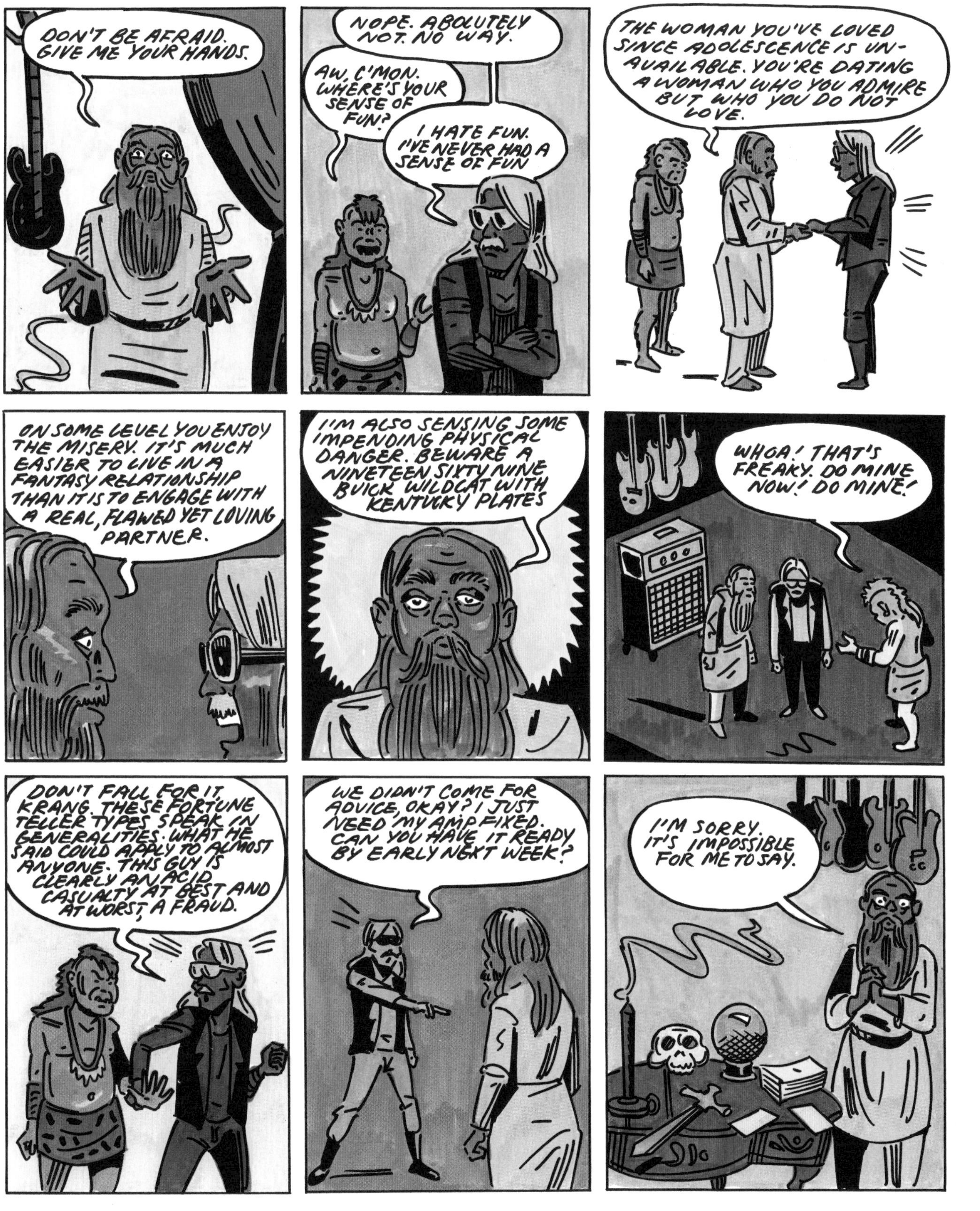
DON'T BE AFRAID. GIVE ME YOUR HANDS.
NOPE. ABOLUTELY NOT. NO WAY.
AW, C'MON. WHERE'S YOUR SENSE OF FUN?
I HATE FUN. I'VE NEVER HAD A SENSE OF FUN
THE WOMAN YOU'VE LOVED SINCE ADOLESCENCE IS UN-AVAILABLE. YOU'RE DATING A WOMAN WHO YOU ADMIRE BUT WHO YOU DO NOT LOVE.
ON SOME LEVEL YOU ENJOY THE MISERY. IT'S MUCH EASIER TO LIVE IN A FANTASY RELATIONSHIP THAN IT IS TO ENGAGE WITH A REAL, FLAWED YET LOVING PARTNER.
I'M ALSO SENSING SOME IMPENDING PHYSICAL DANGER. BEWARE A NINETEEN SIXTY NINE BUICK WILDCAT WITH KENTUCKY PLATES
WHOA! THAT'S FREAKY. DO MINE NOW! DO MINE!
DON'T FALL FOR IT, KRANG. THESE FORTUNE TELLER TYPES SPEAK IN GENERALITIES. WHAT HE SAID COULD APPLY TO ALMOST ANYONE. THIS GUY IS CLEARLY AN ACID CASUALTY AT BEST AND AT WORST, A FRAUD.
WE DIDN'T COME FOR ADVICE, OKAY? I JUST NEED MY AMP FIXED. CAN YOU HAVE IT READY BY EARLY NEXT WEEK?
I'M SORRY. IT'S IMPOSSIBLE FOR ME TO SAY.

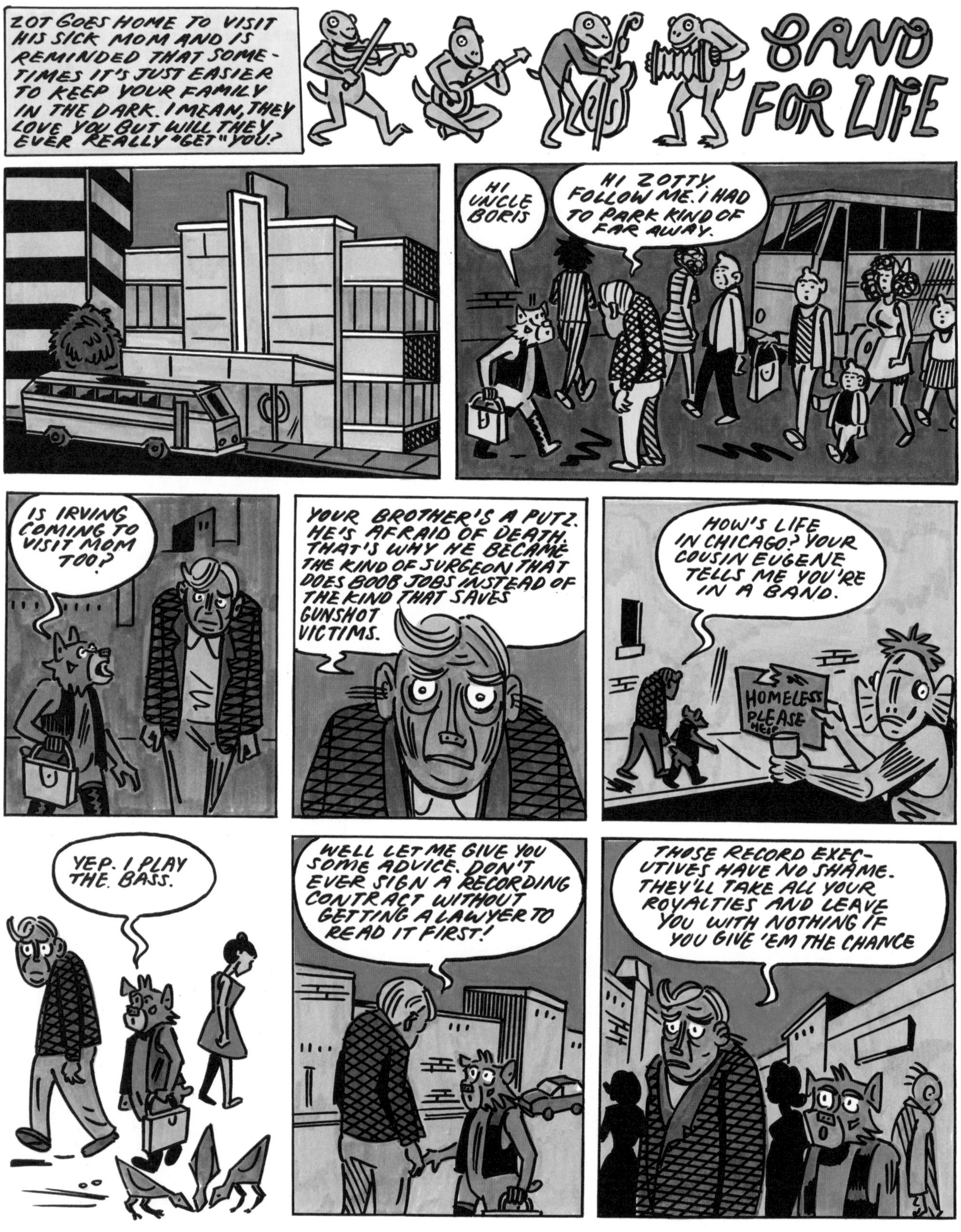
ZOT GOES HOME TO VISIT HIS SICK MOM AND IS REMINDED THAT SOMETIMES IT'S JUST EASIER TO KEEP YOUR FAMILY IN THE DARK. I MEAN, THEY LOVE YOU BUT WILL THEY EVER REALLY "GET" YOU?
BAND FOR LIFE
HI UNCLE BORIS
HI ZOTTY. FOLLOW ME. I HAD TO PARK KIND OF FAR AWAY.
IS IRVING COMING TO VISIT MOM TOO?
YOUR BROTHER'S A PUTZ. HE'S AFRAID OF DEATH. THAT'S WHY HE BECAME THE KIND OF SURGEON THAT DOES BOOB JOBS INSTEAD OF THE KIND THAT SAVES GUNSHOT VICTIMS.
HOW'S LIFE IN CHICAGO? YOUR COUSIN EUGENE TELLS ME YOU'RE IN A BAND.
HOMELESS PLEASE
YEP. I PLAY THE BASS.
WELL LET ME GIVE YOU SOME ADVICE. DON'T EVER SIGN A RECORDING CONTRACT WITHOUT GETTING A LAWYER TO READ IT FIRST!
THOSE RECORD EXECUTIVES HAVE NO SHAME. THEY'LL TAKE ALL YOUR ROYALTIES AND LEAVE YOU WITH NOTHING IF YOU GIVE 'EM THE CHANCE

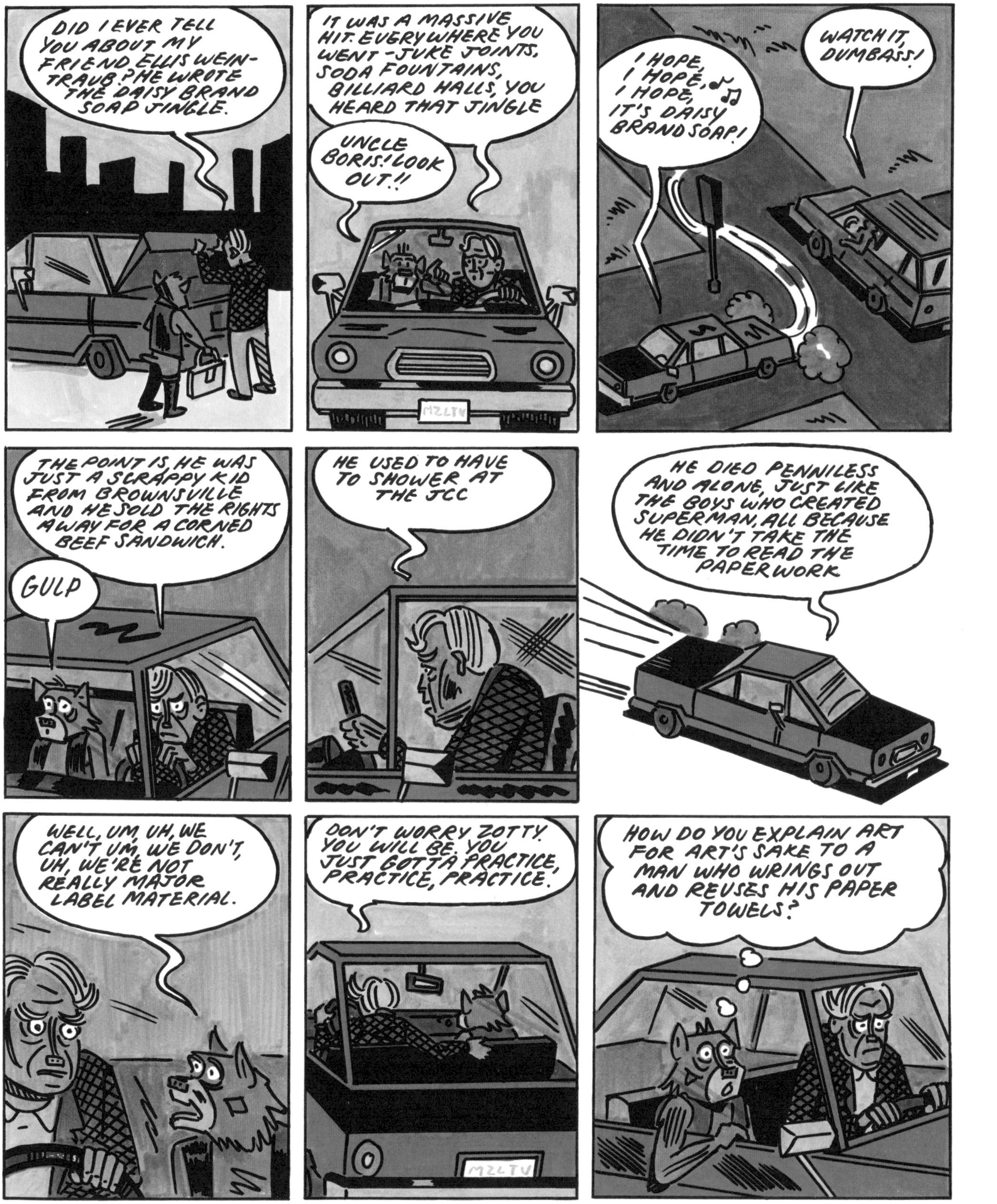
DID I EVER TELL YOU ABOUT MY FRIEND ELLIS WEINTRAUB? HE WROTE THE DAISY BRAND SOAP JINGLE.
IT WAS A MASSIVE HIT. EVERYWHERE YOU WENT - JUKE JOINTS, SODA FOUNTAINS, BILLIARD HALLS, YOU HEARD THAT JINGLE
UNCLE BORIS! LOOK OUT!!
I HOPE, I HOPE, I HOPE, IT'S DAISY BRAND SOAP!
WATCH IT, DUMBASS!
THE POINT IS, HE WAS JUST A SCRAPPY KID FROM BROWNSVILLE AND HE SOLD THE RIGHTS AWAY FOR A CORNED BEEF SANDWICH.
GULP
HE USED TO HAVE TO SHOWER AT THE JCC
HE DIED PENNILESS AND ALONE, JUST LIKE THE BOYS WHO CREATED SUPERMAN, ALL BECAUSE HE DIDN'T TAKE THE TIME TO READ THE PAPERWORK
WELL, UM, UH, WE CAN'T UM, WE DON'T, UH, WE'RE NOT REALLY MAJOR LABEL MATERIAL.
DON'T WORRY ZOTTY. YOU WILL BE. YOU JUST GOTTA PRACTICE, PRACTICE, PRACTICE.
HOW DO YOU EXPLAIN ART FOR ART'S SAKE TO A MAN WHO WRINGS OUT AND REUSES HIS PAPER TOWELS?

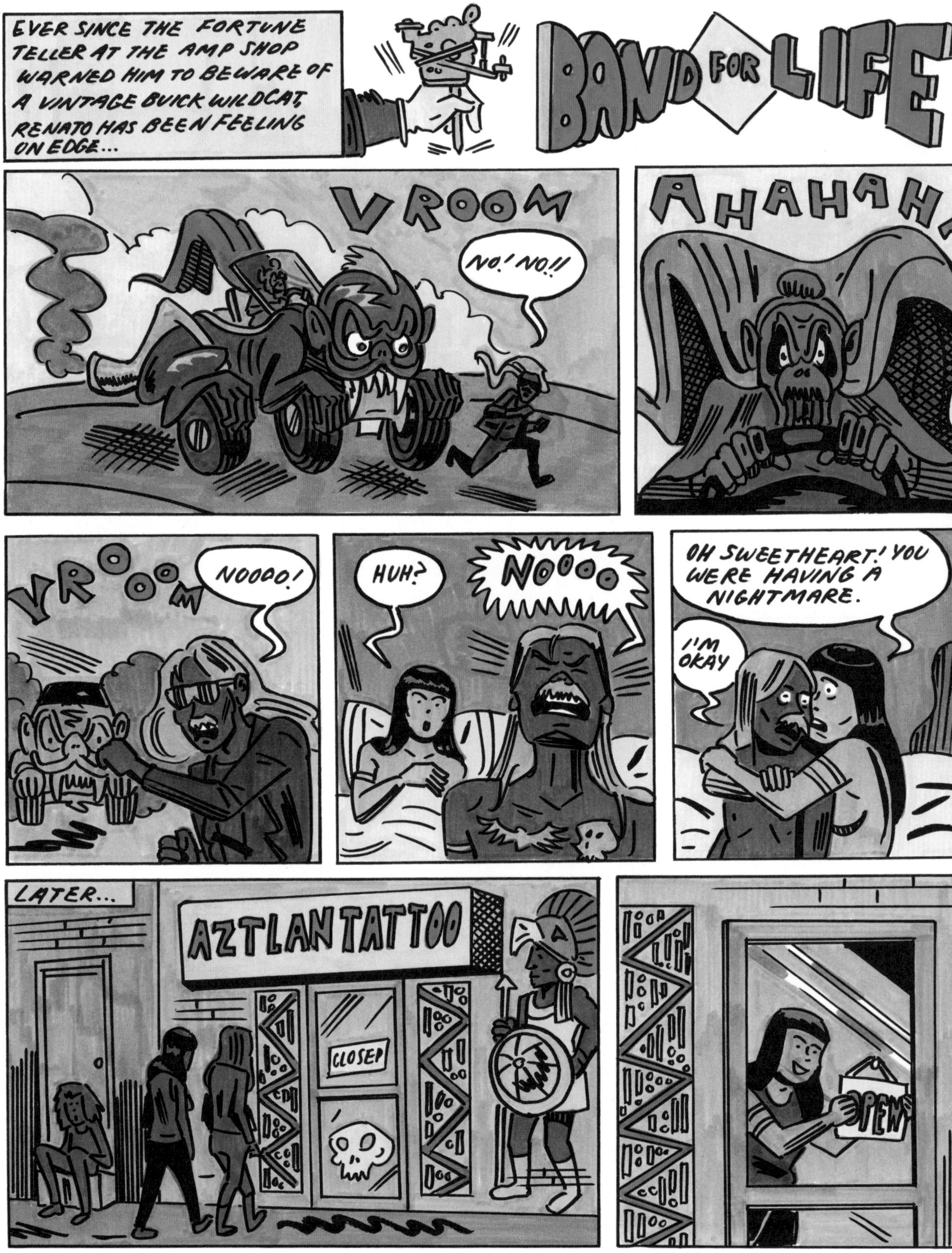
EVER SINCE THE FORTUNE TELLER AT THE AMP SHOP WARNED HIM TO BEWARE OF A VINTAGE BUICK WILDCAT, RENATO HAS BEEN FEELING ON EDGE...
BAND FOR LIFE
VROOM
NO! NO!!
AHAHAHAHA
VROOOM
NOOOO!
HUH?
NOOOO
OH SWEETHEART! YOU WERE HAVING A NIGHTMARE.
I'M OKAY
LATER...
AZTLAN TATTOO
CLOSED
OPEN

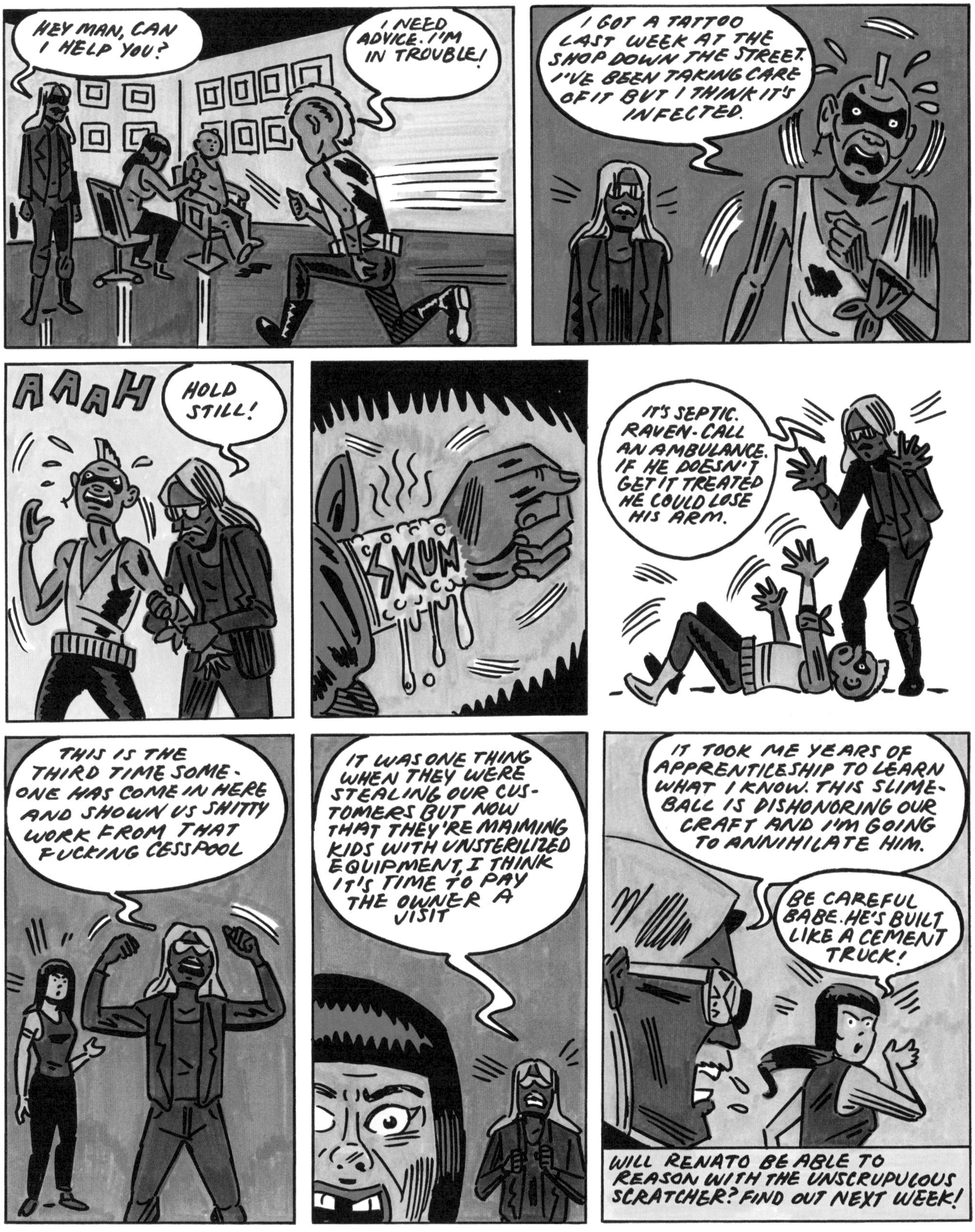
HEY MAN, CAN I HELP YOU?
I NEED ADVICE. I'M IN TROUBLE!
I GOT A TATTOO LAST WEEK AT THE SHOP DOWN THE STREET. I'VE BEEN TAKING CARE OF IT BUT I THINK IT'S INFECTED.
AAAH
HOLD STILL!
SKUM
IT'S SEPTIC. RAVEN- CALL AN AMBULANCE. IF HE DOESN'T GET IT TREATED HE COULD LOSE HIS ARM.
THIS IS THE THIRD TIME SOME-ONE HAS COME IN HERE AND SHOWN US SHITTY WORK FROM THAT FUCKING CESSPOOL
IT WAS ONE THING WHEN THEY WERE STEALING OUR CUS-TOMERS BUT NOW THAT THEY'RE MAIMING KIDS WITH UNSTERILIZED EQUIPMENT, I THINK IT'S TIME TO PAY THE OWNER A VISIT
IT TOOK ME YEARS OF APPRENTICESHIP TO LEARN WHAT I KNOW. THIS SLIME-BALL IS DISHONORING OUR CRAFT AND I'M GOING TO ANNIHILATE HIM.
BE CAREFUL BABE. HE'S BUILT LIKE A CEMENT TRUCK!
WILL RENATO BE ABLE TO REASON WITH THE UNSCRUPULOUS SCRATCHER? FIND OUT NEXT WEEK!

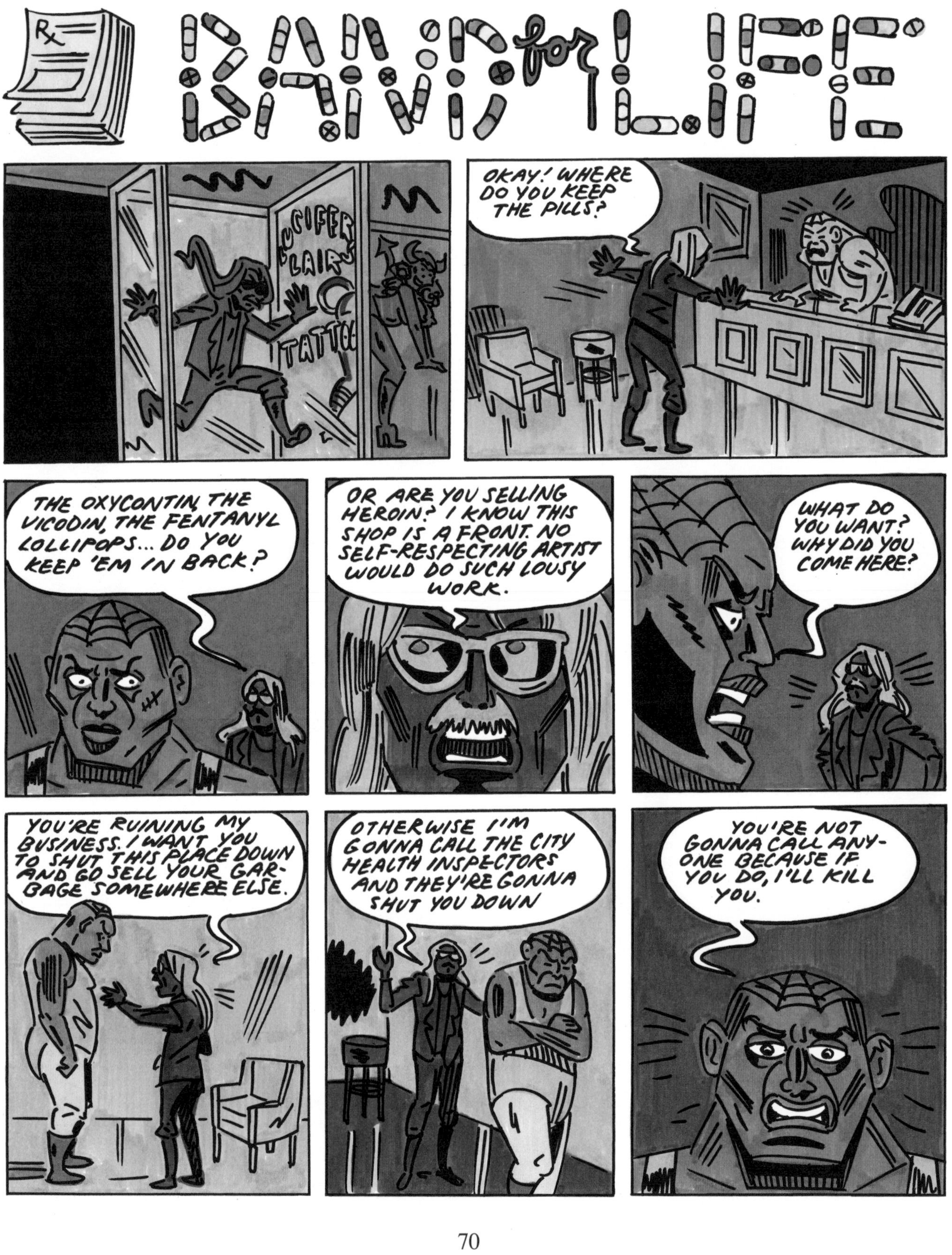
BAND for LIFE
Rx
LUCIFER'S LAIR TATTOO
OKAY! WHERE DO YOU KEEP THE PILLS?
THE OXYCONTIN, THE VICODIN, THE FENTANYL LOLLIPOPS... DO YOU KEEP 'EM IN BACK?
OR ARE YOU SELLING HEROIN? I KNOW THIS SHOP IS A FRONT. NO SELF-RESPECTING ARTIST WOULD DO SUCH LOUSY WORK.
WHAT DO YOU WANT? WHY DID YOU COME HERE?
YOU'RE RUINING MY BUSINESS. I WANT YOU TO SHUT THIS PLACE DOWN AND GO SELL YOUR GARBAGE SOMEWHERE ELSE.
OTHERWISE I'M GONNA CALL THE CITY HEALTH INSPECTORS AND THEY'RE GONNA SHUT YOU DOWN
YOU'RE NOT GONNA CALL ANYONE BECAUSE IF YOU DO, I'LL KILL YOU.

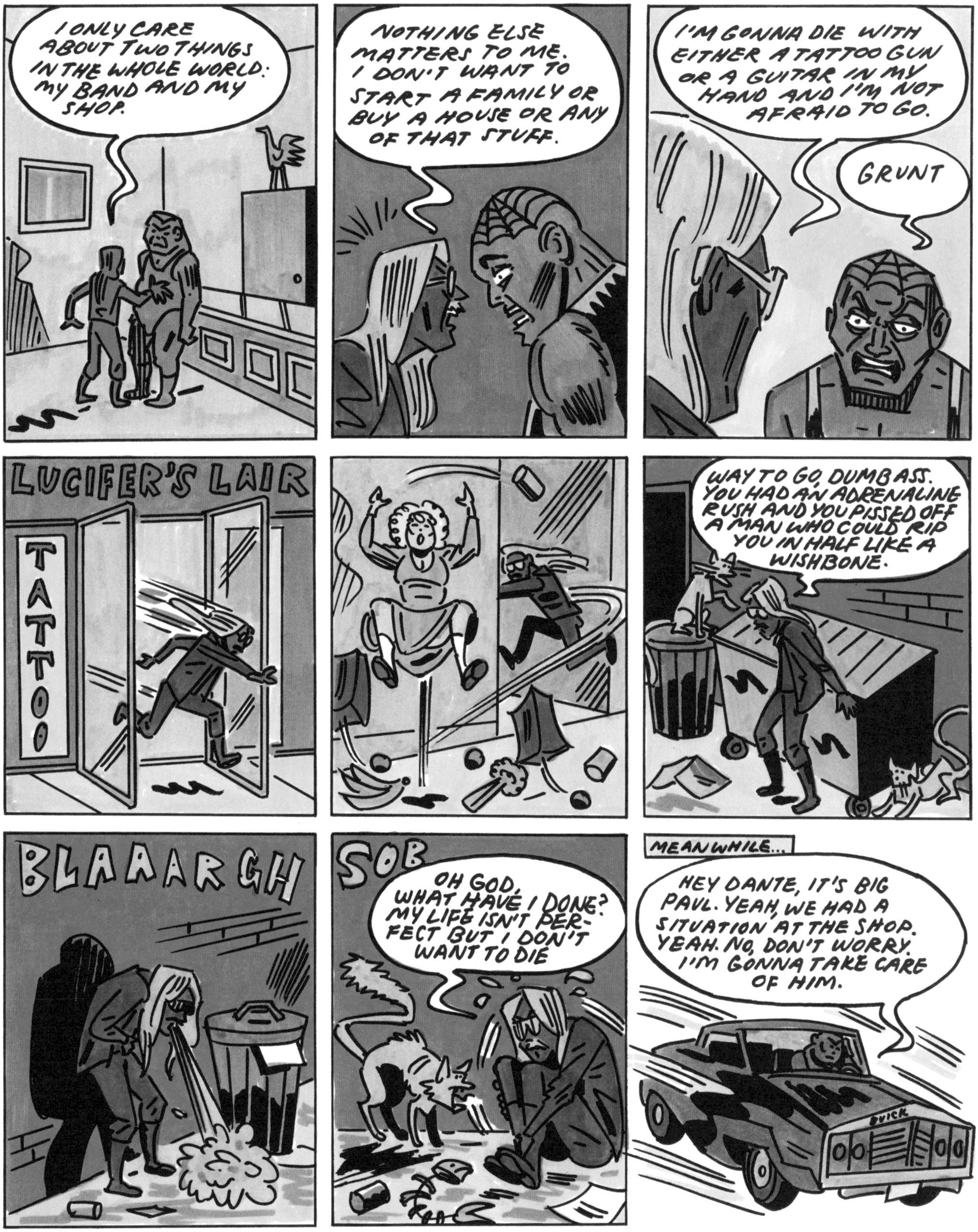

I ONLY CARE ABOUT TWO THINGS IN THE WHOLE WORLD: MY BAND AND MY SHOP.
NOTHING ELSE MATTERS TO ME. I DON'T WANT TO START A FAMILY OR BUY A HOUSE OR ANY OF THAT STUFF.
I'M GONNA DIE WITH EITHER A TATTOO GUN OR A GUITAR IN MY HAND AND I'M NOT AFRAID TO GO.
GRUNT
LUCIFER'S LAIR
TATTOO
WAY TO GO, DUMBASS. YOU HAD AN ADRENALINE RUSH AND YOU PISSED OFF A MAN WHO COULD RIP YOU IN HALF LIKE A WISHBONE.
BLAAARGH
SOB
OH GOD, WHAT HAVE I DONE? MY LIFE ISN'T PERFECT BUT I DON'T WANT TO DIE
MEANWHILE...
HEY DANTE, IT'S BIG PAUL. YEAH, WE HAD A SITUATION AT THE SHOP. YEAH. NO, DON'T WORRY. I'M GONNA TAKE CARE OF HIM.
BUICK

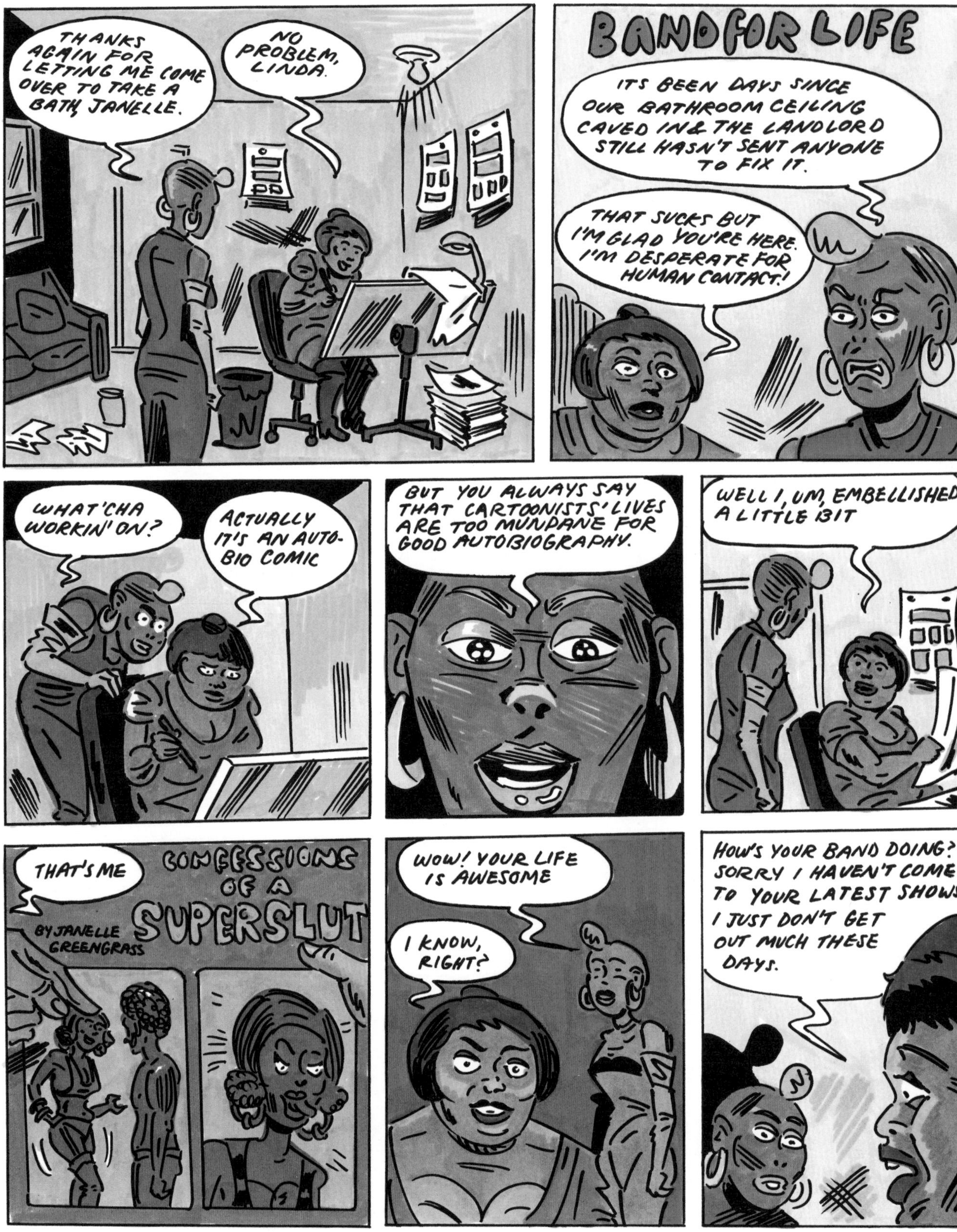
THANKS AGAIN FOR LETTING ME COME OVER TO TAKE A BATH, JANELLE.
NO PROBLEM, LINDA.
BAND FOR LIFE
IT'S BEEN DAYS SINCE OUR BATHROOM CEILING CAVED IN & THE LANDLORD STILL HASN'T SENT ANYONE TO FIX IT.
THAT SUCKS BUT I'M GLAD YOU'RE HERE. I'M DESPERATE FOR HUMAN CONTACT!
WHAT'CHA WORKIN' ON?
ACTUALLY IT'S AN AUTO-BIO COMIC
BUT YOU ALWAYS SAY THAT CARTOONISTS' LIVES ARE TOO MUNDANE FOR GOOD AUTOBIOGRAPHY.
WELL I, UM, EMBELLISHED A LITTLE BIT
THAT'S ME
CONFESSIONS OF A SUPERSLUT
BY JANELLE GREENGRASS
WOW! YOUR LIFE IS AWESOME
I KNOW, RIGHT?
HOW'S YOUR BAND DOING? SORRY I HAVEN'T COME TO YOUR LATEST SHOWS. I JUST DON'T GET OUT MUCH THESE DAYS.

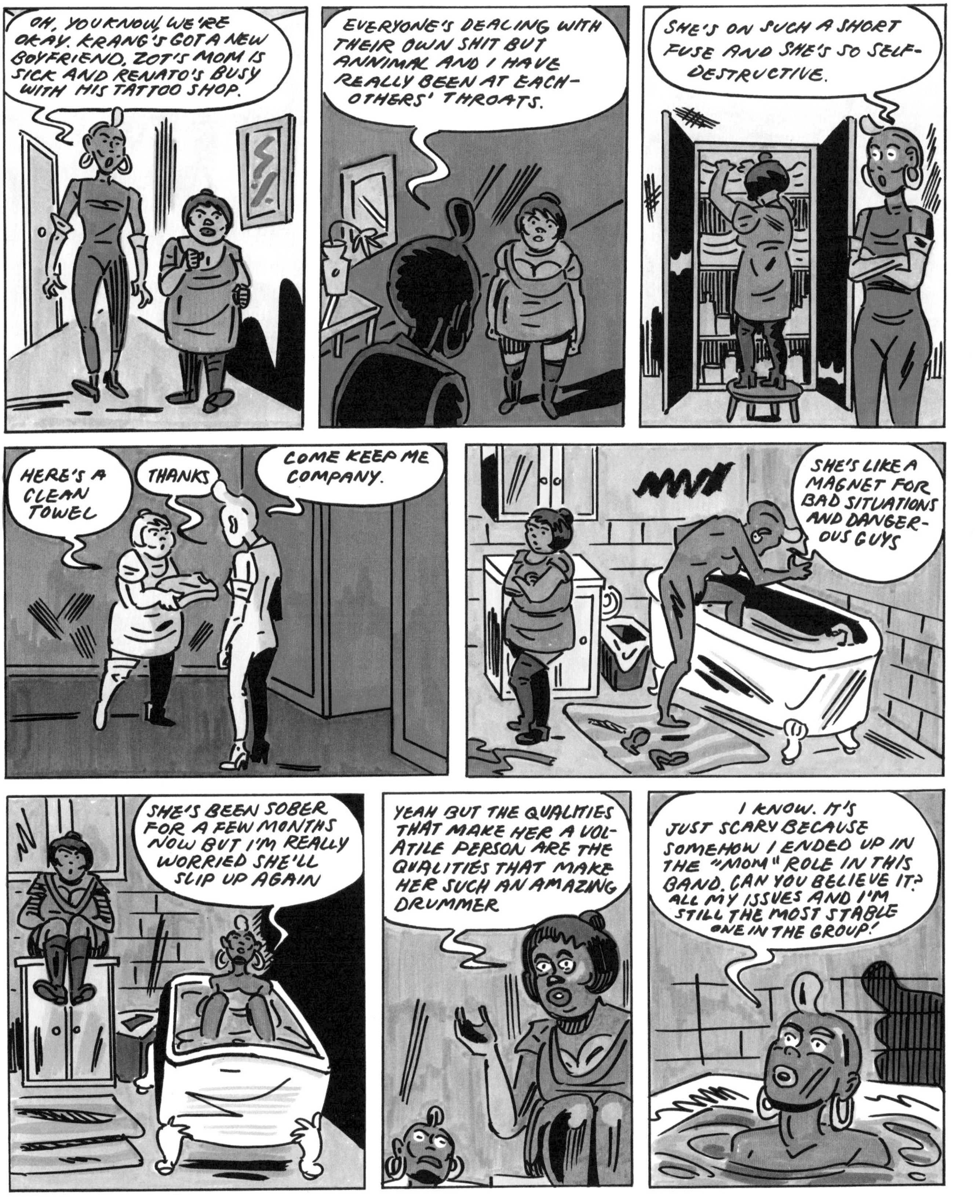
OH, YOU KNOW, WE'RE OKAY. KRANG'S GOT A NEW BOYFRIEND, ZOT'S MOM IS SICK AND RENATO'S BUSY WITH HIS TATTOO SHOP.
EVERYONE'S DEALING WITH THEIR OWN SHIT BUT ANNIMAL AND I HAVE REALLY BEEN AT EACH-OTHERS' THROATS.
SHE'S ON SUCH A SHORT FUSE AND SHE'S SO SELF-DESTRUCTIVE.
HERE'S A CLEAN TOWEL
THANKS
COME KEEP ME COMPANY.
SHE'S LIKE A MAGNET FOR BAD SITUATIONS AND DANGER-OUS GUYS
SHE'S BEEN SOBER FOR A FEW MONTHS NOW BUT I'M REALLY WORRIED SHE'LL SLIP UP AGAIN
YEAH BUT THE QUALITIES THAT MAKE HER A VOL-ATILE PERSON ARE THE QUALITIES THAT MAKE HER SUCH AN AMAZING DRUMMER
I KNOW. IT'S JUST SCARY BECAUSE SOMEHOW I ENDED UP IN THE "MOM" ROLE IN THIS BAND. CAN YOU BELIEVE IT? ALL MY ISSUES AND I'M STILL THE MOST STABLE ONE IN THE GROUP!

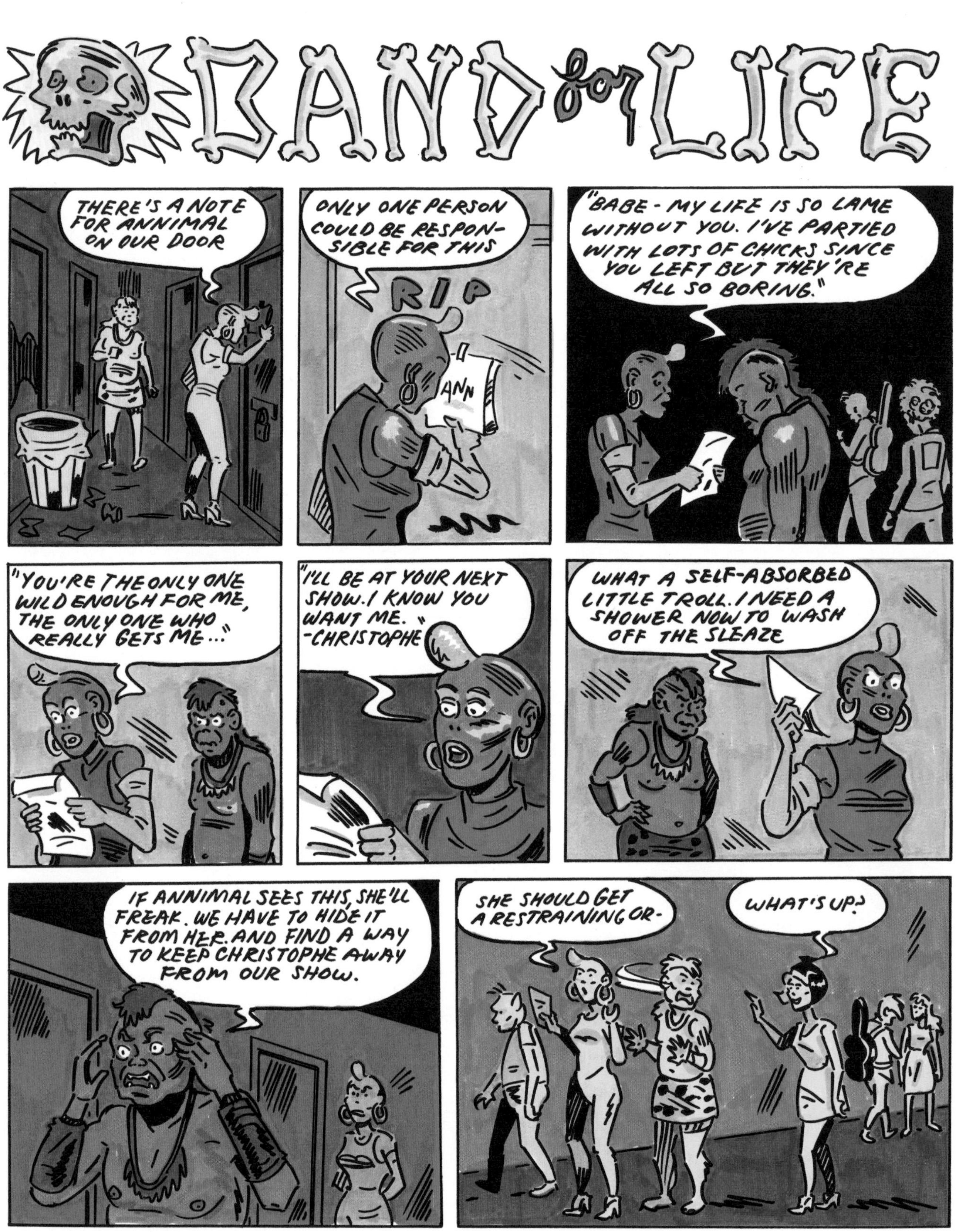
BAND for LIFE
THERE'S A NOTE FOR ANNIMAL ON OUR DOOR
ONLY ONE PERSON COULD BE RESPONSIBLE FOR THIS
RIP
ANN
"BABE - MY LIFE IS SO LAME WITHOUT YOU. I'VE PARTIED WITH LOTS OF CHICKS SINCE YOU LEFT BUT THEY'RE ALL SO BORING."
"YOU'RE THE ONLY ONE WILD ENOUGH FOR ME, THE ONLY ONE WHO REALLY GETS ME..."
"I'LL BE AT YOUR NEXT SHOW. I KNOW YOU WANT ME." -CHRISTOPHE
WHAT A SELF-ABSORBED LITTLE TROLL. I NEED A SHOWER NOW TO WASH OFF THE SLEAZE
IF ANNIMAL SEES THIS, SHE'LL FREAK. WE HAVE TO HIDE IT FROM HER. AND FIND A WAY TO KEEP CHRISTOPHE AWAY FROM OUR SHOW.
SHE SHOULD GET A RESTRAINING OR-
WHAT'S UP?

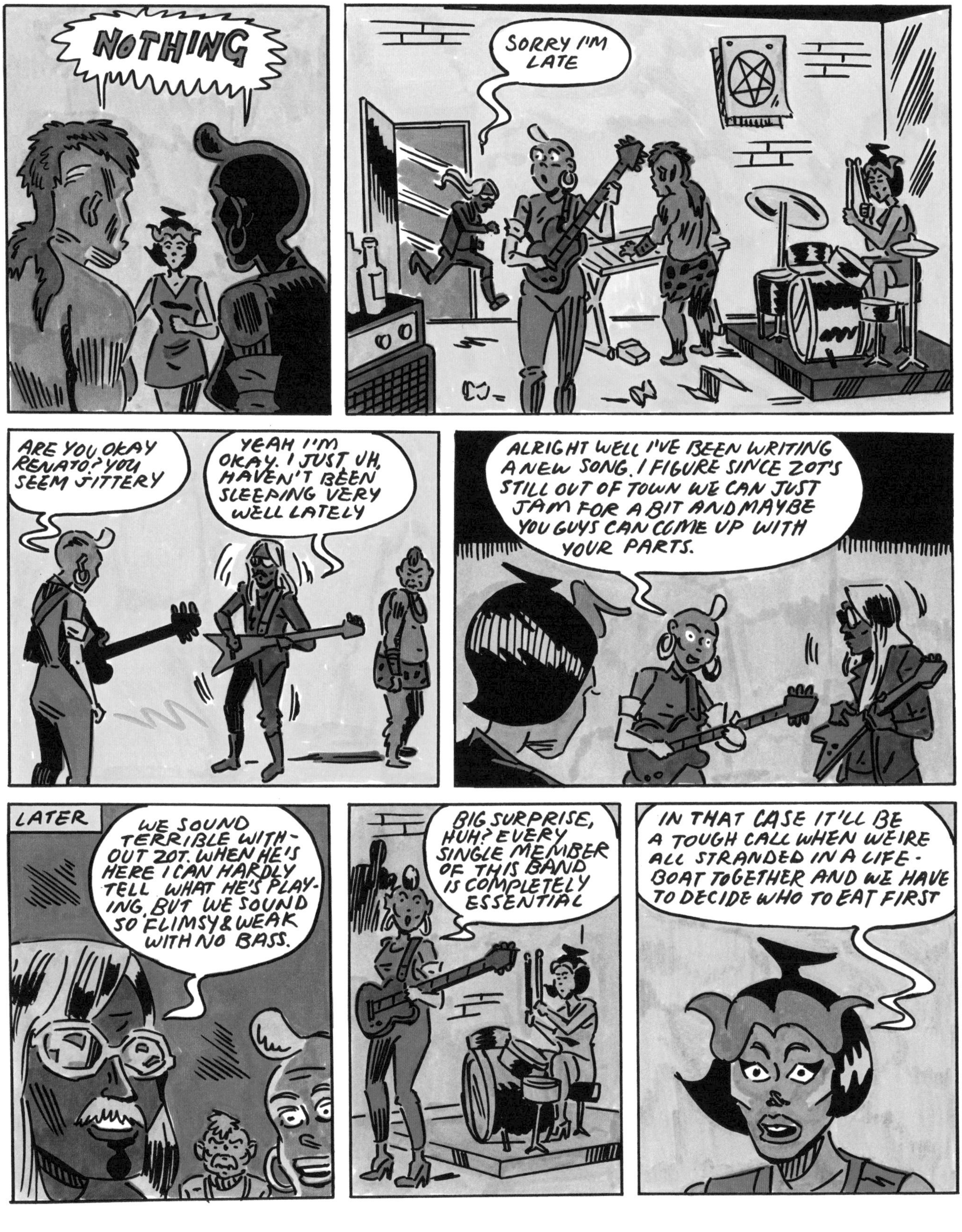
NOTHING
SORRY I'M LATE
ARE YOU OKAY RENATO? YOU SEEM JITTERY
YEAH I'M OKAY. I JUST UH, HAVEN'T BEEN SLEEPING VERY WELL LATELY
ALRIGHT WELL I'VE BEEN WRITING A NEW SONG. I FIGURE SINCE ZOT'S STILL OUT OF TOWN WE CAN JUST JAM FOR A BIT AND MAYBE YOU GUYS CAN COME UP WITH YOUR PARTS.
LATER
WE SOUND TERRIBLE WITH-OUT ZOT. WHEN HE'S HERE I CAN HARDLY TELL WHAT HE'S PLAY-ING, BUT WE SOUND SO FLIMSY & WEAK WITH NO BASS.
BIG SURPRISE, HUH? EVERY SINGLE MEMBER OF THIS BAND IS COMPLETELY ESSENTIAL
IN THAT CASE IT'LL BE A TOUGH CALL WHEN WE'RE ALL STRANDED IN A LIFE-BOAT TOGETHER AND WE HAVE TO DECIDE WHO TO EAT FIRST

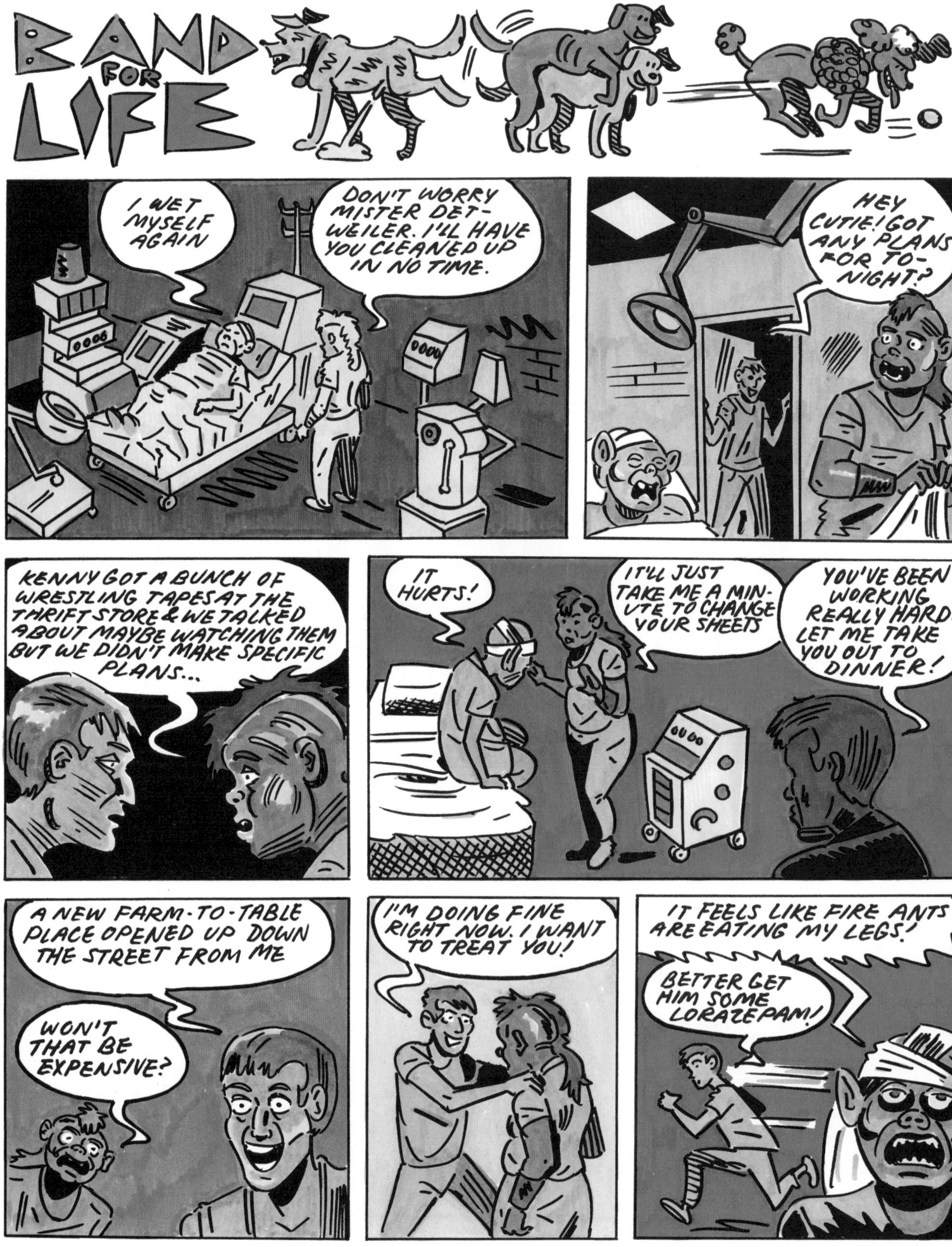
BAND FOR LIFE
I WET MYSELF AGAIN
DON'T WORRY MISTER DETWEILER. I'LL HAVE YOU CLEANED UP IN NO TIME.
HEY CUTIE! GOT ANY PLANS FOR TONIGHT?
KENNY GOT A BUNCH OF WRESTLING TAPES AT THE THRIFT STORE & WE TALKED ABOUT MAYBE WATCHING THEM BUT WE DIDN'T MAKE SPECIFIC PLANS...
IT HURTS!
IT'LL JUST TAKE ME A MINUTE TO CHANGE YOUR SHEETS
YOU'VE BEEN WORKING REALLY HARD. LET ME TAKE YOU OUT TO DINNER!
A NEW FARM-TO-TABLE PLACE OPENED UP DOWN THE STREET FROM ME
WON'T THAT BE EXPENSIVE?
I'M DOING FINE RIGHT NOW. I WANT TO TREAT YOU!
IT FEELS LIKE FIRE ANTS ARE EATING MY LEGS!
BETTER GET HIM SOME LORAZEPAM!

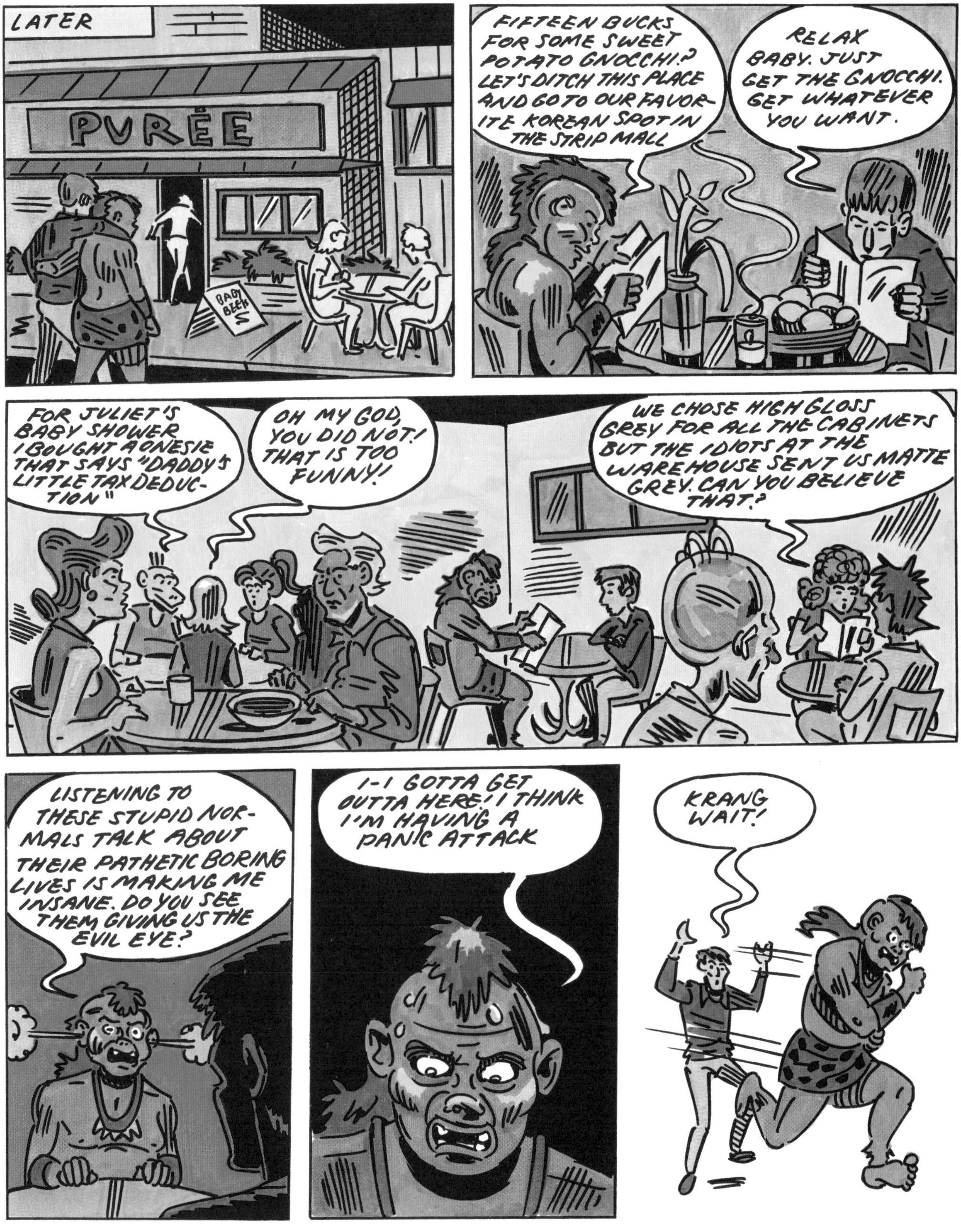
LATER
PURÉE
BABY BEETS $
FIFTEEN BUCKS FOR SOME SWEET POTATO GNOCCHI? LET'S DITCH THIS PLACE AND GO TO OUR FAVORITE KOREAN SPOT IN THE STRIP MALL
RELAX BABY. JUST GET THE GNOCCHI. GET WHATEVER YOU WANT.
FOR JULIET'S BABY SHOWER I BOUGHT A ONESIE THAT SAYS "DADDY'S LITTLE TAX DEDUCTION"
OH MY GOD, YOU DID NOT! THAT IS TOO FUNNY!
WE CHOSE HIGH GLOSS GREY FOR ALL THE CABINETS BUT THE IDIOTS AT THE WAREHOUSE SENT US MATTE GREY. CAN YOU BELIEVE THAT?
LISTENING TO THESE STUPID NORMALS TALK ABOUT THEIR PATHETIC BORING LIVES IS MAKING ME INSANE. DO YOU SEE THEM GIVING US THE EVIL EYE?
I-I GOTTA GET OUTTA HERE! I THINK I'M HAVING A PANIC ATTACK
KRANG WAIT!

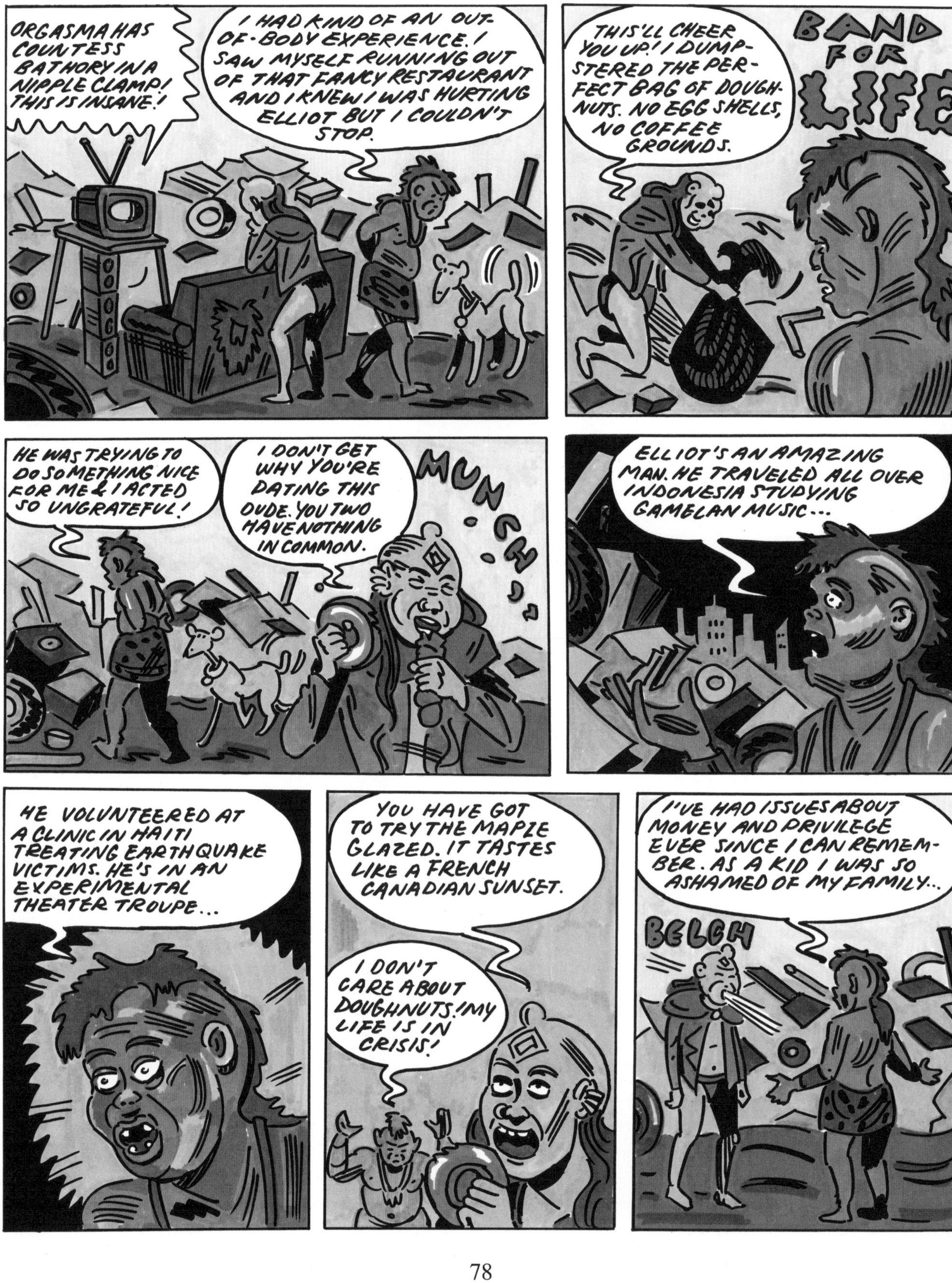
ORGASMA HAS COUNTESS BATHORY IN A NIPPLE CLAMP! THIS IS INSANE!
I HAD KIND OF AN OUT-OF-BODY EXPERIENCE. I SAW MYSELF RUNNING OUT OF THAT FANCY RESTAURANT AND I KNEW I WAS HURTING ELLIOT BUT I COULDN'T STOP.
THIS'LL CHEER YOU UP! I DUMPSTERED THE PERFECT BAG OF DOUGHNUTS. NO EGG SHELLS, NO COFFEE GROUNDS.
BAND FOR LIFE
HE WAS TRYING TO DO SOMETHING NICE FOR ME & I ACTED SO UNGRATEFUL!
I DON'T GET WHY YOU'RE DATING THIS DUDE. YOU TWO HAVE NOTHING IN COMMON.
MUNCH
ELLIOT'S AN AMAZING MAN. HE TRAVELED ALL OVER INDONESIA STUDYING GAMELAN MUSIC...
HE VOLUNTEERED AT A CLINIC IN HAITI TREATING EARTHQUAKE VICTIMS. HE'S IN AN EXPERIMENTAL THEATER TROUPE...
YOU HAVE GOT TO TRY THE MAPLE GLAZED. IT TASTES LIKE A FRENCH CANADIAN SUNSET.
I DON'T CARE ABOUT DOUGHNUTS! MY LIFE IS IN CRISIS!
I'VE HAD ISSUES ABOUT MONEY AND PRIVILEGE EVER SINCE I CAN REMEMBER. AS A KID I WAS SO ASHAMED OF MY FAMILY...
BELCH

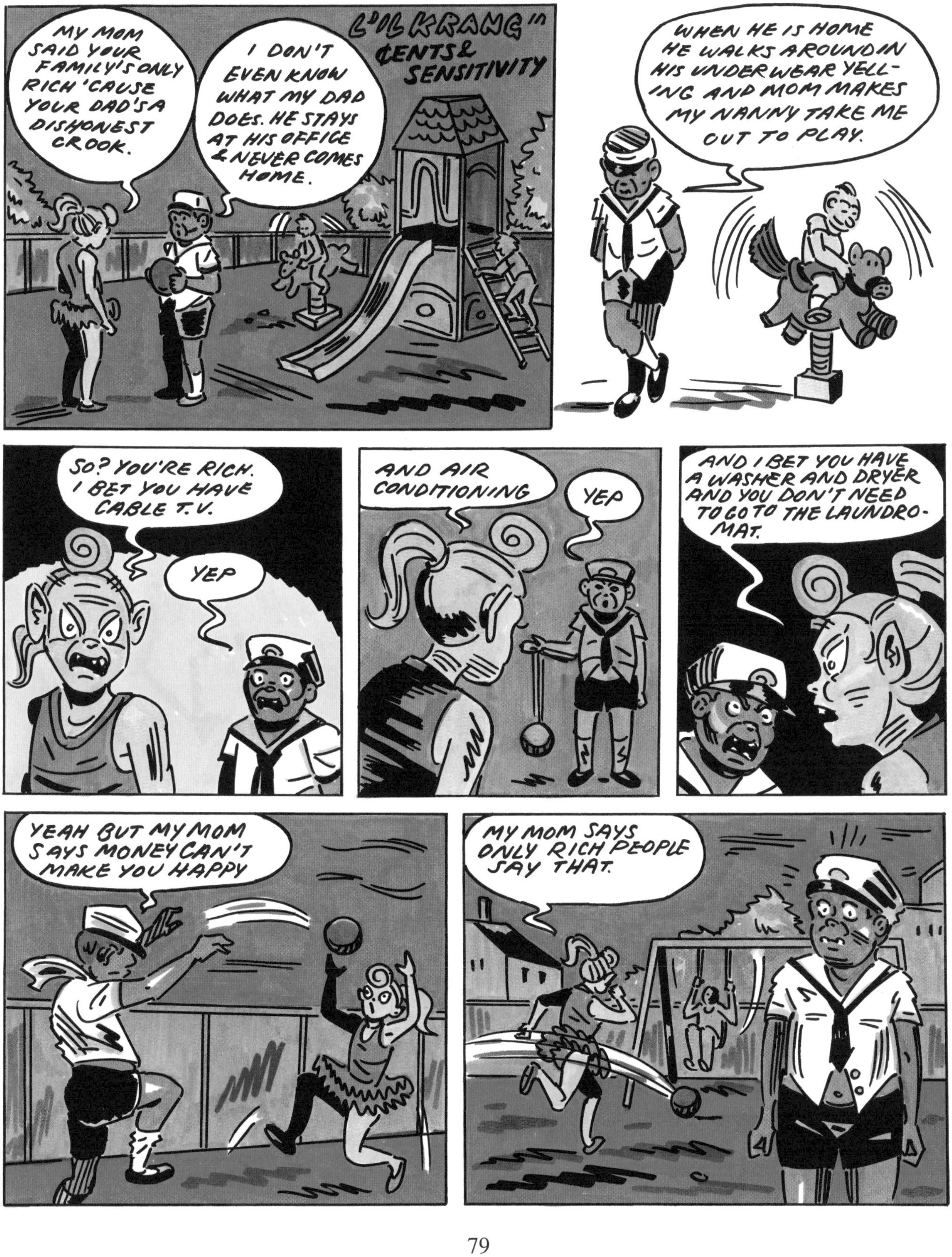
L'IL KRANG" in ¢ENTS & SENSITIVITY
MY MOM SAID YOUR FAMILY'S ONLY RICH 'CAUSE YOUR DAD'S A DISHONEST CROOK.
I DON'T EVEN KNOW WHAT MY DAD DOES. HE STAYS AT HIS OFFICE & NEVER COMES HOME.
WHEN HE IS HOME HE WALKS AROUND IN HIS UNDERWEAR YELLING AND MOM MAKES MY NANNY TAKE ME OUT TO PLAY.
SO? YOU'RE RICH. I BET YOU HAVE CABLE T.V.
YEP
AND AIR CONDITIONING
YEP
AND I BET YOU HAVE A WASHER AND DRYER AND YOU DON'T NEED TO GO TO THE LAUNDROMAT.
YEAH BUT MY MOM SAYS MONEY CAN'T MAKE YOU HAPPY
MY MOM SAYS ONLY RICH PEOPLE SAY THAT.

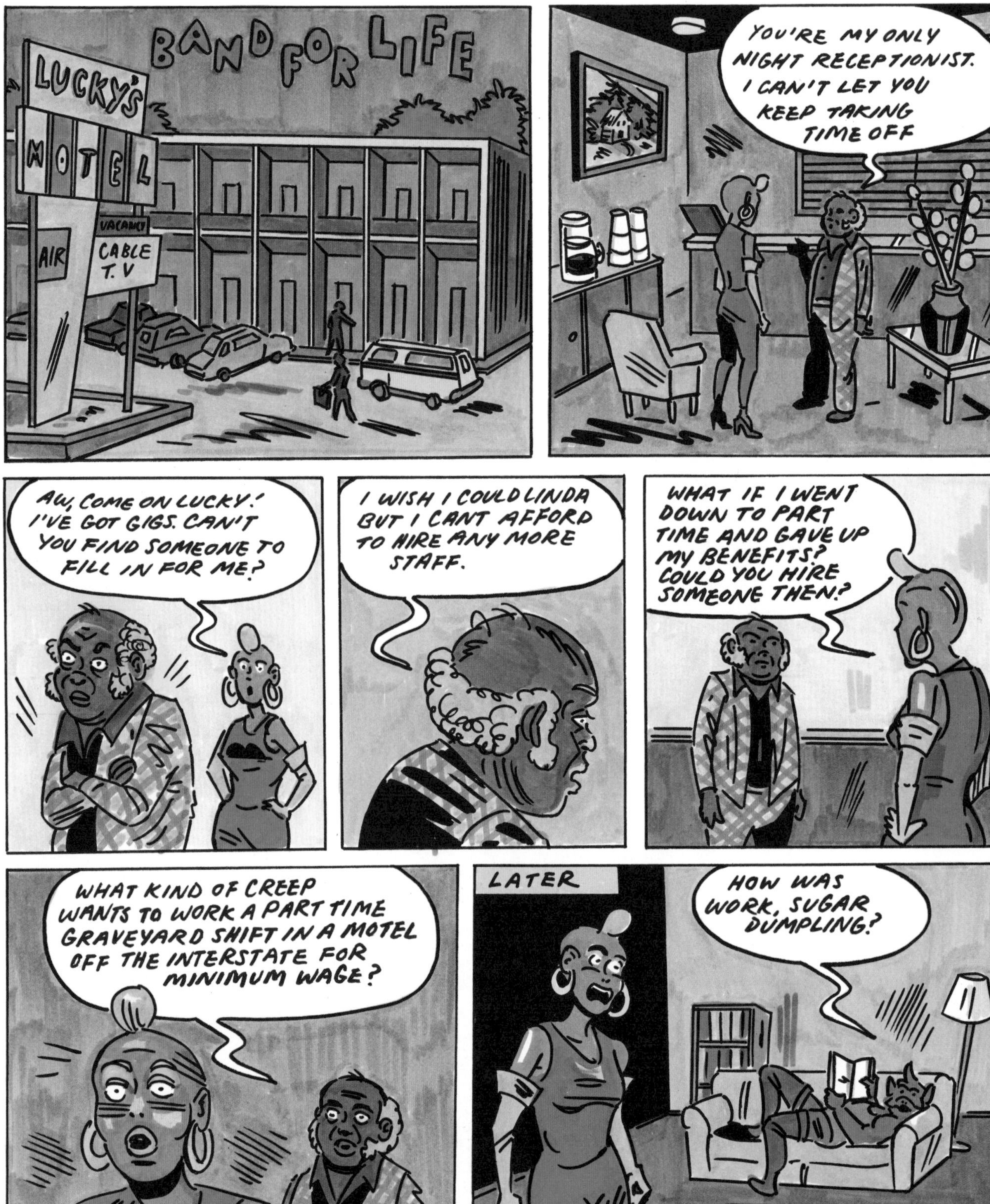
BAND FOR LIFE
LUCKY'S
MOTEL
VACANCY
AIR
CABLE T.V
YOU'RE MY ONLY NIGHT RECEPTIONIST. I CAN'T LET YOU KEEP TAKING TIME OFF
AW, COME ON LUCKY! I'VE GOT GIGS. CAN'T YOU FIND SOMEONE TO FILL IN FOR ME?
I WISH I COULD LINDA BUT I CANT AFFORD TO HIRE ANY MORE STAFF.
WHAT IF I WENT DOWN TO PART TIME AND GAVE UP MY BENEFITS? COULD YOU HIRE SOMEONE THEN?
WHAT KIND OF CREEP WANTS TO WORK A PART TIME GRAVEYARD SHIFT IN A MOTEL OFF THE INTERSTATE FOR MINIMUM WAGE?
LATER
HOW WAS WORK, SUGAR DUMPLING?

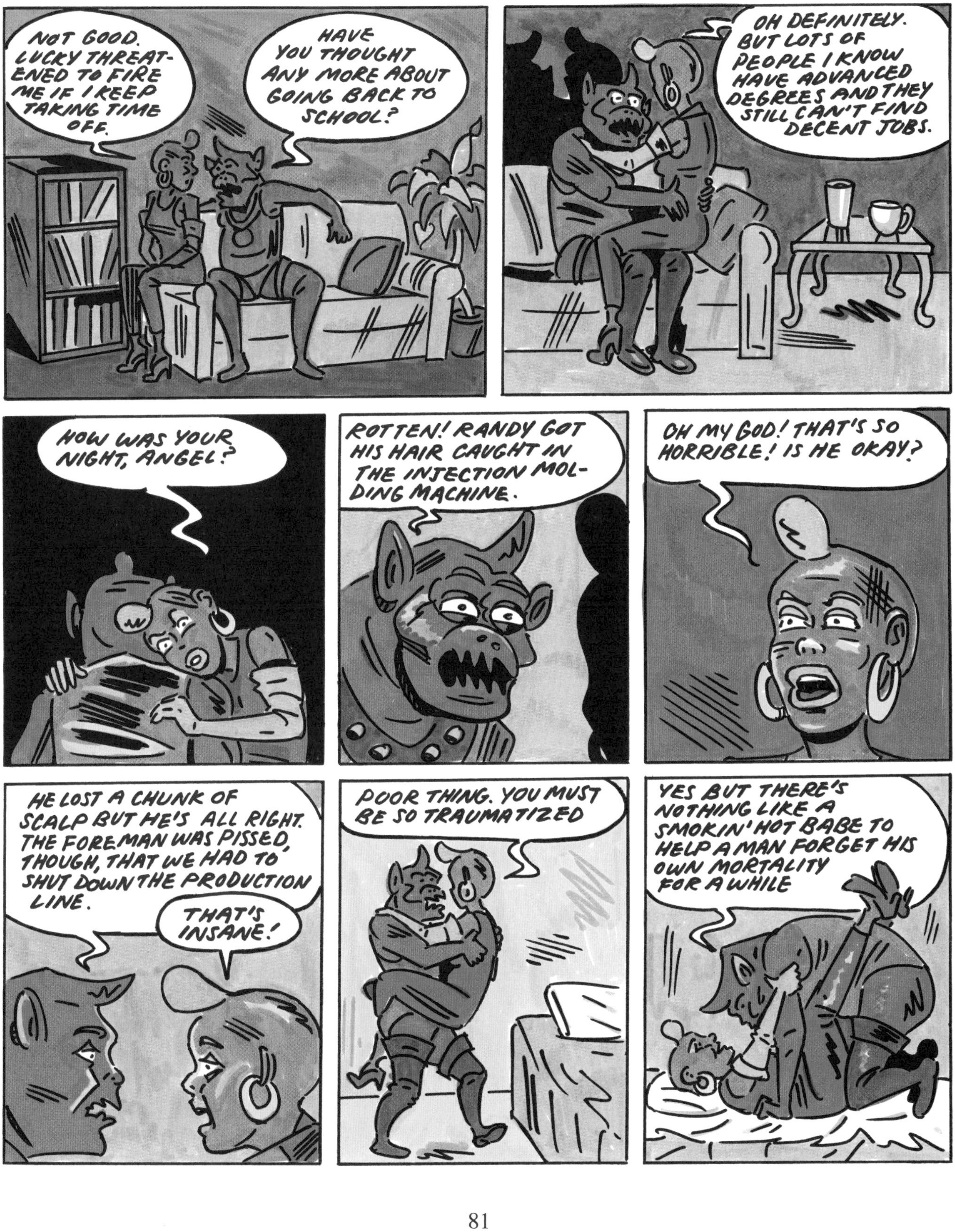
NOT GOOD. LUCKY THREAT-ENED TO FIRE ME IF I KEEP TAKING TIME OFF.
HAVE YOU THOUGHT ANY MORE ABOUT GOING BACK TO SCHOOL?
OH DEFINITELY. BUT LOTS OF PEOPLE I KNOW HAVE ADVANCED DEGREES AND THEY STILL CAN'T FIND DECENT JOBS.
HOW WAS YOUR NIGHT, ANGEL?
ROTTEN! RANDY GOT HIS HAIR CAUGHT IN THE INJECTION MOL-DING MACHINE.
OH MY GOD! THAT'S SO HORRIBLE! IS HE OKAY?
HE LOST A CHUNK OF SCALP BUT HE'S ALL RIGHT. THE FOREMAN WAS PISSED, THOUGH, THAT WE HAD TO SHUT DOWN THE PRODUCTION LINE.
THAT'S INSANE!
POOR THING. YOU MUST BE SO TRAUMATIZED
YES BUT THERE'S NOTHING LIKE A SMOKIN' HOT BABE TO HELP A MAN FORGET HIS OWN MORTALITY FOR A WHILE

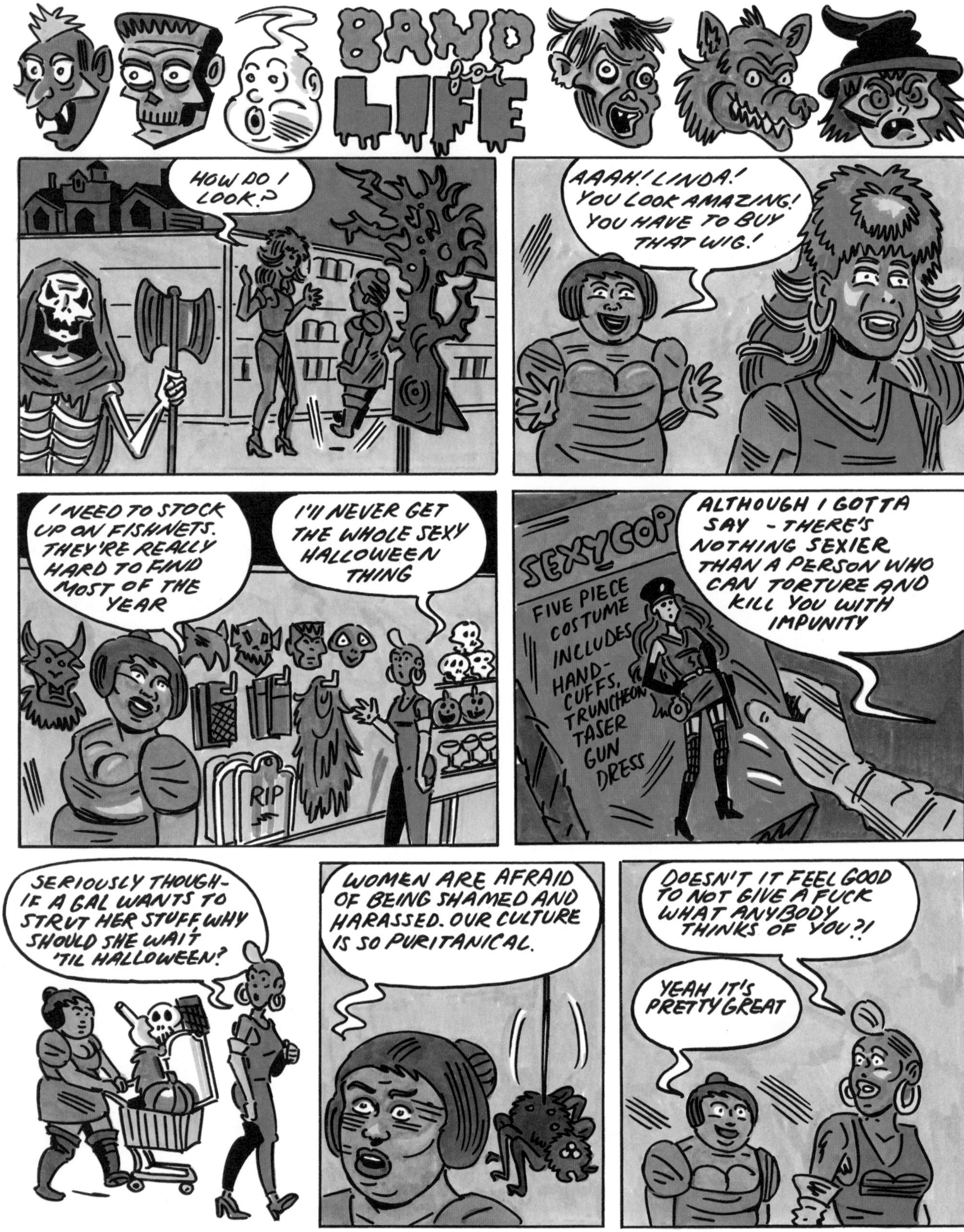
BAND for LIFE
HOW DO I LOOK?
AAAH! LINDA! YOU LOOK AMAZING! YOU HAVE TO BUY THAT WIG!
I NEED TO STOCK UP ON FISHNETS. THEY'RE REALLY HARD TO FIND MOST OF THE YEAR
I'll NEVER GET THE WHOLE SEXY HALLOWEEN THING
RIP
SEXY COP
FIVE PIECE COSTUME INCLUDES HAND-CUFFS, TRUNCHEON TASER GUN DRESS
ALTHOUGH I GOTTA SAY - THERE'S NOTHING SEXIER THAN A PERSON WHO CAN TORTURE AND KILL YOU WITH IMPUNITY
SERIOUSLY THOUGH- IF A GAL WANTS TO STRUT HER STUFF, WHY SHOULD SHE WAIT 'TIL HALLOWEEN?
WOMEN ARE AFRAID OF BEING SHAMED AND HARASSED. OUR CULTURE IS SO PURITANICAL.
DOESN'T IT FEEL GOOD TO NOT GIVE A FUCK WHAT ANYBODY THINKS OF YOU?!
YEAH IT'S PRETTY GREAT

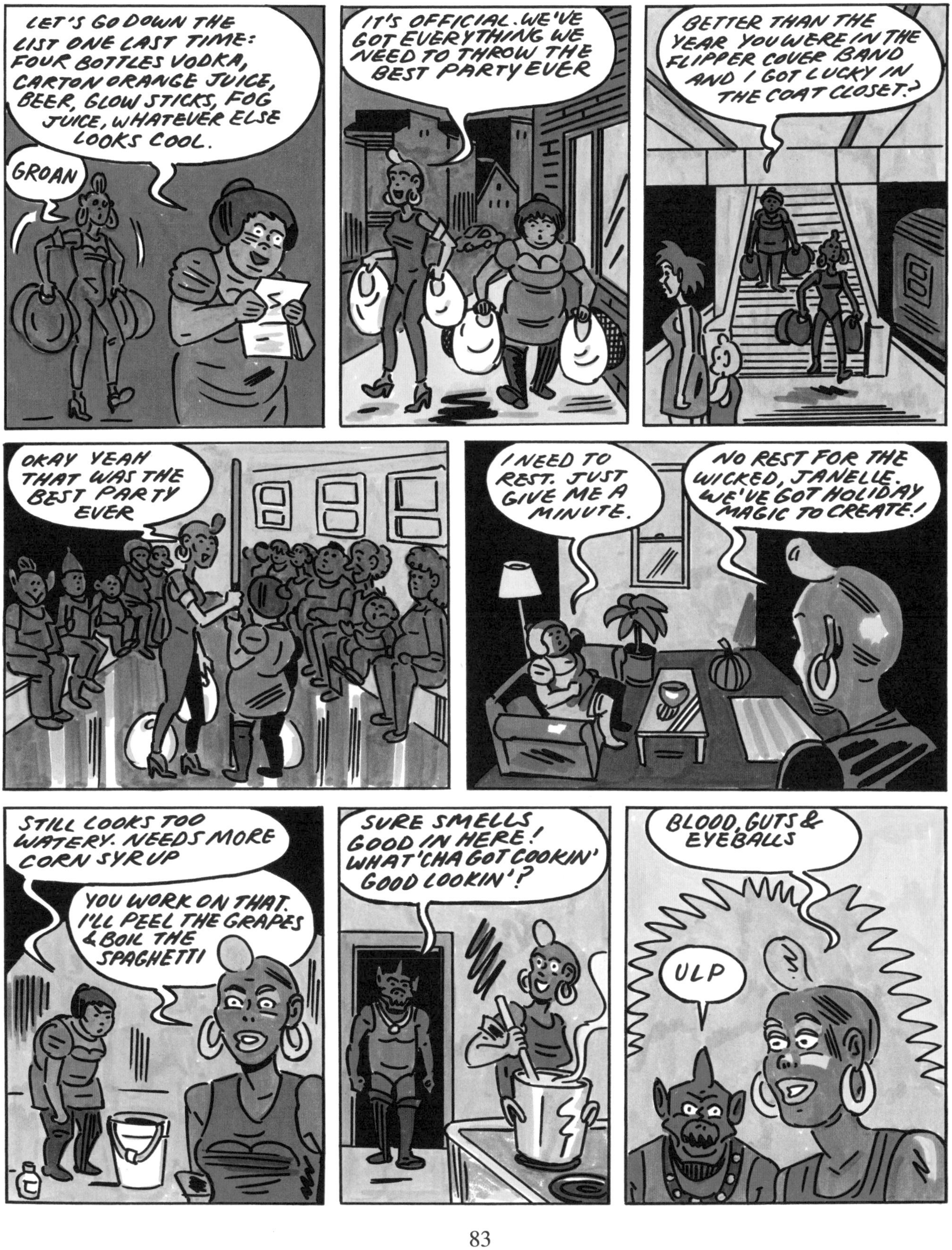
LET'S GO DOWN THE LIST ONE LAST TIME: FOUR BOTTLES VODKA, CARTON ORANGE JUICE, BEER, GLOW STICKS, FOG JUICE, WHATEVER ELSE LOOKS COOL.
GROAN
IT'S OFFICIAL. WE'VE GOT EVERYTHING WE NEED TO THROW THE BEST PARTY EVER
BETTER THAN THE YEAR YOU WERE IN THE FLIPPER COVER BAND AND I GOT LUCKY IN THE COAT CLOSET?
OKAY YEAH THAT WAS THE BEST PARTY EVER
I NEED TO REST. JUST GIVE ME A MINUTE.
NO REST FOR THE WICKED, JANELLE. WE'VE GOT HOLIDAY MAGIC TO CREATE!
STILL LOOKS TOO WATERY. NEEDS MORE CORN SYRUP
YOU WORK ON THAT. I'LL PEEL THE GRAPES & BOIL THE SPAGHETTI
SURE SMELLS GOOD IN HERE! WHAT'CHA GOT COOKIN' GOOD LOOKIN'?
BLOOD, GUTS & EYEBALLS
ULP

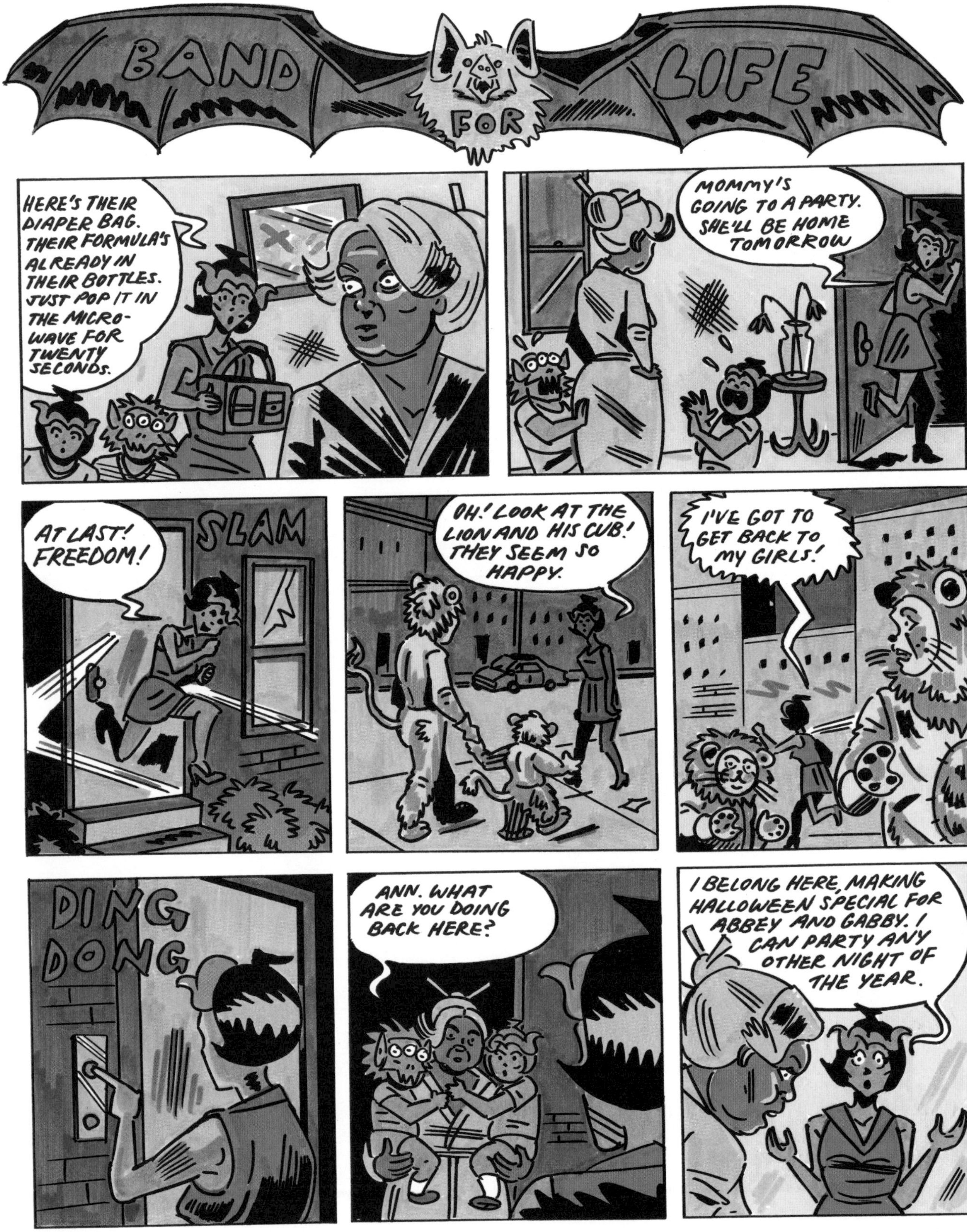
BAND FOR LIFE
HERE'S THEIR DIAPER BAG. THEIR FORMULA'S ALREADY IN THEIR BOTTLES. JUST POP IT IN THE MICRO-WAVE FOR TWENTY SECONDS.
MOMMY'S GOING TO A PARTY. SHE'LL BE HOME TOMORROW
AT LAST! FREEDOM!
SLAM
OH! LOOK AT THE LION AND HIS CUB! THEY SEEM SO HAPPY.
I'VE GOT TO GET BACK TO MY GIRLS!
DING DONG
ANN. WHAT ARE YOU DOING BACK HERE?
I BELONG HERE, MAKING HALLOWEEN SPECIAL FOR ABBEY AND GABBY. I CAN PARTY ANY OTHER NIGHT OF THE YEAR.

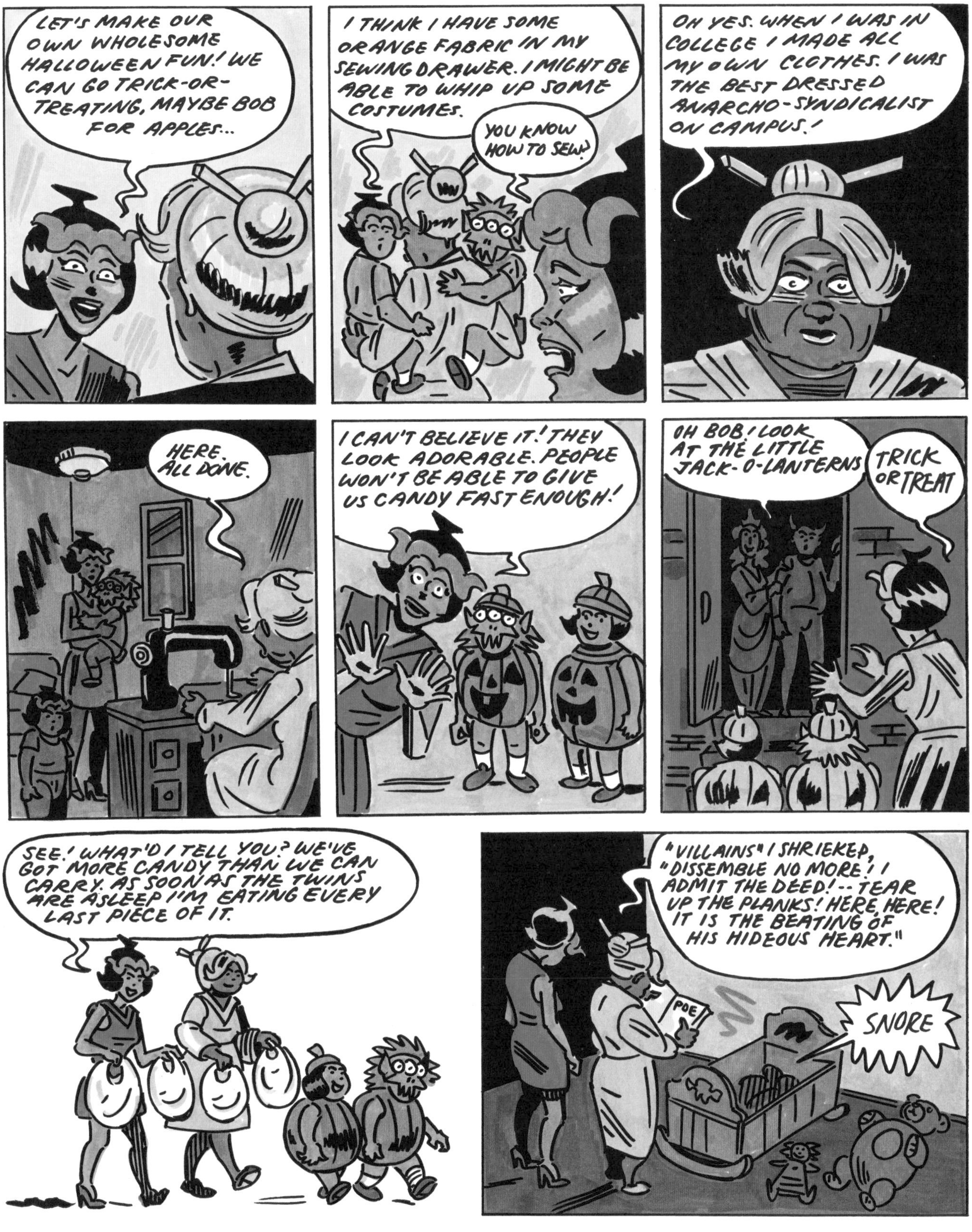
LET'S MAKE OUR OWN WHOLESOME HALLOWEEN FUN! WE CAN GO TRICK-OR-TREATING, MAYBE BOB FOR APPLES...
I THINK I HAVE SOME ORANGE FABRIC IN MY SEWING DRAWER. I MIGHT BE ABLE TO WHIP UP SOME COSTUMES.
YOU KNOW HOW TO SEW?
OH YES. WHEN I WAS IN COLLEGE I MADE ALL MY OWN CLOTHES. I WAS THE BEST DRESSED ANARCHO-SYNDICALIST ON CAMPUS!
HERE. ALL DONE.
I CAN'T BELIEVE IT! THEY LOOK ADORABLE. PEOPLE WON'T BE ABLE TO GIVE US CANDY FAST ENOUGH!
OH BOB! LOOK AT THE LITTLE JACK-O-LANTERNS
TRICK OR TREAT
SEE! WHAT'D I TELL YOU? WE'VE GOT MORE CANDY THAN WE CAN CARRY. AS SOON AS THE TWINS ARE ASLEEP I'M EATING EVERY LAST PIECE OF IT.
"VILLAINS" I SHRIEKED, "DISSEMBLE NO MORE! I ADMIT THE DEED! -- TEAR UP THE PLANKS! HERE, HERE! IT IS THE BEATING OF HIS HIDEOUS HEART."
POE
SNORE

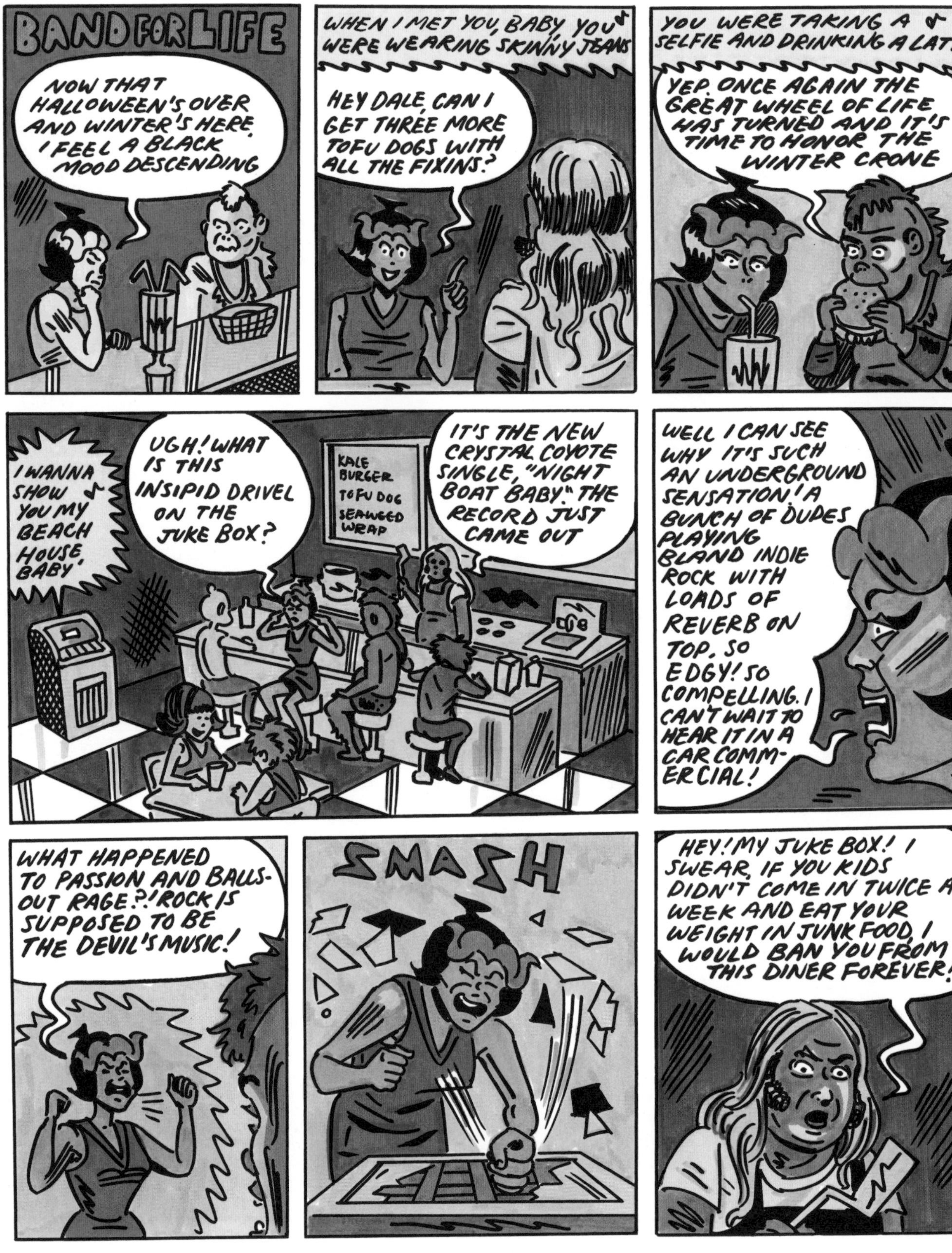
BAND FOR LIFE
NOW THAT HALLOWEEN'S OVER AND WINTER'S HERE, I FEEL A BLACK MOOD DESCENDING
WHEN I MET YOU, BABY YOU WERE WEARING SKINNY JEANS
HEY DALE, CAN I GET THREE MORE TOFU DOGS WITH ALL THE FIXINS?
YOU WERE TAKING A SELFIE AND DRINKING A LATTE
YEP. ONCE AGAIN THE GREAT WHEEL OF LIFE HAS TURNED AND IT'S TIME TO HONOR THE WINTER CRONE
I WANNA SHOW YOU MY BEACH HOUSE, BABY
UGH! WHAT IS THIS INSIPID DRIVEL ON THE JUKE BOX?
KALE BURGER
TOFU DOG
SEAWEED WRAP
IT'S THE NEW CRYSTAL COYOTE SINGLE, "NIGHT BOAT BABY." THE RECORD JUST CAME OUT
WELL I CAN SEE WHY IT'S SUCH AN UNDERGROUND SENSATION! A BUNCH OF DUDES PLAYING BLAND INDIE ROCK WITH LOADS OF REVERB ON TOP. SO EDGY! SO COMPELLING. I CAN'T WAIT TO HEAR IT IN A CAR COMMERCIAL!
WHAT HAPPENED TO PASSION AND BALLS-OUT RAGE?! ROCK IS SUPPOSED TO BE THE DEVIL'S MUSIC!
SMASH
HEY! MY JUKE BOX! I SWEAR, IF YOU KIDS DIDN'T COME IN TWICE A WEEK AND EAT YOUR WEIGHT IN JUNK FOOD, I WOULD BAN YOU FROM THIS DINER FOREVER!

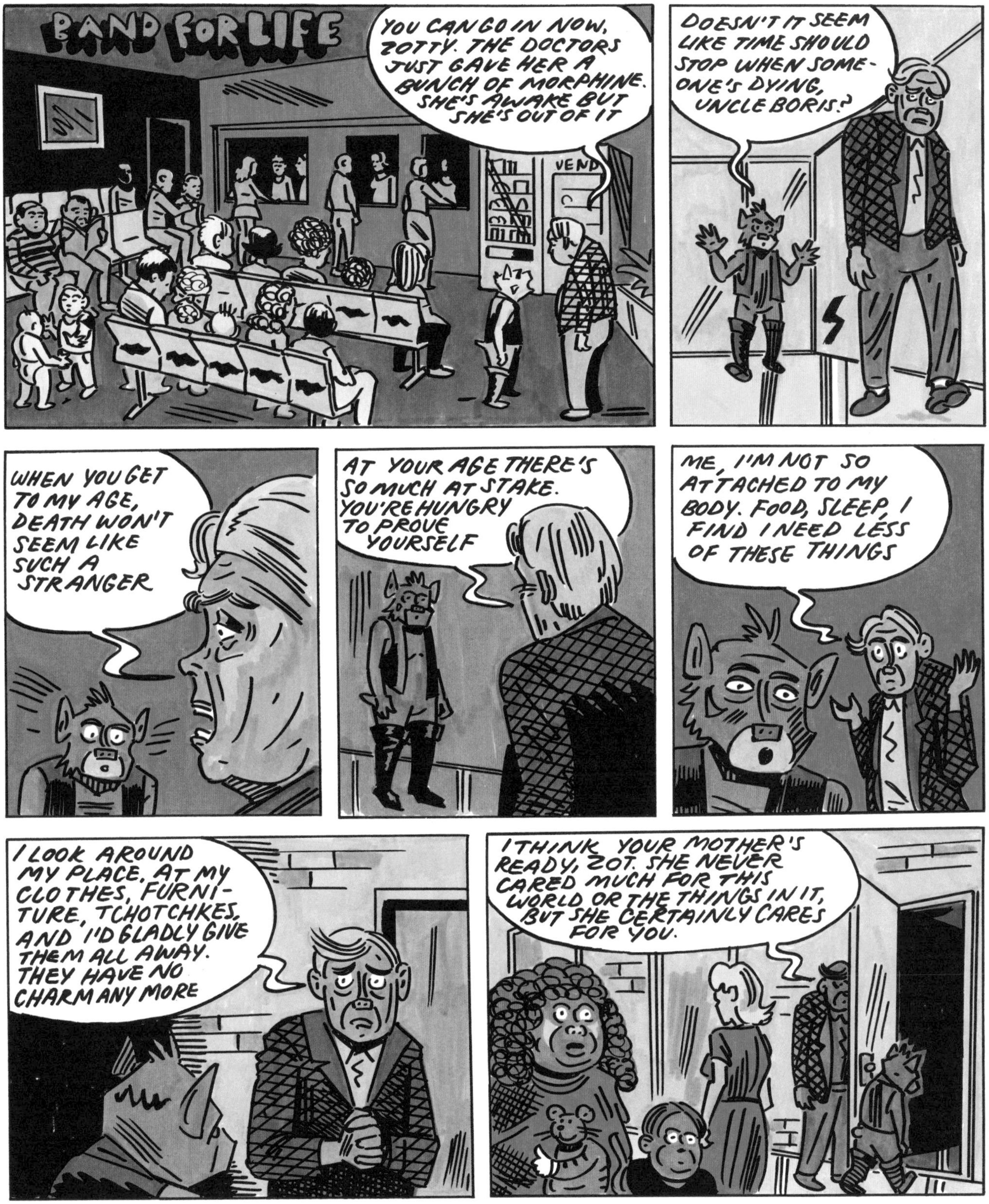
BAND FOR LIFE
YOU CAN GO IN NOW, ZOTTY. THE DOCTORS JUST GAVE HER A BUNCH OF MORPHINE. SHE'S AWAKE BUT SHE'S OUT OF IT
VEND
DOESN'T IT SEEM LIKE TIME SHOULD STOP WHEN SOME-ONE'S DYING, UNCLE BORIS?
WHEN YOU GET TO MY AGE, DEATH WON'T SEEM LIKE SUCH A STRANGER
AT YOUR AGE THERE'S SO MUCH AT STAKE. YOU'RE HUNGRY TO PROVE YOURSELF
ME, I'M NOT SO ATTACHED TO MY BODY. FOOD, SLEEP, I FIND I NEED LESS OF THESE THINGS
I LOOK AROUND MY PLACE, AT MY CLOTHES, FURNI-TURE, TCHOTCHKES, AND I'D GLADLY GIVE THEM ALL AWAY. THEY HAVE NO CHARM ANY MORE
I THINK YOUR MOTHER'S READY, ZOT. SHE NEVER CARED MUCH FOR THIS WORLD OR THE THINGS IN IT, BUT SHE CERTAINLY CARES FOR YOU.

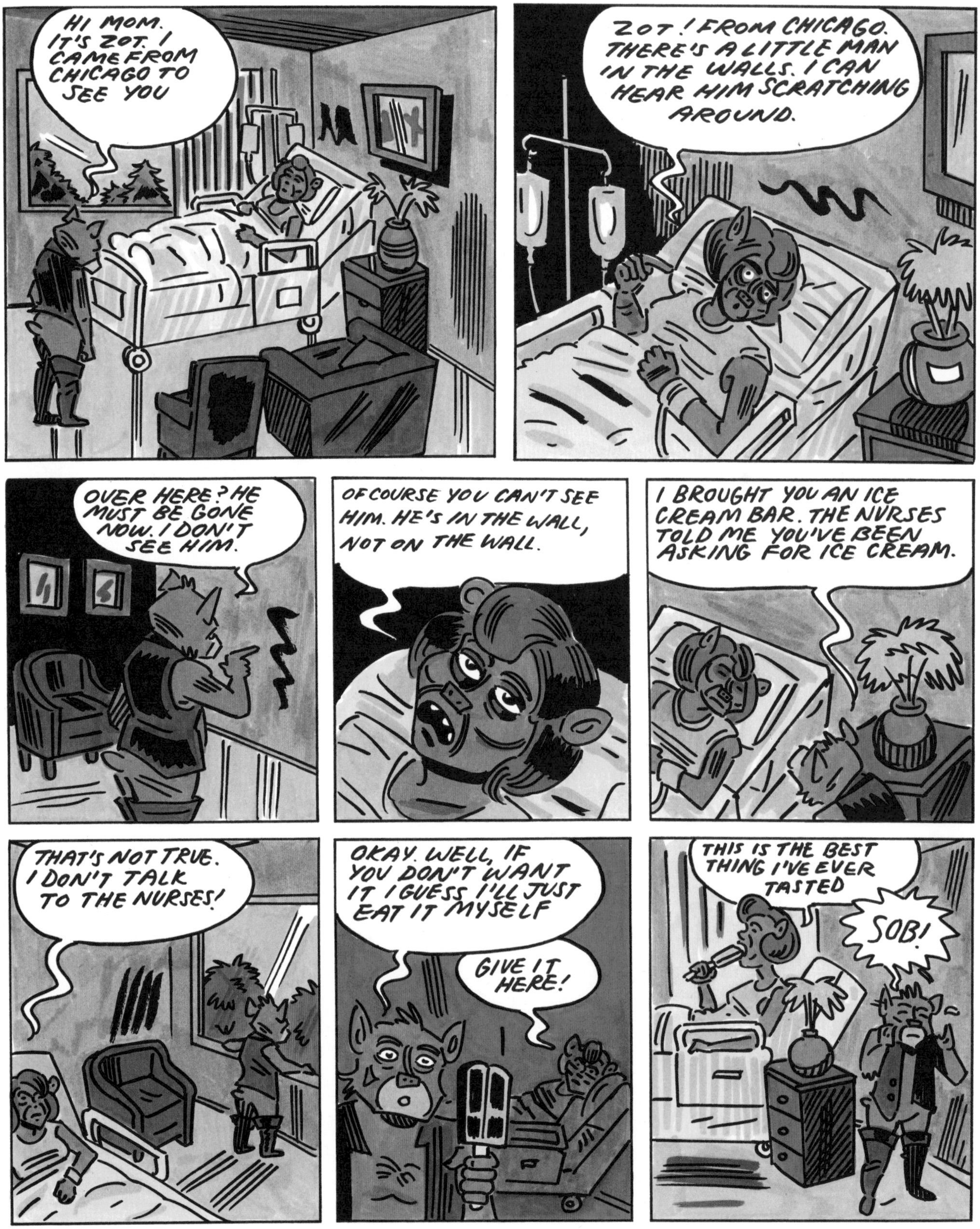
HI MOM. IT'S ZOT. I CAME FROM CHICAGO TO SEE YOU
ZOT! FROM CHICAGO. THERE'S A LITTLE MAN IN THE WALLS. I CAN HEAR HIM SCRATCHING AROUND.
OVER HERE? HE MUST BE GONE NOW. I DON'T SEE HIM.
OF COURSE YOU CAN'T SEE HIM. HE'S IN THE WALL, NOT ON THE WALL.
I BROUGHT YOU AN ICE CREAM BAR. THE NURSES TOLD ME YOU'VE BEEN ASKING FOR ICE CREAM.
THAT'S NOT TRUE. I DON'T TALK TO THE NURSES!
OKAY. WELL, IF YOU DON'T WANT IT I GUESS I'LL JUST EAT IT MYSELF
GIVE IT HERE!
THIS IS THE BEST THING I'VE EVER TASTED
SOB!

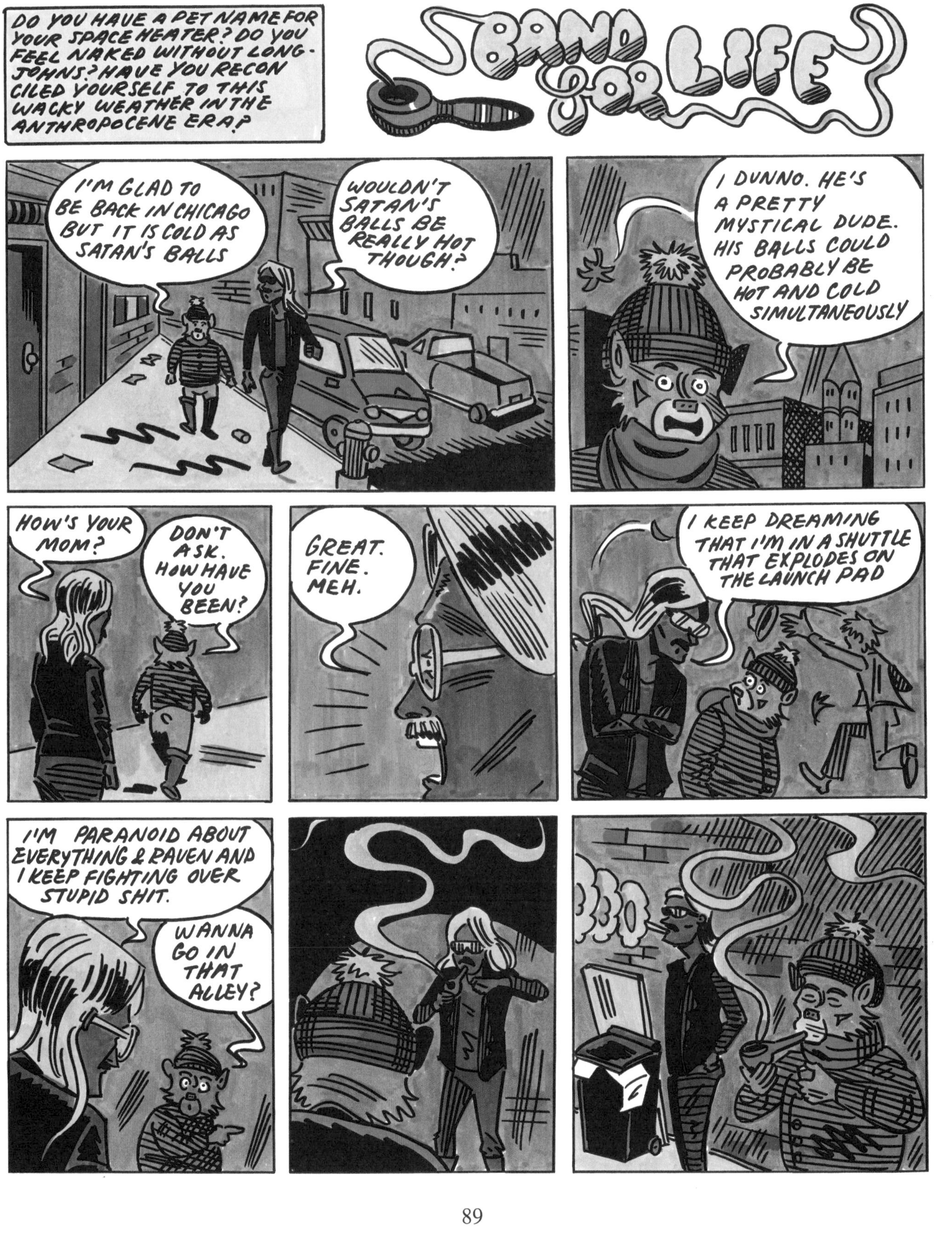
DO YOU HAVE A PET NAME FOR YOUR SPACE HEATER? DO YOU FEEL NAKED WITHOUT LONG-JOHNS? HAVE YOU RECONCILED YOURSELF TO THIS WACKY WEATHER IN THE ANTHROPOCENE ERA?
BAND FOR LIFE
I'M GLAD TO BE BACK IN CHICAGO BUT IT IS COLD AS SATAN'S BALLS
WOULDN'T SATAN'S BALLS BE REALLY HOT THOUGH?
I DUNNO. HE'S A PRETTY MYSTICAL DUDE. HIS BALLS COULD PROBABLY BE HOT AND COLD SIMULTANEOUSLY
HOW'S YOUR MOM?
DON'T ASK. HOW HAVE YOU BEEN?
GREAT. FINE. MEH.
I KEEP DREAMING THAT I'M IN A SHUTTLE THAT EXPLODES ON THE LAUNCH PAD
I'M PARANOID ABOUT EVERYTHING & RAVEN AND I KEEP FIGHTING OVER STUPID SHIT.
WANNA GO IN THAT ALLEY?

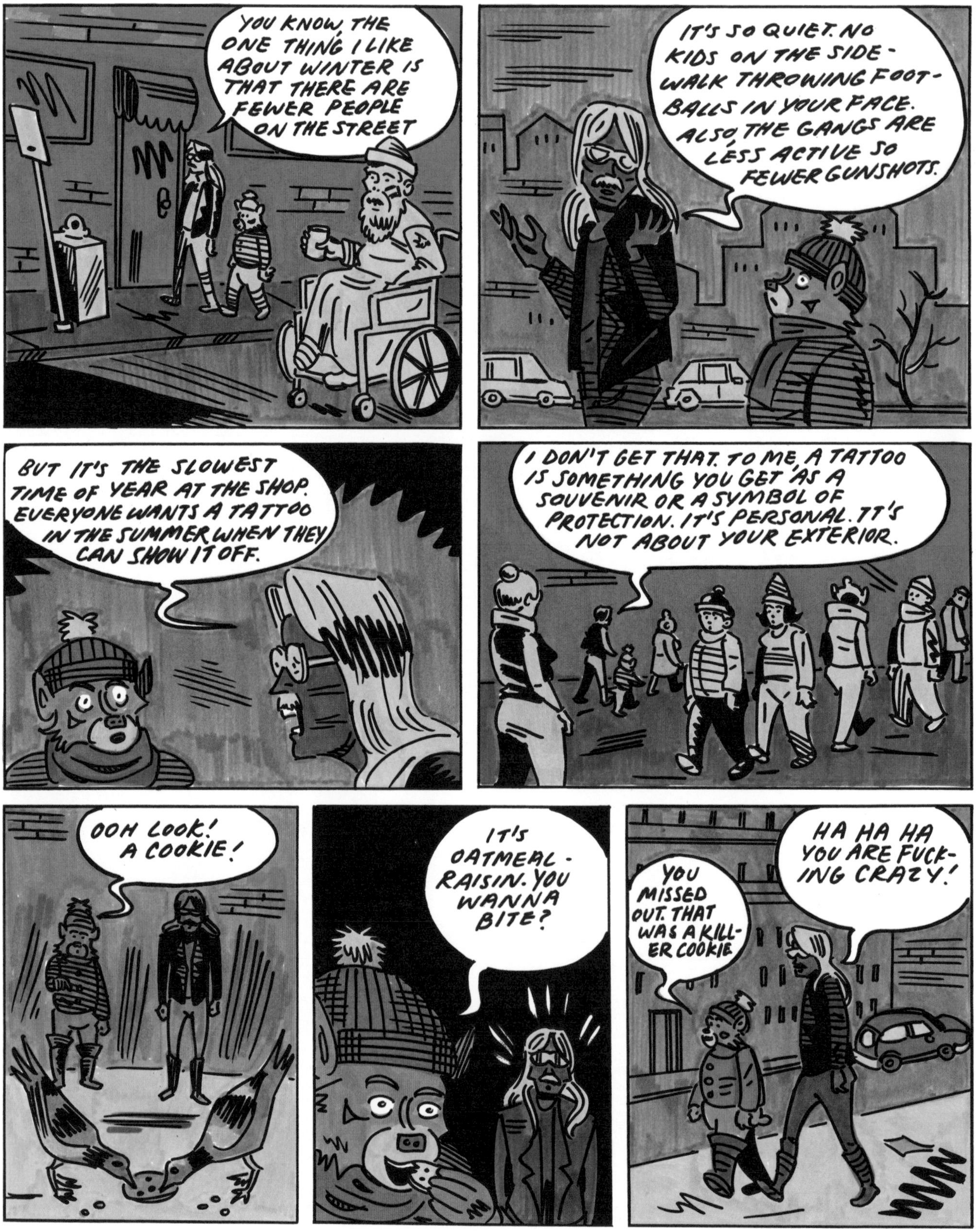
YOU KNOW, THE ONE THING I LIKE ABOUT WINTER IS THAT THERE ARE FEWER PEOPLE ON THE STREET
IT'S SO QUIET. NO KIDS ON THE SIDE-WALK THROWING FOOT-BALLS IN YOUR FACE. ALSO, THE GANGS ARE LESS ACTIVE SO FEWER GUNSHOTS.
BUT IT'S THE SLOWEST TIME OF YEAR AT THE SHOP. EVERYONE WANTS A TATTOO IN THE SUMMER WHEN THEY CAN SHOW IT OFF.
I DON'T GET THAT. TO ME, A TATTOO IS SOMETHING YOU GET AS A SOUVENIR OR A SYMBOL OF PROTECTION. IT'S PERSONAL. IT'S NOT ABOUT YOUR EXTERIOR.
OOH LOOK! A COOKIE!
IT'S OATMEAL-RAISIN. YOU WANNA BITE?
YOU MISSED OUT. THAT WAS A KILL-ER COOKIE
HA HA HA YOU ARE FUCK-ING CRAZY!

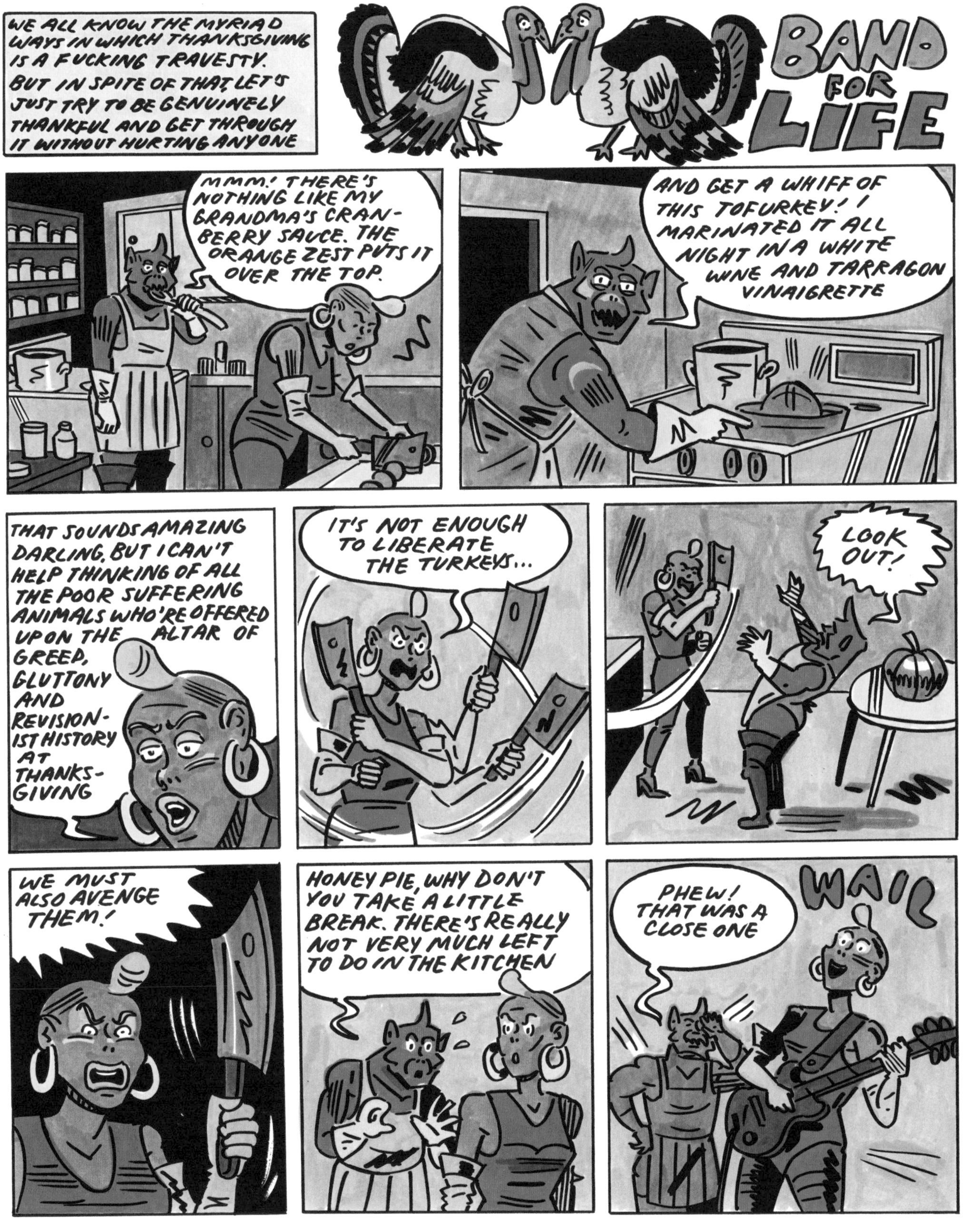
WE ALL KNOW THE MYRIAD WAYS IN WHICH THANKSGIVING IS A FUCKING TRAVESTY. BUT IN SPITE OF THAT, LET'S JUST TRY TO BE GENUINELY THANKFUL AND GET THROUGH IT WITHOUT HURTING ANYONE
BAND FOR LIFE
MMM! THERE'S NOTHING LIKE MY GRANDMA'S CRANBERRY SAUCE. THE ORANGE ZEST PUTS IT OVER THE TOP.
AND GET A WHIFF OF THIS TOFURKEY! I MARINATED IT ALL NIGHT IN A WHITE WINE AND TARRAGON VINAIGRETTE
THAT SOUNDS AMAZING DARLING, BUT I CAN'T HELP THINKING OF ALL THE POOR SUFFERING ANIMALS WHO'RE OFFERED UP ON THE ALTAR OF GREED, GLUTTONY AND REVISIONIST HISTORY AT THANKSGIVING
IT'S NOT ENOUGH TO LIBERATE THE TURKEYS...
LOOK OUT!
WE MUST ALSO AVENGE THEM!
HONEY PIE, WHY DON'T YOU TAKE A LITTLE BREAK. THERE'S REALLY NOT VERY MUCH LEFT TO DO IN THE KITCHEN
PHEW! THAT WAS A CLOSE ONE
WAIL

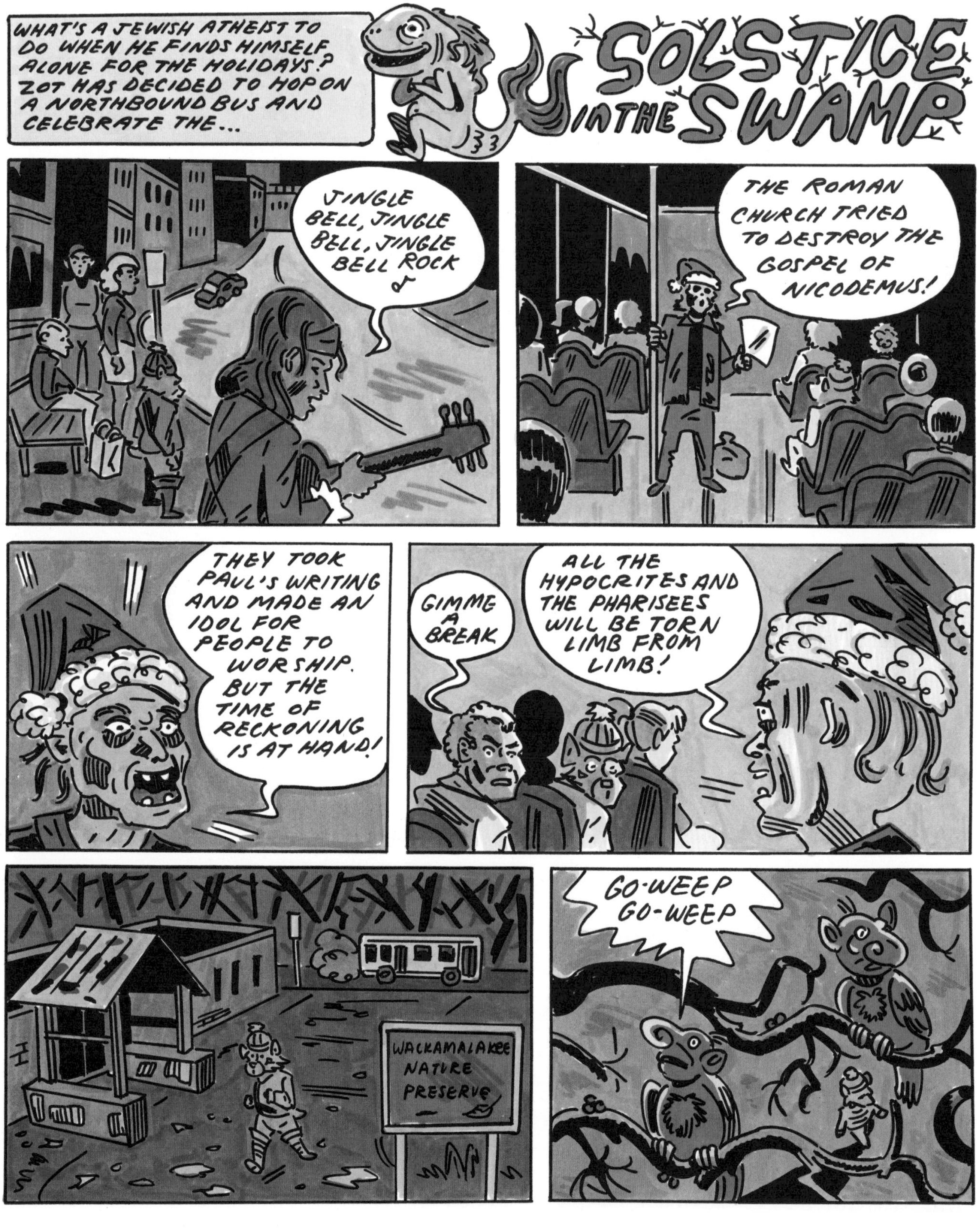
WHAT'S A JEWISH ATHEIST TO DO WHEN HE FINDS HIMSELF ALONE FOR THE HOLIDAYS? ZOT HAS DECIDED TO HOP ON A NORTHBOUND BUS AND CELEBRATE THE...
SOLSTICE IN THE SWAMP
JINGLE BELL, JINGLE BELL, JINGLE BELL ROCK
THE ROMAN CHURCH TRIED TO DESTROY THE GOSPEL OF NICODEMUS!
THEY TOOK PAUL'S WRITING AND MADE AN IDOL FOR PEOPLE TO WORSHIP. BUT THE TIME OF RECKONING IS AT HAND!
ALL THE HYPOCRITES AND THE PHARISEES WILL BE TORN LIMB FROM LIMB!
GIMME A BREAK
WACKAMALAKEE NATURE PRESERVE
GO-WEEP GO-WEEP

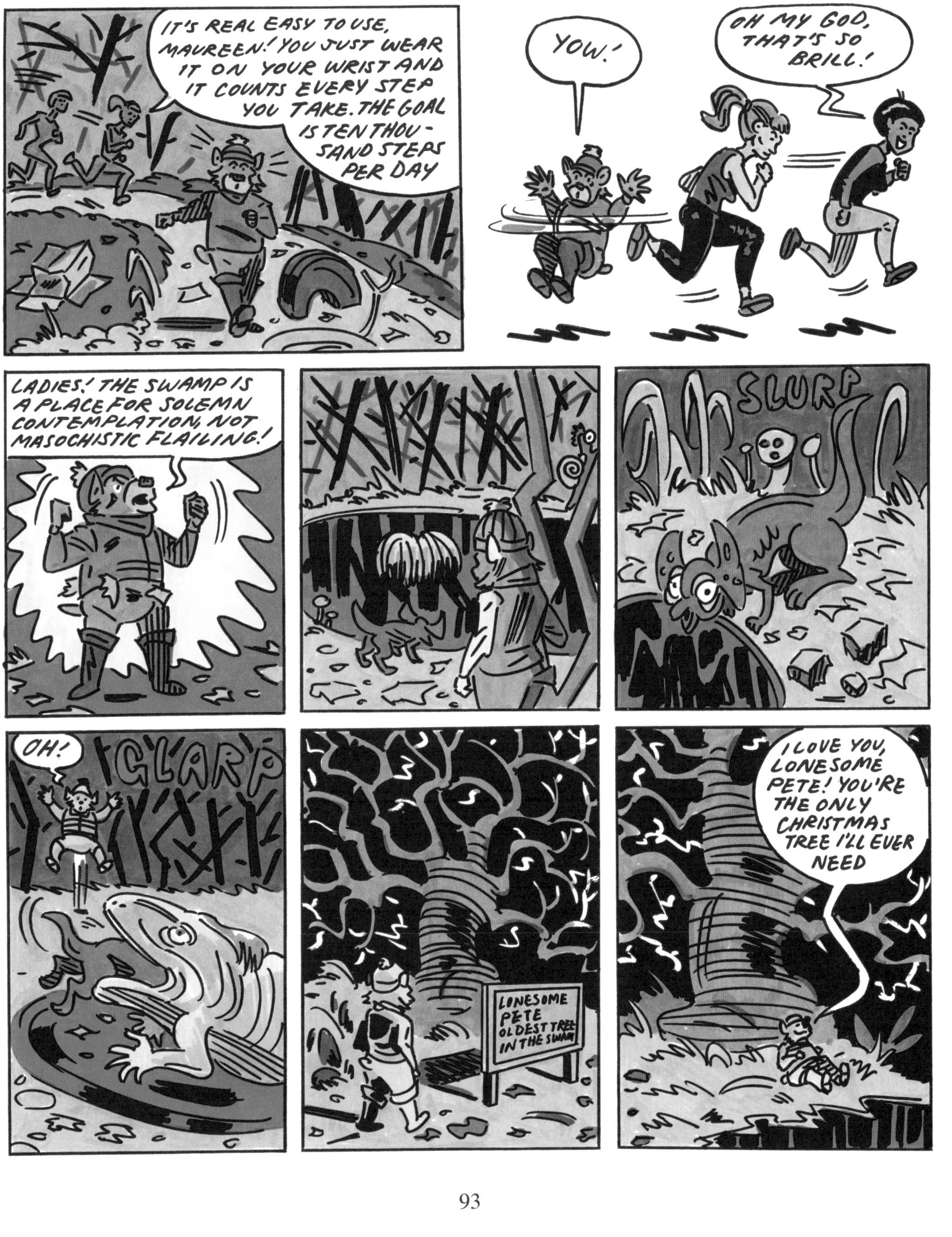
IT'S REAL EASY TO USE, MAUREEN! YOU JUST WEAR IT ON YOUR WRIST AND IT COUNTS EVERY STEP YOU TAKE. THE GOAL IS TEN THOUSAND STEPS PER DAY
YOW!
OH MY GOD, THAT'S SO BRILL!
LADIES! THE SWAMP IS A PLACE FOR SOLEMN CONTEMPLATION, NOT MASOCHISTIC FLAILING!
SLURP
OH!
GLARP
LONESOME PETE OLDEST TREE IN THE SWAMP
I LOVE YOU, LONESOME PETE! YOU'RE THE ONLY CHRISTMAS TREE I'LL EVER NEED

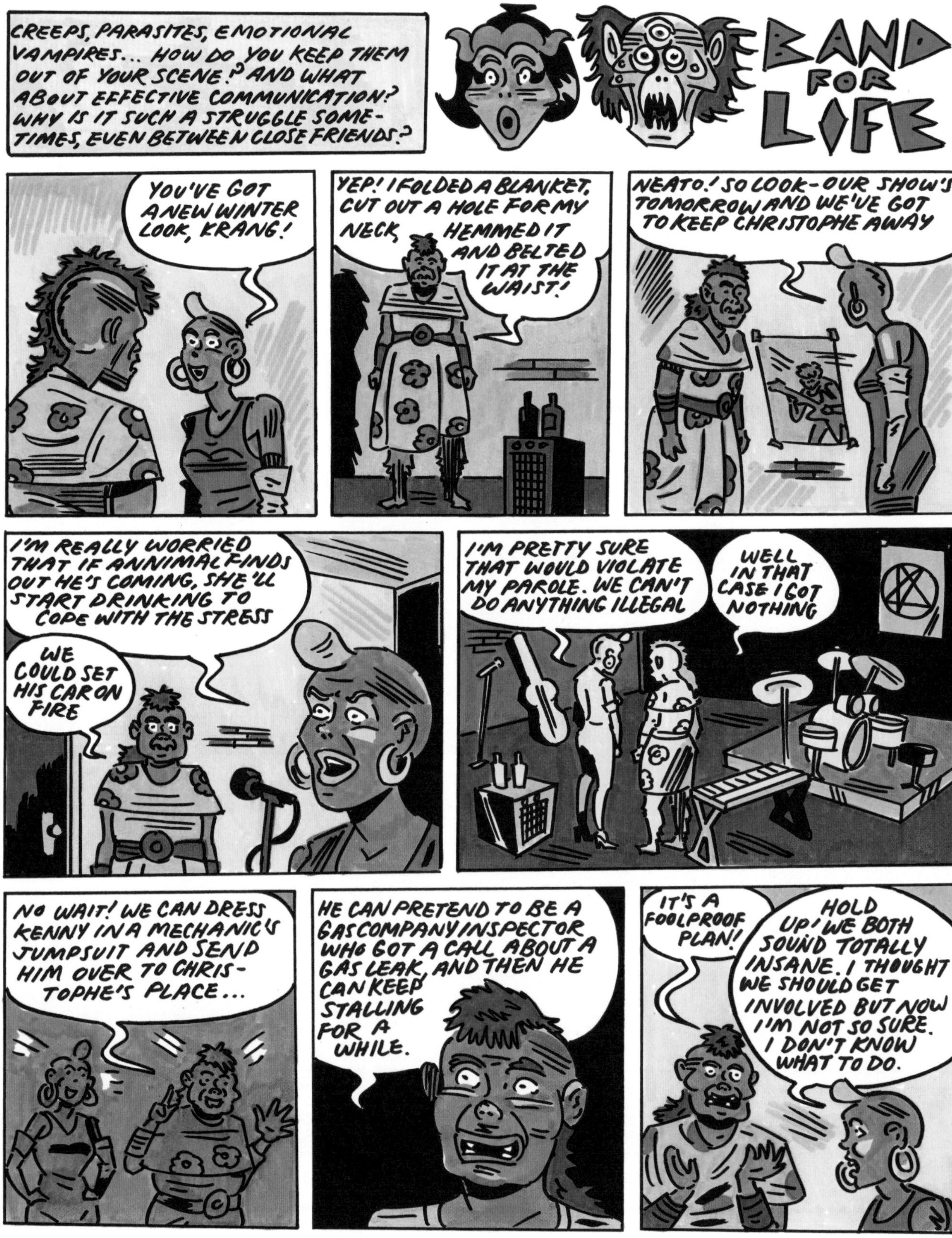
CREEPS, PARASITES, EMOTIONAL VAMPIRES... HOW DO YOU KEEP THEM OUT OF YOUR SCENE? AND WHAT ABOUT EFFECTIVE COMMUNICATION? WHY IS IT SUCH A STRUGGLE SOMETIMES, EVEN BETWEEN CLOSE FRIENDS?
BAND FOR LIFE
YOU'VE GOT A NEW WINTER LOOK, KRANG!
YEP! I FOLDED A BLANKET, CUT OUT A HOLE FOR MY NECK, HEMMED IT AND BELTED IT AT THE WAIST!
NEATO! SO LOOK- OUR SHOW'S TOMORROW AND WE'VE GOT TO KEEP CHRISTOPHE AWAY
I'M REALLY WORRIED THAT IF ANNIMAL FINDS OUT HE'S COMING, SHE'LL START DRINKING TO COPE WITH THE STRESS
WE COULD SET HIS CAR ON FIRE
I'M PRETTY SURE THAT WOULD VIOLATE MY PAROLE. WE CAN'T DO ANYTHING ILLEGAL
WELL IN THAT CASE I GOT NOTHING
NO WAIT! WE CAN DRESS KENNY IN A MECHANIC'S JUMPSUIT AND SEND HIM OVER TO CHRISTOPHE'S PLACE...
HE CAN PRETEND TO BE A GAS COMPANY INSPECTOR WHO GOT A CALL ABOUT A GAS LEAK, AND THEN HE CAN KEEP STALLING FOR A WHILE.
IT'S A FOOLPROOF PLAN!
HOLD UP! WE BOTH SOUND TOTALLY INSANE. I THOUGHT WE SHOULD GET INVOLVED BUT NOW I'M NOT SO SURE. I DON'T KNOW WHAT TO DO.

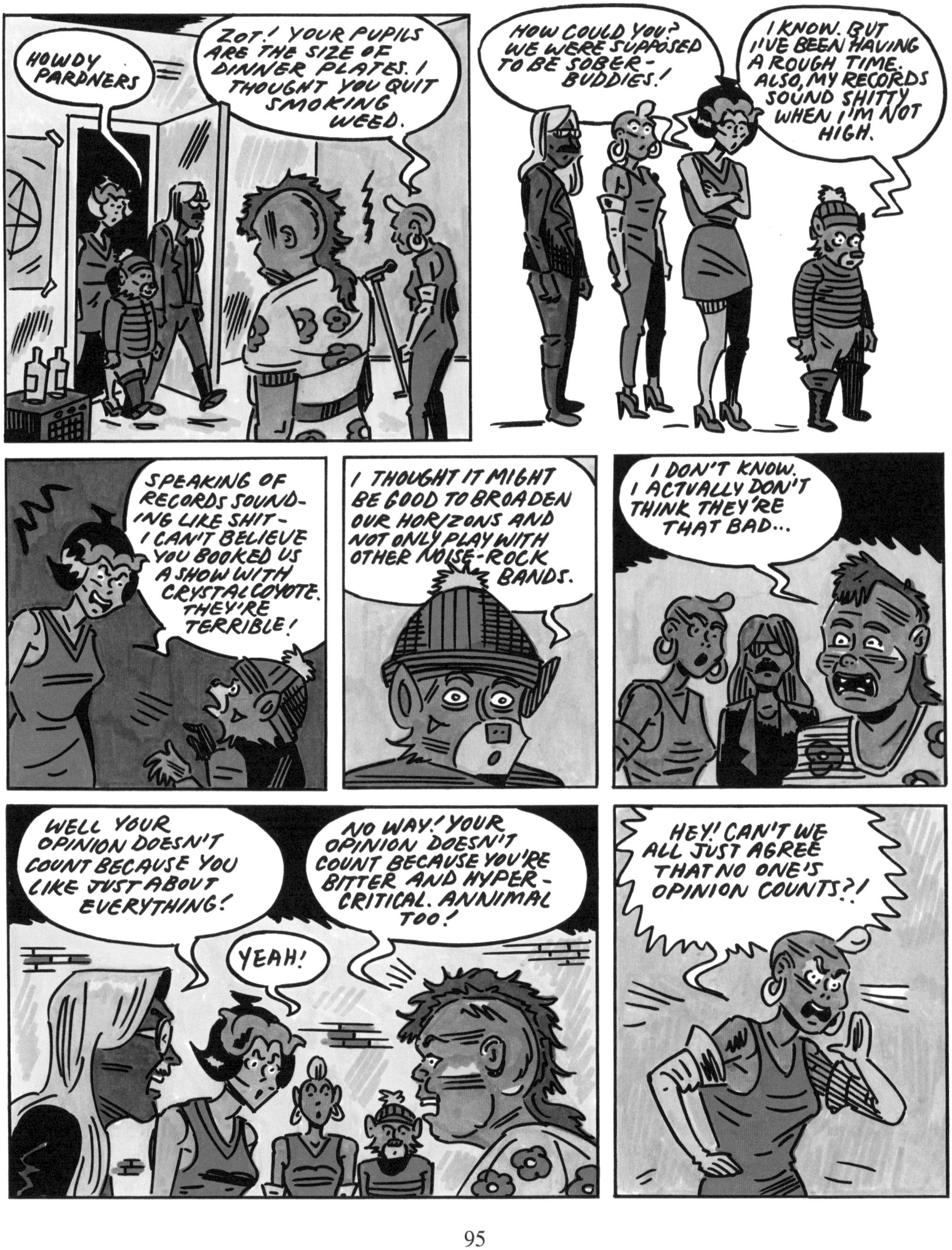
HOWDY PARDNERS
ZOT! YOUR PUPILS ARE THE SIZE OF DINNER PLATES. I THOUGHT YOU QUIT SMOKING WEED.
HOW COULD YOU? WE WERE SUPPOSED TO BE SOBER-BUDDIES!
I KNOW. BUT I'VE BEEN HAVING A ROUGH TIME. ALSO, MY RECORDS SOUND SHITTY WHEN I'M NOT HIGH.
SPEAKING OF RECORDS SOUNDING LIKE SHIT- I CAN'T BELIEVE YOU BOOKED US A SHOW WITH CRYSTAL COYOTE. THEY'RE TERRIBLE!
I THOUGHT IT MIGHT BE GOOD TO BROADEN OUR HORIZONS AND NOT ONLY PLAY WITH OTHER NOISE-ROCK BANDS.
I DON'T KNOW. I ACTUALLY DON'T THINK THEY'RE THAT BAD...
WELL YOUR OPINION DOESN'T COUNT BECAUSE YOU LIKE JUST ABOUT EVERYTHING!
YEAH!
NO WAY! YOUR OPINION DOESN'T COUNT BECAUSE YOU'RE BITTER AND HYPER-CRITICAL. ANNIMAL TOO!
HEY! CAN'T WE ALL JUST AGREE THAT NO ONE'S OPINION COUNTS?!

DAVID   KEN   COREY   DAVE   KIRK

CRYSTAL COYOTE: HUNKS WITH CATCHY HOOKS OR SCHMUCKS WITH SILLY HAIR? ARE THE SUCCESSFUL ALWAYS DESERVING? ARE THE DESERVING ALWAYS SUCCESSFUL?

BAND FOR LIFE

I GUESS I JUST DON'T UNDERSTAND WHY CERTAIN BANDS GET SO BIG WHILE OTHERS DON'T

I'M NOT JEALOUS OF CRYSTAL COYOTE. I JUST SERIOUSLY DON'T UNDERSTAND WHY THEY'RE POPULAR. IS IT 'CAUSE THEY'RE CUTE? WE'RE CUTE!

WELL... THEY PROBABLY HAVE A PUBLICIST AND A BOOKING AGENT

YEAH BUT HOW DID THEY GET THOSE THINGS IN THE FIRST PLACE?

HOW SHOULD I KNOW?

AND WHO CARES? WE JUST HAVE TO MAKE THE MUSIC WE WANNA MAKE. THE SECOND YOU START MAKING ARTISTIC CHOICES BASED ON MONEY OR FAME, YOU'RE TOTALLY SCREWED.

YEAH BUT I DON'T THINK THERE'S AN INVERSE CORRELATION BETWEEN TALENT AND POPULARITY. LOTS OF BRILLIANT MUSICIANS ARE POPULAR

KRANG ARE YOU A FUCKING NARC? YOU SOUND LIKE A NARC RIGHT NOW

CAPTAIN BEEFHEART, SLY STONE, BOWIE, ZAPPA...

YEAH, POPULAR IN THE 'SEVENTIES. TECHNOLOGY HAS CHANGED EVERYTHING

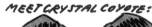

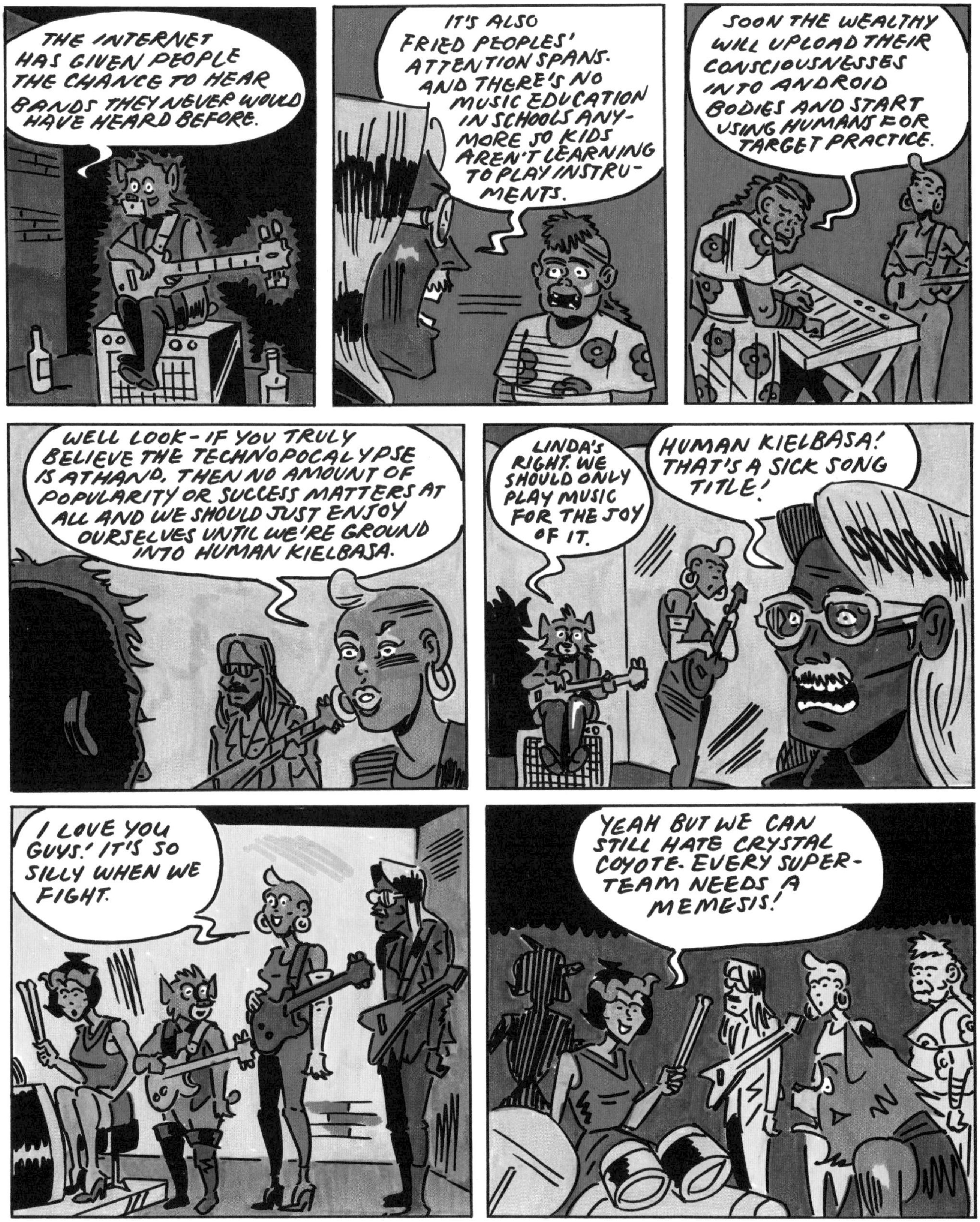
THE INTERNET HAS GIVEN PEOPLE THE CHANCE TO HEAR BANDS THEY NEVER WOULD HAVE HEARD BEFORE.
IT'S ALSO FRIED PEOPLES' ATTENTION SPANS. AND THERE'S NO MUSIC EDUCATION IN SCHOOLS ANY-MORE SO KIDS AREN'T LEARNING TO PLAY INSTRU-MENTS.
SOON THE WEALTHY WILL UPLOAD THEIR CONSCIOUSNESSES INTO ANDROID BODIES AND START USING HUMANS FOR TARGET PRACTICE.
WELL LOOK - IF YOU TRULY BELIEVE THE TECHNOPOCALYPSE IS AT HAND, THEN NO AMOUNT OF POPULARITY OR SUCCESS MATTERS AT ALL AND WE SHOULD JUST ENJOY OURSELVES UNTIL WE'RE GROUND INTO HUMAN KIELBASA.
LINDA'S RIGHT. WE SHOULD ONLY PLAY MUSIC FOR THE JOY OF IT.
HUMAN KIELBASA! THAT'S A SICK SONG TITLE!
I LOVE YOU GUYS! IT'S SO SILLY WHEN WE FIGHT.
YEAH BUT WE CAN STILL HATE CRYSTAL COYOTE - EVERY SUPER-TEAM NEEDS A MEMESIS!

BAND FOR LIFE

GUNTIT

LOOKS LIKE OUR NEMESIS BAND IS ALREADY HERE. AND THEY HAVE VANITY PLATES. WOOF.

looking for true sat

CRSTLCI

JUST LOAD STRAIGHT INTO THE BASEMENT AND SET UP. THE ORDER IS YOU GUYS, LORD VOMIT, THEN CRYSTAL COYOTE.

THANKS ALVIN

HOLD IT STEADY! IT'S TILTING TO THE RIGHT

I'M TRYING!

FUCK ALL REPUBLICANS

SMASH

OH MY GOD! MY AMP. I JUST HAD IT FIXED!

I'M FINE RENATO. THANKS FOR ASKING

THIS IS OUR FAULT SO WHY DON'T YOU BORROW AN AMP FROM LORD VOMIT FOR TONIGHT AND THEN ME AND KRANG CAN TAKE IT TO GET FIXED AGAIN

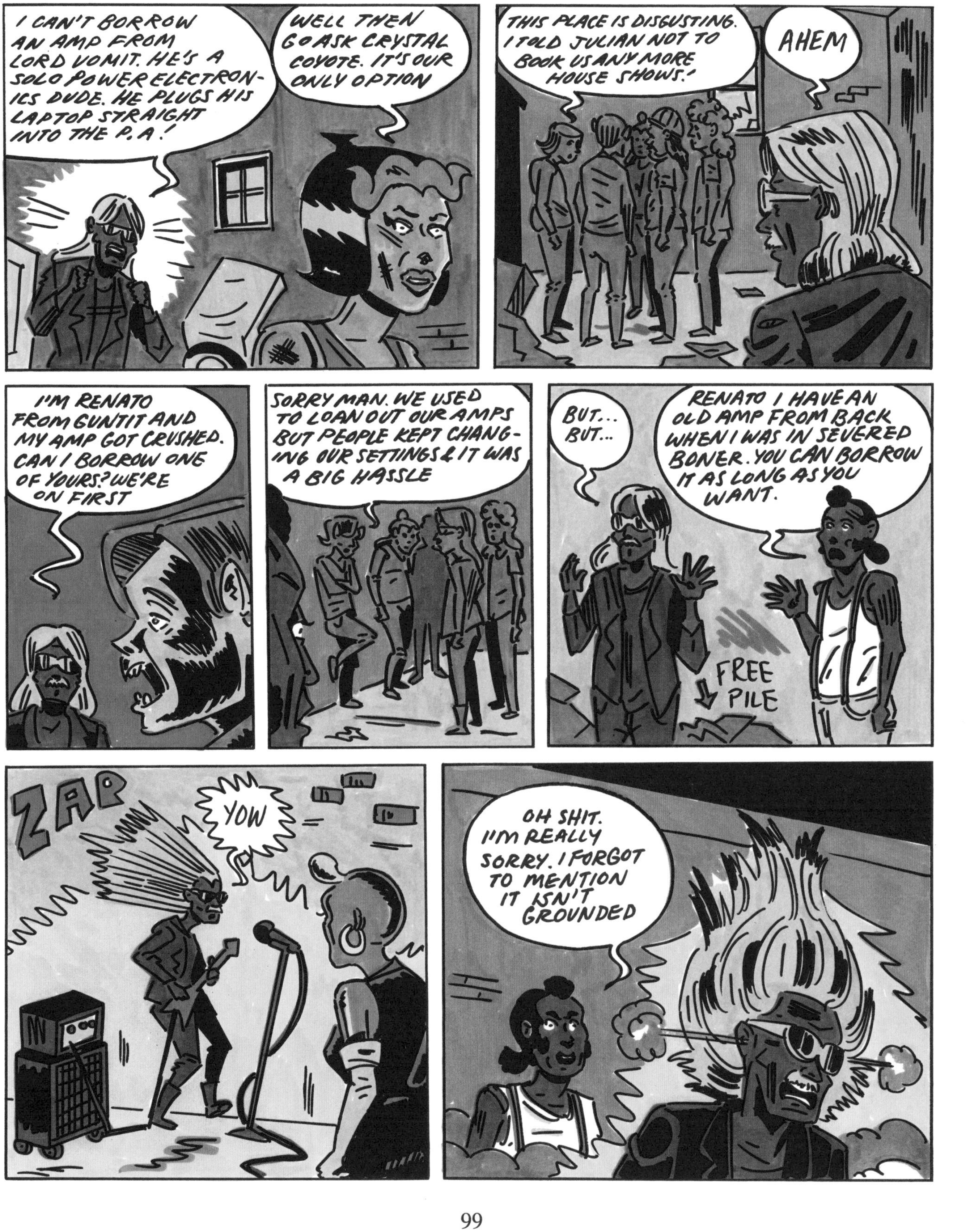
I CAN'T BORROW AN AMP FROM LORD VOMIT. HE'S A SOLO POWER ELECTRONICS DUDE. HE PLUGS HIS LAPTOP STRAIGHT INTO THE P.A.!
WELL THEN GO ASK CRYSTAL COYOTE. IT'S OUR ONLY OPTION
THIS PLACE IS DISGUSTING. I TOLD JULIAN NOT TO BOOK US ANY MORE HOUSE SHOWS.!
AHEM
I'M RENATO FROM GUNTIT AND MY AMP GOT CRUSHED. CAN I BORROW ONE OF YOURS? WE'RE ON FIRST
SORRY MAN. WE USED TO LOAN OUT OUR AMPS BUT PEOPLE KEPT CHANGING OUR SETTINGS & IT WAS A BIG HASSLE
BUT... BUT...
RENATO I HAVE AN OLD AMP FROM BACK WHEN I WAS IN SEVERED BONER. YOU CAN BORROW IT AS LONG AS YOU WANT.
FREE PILE
ZAP
YOW
OH SHIT. I'M REALLY SORRY. I FORGOT TO MENTION IT ISN'T GROUNDED

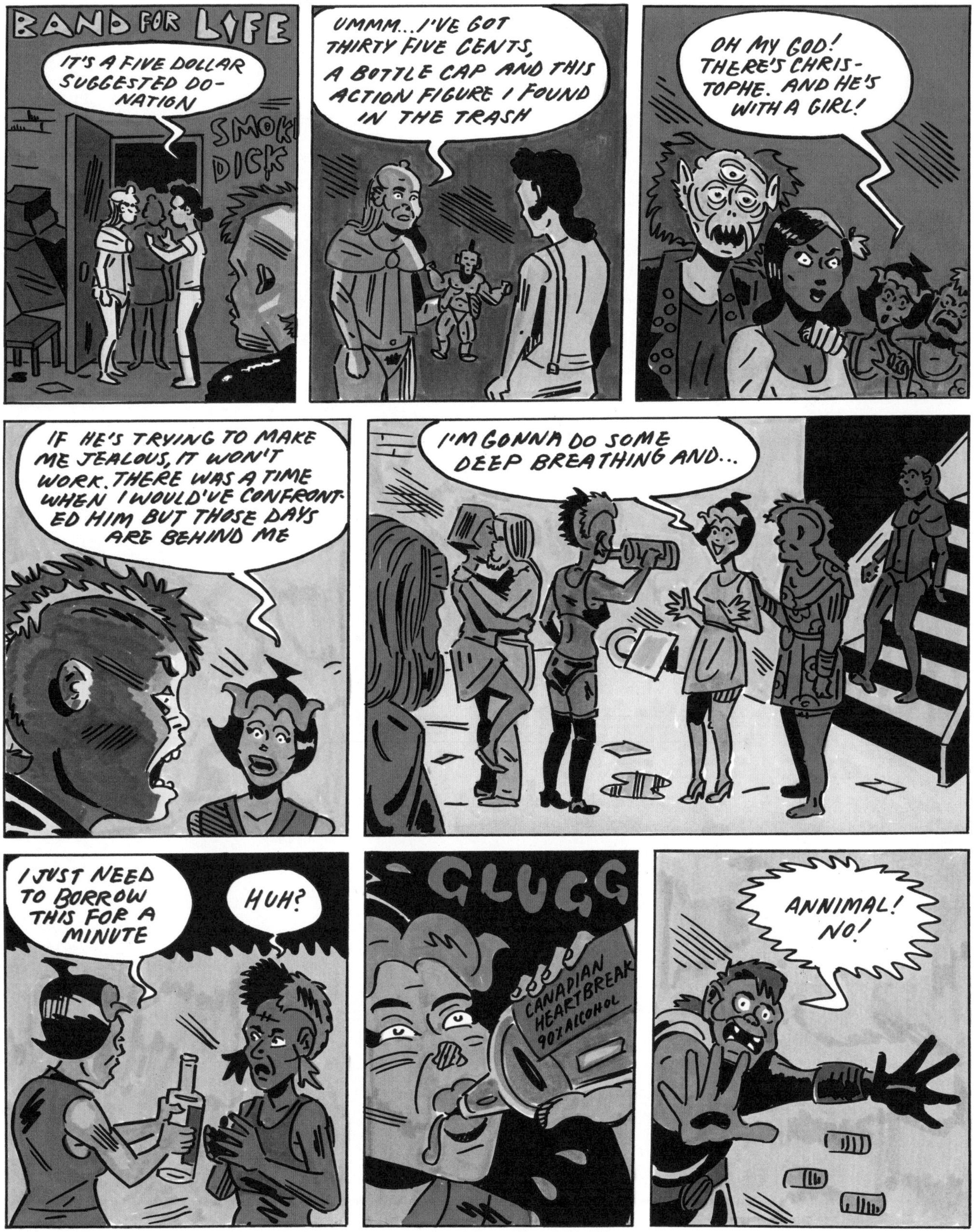
BAND FOR LIFE
IT'S A FIVE DOLLAR SUGGESTED DO-NATION
SMOKI DICK
UMMM...I'VE GOT THIRTY FIVE CENTS, A BOTTLE CAP AND THIS ACTION FIGURE I FOUND IN THE TRASH
OH MY GOD! THERE'S CHRIS-TOPHE. AND HE'S WITH A GIRL!
IF HE'S TRYING TO MAKE ME JEALOUS, IT WON'T WORK. THERE WAS A TIME WHEN I WOULD'VE CONFRONT-ED HIM BUT THOSE DAYS ARE BEHIND ME
I'M GONNA DO SOME DEEP BREATHING AND...
I JUST NEED TO BORROW THIS FOR A MINUTE
HUH?
GLUGG
CANADIAN HEARTBREAK 90% ALCOHOL
ANNIMAL! NO!

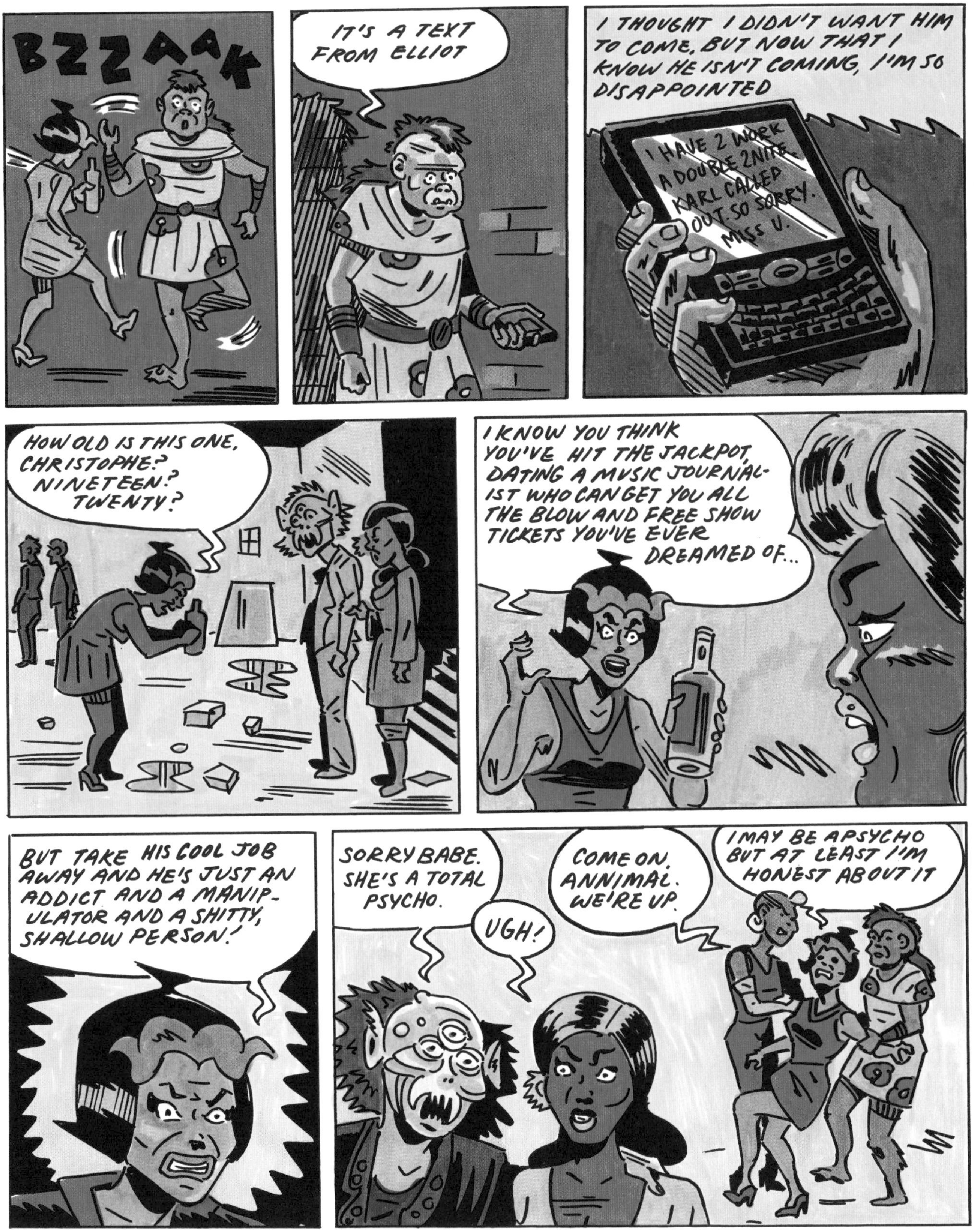
BZZAAK
IT'S A TEXT FROM ELLIOT
I THOUGHT I DIDN'T WANT HIM TO COME. BUT NOW THAT I KNOW HE ISN'T COMING, I'M SO DISAPPOINTED
I HAVE 2 WORK A DOUBLE 2NITE KARL CALLED OUT. SO SORRY. MISS U.
HOW OLD IS THIS ONE, CHRISTOPHE? NINETEEN? TWENTY?
I KNOW YOU THINK YOU'VE HIT THE JACKPOT, DATING A MUSIC JOURNALIST WHO CAN GET YOU ALL THE BLOW AND FREE SHOW TICKETS YOU'VE EVER DREAMED OF...
BUT TAKE HIS COOL JOB AWAY AND HE'S JUST AN ADDICT AND A MANIPULATOR AND A SHITTY, SHALLOW PERSON!
SORRY BABE. SHE'S A TOTAL PSYCHO.
UGH!
COME ON, ANNIMAL. WE'RE UP.
I MAY BE A PSYCHO BUT AT LEAST I'M HONEST ABOUT IT

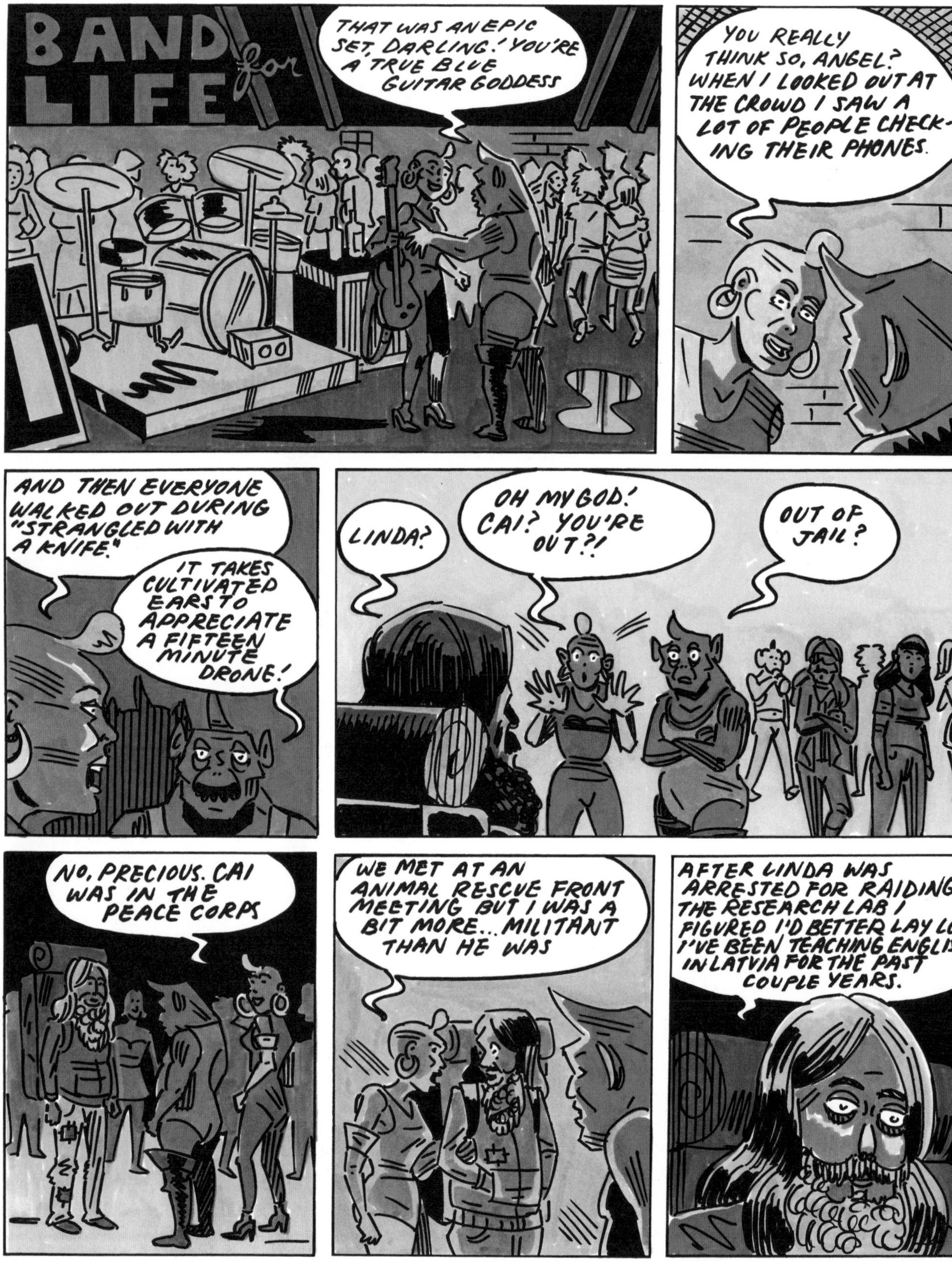
BAND for LIFE
THAT WAS AN EPIC SET, DARLING! YOU'RE A TRUE BLUE GUITAR GODDESS
YOU REALLY THINK SO, ANGEL? WHEN I LOOKED OUT AT THE CROWD I SAW A LOT OF PEOPLE CHECKING THEIR PHONES.
AND THEN EVERYONE WALKED OUT DURING "STRANGLED WITH A KNIFE."
IT TAKES CULTIVATED EARS TO APPRECIATE A FIFTEEN MINUTE DRONE!
LINDA?
OH MY GOD! CAI? YOU'RE OUT?!
OUT OF JAIL?
NO, PRECIOUS. CAI WAS IN THE PEACE CORPS
WE MET AT AN ANIMAL RESCUE FRONT MEETING BUT I WAS A BIT MORE... MILITANT THAN HE WAS
AFTER LINDA WAS ARRESTED FOR RAIDING THE RESEARCH LAB I FIGURED I'D BETTER LAY LOW. I'VE BEEN TEACHING ENGLISH IN LATVIA FOR THE PAST COUPLE YEARS.

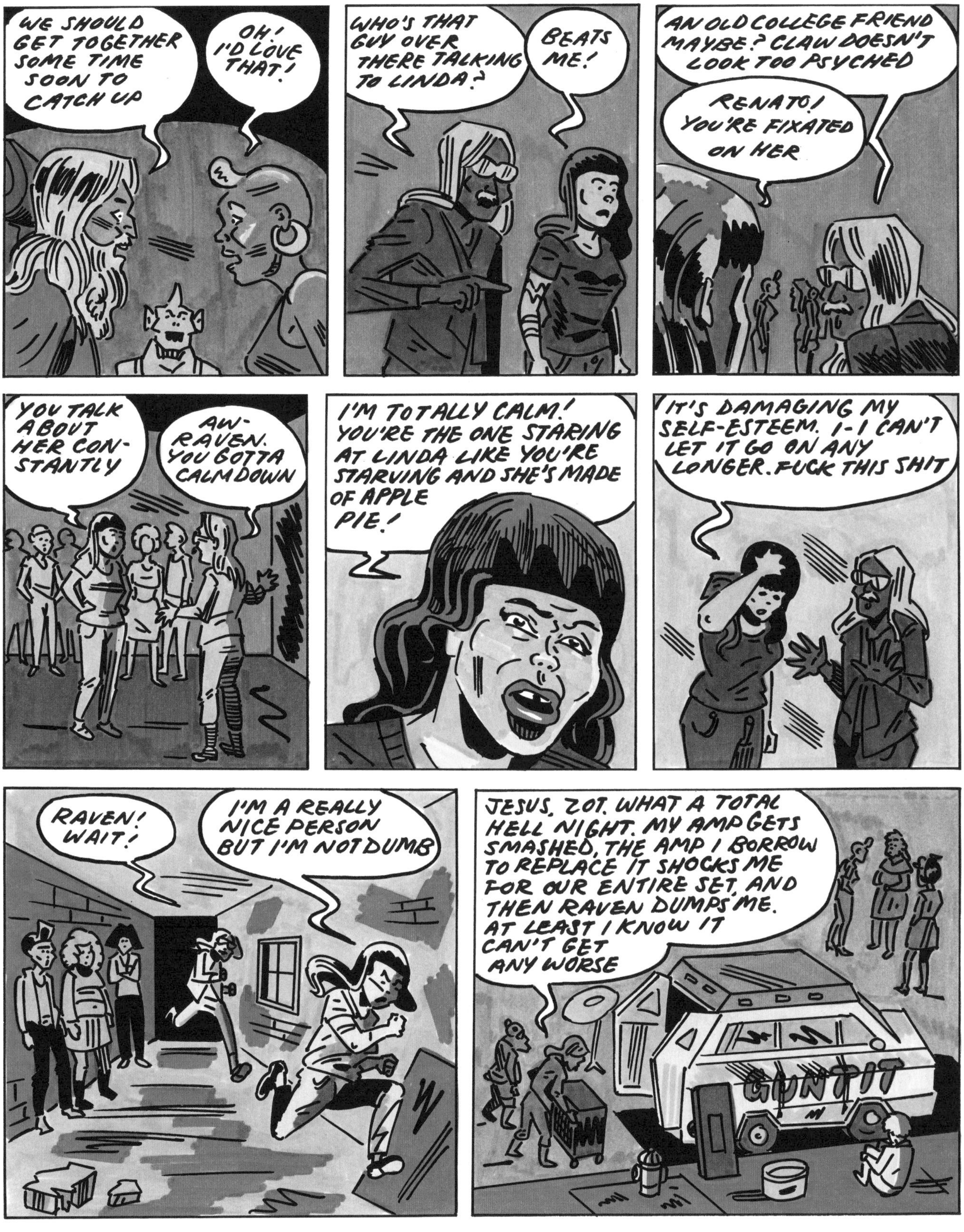
WE SHOULD GET TOGETHER SOME TIME SOON TO CATCH UP
OH! I'D LOVE THAT!
WHO'S THAT GUY OVER THERE TALKING TO LINDA?
BEATS ME!
AN OLD COLLEGE FRIEND MAYBE? CLAW DOESN'T LOOK TOO PSYCHED
RENATO! YOU'RE FIXATED ON HER
YOU TALK ABOUT HER CON-STANTLY
AW-RAVEN. YOU GOTTA CALM DOWN
I'M TOTALLY CALM! YOU'RE THE ONE STARING AT LINDA LIKE YOU'RE STARVING AND SHE'S MADE OF APPLE PIE!
IT'S DAMAGING MY SELF-ESTEEM. I-I CAN'T LET IT GO ON ANY LONGER. FUCK THIS SHIT
RAVEN! WAIT!
I'M A REALLY NICE PERSON BUT I'M NOT DUMB
JESUS, ZOT. WHAT A TOTAL HELL NIGHT. MY AMP GETS SMASHED, THE AMP I BORROW TO REPLACE IT SHOCKS ME FOR OUR ENTIRE SET, AND THEN RAVEN DUMPS ME. AT LEAST I KNOW IT CAN'T GET ANY WORSE

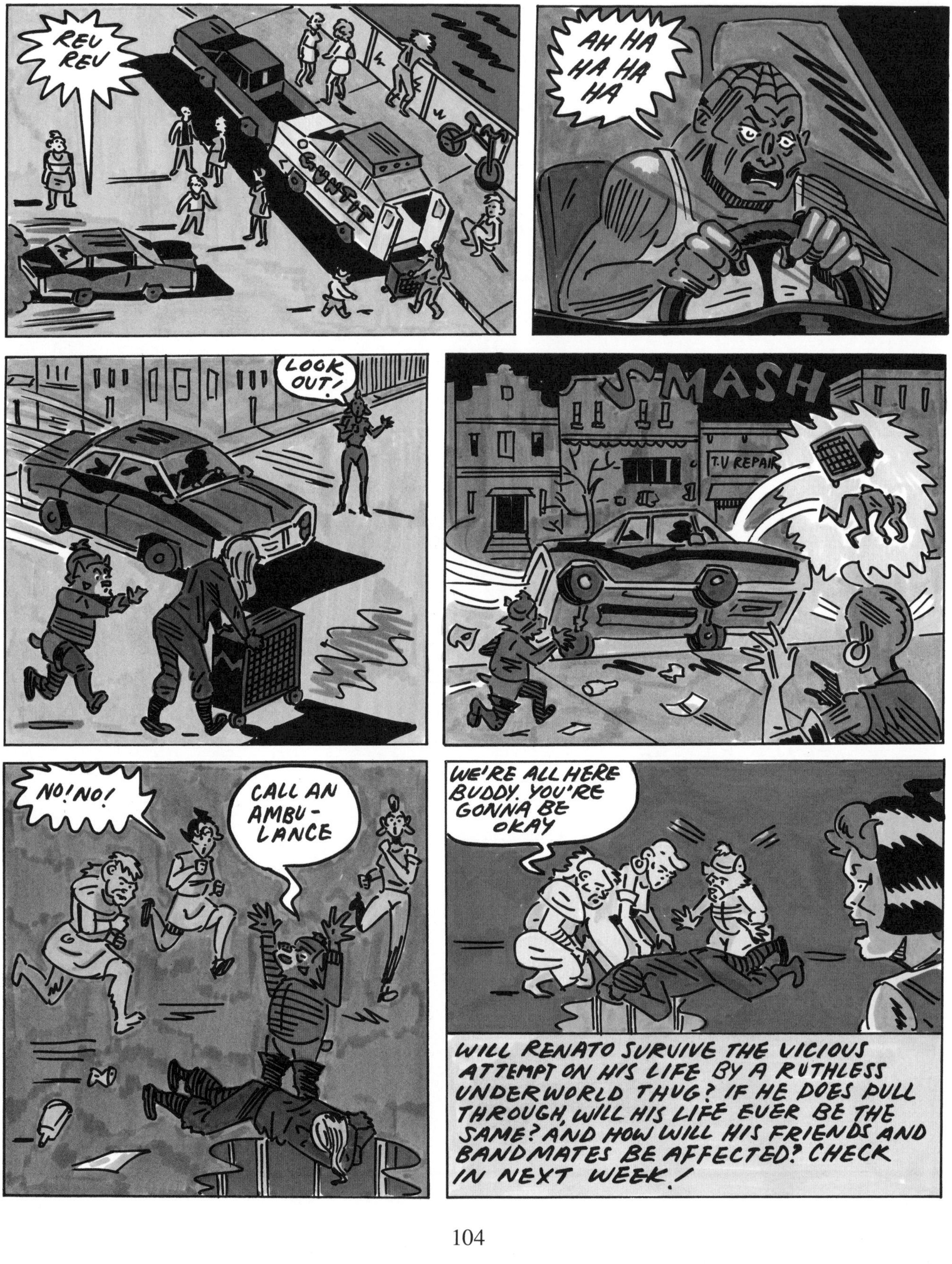

REV REV
AH HA HA HA HA
LOOK OUT!
SMASH
T.V REPAIR
NO! NO!
CALL AN AMBU-LANCE
WE'RE ALL HERE BUDDY. YOU'RE GONNA BE OKAY
WILL RENATO SURVIVE THE VICIOUS ATTEMPT ON HIS LIFE BY A RUTHLESS UNDERWORLD THUG? IF HE DOES PULL THROUGH, WILL HIS LIFE EVER BE THE SAME? AND HOW WILL HIS FRIENDS AND BANDMATES BE AFFECTED? CHECK IN NEXT WEEK!

BAND FOR LIFE

I DON'T KNOW WHAT TO EXPECT. KRANG SAYS HE LOOKS PRETTY BAD

WELL, HE'S GOT A FRACTURED SKULL AND A BROKEN LEG. BUT AT LEAST IT'S NOT IRON LUNG BAD. OR BRAIN IN A JAR BAD...

THE NEXT TIME I'M IN A HOSPITAL, I HOPE IT'S 'CAUSE SOMEONE IS GIVING BIRTH

HEY SHREDDER! YOU LOOK GOOD. HOW YA' FEELIN'?

I WISH HE'D PUT THE CAR IN REVERSE AND FINISHED THE JOB!

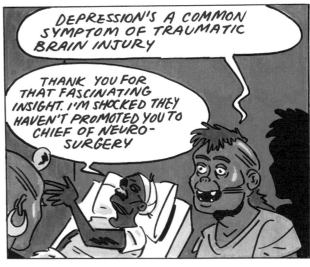

DEPRESSION'S A COMMON SYMPTOM OF TRAUMATIC BRAIN INJURY

THANK YOU FOR THAT FASCINATING INSIGHT. I'M SHOCKED THEY HAVEN'T PROMOTED YOU TO CHIEF OF NEUROSURGERY

THEY CAUGHT HIM, YOU KNOW, THE GUY THAT HIT YOU

IT WAS WILD! A DETECTIVE CAME WHILE YOU WERE UNCONSCIOUS AND ASKED US ALL A BUNCH OF QUESTIONS ABOUT WHAT HE LOOKED LIKE AND WHAT KIND OF CAR HE WAS DRIVING

HIS NAME IS PAVEL SARNOCHINSKI, "BIG PAUL." HE WAS WORKING WITH A CROOKED DOCTOR TO SELL PILLS OUT OF THREE DIFFERENT TATTOO SHOPS

105

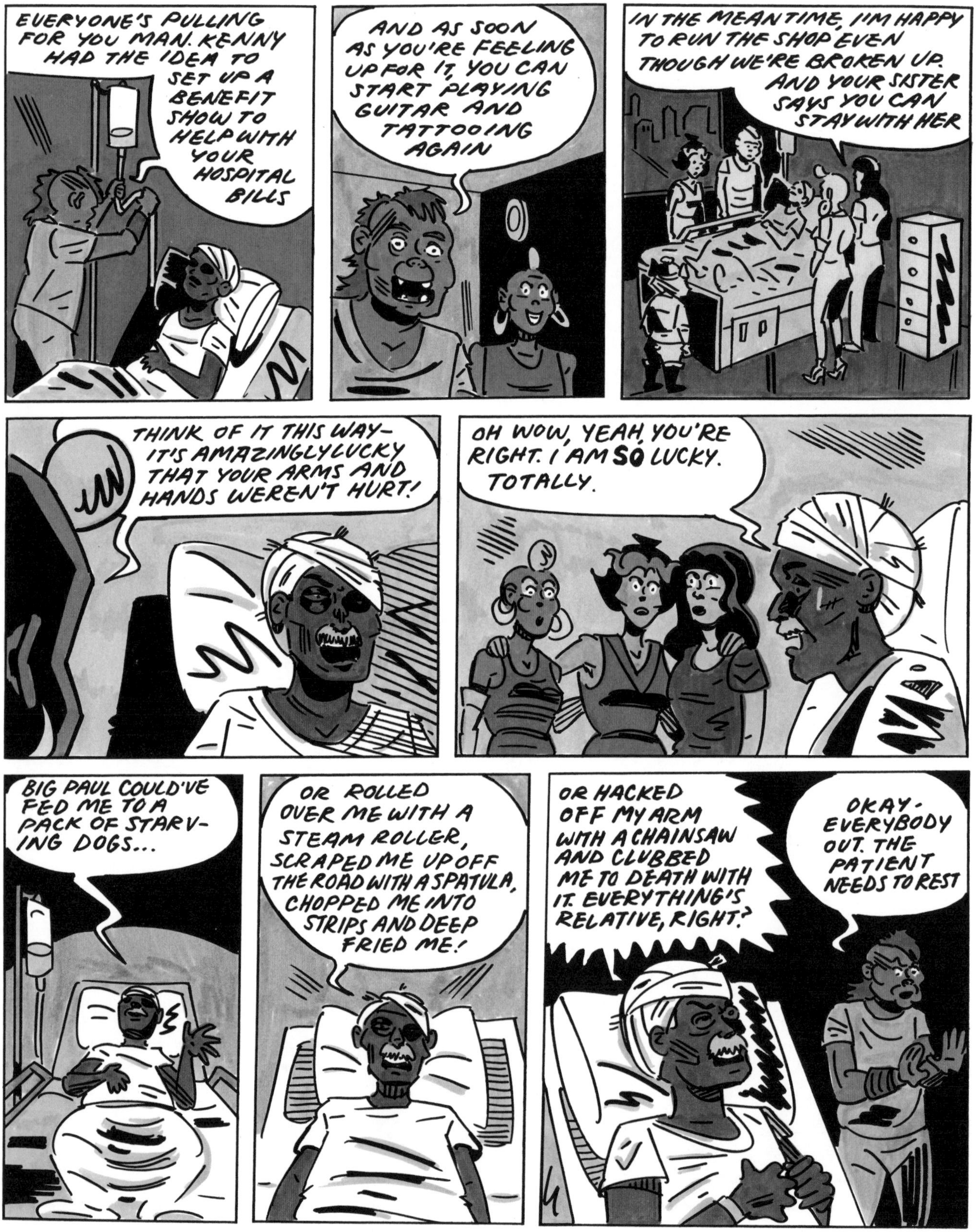
EVERYONE'S PULLING FOR YOU MAN. KENNY HAD THE IDEA TO SET UP A BENEFIT SHOW TO HELP WITH YOUR HOSPITAL BILLS
AND AS SOON AS YOU'RE FEELING UP FOR IT, YOU CAN START PLAYING GUITAR AND TATTOOING AGAIN
IN THE MEANTIME, I'M HAPPY TO RUN THE SHOP EVEN THOUGH WE'RE BROKEN UP.
AND YOUR SISTER SAYS YOU CAN STAY WITH HER
THINK OF IT THIS WAY- IT'S AMAZINGLY LUCKY THAT YOUR ARMS AND HANDS WEREN'T HURT!
OH WOW, YEAH, YOU'RE RIGHT. I AM **SO** LUCKY. TOTALLY.
BIG PAUL COULD'VE FED ME TO A PACK OF STARV-ING DOGS...
OR ROLLED OVER ME WITH A STEAM ROLLER, SCRAPED ME UP OFF THE ROAD WITH A SPATULA, CHOPPED ME INTO STRIPS AND DEEP FRIED ME!
OR HACKED OFF MY ARM WITH A CHAINSAW AND CLUBBED ME TO DEATH WITH IT. EVERYTHING'S RELATIVE, RIGHT?
OKAY- EVERYBODY OUT. THE PATIENT NEEDS TO REST

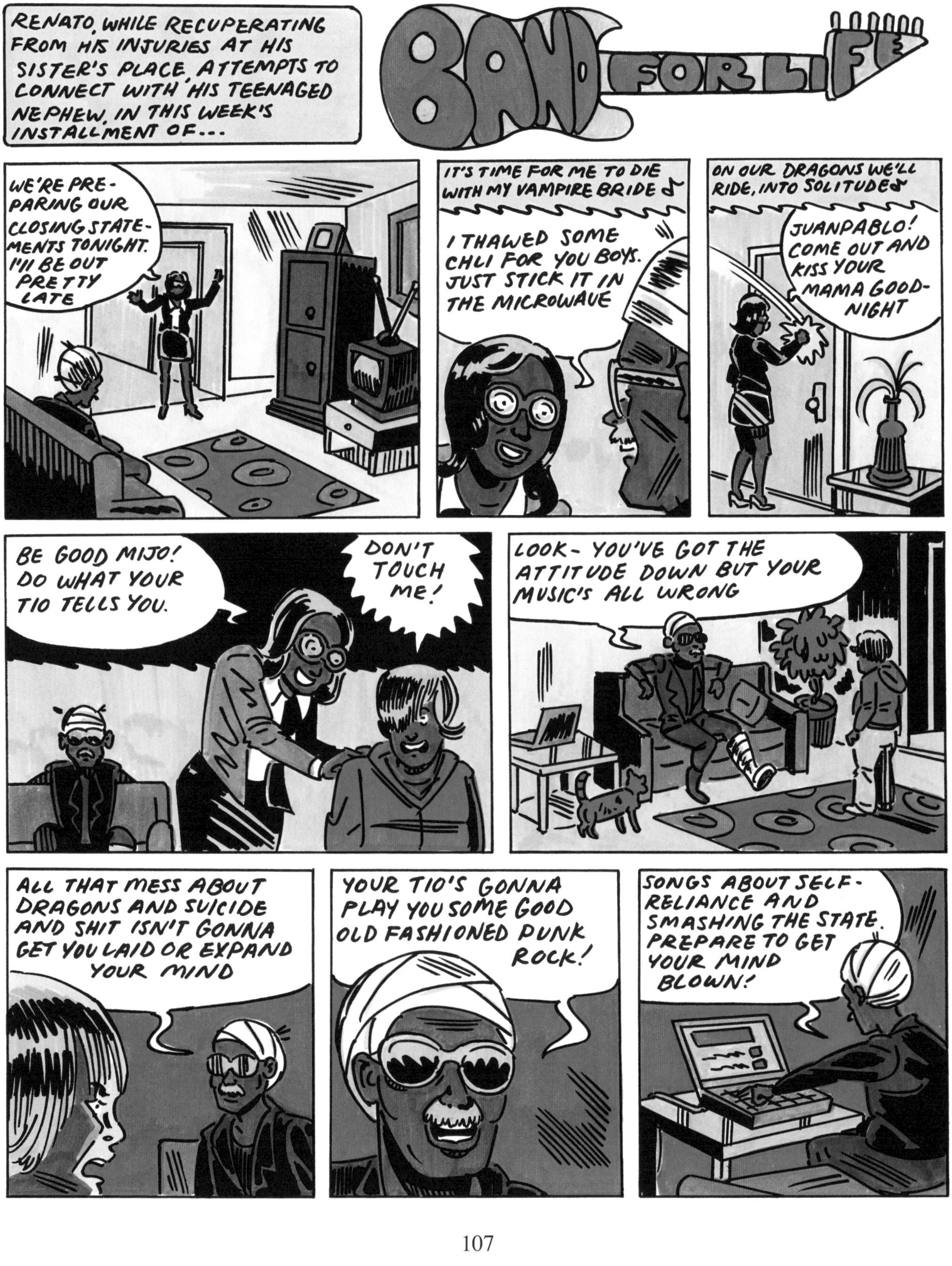
RENATO, WHILE RECUPERATING FROM HIS INJURIES AT HIS SISTER'S PLACE, ATTEMPTS TO CONNECT WITH HIS TEENAGED NEPHEW, IN THIS WEEK'S INSTALLMENT OF...
BAND FOR LIFE
WE'RE PREPARING OUR CLOSING STATEMENTS TONIGHT. I'll BE OUT PRETTY LATE
IT'S TIME FOR ME TO DIE WITH MY VAMPIRE BRIDE ♪
I THAWED SOME CHLI FOR YOU BOYS. JUST STICK IT IN THE MICROWAVE
ON OUR DRAGONS WE'LL RIDE, INTO SOLITUDE ♪
JUANPABLO! COME OUT AND KISS YOUR MAMA GOODNIGHT
BE GOOD MIJO! DO WHAT YOUR TIO TELLS YOU.
DON'T TOUCH ME!
LOOK- YOU'VE GOT THE ATTITUDE DOWN BUT YOUR MUSIC'S ALL WRONG
ALL THAT MESS ABOUT DRAGONS AND SUICIDE AND SHIT ISN'T GONNA GET YOU LAID OR EXPAND YOUR MIND
YOUR TIO'S GONNA PLAY YOU SOME GOOD OLD FASHIONED PUNK ROCK!
SONGS ABOUT SELF-RELIANCE AND SMASHING THE STATE. PREPARE TO GET YOUR MIND BLOWN!

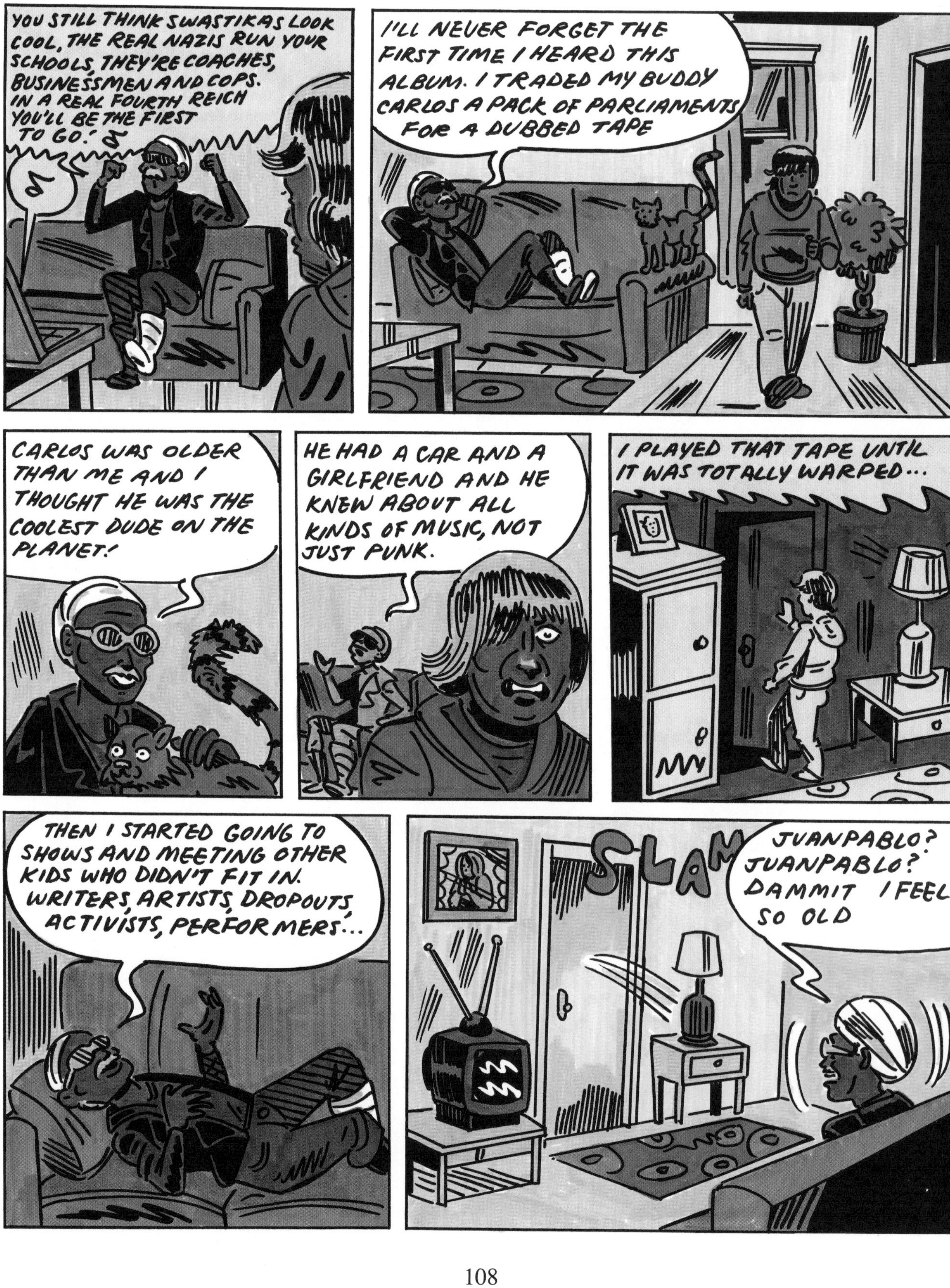
YOU STILL THINK SWASTIKAS LOOK COOL, THE REAL NAZIS RUN YOUR SCHOOLS, THEY'RE COACHES, BUSINESSMEN AND COPS. IN A REAL FOURTH REICH YOU'LL BE THE FIRST TO GO!
I'LL NEVER FORGET THE FIRST TIME I HEARD THIS ALBUM. I TRADED MY BUDDY CARLOS A PACK OF PARLIAMENTS FOR A DUBBED TAPE
CARLOS WAS OLDER THAN ME AND I THOUGHT HE WAS THE COOLEST DUDE ON THE PLANET!
HE HAD A CAR AND A GIRLFRIEND AND HE KNEW ABOUT ALL KINDS OF MUSIC, NOT JUST PUNK.
I PLAYED THAT TAPE UNTIL IT WAS TOTALLY WARPED...
THEN I STARTED GOING TO SHOWS AND MEETING OTHER KIDS WHO DIDN'T FIT IN. WRITERS, ARTISTS, DROPOUTS, ACTIVISTS, PERFORMERS...
SLAM
JUANPABLO? JUANPABLO? DAMMIT I FEEL SO OLD

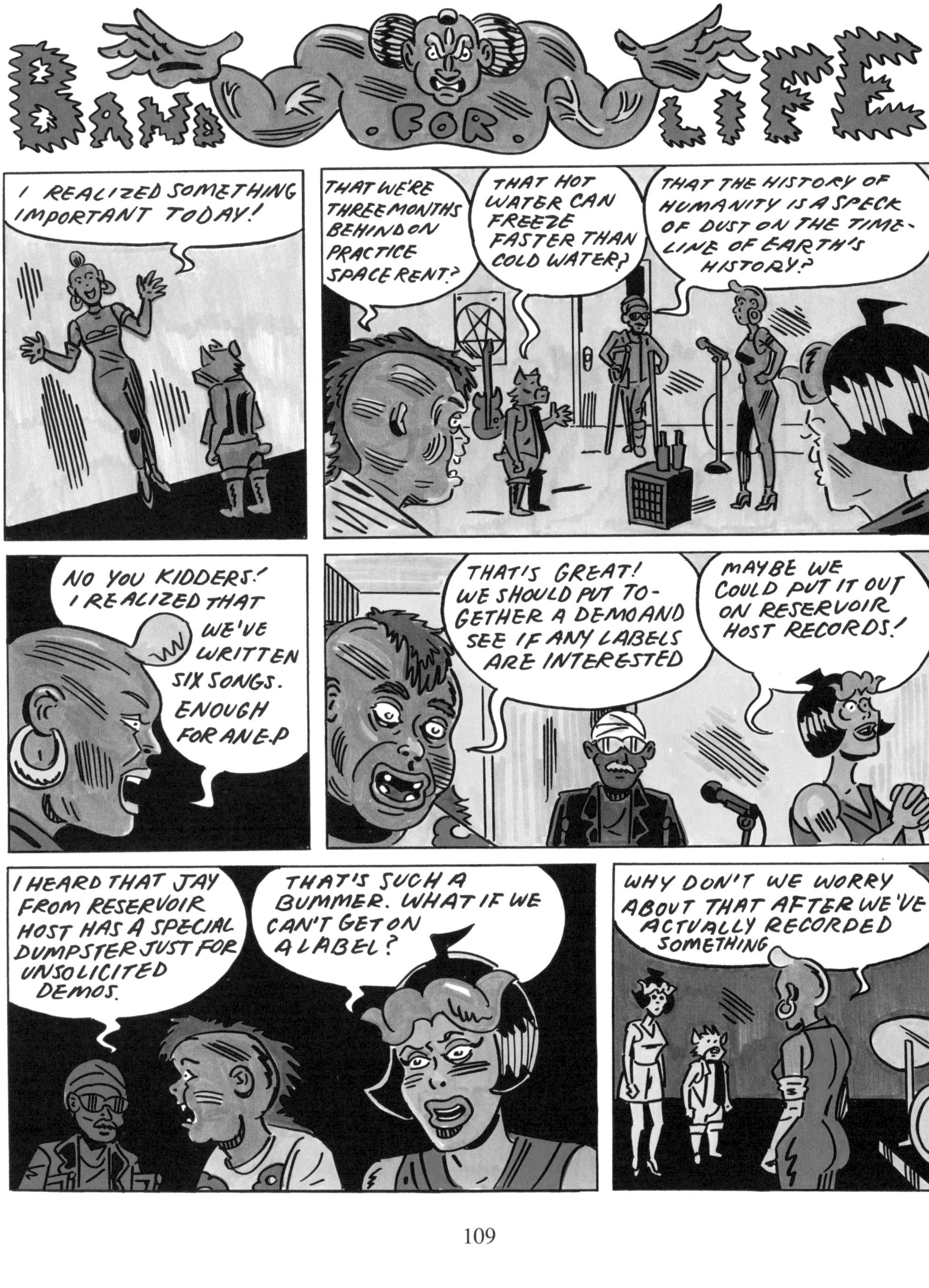
BAND FOR LIFE
I REALIZED SOMETHING IMPORTANT TODAY!
THAT WE'RE THREE MONTHS BEHIND ON PRACTICE SPACE RENT?
THAT HOT WATER CAN FREEZE FASTER THAN COLD WATER?
THAT THE HISTORY OF HUMANITY IS A SPECK OF DUST ON THE TIME-LINE OF EARTH'S HISTORY?
NO YOU KIDDERS! I REALIZED THAT WE'VE WRITTEN SIX SONGS. ENOUGH FOR AN E.P
THAT'S GREAT! WE SHOULD PUT TO-GETHER A DEMO AND SEE IF ANY LABELS ARE INTERESTED
MAYBE WE COULD PUT IT OUT ON RESERVOIR HOST RECORDS!
I HEARD THAT JAY FROM RESERVOIR HOST HAS A SPECIAL DUMPSTER JUST FOR UNSOLICITED DEMOS.
THAT'S SUCH A BUMMER. WHAT IF WE CAN'T GET ON A LABEL?
WHY DON'T WE WORRY ABOUT THAT AFTER WE'VE ACTUALLY RECORDED SOMETHING

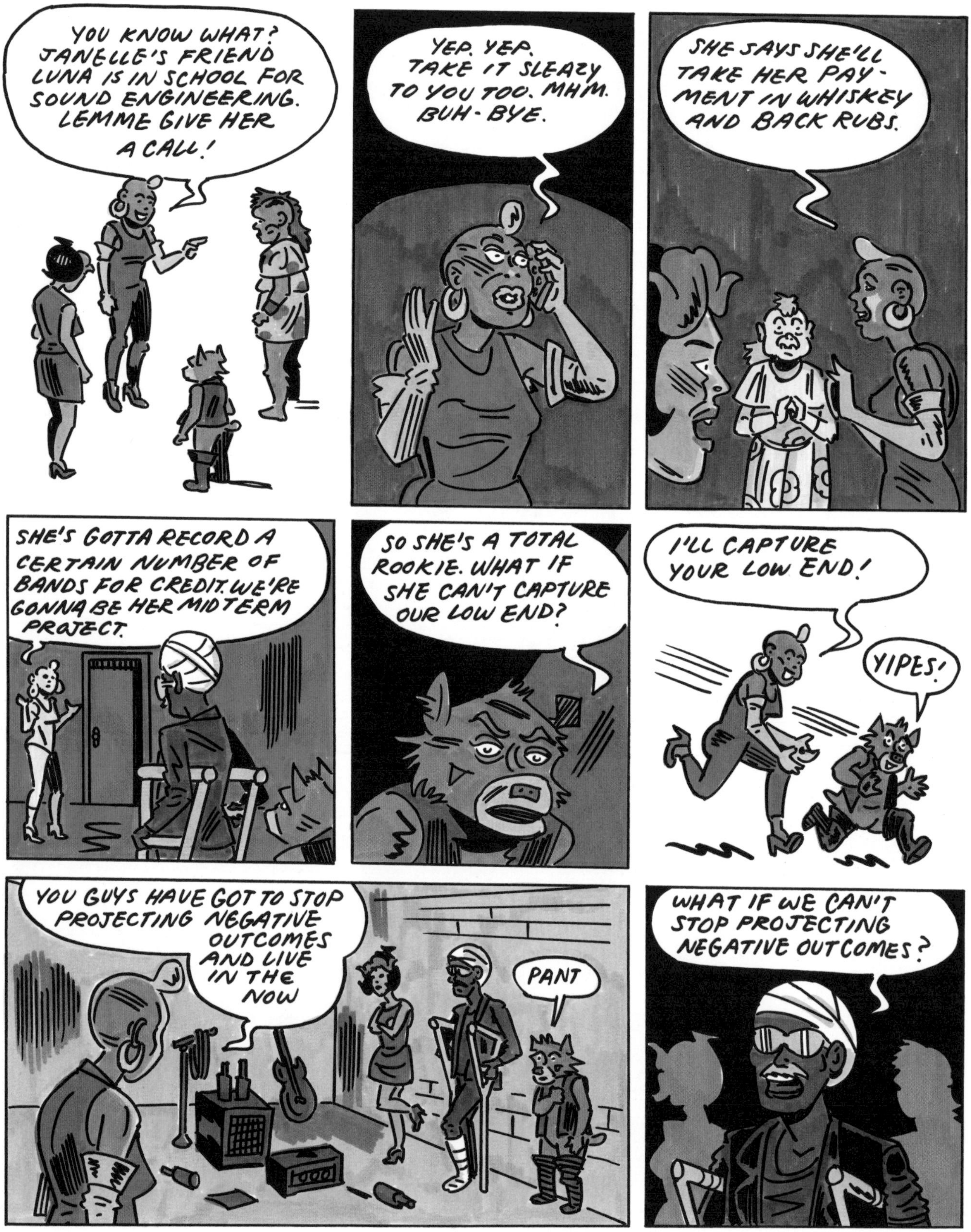
YOU KNOW WHAT? JANELLE'S FRIEND LUNA IS IN SCHOOL FOR SOUND ENGINEERING. LEMME GIVE HER A CALL!
YEP. YEP. TAKE IT SLEAZY TO YOU TOO. MHM. BUH-BYE.
SHE SAYS SHE'LL TAKE HER PAY-MENT IN WHISKEY AND BACK RUBS.
SHE'S GOTTA RECORD A CERTAIN NUMBER OF BANDS FOR CREDIT. WE'RE GONNA BE HER MIDTERM PROJECT.
SO SHE'S A TOTAL ROOKIE. WHAT IF SHE CAN'T CAPTURE OUR LOW END?
I'LL CAPTURE YOUR LOW END!
YIPES!
YOU GUYS HAVE GOT TO STOP PROJECTING NEGATIVE OUTCOMES AND LIVE IN THE NOW
PANT
WHAT IF WE CAN'T STOP PROJECTING NEGATIVE OUTCOMES?

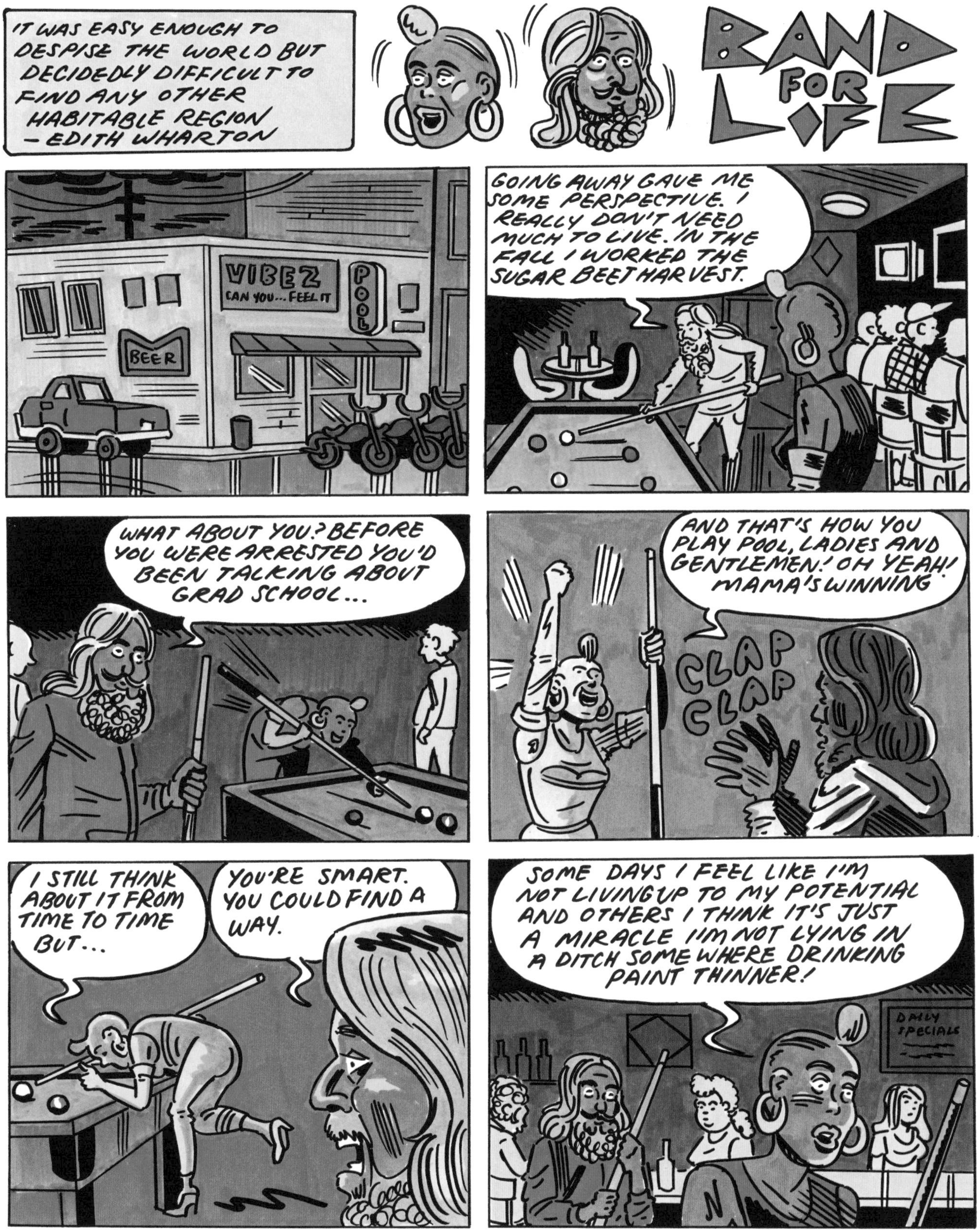
IT WAS EASY ENOUGH TO DESPISE THE WORLD BUT DECIDEDLY DIFFICULT TO FIND ANY OTHER HABITABLE REGION – EDITH WHARTON
BAND FOR LIFE
VIBEZ CAN YOU... FEEL IT
POOL
BEER
GOING AWAY GAVE ME SOME PERSPECTIVE. I REALLY DON'T NEED MUCH TO LIVE. IN THE FALL I WORKED THE SUGAR BEET HARVEST.
WHAT ABOUT YOU? BEFORE YOU WERE ARRESTED YOU'D BEEN TALKING ABOUT GRAD SCHOOL...
AND THAT'S HOW YOU PLAY POOL, LADIES AND GENTLEMEN! OH YEAH! MAMA'S WINNING
CLAP CLAP
I STILL THINK ABOUT IT FROM TIME TO TIME BUT...
YOU'RE SMART. YOU COULD FIND A WAY.
SOME DAYS I FEEL LIKE I'M NOT LIVING UP TO MY POTENTIAL AND OTHERS I THINK IT'S JUST A MIRACLE I'M NOT LYING IN A DITCH SOMEWHERE DRINKING PAINT THINNER!
DAILY SPECIALS

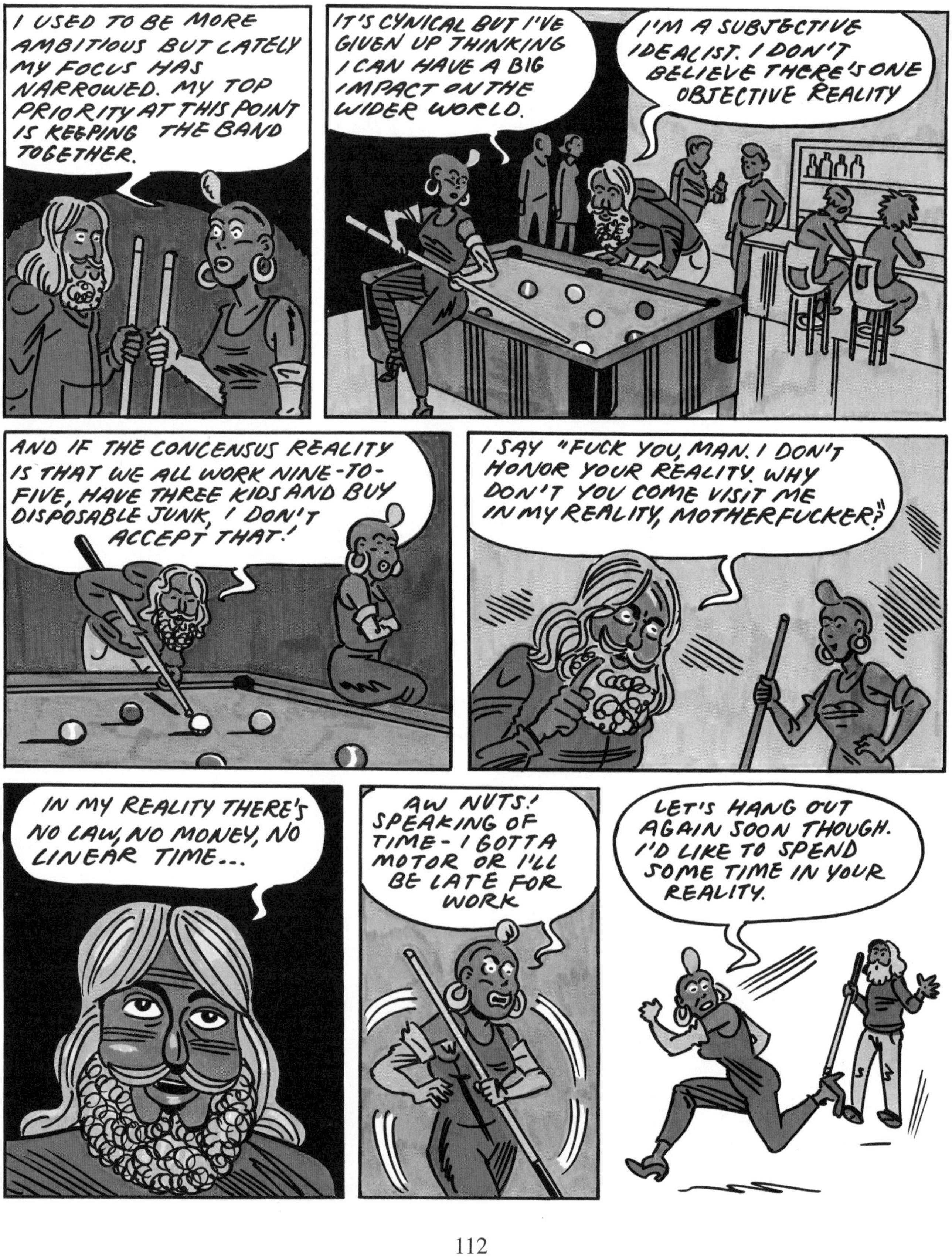
I USED TO BE MORE AMBITIOUS BUT LATELY MY FOCUS HAS NARROWED. MY TOP PRIORITY AT THIS POINT IS KEEPING THE BAND TOGETHER.
IT'S CYNICAL BUT I'VE GIVEN UP THINKING I CAN HAVE A BIG IMPACT ON THE WIDER WORLD.
I'M A SUBJECTIVE IDEALIST. I DON'T BELIEVE THERE'S ONE OBJECTIVE REALITY
AND IF THE CONCENSUS REALITY IS THAT WE ALL WORK NINE-TO-FIVE, HAVE THREE KIDS AND BUY DISPOSABLE JUNK, I DON'T ACCEPT THAT!
I SAY "FUCK YOU, MAN. I DON'T HONOR YOUR REALITY. WHY DON'T YOU COME VISIT ME IN MY REALITY, MOTHERFUCKER?"
IN MY REALITY THERE'S NO LAW, NO MONEY, NO LINEAR TIME...
AW NUTS! SPEAKING OF TIME- I GOTTA MOTOR OR I'LL BE LATE FOR WORK
LET'S HANG OUT AGAIN SOON THOUGH. I'D LIKE TO SPEND SOME TIME IN YOUR REALITY.

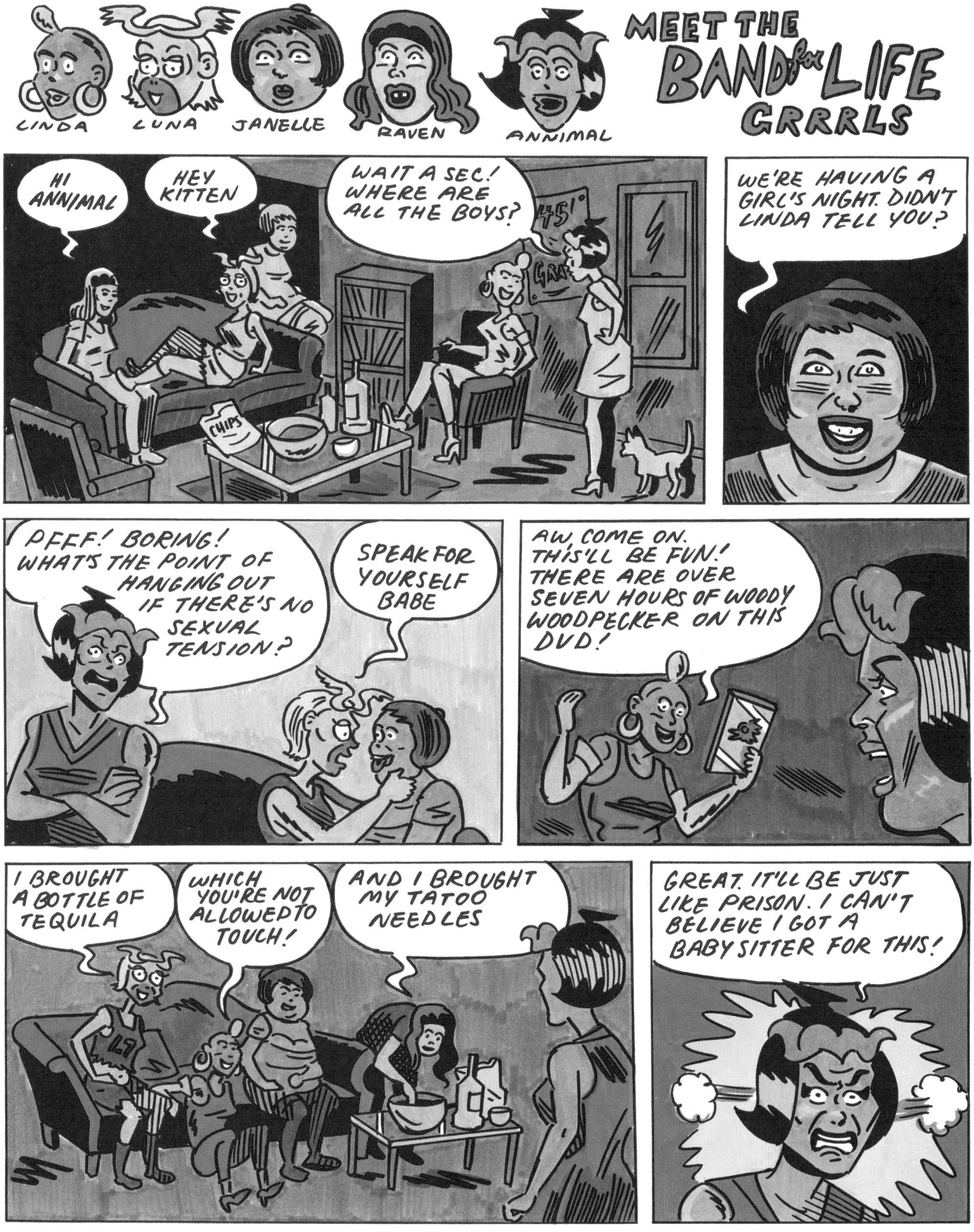
MEET THE BAND for LIFE GRRRLS
LINDA
LUNA
JANELLE
RAVEN
ANNIMAL
HI ANNIMAL
HEY KITTEN
WAIT A SEC! WHERE ARE ALL THE BOYS?
CHIPS
WE'RE HAVING A GIRL'S NIGHT. DIDN'T LINDA TELL YOU?
PFFF! BORING! WHAT'S THE POINT OF HANGING OUT IF THERE'S NO SEXUAL TENSION?
SPEAK FOR YOURSELF BABE
AW, COME ON. THIS'LL BE FUN! THERE ARE OVER SEVEN HOURS OF WOODY WOODPECKER ON THIS DVD!
I BROUGHT A BOTTLE OF TEQUILA
WHICH YOU'RE NOT ALLOWED TO TOUCH!
AND I BROUGHT MY TATOO NEEDLES
GREAT. IT'LL BE JUST LIKE PRISON. I CAN'T BELIEVE I GOT A BABY SITTER FOR THIS!

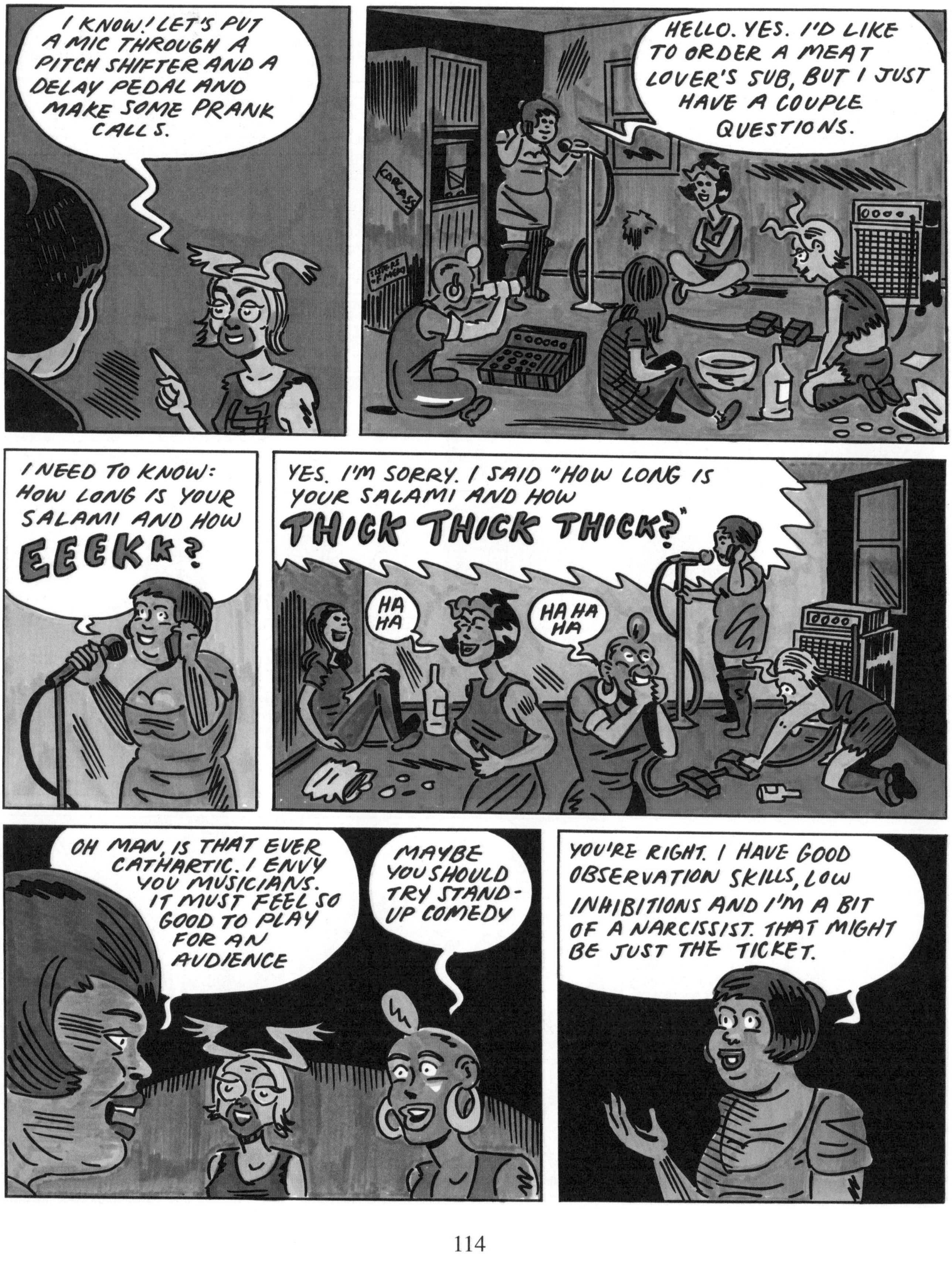
I KNOW! LET'S PUT A MIC THROUGH A PITCH SHIFTER AND A DELAY PEDAL AND MAKE SOME PRANK CALLS.
HELLO. YES. I'D LIKE TO ORDER A MEAT LOVER'S SUB, BUT I JUST HAVE A COUPLE QUESTIONS.
CARCASS
I NEED TO KNOW: HOW LONG IS YOUR SALAMI AND HOW EEEKK?
YES. I'M SORRY. I SAID "HOW LONG IS YOUR SALAMI AND HOW THICK THICK THICK?"
HA HA
HA HA HA
OH MAN, IS THAT EVER CATHARTIC. I ENVY YOU MUSICIANS. IT MUST FEEL SO GOOD TO PLAY FOR AN AUDIENCE
MAYBE YOU SHOULD TRY STAND-UP COMEDY
YOU'RE RIGHT. I HAVE GOOD OBSERVATION SKILLS, LOW INHIBITIONS AND I'M A BIT OF A NARCISSIST. THAT MIGHT BE JUST THE TICKET.

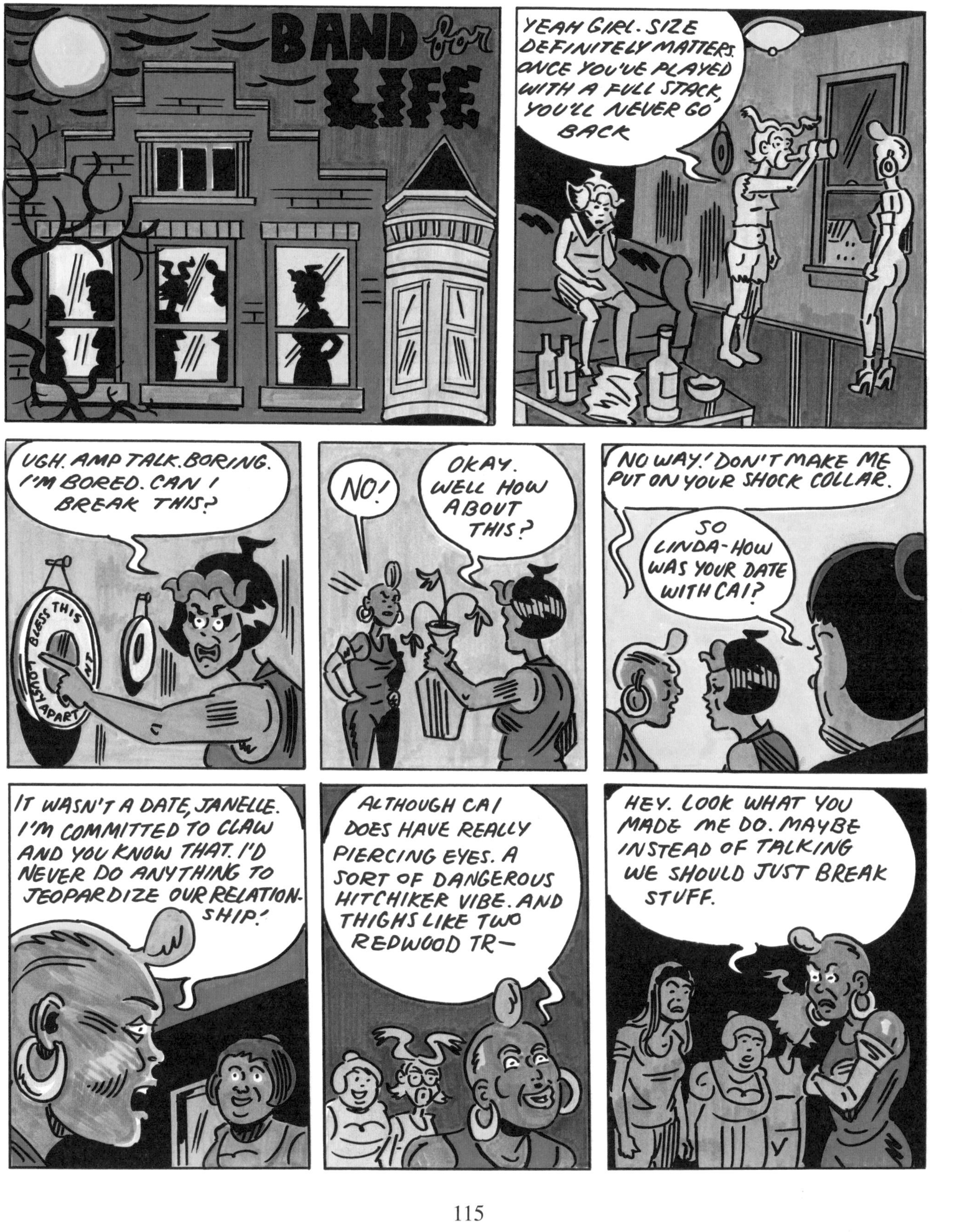
BAND for LIFE
YEAH GIRL. SIZE DEFINITELY MATTERS. ONCE YOU'VE PLAYED WITH A FULL STACK, YOU'LL NEVER GO BACK
UGH. AMP TALK. BORING. I'M BORED. CAN I BREAK THIS?
BLESS THIS LOUSY APARTMENT
NO!
OKAY. WELL HOW ABOUT THIS?
NO WAY! DON'T MAKE ME PUT ON YOUR SHOCK COLLAR.
SO LINDA- HOW WAS YOUR DATE WITH CAI?
IT WASN'T A DATE, JANELLE. I'M COMMITTED TO CLAW AND YOU KNOW THAT. I'D NEVER DO ANYTHING TO JEOPARDIZE OUR RELATIONSHIP!
ALTHOUGH CAI DOES HAVE REALLY PIERCING EYES. A SORT OF DANGEROUS HITCHIKER VIBE. AND THIGHS LIKE TWO REDWOOD TR—
HEY. LOOK WHAT YOU MADE ME DO. MAYBE INSTEAD OF TALKING WE SHOULD JUST BREAK STUFF.

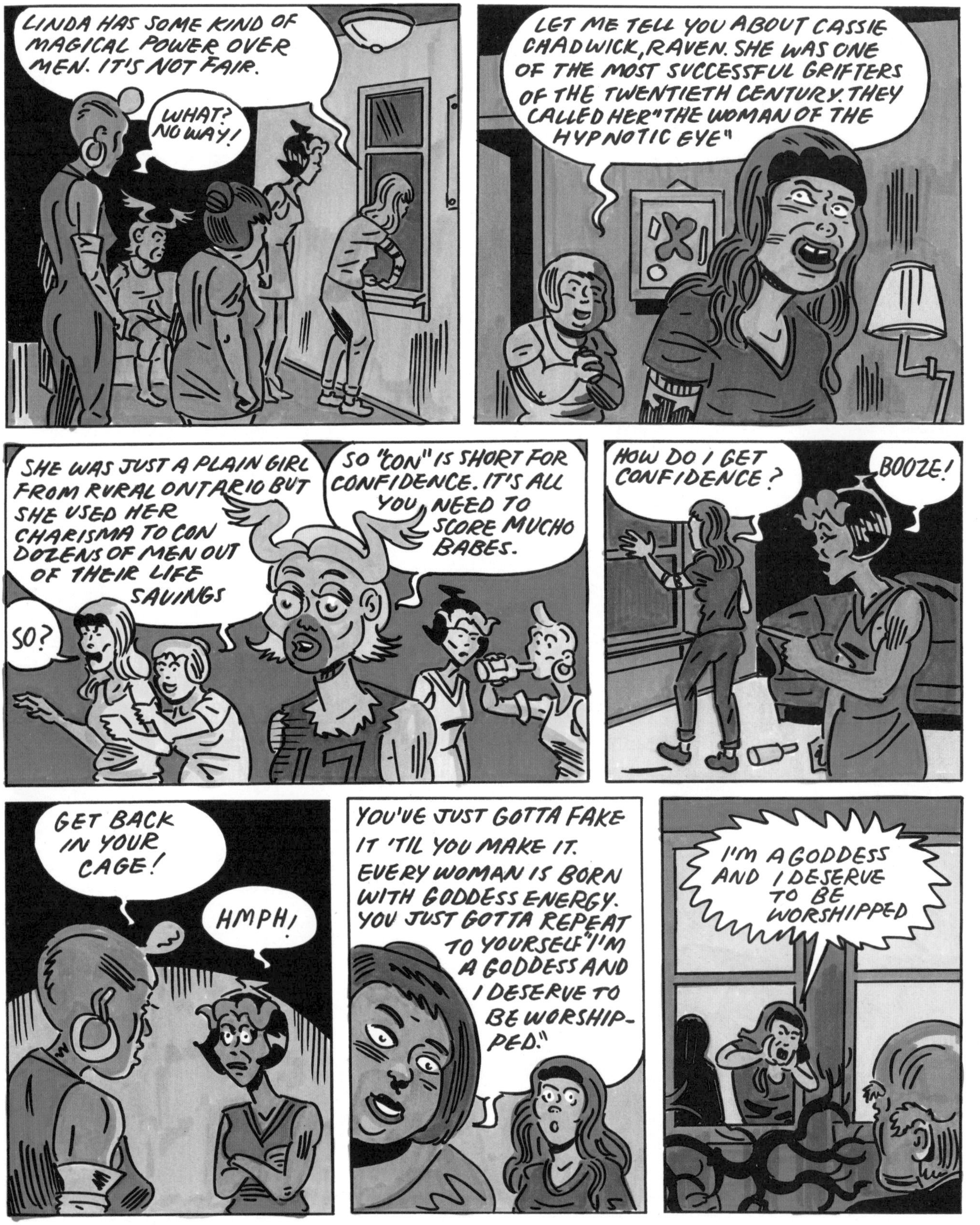
LINDA HAS SOME KIND OF MAGICAL POWER OVER MEN. IT'S NOT FAIR.
WHAT? NO WAY!
LET ME TELL YOU ABOUT CASSIE CHADWICK, RAVEN. SHE WAS ONE OF THE MOST SUCCESSFUL GRIFTERS OF THE TWENTIETH CENTURY. THEY CALLED HER "THE WOMAN OF THE HYPNOTIC EYE"
SHE WAS JUST A PLAIN GIRL FROM RURAL ONTARIO BUT SHE USED HER CHARISMA TO CON DOZENS OF MEN OUT OF THEIR LIFE SAVINGS
SO?
SO "CON" IS SHORT FOR CONFIDENCE. IT'S ALL YOU NEED TO SCORE MUCHO BABES.
HOW DO I GET CONFIDENCE?
BOOZE!
GET BACK IN YOUR CAGE!
HMPH!
YOU'VE JUST GOTTA FAKE IT 'TIL YOU MAKE IT. EVERY WOMAN IS BORN WITH GODDESS ENERGY. YOU JUST GOTTA REPEAT TO YOURSELF "I'M A GODDESS AND I DESERVE TO BE WORSHIP-PED."
I'M A GODDESS AND I DESERVE TO BE WORSHIPPED

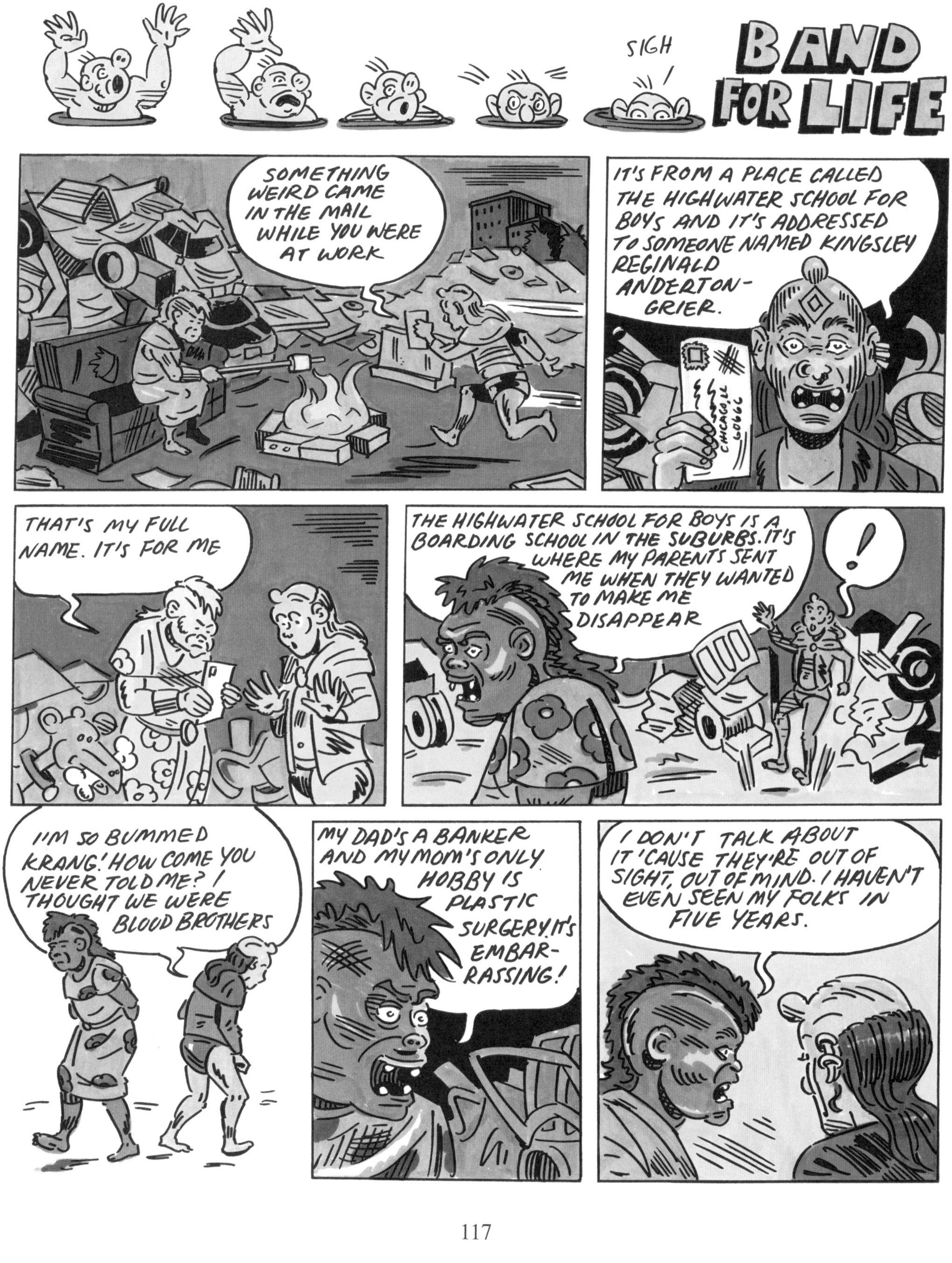
SIGH
BAND FOR LIFE
SOMETHING WEIRD CAME IN THE MAIL WHILE YOU WERE AT WORK
IT'S FROM A PLACE CALLED THE HIGHWATER SCHOOL FOR BOYS AND IT'S ADDRESSED TO SOMEONE NAMED KINGSLEY REGINALD ANDERTON-GRIER.
THAT'S MY FULL NAME. IT'S FOR ME
THE HIGHWATER SCHOOL FOR BOYS IS A BOARDING SCHOOL IN THE SUBURBS. IT'S WHERE MY PARENTS SENT ME WHEN THEY WANTED TO MAKE ME DISAPPEAR
!
I'M SO BUMMED KRANG! HOW COME YOU NEVER TOLD ME? I THOUGHT WE WERE BLOOD BROTHERS
MY DAD'S A BANKER AND MY MOM'S ONLY HOBBY IS PLASTIC SURGERY. IT'S EMBARRASSING!
I DON'T TALK ABOUT IT 'CAUSE THEY'RE OUT OF SIGHT, OUT OF MIND. I HAVEN'T EVEN SEEN MY FOLKS IN FIVE YEARS.

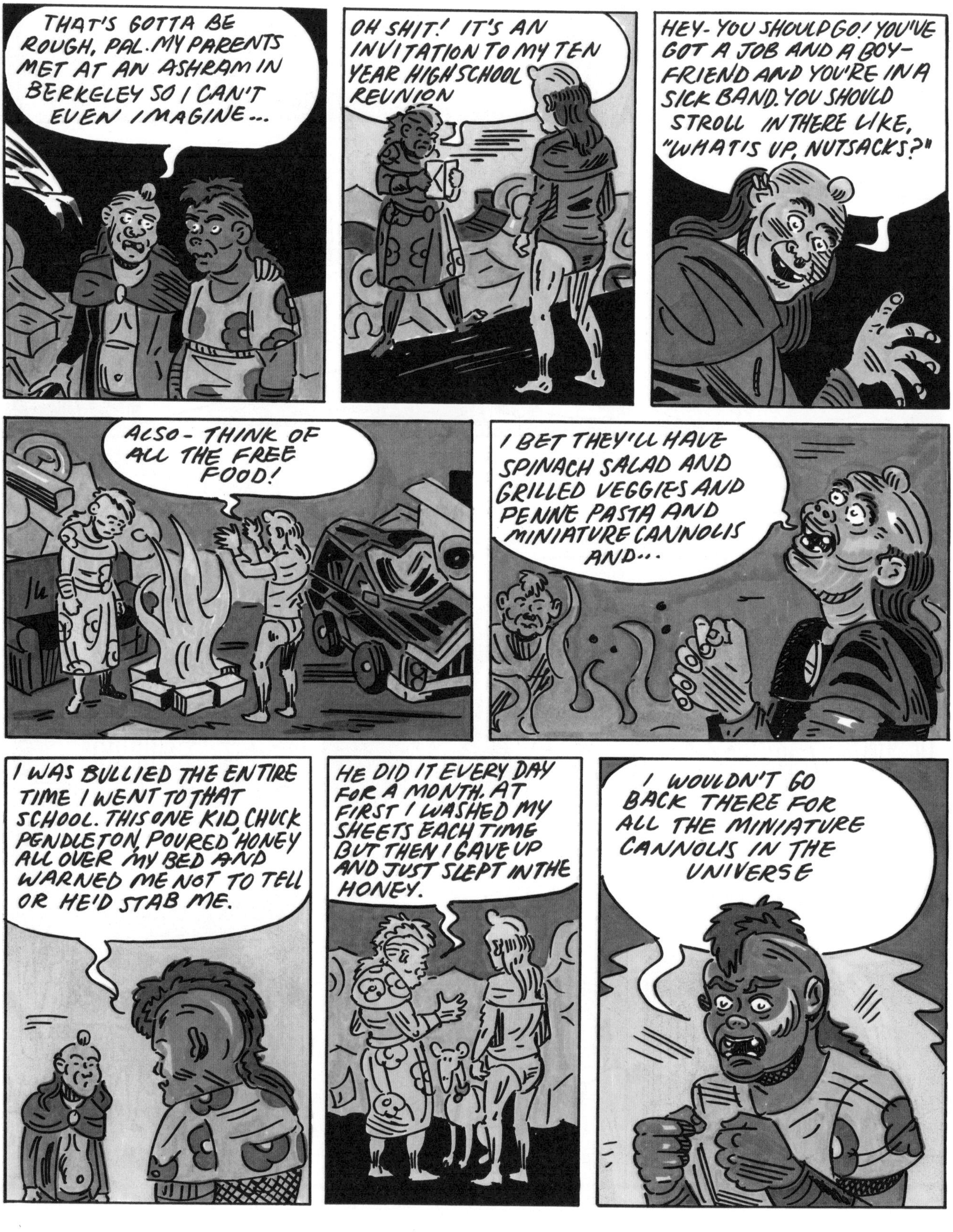
THAT'S GOTTA BE ROUGH, PAL. MY PARENTS MET AT AN ASHRAM IN BERKELEY SO I CAN'T EVEN IMAGINE...
OH SHIT! IT'S AN INVITATION TO MY TEN YEAR HIGH SCHOOL REUNION
HEY- YOU SHOULD GO! YOU'VE GOT A JOB AND A BOY-FRIEND AND YOU'RE IN A SICK BAND. YOU SHOULD STROLL IN THERE LIKE, "WHAT'S UP, NUTSACKS?"
ALSO- THINK OF ALL THE FREE FOOD!
I BET THEY'LL HAVE SPINACH SALAD AND GRILLED VEGGIES AND PENNE PASTA AND MINIATURE CANNOLIS AND...
I WAS BULLIED THE ENTIRE TIME I WENT TO THAT SCHOOL. THIS ONE KID, CHUCK PENDLETON, POURED HONEY ALL OVER MY BED AND WARNED ME NOT TO TELL OR HE'D STAB ME.
HE DID IT EVERY DAY FOR A MONTH. AT FIRST I WASHED MY SHEETS EACH TIME BUT THEN I GAVE UP AND JUST SLEPT IN THE HONEY.
I WOULDN'T GO BACK THERE FOR ALL THE MINIATURE CANNOLIS IN THE UNIVERSE

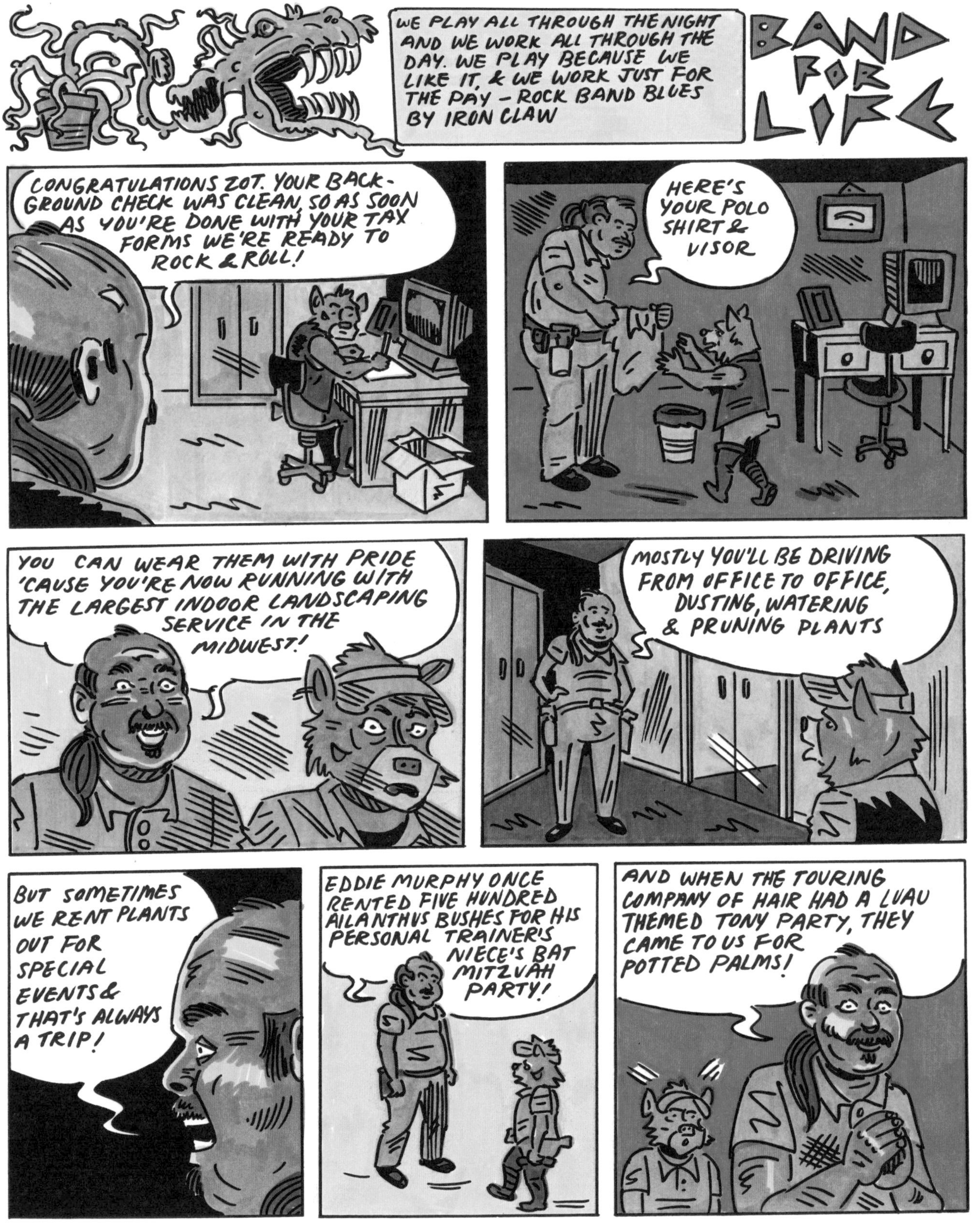
WE PLAY ALL THROUGH THE NIGHT AND WE WORK ALL THROUGH THE DAY. WE PLAY BECAUSE WE LIKE IT, & WE WORK JUST FOR THE PAY - ROCK BAND BLUES BY IRON CLAW
BAND FOR LIFE
CONGRATULATIONS ZOT. YOUR BACKGROUND CHECK WAS CLEAN, SO AS SOON AS YOU'RE DONE WITH YOUR TAX FORMS WE'RE READY TO ROCK & ROLL!
HERE'S YOUR POLO SHIRT & VISOR
YOU CAN WEAR THEM WITH PRIDE 'CAUSE YOU'RE NOW RUNNING WITH THE LARGEST INDOOR LANDSCAPING SERVICE IN THE MIDWEST!
MOSTLY YOU'LL BE DRIVING FROM OFFICE TO OFFICE, DUSTING, WATERING & PRUNING PLANTS
BUT SOMETIMES WE RENT PLANTS OUT FOR SPECIAL EVENTS & THAT'S ALWAYS A TRIP!
EDDIE MURPHY ONCE RENTED FIVE HUNDRED AILANTHUS BUSHES FOR HIS PERSONAL TRAINER'S NIECE'S BAT MITZVAH PARTY!
AND WHEN THE TOURING COMPANY OF HAIR HAD A LUAU THEMED TONY PARTY, THEY CAME TO US FOR POTTED PALMS!

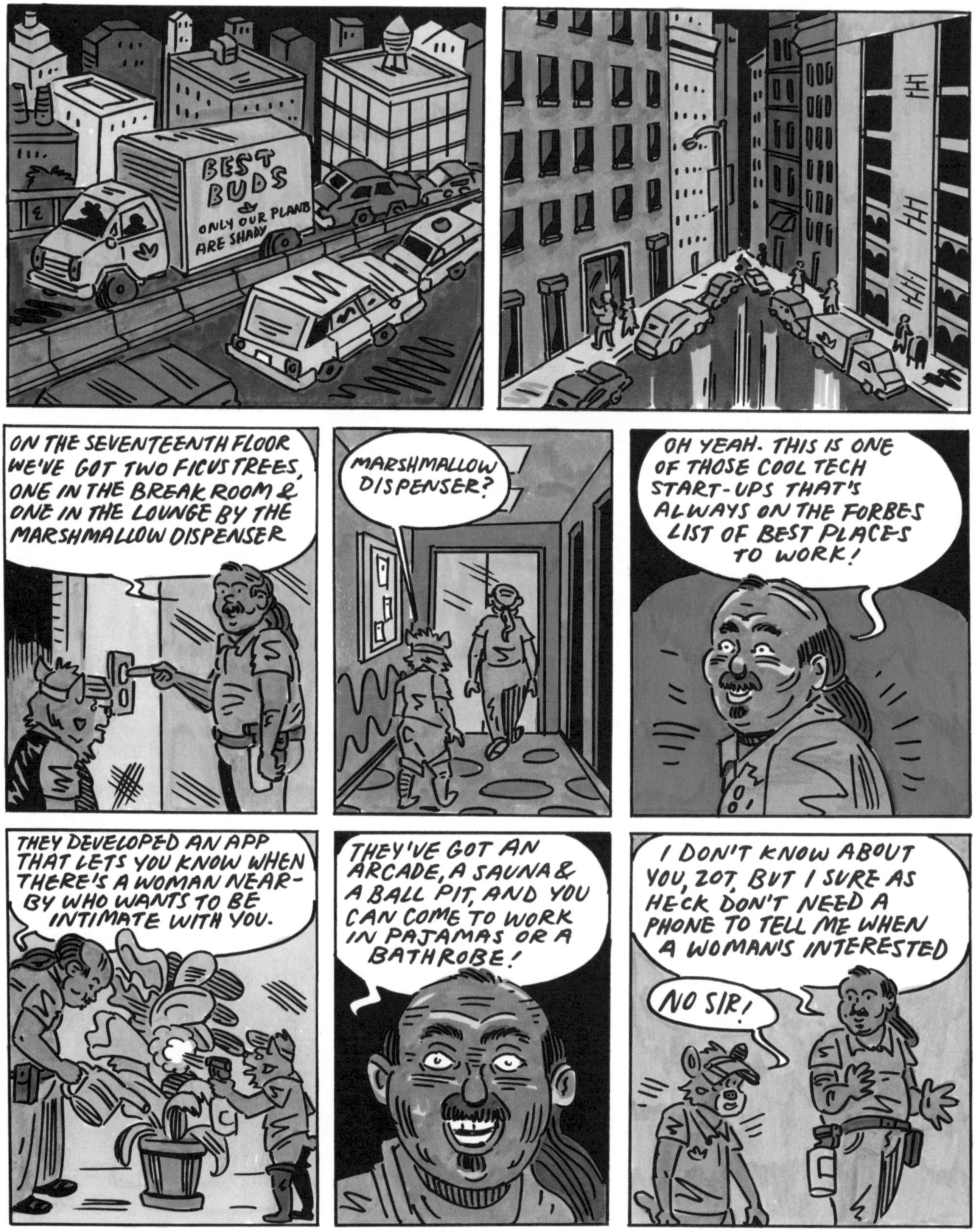
BEST BUDS
ONLY OUR PLANTS ARE SHADY
ON THE SEVENTEENTH FLOOR WE'VE GOT TWO FICUS TREES, ONE IN THE BREAK ROOM & ONE IN THE LOUNGE BY THE MARSHMALLOW DISPENSER
MARSHMALLOW DISPENSER?
OH YEAH. THIS IS ONE OF THOSE COOL TECH START-UPS THAT'S ALWAYS ON THE FORBES LIST OF BEST PLACES TO WORK!
THEY DEVELOPED AN APP THAT LETS YOU KNOW WHEN THERE'S A WOMAN NEAR-BY WHO WANTS TO BE INTIMATE WITH YOU.
THEY'VE GOT AN ARCADE, A SAUNA & A BALL PIT, AND YOU CAN COME TO WORK IN PAJAMAS OR A BATHROBE!
I DON'T KNOW ABOUT YOU, ZOT, BUT I SURE AS HECK DON'T NEED A PHONE TO TELL ME WHEN A WOMAN'S INTERESTED
NO SIR!

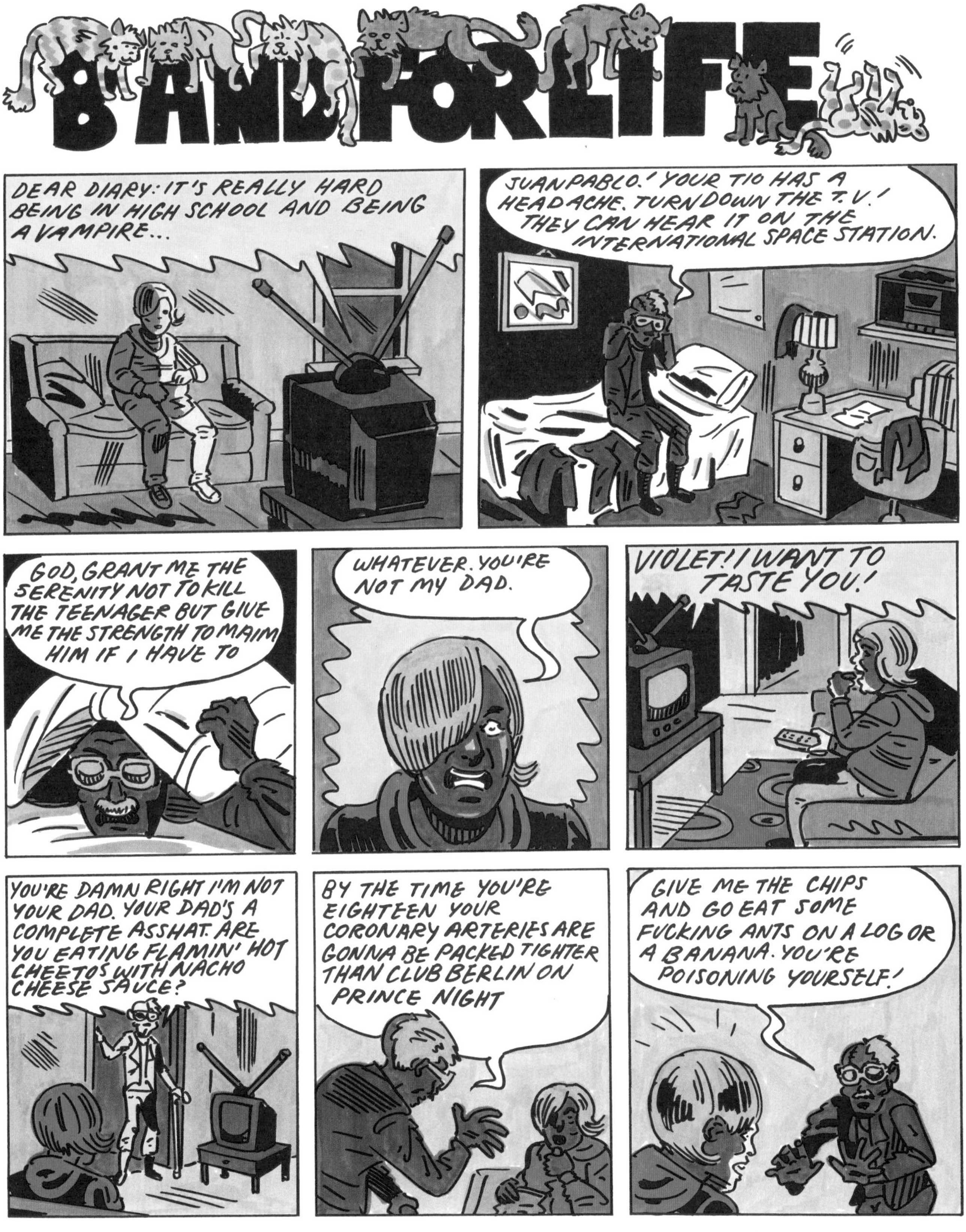
BAND FOR LIFE
DEAR DIARY: IT'S REALLY HARD BEING IN HIGH SCHOOL AND BEING A VAMPIRE...
JUAN PABLO! YOUR TIO HAS A HEADACHE. TURN DOWN THE T.V.! THEY CAN HEAR IT ON THE INTERNATIONAL SPACE STATION.
GOD, GRANT ME THE SERENITY NOT TO KILL THE TEENAGER BUT GIVE ME THE STRENGTH TO MAIM HIM IF I HAVE TO
WHATEVER. YOU'RE NOT MY DAD.
VIOLET! I WANT TO TASTE YOU!
YOU'RE DAMN RIGHT I'M NOT YOUR DAD. YOUR DAD'S A COMPLETE ASSHAT. ARE YOU EATING FLAMIN' HOT CHEETOS WITH NACHO CHEESE SAUCE?
BY THE TIME YOU'RE EIGHTEEN YOUR CORONARY ARTERIES ARE GONNA BE PACKED TIGHTER THAN CLUB BERLIN ON PRINCE NIGHT
GIVE ME THE CHIPS AND GO EAT SOME FUCKING ANTS ON A LOG OR A BANANA. YOU'RE POISONING YOURSELF!

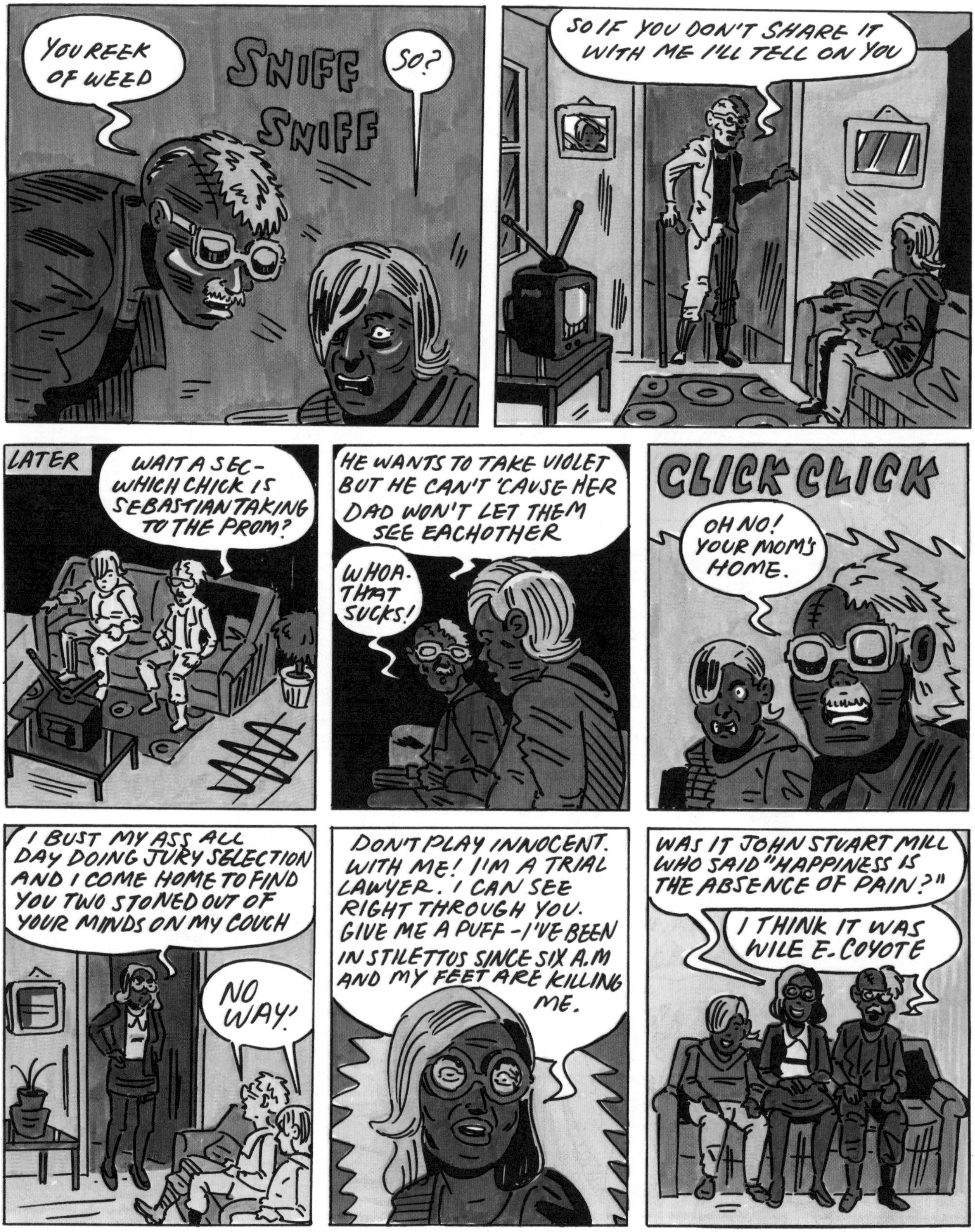
YOU REEK OF WEED
SNIFF SNIFF
SO?
SO IF YOU DON'T SHARE IT WITH ME I'LL TELL ON YOU
LATER
WAIT A SEC- WHICH CHICK IS SEBASTIAN TAKING TO THE PROM?
HE WANTS TO TAKE VIOLET BUT HE CAN'T 'CAUSE HER DAD WON'T LET THEM SEE EACHOTHER
WHOA. THAT SUCKS!
CLICK CLICK
OH NO! YOUR MOM'S HOME.
I BUST MY ASS ALL DAY DOING JURY SELECTION AND I COME HOME TO FIND YOU TWO STONED OUT OF YOUR MINDS ON MY COUCH
NO WAY!
DON'T PLAY INNOCENT. WITH ME! I'M A TRIAL LAWYER. I CAN SEE RIGHT THROUGH YOU. GIVE ME A PUFF - I'VE BEEN IN STILETTOS SINCE SIX A.M AND MY FEET ARE KILLING ME.
WAS IT JOHN STUART MILL WHO SAID "HAPPINESS IS THE ABSENCE OF PAIN?"
I THINK IT WAS WILE E. COYOTE

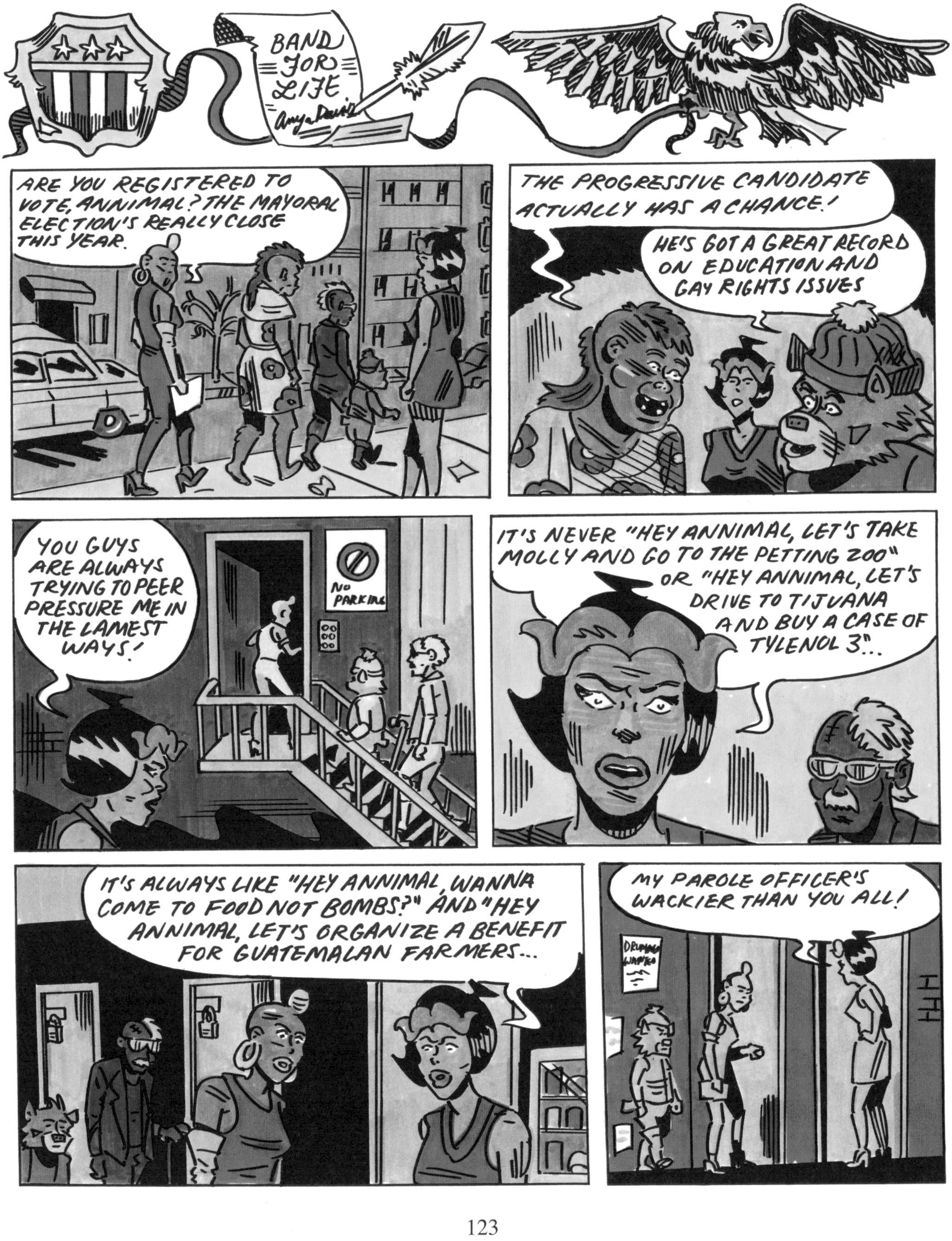
BAND FOR LIFE
ARE YOU REGISTERED TO VOTE, ANNIMAL? THE MAYORAL ELECTION'S REALLY CLOSE THIS YEAR.
THE PROGRESSIVE CANDIDATE ACTUALLY HAS A CHANCE!
HE'S GOT A GREAT RECORD ON EDUCATION AND GAY RIGHTS ISSUES
YOU GUYS ARE ALWAYS TRYING TO PEER PRESSURE ME IN THE LAMEST WAYS!
NO PARKING
IT'S NEVER "HEY ANNIMAL, LET'S TAKE MOLLY AND GO TO THE PETTING ZOO" OR "HEY ANNIMAL, LET'S DRIVE TO TIJUANA AND BUY A CASE OF TYLENOL 3"...
IT'S ALWAYS LIKE "HEY ANNIMAL, WANNA COME TO FOOD NOT BOMBS?" AND "HEY ANNIMAL, LET'S ORGANIZE A BENEFIT FOR GUATEMALAN FARMERS...
MY PAROLE OFFICER'S WACKIER THAN YOU ALL!

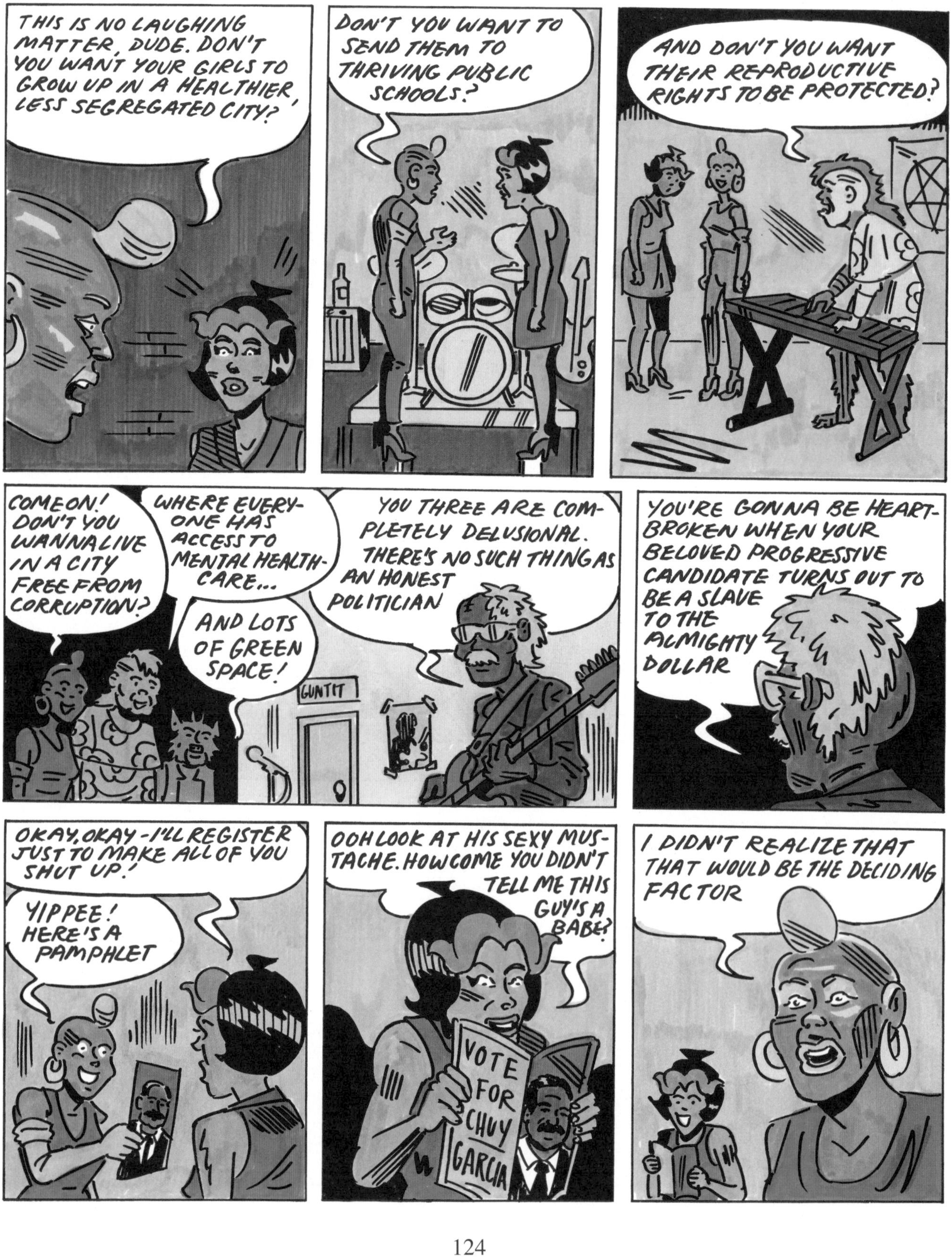
THIS IS NO LAUGHING MATTER, DUDE. DON'T YOU WANT YOUR GIRLS TO GROW UP IN A HEALTHIER, LESS SEGREGATED CITY?
DON'T YOU WANT TO SEND THEM TO THRIVING PUBLIC SCHOOLS?
AND DON'T YOU WANT THEIR REPRODUCTIVE RIGHTS TO BE PROTECTED?
COMEON! DON'T YOU WANNA LIVE IN A CITY FREE FROM CORRUPTION?
WHERE EVERY-ONE HAS ACCESS TO MENTAL HEALTH-CARE...
AND LOTS OF GREEN SPACE!
YOU THREE ARE COM-PLETELY DELUSIONAL. THERE'S NO SUCH THING AS AN HONEST POLITICIAN
GUNTIT
YOU'RE GONNA BE HEART-BROKEN WHEN YOUR BELOVED PROGRESSIVE CANDIDATE TURNS OUT TO BE A SLAVE TO THE ALMIGHTY DOLLAR
OKAY, OKAY - I'LL REGISTER JUST TO MAKE ALL OF YOU SHUT UP!
YIPPEE! HERE'S A PAMPHLET
OOH LOOK AT HIS SEXY MUS-TACHE. HOW COME YOU DIDN'T TELL ME THIS GUY'S A BABE?
VOTE FOR CHUY GARCIA
I DIDN'T REALIZE THAT THAT WOULD BE THE DECIDING FACTOR

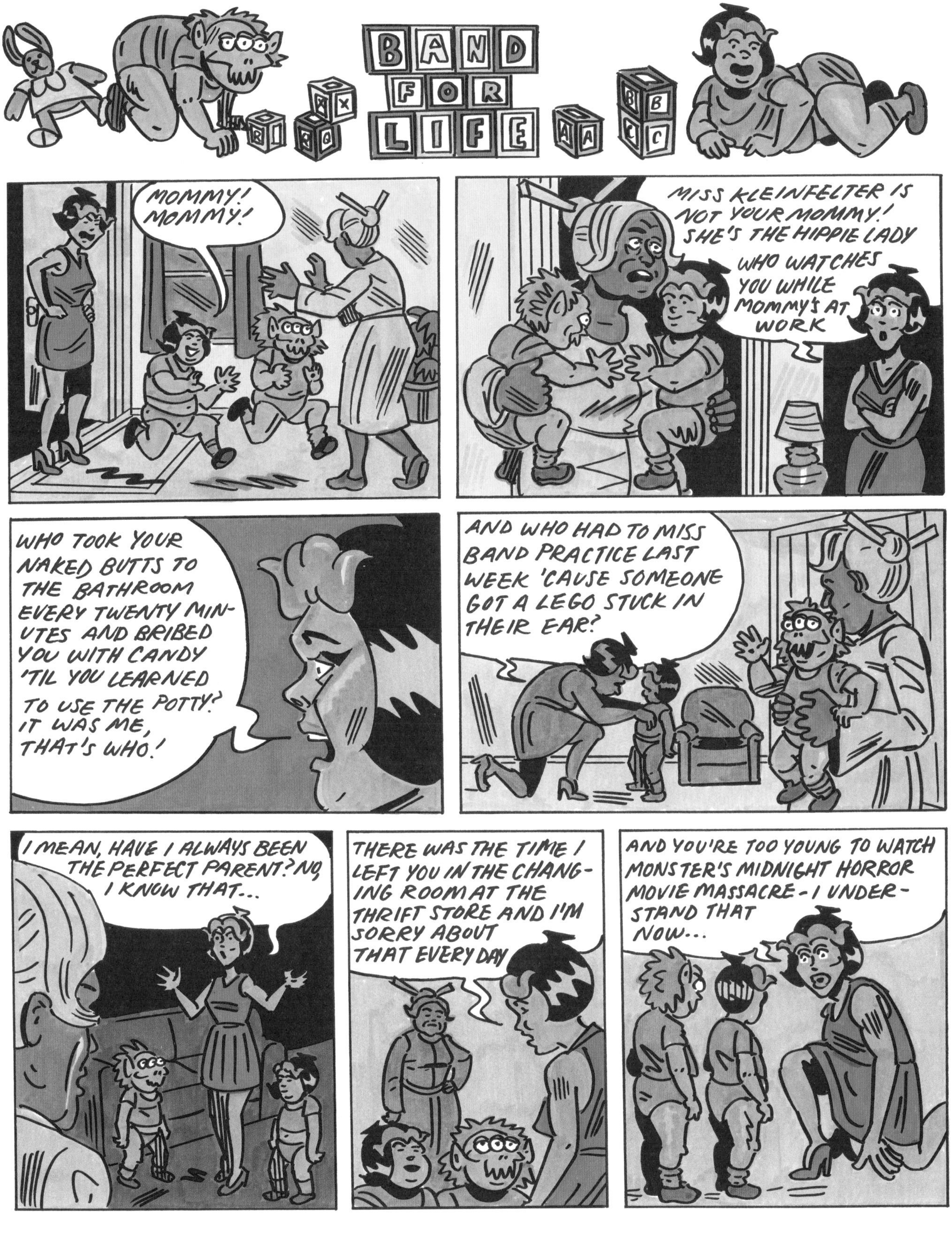
BAND FOR LIFE
MOMMY! MOMMY!
MISS KLEINFELTER IS NOT YOUR MOMMY! SHE'S THE HIPPIE LADY
WHO WATCHES YOU WHILE MOMMY'S AT WORK
WHO TOOK YOUR NAKED BUTTS TO THE BATHROOM EVERY TWENTY MINUTES AND BRIBED YOU WITH CANDY 'TIL YOU LEARNED TO USE THE POTTY? IT WAS ME, THAT'S WHO!
AND WHO HAD TO MISS BAND PRACTICE LAST WEEK 'CAUSE SOMEONE GOT A LEGO STUCK IN THEIR EAR?
I MEAN, HAVE I ALWAYS BEEN THE PERFECT PARENT? NO, I KNOW THAT...
THERE WAS THE TIME I LEFT YOU IN THE CHANGING ROOM AT THE THRIFT STORE AND I'M SORRY ABOUT THAT EVERY DAY
AND YOU'RE TOO YOUNG TO WATCH MONSTER'S MIDNIGHT HORROR MOVIE MASSACRE - I UNDERSTAND THAT NOW...

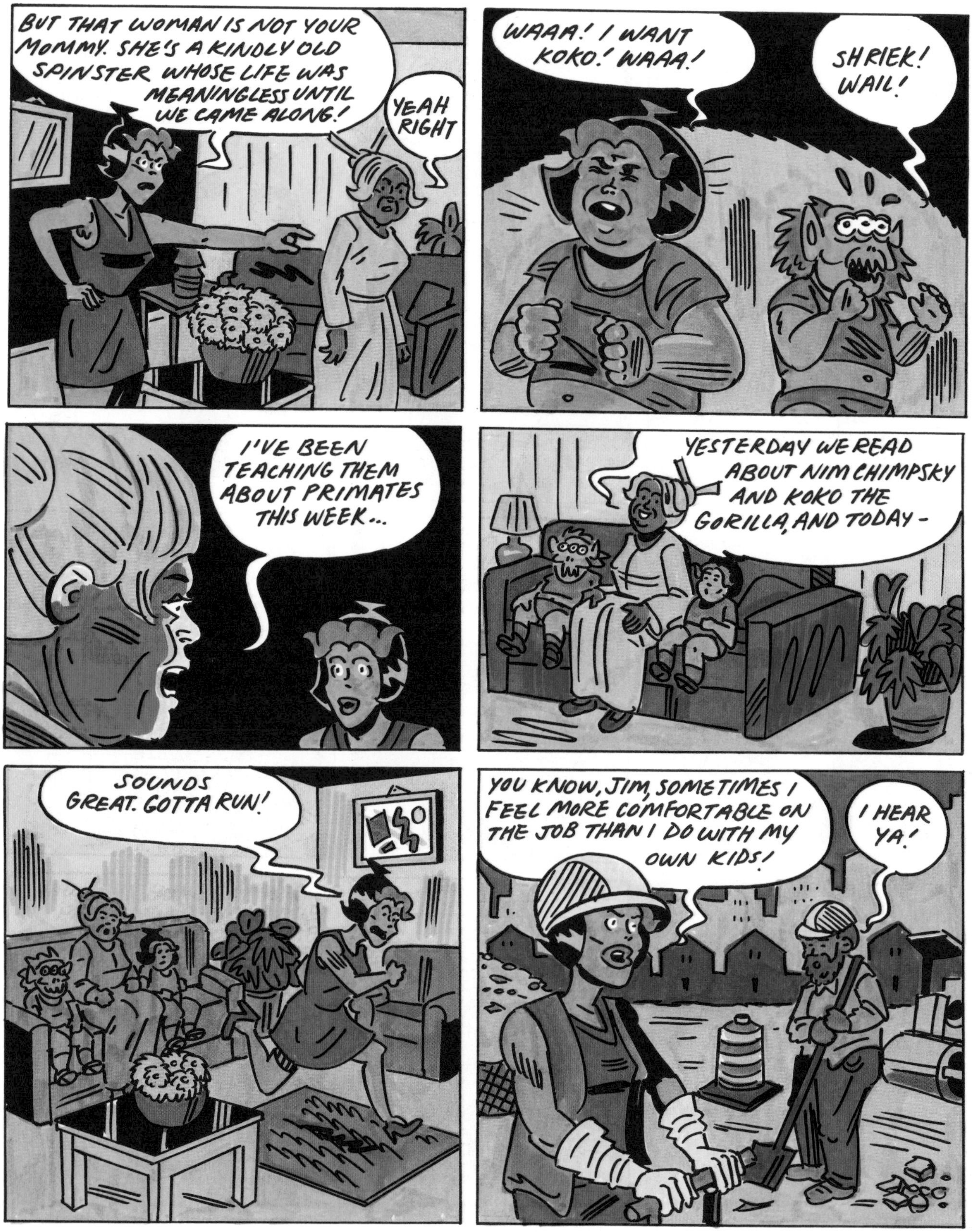
BUT THAT WOMAN IS NOT YOUR MOMMY. SHE'S A KINDLY OLD SPINSTER WHOSE LIFE WAS MEANINGLESS UNTIL WE CAME ALONG!
YEAH RIGHT
WAAA! I WANT KOKO! WAAA!
SHRIEK! WAIL!
I'VE BEEN TEACHING THEM ABOUT PRIMATES THIS WEEK...
YESTERDAY WE READ ABOUT NIM CHIMPSKY AND KOKO THE GORILLA, AND TODAY -
SOUNDS GREAT. GOTTA RUN!
YOU KNOW, JIM, SOMETIMES I FEEL MORE COMFORTABLE ON THE JOB THAN I DO WITH MY OWN KIDS!
I HEAR YA!

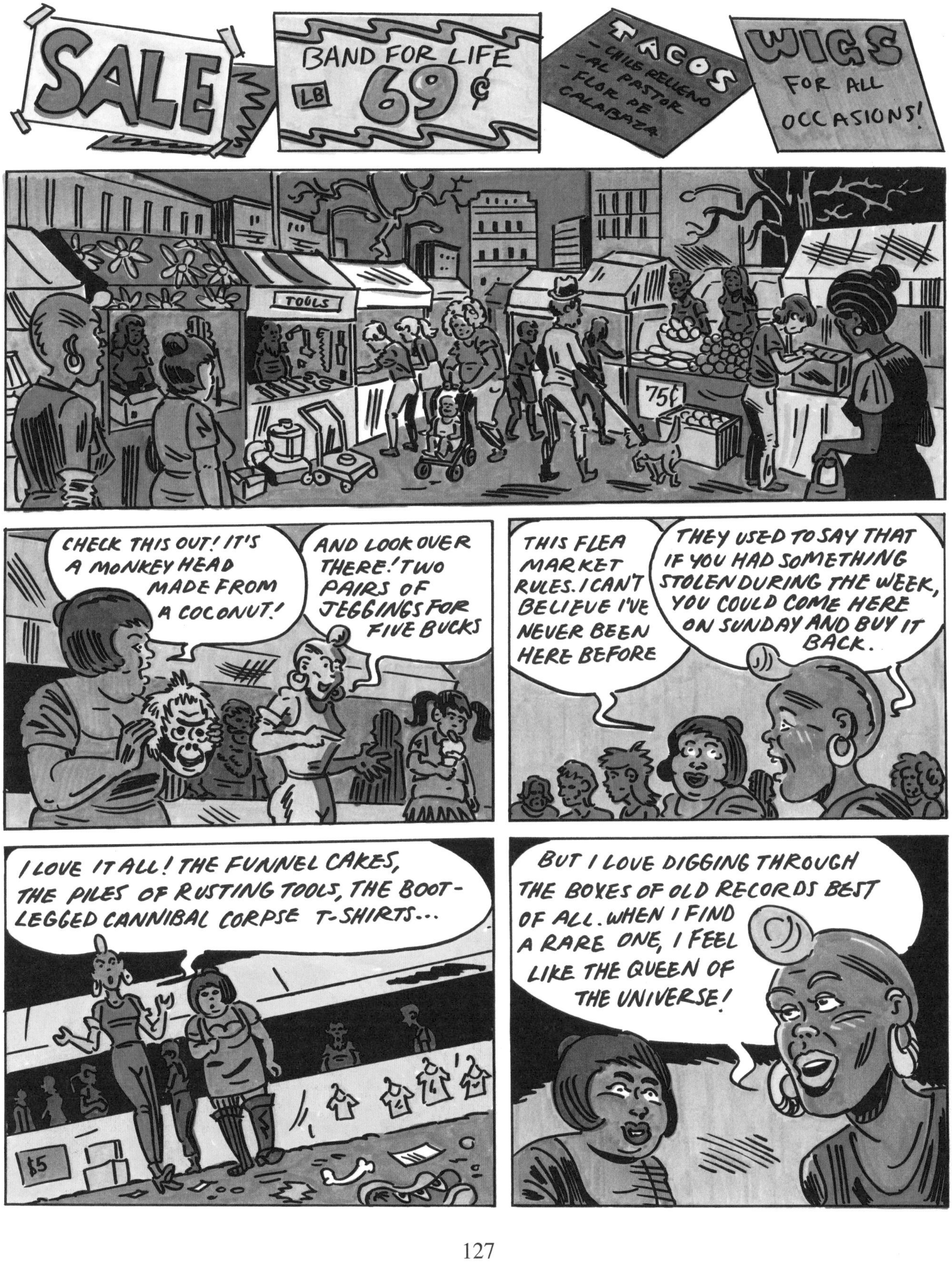
SALE
BAND FOR LIFE
LB 69¢
TACOS
-CHILE RELLENO
-AL PASTOR
-FLOR DE CALABAZA
WIGS
FOR ALL OCCASIONS!
TOOLS
75¢
CHECK THIS OUT! IT'S A MONKEY HEAD MADE FROM A COCONUT!
AND LOOK OVER THERE! TWO PAIRS OF JEGGINGS FOR FIVE BUCKS
THIS FLEA MARKET RULES. I CAN'T BELIEVE I'VE NEVER BEEN HERE BEFORE
THEY USED TO SAY THAT IF YOU HAD SOMETHING STOLEN DURING THE WEEK, YOU COULD COME HERE ON SUNDAY AND BUY IT BACK.
I LOVE IT ALL! THE FUNNEL CAKES, THE PILES OF RUSTING TOOLS, THE BOOT-LEGGED CANNIBAL CORPSE T-SHIRTS...
$5
BUT I LOVE DIGGING THROUGH THE BOXES OF OLD RECORDS BEST OF ALL. WHEN I FIND A RARE ONE, I FEEL LIKE THE QUEEN OF THE UNIVERSE!

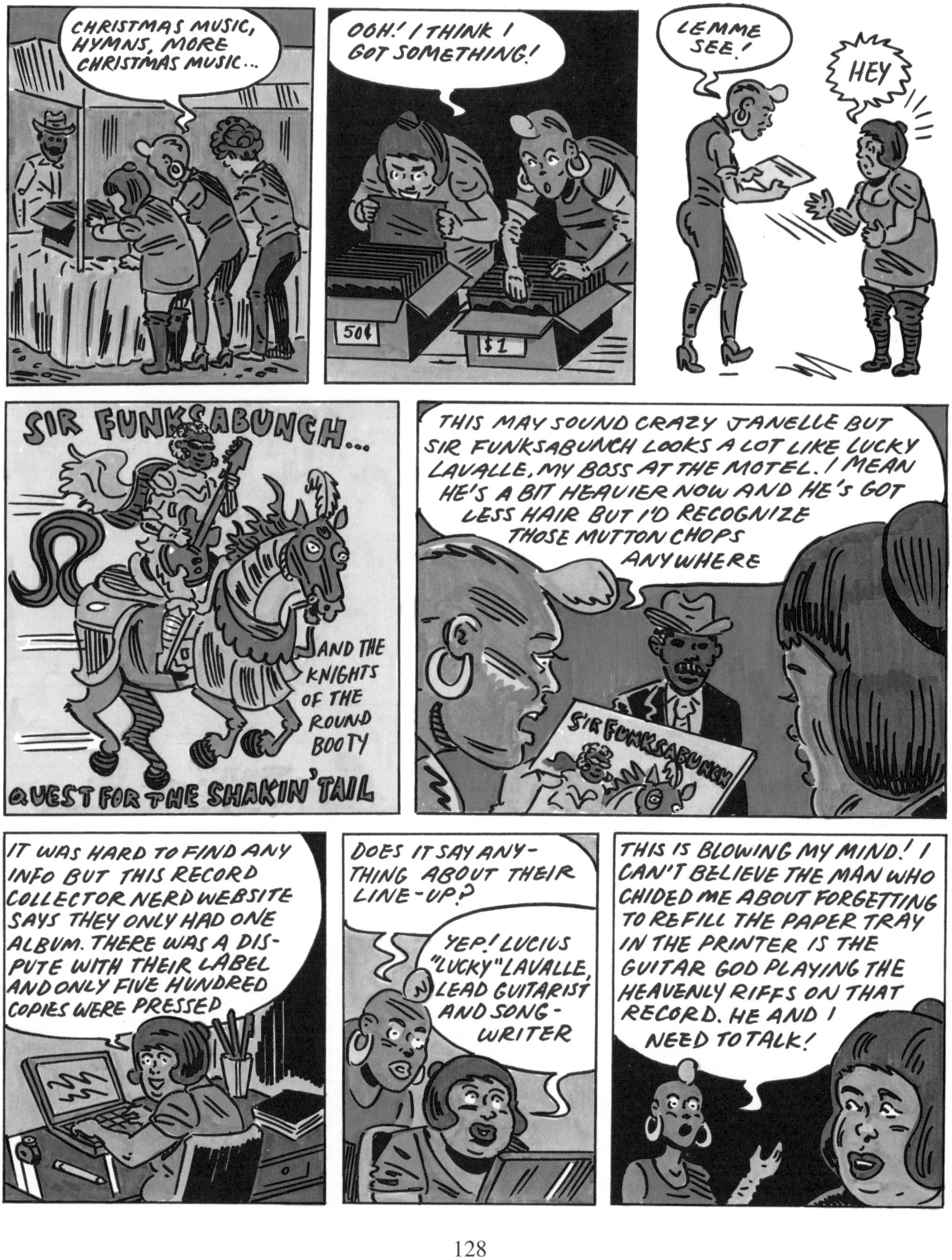
CHRISTMAS MUSIC, HYMNS, MORE CHRISTMAS MUSIC...
OOH! I THINK I GOT SOMETHING!
50¢
$1
LEMME SEE!
HEY
SIR FUNKSABUNCH...
AND THE KNIGHTS OF THE ROUND BOOTY
QUEST FOR THE SHAKIN' TAIL
THIS MAY SOUND CRAZY JANELLE BUT SIR FUNKSABUNCH LOOKS A LOT LIKE LUCKY LAVALLE, MY BOSS AT THE MOTEL. I MEAN HE'S A BIT HEAVIER NOW AND HE'S GOT LESS HAIR BUT I'D RECOGNIZE THOSE MUTTON CHOPS ANYWHERE
SIR FUNKSABUNCH
IT WAS HARD TO FIND ANY INFO BUT THIS RECORD COLLECTOR NERD WEBSITE SAYS THEY ONLY HAD ONE ALBUM. THERE WAS A DISPUTE WITH THEIR LABEL AND ONLY FIVE HUNDRED COPIES WERE PRESSED
DOES IT SAY ANYTHING ABOUT THEIR LINE-UP?
YEP! LUCIUS "LUCKY" LAVALLE, LEAD GUITARIST AND SONGWRITER
THIS IS BLOWING MY MIND! I CAN'T BELIEVE THE MAN WHO CHIDED ME ABOUT FORGETTING TO REFILL THE PAPER TRAY IN THE PRINTER IS THE GUITAR GOD PLAYING THE HEAVENLY RIFFS ON THAT RECORD. HE AND I NEED TO TALK!

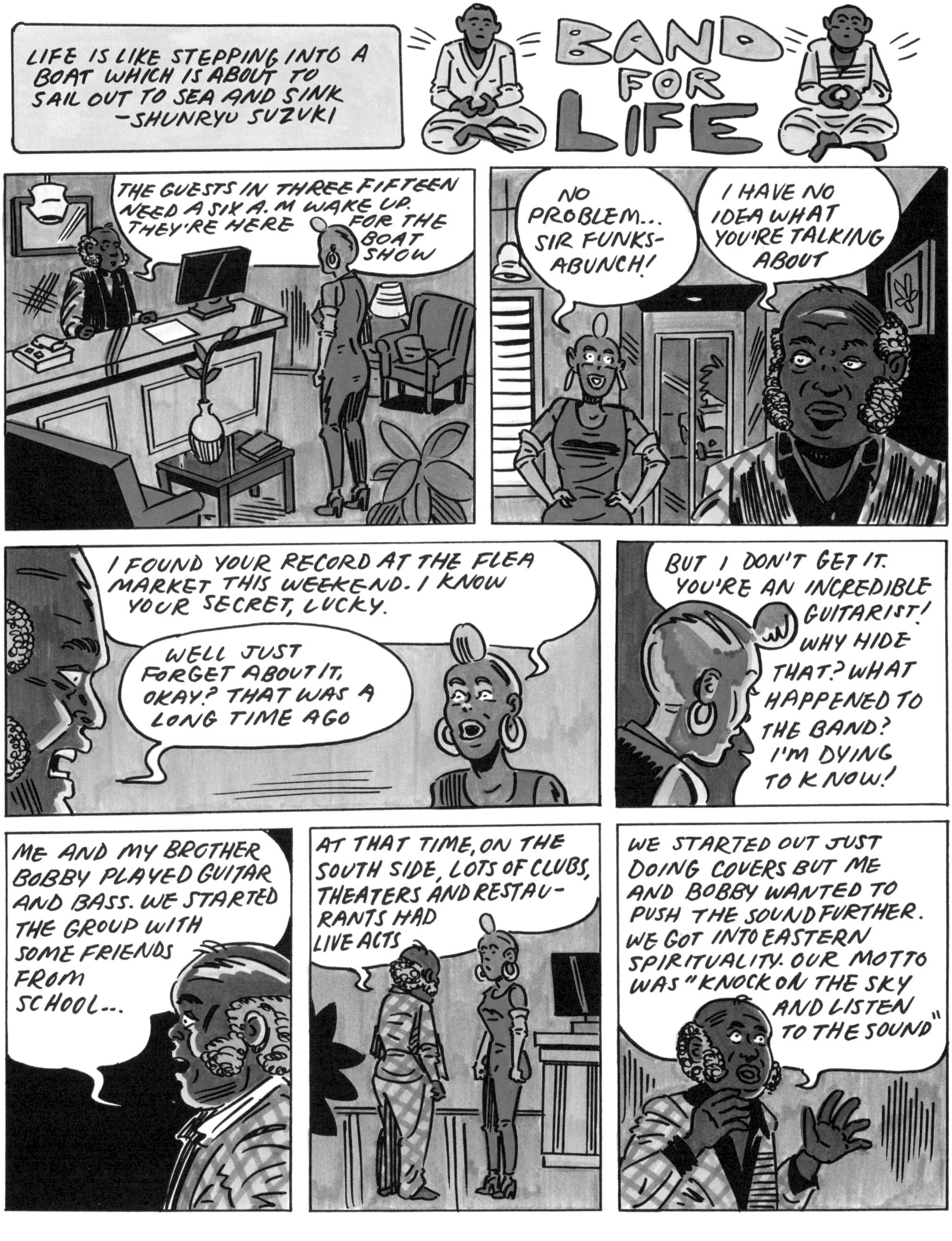
LIFE IS LIKE STEPPING INTO A BOAT WHICH IS ABOUT TO SAIL OUT TO SEA AND SINK
—SHUNRYU SUZUKI
BAND FOR LIFE
THE GUESTS IN THREE FIFTEEN NEED A SIX A.M WAKE UP. THEY'RE HERE FOR THE BOAT SHOW
NO PROBLEM... SIR FUNKS-ABUNCH!
I HAVE NO IDEA WHAT YOU'RE TALKING ABOUT
I FOUND YOUR RECORD AT THE FLEA MARKET THIS WEEKEND. I KNOW YOUR SECRET, LUCKY.
WELL JUST FORGET ABOUT IT, OKAY? THAT WAS A LONG TIME AGO
BUT I DON'T GET IT. YOU'RE AN INCREDIBLE GUITARIST! WHY HIDE THAT? WHAT HAPPENED TO THE BAND? I'M DYING TO KNOW!
ME AND MY BROTHER BOBBY PLAYED GUITAR AND BASS. WE STARTED THE GROUP WITH SOME FRIENDS FROM SCHOOL...
AT THAT TIME, ON THE SOUTH SIDE, LOTS OF CLUBS, THEATERS AND RESTAU-RANTS HAD LIVE ACTS
WE STARTED OUT JUST DOING COVERS BUT ME AND BOBBY WANTED TO PUSH THE SOUND FURTHER. WE GOT INTO EASTERN SPIRITUALITY. OUR MOTTO WAS "KNOCK ON THE SKY AND LISTEN TO THE SOUND"

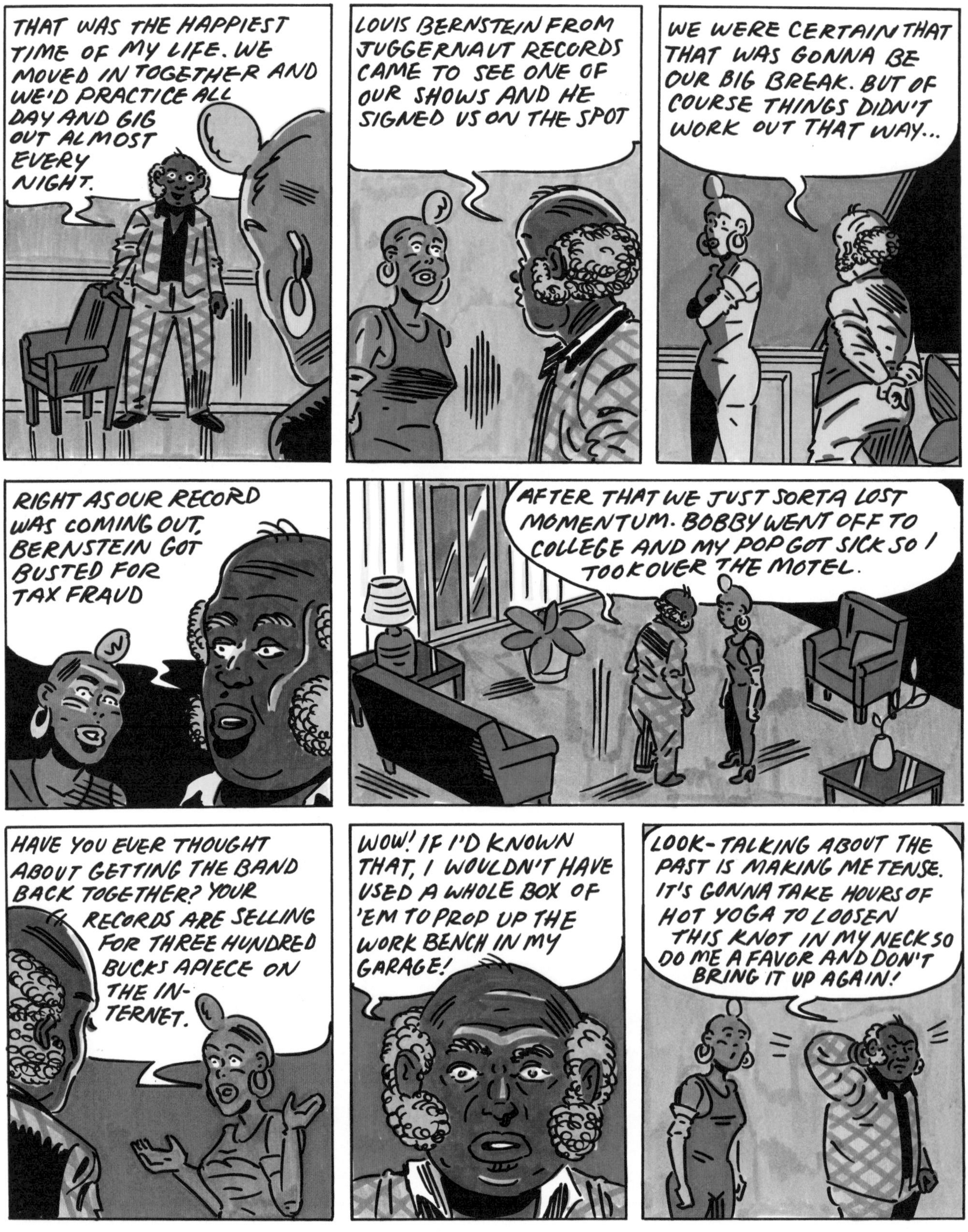
THAT WAS THE HAPPIEST TIME OF MY LIFE. WE MOVED IN TOGETHER AND WE'D PRACTICE ALL DAY AND GIG OUT ALMOST EVERY NIGHT.
LOUIS BERNSTEIN FROM JUGGERNAUT RECORDS CAME TO SEE ONE OF OUR SHOWS AND HE SIGNED US ON THE SPOT
WE WERE CERTAIN THAT THAT WAS GONNA BE OUR BIG BREAK. BUT OF COURSE THINGS DIDN'T WORK OUT THAT WAY...
RIGHT AS OUR RECORD WAS COMING OUT, BERNSTEIN GOT BUSTED FOR TAX FRAUD
AFTER THAT WE JUST SORTA LOST MOMENTUM. BOBBY WENT OFF TO COLLEGE AND MY POP GOT SICK SO I TOOK OVER THE MOTEL.
HAVE YOU EVER THOUGHT ABOUT GETTING THE BAND BACK TOGETHER? YOUR RECORDS ARE SELLING FOR THREE HUNDRED BUCKS APIECE ON THE IN-TERNET.
WOW! IF I'D KNOWN THAT, I WOULDN'T HAVE USED A WHOLE BOX OF 'EM TO PROP UP THE WORK BENCH IN MY GARAGE!
LOOK- TALKING ABOUT THE PAST IS MAKING ME TENSE. IT'S GONNA TAKE HOURS OF HOT YOGA TO LOOSEN THIS KNOT IN MY NECK SO DO ME A FAVOR AND DON'T BRING IT UP AGAIN!

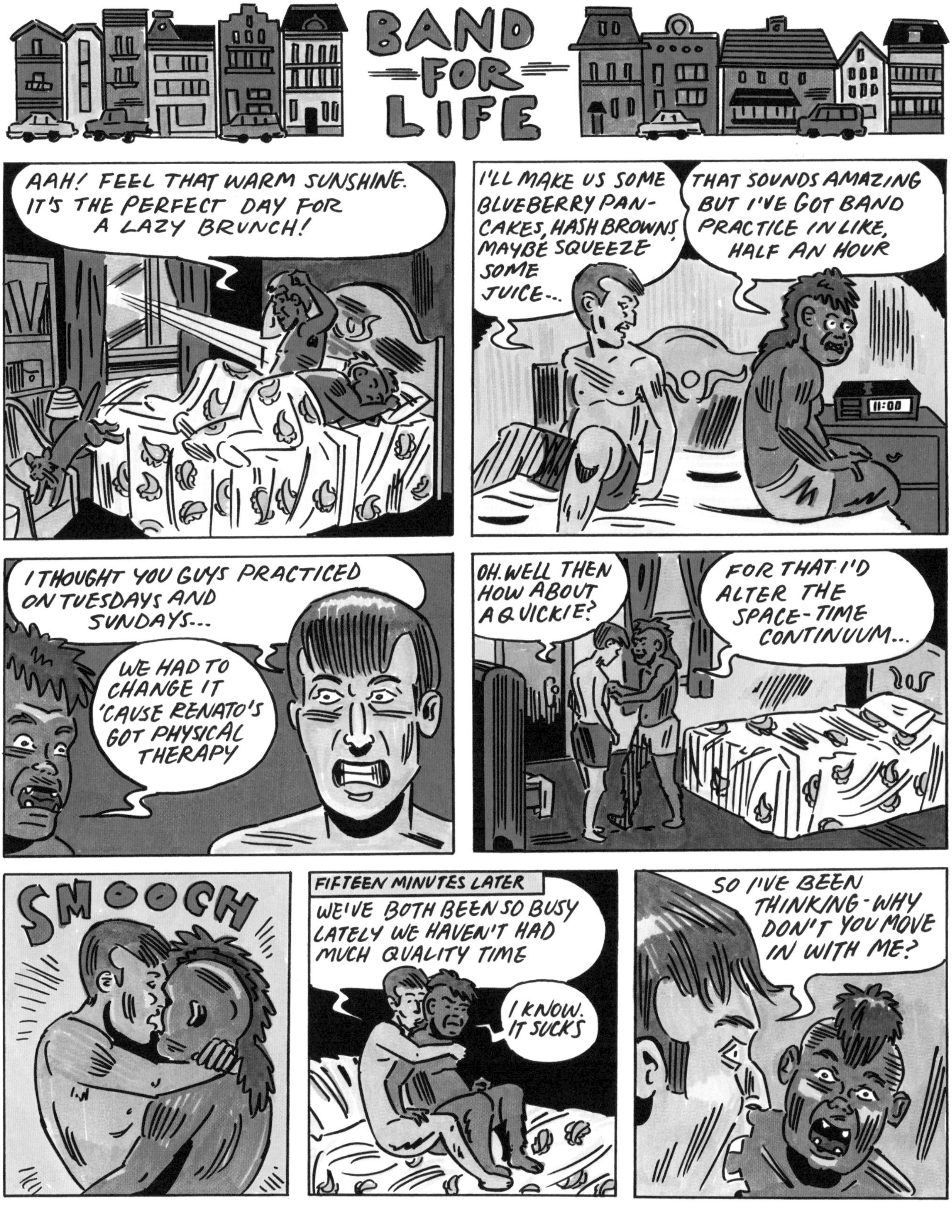
BAND FOR LIFE
AAH! FEEL THAT WARM SUNSHINE. IT'S THE PERFECT DAY FOR A LAZY BRUNCH!
I'LL MAKE US SOME BLUEBERRY PANCAKES, HASH BROWNS, MAYBE SQUEEZE SOME JUICE...
THAT SOUNDS AMAZING BUT I'VE GOT BAND PRACTICE IN LIKE, HALF AN HOUR
11:00
I THOUGHT YOU GUYS PRACTICED ON TUESDAYS AND SUNDAYS...
WE HAD TO CHANGE IT 'CAUSE RENATO'S GOT PHYSICAL THERAPY
OH. WELL THEN HOW ABOUT A QUICKIE?
FOR THAT I'D ALTER THE SPACE-TIME CONTINUUM...
SMOOCH
FIFTEEN MINUTES LATER
WE'VE BOTH BEEN SO BUSY LATELY WE HAVEN'T HAD MUCH QUALITY TIME
I KNOW. IT SUCKS
SO I'VE BEEN THINKING - WHY DON'T YOU MOVE IN WITH ME?

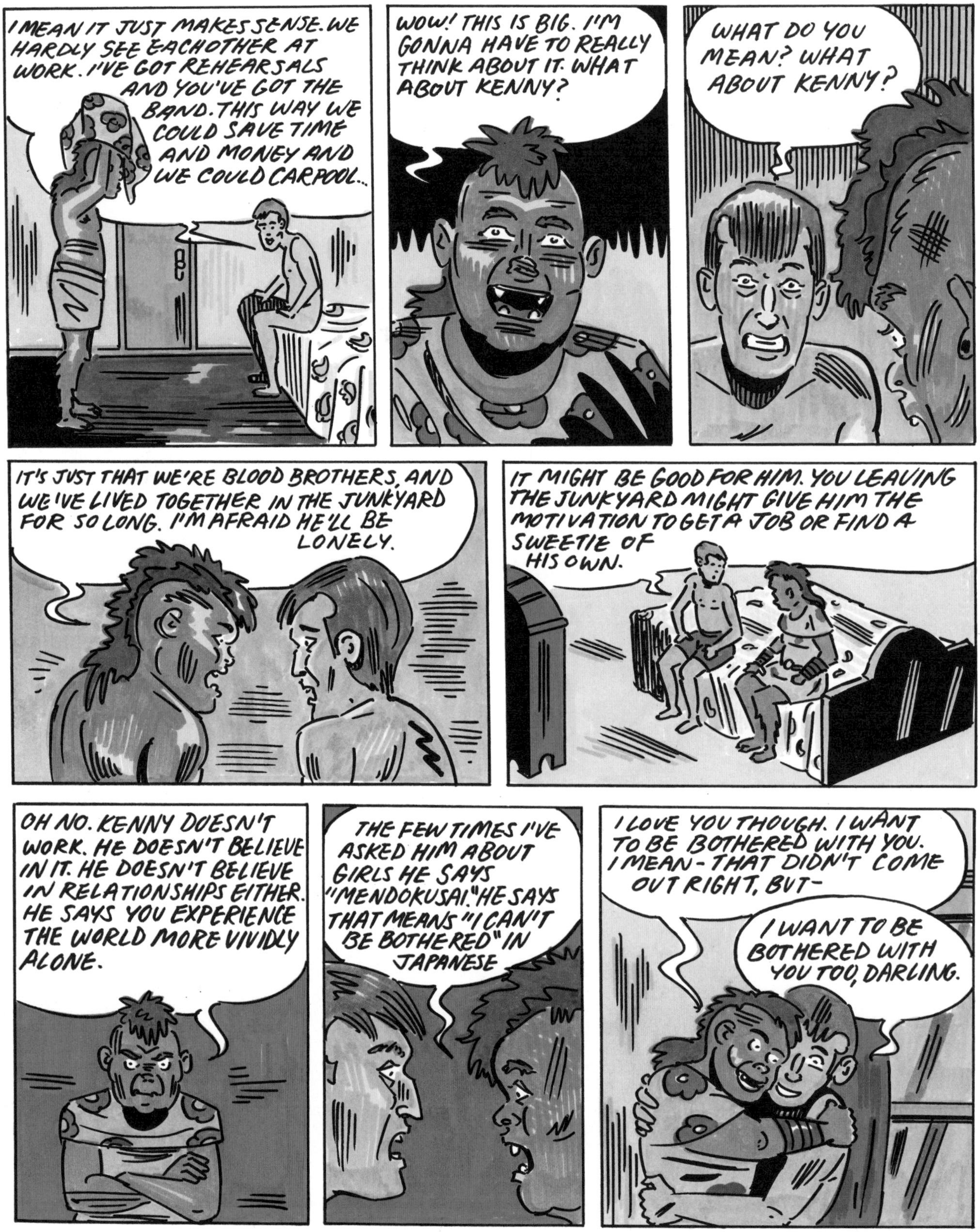
I MEAN IT JUST MAKES SENSE. WE HARDLY SEE EACHOTHER AT WORK. I'VE GOT REHEARSALS AND YOU'VE GOT THE BAND. THIS WAY WE COULD SAVE TIME AND MONEY AND WE COULD CARPOOL...
WOW! THIS IS BIG. I'M GONNA HAVE TO REALLY THINK ABOUT IT. WHAT ABOUT KENNY?
WHAT DO YOU MEAN? WHAT ABOUT KENNY?
IT'S JUST THAT WE'RE BLOOD BROTHERS, AND WE'VE LIVED TOGETHER IN THE JUNKYARD FOR SO LONG. I'M AFRAID HE'LL BE LONELY.
IT MIGHT BE GOOD FOR HIM. YOU LEAVING THE JUNKYARD MIGHT GIVE HIM THE MOTIVATION TO GET A JOB OR FIND A SWEETIE OF HIS OWN.
OH NO. KENNY DOESN'T WORK. HE DOESN'T BELIEVE IN IT. HE DOESN'T BELIEVE IN RELATIONSHIPS EITHER. HE SAYS YOU EXPERIENCE THE WORLD MORE VIVIDLY ALONE.
THE FEW TIMES I'VE ASKED HIM ABOUT GIRLS HE SAYS "MENDOKUSAI." HE SAYS THAT MEANS "I CAN'T BE BOTHERED" IN JAPANESE
I LOVE YOU THOUGH. I WANT TO BE BOTHERED WITH YOU. I MEAN - THAT DIDN'T COME OUT RIGHT, BUT-
I WANT TO BE BOTHERED WITH YOU TOO, DARLING.

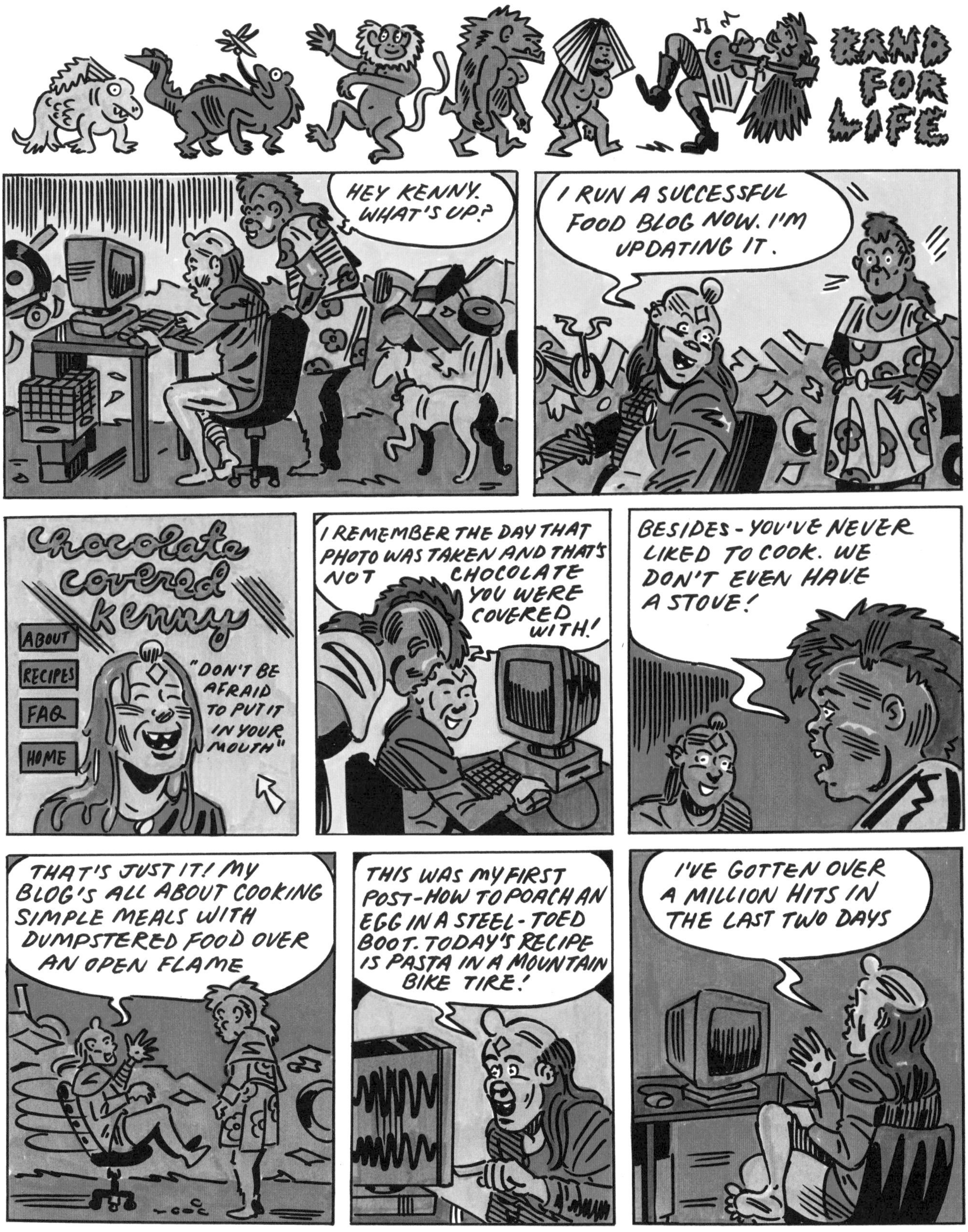
BAND FOR LIFE
HEY KENNY. WHAT'S UP?
I RUN A SUCCESSFUL FOOD BLOG NOW. I'M UPDATING IT.
chocolate covered kenny
ABOUT
RECIPES
FAQ
HOME
"DON'T BE AFRAID TO PUT IT IN YOUR MOUTH"
I REMEMBER THE DAY THAT PHOTO WAS TAKEN AND THAT'S NOT CHOCOLATE YOU WERE COVERED WITH!
BESIDES - YOU'VE NEVER LIKED TO COOK. WE DON'T EVEN HAVE A STOVE!
THAT'S JUST IT! MY BLOG'S ALL ABOUT COOKING SIMPLE MEALS WITH DUMPSTERED FOOD OVER AN OPEN FLAME
THIS WAS MY FIRST POST-HOW TO POACH AN EGG IN A STEEL-TOED BOOT. TODAY'S RECIPE IS PASTA IN A MOUNTAIN BIKE TIRE!
I'VE GOTTEN OVER A MILLION HITS IN THE LAST TWO DAYS

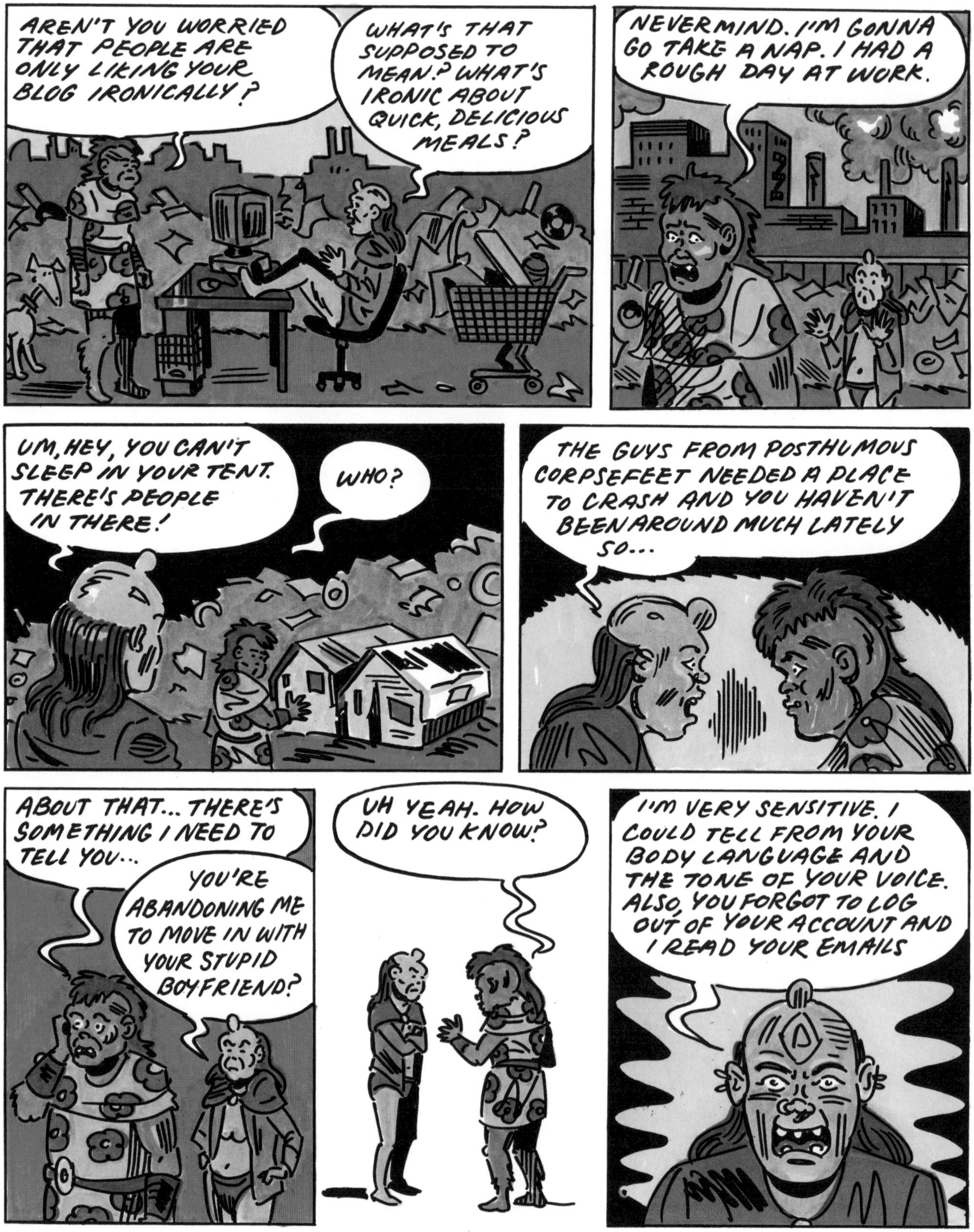
AREN'T YOU WORRIED THAT PEOPLE ARE ONLY LIKING YOUR BLOG IRONICALLY?
WHAT'S THAT SUPPOSED TO MEAN? WHAT'S IRONIC ABOUT QUICK, DELICIOUS MEALS?
NEVERMIND. I'M GONNA GO TAKE A NAP. I HAD A ROUGH DAY AT WORK.
UM, HEY, YOU CAN'T SLEEP IN YOUR TENT. THERE'S PEOPLE IN THERE!
WHO?
THE GUYS FROM POSTHUMOUS CORPSEFEET NEEDED A PLACE TO CRASH AND YOU HAVEN'T BEEN AROUND MUCH LATELY SO...
ABOUT THAT... THERE'S SOMETHING I NEED TO TELL YOU...
YOU'RE ABANDONING ME TO MOVE IN WITH YOUR STUPID BOYFRIEND?
UH YEAH. HOW DID YOU KNOW?
I'M VERY SENSITIVE. I COULD TELL FROM YOUR BODY LANGUAGE AND THE TONE OF YOUR VOICE. ALSO, YOU FORGOT TO LOG OUT OF YOUR ACCOUNT AND I READ YOUR EMAILS

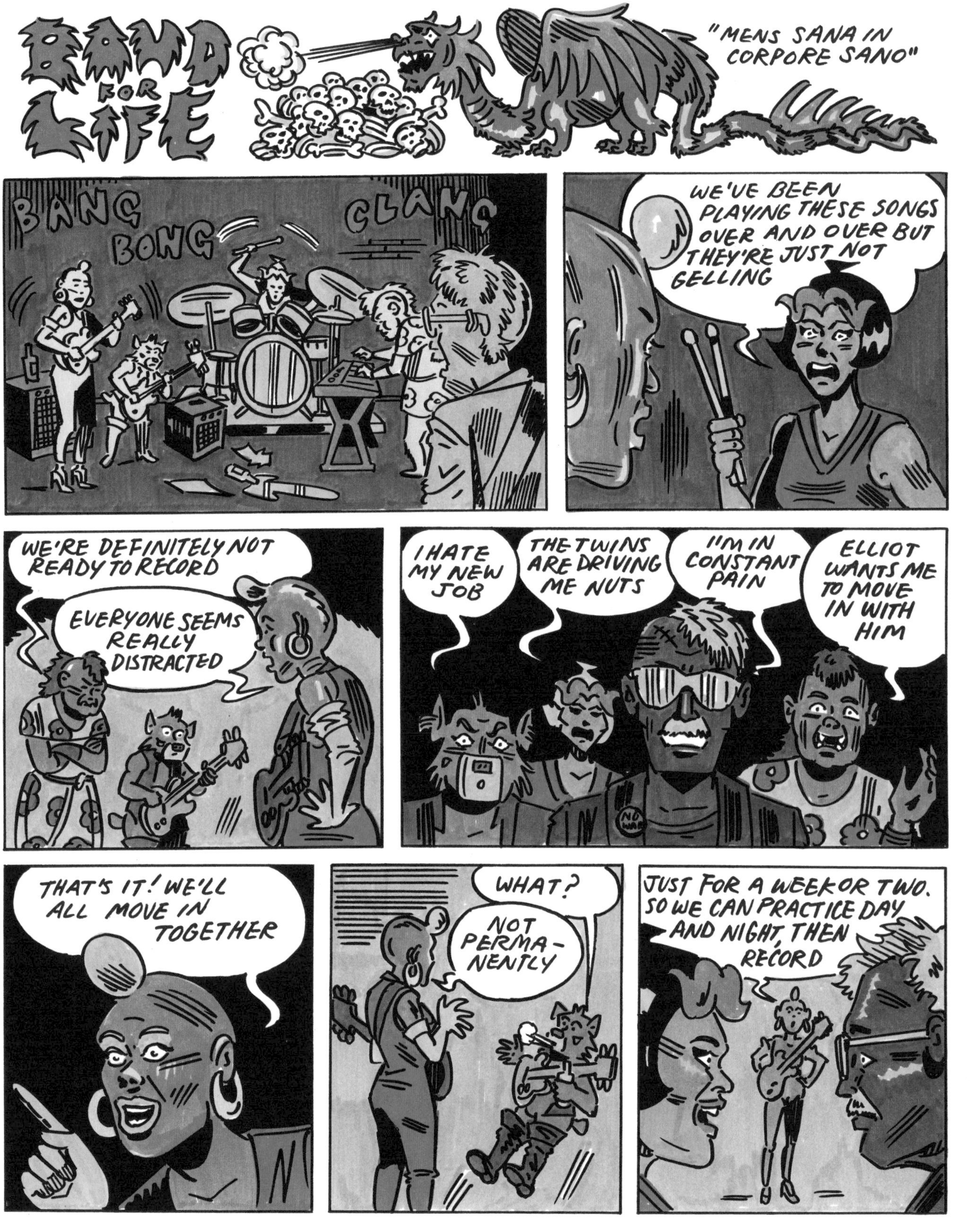
BAND FOR LIFE
"MENS SANA IN CORPORE SANO"
BANG
BONG
CLANG
WE'VE BEEN PLAYING THESE SONGS OVER AND OVER BUT THEY'RE JUST NOT GELLING
WE'RE DEFINITELY NOT READY TO RECORD
EVERYONE SEEMS REALLY DISTRACTED
I HATE MY NEW JOB
THE TWINS ARE DRIVING ME NUTS
I'M IN CONSTANT PAIN
ELLIOT WANTS ME TO MOVE IN WITH HIM
NO WAR
THAT'S IT! WE'LL ALL MOVE IN TOGETHER
WHAT?
NOT PERMA-NENTLY
JUST FOR A WEEK OR TWO. SO WE CAN PRACTICE DAY AND NIGHT, THEN RECORD

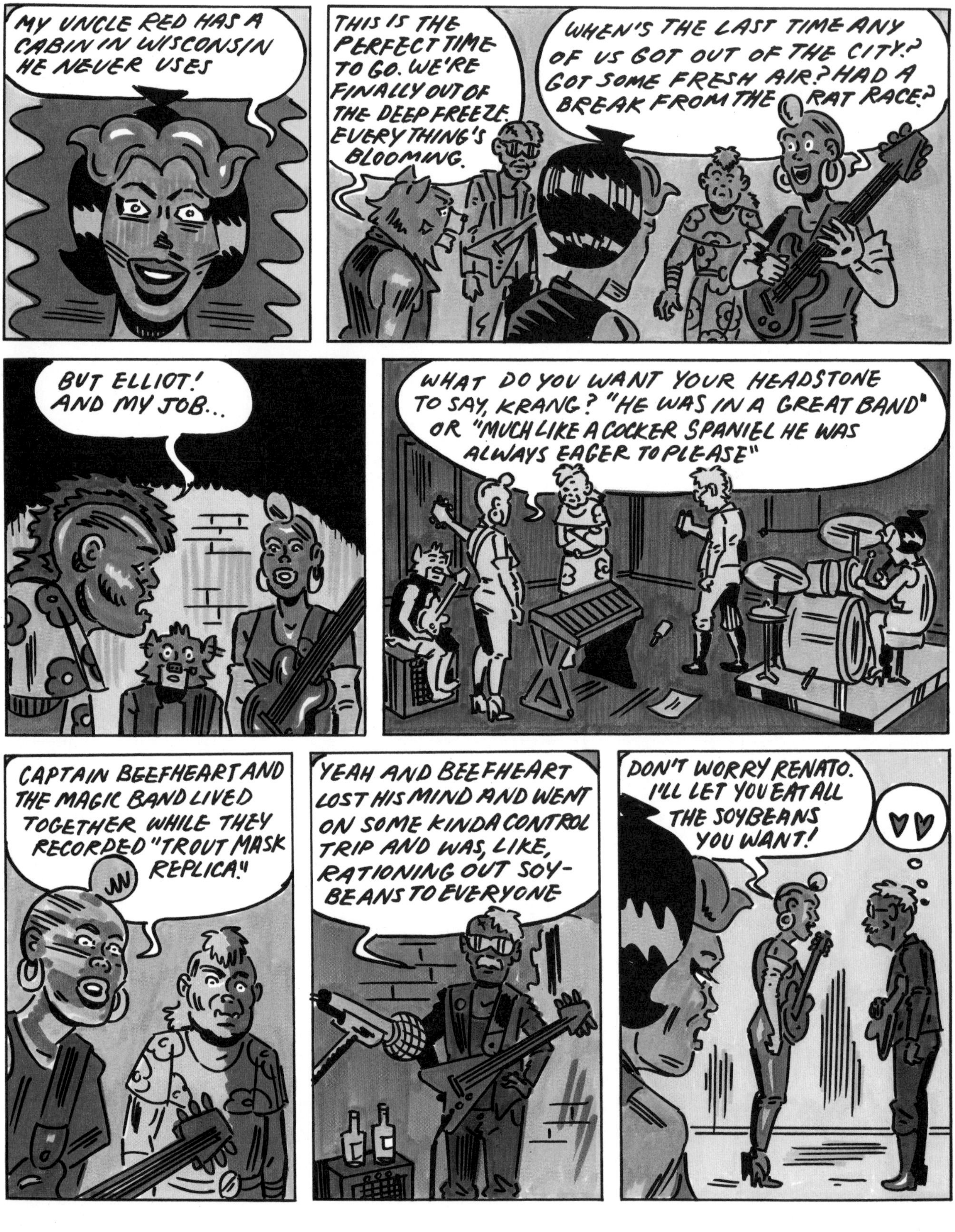
MY UNCLE RED HAS A CABIN IN WISCONSIN HE NEVER USES
THIS IS THE PERFECT TIME TO GO. WE'RE FINALLY OUT OF THE DEEP FREEZE. EVERYTHING'S BLOOMING.
WHEN'S THE LAST TIME ANY OF US GOT OUT OF THE CITY? GOT SOME FRESH AIR? HAD A BREAK FROM THE RAT RACE?
BUT ELLIOT! AND MY JOB...
WHAT DO YOU WANT YOUR HEADSTONE TO SAY, KRANG? "HE WAS IN A GREAT BAND" OR "MUCH LIKE A COCKER SPANIEL HE WAS ALWAYS EAGER TO PLEASE"
CAPTAIN BEEFHEART AND THE MAGIC BAND LIVED TOGETHER WHILE THEY RECORDED "TROUT MASK REPLICA."
YEAH AND BEEFHEART LOST HIS MIND AND WENT ON SOME KINDA CONTROL TRIP AND WAS, LIKE, RATIONING OUT SOY-BEANS TO EVERYONE
DON'T WORRY RENATO. I'LL LET YOU EAT ALL THE SOYBEANS YOU WANT!

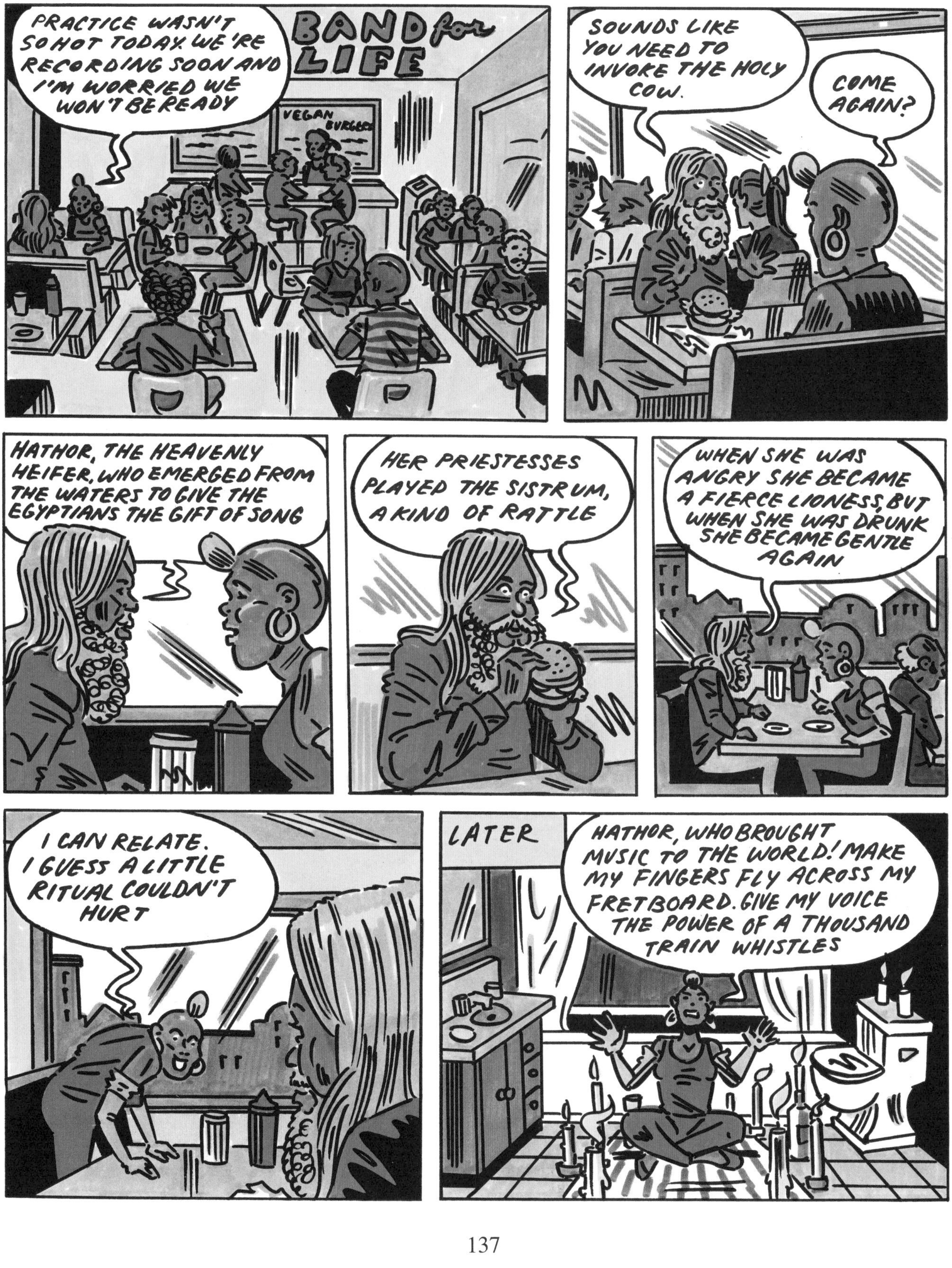
BAND for LIFE
PRACTICE WASN'T SO HOT TODAY. WE'RE RECORDING SOON AND I'M WORRIED WE WON'T BE READY
VEGAN BURGERS
SOUNDS LIKE YOU NEED TO INVOKE THE HOLY COW.
COME AGAIN?
HATHOR, THE HEAVENLY HEIFER, WHO EMERGED FROM THE WATERS TO GIVE THE EGYPTIANS THE GIFT OF SONG
HER PRIESTESSES PLAYED THE SISTRUM, A KIND OF RATTLE
WHEN SHE WAS ANGRY SHE BECAME A FIERCE LIONESS, BUT WHEN SHE WAS DRUNK SHE BECAME GENTLE AGAIN
I CAN RELATE. I GUESS A LITTLE RITUAL COULDN'T HURT
LATER
HATHOR, WHO BROUGHT MUSIC TO THE WORLD! MAKE MY FINGERS FLY ACROSS MY FRETBOARD. GIVE MY VOICE THE POWER OF A THOUSAND TRAIN WHISTLES

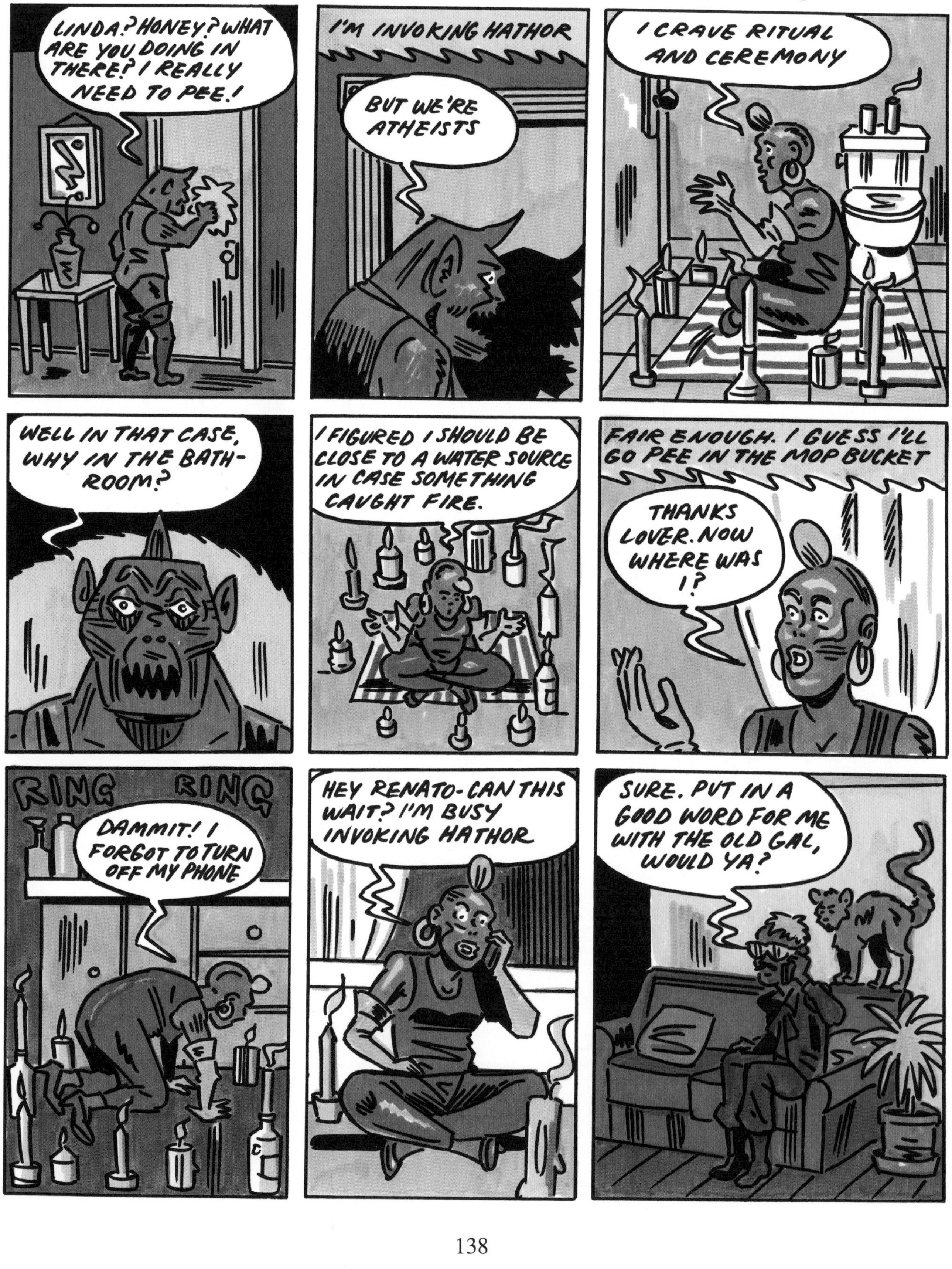
LINDA? HONEY? WHAT ARE YOU DOING IN THERE? I REALLY NEED TO PEE!
I'M INVOKING HATHOR
BUT WE'RE ATHEISTS
I CRAVE RITUAL AND CEREMONY
WELL IN THAT CASE, WHY IN THE BATH-ROOM?
I FIGURED I SHOULD BE CLOSE TO A WATER SOURCE IN CASE SOMETHING CAUGHT FIRE.
FAIR ENOUGH. I GUESS I'LL GO PEE IN THE MOP BUCKET
THANKS LOVER. NOW WHERE WAS I?
RING RING
DAMMIT! I FORGOT TO TURN OFF MY PHONE
HEY RENATO- CAN THIS WAIT? I'M BUSY INVOKING HATHOR
SURE. PUT IN A GOOD WORD FOR ME WITH THE OLD GAL, WOULD YA?

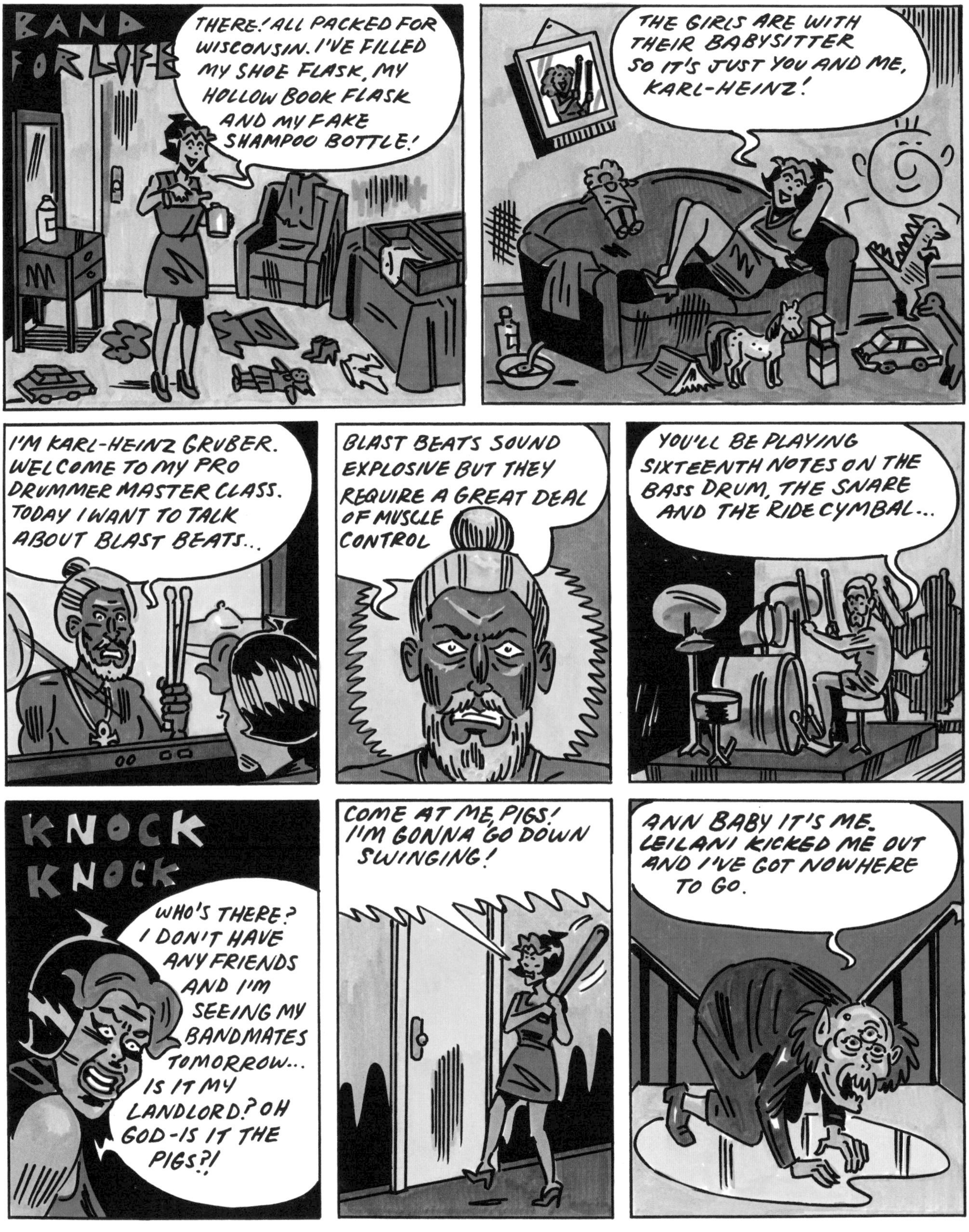
BAND FOR LIFE
THERE! ALL PACKED FOR WISCONSIN. I'VE FILLED MY SHOE FLASK, MY HOLLOW BOOK FLASK AND MY FAKE SHAMPOO BOTTLE!
THE GIRLS ARE WITH THEIR BABYSITTER SO IT'S JUST YOU AND ME, KARL-HEINZ!
I'M KARL-HEINZ GRUBER. WELCOME TO MY PRO DRUMMER MASTER CLASS. TODAY I WANT TO TALK ABOUT BLAST BEATS...
BLAST BEATS SOUND EXPLOSIVE BUT THEY REQUIRE A GREAT DEAL OF MUSCLE CONTROL
YOU'LL BE PLAYING SIXTEENTH NOTES ON THE BASS DRUM, THE SNARE AND THE RIDE CYMBAL...
KNOCK KNOCK
WHO'S THERE? I DON'T HAVE ANY FRIENDS AND I'M SEEING MY BANDMATES TOMORROW... IS IT MY LANDLORD? OH GOD-IS IT THE PIGS?!
COME AT ME, PIGS! I'M GONNA GO DOWN SWINGING!
ANN BABY IT'S ME. LEILANI KICKED ME OUT AND I'VE GOT NOWHERE TO GO.

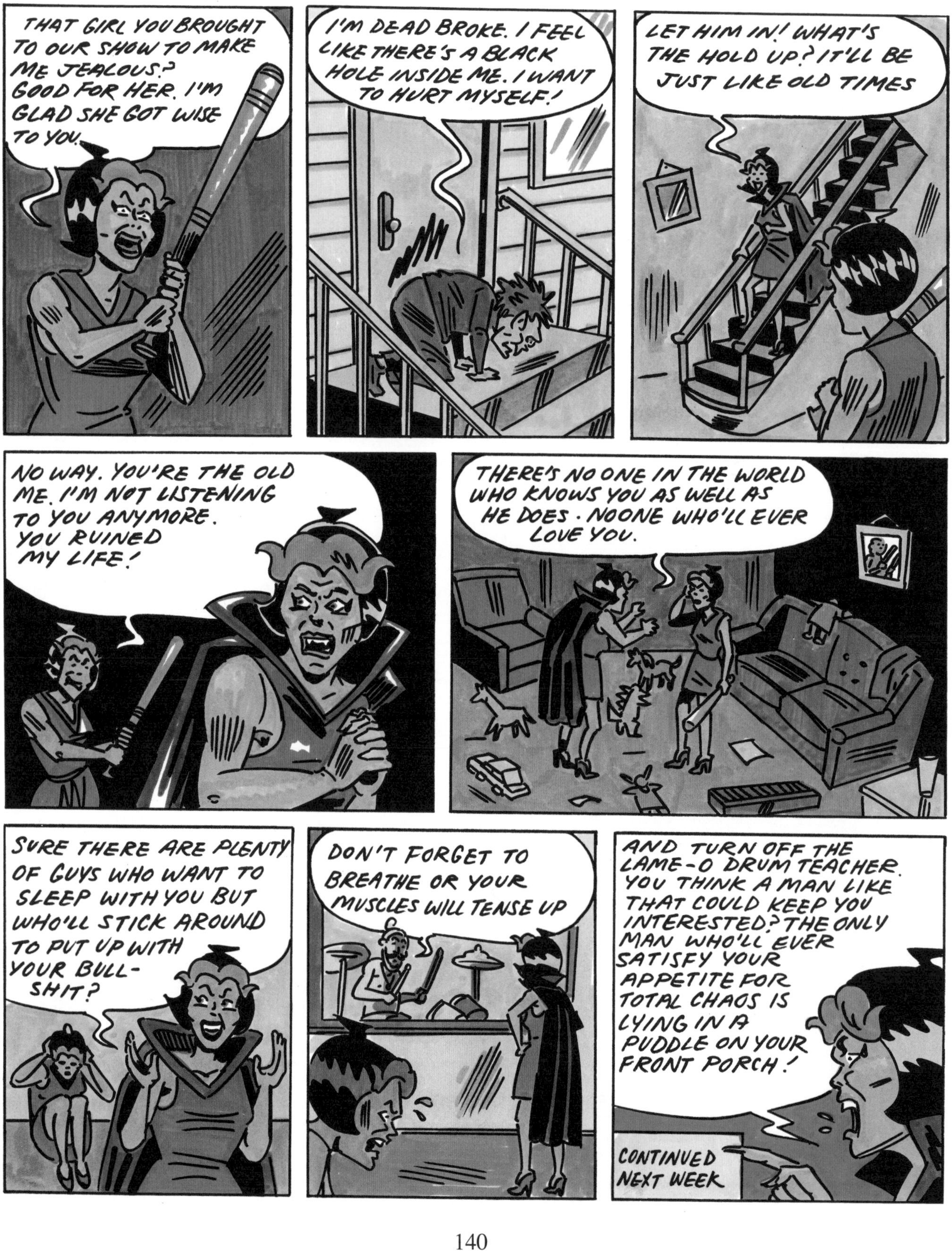
THAT GIRL YOU BROUGHT TO OUR SHOW TO MAKE ME JEALOUS? GOOD FOR HER. I'M GLAD SHE GOT WISE TO YOU.
I'M DEAD BROKE. I FEEL LIKE THERE'S A BLACK HOLE INSIDE ME. I WANT TO HURT MYSELF!
LET HIM IN! WHAT'S THE HOLD UP? IT'LL BE JUST LIKE OLD TIMES
NO WAY. YOU'RE THE OLD ME. I'M NOT LISTENING TO YOU ANYMORE. YOU RUINED MY LIFE!
THERE'S NO ONE IN THE WORLD WHO KNOWS YOU AS WELL AS HE DOES. NOONE WHO'LL EVER LOVE YOU.
SURE THERE ARE PLENTY OF GUYS WHO WANT TO SLEEP WITH YOU BUT WHO'LL STICK AROUND TO PUT UP WITH YOUR BULL-SHIT?
DON'T FORGET TO BREATHE OR YOUR MUSCLES WILL TENSE UP
AND TURN OFF THE LAME-O DRUM TEACHER. YOU THINK A MAN LIKE THAT COULD KEEP YOU INTERESTED? THE ONLY MAN WHO'LL EVER SATISFY YOUR APPETITE FOR TOTAL CHAOS IS LYING IN A PUDDLE ON YOUR FRONT PORCH!
CONTINUED NEXT WEEK

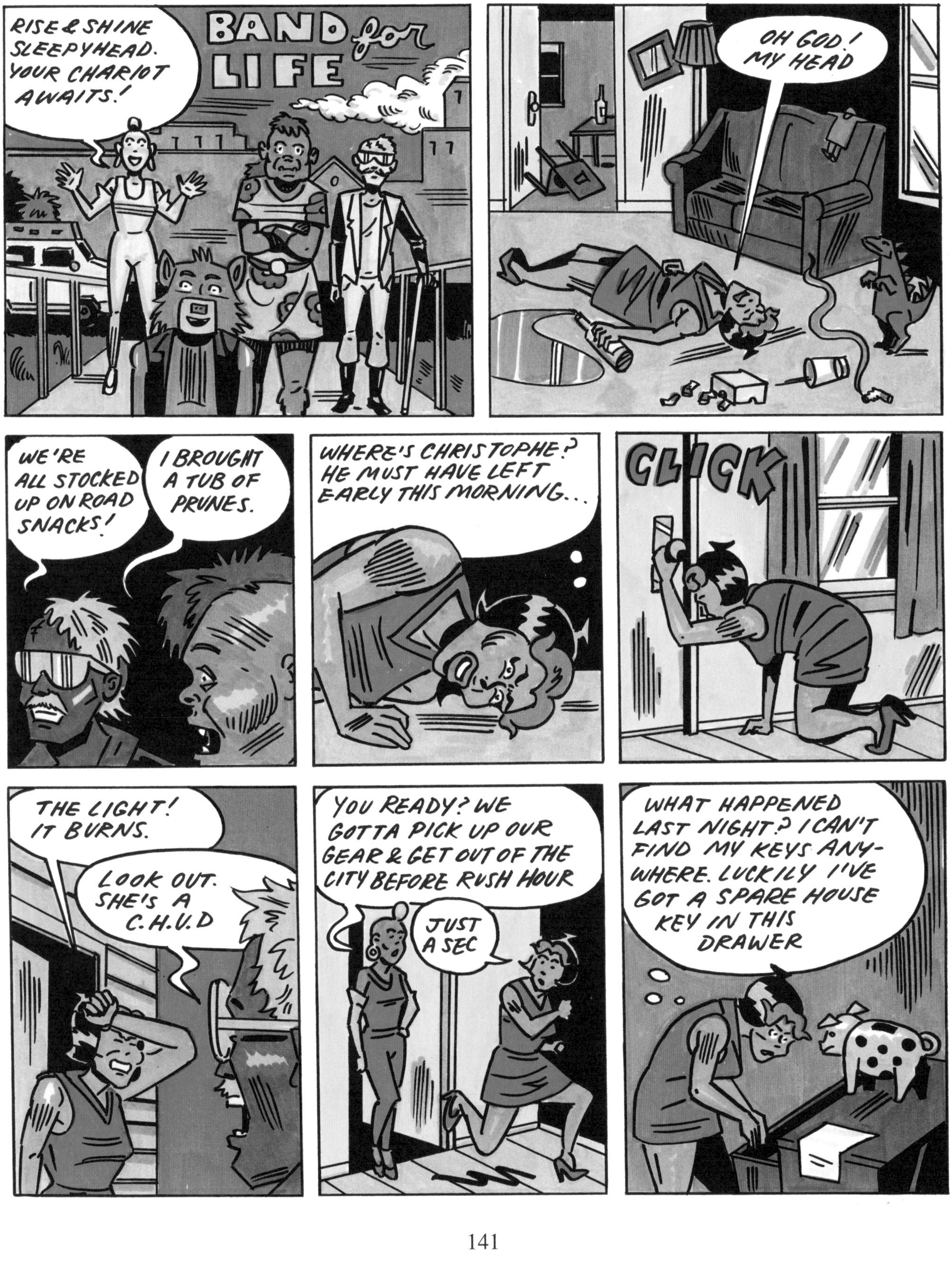
RISE & SHINE SLEEPYHEAD. YOUR CHARIOT AWAITS!
BAND for LIFE
OH GOD! MY HEAD
WE'RE ALL STOCKED UP ON ROAD SNACKS!
I BROUGHT A TUB OF PRUNES.
WHERE'S CHRISTOPHE? HE MUST HAVE LEFT EARLY THIS MORNING...
CLICK
THE LIGHT! IT BURNS.
LOOK OUT. SHE'S A C.H.U.D
YOU READY? WE GOTTA PICK UP OUR GEAR & GET OUT OF THE CITY BEFORE RUSH HOUR
JUST A SEC
WHAT HAPPENED LAST NIGHT? I CAN'T FIND MY KEYS ANYWHERE. LUCKILY I'VE GOT A SPARE HOUSE KEY IN THIS DRAWER

SO ARE WE GONNA BE CAPTURED BY HILLBILLIES OR MENACED BY THE UNDEAD IN THIS CABIN? I'M TAKING BETS.
THIS IS THE MIDWEST. DO WE EVEN HAVE HILLBILLIES?
PLENTY OF HICKS. NO HILLBILL-AAH!
OUR PRACTICE SPACE IS WIDE OPEN AND ALL OUR GEAR IS GONE!
MY SWEET CAROLINE! MY BEAUTIFUL BASS. I'LL NEVER CARESS YOUR ROSEWOOD CURVES AGAIN
IF NONE OF THE LOCKS WERE BROKEN, IT HAD TO BE AN INSIDE JOB!
SOB
I BET IT WAS PEGHEAD, THE MAINTENANCE MAN!
HOLY SHIT YOU'RE RIGHT! I ALWAYS ASSUMED HE WAS A HARMLESS OLD ACID CASUALTY. BUT THAT MUST BE A CLEVER RUSE!
I'M GONNA GO PUNCH HIM IN THE THROAT!
I'M GONNA LIGHT ALL HIS BODY HAIR ON FIRE!
WAIT YOU GUYS. I, UM, WELL, UH, I THINK I KNOW WHO DID THIS. HIS NAME RHYMES WITH "PISSED OFF"
WILL GUNTIT RECOVER THEIR STOLEN GEAR? FIND OUT NEXT WEEK!

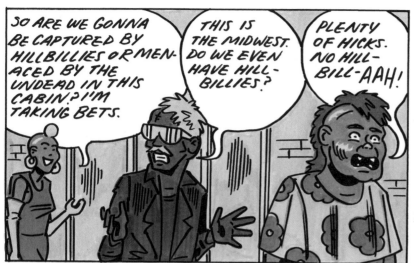

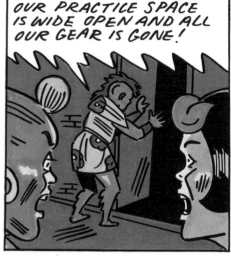

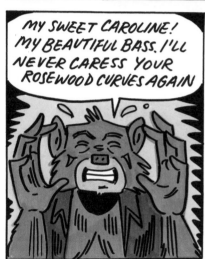

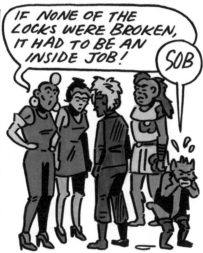

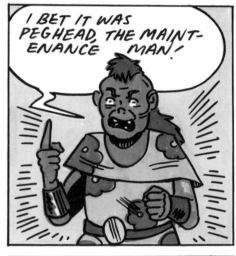

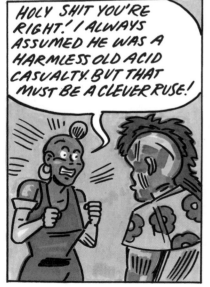

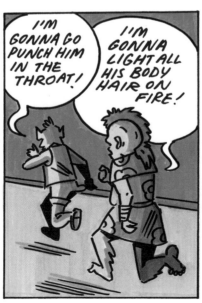

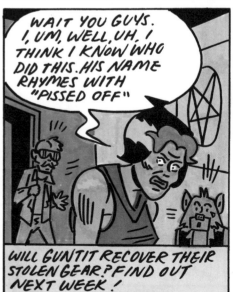

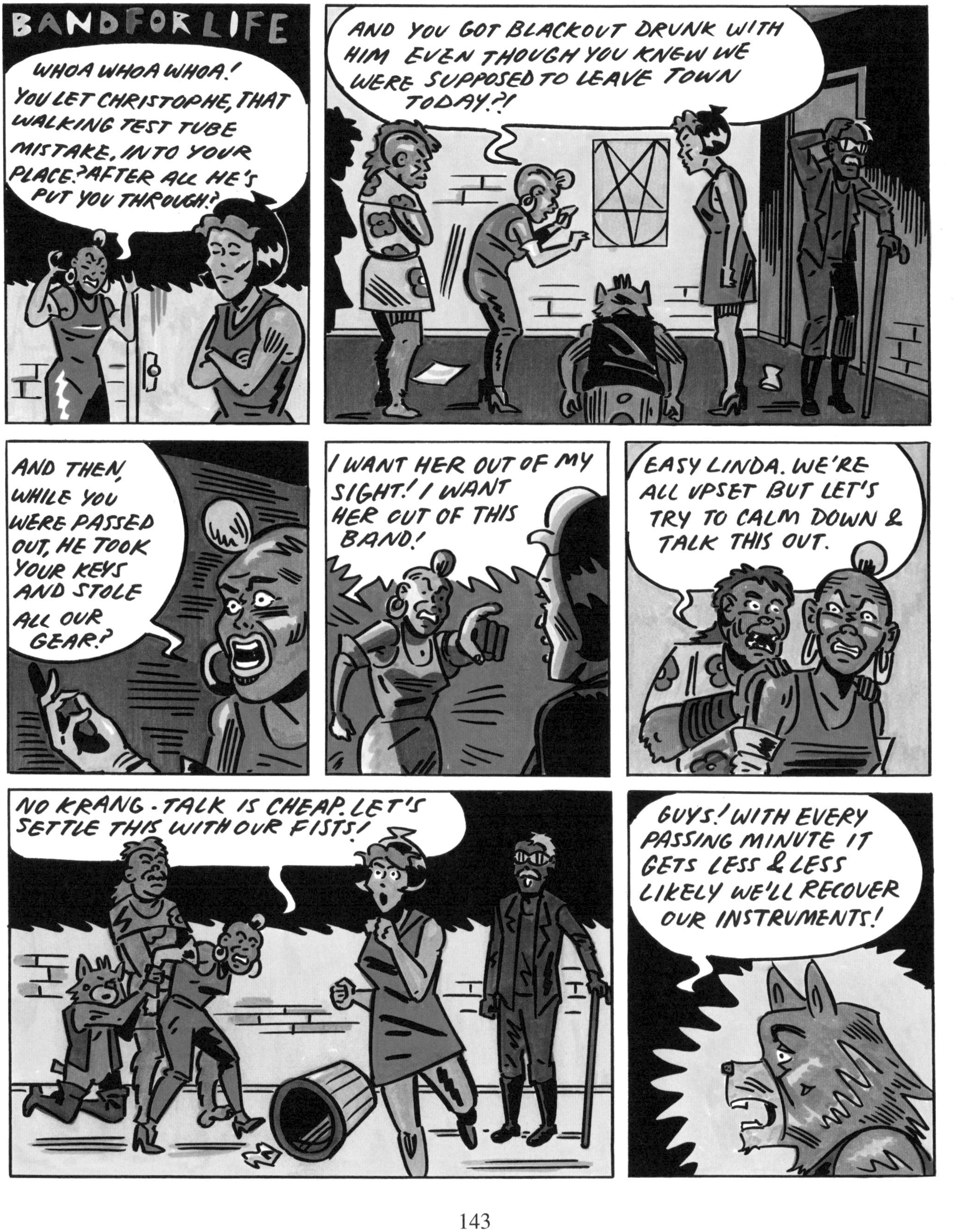
BANDFORLIFE
WHOA WHOA WHOA! YOU LET CHRISTOPHE, THAT WALKING TEST TUBE MISTAKE, INTO YOUR PLACE? AFTER ALL HE'S PUT YOU THROUGH?
AND YOU GOT BLACKOUT DRUNK WITH HIM EVEN THOUGH YOU KNEW WE WERE SUPPOSED TO LEAVE TOWN TODAY?!
AND THEN, WHILE YOU WERE PASSED OUT, HE TOOK YOUR KEYS AND STOLE ALL OUR GEAR?
I WANT HER OUT OF MY SIGHT! I WANT HER OUT OF THIS BAND!
EASY LINDA. WE'RE ALL UPSET BUT LET'S TRY TO CALM DOWN & TALK THIS OUT.
NO KRANG - TALK IS CHEAP. LET'S SETTLE THIS WITH OUR FISTS!
GUYS! WITH EVERY PASSING MINUTE IT GETS LESS & LESS LIKELY WE'LL RECOVER OUR INSTRUMENTS!

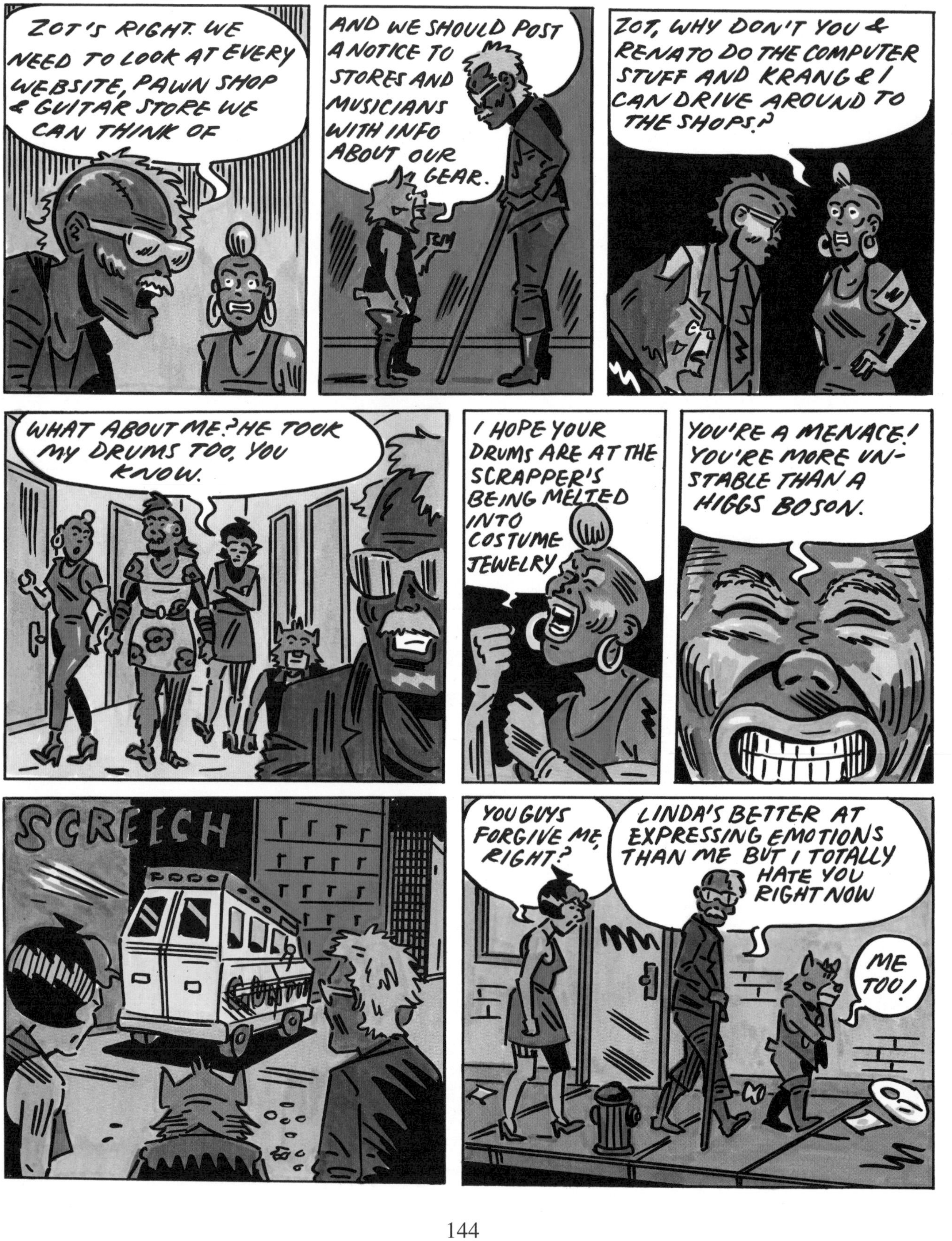
ZOT'S RIGHT. WE NEED TO LOOK AT EVERY WEBSITE, PAWN SHOP & GUITAR STORE WE CAN THINK OF
AND WE SHOULD POST A NOTICE TO STORES AND MUSICIANS WITH INFO ABOUT OUR GEAR.
ZOT, WHY DON'T YOU & RENATO DO THE COMPUTER STUFF AND KRANG & I CAN DRIVE AROUND TO THE SHOPS?
WHAT ABOUT ME? HE TOOK MY DRUMS TOO, YOU KNOW.
I HOPE YOUR DRUMS ARE AT THE SCRAPPER'S BEING MELTED INTO COSTUME JEWELRY
YOU'RE A MENACE! YOU'RE MORE UN-STABLE THAN A HIGGS BOSON.
SCREECH
YOU GUYS FORGIVE ME, RIGHT?
LINDA'S BETTER AT EXPRESSING EMOTIONS THAN ME BUT I TOTALLY HATE YOU RIGHT NOW
ME TOO!

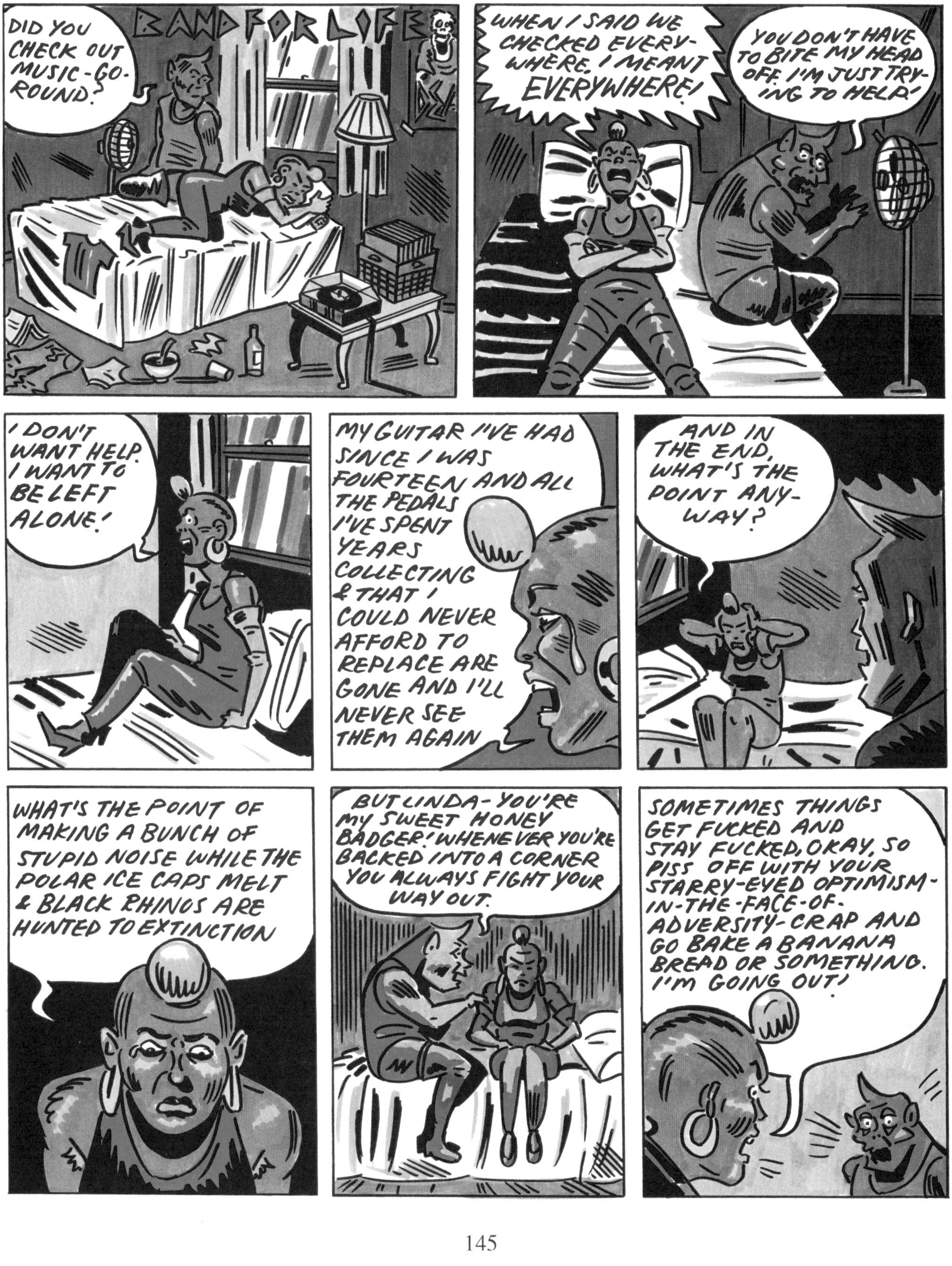
BAND FOR LIFE
DID YOU CHECK OUT MUSIC-GO-ROUND?
WHEN I SAID WE CHECKED EVERYWHERE, I MEANT EVERYWHERE!
YOU DON'T HAVE TO BITE MY HEAD OFF. I'M JUST TRYING TO HELP!
I DON'T WANT HELP. I WANT TO BE LEFT ALONE!
MY GUITAR I'VE HAD SINCE I WAS FOURTEEN AND ALL THE PEDALS I'VE SPENT YEARS COLLECTING & THAT I COULD NEVER AFFORD TO REPLACE ARE GONE AND I'LL NEVER SEE THEM AGAIN
AND IN THE END, WHAT'S THE POINT ANYWAY?
WHAT'S THE POINT OF MAKING A BUNCH OF STUPID NOISE WHILE THE POLAR ICE CAPS MELT & BLACK RHINOS ARE HUNTED TO EXTINCTION
BUT LINDA- YOU'RE MY SWEET HONEY BADGER! WHENEVER YOU'RE BACKED INTO A CORNER YOU ALWAYS FIGHT YOUR WAY OUT.
SOMETIMES THINGS GET FUCKED AND STAY FUCKED, OKAY, SO PISS OFF WITH YOUR STARRY-EYED OPTIMISM-IN-THE-FACE-OF-ADVERSITY-CRAP AND GO BAKE A BANANA BREAD OR SOMETHING. I'M GOING OUT!

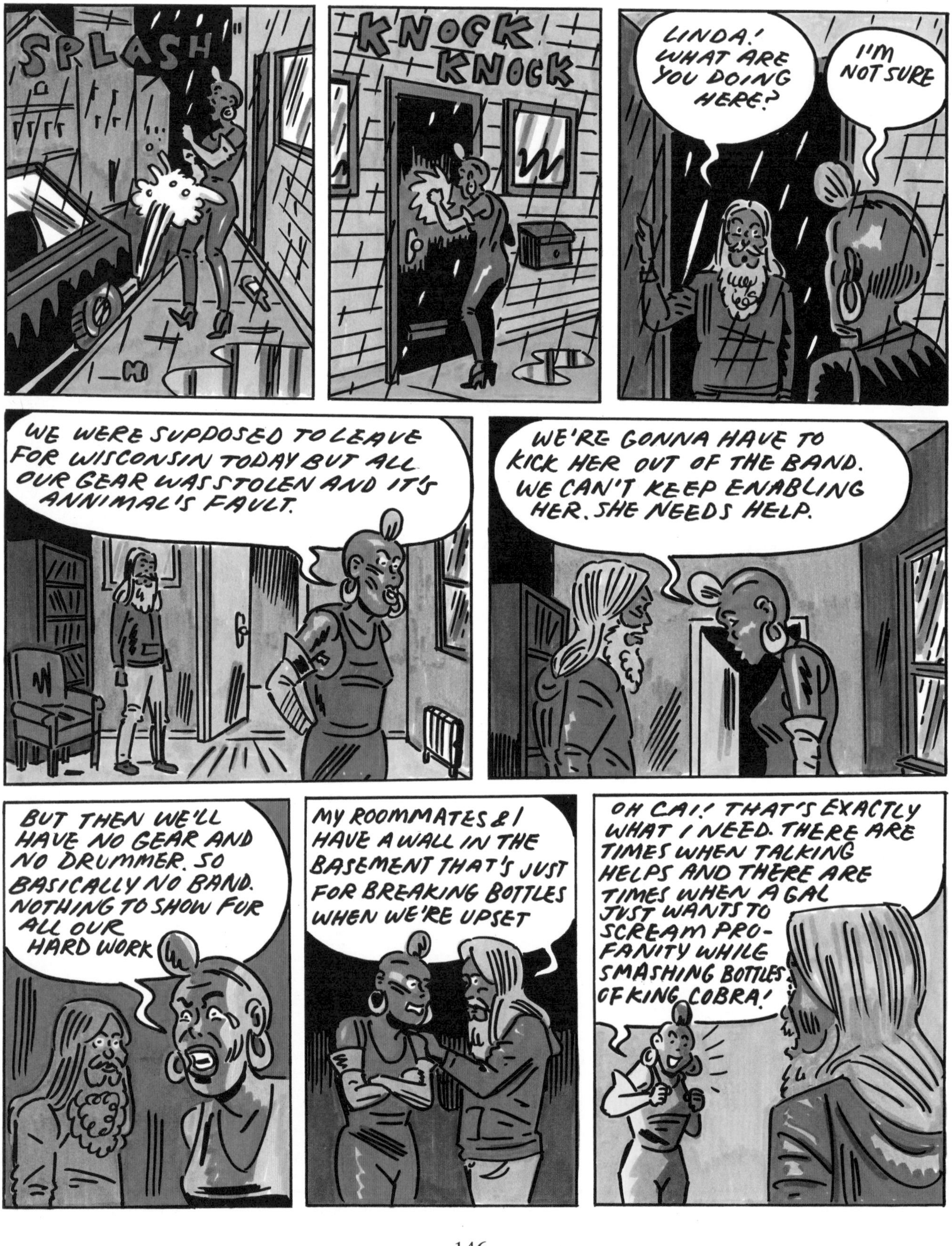
SPLASH
KNOCK KNOCK
LINDA! WHAT ARE YOU DOING HERE?
I'M NOT SURE
WE WERE SUPPOSED TO LEAVE FOR WISCONSIN TODAY BUT ALL OUR GEAR WAS STOLEN AND IT'S ANNIMAL'S FAULT.
WE'RE GONNA HAVE TO KICK HER OUT OF THE BAND. WE CAN'T KEEP ENABLING HER. SHE NEEDS HELP.
BUT THEN WE'LL HAVE NO GEAR AND NO DRUMMER. SO BASICALLY NO BAND. NOTHING TO SHOW FOR ALL OUR HARD WORK
MY ROOMMATES & I HAVE A WALL IN THE BASEMENT THAT'S JUST FOR BREAKING BOTTLES WHEN WE'RE UPSET
OH CAI! THAT'S EXACTLY WHAT I NEED. THERE ARE TIMES WHEN TALKING HELPS AND THERE ARE TIMES WHEN A GAL JUST WANTS TO SCREAM PRO-FANITY WHILE SMASHING BOTTLES OF KING COBRA!

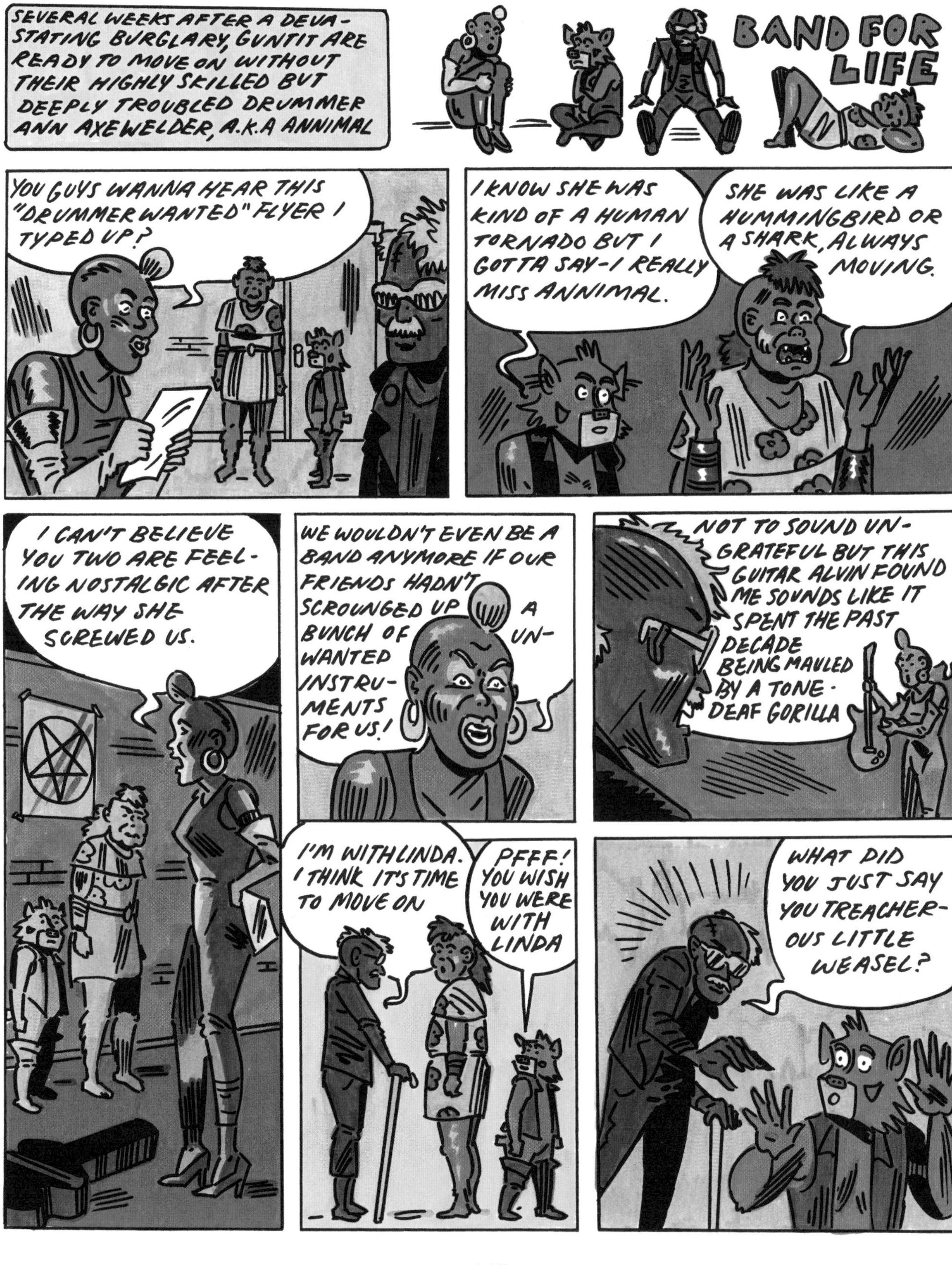
SEVERAL WEEKS AFTER A DEVA-STATING BURGLARY, GUNTIT ARE READY TO MOVE ON WITHOUT THEIR HIGHLY SKILLED BUT DEEPLY TROUBLED DRUMMER ANN AXEWELDER, A.K.A ANNIMAL
BAND FOR LIFE
YOU GUYS WANNA HEAR THIS "DRUMMER WANTED" FLYER I TYPED UP?
I KNOW SHE WAS KIND OF A HUMAN TORNADO BUT I GOTTA SAY-I REALLY MISS ANNIMAL.
SHE WAS LIKE A HUMMINGBIRD OR A SHARK, ALWAYS MOVING.
I CAN'T BELIEVE YOU TWO ARE FEEL-ING NOSTALGIC AFTER THE WAY SHE SCREWED US.
WE WOULDN'T EVEN BE A BAND ANYMORE IF OUR FRIENDS HADN'T SCROUNGED UP A BUNCH OF UN-WANTED INSTRU-MENTS FOR US!
NOT TO SOUND UN-GRATEFUL BUT THIS GUITAR ALVIN FOUND ME SOUNDS LIKE IT SPENT THE PAST DECADE BEING MAULED BY A TONE-DEAF GORILLA
I'M WITH LINDA. I THINK IT'S TIME TO MOVE ON
PFFF! YOU WISH YOU WERE WITH LINDA
WHAT DID YOU JUST SAY YOU TREACHER-OUS LITTLE WEASEL?

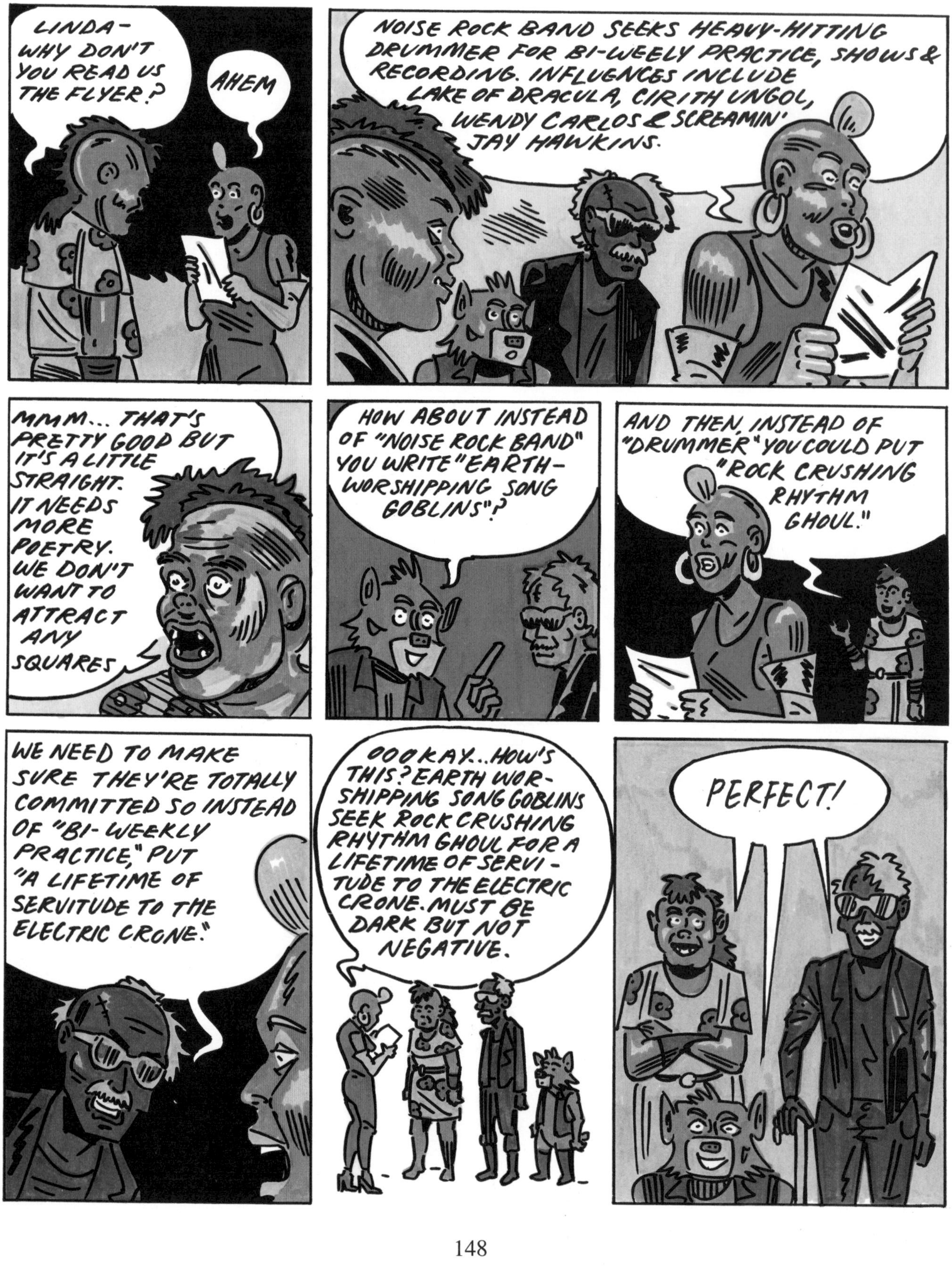
LINDA- WHY DON'T YOU READ US THE FLYER?
AHEM
NOISE ROCK BAND SEEKS HEAVY-HITTING DRUMMER FOR BI-WEELY PRACTICE, SHOWS & RECORDING. INFLUENCES INCLUDE LAKE OF DRACULA, CIRITH UNGOL, WENDY CARLOS & SCREAMIN' JAY HAWKINS.
MMM... THAT'S PRETTY GOOD BUT IT'S A LITTLE STRAIGHT. IT NEEDS MORE POETRY. WE DON'T WANT TO ATTRACT ANY SQUARES
HOW ABOUT INSTEAD OF "NOISE ROCK BAND" YOU WRITE "EARTH-WORSHIPPING SONG GOBLINS"?
AND THEN, INSTEAD OF "DRUMMER" YOU COULD PUT "ROCK CRUSHING RHYTHM GHOUL."
WE NEED TO MAKE SURE THEY'RE TOTALLY COMMITTED SO INSTEAD OF "BI-WEEKLY PRACTICE," PUT "A LIFETIME OF SERVITUDE TO THE ELECTRIC CRONE."
OOOKAY... HOW'S THIS? EARTH WOR-SHIPPING SONG GOBLINS SEEK ROCK CRUSHING RHYTHM GHOUL FOR A LIFETIME OF SERVI-TUDE TO THE ELECTRIC CRONE. MUST BE DARK BUT NOT NEGATIVE.
PERFECT!

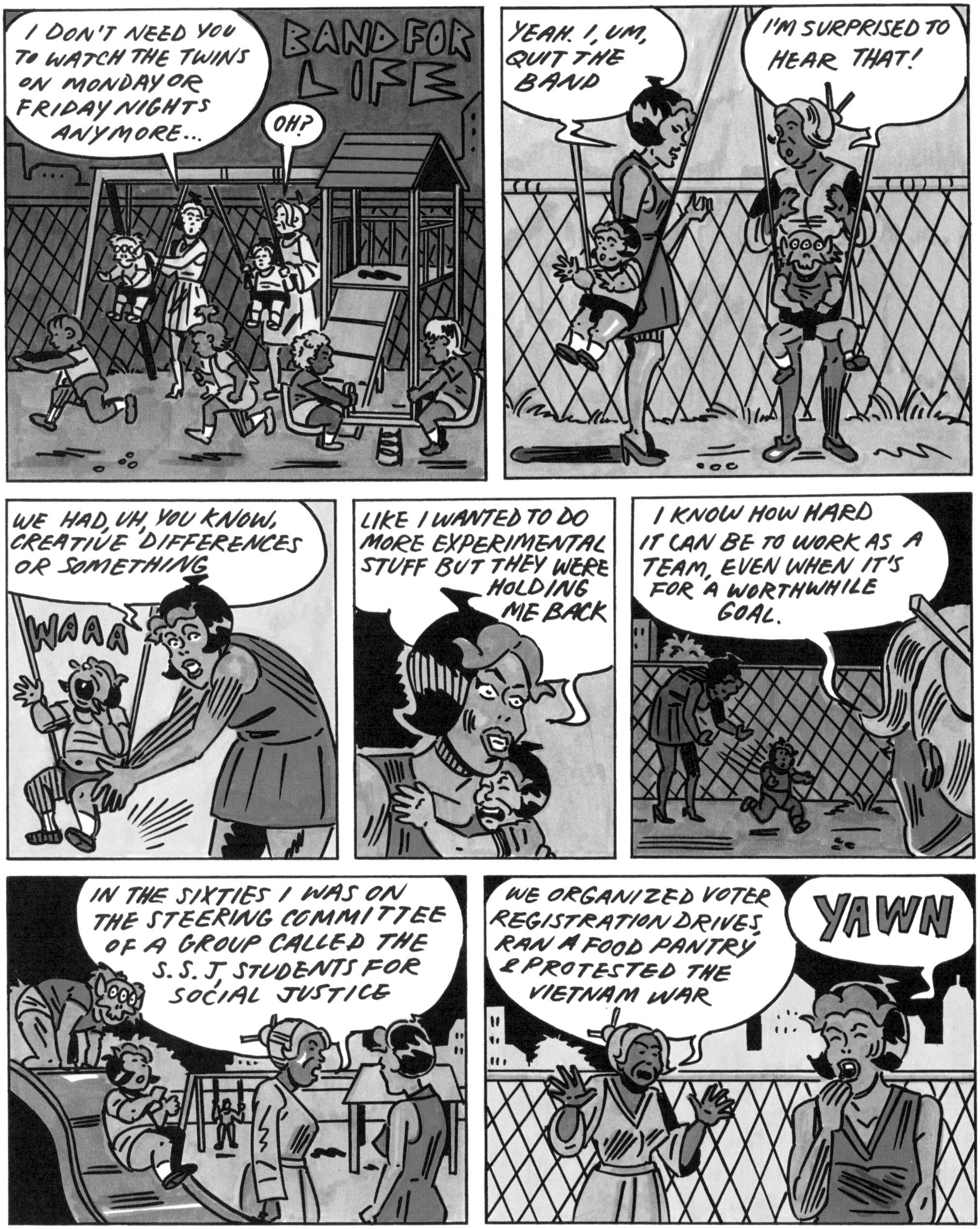
I DON'T NEED YOU TO WATCH THE TWINS ON MONDAY OR FRIDAY NIGHTS ANYMORE...
BAND FOR LIFE
OH?
YEAH. I, UM, QUIT THE BAND
I'M SURPRISED TO HEAR THAT!
WE HAD, UH, YOU KNOW, CREATIVE DIFFERENCES OR SOMETHING
WAAA
LIKE I WANTED TO DO MORE EXPERIMENTAL STUFF BUT THEY WERE HOLDING ME BACK
I KNOW HOW HARD IT CAN BE TO WORK AS A TEAM, EVEN WHEN IT'S FOR A WORTHWHILE GOAL.
IN THE SIXTIES I WAS ON THE STEERING COMMITTEE OF A GROUP CALLED THE S.S.J, STUDENTS FOR SOCIAL JUSTICE
WE ORGANIZED VOTER REGISTRATION DRIVES, RAN A FOOD PANTRY & PROTESTED THE VIETNAM WAR
YAWN

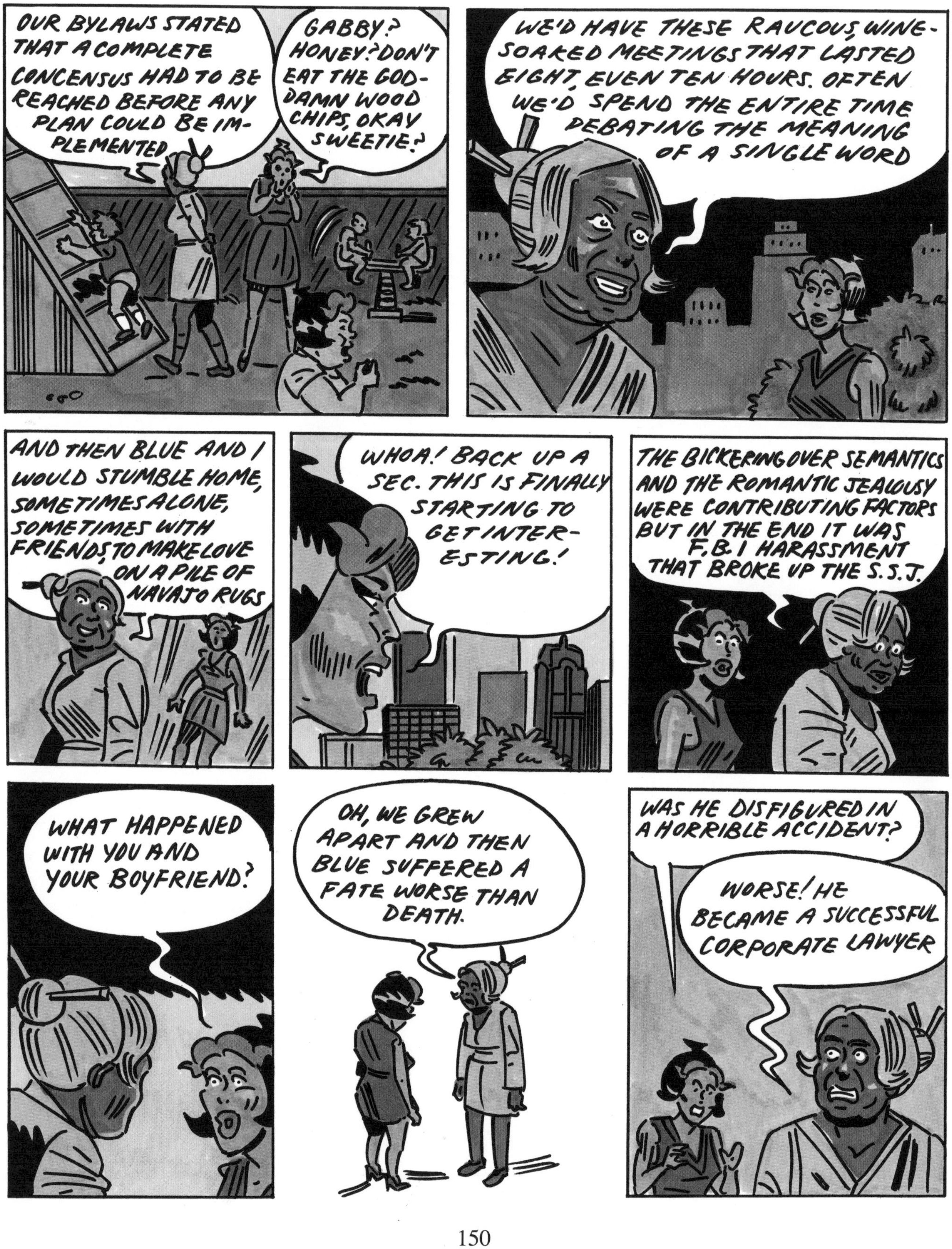
OUR BYLAWS STATED THAT A COMPLETE CONCENSUS HAD TO BE REACHED BEFORE ANY PLAN COULD BE IMPLEMENTED
GABBY? HONEY? DON'T EAT THE GOD-DAMN WOOD CHIPS, OKAY SWEETIE?
WE'D HAVE THESE RAUCOUS, WINE-SOAKED MEETINGS THAT LASTED EIGHT, EVEN TEN HOURS. OFTEN WE'D SPEND THE ENTIRE TIME DEBATING THE MEANING OF A SINGLE WORD
AND THEN BLUE AND I WOULD STUMBLE HOME, SOMETIMES ALONE, SOMETIMES WITH FRIENDS, TO MAKE LOVE ON A PILE OF NAVAJO RUGS
WHOA! BACK UP A SEC. THIS IS FINALLY STARTING TO GET INTERESTING!
THE BICKERING OVER SEMANTICS AND THE ROMANTIC JEALOUSY WERE CONTRIBUTING FACTORS BUT IN THE END IT WAS F.B.I HARASSMENT THAT BROKE UP THE S.S.J.
WHAT HAPPENED WITH YOU AND YOUR BOYFRIEND?
OH, WE GREW APART AND THEN BLUE SUFFERED A FATE WORSE THAN DEATH.
WAS HE DISFIGURED IN A HORRIBLE ACCIDENT?
WORSE! HE BECAME A SUCCESSFUL CORPORATE LAWYER

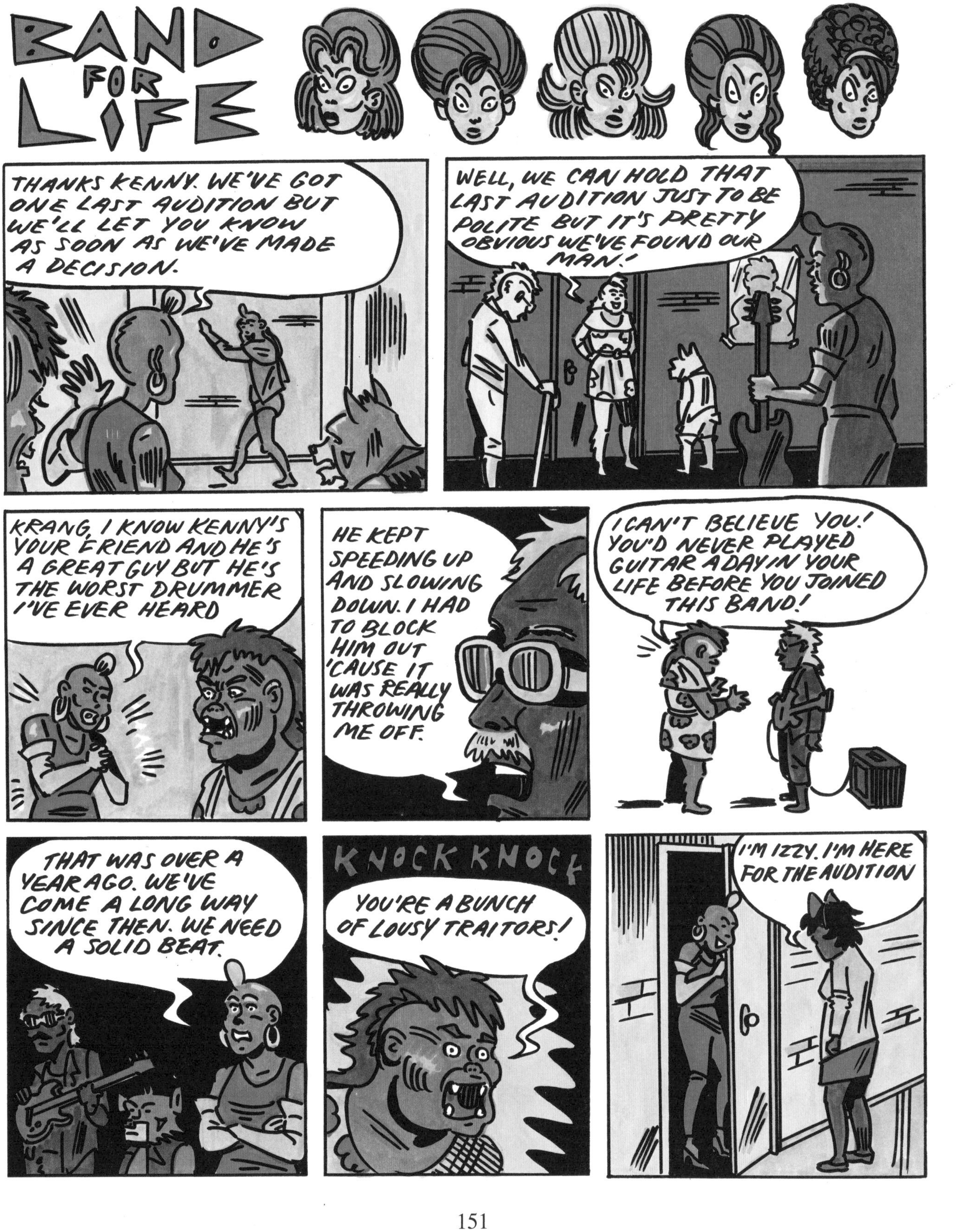
BAND FOR LIFE
THANKS KENNY. WE'VE GOT ONE LAST AUDITION BUT WE'LL LET YOU KNOW AS SOON AS WE'VE MADE A DECISION.
WELL, WE CAN HOLD THAT LAST AUDITION JUST TO BE POLITE BUT IT'S PRETTY OBVIOUS WE'VE FOUND OUR MAN!
KRANG, I KNOW KENNY'S YOUR FRIEND AND HE'S A GREAT GUY BUT HE'S THE WORST DRUMMER I'VE EVER HEARD
HE KEPT SPEEDING UP AND SLOWING DOWN. I HAD TO BLOCK HIM OUT 'CAUSE IT WAS REALLY THROWING ME OFF.
I CAN'T BELIEVE YOU! YOU'D NEVER PLAYED GUITAR A DAY IN YOUR LIFE BEFORE YOU JOINED THIS BAND!
THAT WAS OVER A YEAR AGO. WE'VE COME A LONG WAY SINCE THEN. WE NEED A SOLID BEAT.
KNOCK KNOCK
YOU'RE A BUNCH OF LOUSY TRAITORS!
I'M IZZY. I'M HERE FOR THE AUDITION

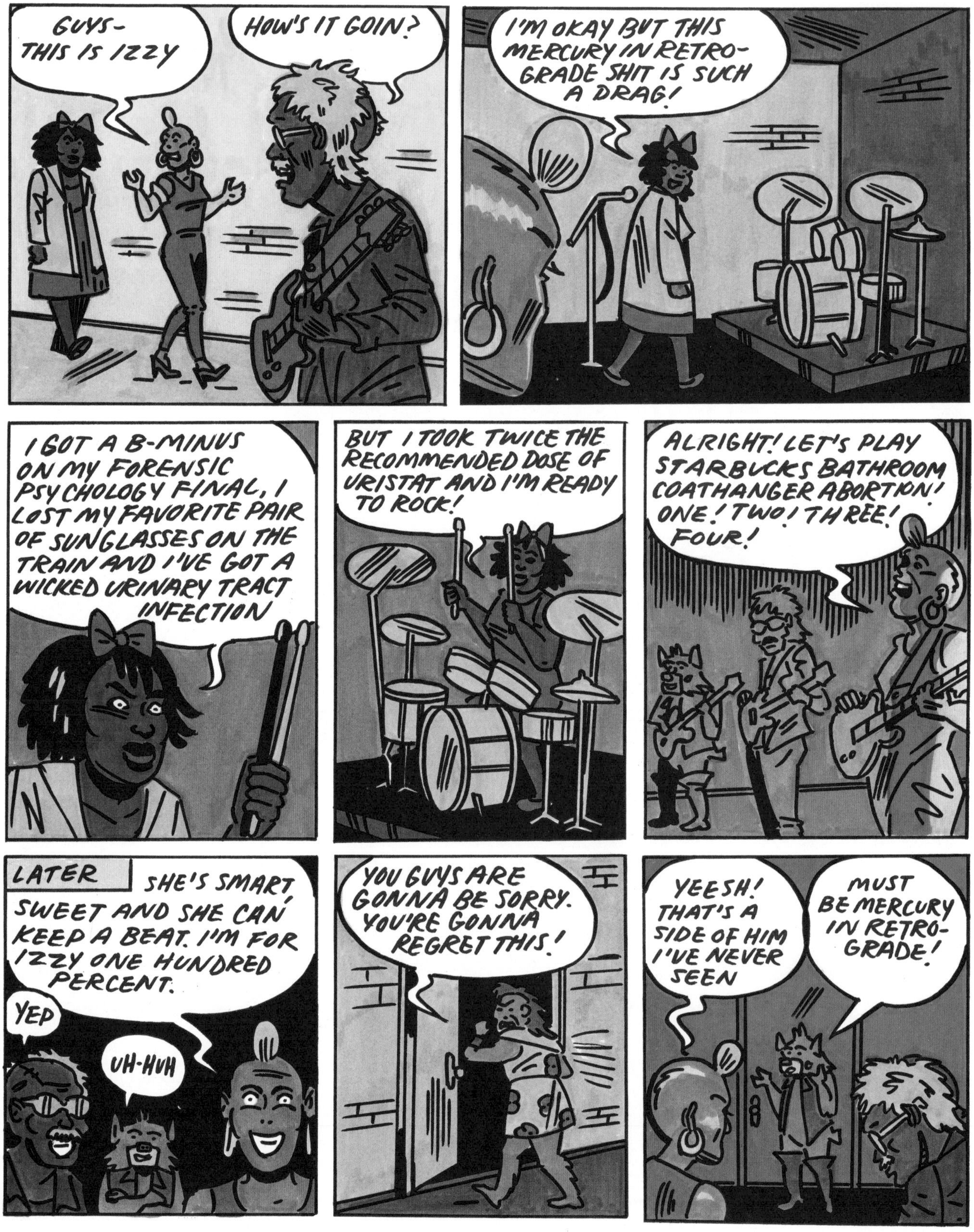
GUYS- THIS IS IZZY
HOW'S IT GOIN?
I'M OKAY BUT THIS MERCURY IN RETRO-GRADE SHIT IS SUCH A DRAG!
I GOT A B-MINUS ON MY FORENSIC PSYCHOLOGY FINAL, I LOST MY FAVORITE PAIR OF SUNGLASSES ON THE TRAIN AND I'VE GOT A WICKED URINARY TRACT INFECTION
BUT I TOOK TWICE THE RECOMMENDED DOSE OF URISTAT AND I'M READY TO ROCK!
ALRIGHT! LET'S PLAY STARBUCKS BATHROOM COATHANGER ABORTION! ONE! TWO! THREE! FOUR!
LATER
SHE'S SMART, SWEET AND SHE CAN KEEP A BEAT. I'M FOR IZZY ONE HUNDRED PERCENT.
YEP
UH-HUH
YOU GUYS ARE GONNA BE SORRY. YOU'RE GONNA REGRET THIS!
YEESH! THAT'S A SIDE OF HIM I'VE NEVER SEEN
MUST BE MERCURY IN RETRO-GRADE!

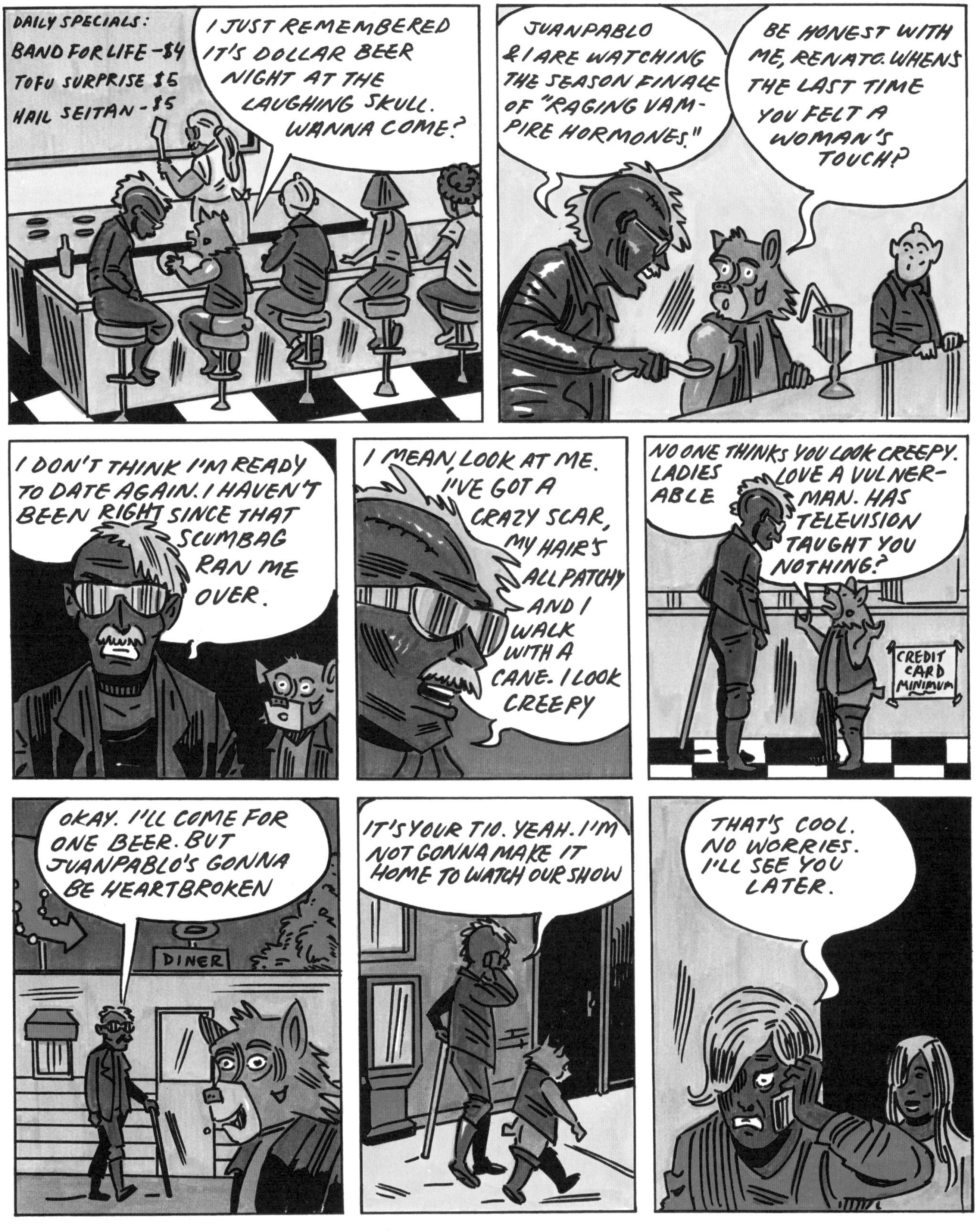
DAILY SPECIALS:
BAND FOR LIFE -$4
TOFU SURPRISE $5
HAIL SEITAN -$5
I JUST REMEMBERED IT'S DOLLAR BEER NIGHT AT THE LAUGHING SKULL. WANNA COME?
JUANPABLO & I ARE WATCHING THE SEASON FINALE OF "RAGING VAMPIRE HORMONES."
BE HONEST WITH ME, RENATO. WHENS THE LAST TIME YOU FELT A WOMAN'S TOUCH?
I DON'T THINK I'M READY TO DATE AGAIN. I HAVEN'T BEEN RIGHT SINCE THAT SCUMBAG RAN ME OVER.
I MEAN, LOOK AT ME. I'VE GOT A CRAZY SCAR, MY HAIR'S ALL PATCHY AND I WALK WITH A CANE. I LOOK CREEPY
NO ONE THINKS YOU LOOK CREEPY. LADIES LOVE A VULNERABLE MAN. HAS TELEVISION TAUGHT YOU NOTHING?
CREDIT CARD MINIMUM
OKAY. I'LL COME FOR ONE BEER. BUT JUANPABLO'S GONNA BE HEARTBROKEN
DINER
IT'S YOUR TIO. YEAH. I'M NOT GONNA MAKE IT HOME TO WATCH OUR SHOW
THAT'S COOL. NO WORRIES. I'LL SEE YOU LATER.

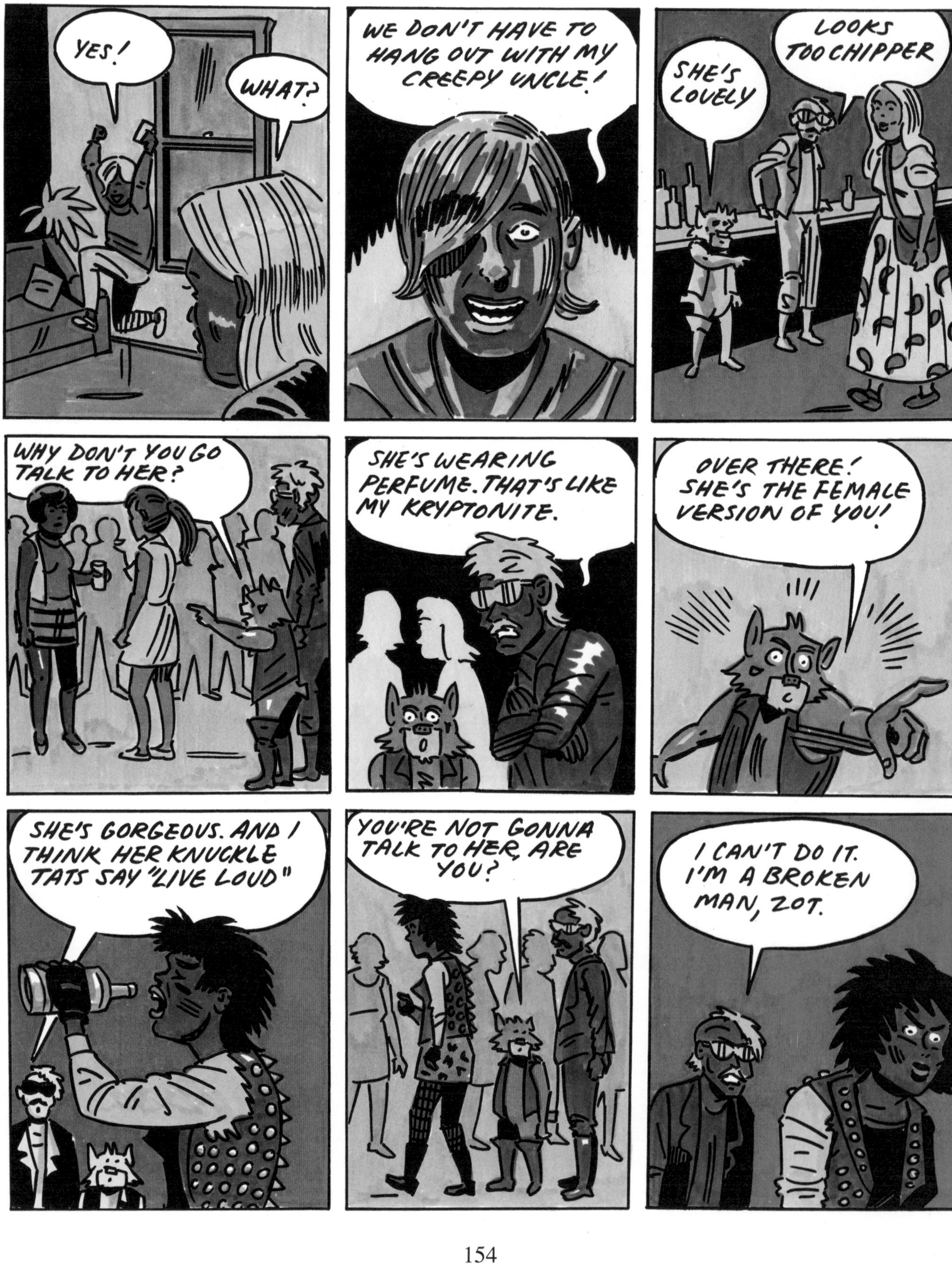
YES!
WHAT?
WE DON'T HAVE TO HANG OUT WITH MY CREEPY UNCLE!
SHE'S LOVELY
LOOKS TOO CHIPPER
WHY DON'T YOU GO TALK TO HER?
SHE'S WEARING PERFUME. THAT'S LIKE MY KRYPTONITE.
OVER THERE! SHE'S THE FEMALE VERSION OF YOU!
SHE'S GORGEOUS. AND I THINK HER KNUCKLE TATS SAY "LIVE LOUD"
YOU'RE NOT GONNA TALK TO HER, ARE YOU?
I CAN'T DO IT. I'M A BROKEN MAN, ZOT.

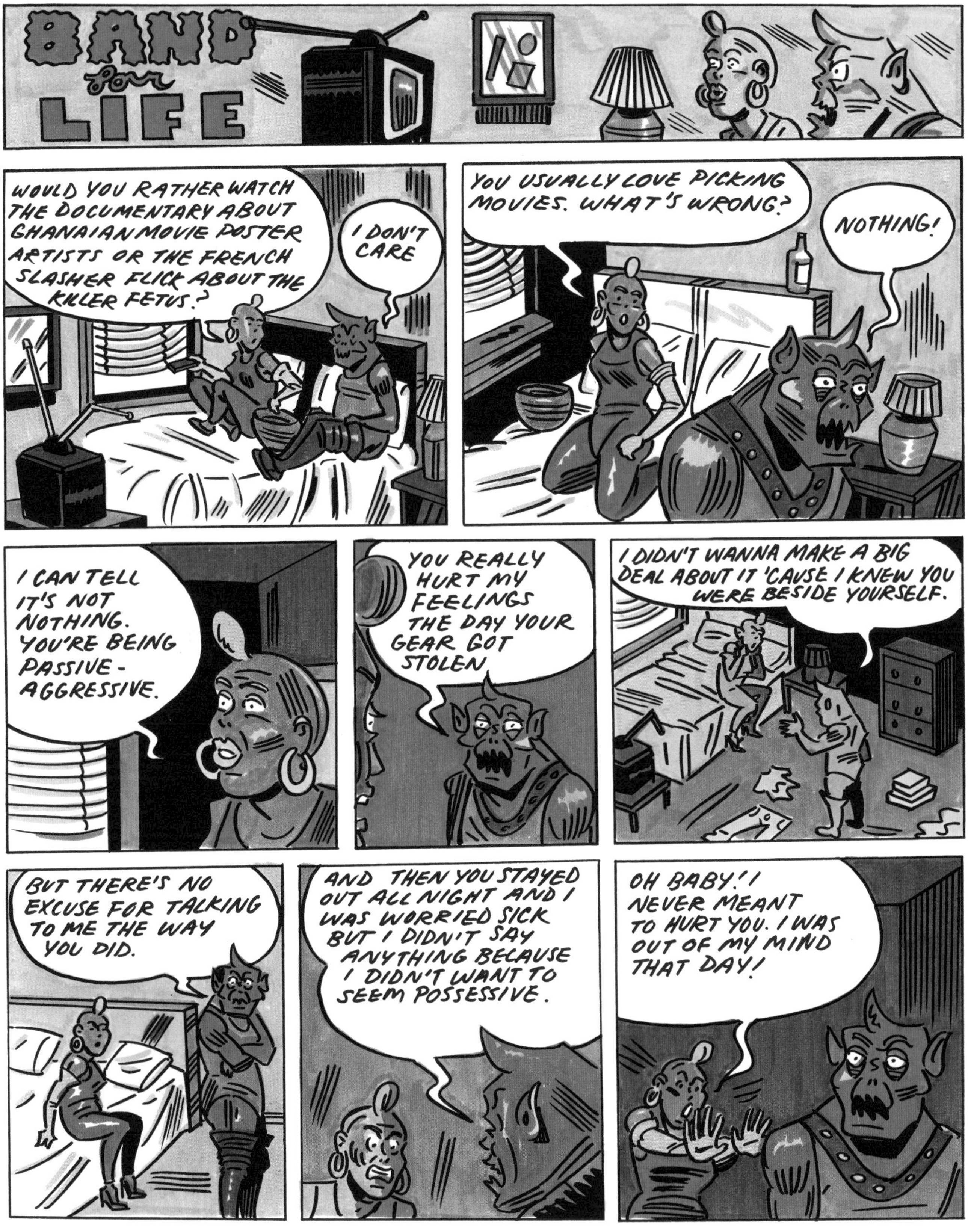
BAND for LIFE
WOULD YOU RATHER WATCH THE DOCUMENTARY ABOUT GHANAIAN MOVIE POSTER ARTISTS OR THE FRENCH SLASHER FLICK ABOUT THE KILLER FETUS?
I DON'T CARE
YOU USUALLY LOVE PICKING MOVIES. WHAT'S WRONG?
NOTHING!
I CAN TELL IT'S NOT NOTHING. YOU'RE BEING PASSIVE-AGGRESSIVE.
YOU REALLY HURT MY FEELINGS THE DAY YOUR GEAR GOT STOLEN.
I DIDN'T WANNA MAKE A BIG DEAL ABOUT IT 'CAUSE I KNEW YOU WERE BESIDE YOURSELF.
BUT THERE'S NO EXCUSE FOR TALKING TO ME THE WAY YOU DID.
AND THEN YOU STAYED OUT ALL NIGHT AND I WAS WORRIED SICK BUT I DIDN'T SAY ANYTHING BECAUSE I DIDN'T WANT TO SEEM POSSESSIVE.
OH BABY! I NEVER MEANT TO HURT YOU. I WAS OUT OF MY MIND THAT DAY!

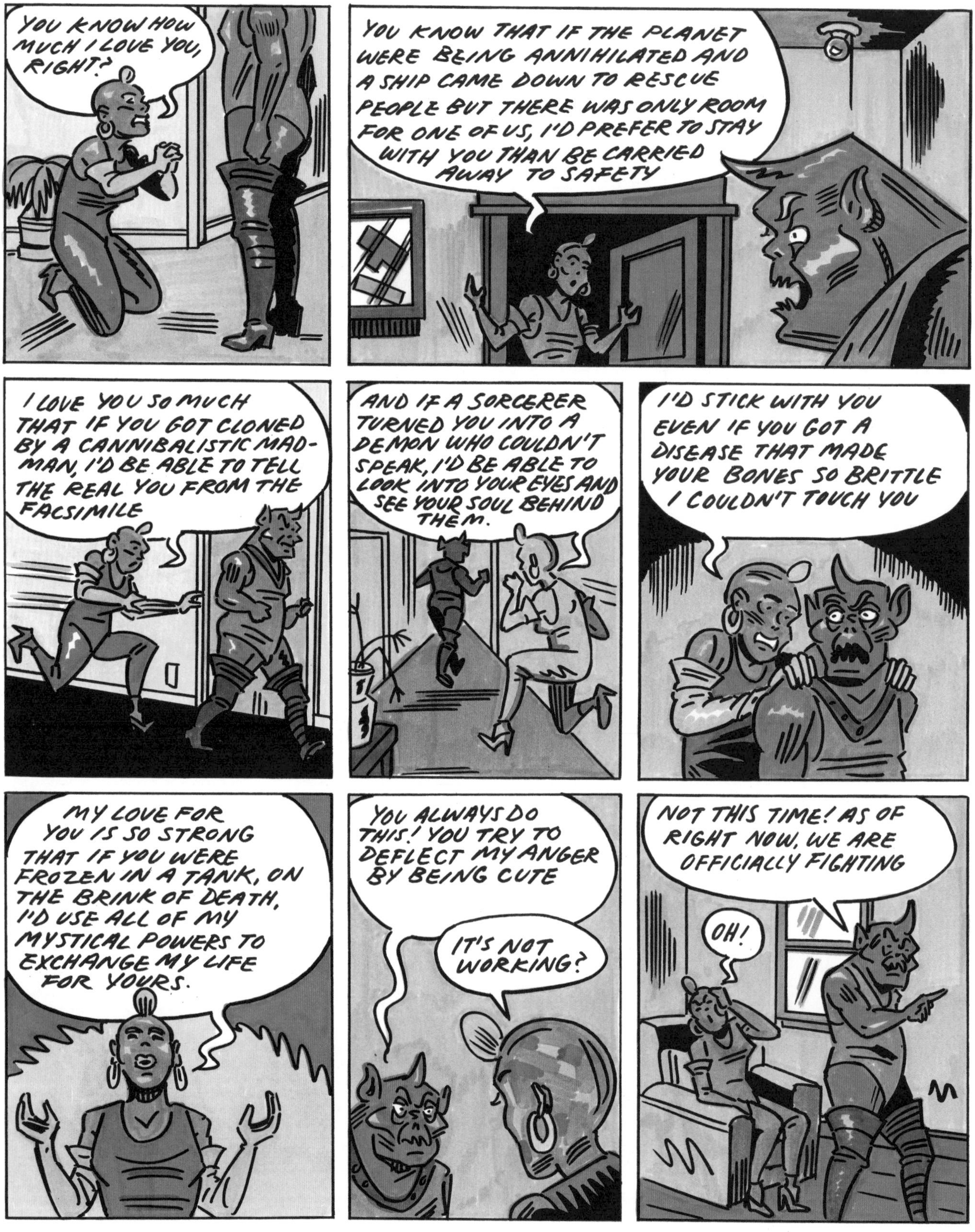
YOU KNOW HOW MUCH I LOVE YOU, RIGHT?
YOU KNOW THAT IF THE PLANET WERE BEING ANNIHILATED AND A SHIP CAME DOWN TO RESCUE PEOPLE BUT THERE WAS ONLY ROOM FOR ONE OF US, I'D PREFER TO STAY WITH YOU THAN BE CARRIED AWAY TO SAFETY
I LOVE YOU SO MUCH THAT IF YOU GOT CLONED BY A CANNIBALISTIC MAD-MAN, I'D BE ABLE TO TELL THE REAL YOU FROM THE FACSIMILE
AND IF A SORCERER TURNED YOU INTO A DEMON WHO COULDN'T SPEAK, I'D BE ABLE TO LOOK INTO YOUR EYES AND SEE YOUR SOUL BEHIND THEM.
I'D STICK WITH YOU EVEN IF YOU GOT A DISEASE THAT MADE YOUR BONES SO BRITTLE I COULDN'T TOUCH YOU
MY LOVE FOR YOU IS SO STRONG THAT IF YOU WERE FROZEN IN A TANK, ON THE BRINK OF DEATH, I'D USE ALL OF MY MYSTICAL POWERS TO EXCHANGE MY LIFE FOR YOURS.
YOU ALWAYS DO THIS! YOU TRY TO DEFLECT MY ANGER BY BEING CUTE
IT'S NOT WORKING?
NOT THIS TIME! AS OF RIGHT NOW, WE ARE OFFICIALLY FIGHTING
OH!

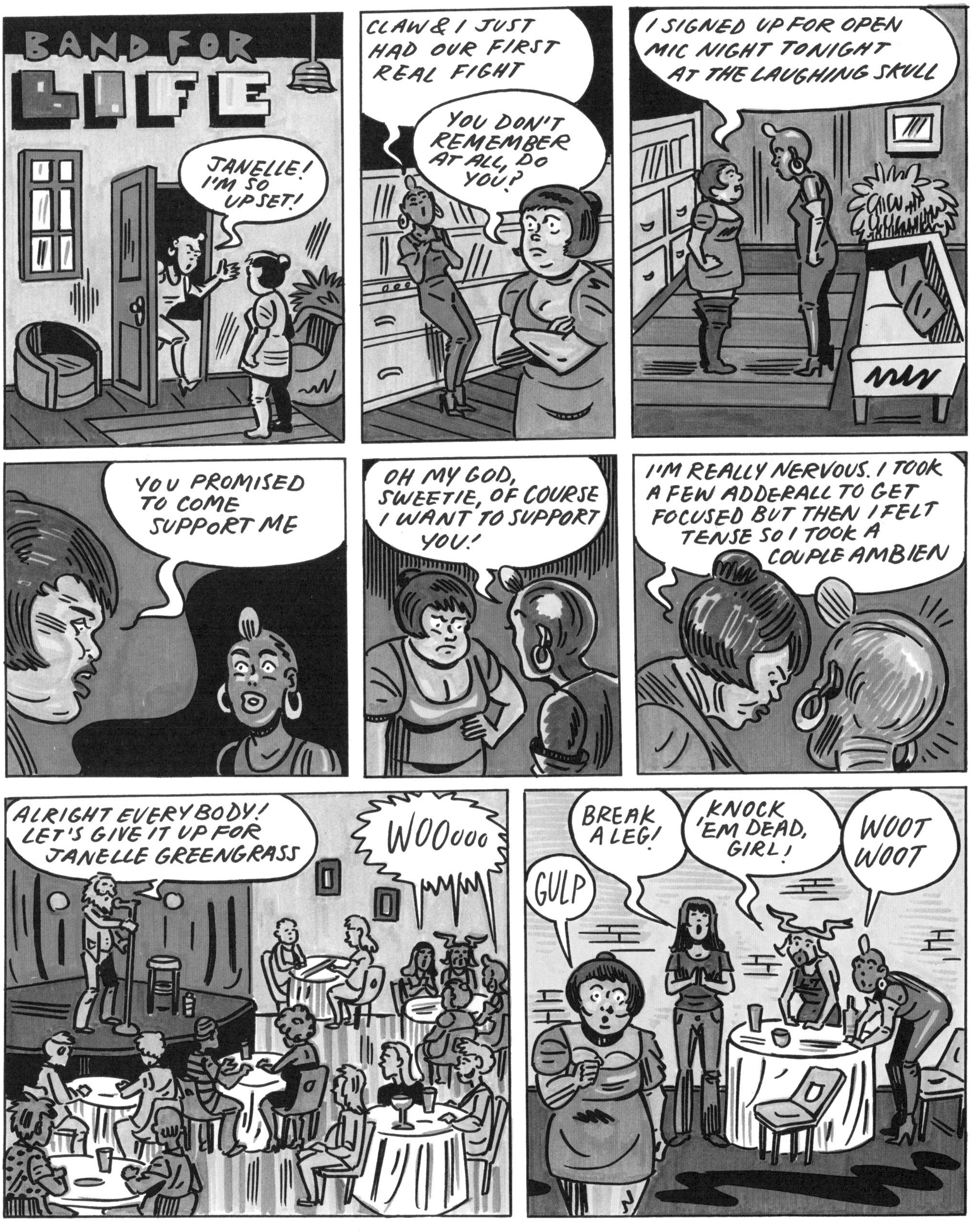
BAND FOR LIFE
JANELLE! I'M SO UPSET!
CLAW & I JUST HAD OUR FIRST REAL FIGHT
YOU DON'T REMEMBER AT ALL, DO YOU?
I SIGNED UP FOR OPEN MIC NIGHT TONIGHT AT THE LAUGHING SKULL
YOU PROMISED TO COME SUPPORT ME
OH MY GOD, SWEETIE, OF COURSE I WANT TO SUPPORT YOU!
I'M REALLY NERVOUS. I TOOK A FEW ADDERALL TO GET FOCUSED BUT THEN I FELT TENSE SO I TOOK A COUPLE AMBIEN
ALRIGHT EVERYBODY! LET'S GIVE IT UP FOR JANELLE GREENGRASS
WOOuuu
GULP
BREAK A LEG!
KNOCK 'EM DEAD, GIRL!
WOOT WOOT

I LOVE THE THEORY THAT THERE ARE AN INFINITE NUMBER OF UNIVERSES BUT THEY'RE ALL ISOLATED FROM ONE ANOTHER.

AND TO US, THE ACTUAL WORLD IS THE WORLD WE KNOW, BUT THERE ARE OTHER WORLDS WHERE ELEPHANTS ARE THE SIZE OF CATS AND EVERYONE'S KNEES AND ELBOWS ARE BACKWARDS.

NO ONE'S LAUGHING

SHE'S BOMBING

WE GOTTA DO SOMETHING!

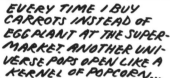

EVERY TIME I BUY CARROTS INSTEAD OF EGGPLANT AT THE SUPERMARKET, ANOTHER UNIVERSE POPS OPEN LIKE A KERNEL OF POPCORN...

YEAH

WOOoo

AND IN THAT UNIVERSE, I BUY THE EGGPLANT. IT'S LIKE "CHOOSE YOUR OWN ADVENTURE" ON A COSMIC SCALE, AND SOME OF IT'S MUNDANE BUT SOME OF IT IS FUCKING TERRIFYING!

HAHAHA

OW

LIKE THERE ARE THOUSANDS OF POSSIBLE WORLDS WHERE I DIE SPECTACULARLY, AND THEY STARTED RADIATING OUT AROUND ME FROM THE MOMENT I WAS BORN. SO THERE'S A WORLD WHERE I CHOKE TO DEATH ON AN ALPHABET BLOCK...

AND THERE'S A WORLD WHERE I EAT A LIT FIRECRACKER AND ONE WHERE I TRY TO JUMP A ROW OF BURNING CARS IN A MONSTER TRUCK WITH A RATTLESNAKE IN THE CAB.

WE LOVE YOU!

GO BABY GO!

THEN THERE ARE OTHER, STRANGER WORLDS THAT ARE LESS LIKE OUR OWN. IN ONE OF THEM, THERE'S A VERSION OF ME THAT HAS FOUR MASSIVE SWINGING BLUE DICKS...

FUCK YEAH

AND THREE PAIRS OF TITS. AND THIS LONG SILKY RED HAIR THAT FLOWS BEHIND ME WHEN I WALK, LIKE IN A SHAMPOO COMMERCIAL.

WOOO

HAHAHA

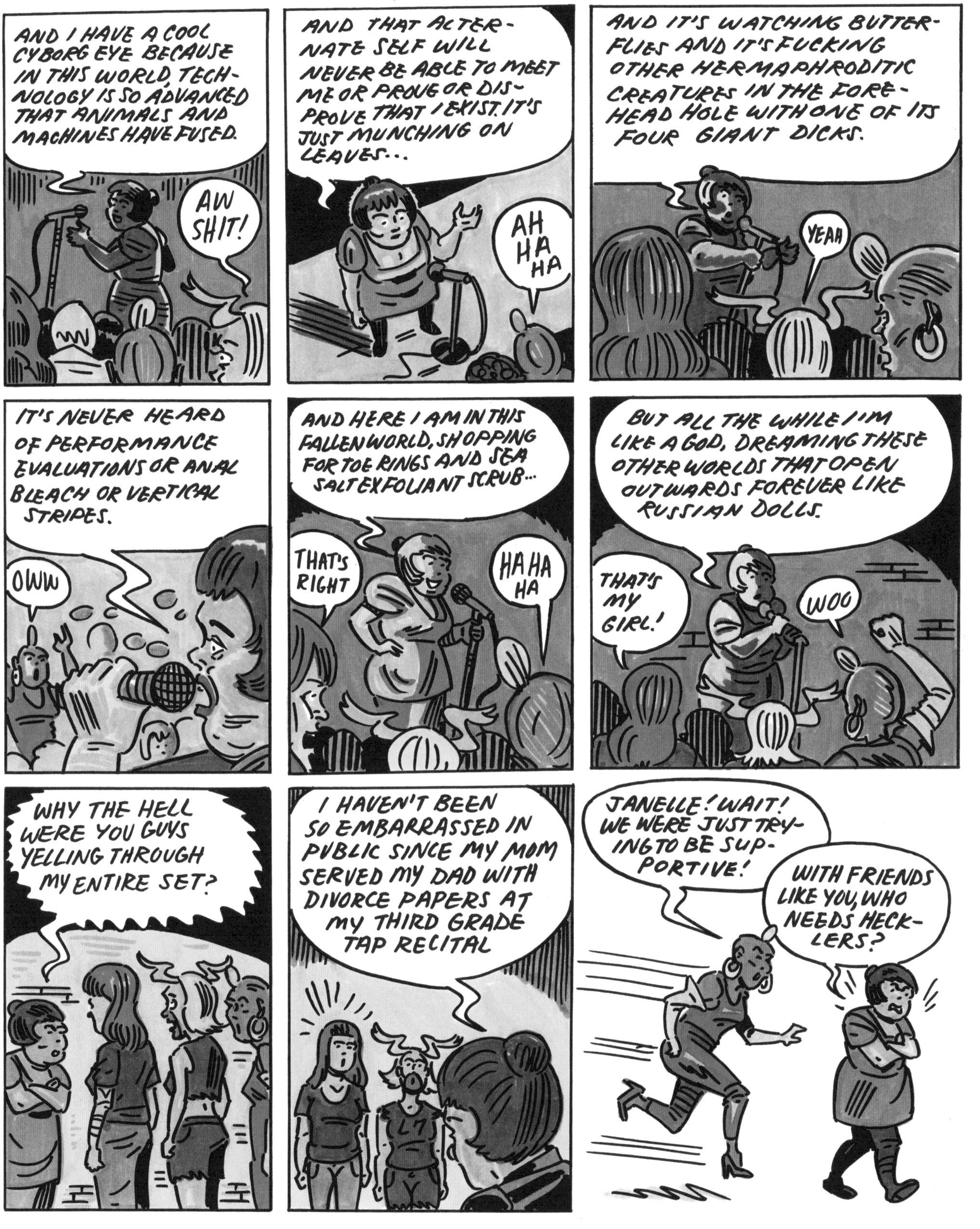
AND I HAVE A COOL CYBORG EYE BECAUSE IN THIS WORLD, TECHNOLOGY IS SO ADVANCED THAT ANIMALS AND MACHINES HAVE FUSED.
AW SHIT!
AND THAT ALTERNATE SELF WILL NEVER BE ABLE TO MEET ME OR PROVE OR DISPROVE THAT I EXIST. IT'S JUST MUNCHING ON LEAVES...
AH HA HA
AND IT'S WATCHING BUTTERFLIES AND IT'S FUCKING OTHER HERMAPHRODITIC CREATURES IN THE FOREHEAD HOLE WITH ONE OF ITS FOUR GIANT DICKS.
YEAH
IT'S NEVER HEARD OF PERFORMANCE EVALUATIONS OR ANAL BLEACH OR VERTICAL STRIPES.
OWW
AND HERE I AM IN THIS FALLEN WORLD, SHOPPING FOR TOE RINGS AND SEA SALT EXFOLIANT SCRUB...
THAT'S RIGHT
HA HA HA
BUT ALL THE WHILE I'M LIKE A GOD, DREAMING THESE OTHER WORLDS THAT OPEN OUTWARDS FOREVER LIKE RUSSIAN DOLLS.
THAT'S MY GIRL!
WOO
WHY THE HELL WERE YOU GUYS YELLING THROUGH MY ENTIRE SET?
I HAVEN'T BEEN SO EMBARRASSED IN PUBLIC SINCE MY MOM SERVED MY DAD WITH DIVORCE PAPERS AT MY THIRD GRADE TAP RECITAL
JANELLE! WAIT! WE WERE JUST TRYING TO BE SUPPORTIVE!
WITH FRIENDS LIKE YOU, WHO NEEDS HECKLERS?

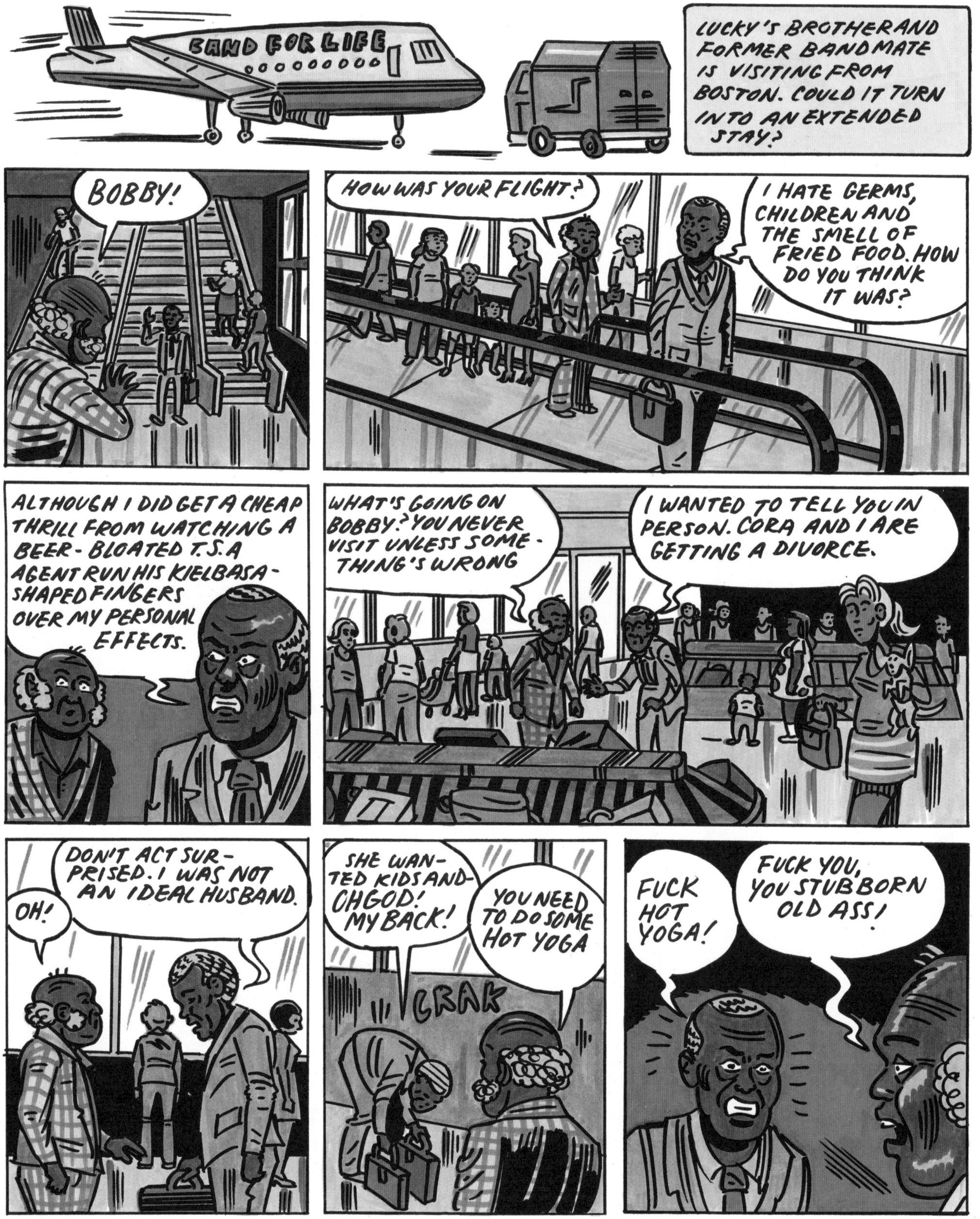
BAND FOR LIFE
LUCKY'S BROTHER AND FORMER BANDMATE IS VISITING FROM BOSTON. COULD IT TURN INTO AN EXTENDED STAY?
BOBBY!
HOW WAS YOUR FLIGHT?
I HATE GERMS, CHILDREN AND THE SMELL OF FRIED FOOD. HOW DO YOU THINK IT WAS?
ALTHOUGH I DID GET A CHEAP THRILL FROM WATCHING A BEER-BLOATED T.S.A AGENT RUN HIS KIELBASA-SHAPED FINGERS OVER MY PERSONAL EFFECTS.
WHAT'S GOING ON BOBBY? YOU NEVER VISIT UNLESS SOMETHING'S WRONG
I WANTED TO TELL YOU IN PERSON. CORA AND I ARE GETTING A DIVORCE.
OH!
DON'T ACT SURPRISED. I WAS NOT AN IDEAL HUSBAND.
SHE WANTED KIDS AND- OHGOD! MY BACK!
CRAK
YOU NEED TO DO SOME HOT YOGA
FUCK HOT YOGA!
FUCK YOU, YOU STUBBORN OLD ASS!

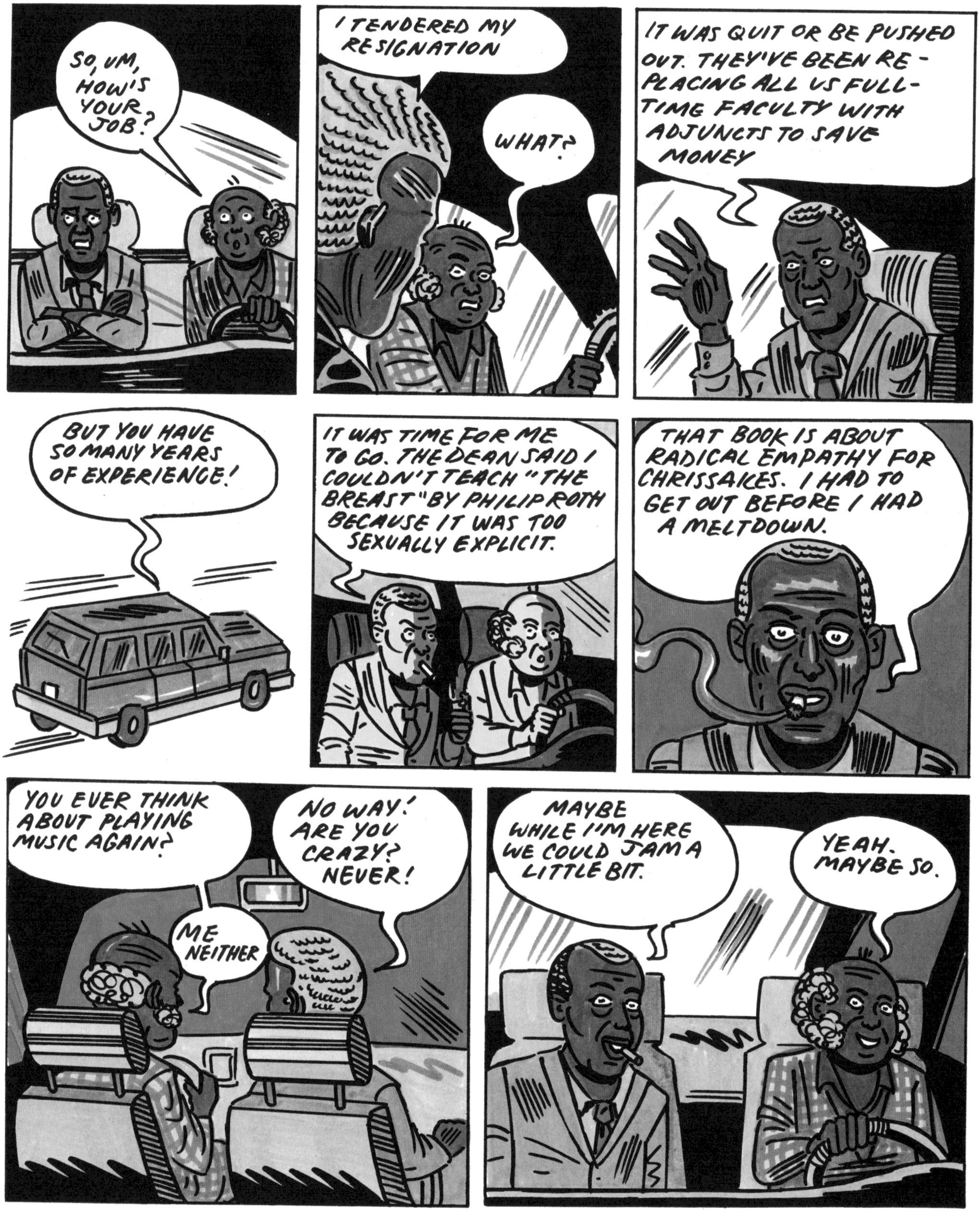

SO, UM, HOW'S YOUR JOB?
I TENDERED MY RESIGNATION
WHAT?
IT WAS QUIT OR BE PUSHED OUT. THEY'VE BEEN REPLACING ALL US FULL-TIME FACULTY WITH ADJUNCTS TO SAVE MONEY
BUT YOU HAVE SO MANY YEARS OF EXPERIENCE!
IT WAS TIME FOR ME TO GO. THE DEAN SAID I COULDN'T TEACH "THE BREAST" BY PHILIP ROTH BECAUSE IT WAS TOO SEXUALLY EXPLICIT.
THAT BOOK IS ABOUT RADICAL EMPATHY FOR CHRISSAKES. I HAD TO GET OUT BEFORE I HAD A MELTDOWN.
YOU EVER THINK ABOUT PLAYING MUSIC AGAIN?
NO WAY! ARE YOU CRAZY? NEVER!
ME NEITHER
MAYBE WHILE I'M HERE WE COULD JAM A LITTLE BIT.
YEAH. MAYBE SO.

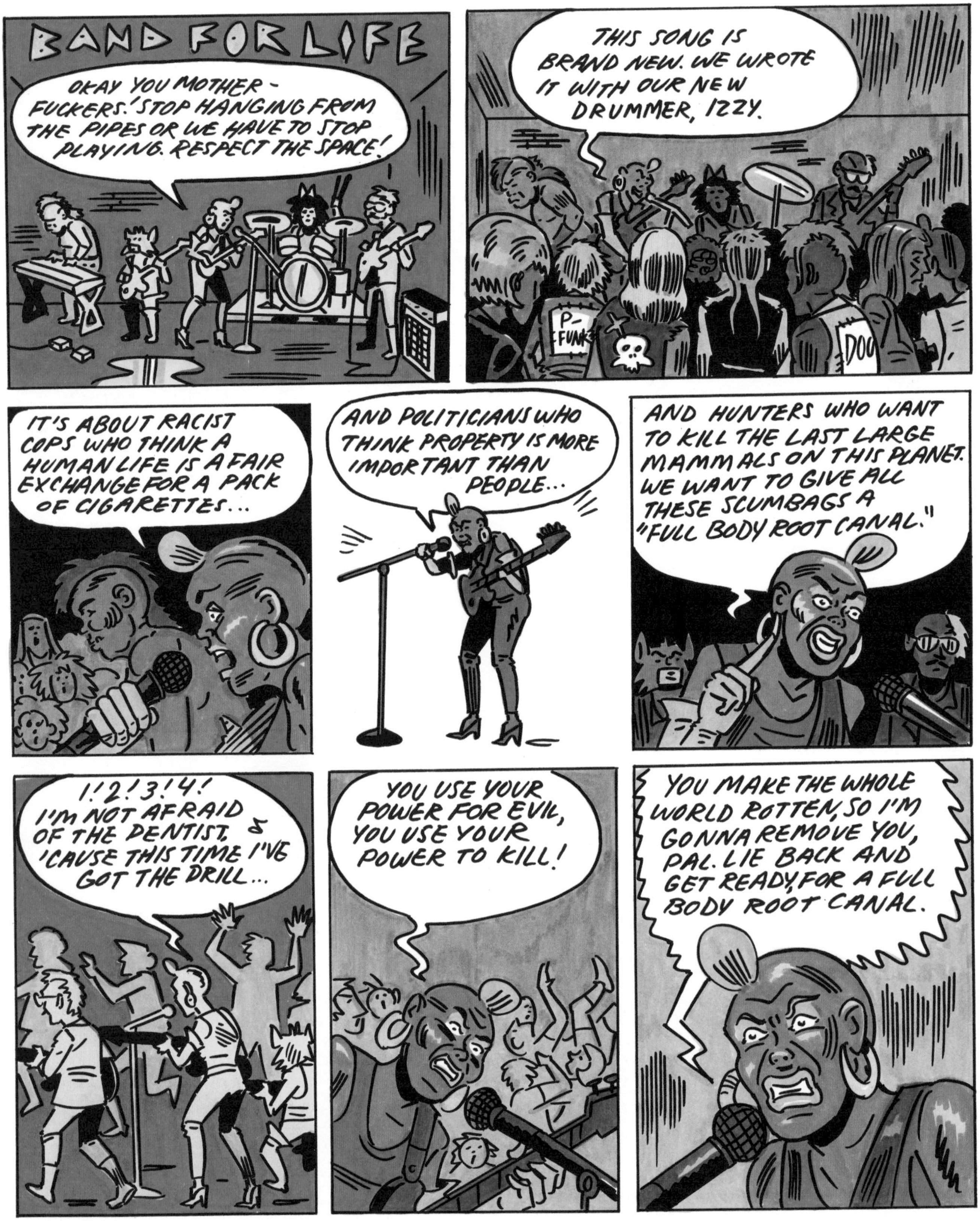
BAND FOR LIFE
OKAY YOU MOTHER-FUCKERS! STOP HANGING FROM THE PIPES OR WE HAVE TO STOP PLAYING. RESPECT THE SPACE!
THIS SONG IS BRAND NEW. WE WROTE IT WITH OUR NEW DRUMMER, IZZY.
P-FUNK
DOO
IT'S ABOUT RACIST COPS WHO THINK A HUMAN LIFE IS A FAIR EXCHANGE FOR A PACK OF CIGARETTES...
AND POLITICIANS WHO THINK PROPERTY IS MORE IMPORTANT THAN PEOPLE...
AND HUNTERS WHO WANT TO KILL THE LAST LARGE MAMMALS ON THIS PLANET. WE WANT TO GIVE ALL THESE SCUMBAGS A "FULL BODY ROOT CANAL."
1! 2! 3! 4! I'M NOT AFRAID OF THE DENTIST, 'CAUSE THIS TIME I'VE GOT THE DRILL...
YOU USE YOUR POWER FOR EVIL, YOU USE YOUR POWER TO KILL!
YOU MAKE THE WHOLE WORLD ROTTEN, SO I'M GONNA REMOVE YOU, PAL. LIE BACK AND GET READY FOR A FULL BODY ROOT CANAL.

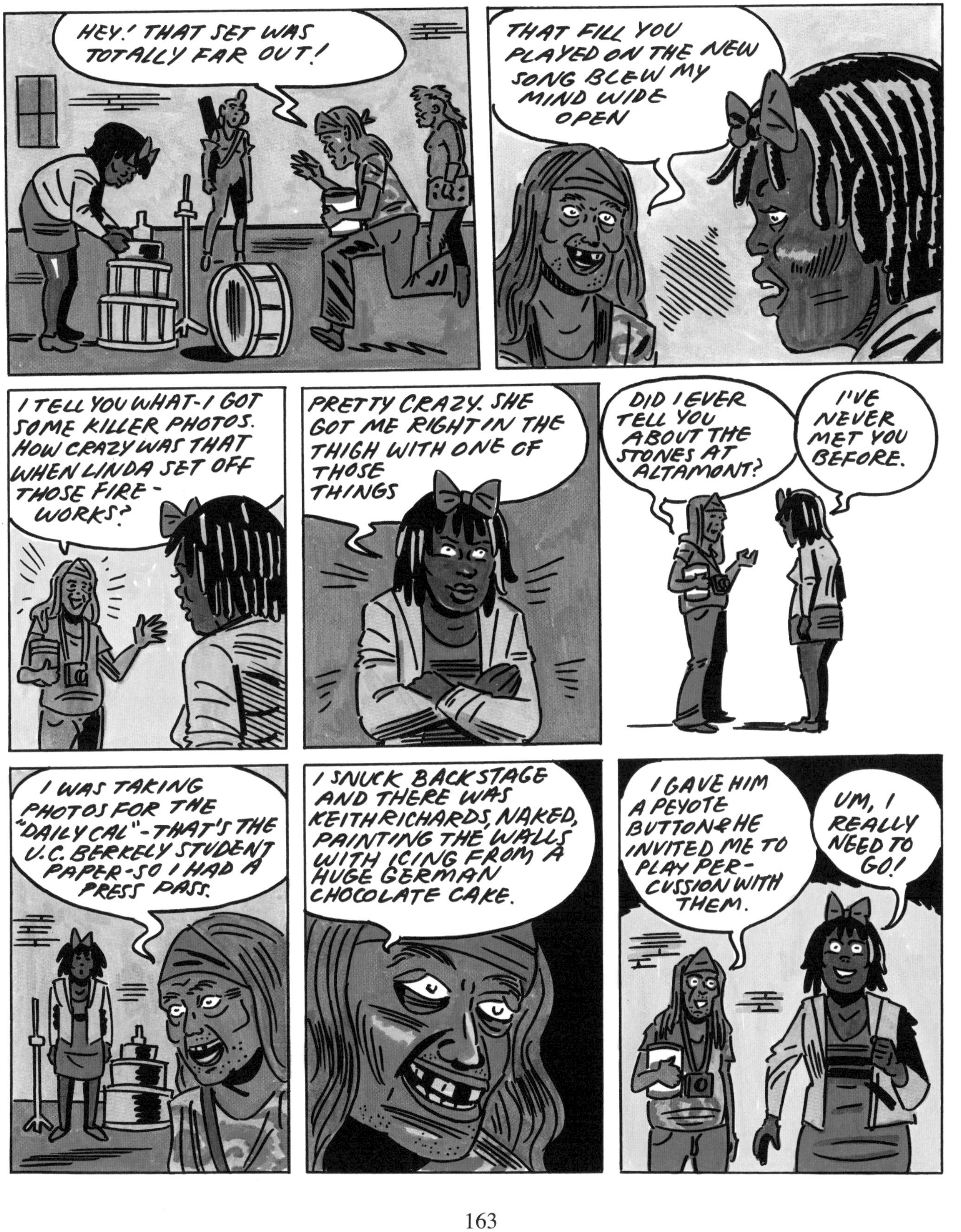
HEY! THAT SET WAS TOTALLY FAR OUT!
THAT FILL YOU PLAYED ON THE NEW SONG BLEW MY MIND WIDE OPEN
I TELL YOU WHAT- I GOT SOME KILLER PHOTOS. HOW CRAZY WAS THAT WHEN LINDA SET OFF THOSE FIRE-WORKS?
PRETTY CRAZY. SHE GOT ME RIGHT IN THE THIGH WITH ONE OF THOSE THINGS
DID I EVER TELL YOU ABOUT THE STONES AT ALTAMONT?
I'VE NEVER MET YOU BEFORE.
I WAS TAKING PHOTOS FOR THE "DAILY CAL"- THAT'S THE U.C. BERKELY STUDENT PAPER- SO I HAD A PRESS PASS.
I SNUCK BACKSTAGE AND THERE WAS KEITH RICHARDS, NAKED, PAINTING THE WALLS WITH ICING FROM A HUGE GERMAN CHOCOLATE CAKE.
I GAVE HIM A PEYOTE BUTTON & HE INVITED ME TO PLAY PER-CUSSION WITH THEM.
UM, I REALLY NEED TO GO!

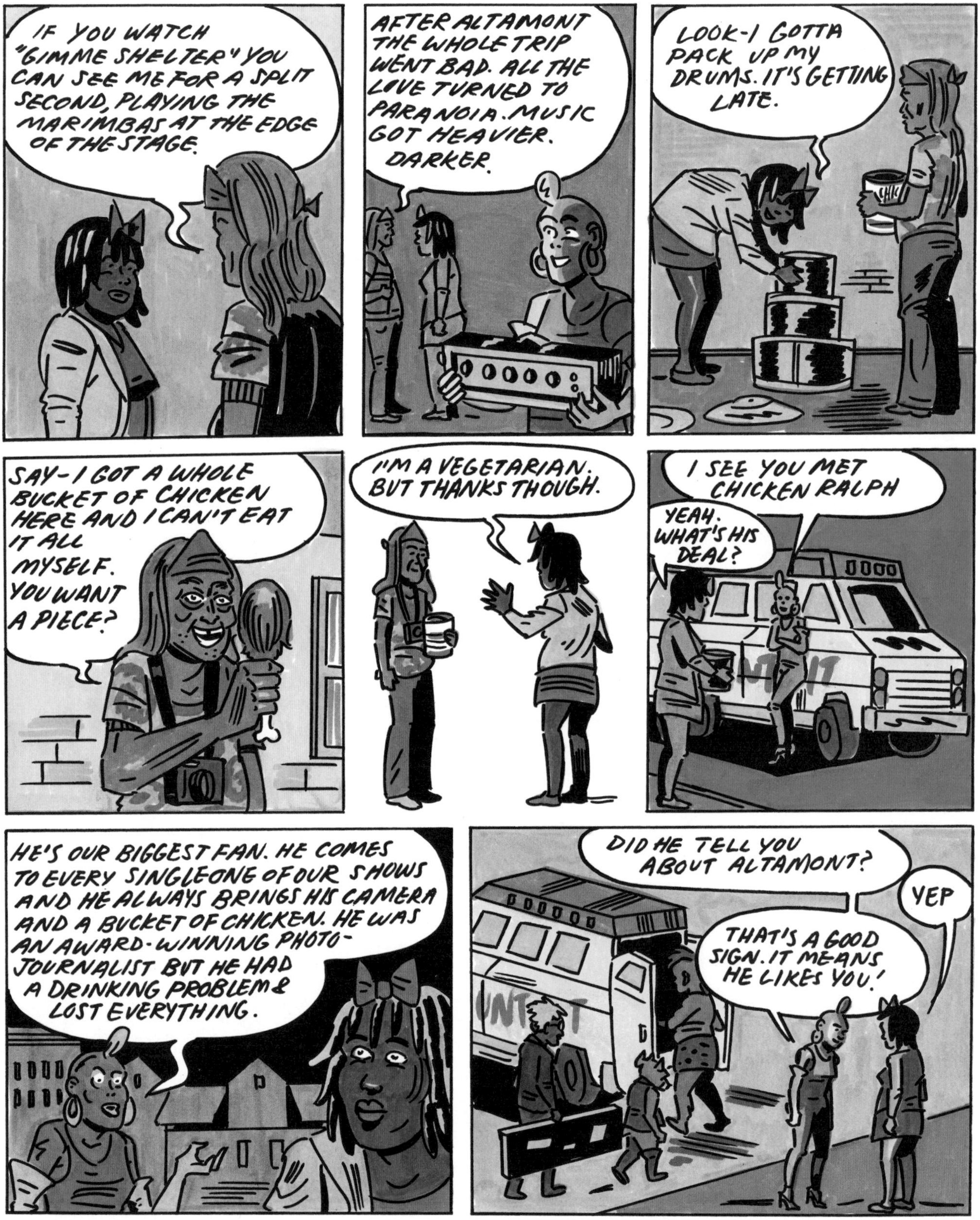
IF YOU WATCH "GIMME SHELTER" YOU CAN SEE ME FOR A SPLIT SECOND, PLAYING THE MARIMBAS AT THE EDGE OF THE STAGE.
AFTER ALTAMONT THE WHOLE TRIP WENT BAD. ALL THE LOVE TURNED TO PARANOIA. MUSIC GOT HEAVIER. DARKER.
LOOK-I GOTTA PACK UP MY DRUMS. IT'S GETTING LATE.
SAY-I GOT A WHOLE BUCKET OF CHICKEN HERE AND I CAN'T EAT IT ALL MYSELF. YOU WANT A PIECE?
I'M A VEGETARIAN. BUT THANKS THOUGH.
I SEE YOU MET CHICKEN RALPH
YEAH. WHAT'S HIS DEAL?
HE'S OUR BIGGEST FAN. HE COMES TO EVERY SINGLE ONE OF OUR SHOWS AND HE ALWAYS BRINGS HIS CAMERA AND A BUCKET OF CHICKEN. HE WAS AN AWARD-WINNING PHOTO-JOURNALIST BUT HE HAD A DRINKING PROBLEM & LOST EVERYTHING.
DID HE TELL YOU ABOUT ALTAMONT?
YEP
THAT'S A GOOD SIGN. IT MEANS HE LIKES YOU!

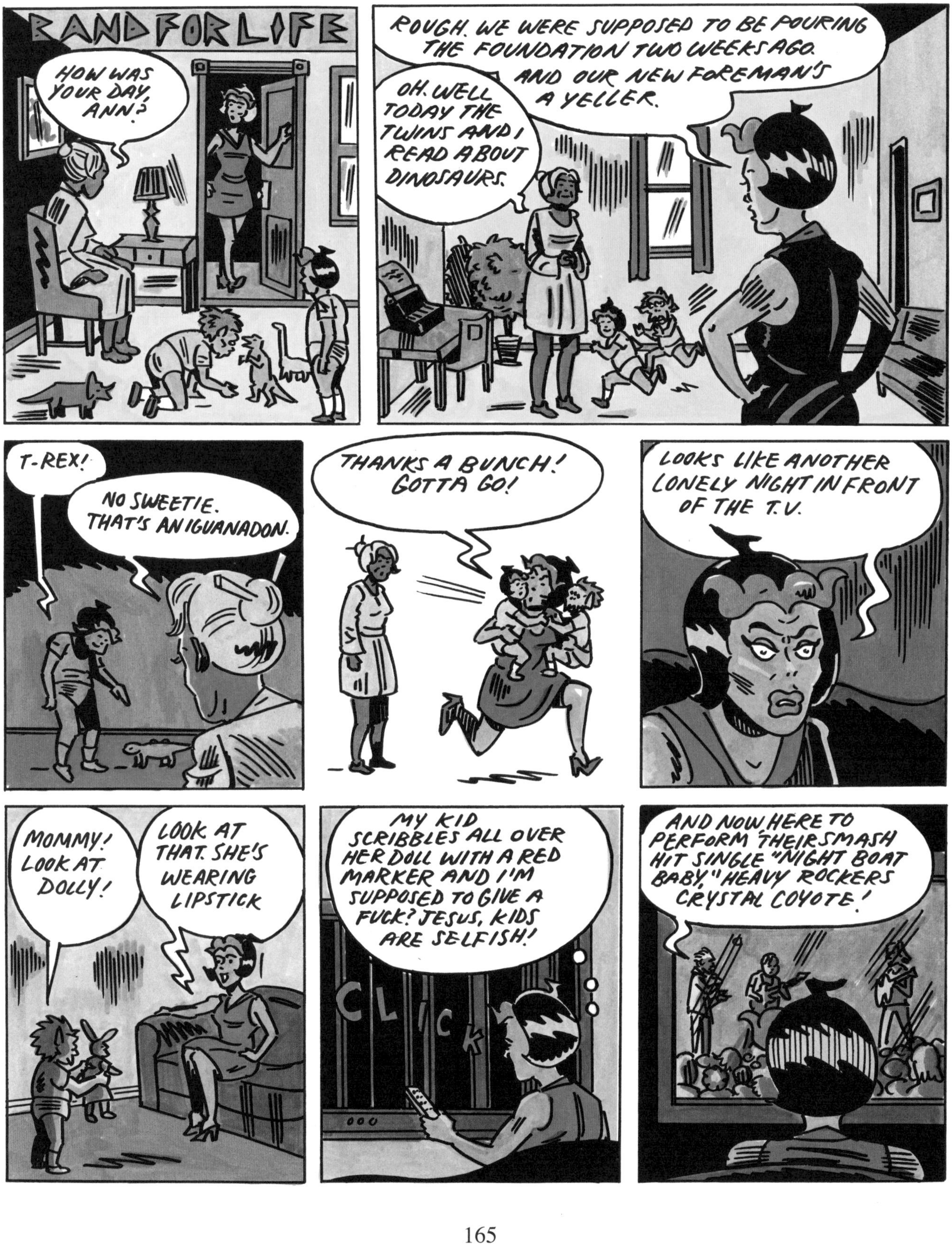
BAND FOR LIFE
HOW WAS YOUR DAY, ANN?
ROUGH. WE WERE SUPPOSED TO BE POURING THE FOUNDATION TWO WEEKS AGO.
AND OUR NEW FOREMAN'S A YELLER.
OH. WELL TODAY THE TWINS AND I READ ABOUT DINOSAURS.
T-REX!
NO SWEETIE. THAT'S AN IGUANADON.
THANKS A BUNCH! GOTTA GO!
LOOKS LIKE ANOTHER LONELY NIGHT IN FRONT OF THE T.V.
MOMMY! LOOK AT DOLLY!
LOOK AT THAT. SHE'S WEARING LIPSTICK
MY KID SCRIBBLES ALL OVER HER DOLL WITH A RED MARKER AND I'M SUPPOSED TO GIVE A FUCK? JESUS, KIDS ARE SELFISH!
CLICK
AND NOW HERE TO PERFORM THEIR SMASH HIT SINGLE "NIGHT BOAT BABY," HEAVY ROCKERS CRYSTAL COYOTE!

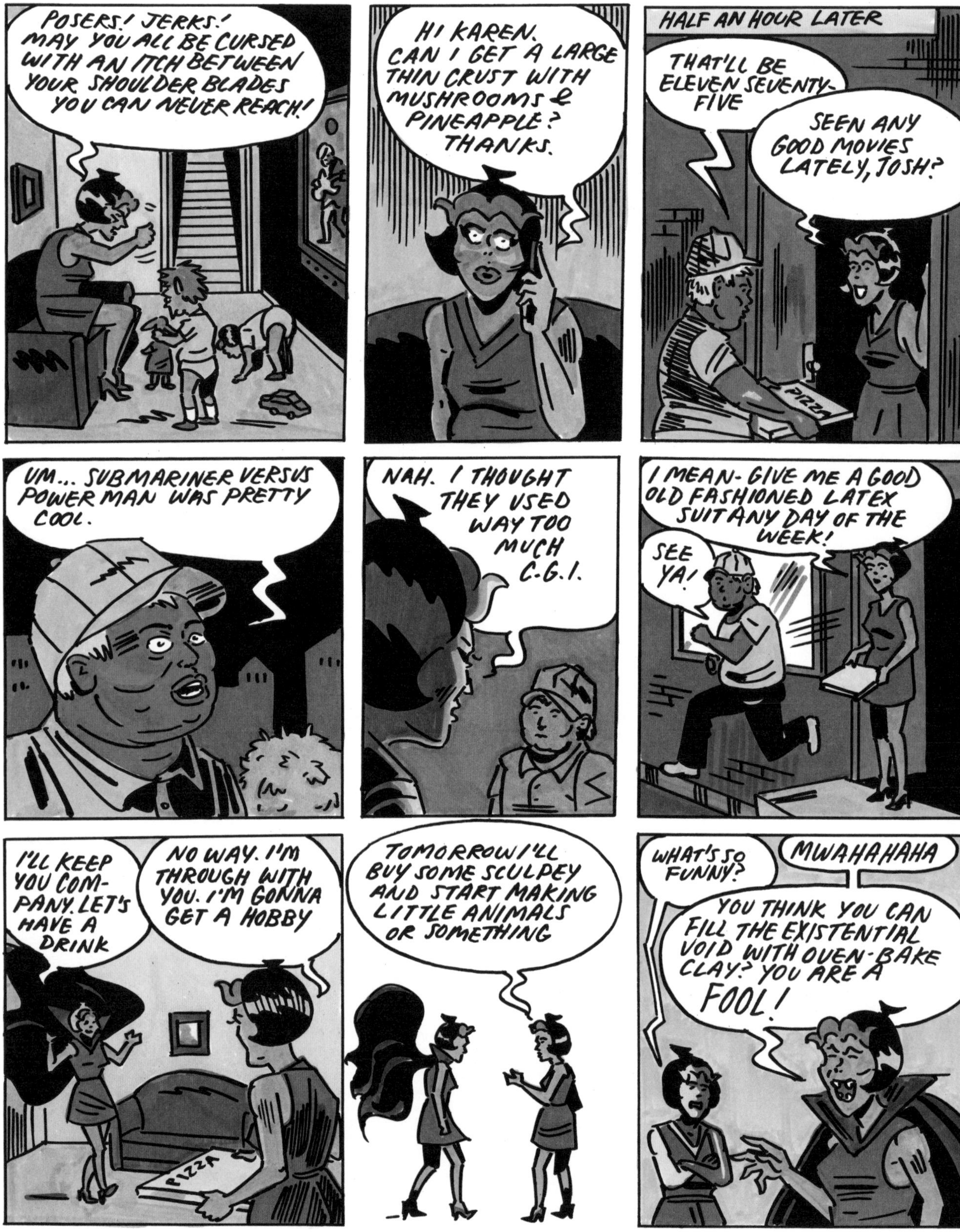
POSERS! JERKS! MAY YOU ALL BE CURSED WITH AN ITCH BETWEEN YOUR SHOULDER BLADES YOU CAN NEVER REACH!
HI KAREN. CAN I GET A LARGE THIN CRUST WITH MUSHROOMS & PINEAPPLE? THANKS.
HALF AN HOUR LATER
THAT'LL BE ELEVEN SEVENTY-FIVE
SEEN ANY GOOD MOVIES LATELY, JOSH?
PIZZA
UM... SUBMARINER VERSUS POWER MAN WAS PRETTY COOL.
NAH. I THOUGHT THEY USED WAY TOO MUCH C.G.I.
I MEAN- GIVE ME A GOOD OLD FASHIONED LATEX SUIT ANY DAY OF THE WEEK!
SEE YA!
I'LL KEEP YOU COMPANY. LET'S HAVE A DRINK
NO WAY. I'M THROUGH WITH YOU. I'M GONNA GET A HOBBY
PIZZA
TOMORROW I'LL BUY SOME SCULPEY AND START MAKING LITTLE ANIMALS OR SOMETHING
WHAT'S SO FUNNY?
MWAHAHAHA
YOU THINK YOU CAN FILL THE EXISTENTIAL VOID WITH OVEN-BAKE CLAY? YOU ARE A FOOL!

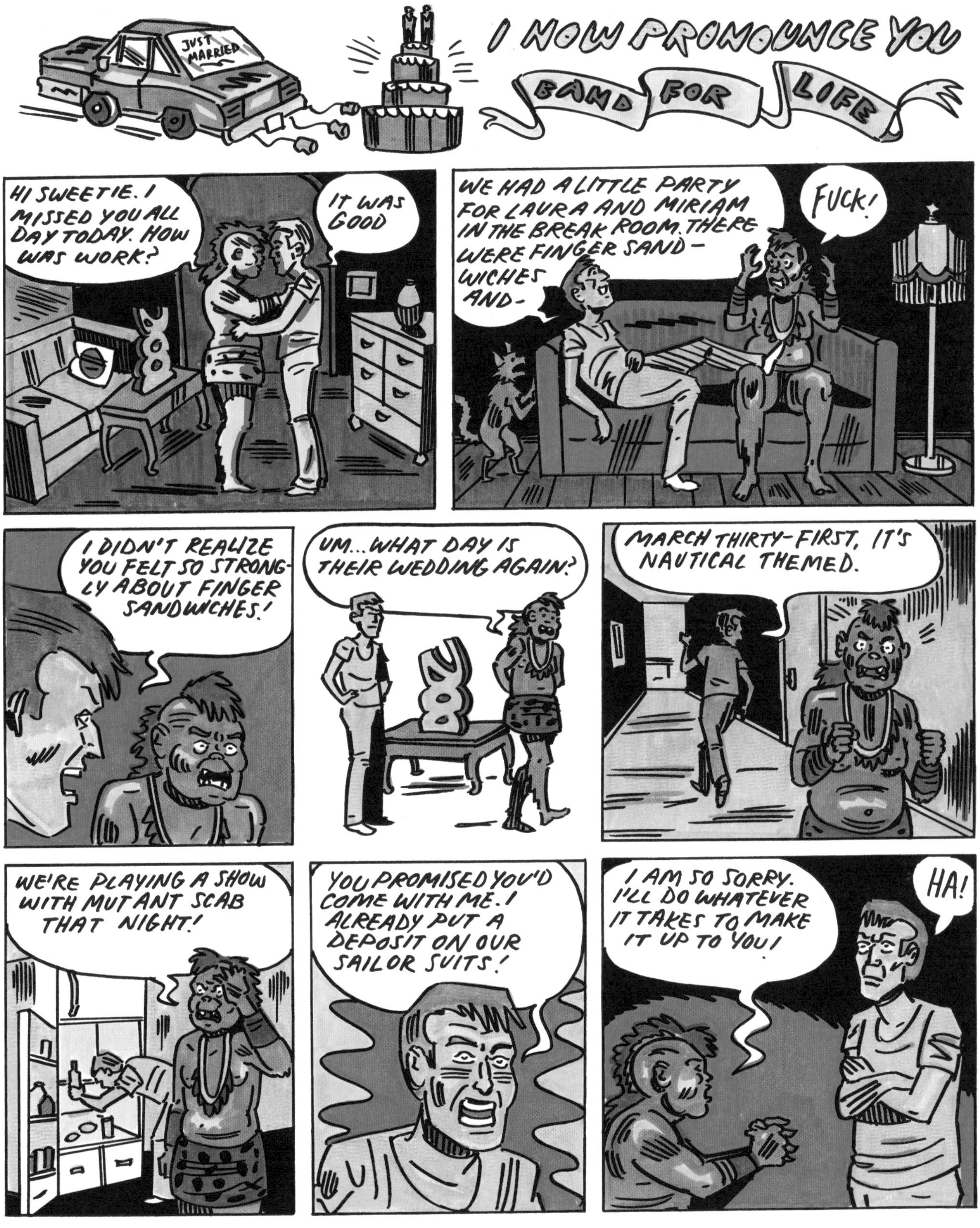
JUST MARRIED
I NOW PRONOUNCE YOU
BAND FOR LIFE
HI SWEETIE. I MISSED YOU ALL DAY TODAY. HOW WAS WORK?
IT WAS GOOD
WE HAD A LITTLE PARTY FOR LAURA AND MIRIAM IN THE BREAK ROOM. THERE WERE FINGER SAND-WICHES AND-
FUCK!
I DIDN'T REALIZE YOU FELT SO STRONGLY ABOUT FINGER SANDWICHES!
UM... WHAT DAY IS THEIR WEDDING AGAIN?
MARCH THIRTY-FIRST, IT'S NAUTICAL THEMED.
WE'RE PLAYING A SHOW WITH MUTANT SCAB THAT NIGHT!
YOU PROMISED YOU'D COME WITH ME. I ALREADY PUT A DEPOSIT ON OUR SAILOR SUITS!
I AM SO SORRY. I'LL DO WHATEVER IT TAKES TO MAKE IT UP TO YOU!
HA!

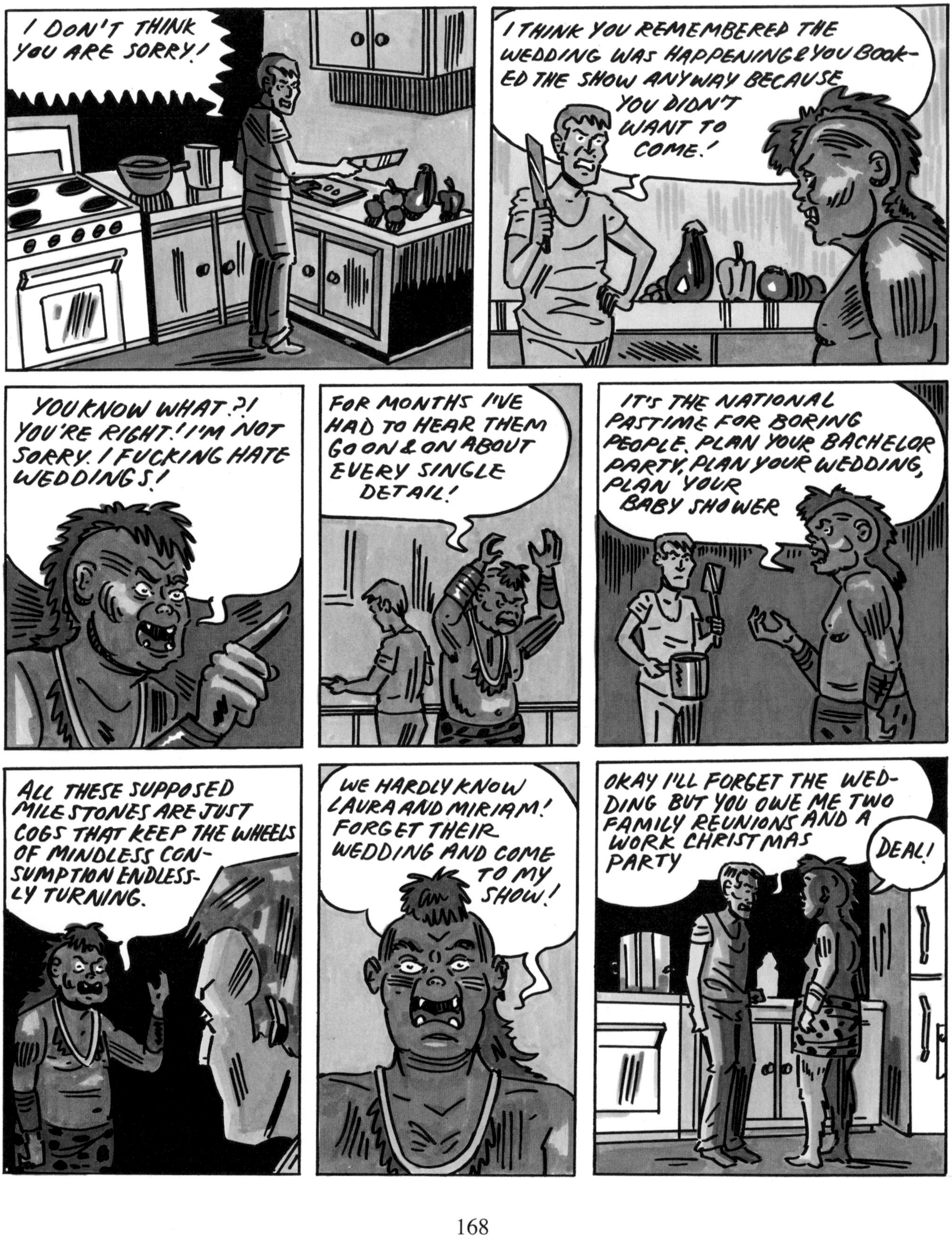
I DON'T THINK YOU ARE SORRY!
I THINK YOU REMEMBERED THE WEDDING WAS HAPPENING & YOU BOOKED THE SHOW ANYWAY BECAUSE YOU DIDN'T WANT TO COME!
YOU KNOW WHAT?! YOU'RE RIGHT! I'M NOT SORRY. I FUCKING HATE WEDDINGS!
FOR MONTHS I'VE HAD TO HEAR THEM GO ON & ON ABOUT EVERY SINGLE DETAIL!
IT'S THE NATIONAL PASTIME FOR BORING PEOPLE. PLAN YOUR BACHELOR PARTY, PLAN YOUR WEDDING, PLAN YOUR BABY SHOWER
ALL THESE SUPPOSED MILESTONES ARE JUST COGS THAT KEEP THE WHEELS OF MINDLESS CONSUMPTION ENDLESSLY TURNING.
WE HARDLY KNOW LAURA AND MIRIAM! FORGET THEIR WEDDING AND COME TO MY SHOW!
OKAY I'LL FORGET THE WEDDING BUT YOU OWE ME TWO FAMILY REUNIONS AND A WORK CHRISTMAS PARTY
DEAL!

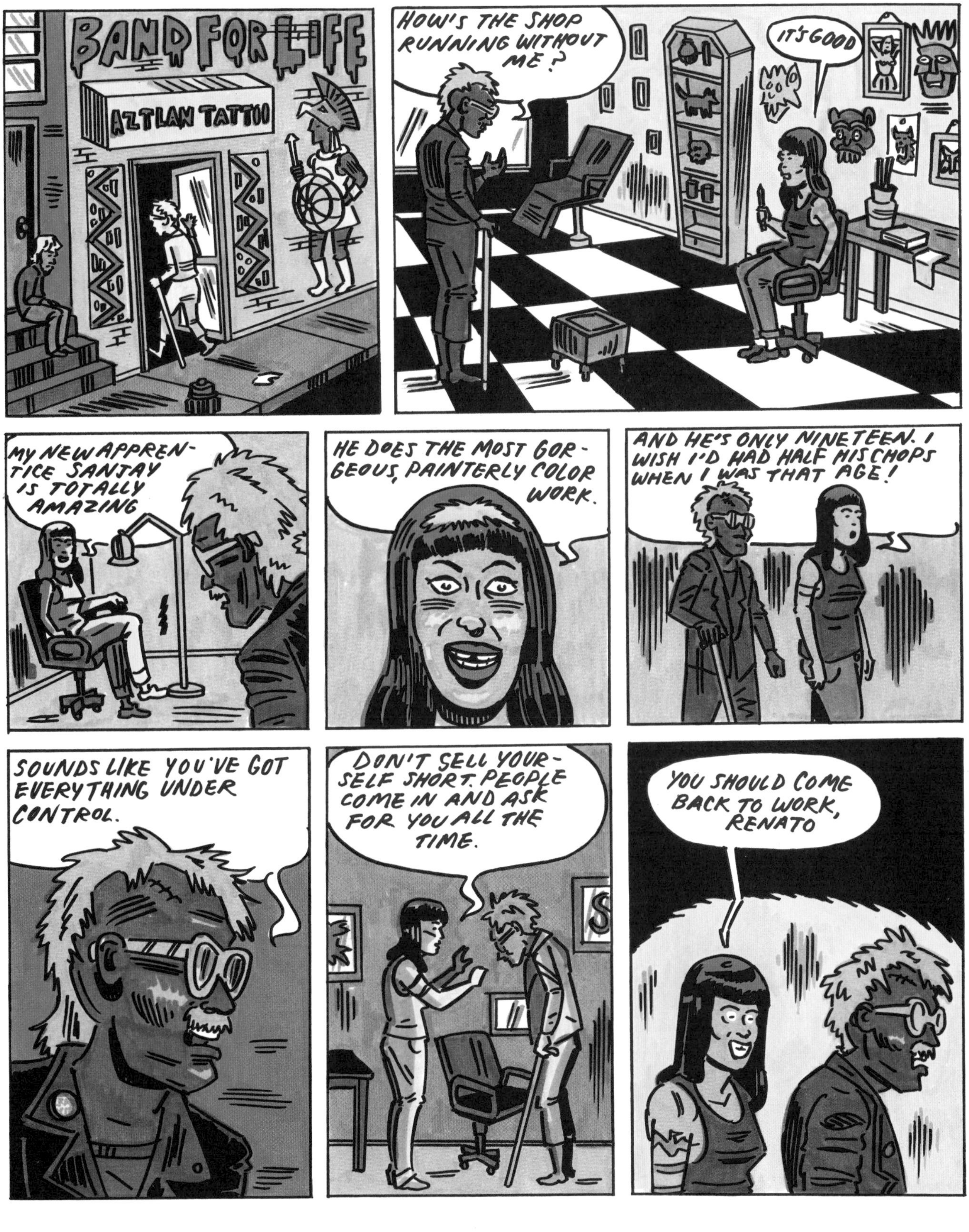
BAND FOR LIFE
AZTLAN TATTOO
HOW'S THE SHOP RUNNING WITHOUT ME?
IT'S GOOD
MY NEW APPRENTICE SANJAY IS TOTALLY AMAZING
HE DOES THE MOST GORGEOUS, PAINTERLY COLOR WORK.
AND HE'S ONLY NINETEEN. I WISH I'D HAD HALF HIS CHOPS WHEN I WAS THAT AGE!
SOUNDS LIKE YOU'VE GOT EVERYTHING UNDER CONTROL.
DON'T SELL YOURSELF SHORT. PEOPLE COME IN AND ASK FOR YOU ALL THE TIME.
YOU SHOULD COME BACK TO WORK, RENATO

I'M TOO RUSTY. I SHOULD DO SOME WORK ON MYSELF TO GET MY CONFIDENCE BACK

YOU CAN PRACTICE ON ME. FINISH UP MY BACK PIECE.

I'M STILL GETTING REALLY INTENSE HEADACHES.

IN THAT CASE YOU COULD ANSWER THE PHONE OR DRAW SOME FLASH.

I'M JUST NOT READY, OKAY?!

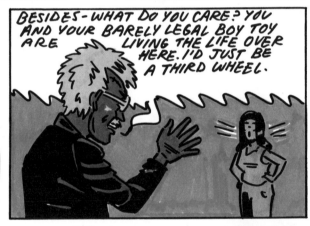

BESIDES— WHAT DO YOU CARE? YOU AND YOUR BARELY LEGAL BOY TOY ARE LIVING THE LIFE OVER HERE. I'D JUST BE A THIRD WHEEL.

IF YOU'RE NOT CAREFUL YOU'RE GONNA END UP LIKE MY NEIGHBOR DAN WHO SITS ON HIS PORCH CRYING, SINGING AND SPITTING INTO A CAN ALL DAY.

I DON'T NEED YOUR PITY, OKAY? YOU DON'T HAVE TO TREAT ME LIKE A CHARITY CASE. IT'S CREEPY.

WOULD YOU PREFER I TREAT YOU WITH BARELY CONCEALED CONTEMPT?

YES!

FINE

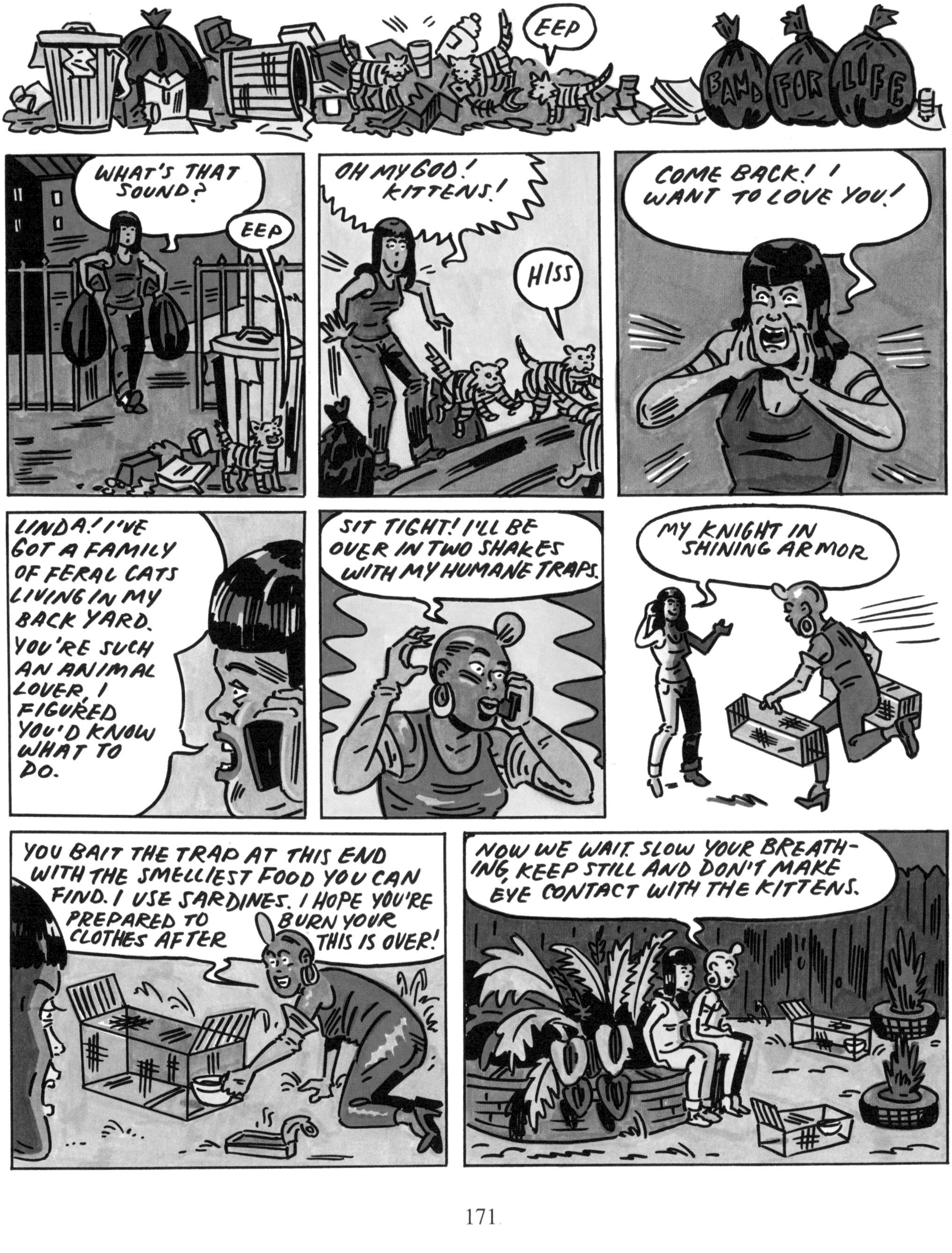
EEP
BAND FOR LIFE
WHAT'S THAT SOUND?
EEP
OH MY GOD! KITTENS!
HISS
COME BACK! I WANT TO LOVE YOU!
LINDA! I'VE GOT A FAMILY OF FERAL CATS LIVING IN MY BACK YARD. YOU'RE SUCH AN ANIMAL LOVER, I FIGURED YOU'D KNOW WHAT TO DO.
SIT TIGHT! I'LL BE OVER IN TWO SHAKES WITH MY HUMANE TRAPS.
MY KNIGHT IN SHINING ARMOR
YOU BAIT THE TRAP AT THIS END WITH THE SMELLIEST FOOD YOU CAN FIND. I USE SARDINES. I HOPE YOU'RE PREPARED TO BURN YOUR CLOTHES AFTER THIS IS OVER!
NOW WE WAIT. SLOW YOUR BREATHING, KEEP STILL AND DON'T MAKE EYE CONTACT WITH THE KITTENS.

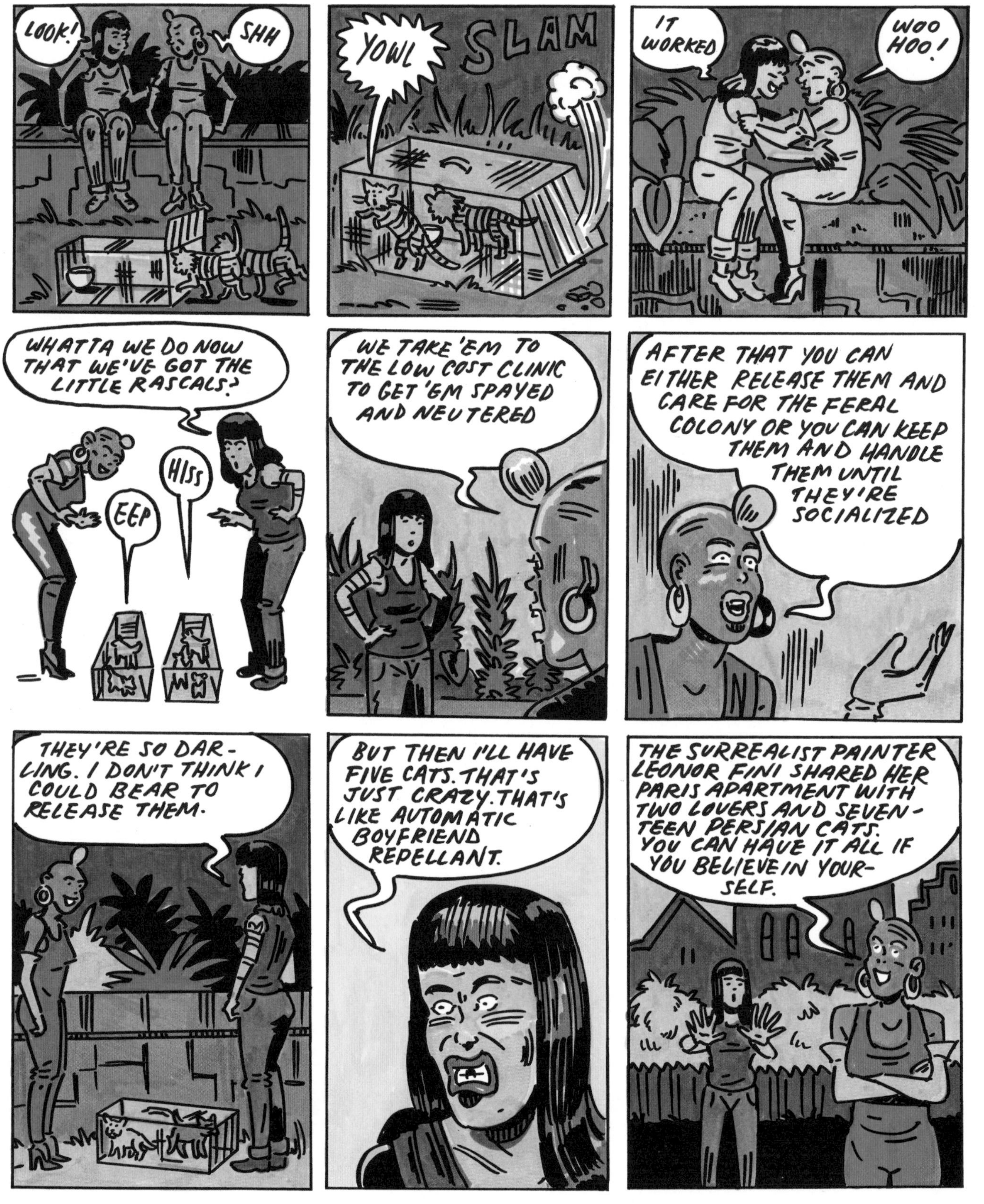
LOOK!
SHH
YOWL
SLAM
IT WORKED
WOO HOO!
WHATTA WE DO NOW THAT WE'VE GOT THE LITTLE RASCALS?
EEP
HISS
WE TAKE 'EM TO THE LOW COST CLINIC TO GET 'EM SPAYED AND NEUTERED
AFTER THAT YOU CAN EITHER RELEASE THEM AND CARE FOR THE FERAL COLONY OR YOU CAN KEEP THEM AND HANDLE THEM UNTIL THEY'RE SOCIALIZED
THEY'RE SO DARLING. I DON'T THINK I COULD BEAR TO RELEASE THEM.
BUT THEN I'LL HAVE FIVE CATS. THAT'S JUST CRAZY. THAT'S LIKE AUTOMATIC BOYFRIEND REPELLANT.
THE SURREALIST PAINTER LEONOR FINI SHARED HER PARIS APARTMENT WITH TWO LOVERS AND SEVENTEEN PERSIAN CATS. YOU CAN HAVE IT ALL IF YOU BELIEVE IN YOURSELF.

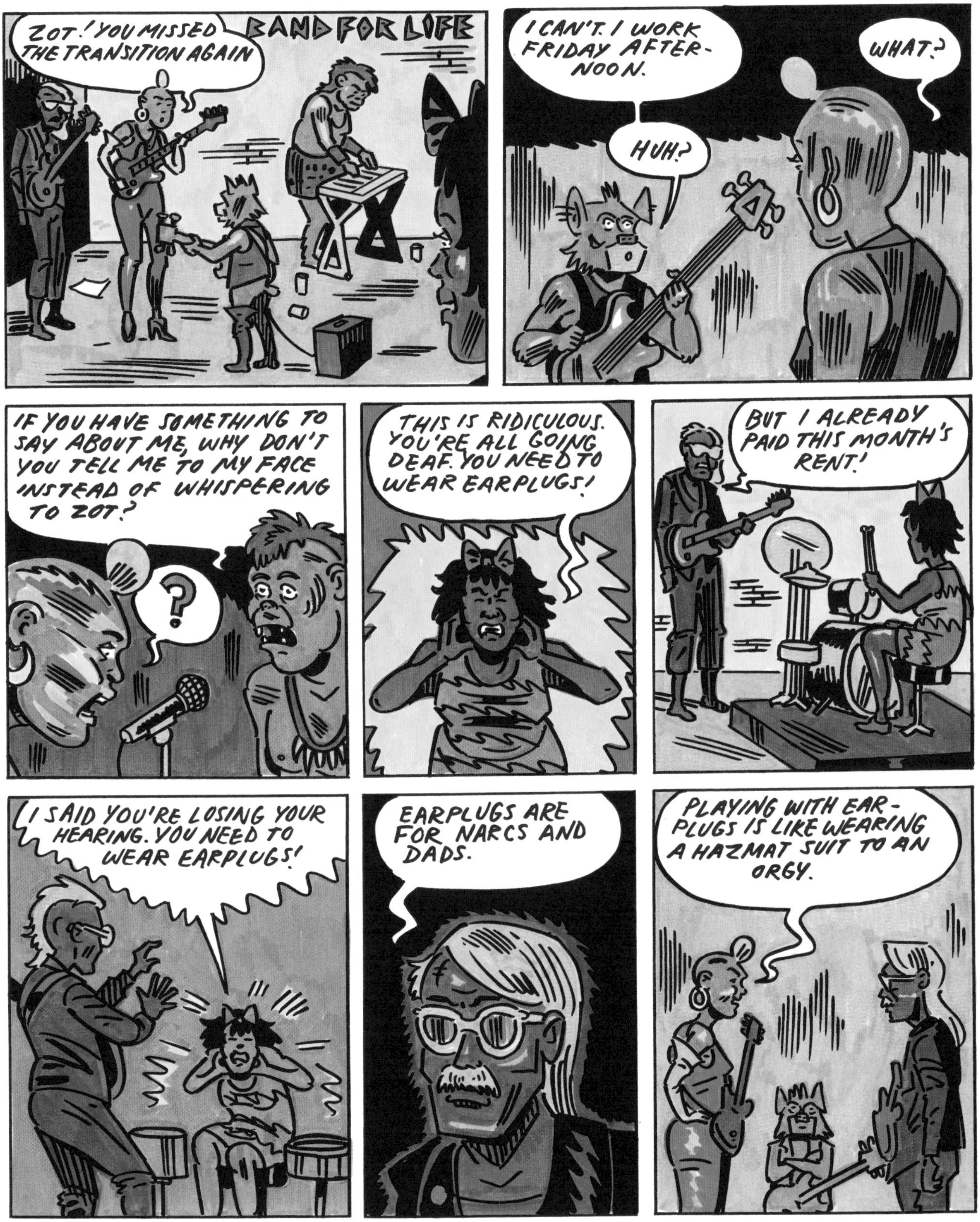
BAND FOR LIFE
ZOT! YOU MISSED THE TRANSITION AGAIN
I CAN'T. I WORK FRIDAY AFTER-NOON.
HUH?
WHAT?
IF YOU HAVE SOMETHING TO SAY ABOUT ME, WHY DON'T YOU TELL ME TO MY FACE INSTEAD OF WHISPERING TO ZOT?
?
THIS IS RIDICULOUS. YOU'RE ALL GOING DEAF. YOU NEED TO WEAR EARPLUGS!
BUT I ALREADY PAID THIS MONTH'S RENT!
I SAID YOU'RE LOSING YOUR HEARING. YOU NEED TO WEAR EARPLUGS!
EARPLUGS ARE FOR NARCS AND DADS.
PLAYING WITH EAR-PLUGS IS LIKE WEARING A HAZMAT SUIT TO AN ORGY.

YOU NUT BARS ARE THINKING IN THE SHORT TERM. WHAT ABOUT WHEN WE'RE OLDER?

I'M STILL COMING TO TERMS WITH THE FACT THAT I'LL PROBABLY LIVE PAST THE AGE OF THIRTY.

IN A LOT OF WAYS I'M THE SAME PERSON I WAS AT TWELVE. MY INTERESTS HAVEN'T REALLY CHANGED.

UH-HUH

IN TENSE SITUATIONS I STILL ACT LIKE A CORNERED, MISERABLE KID. I TALK ABOUT IT A LOT IN THERAPY.

OUR BODIES ARE VESSELS AND SOUND TRAVELS THROUGH US. I WANT TO PRESERVE MY VESSEL SO I CAN BE A CONDUIT FOR AS LONG AS I LIVE.

LEE "SCRATCH" PERRY SAID HE CREATED THE BEAT OF DUB TO MIMIC THE RHYTHM OF THE HUMAN HEART. HE'S ALMOST EIGHTY AND STILL PERFORMING. MAYBE THE MUSIC IS KEEPING HIM ALIVE.

OH WOW MAN, THAT'S ALL REALLY BEAUTIFUL!

RENATO, IS THAT A TEAR IN YOUR EYE?

SURE. WHY NOT? IT'S FIVE O'CLOCK SOMEWHERE, RIGHT?

HUH?

WHAT?

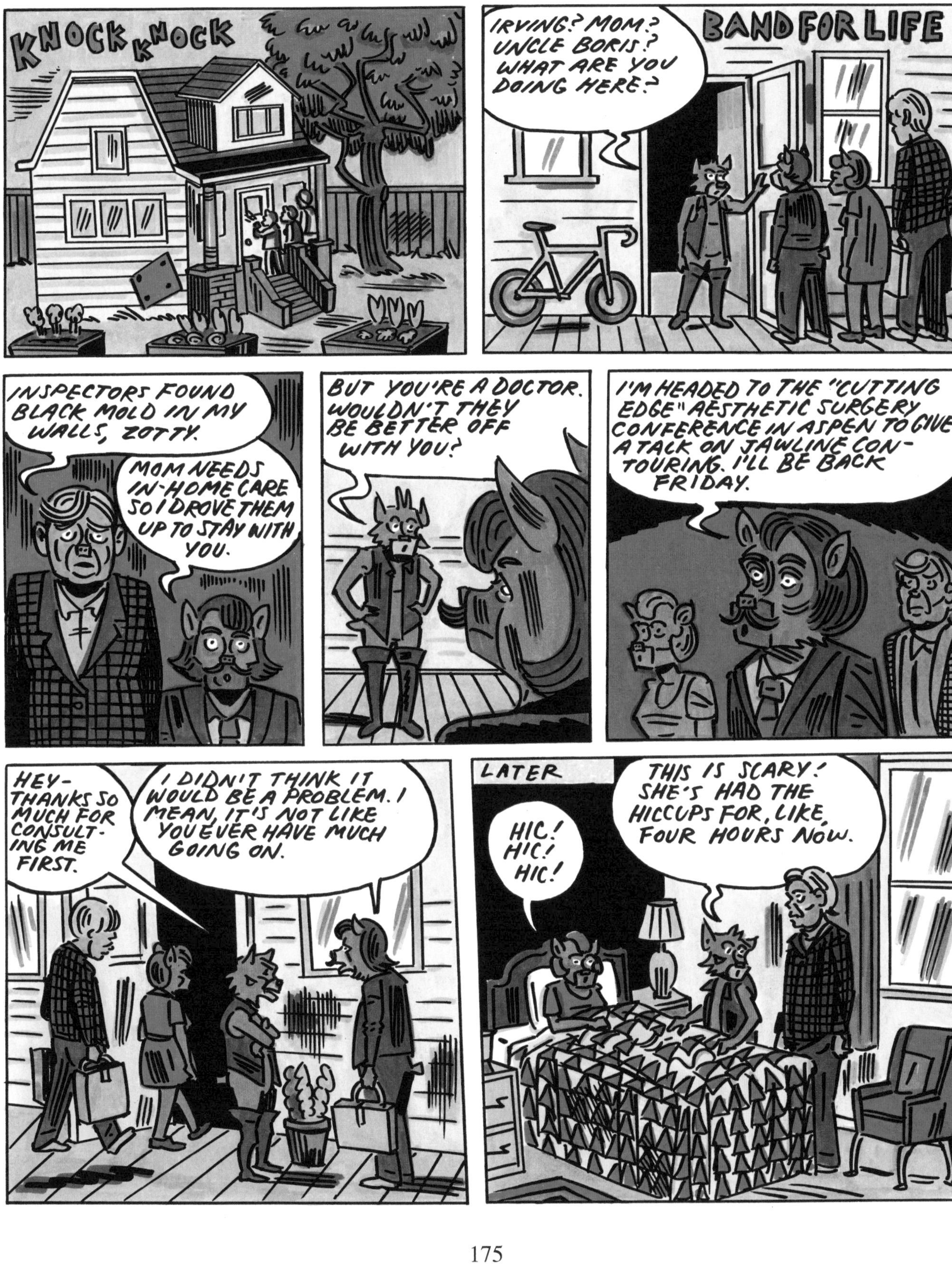

KNOCK KNOCK
BAND FOR LIFE
IRVING? MOM? UNCLE BORIS? WHAT ARE YOU DOING HERE?
INSPECTORS FOUND BLACK MOLD IN MY WALLS, ZOTTY.
MOM NEEDS IN-HOME CARE SO I DROVE THEM UP TO STAY WITH YOU.
BUT YOU'RE A DOCTOR. WOULDN'T THEY BE BETTER OFF WITH YOU?
I'M HEADED TO THE "CUTTING EDGE" AESTHETIC SURGERY CONFERENCE IN ASPEN TO GIVE A TALK ON JAWLINE CONTOURING. I'LL BE BACK FRIDAY.
HEY- THANKS SO MUCH FOR CONSULTING ME FIRST.
I DIDN'T THINK IT WOULD BE A PROBLEM. I MEAN, IT'S NOT LIKE YOU EVER HAVE MUCH GOING ON.
LATER
HIC! HIC! HIC!
THIS IS SCARY! SHE'S HAD THE HICCUPS FOR, LIKE, FOUR HOURS NOW.

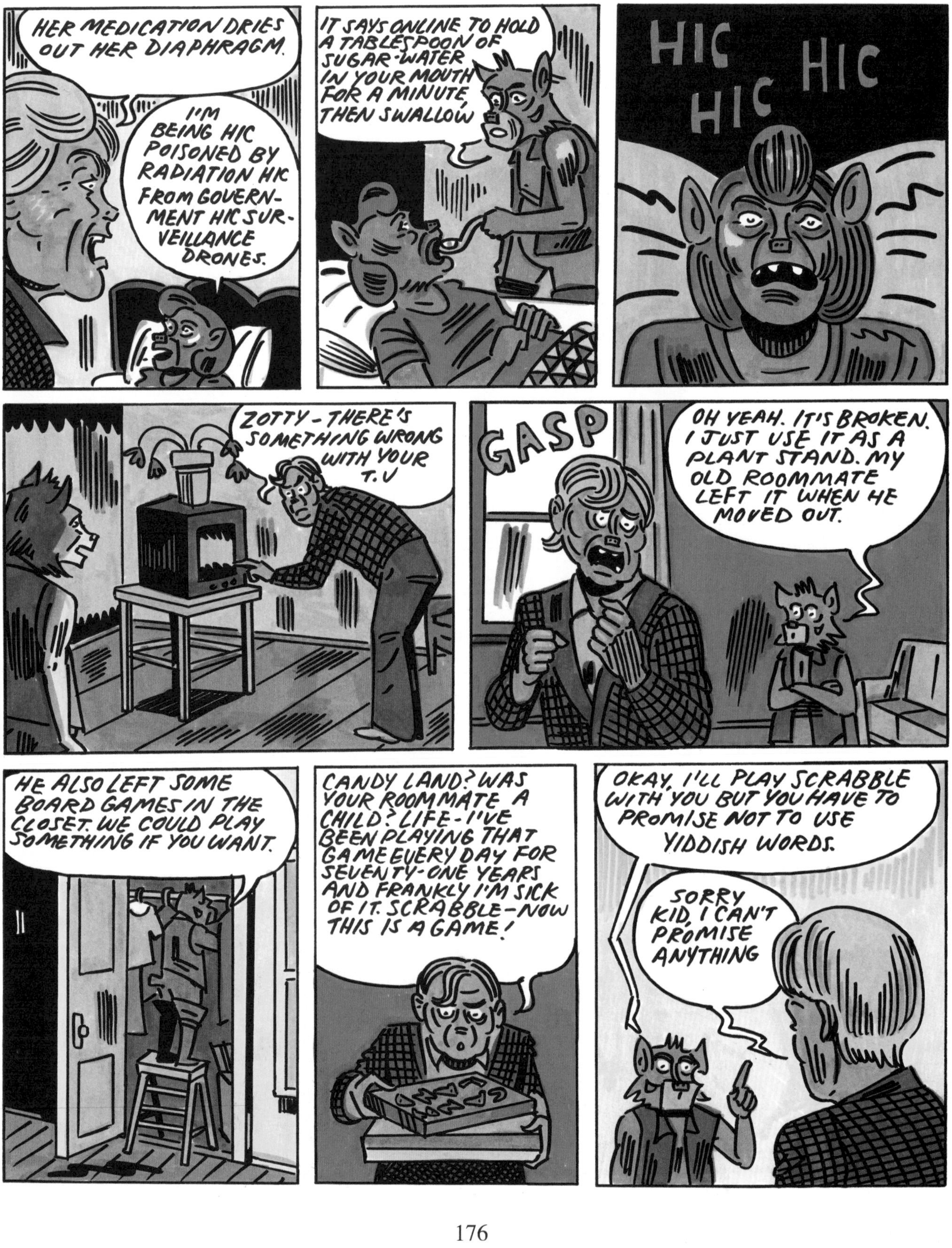
HER MEDICATION DRIES OUT HER DIAPHRAGM.
I'M BEING HIC POISONED BY RADIATION HIC FROM GOVERNMENT HIC SURVEILLANCE DRONES.
IT SAYS ONLINE TO HOLD A TABLESPOON OF SUGAR-WATER IN YOUR MOUTH FOR A MINUTE, THEN SWALLOW
HIC HIC HIC
ZOTTY - THERE'S SOMETHING WRONG WITH YOUR T.V
GASP
OH YEAH. IT'S BROKEN. I JUST USE IT AS A PLANT STAND. MY OLD ROOMMATE LEFT IT WHEN HE MOVED OUT.
HE ALSO LEFT SOME BOARD GAMES IN THE CLOSET. WE COULD PLAY SOMETHING IF YOU WANT.
CANDY LAND? WAS YOUR ROOMMATE A CHILD? LIFE- I'VE BEEN PLAYING THAT GAME EVERY DAY FOR SEVENTY-ONE YEARS AND FRANKLY I'M SICK OF IT. SCRABBLE- NOW THIS IS A GAME!
OKAY, I'LL PLAY SCRABBLE WITH YOU BUT YOU HAVE TO PROMISE NOT TO USE YIDDISH WORDS.
SORRY KID, I CAN'T PROMISE ANYTHING

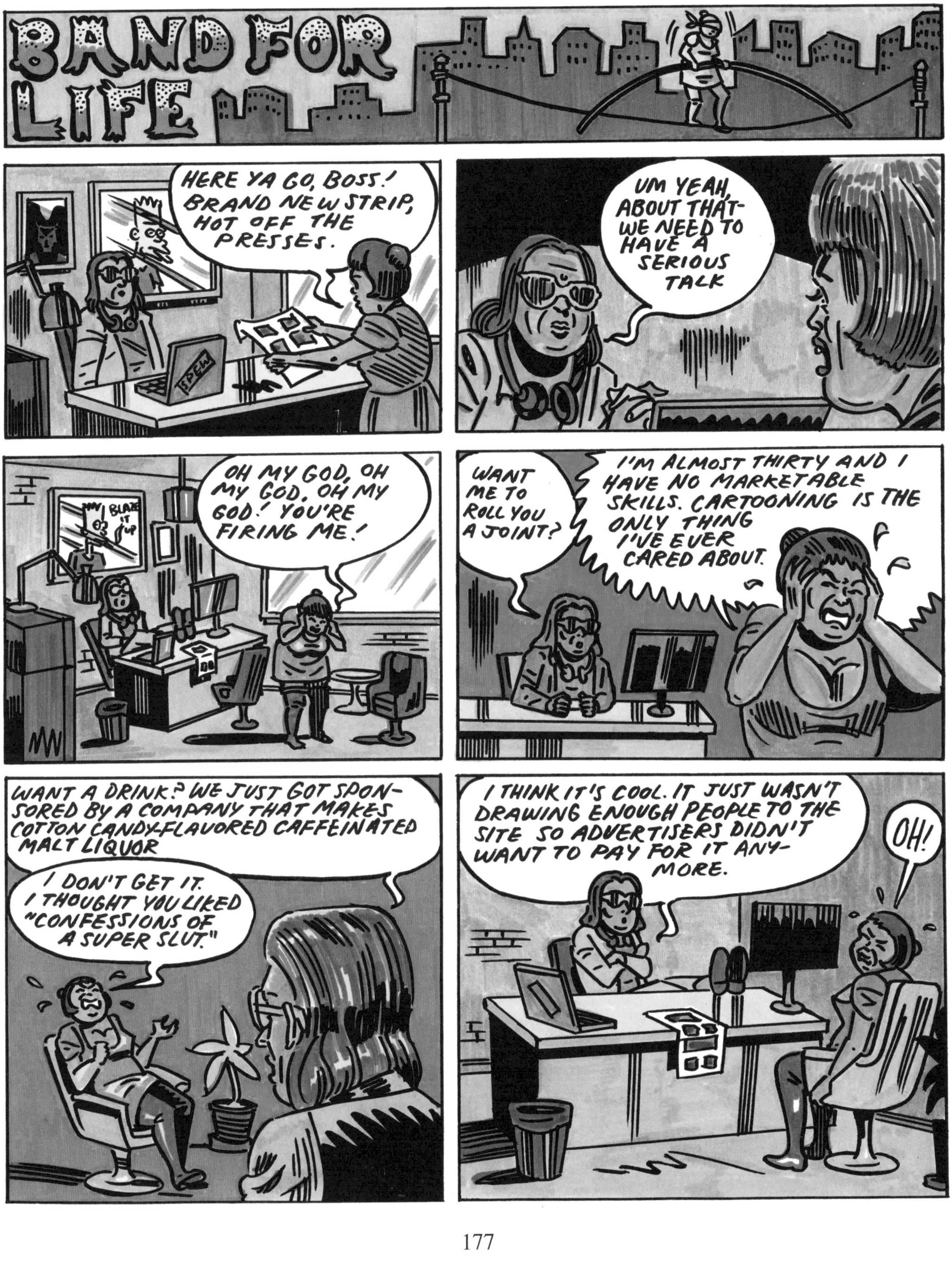
BAND FOR LIFE
HERE YA GO, BOSS! BRAND NEW STRIP, HOT OFF THE PRESSES.
SPEW
UM YEAH, ABOUT THAT- WE NEED TO HAVE A SERIOUS TALK
OH MY GOD, OH MY GOD, OH MY GOD! YOU'RE FIRING ME!
BLAZE IT UP
WANT ME TO ROLL YOU A JOINT?
I'M ALMOST THIRTY AND I HAVE NO MARKETABLE SKILLS. CARTOONING IS THE ONLY THING I'VE EVER CARED ABOUT.
WANT A DRINK? WE JUST GOT SPONSORED BY A COMPANY THAT MAKES COTTON CANDY-FLAVORED CAFFEINATED MALT LIQUOR
I DON'T GET IT. I THOUGHT YOU LIKED "CONFESSIONS OF A SUPER SLUT."
I THINK IT'S COOL. IT JUST WASN'T DRAWING ENOUGH PEOPLE TO THE SITE SO ADVERTISERS DIDN'T WANT TO PAY FOR IT ANYMORE.
OH!

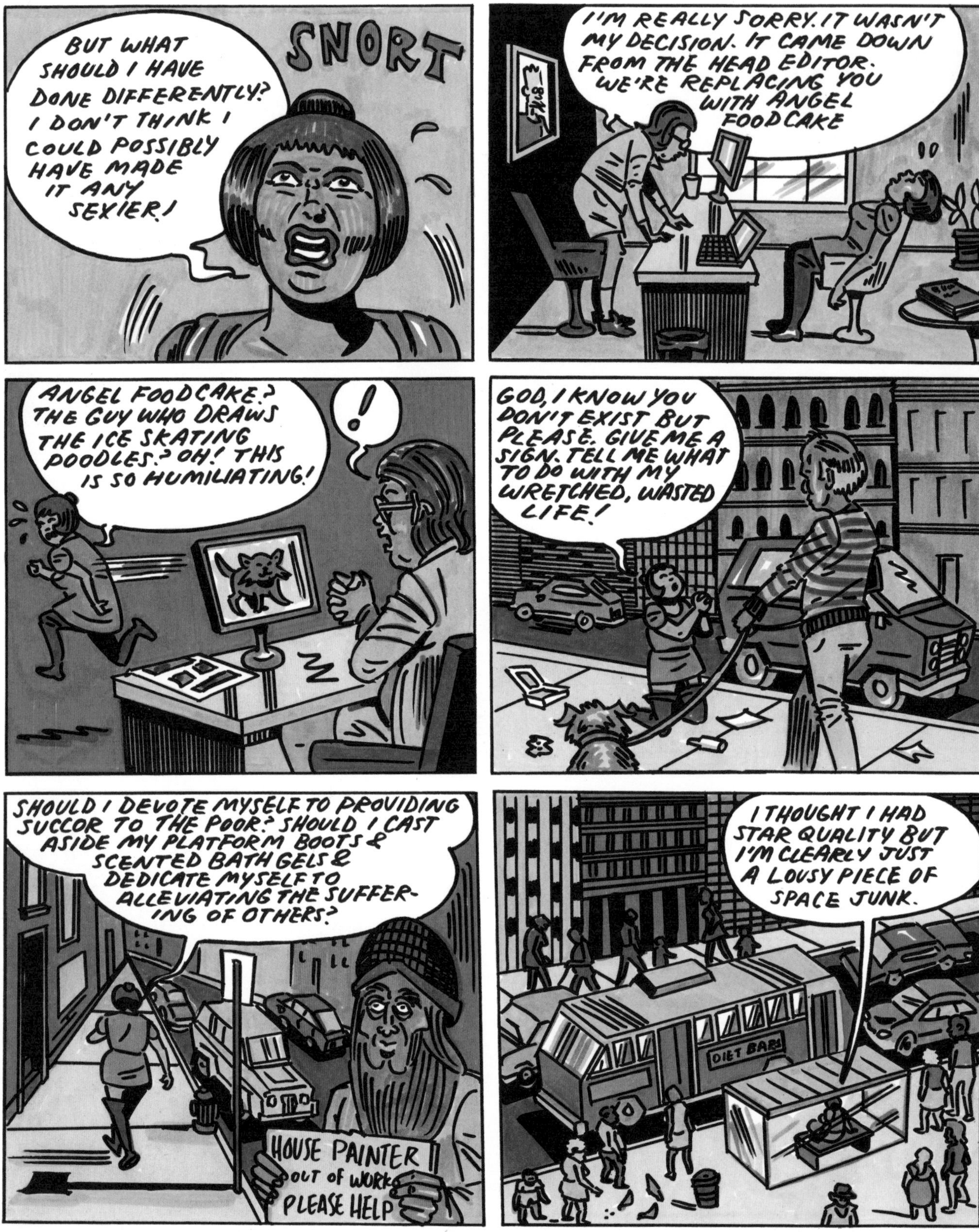
BUT WHAT SHOULD I HAVE DONE DIFFERENTLY? I DON'T THINK I COULD POSSIBLY HAVE MADE IT ANY SEXIER!
SNORT
I'M REALLY SORRY. IT WASN'T MY DECISION. IT CAME DOWN FROM THE HEAD EDITOR. WE'RE REPLACING YOU WITH ANGEL FOODCAKE
ANGEL FOODCAKE? THE GUY WHO DRAWS THE ICE SKATING POODLES? OH! THIS IS SO HUMILIATING!
!
GOD, I KNOW YOU DON'T EXIST BUT PLEASE. GIVE ME A SIGN. TELL ME WHAT TO DO WITH MY WRETCHED, WASTED LIFE!
SHOULD I DEVOTE MYSELF TO PROVIDING SUCCOR TO THE POOR? SHOULD I CAST ASIDE MY PLATFORM BOOTS & SCENTED BATH GELS & DEDICATE MYSELF TO ALLEVIATING THE SUFFERING OF OTHERS?
HOUSE PAINTER OUT OF WORK PLEASE HELP
I THOUGHT I HAD STAR QUALITY BUT I'M CLEARLY JUST A LOUSY PIECE OF SPACE JUNK.
DIET BARS

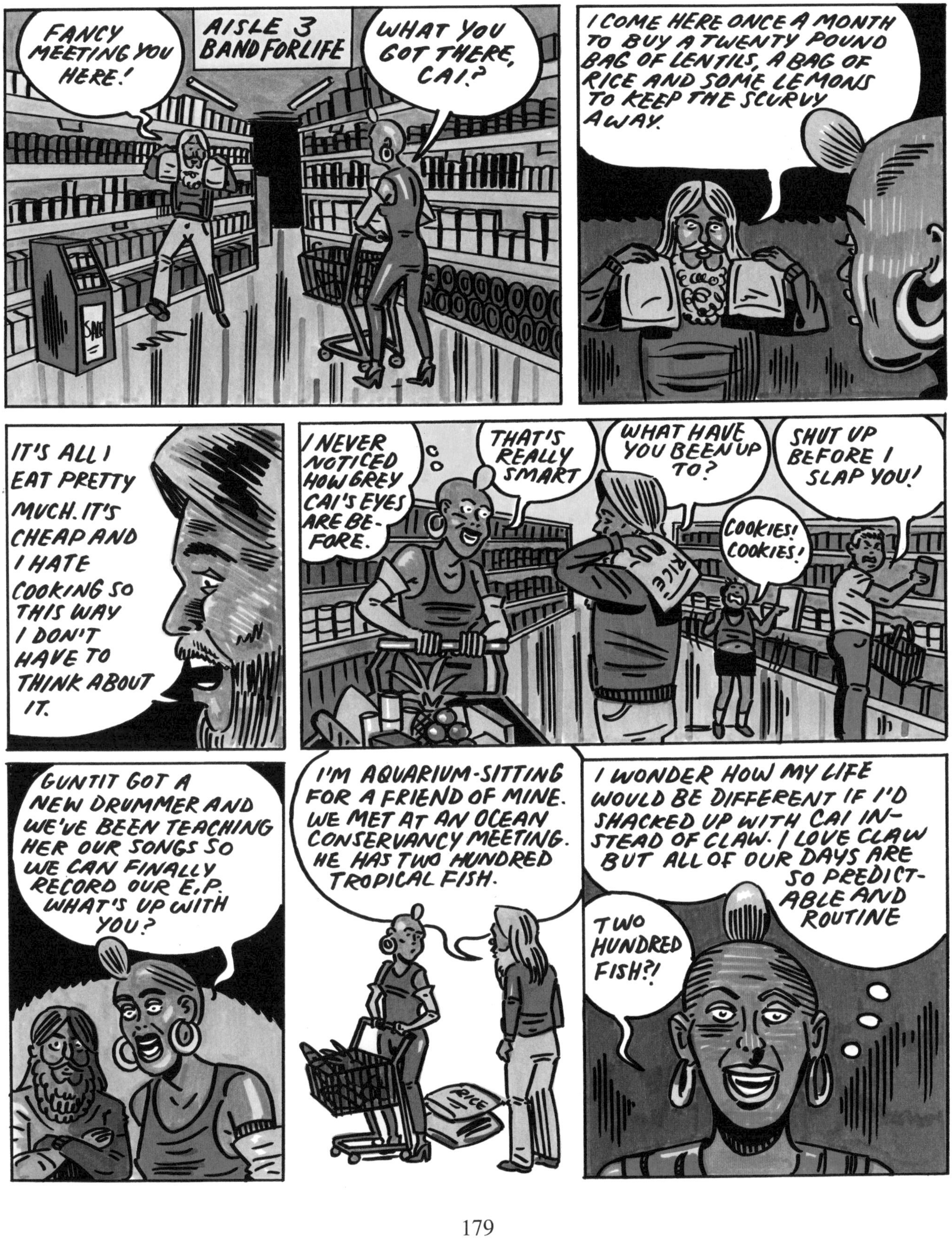
FANCY MEETING YOU HERE!
AISLE 3 BAND FOR LIFE
WHAT YOU GOT THERE, CAI?
I COME HERE ONCE A MONTH TO BUY A TWENTY POUND BAG OF LENTILS, A BAG OF RICE AND SOME LEMONS TO KEEP THE SCURVY AWAY.
IT'S ALL I EAT PRETTY MUCH. IT'S CHEAP AND I HATE COOKING SO THIS WAY I DON'T HAVE TO THINK ABOUT IT.
I NEVER NOTICED HOW GREY CAI'S EYES ARE BEFORE.
THAT'S REALLY SMART
WHAT HAVE YOU BEEN UP TO?
SHUT UP BEFORE I SLAP YOU!
COOKIES! COOKIES!
RICE
GUNTIT GOT A NEW DRUMMER AND WE'VE BEEN TEACHING HER OUR SONGS SO WE CAN FINALLY RECORD OUR E.P. WHAT'S UP WITH YOU?
I'M AQUARIUM-SITTING FOR A FRIEND OF MINE. WE MET AT AN OCEAN CONSERVANCY MEETING. HE HAS TWO HUNDRED TROPICAL FISH.
RICE
I WONDER HOW MY LIFE WOULD BE DIFFERENT IF I'D SHACKED UP WITH CAI INSTEAD OF CLAW. I LOVE CLAW BUT ALL OF OUR DAYS ARE SO PREDICTABLE AND ROUTINE
TWO HUNDRED FISH?!

IT'S INCREDIBLE. HE HAS EELS, FLATFISH, THESE GORGEOUS ORANGE & WHITE CLOWN FISH...

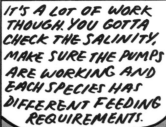

IT'S A LOT OF WORK THOUGH. YOU GOTTA CHECK THE SALINITY, MAKE SURE THE PUMPS ARE WORKING AND EACH SPECIES HAS DIFFERENT FEEDING REQUIREMENTS.

I WOULD NEVER WANT THAT KIND OF COMMITMENT LONG TERM.

RIGHT. CAI'S ALLERGIC TO COMMITMENT. THAT'S WHY YOU'D BE A LOUSY MATCH.

SOUNDS LIKE A LOT OF WORK!

CAI'S SO SELF-FOCUSED. IF I WERE WITH HIM I'D HAVE TO PUT MY OWN GOALS ASIDE. AND IF WE WERE ALWAYS MOVING I WOULDN'T BE ABLE TO KEEP THE BAND TOGETHER.

HOW'S CLAW?

CLAW? HE'S GREAT. WE'VE NEVER BEEN HAPPIER. HE'S DOING SO WELL. REALLY REALLY WELL

CLAW SUPPORTS ME, EVEN AFTER SEEING ME AT MY WORST. AND MY WORST IS WORSE THAN OTHER PEOPLES' WORST.

GLUTEN FREE CAT LITTER

HEY- I'D BETTER GO. BUT YOU SHOULD COME HANG OUT WITH ME AND THE FISH SOMETIME.

SALE

LISTEN HERE BUSTER! ONE TIME, WHEN I HAD THE STOMACH FLU, CLAW SPENT AN ENTIRE EVENING CLEANING A PUKE STAIN OUT OF MY FAVORITE DRESS WITH SALT AND A TOOTHBRUSH. SO IT WOULD TAKE MORE THAN A FEW CLOWNFISH TO GET IN MY PANTS

WHAT?!

LOW FAT TAMPONS

LOW SODIUM SALT

SALE

180

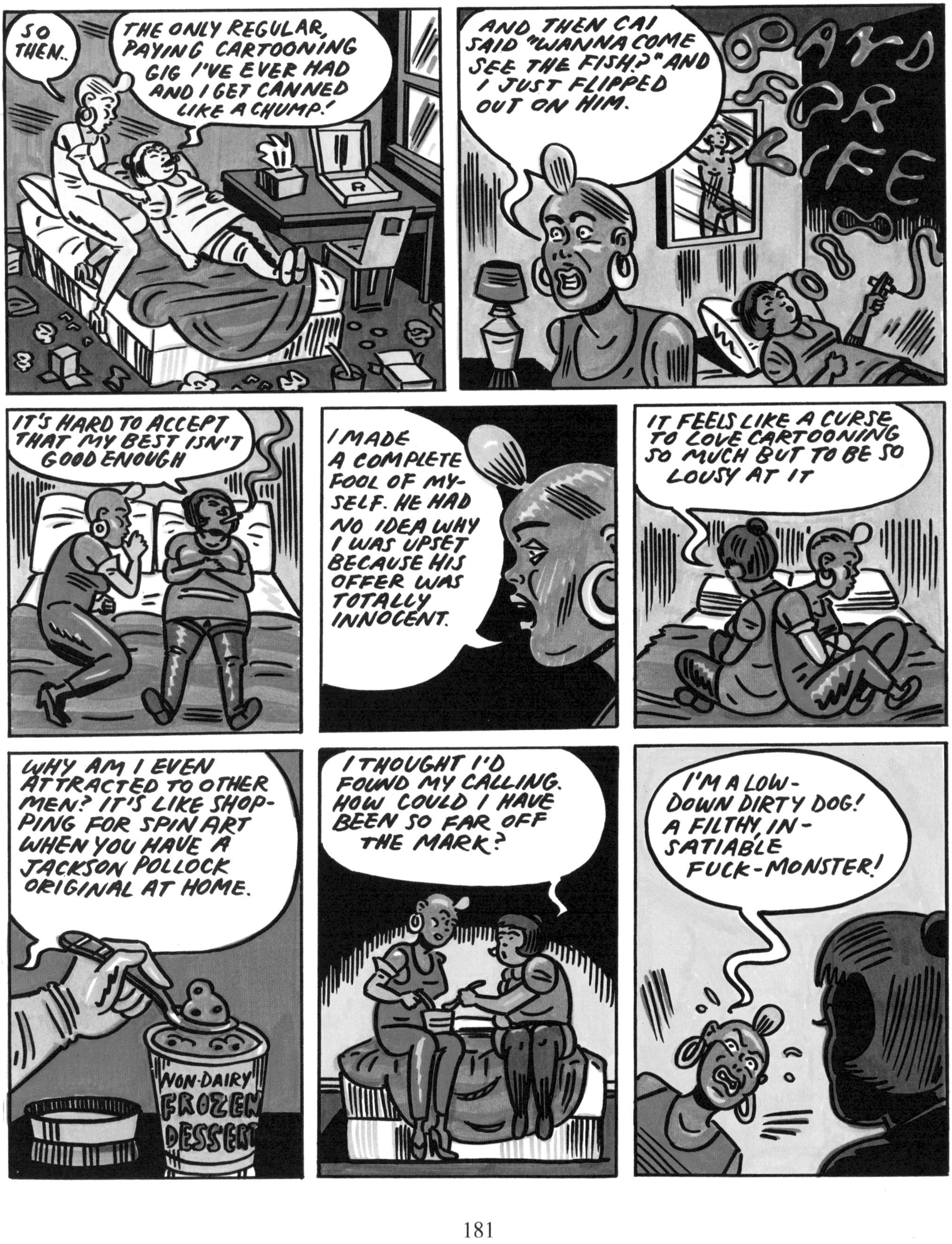
SO THEN..
THE ONLY REGULAR, PAYING CARTOONING GIG I'VE EVER HAD AND I GET CANNED LIKE A CHUMP!
AND THEN CAI SAID "WANNA COME SEE THE FISH?" AND I JUST FLIPPED OUT ON HIM.
PAID FOR LIFE
IT'S HARD TO ACCEPT THAT MY BEST ISN'T GOOD ENOUGH
I MADE A COMPLETE FOOL OF MY-SELF. HE HAD NO IDEA WHY I WAS UPSET BECAUSE HIS OFFER WAS TOTALLY INNOCENT.
IT FEELS LIKE A CURSE TO LOVE CARTOONING SO MUCH BUT TO BE SO LOUSY AT IT
WHY AM I EVEN ATTRACTED TO OTHER MEN? IT'S LIKE SHOP-PING FOR SPIN ART WHEN YOU HAVE A JACKSON POLLOCK ORIGINAL AT HOME.
NON-DAIRY FROZEN DESSERT
I THOUGHT I'D FOUND MY CALLING. HOW COULD I HAVE BEEN SO FAR OFF THE MARK?
I'M A LOW-DOWN DIRTY DOG! A FILTHY, IN-SATIABLE FUCK-MONSTER!

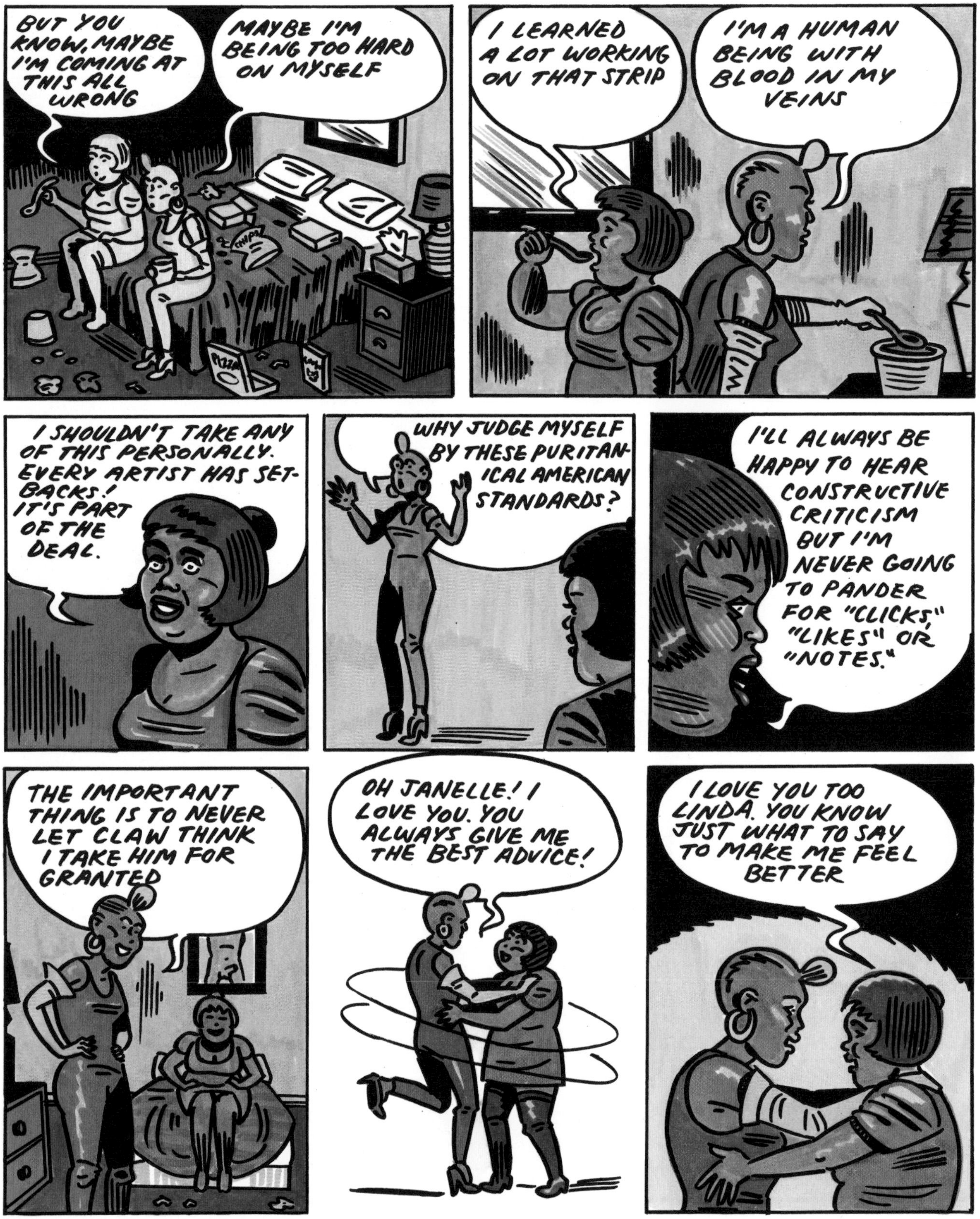

BUT YOU KNOW, MAYBE I'M COMING AT THIS ALL WRONG
MAYBE I'M BEING TOO HARD ON MYSELF
PIZZA
I LEARNED A LOT WORKING ON THAT STRIP
I'M A HUMAN BEING WITH BLOOD IN MY VEINS
I SHOULDN'T TAKE ANY OF THIS PERSONALLY. EVERY ARTIST HAS SET-BACKS! IT'S PART OF THE DEAL.
WHY JUDGE MYSELF BY THESE PURITAN-ICAL AMERICAN STANDARDS?
I'LL ALWAYS BE HAPPY TO HEAR CONSTRUCTIVE CRITICISM BUT I'M NEVER GOING TO PANDER FOR "CLICKS," "LIKES" OR "NOTES."
THE IMPORTANT THING IS TO NEVER LET CLAW THINK I TAKE HIM FOR GRANTED
OH JANELLE! I LOVE YOU. YOU ALWAYS GIVE ME THE BEST ADVICE!
I LOVE YOU TOO LINDA. YOU KNOW JUST WHAT TO SAY TO MAKE ME FEEL BETTER

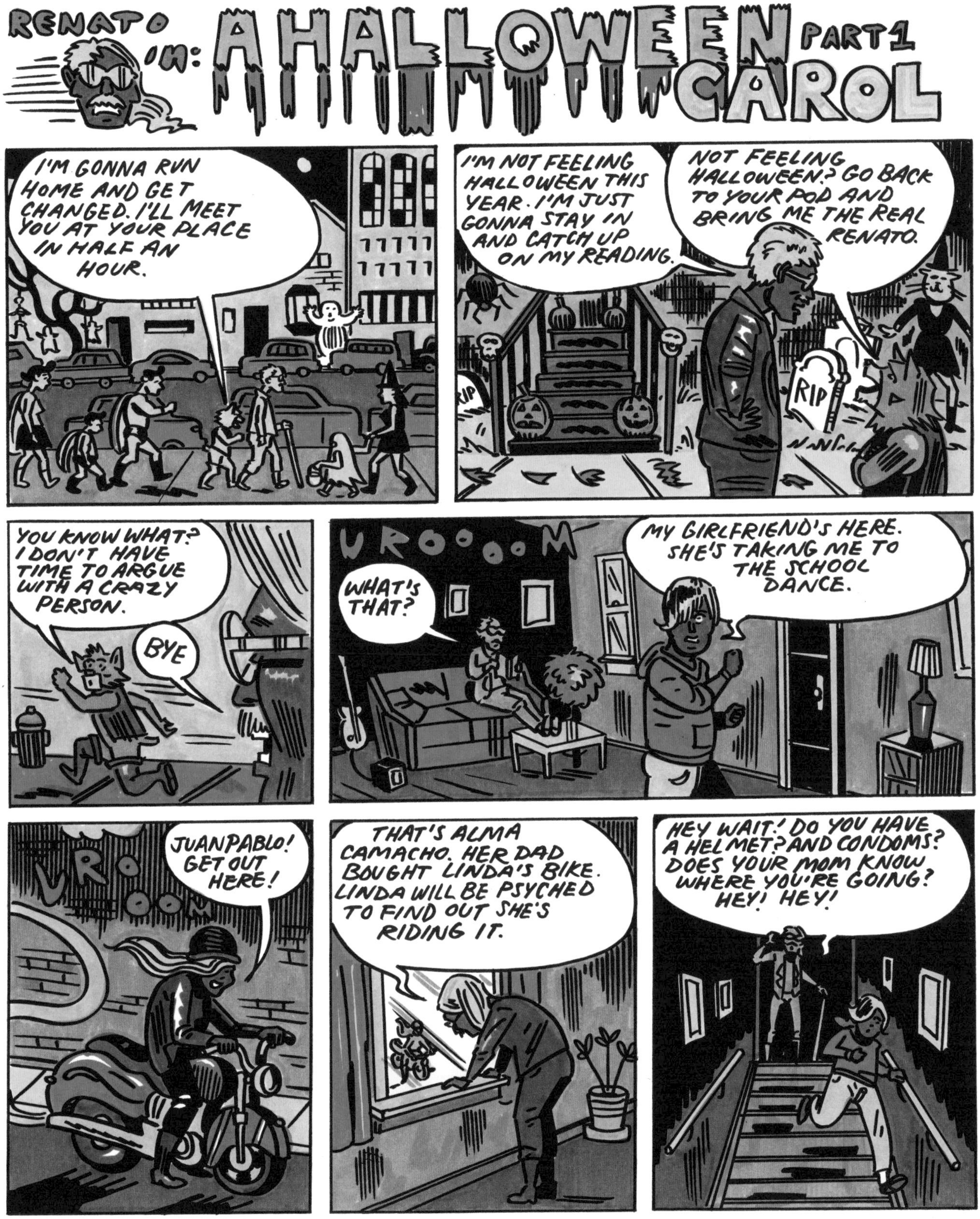
RENATO IN: A HALLOWEEN CAROL PART 1
I'M GONNA RUN HOME AND GET CHANGED. I'LL MEET YOU AT YOUR PLACE IN HALF AN HOUR.
I'M NOT FEELING HALLOWEEN THIS YEAR. I'M JUST GONNA STAY IN AND CATCH UP ON MY READING.
NOT FEELING HALLOWEEN? GO BACK TO YOUR POD AND BRING ME THE REAL RENATO.
RIP
RIP
YOU KNOW WHAT? I DON'T HAVE TIME TO ARGUE WITH A CRAZY PERSON.
BYE
UROOOOM
WHAT'S THAT?
MY GIRLFRIEND'S HERE. SHE'S TAKING ME TO THE SCHOOL DANCE.
UROOON
JUANPABLO! GET OUT HERE!
THAT'S ALMA CAMACHO. HER DAD BOUGHT LINDA'S BIKE. LINDA WILL BE PSYCHED TO FIND OUT SHE'S RIDING IT.
HEY WAIT! DO YOU HAVE A HELMET? AND CONDOMS? DOES YOUR MOM KNOW WHERE YOU'RE GOING? HEY! HEY!

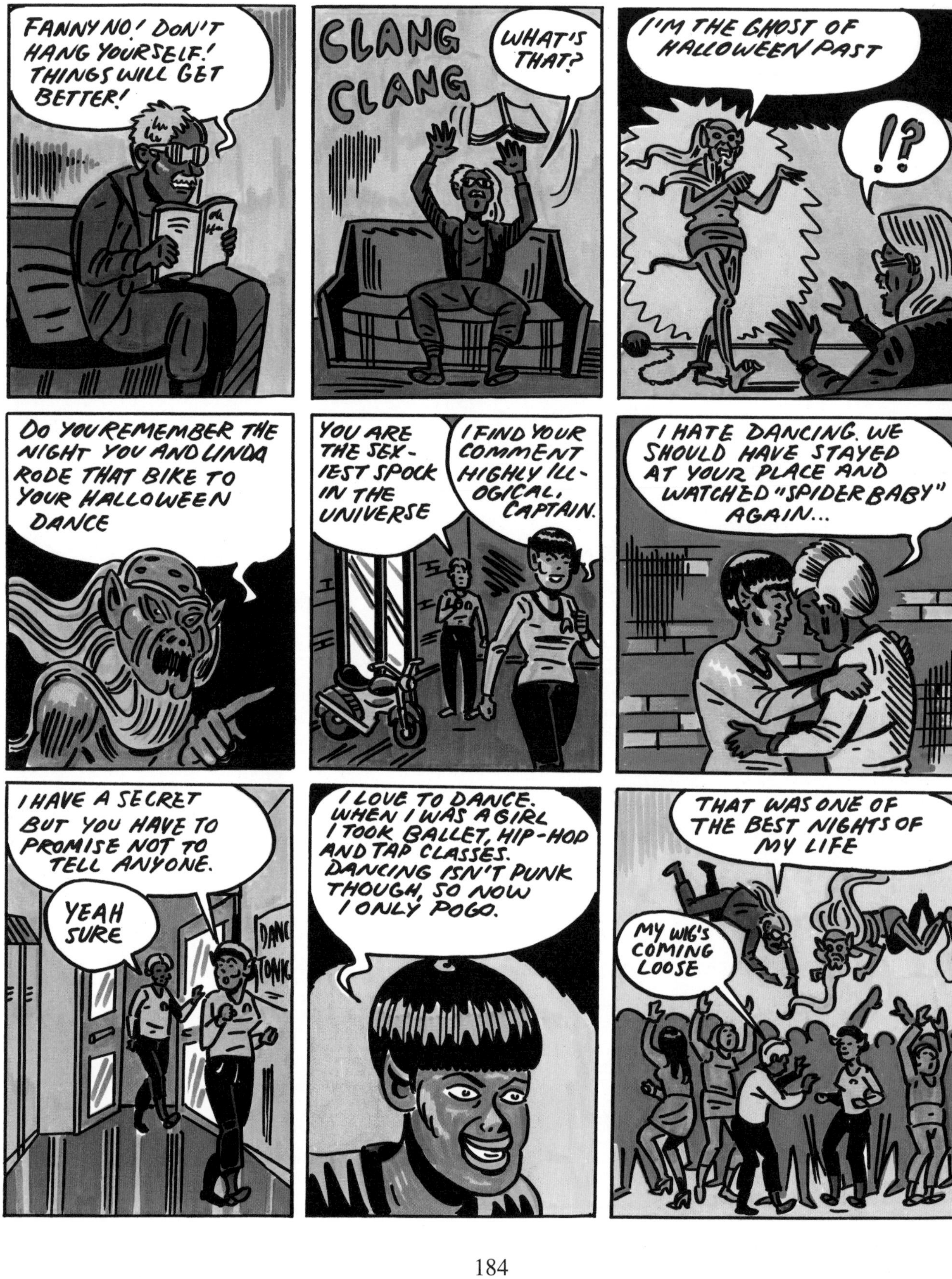
FANNY NO! DON'T HANG YOURSELF! THINGS WILL GET BETTER!
CLANG CLANG
WHAT'S THAT?
I'M THE GHOST OF HALLOWEEN PAST
!?
DO YOU REMEMBER THE NIGHT YOU AND LINDA RODE THAT BIKE TO YOUR HALLOWEEN DANCE
YOU ARE THE SEXIEST SPOCK IN THE UNIVERSE
I FIND YOUR COMMENT HIGHLY ILLOGICAL, CAPTAIN.
I HATE DANCING. WE SHOULD HAVE STAYED AT YOUR PLACE AND WATCHED "SPIDER BABY" AGAIN...
I HAVE A SECRET BUT YOU HAVE TO PROMISE NOT TO TELL ANYONE.
YEAH SURE
DANC
TONIC
I LOVE TO DANCE. WHEN I WAS A GIRL I TOOK BALLET, HIP-HOP AND TAP CLASSES. DANCING ISN'T PUNK THOUGH, SO NOW I ONLY POGO.
THAT WAS ONE OF THE BEST NIGHTS OF MY LIFE
MY WIG'S COMING LOOSE

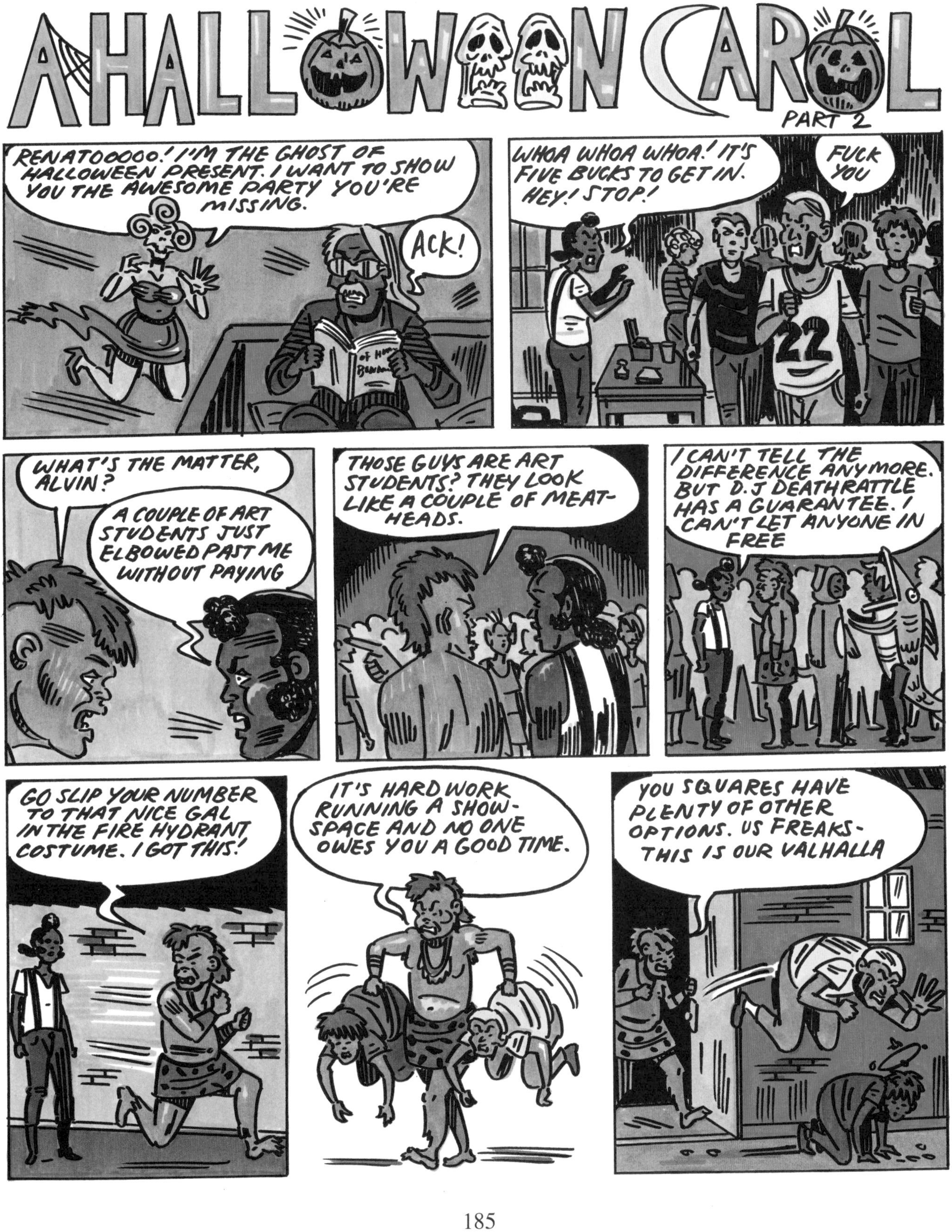

A HALLOWEEN CAROL
PART 2
RENATOOOOO! I'M THE GHOST OF HALLOWEEN PRESENT. I WANT TO SHOW YOU THE AWESOME PARTY YOU'RE MISSING.
ACK!
WHOA WHOA WHOA! IT'S FIVE BUCKS TO GET IN. HEY! STOP!
FUCK YOU
22
WHAT'S THE MATTER, ALVIN?
A COUPLE OF ART STUDENTS JUST ELBOWED PAST ME WITHOUT PAYING
THOSE GUYS ARE ART STUDENTS? THEY LOOK LIKE A COUPLE OF MEAT-HEADS.
I CAN'T TELL THE DIFFERENCE ANYMORE. BUT D.J DEATHRATTLE HAS A GUARANTEE. I CAN'T LET ANYONE IN FREE
GO SLIP YOUR NUMBER TO THAT NICE GAL IN THE FIRE HYDRANT COSTUME. I GOT THIS!
IT'S HARD WORK RUNNING A SHOW-SPACE AND NO ONE OWES YOU A GOOD TIME.
YOU SQUARES HAVE PLENTY OF OTHER OPTIONS. US FREAKS- THIS IS OUR VALHALLA

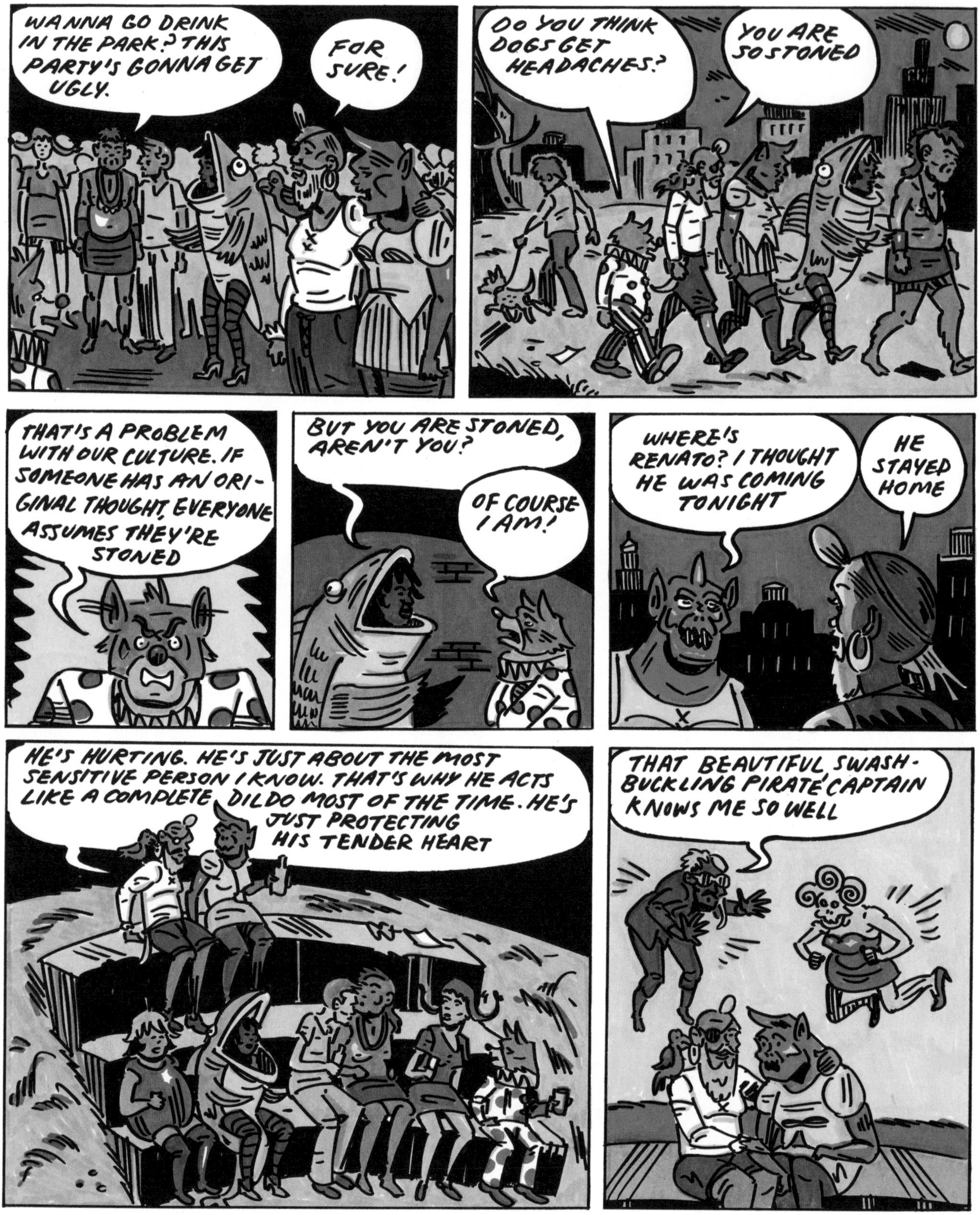
WANNA GO DRINK IN THE PARK? THIS PARTY'S GONNA GET UGLY.
FOR SURE!
DO YOU THINK DOGS GET HEADACHES?
YOU ARE SO STONED
THAT'S A PROBLEM WITH OUR CULTURE. IF SOMEONE HAS AN ORIGINAL THOUGHT, EVERYONE ASSUMES THEY'RE STONED
BUT YOU ARE STONED, AREN'T YOU?
OF COURSE I AM!
WHERE'S RENATO? I THOUGHT HE WAS COMING TONIGHT
HE STAYED HOME
HE'S HURTING. HE'S JUST ABOUT THE MOST SENSITIVE PERSON I KNOW. THAT'S WHY HE ACTS LIKE A COMPLETE DILDO MOST OF THE TIME. HE'S JUST PROTECTING HIS TENDER HEART
THAT BEAUTIFUL SWASH-BUCKLING PIRATE CAPTAIN KNOWS ME SO WELL

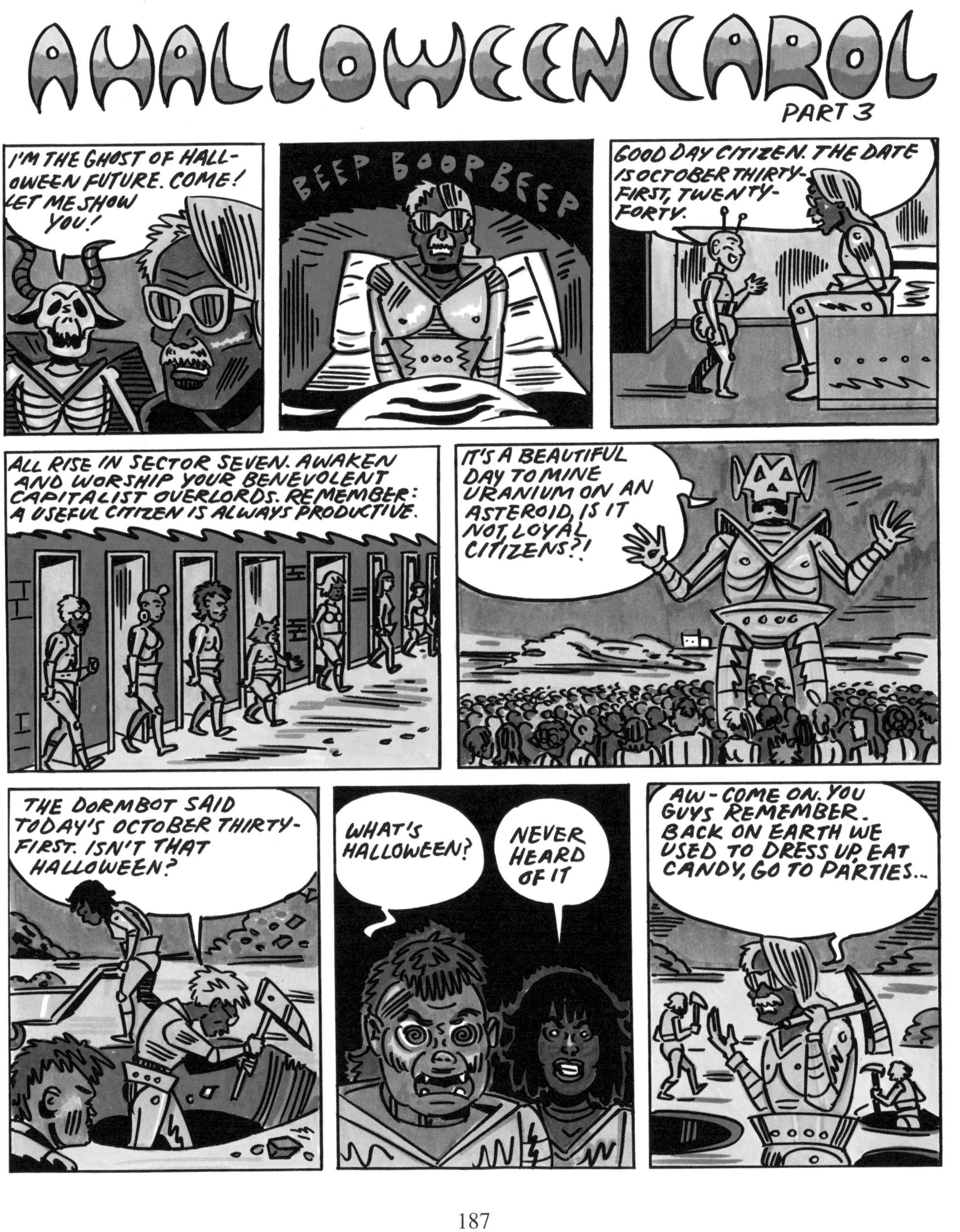
A HALLOWEEN CAROL
PART 3
I'M THE GHOST OF HALLOWEEN FUTURE. COME! LET ME SHOW YOU!
BEEP BOOP BEEP
GOOD DAY CITIZEN. THE DATE IS OCTOBER THIRTY-FIRST, TWENTY-FORTY.
ALL RISE IN SECTOR SEVEN. AWAKEN AND WORSHIP YOUR BENEVOLENT CAPITALIST OVERLORDS. REMEMBER: A USEFUL CITIZEN IS ALWAYS PRODUCTIVE.
IT'S A BEAUTIFUL DAY TO MINE URANIUM ON AN ASTEROID, IS IT NOT, LOYAL CITIZENS?!
THE DORMBOT SAID TODAY'S OCTOBER THIRTY-FIRST. ISN'T THAT HALLOWEEN?
WHAT'S HALLOWEEN?
NEVER HEARD OF IT
AW-COME ON. YOU GUYS REMEMBER. BACK ON EARTH WE USED TO DRESS UP, EAT CANDY, GO TO PARTIES...

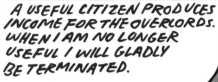

A USEFUL CITIZEN PRODUCES INCOME FOR THE OVERLORDS. WHEN I AM NO LONGER USEFUL I WILL GLADLY BE TERMINATED.

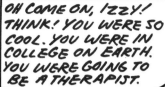

OH COME ON, IZZY! THINK! YOU WERE SO COOL. YOU WERE IN COLLEGE ON EARTH. YOU WERE GOING TO BE A THERAPIST.

YOU ADORED SAMUEL R. DELANEY AND YOU CARRIED A PACK OF TAROT CARDS IN AN OLD BASMATI RICE BAG.

YOU LOVED DRUMMING. YOUR FAVORITE FOOD WAS BIBIMBAP AND YOU HAD AN AMAZING COLLECTION OF HAIR BOWS.

TRAITOR IN SECTOR SEVEN! TRAITOR IN SECTOR SEVEN!

THE PUNISHMENT FOR TREASON IS INSTANT DEATH!

KAFOOSH

OH MY GOD! IS THAT REALLY MY FUTURE? THAT IS... UNSPEAKABLY HORRIBLE

MAYBE IT IS, MAYBE IT ISN'T. JUST REMEMBER: HALLOWEEN IS A TIME TO GIVE THANKS AND LET YOUR LOVED ONES KNOW YOU CARE FOR THEM.

188

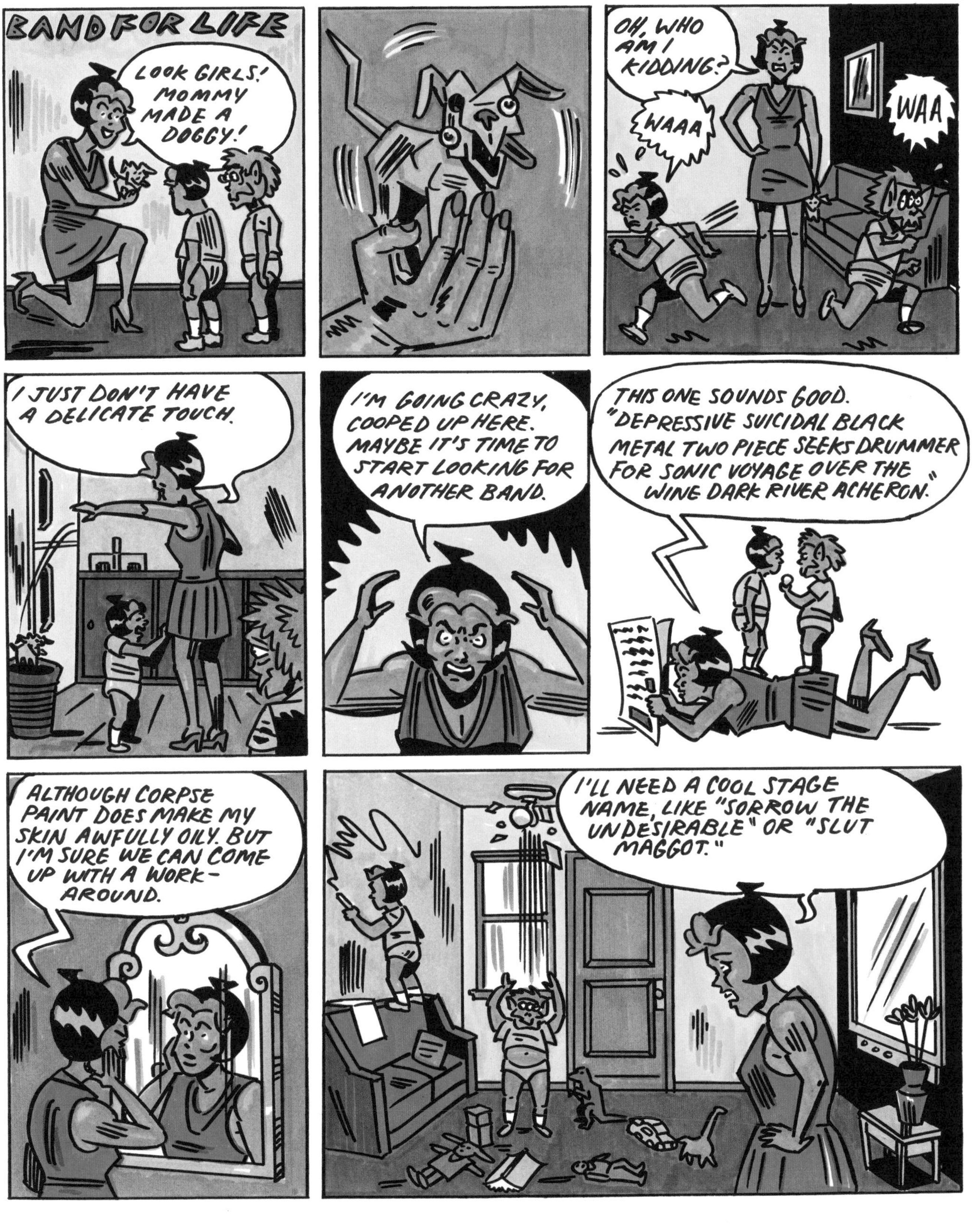
BAND FOR LIFE
LOOK GIRLS! MOMMY MADE A DOGGY!
OH, WHO AM I KIDDING?
WAAA
WAA
I JUST DON'T HAVE A DELICATE TOUCH.
I'M GOING CRAZY, COOPED UP HERE. MAYBE IT'S TIME TO START LOOKING FOR ANOTHER BAND.
THIS ONE SOUNDS GOOD. "DEPRESSIVE SUICIDAL BLACK METAL TWO PIECE SEEKS DRUMMER FOR SONIC VOYAGE OVER THE WINE DARK RIVER ACHERON."
ALTHOUGH CORPSE PAINT DOES MAKE MY SKIN AWFULLY OILY. BUT I'M SURE WE CAN COME UP WITH A WORK-AROUND.
I'LL NEED A COOL STAGE NAME, LIKE "SORROW THE UNDESIRABLE" OR "SLUT MAGGOT."

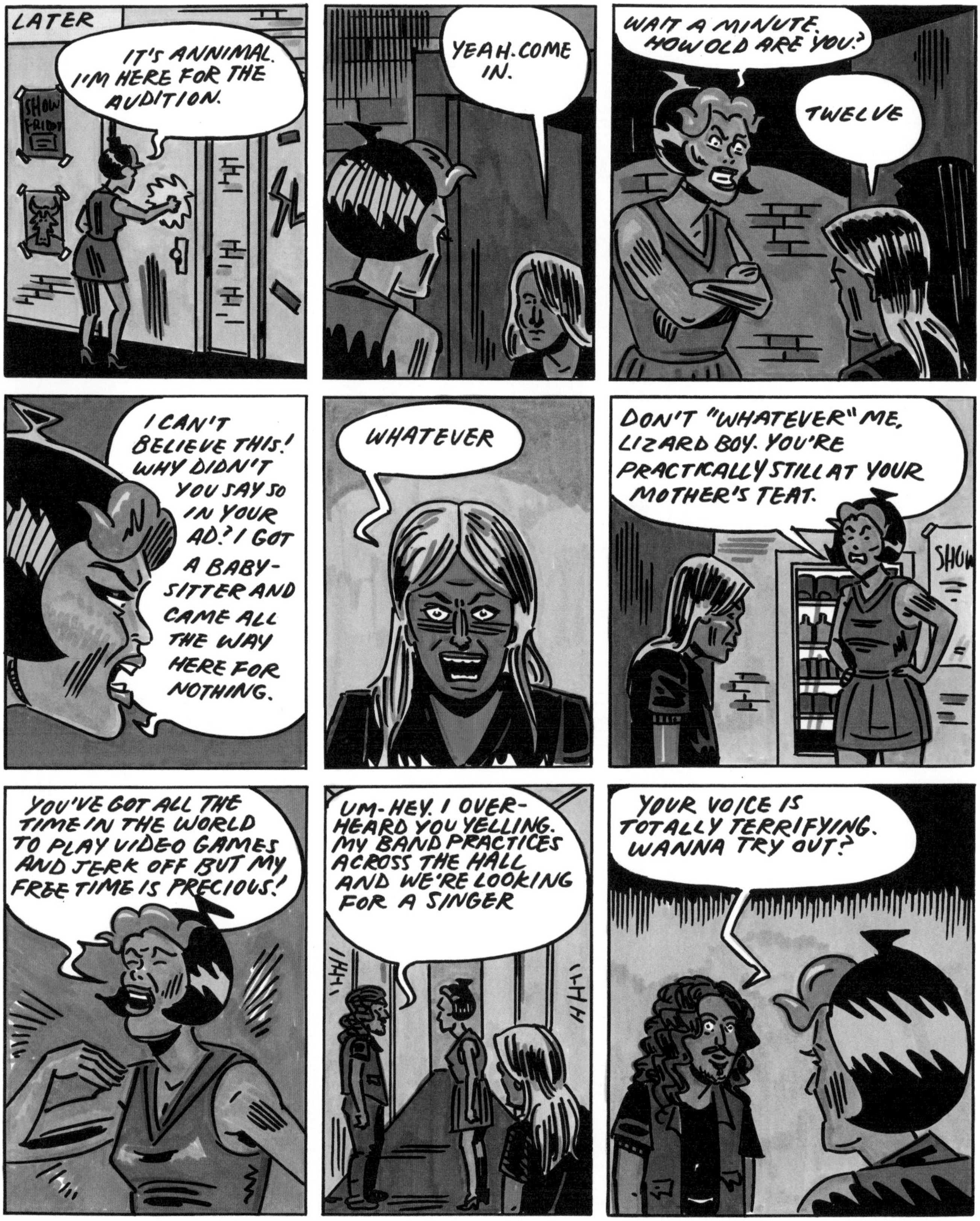
LATER
IT'S ANNIMAL. I'M HERE FOR THE AUDITION.
SHOW FRIDAY
YEAH. COME IN.
WAIT A MINUTE. HOW OLD ARE YOU?
TWELVE
I CAN'T BELIEVE THIS! WHY DIDN'T YOU SAY SO IN YOUR AD? I GOT A BABY-SITTER AND CAME ALL THE WAY HERE FOR NOTHING.
WHATEVER
DON'T "WHATEVER" ME, LIZARD BOY. YOU'RE PRACTICALLY STILL AT YOUR MOTHER'S TEAT.
YOU'VE GOT ALL THE TIME IN THE WORLD TO PLAY VIDEO GAMES AND JERK OFF BUT MY FREE TIME IS PRECIOUS!
UM-HEY. I OVER-HEARD YOU YELLING. MY BAND PRACTICES ACROSS THE HALL AND WE'RE LOOKING FOR A SINGER
YOUR VOICE IS TOTALLY TERRIFYING. WANNA TRY OUT?

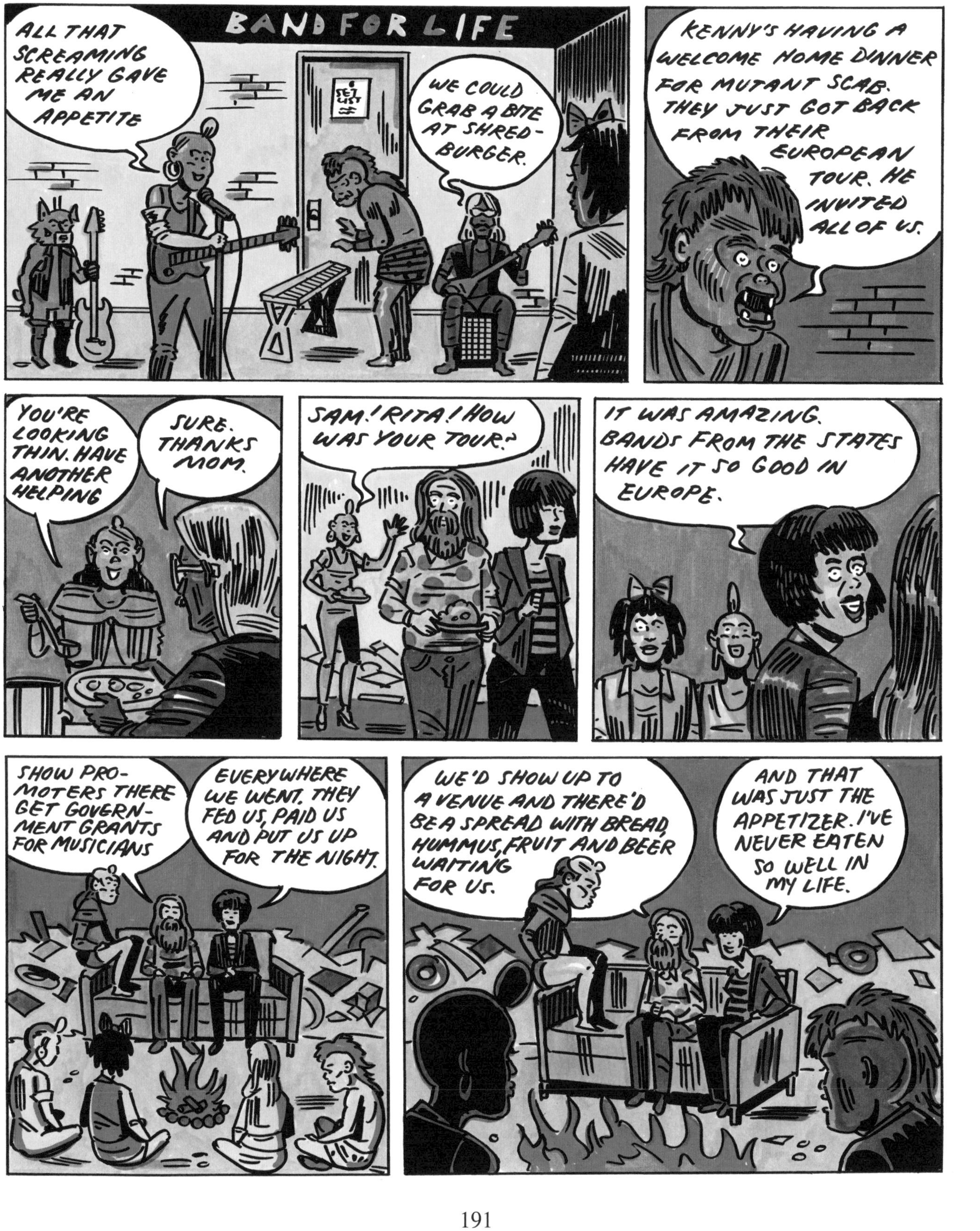
BAND FOR LIFE
ALL THAT SCREAMING REALLY GAVE ME AN APPETITE
WE COULD GRAB A BITE AT SHRED-BURGER.
KENNY'S HAVING A WELCOME HOME DINNER FOR MUTANT SCAB. THEY JUST GOT BACK FROM THEIR EUROPEAN TOUR. HE INVITED ALL OF US.
YOU'RE LOOKING THIN. HAVE ANOTHER HELPING
SURE. THANKS MOM.
SAM! RITA! HOW WAS YOUR TOUR?
IT WAS AMAZING. BANDS FROM THE STATES HAVE IT SO GOOD IN EUROPE.
SHOW PROMOTERS THERE GET GOVERNMENT GRANTS FOR MUSICIANS
EVERYWHERE WE WENT. THEY FED US, PAID US AND PUT US UP FOR THE NIGHT.
WE'D SHOW UP TO A VENUE AND THERE'D BE A SPREAD WITH BREAD, HUMMUS, FRUIT AND BEER WAITING FOR US.
AND THAT WAS JUST THE APPETIZER. I'VE NEVER EATEN SO WELL IN MY LIFE.

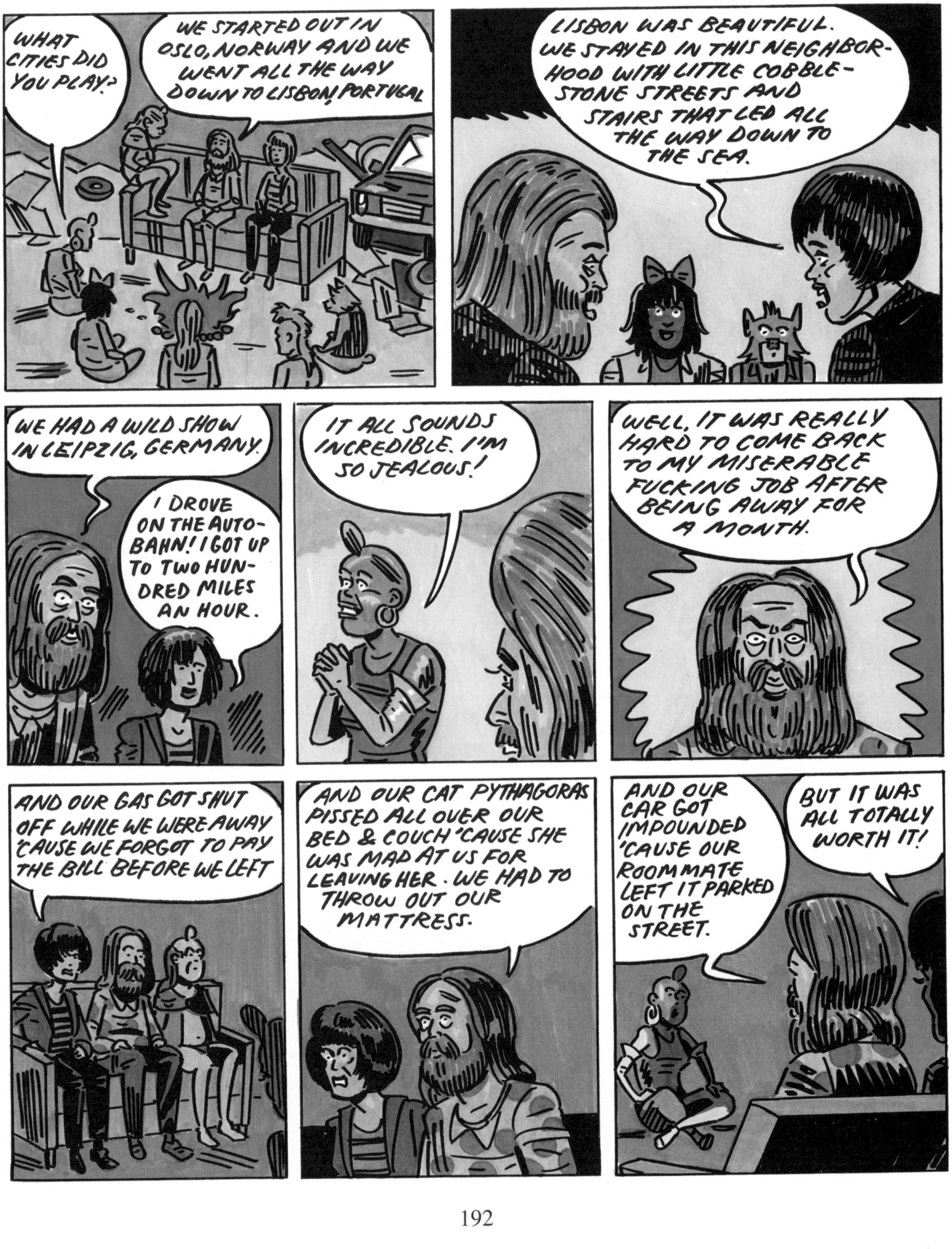
WHAT CITIES DID YOU PLAY?
WE STARTED OUT IN OSLO, NORWAY AND WE WENT ALL THE WAY DOWN TO LISBON, PORTUGAL
LISBON WAS BEAUTIFUL. WE STAYED IN THIS NEIGHBORHOOD WITH LITTLE COBBLESTONE STREETS AND STAIRS THAT LED ALL THE WAY DOWN TO THE SEA.
WE HAD A WILD SHOW IN LEIPZIG, GERMANY.
I DROVE ON THE AUTOBAHN! I GOT UP TO TWO HUNDRED MILES AN HOUR.
IT ALL SOUNDS INCREDIBLE. I'M SO JEALOUS!
WELL, IT WAS REALLY HARD TO COME BACK TO MY MISERABLE FUCKING JOB AFTER BEING AWAY FOR A MONTH.
AND OUR GAS GOT SHUT OFF WHILE WE WERE AWAY 'CAUSE WE FORGOT TO PAY THE BILL BEFORE WE LEFT
AND OUR CAT PYTHAGORAS PISSED ALL OVER OUR BED & COUCH 'CAUSE SHE WAS MAD AT US FOR LEAVING HER. WE HAD TO THROW OUT OUR MATTRESS.
AND OUR CAR GOT IMPOUNDED 'CAUSE OUR ROOMMATE LEFT IT PARKED ON THE STREET.
BUT IT WAS ALL TOTALLY WORTH IT!

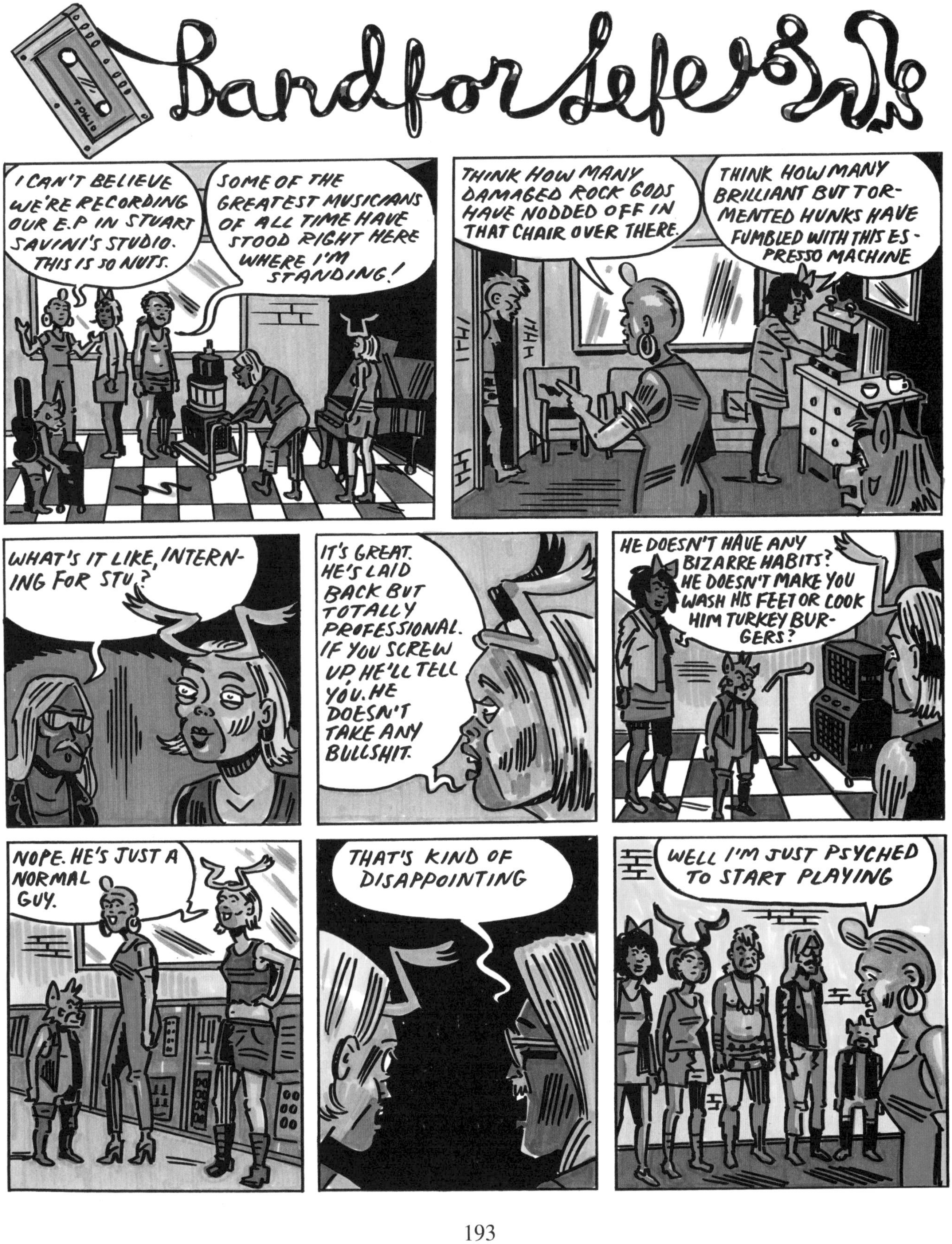
Band for Life
I CAN'T BELIEVE WE'RE RECORDING OUR E.P IN STUART SAVINI'S STUDIO. THIS IS SO NUTS.
SOME OF THE GREATEST MUSICIANS OF ALL TIME HAVE STOOD RIGHT HERE WHERE I'M STANDING!
THINK HOW MANY DAMAGED ROCK GODS HAVE NODDED OFF IN THAT CHAIR OVER THERE.
THINK HOW MANY BRILLIANT BUT TORMENTED HUNKS HAVE FUMBLED WITH THIS ESPRESSO MACHINE
WHAT'S IT LIKE, INTERNING FOR STU?
IT'S GREAT. HE'S LAID BACK BUT TOTALLY PROFESSIONAL. IF YOU SCREW UP, HE'LL TELL YOU. HE DOESN'T TAKE ANY BULLSHIT.
HE DOESN'T HAVE ANY BIZARRE HABITS? HE DOESN'T MAKE YOU WASH HIS FEET OR COOK HIM TURKEY BURGERS?
NOPE. HE'S JUST A NORMAL GUY.
THAT'S KIND OF DISAPPOINTING
WELL I'M JUST PSYCHED TO START PLAYING

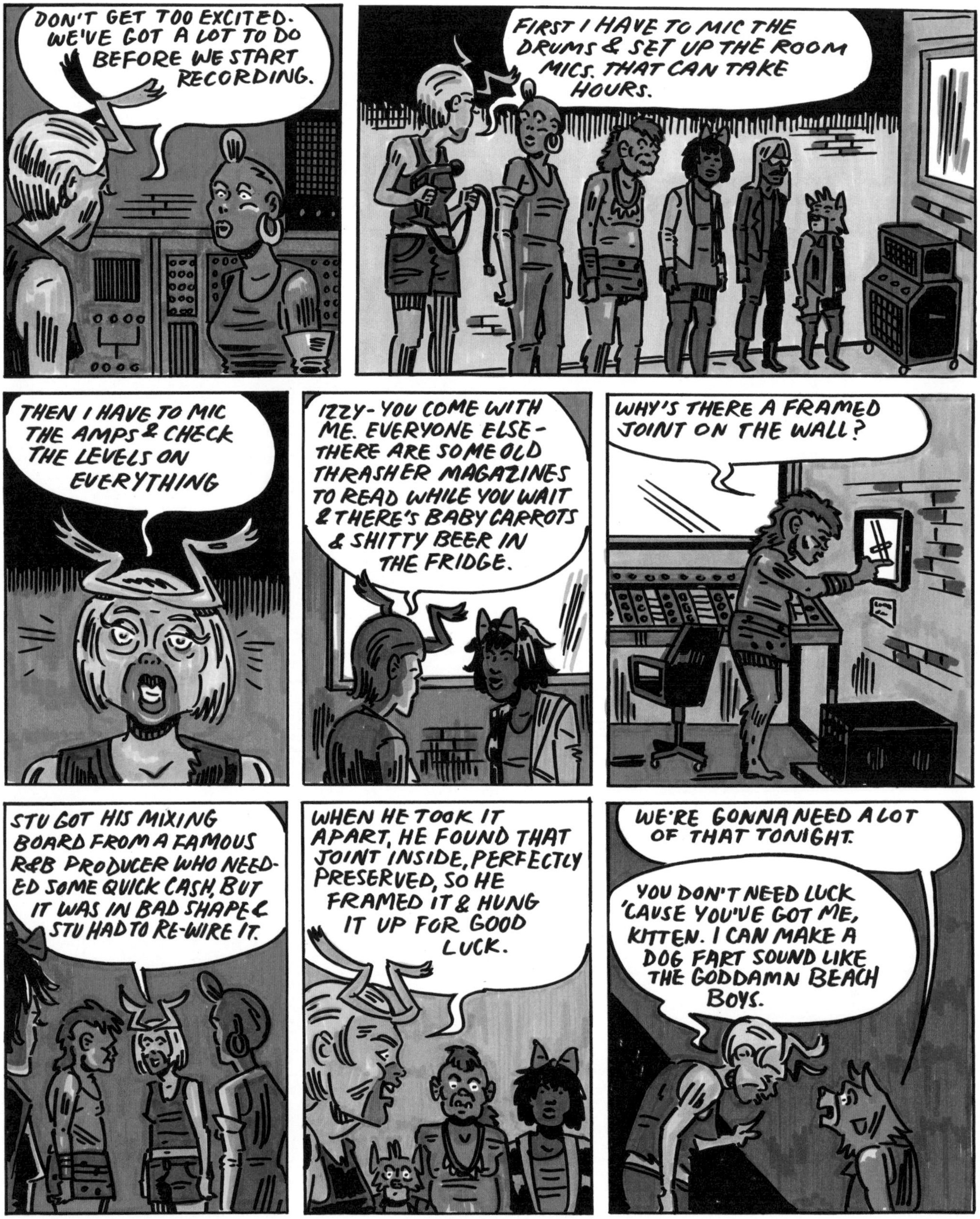
DON'T GET TOO EXCITED. WE'VE GOT A LOT TO DO BEFORE WE START RECORDING.
FIRST I HAVE TO MIC THE DRUMS & SET UP THE ROOM MICS. THAT CAN TAKE HOURS.
THEN I HAVE TO MIC THE AMPS & CHECK THE LEVELS ON EVERYTHING
IZZY- YOU COME WITH ME. EVERYONE ELSE- THERE ARE SOME OLD THRASHER MAGAZINES TO READ WHILE YOU WAIT & THERE'S BABY CARROTS & SHITTY BEER IN THE FRIDGE.
WHY'S THERE A FRAMED JOINT ON THE WALL?
STU GOT HIS MIXING BOARD FROM A FAMOUS R&B PRODUCER WHO NEEDED SOME QUICK CASH, BUT IT WAS IN BAD SHAPE & STU HAD TO RE-WIRE IT.
WHEN HE TOOK IT APART, HE FOUND THAT JOINT INSIDE, PERFECTLY PRESERVED, SO HE FRAMED IT & HUNG IT UP FOR GOOD LUCK.
WE'RE GONNA NEED A LOT OF THAT TONIGHT.
YOU DON'T NEED LUCK 'CAUSE YOU'VE GOT ME, KITTEN. I CAN MAKE A DOG FART SOUND LIKE THE GODDAMN BEACH BOYS.

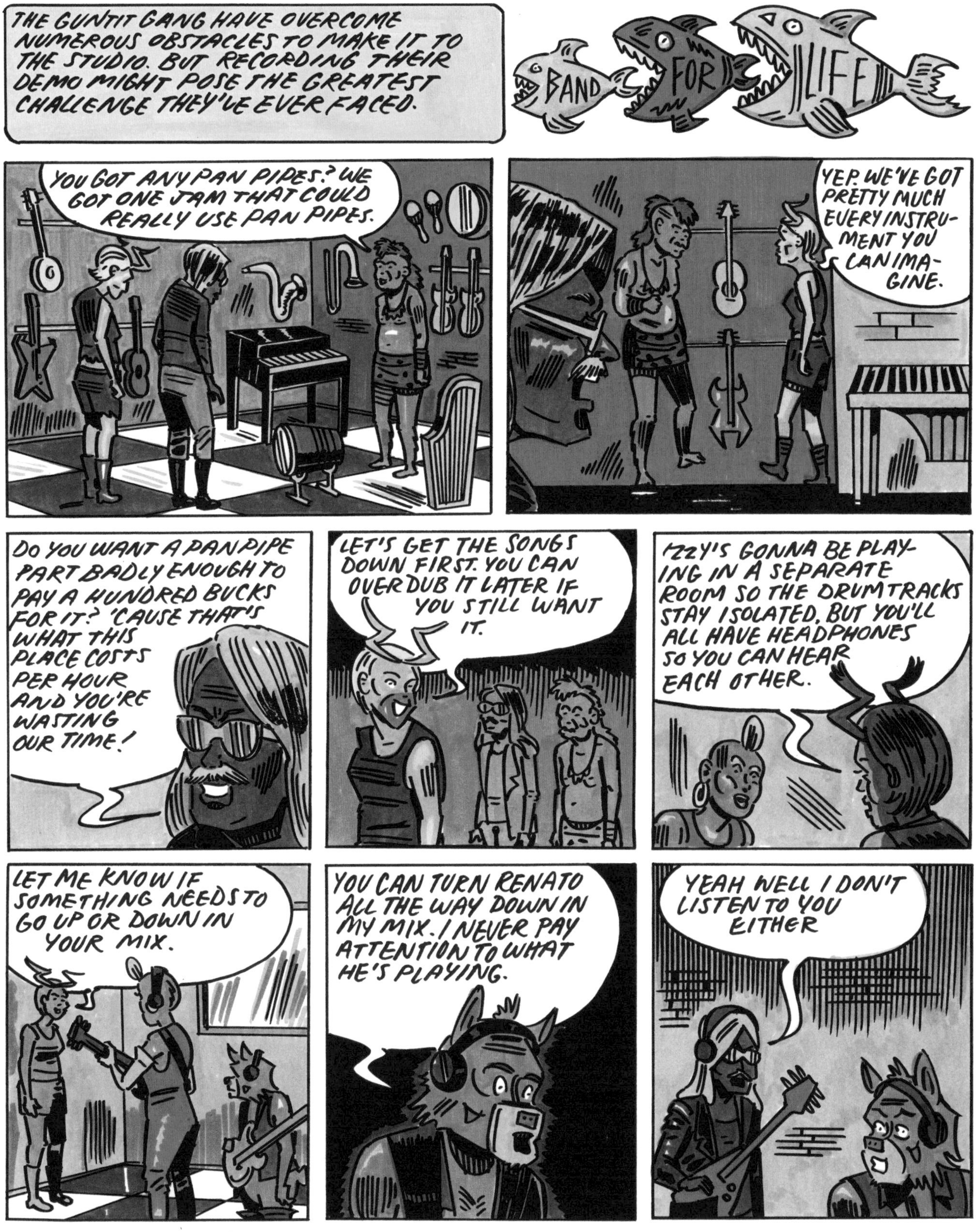
THE GUNTIT GANG HAVE OVERCOME NUMEROUS OBSTACLES TO MAKE IT TO THE STUDIO. BUT RECORDING THEIR DEMO MIGHT POSE THE GREATEST CHALLENGE THEY'VE EVER FACED.
BAND FOR LIFE
YOU GOT ANY PAN PIPES? WE GOT ONE JAM THAT COULD REALLY USE PAN PIPES.
YEP. WE'VE GOT PRETTY MUCH EVERY INSTRUMENT YOU CAN IMAGINE.
DO YOU WANT A PAN PIPE PART BADLY ENOUGH TO PAY A HUNDRED BUCKS FOR IT? 'CAUSE THAT'S WHAT THIS PLACE COSTS PER HOUR AND YOU'RE WASTING OUR TIME!
LET'S GET THE SONGS DOWN FIRST. YOU CAN OVERDUB IT LATER IF YOU STILL WANT IT.
IZZY'S GONNA BE PLAYING IN A SEPARATE ROOM SO THE DRUM TRACKS STAY ISOLATED. BUT YOU'LL ALL HAVE HEADPHONES SO YOU CAN HEAR EACH OTHER.
LET ME KNOW IF SOMETHING NEEDS TO GO UP OR DOWN IN YOUR MIX.
YOU CAN TURN RENATO ALL THE WAY DOWN IN MY MIX. I NEVER PAY ATTENTION TO WHAT HE'S PLAYING.
YEAH WELL I DON'T LISTEN TO YOU EITHER

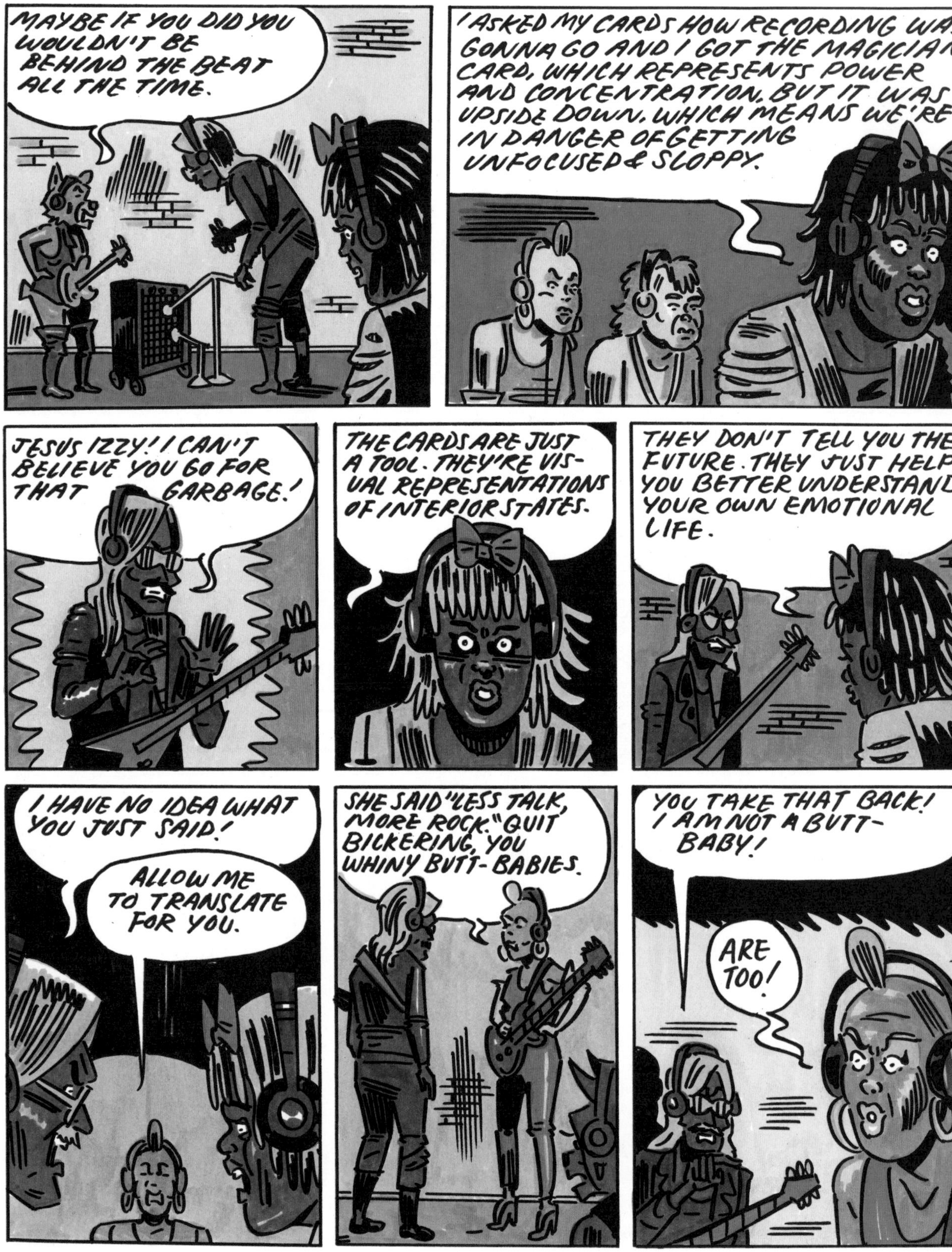
MAYBE IF YOU DID YOU WOULDN'T BE BEHIND THE BEAT ALL THE TIME.
I ASKED MY CARDS HOW RECORDING WAS GONNA GO AND I GOT THE MAGICIAN CARD, WHICH REPRESENTS POWER AND CONCENTRATION. BUT IT WAS UPSIDE DOWN, WHICH MEANS WE'RE IN DANGER OF GETTING UNFOCUSED & SLOPPY.
JESUS IZZY! I CAN'T BELIEVE YOU GO FOR THAT GARBAGE!
THE CARDS ARE JUST A TOOL. THEY'RE VISUAL REPRESENTATIONS OF INTERIOR STATES.
THEY DON'T TELL YOU THE FUTURE. THEY JUST HELP YOU BETTER UNDERSTAND YOUR OWN EMOTIONAL LIFE.
I HAVE NO IDEA WHAT YOU JUST SAID!
ALLOW ME TO TRANSLATE FOR YOU.
SHE SAID "LESS TALK, MORE ROCK." QUIT BICKERING, YOU WHINY BUTT-BABIES.
YOU TAKE THAT BACK! I AM NOT A BUTT-BABY!
ARE TOO!

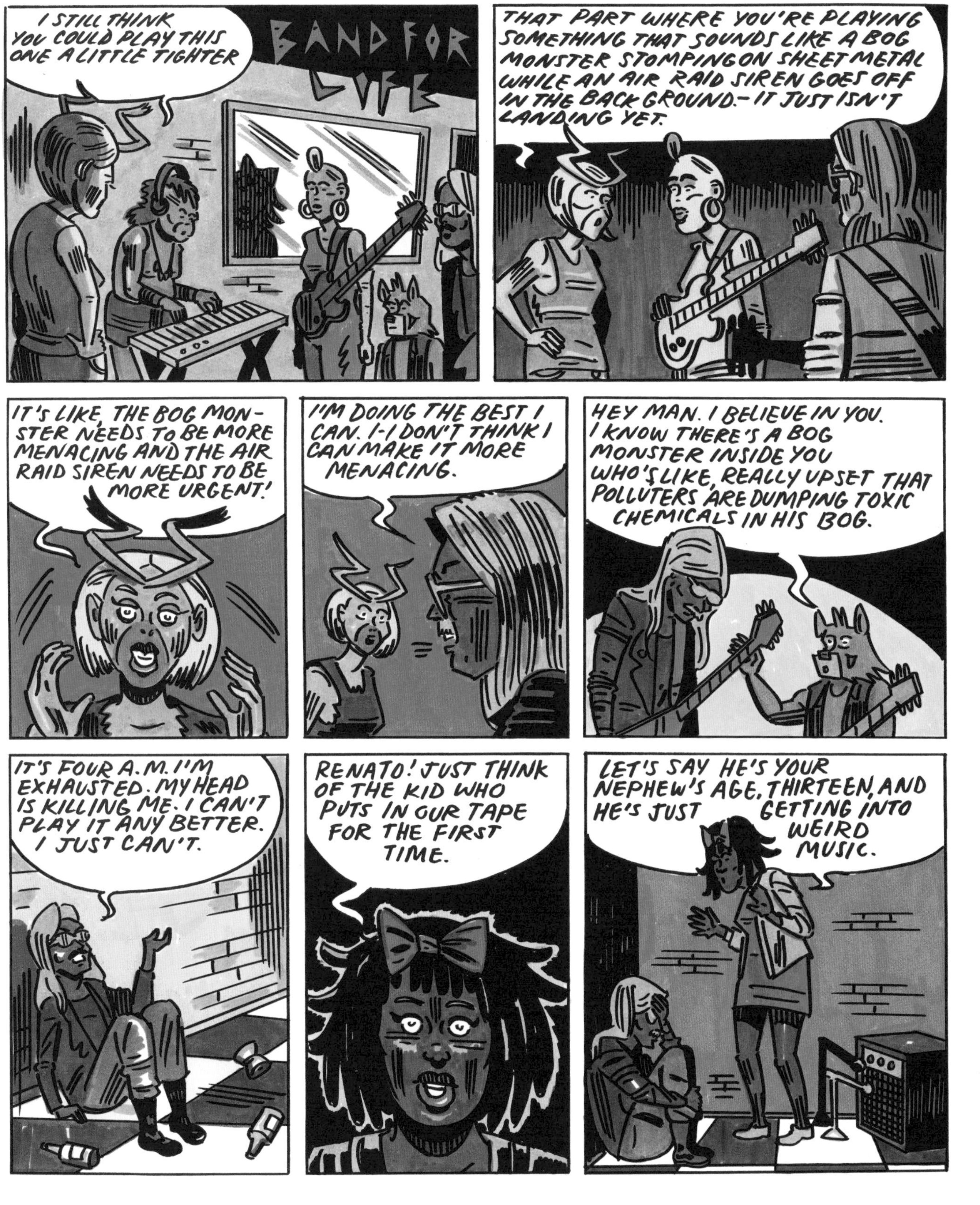

I STILL THINK YOU COULD PLAY THIS ONE A LITTLE TIGHTER
BAND FOR LIFE
THAT PART WHERE YOU'RE PLAYING SOMETHING THAT SOUNDS LIKE A BOG MONSTER STOMPING ON SHEET METAL WHILE AN AIR RAID SIREN GOES OFF IN THE BACKGROUND.– IT JUST ISN'T LANDING YET.
IT'S LIKE, THE BOG MON-STER NEEDS TO BE MORE MENACING AND THE AIR RAID SIREN NEEDS TO BE MORE URGENT!
I'M DOING THE BEST I CAN. I-I DON'T THINK I CAN MAKE IT MORE MENACING.
HEY MAN. I BELIEVE IN YOU. I KNOW THERE'S A BOG MONSTER INSIDE YOU WHO'S LIKE, REALLY UPSET THAT POLLUTERS ARE DUMPING TOXIC CHEMICALS IN HIS BOG.
IT'S FOUR A.M. I'M EXHAUSTED. MY HEAD IS KILLING ME. I CAN'T PLAY IT ANY BETTER. I JUST CAN'T.
RENATO! JUST THINK OF THE KID WHO PUTS IN OUR TAPE FOR THE FIRST TIME.
LET'S SAY HE'S YOUR NEPHEW'S AGE, THIRTEEN, AND HE'S JUST GETTING INTO WEIRD MUSIC.

ALL HIS LIFE THIS KID HAS FELT LIKE A VISITOR FROM MARS ON A WORK VISA. LIKE A MUTT AT THE WESTMINSTER KENNEL CLUB...

WHEN THE OTHER KIDS WERE READING "JAMES AND THE GIANT PEACH" HE WAS READING "APOCALYPSE CULTURE."

WHEN THE OTHER KIDS WERE PLAYING VIDEO GAMES HE WAS BUILDING A SCALE MODEL OF THE TEMPLE OF HATSHEPSUT OUT OF TOOTHPICKS

WHEN THE OTHER KIDS WERE WRITING TO SANTA, HE WAS WRITING TO JOHN WATERS.

THIS KID PUTS OUR TAPE IN HIS BEAT UP OLD WALKMAN AND PRESSES PLAY. ARE WE GONNA BLOW HIS MIND? ARE WE GONNA FREAK HIM OUT?

OR ARE WE GONNA DISAPPOINT HIM JUST LIKE EVERYONE ELSE IN HIS LIFE?

NO! NEVER! WE'RE GONNA GET THIS PART RIGHT OR DIE TRYING!

YOU'VE GOT THE POWER OF PERSUASION, IZ. IF YOU STARTED A CULT, I'D DEFINITELY JOIN

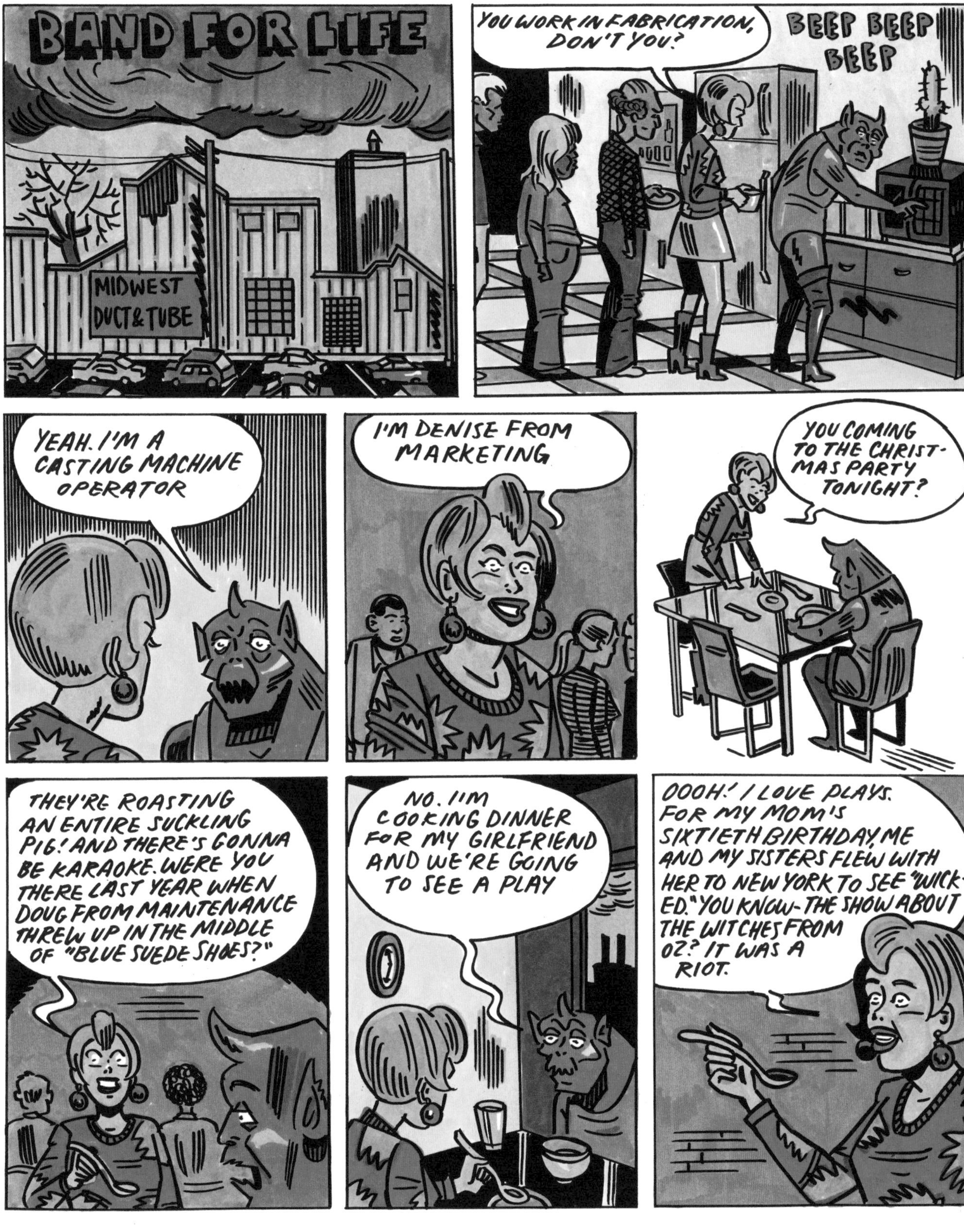
BAND FOR LIFE
MIDWEST DUCT & TUBE
YOU WORK IN FABRICATION, DON'T YOU?
BEEP BEEP BEEP
YEAH. I'M A CASTING MACHINE OPERATOR
I'M DENISE FROM MARKETING
YOU COMING TO THE CHRISTMAS PARTY TONIGHT?
THEY'RE ROASTING AN ENTIRE SUCKLING PIG! AND THERE'S GONNA BE KARAOKE. WERE YOU THERE LAST YEAR WHEN DOUG FROM MAINTENANCE THREW UP IN THE MIDDLE OF "BLUE SUEDE SHOES?"
NO. I'M COOKING DINNER FOR MY GIRLFRIEND AND WE'RE GOING TO SEE A PLAY
OOOH! I LOVE PLAYS. FOR MY MOM'S SIXTIETH BIRTHDAY, ME AND MY SISTERS FLEW WITH HER TO NEW YORK TO SEE "WICKED." YOU KNOW- THE SHOW ABOUT THE WITCHES FROM OZ? IT WAS A RIOT.

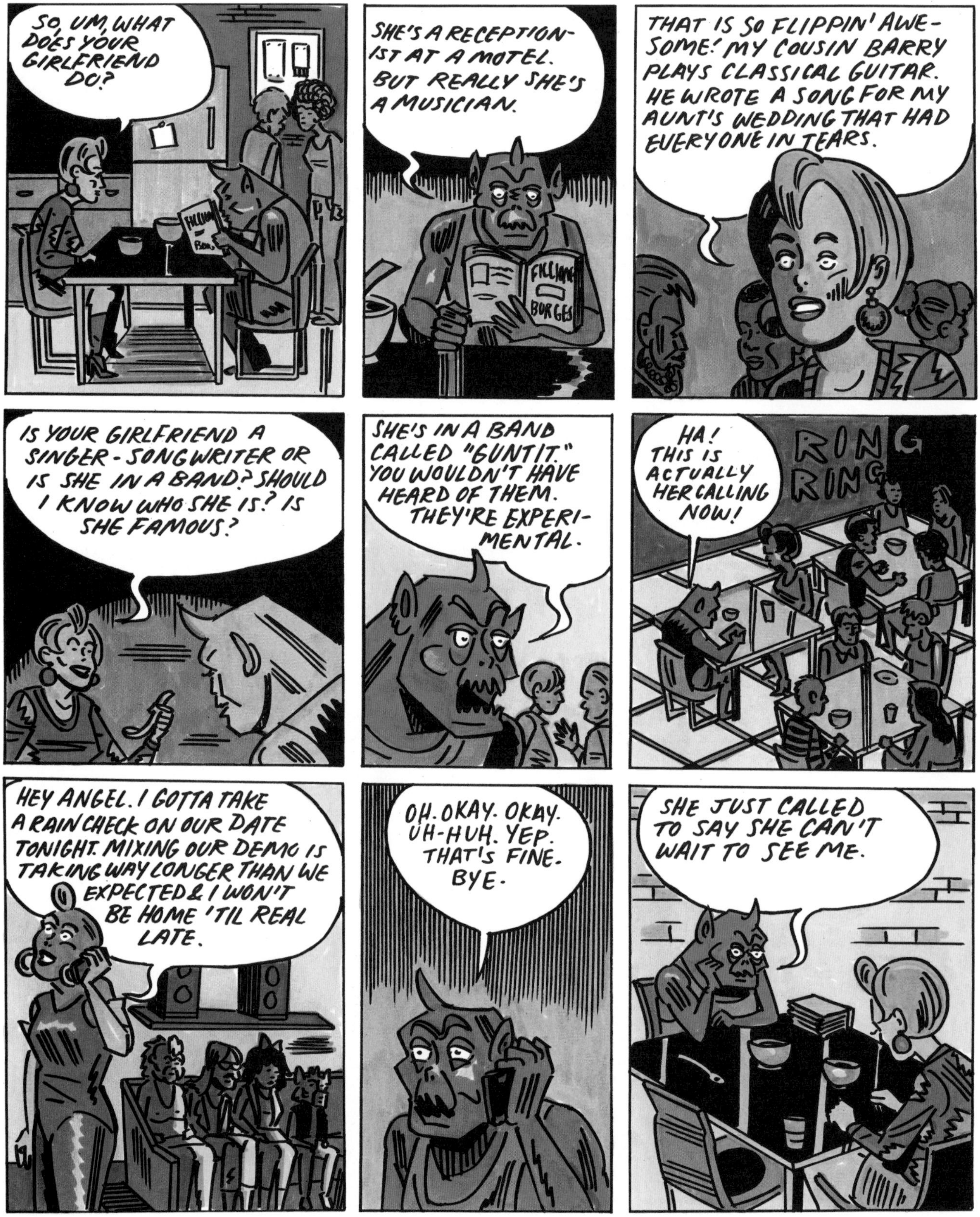
SO, UM, WHAT DOES YOUR GIRLFRIEND DO?
FICCIONES BORGES
SHE'S A RECEPTIONIST AT A MOTEL. BUT REALLY SHE'S A MUSICIAN.
THAT IS SO FLIPPIN' AWESOME! MY COUSIN BARRY PLAYS CLASSICAL GUITAR. HE WROTE A SONG FOR MY AUNT'S WEDDING THAT HAD EVERYONE IN TEARS.
IS YOUR GIRLFRIEND A SINGER-SONGWRITER OR IS SHE IN A BAND? SHOULD I KNOW WHO SHE IS? IS SHE FAMOUS?
SHE'S IN A BAND CALLED "GUNTIT." YOU WOULDN'T HAVE HEARD OF THEM. THEY'RE EXPERIMENTAL.
HA! THIS IS ACTUALLY HER CALLING NOW!
RING RING
HEY ANGEL. I GOTTA TAKE A RAIN CHECK ON OUR DATE TONIGHT. MIXING OUR DEMO IS TAKING WAY LONGER THAN WE EXPECTED & I WON'T BE HOME 'TIL REAL LATE.
OH. OKAY. OKAY. UH-HUH. YEP. THAT'S FINE. BYE.
SHE JUST CALLED TO SAY SHE CAN'T WAIT TO SEE ME.

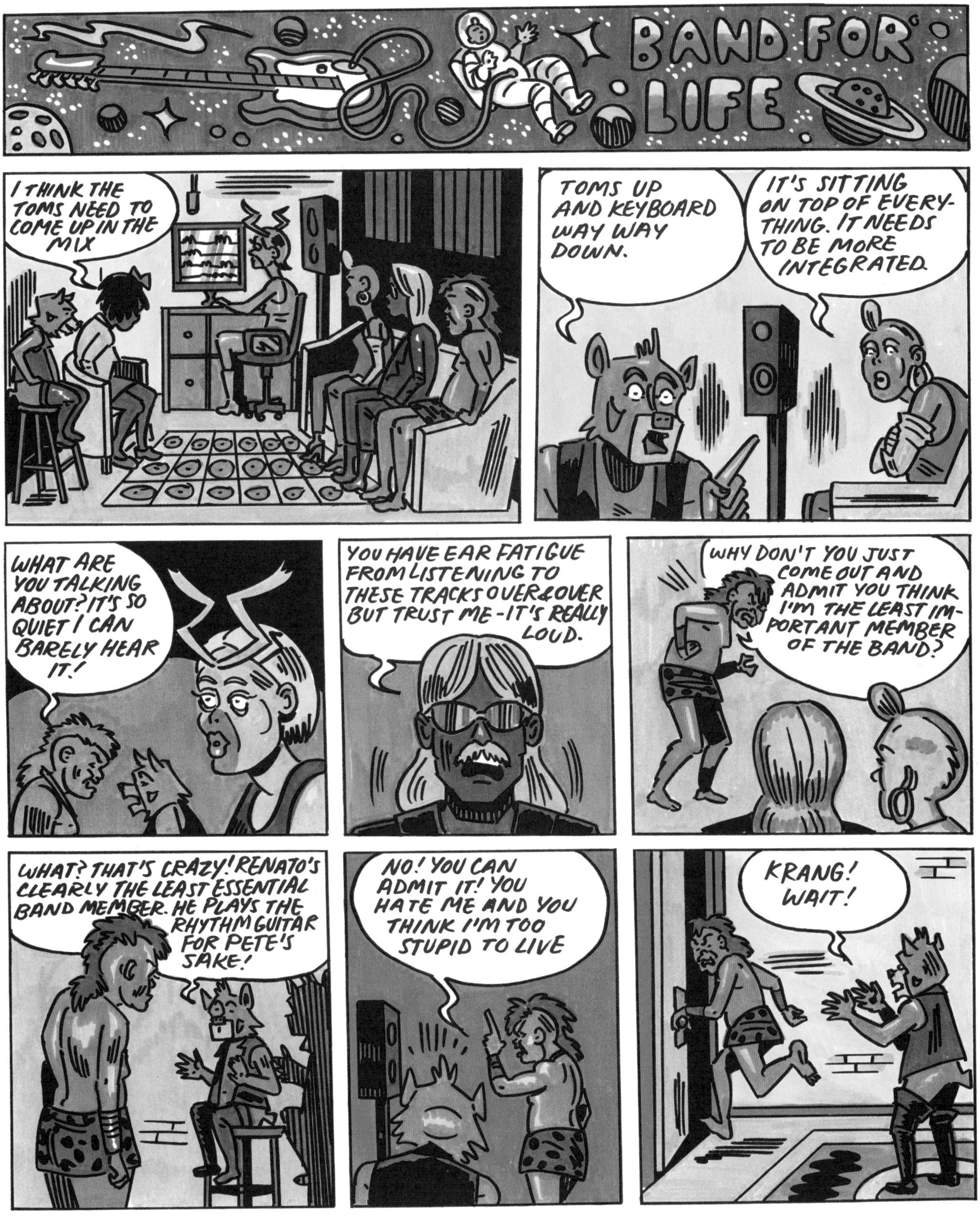
BAND FOR LIFE
I THINK THE TOMS NEED TO COME UP IN THE MIX
TOMS UP AND KEYBOARD WAY WAY DOWN.
IT'S SITTING ON TOP OF EVERY-THING. IT NEEDS TO BE MORE INTEGRATED.
WHAT ARE YOU TALKING ABOUT? IT'S SO QUIET I CAN BARELY HEAR IT!
YOU HAVE EAR FATIGUE FROM LISTENING TO THESE TRACKS OVER & OVER BUT TRUST ME - IT'S REALLY LOUD.
WHY DON'T YOU JUST COME OUT AND ADMIT YOU THINK I'M THE LEAST IM-PORTANT MEMBER OF THE BAND?
WHAT? THAT'S CRAZY! RENATO'S CLEARLY THE LEAST ESSENTIAL BAND MEMBER. HE PLAYS THE RHYTHM GUITAR FOR PETE'S SAKE!
NO! YOU CAN ADMIT IT! YOU HATE ME AND YOU THINK I'M TOO STUPID TO LIVE
KRANG! WAIT!

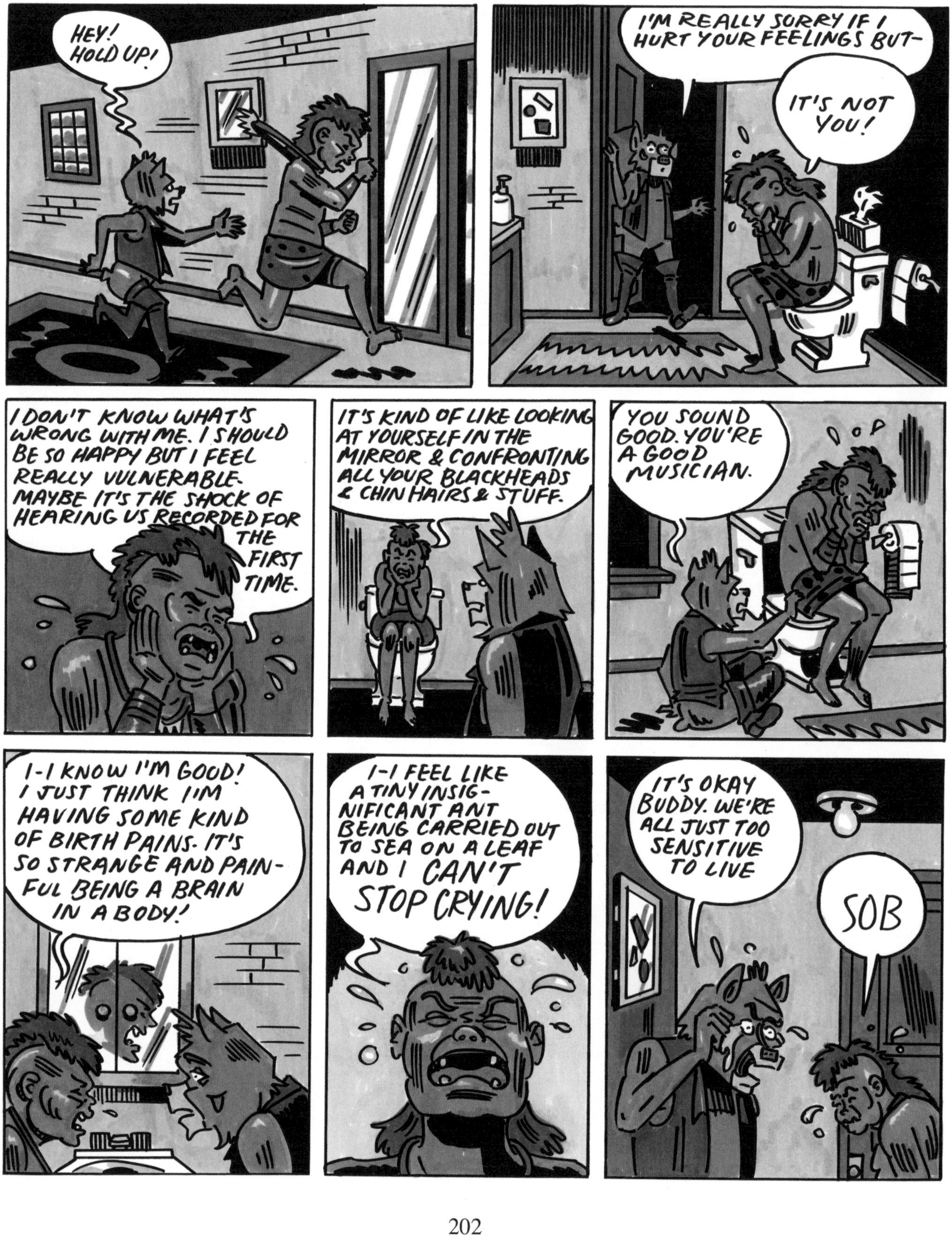
HEY! HOLD UP!
I'M REALLY SORRY IF I HURT YOUR FEELINGS BUT-
IT'S NOT YOU!
I DON'T KNOW WHAT'S WRONG WITH ME. I SHOULD BE SO HAPPY BUT I FEEL REALLY VULNERABLE. MAYBE IT'S THE SHOCK OF HEARING US RECORDED FOR THE FIRST TIME.
IT'S KIND OF LIKE LOOKING AT YOURSELF IN THE MIRROR & CONFRONTING ALL YOUR BLACKHEADS & CHIN HAIRS & STUFF.
YOU SOUND GOOD. YOU'RE A GOOD MUSICIAN.
I-I KNOW I'M GOOD! I JUST THINK I'M HAVING SOME KIND OF BIRTH PAINS. IT'S SO STRANGE AND PAIN-FUL BEING A BRAIN IN A BODY!
I-I FEEL LIKE A TINY INSIG-NIFICANT ANT BEING CARRIED OUT TO SEA ON A LEAF AND I CAN'T STOP CRYING!
IT'S OKAY BUDDY. WE'RE ALL JUST TOO SENSITIVE TO LIVE
SOB

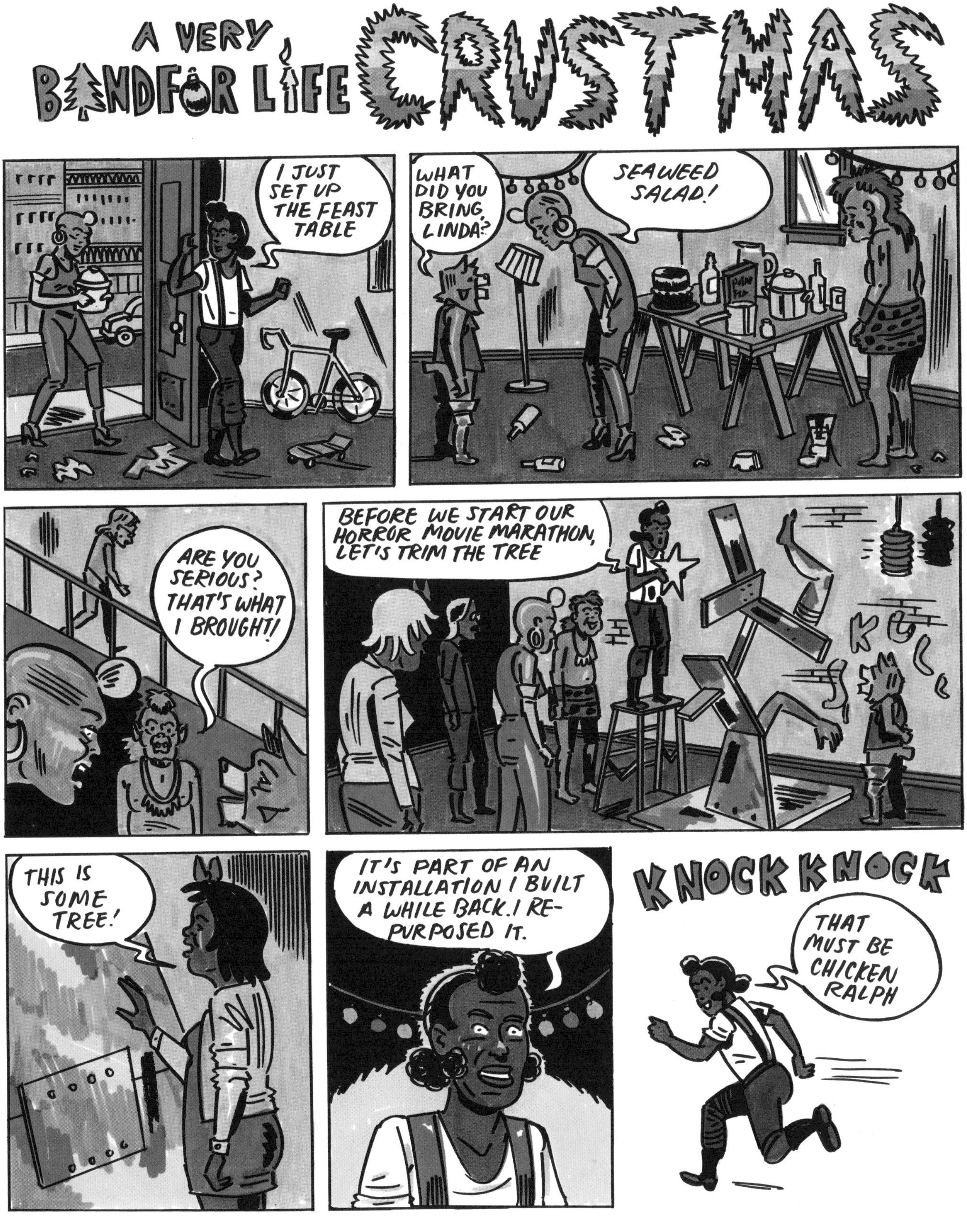
A VERY BAND FOR LIFE CRUSTMAS
I JUST SET UP THE FEAST TABLE
WHAT DID YOU BRING, LINDA?
SEAWEED SALAD!
ARE YOU SERIOUS? THAT'S WHAT I BROUGHT!
BEFORE WE START OUR HORROR MOVIE MARATHON, LET'S TRIM THE TREE
THIS IS SOME TREE!
IT'S PART OF AN INSTALLATION I BUILT A WHILE BACK. I RE-PURPOSED IT.
KNOCK KNOCK
THAT MUST BE CHICKEN RALPH

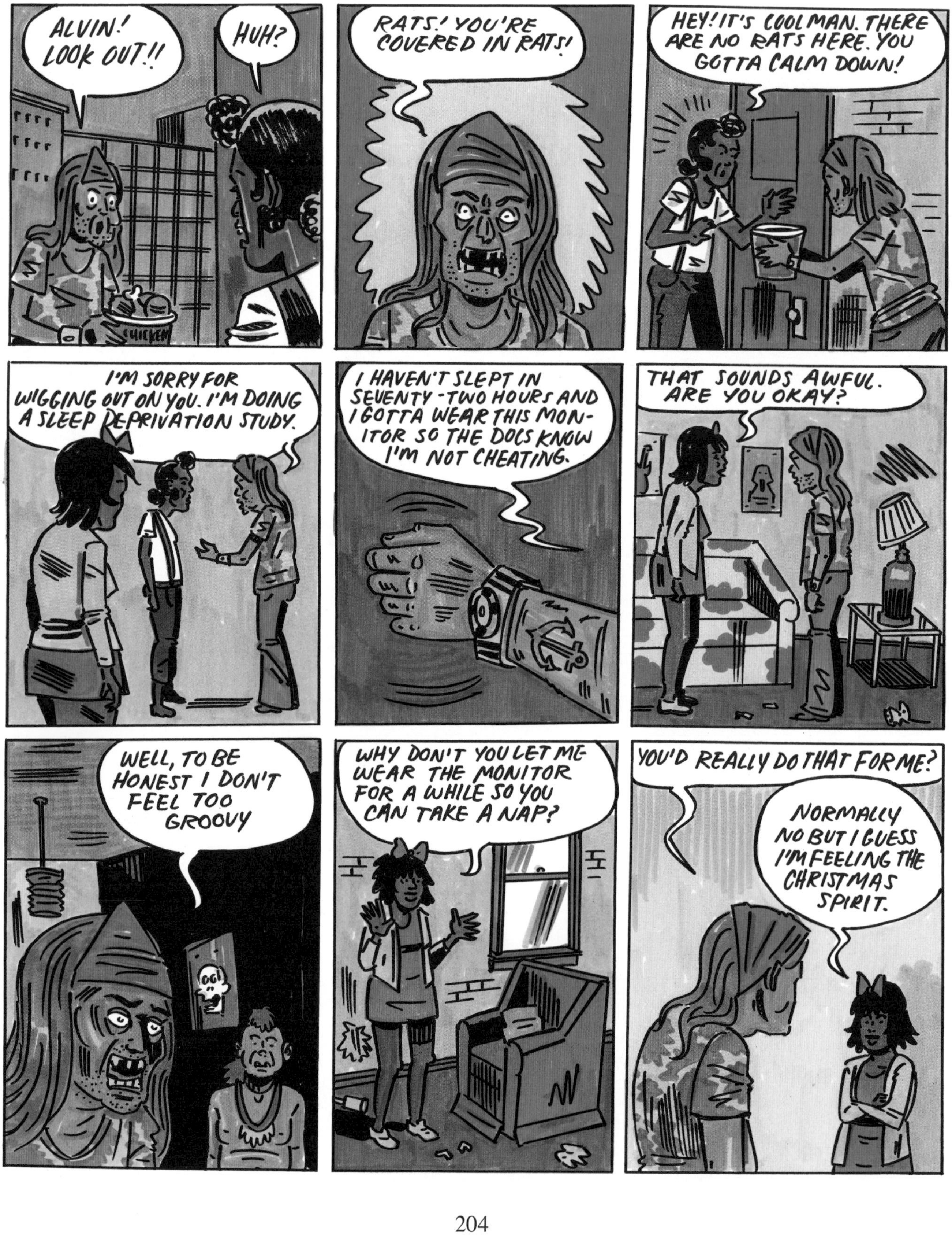
ALVIN! LOOK OUT!!
HUH?
CHICKEN
RATS! YOU'RE COVERED IN RATS!
HEY! IT'S COOL MAN. THERE ARE NO RATS HERE. YOU GOTTA CALM DOWN!
I'M SORRY FOR WIGGING OUT ON YOU. I'M DOING A SLEEP DEPRIVATION STUDY.
I HAVEN'T SLEPT IN SEVENTY-TWO HOURS AND I GOTTA WEAR THIS MONITOR SO THE DOCS KNOW I'M NOT CHEATING.
THAT SOUNDS AWFUL. ARE YOU OKAY?
WELL, TO BE HONEST I DON'T FEEL TOO GROOVY
WHY DON'T YOU LET ME WEAR THE MONITOR FOR A WHILE SO YOU CAN TAKE A NAP?
YOU'D REALLY DO THAT FOR ME?
NORMALLY NO BUT I GUESS I'M FEELING THE CHRISTMAS SPIRIT.

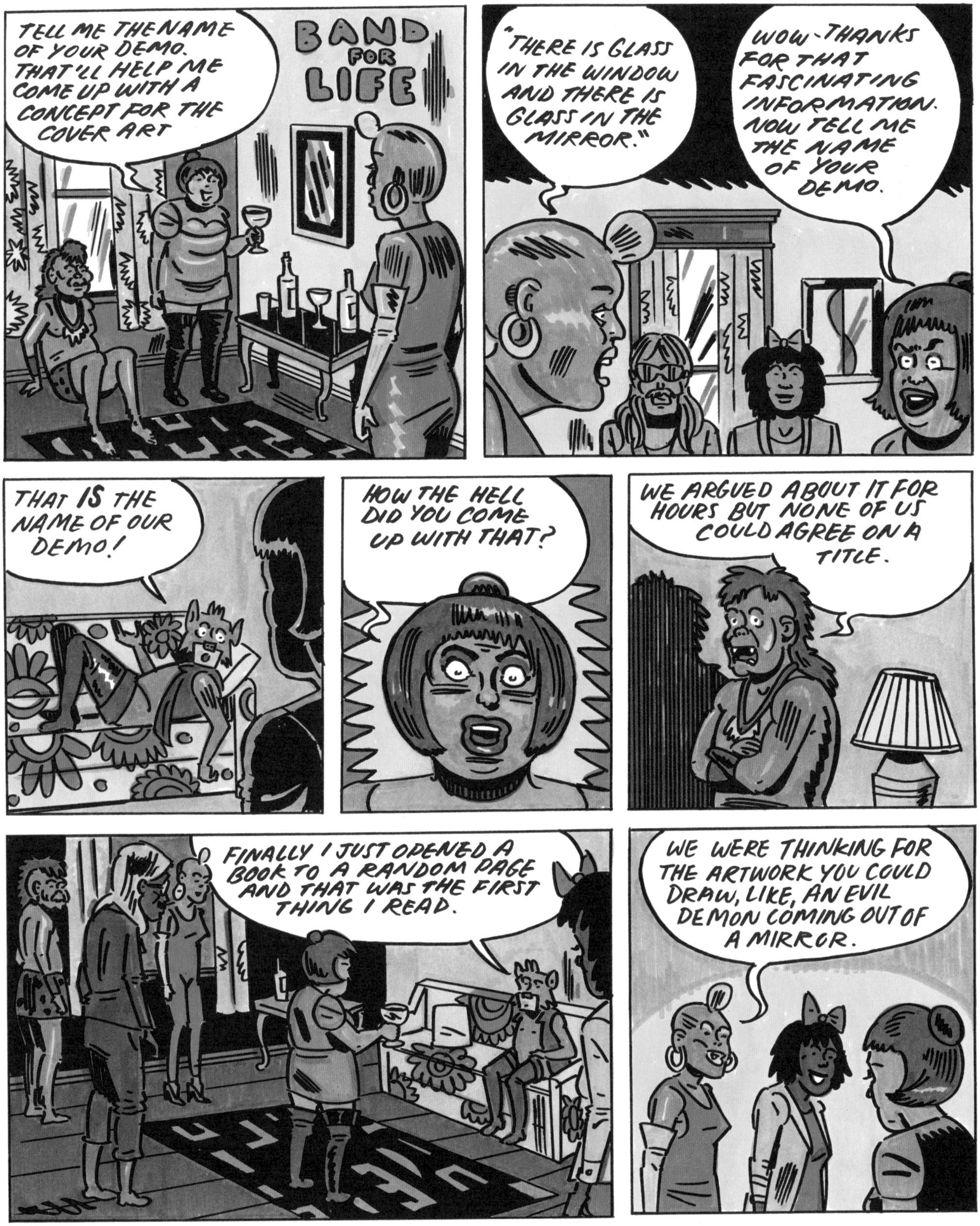
BAND FOR LIFE
TELL ME THE NAME OF YOUR DEMO. THAT'LL HELP ME COME UP WITH A CONCEPT FOR THE COVER ART
"THERE IS GLASS IN THE WINDOW AND THERE IS GLASS IN THE MIRROR."
WOW-THANKS FOR THAT FASCINATING INFORMATION. NOW TELL ME THE NAME OF YOUR DEMO.
THAT IS THE NAME OF OUR DEMO!
HOW THE HELL DID YOU COME UP WITH THAT?
WE ARGUED ABOUT IT FOR HOURS BUT NONE OF US COULD AGREE ON A TITLE.
FINALLY I JUST OPENED A BOOK TO A RANDOM PAGE AND THAT WAS THE FIRST THING I READ.
WE WERE THINKING FOR THE ARTWORK YOU COULD DRAW, LIKE, AN EVIL DEMON COMING OUT OF A MIRROR.

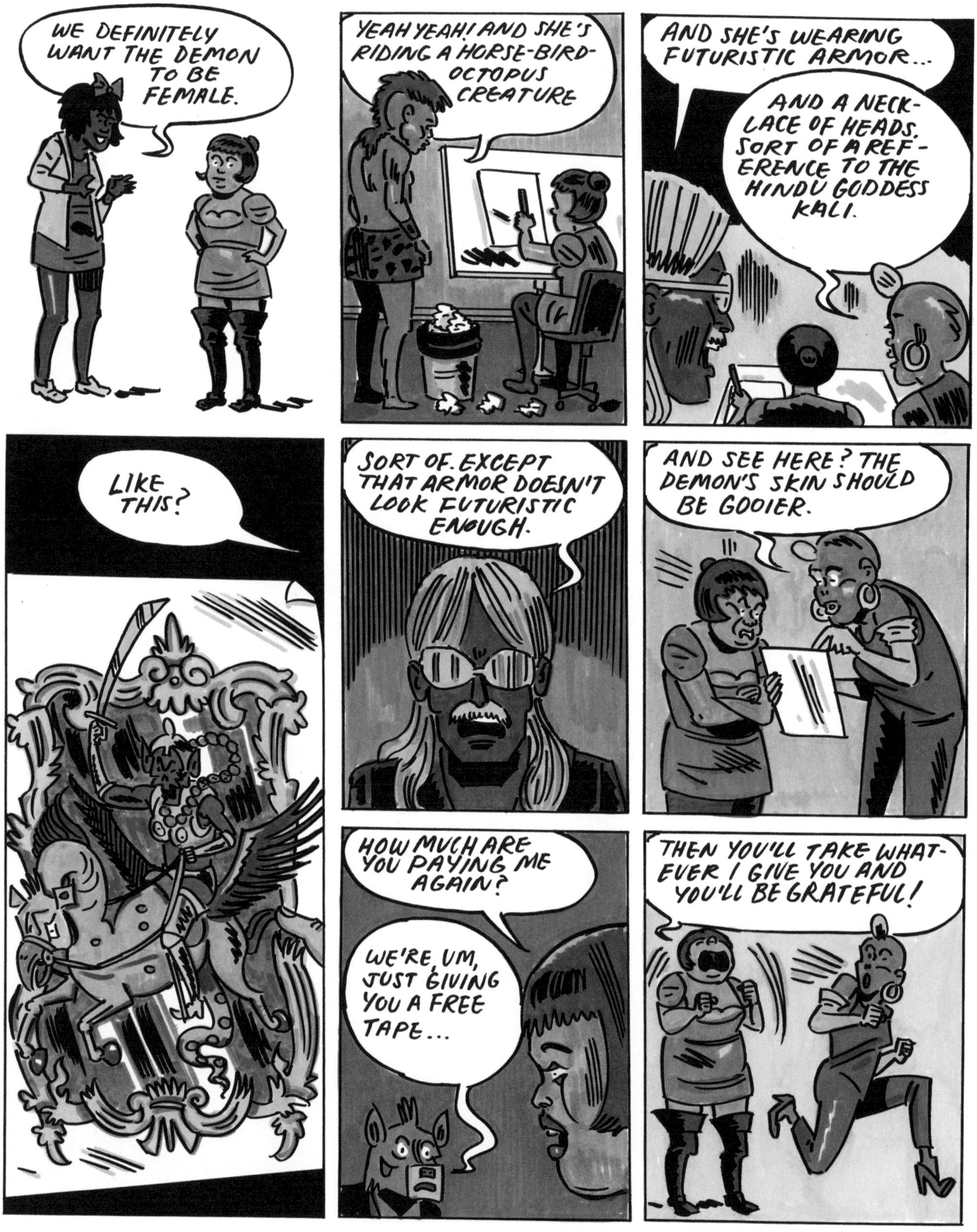
WE DEFINITELY WANT THE DEMON TO BE FEMALE.
YEAH YEAH! AND SHE'S RIDING A HORSE-BIRD-OCTOPUS CREATURE
AND SHE'S WEARING FUTURISTIC ARMOR...
AND A NECKLACE OF HEADS. SORT OF A REFERENCE TO THE HINDU GODDESS KALI.
LIKE THIS?
SORT OF. EXCEPT THAT ARMOR DOESN'T LOOK FUTURISTIC ENOUGH.
AND SEE HERE? THE DEMON'S SKIN SHOULD BE GOOIER.
HOW MUCH ARE YOU PAYING ME AGAIN?
WE'RE, UM, JUST GIVING YOU A FREE TAPE...
THEN YOU'LL TAKE WHATEVER I GIVE YOU AND YOU'LL BE GRATEFUL!

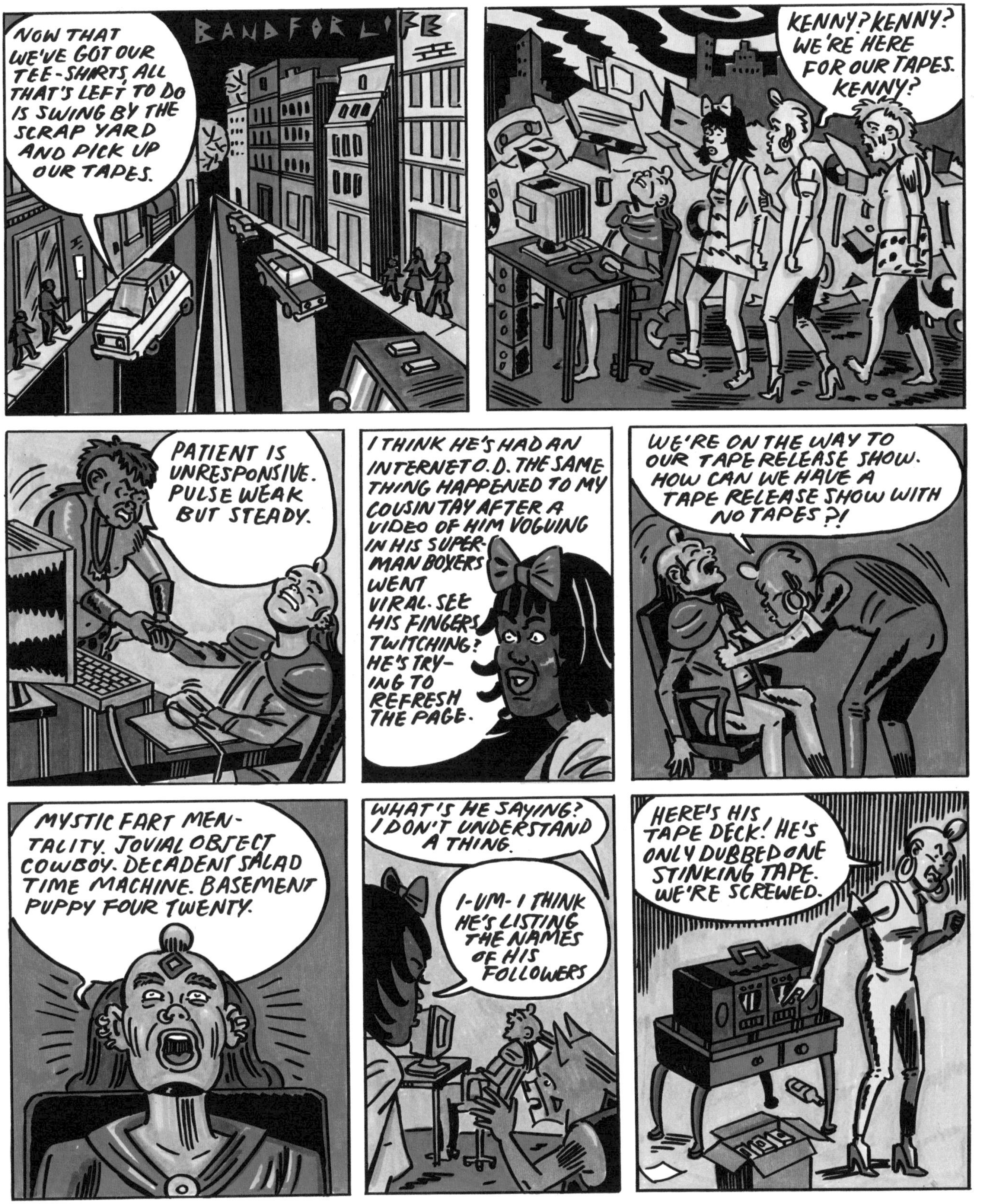
BAND FOR LIFE
NOW THAT WE'VE GOT OUR TEE-SHIRTS, ALL THAT'S LEFT TO DO IS SWING BY THE SCRAP YARD AND PICK UP OUR TAPES.
KENNY? KENNY? WE'RE HERE FOR OUR TAPES. KENNY?
PATIENT IS UNRESPONSIVE. PULSE WEAK BUT STEADY.
I THINK HE'S HAD AN INTERNET O.D. THE SAME THING HAPPENED TO MY COUSIN TAY AFTER A VIDEO OF HIM VOGUING IN HIS SUPER-MAN BOXERS WENT VIRAL. SEE HIS FINGERS TWITCHING? HE'S TRY-ING TO REFRESH THE PAGE.
WE'RE ON THE WAY TO OUR TAPE RELEASE SHOW. HOW CAN WE HAVE A TAPE RELEASE SHOW WITH NO TAPES?!
MYSTIC FART MEN-TALITY. JOVIAL OBJECT COWBOY. DECADENT SALAD TIME MACHINE. BASEMENT PUPPY FOUR TWENTY.
WHAT'S HE SAYING? I DON'T UNDERSTAND A THING.
I-UM- I THINK HE'S LISTING THE NAMES OF HIS FOLLOWERS
HERE'S HIS TAPE DECK! HE'S ONLY DUBBED ONE STINKING TAPE. WE'RE SCREWED.

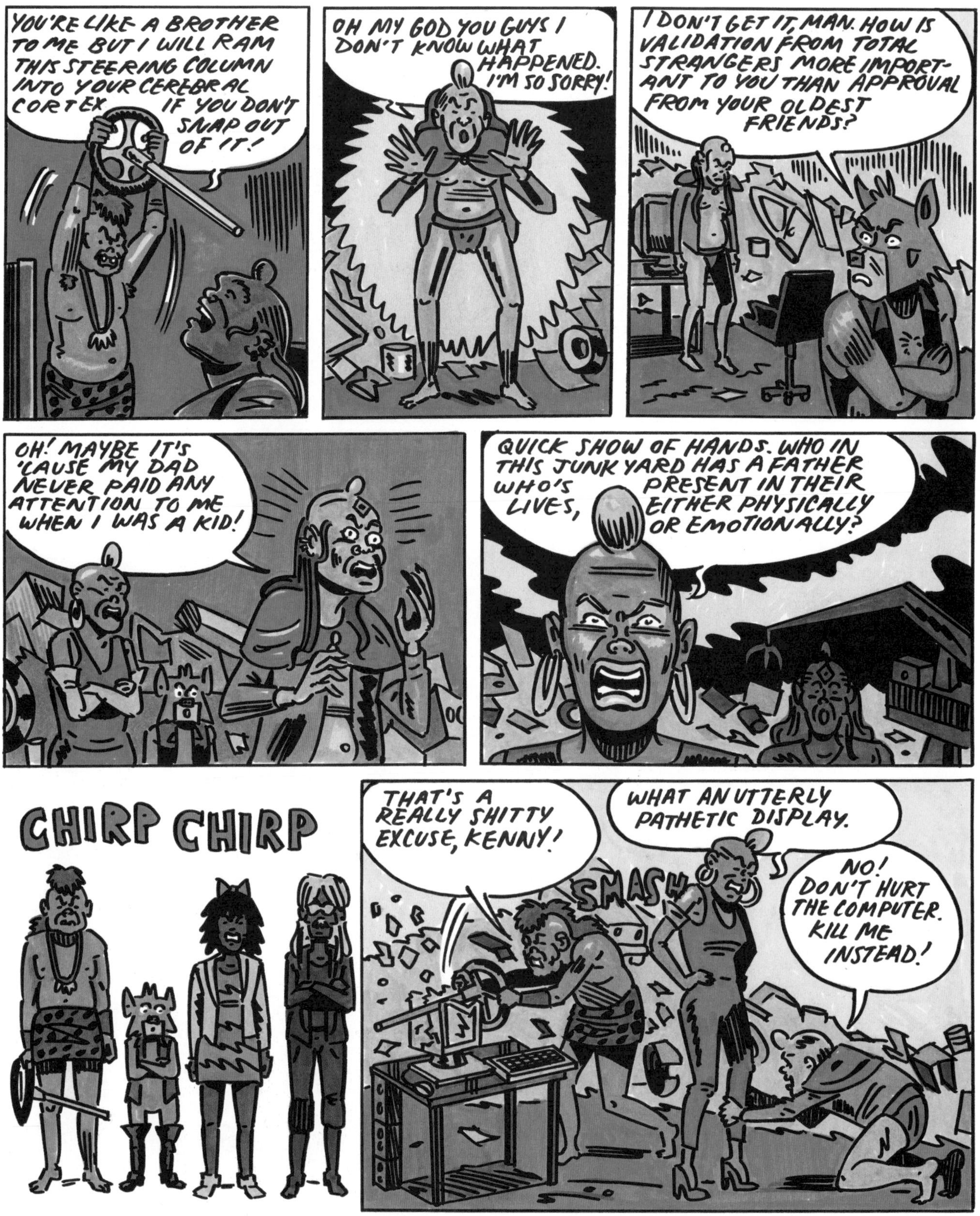
YOU'RE LIKE A BROTHER TO ME BUT I WILL RAM THIS STEERING COLUMN INTO YOUR CEREBRAL CORTEX IF YOU DON'T SNAP OUT OF IT!
OH MY GOD YOU GUYS I DON'T KNOW WHAT HAPPENED. I'M SO SORRY!
I DON'T GET IT, MAN. HOW IS VALIDATION FROM TOTAL STRANGERS MORE IMPORTANT TO YOU THAN APPROVAL FROM YOUR OLDEST FRIENDS?
OH! MAYBE IT'S 'CAUSE MY DAD NEVER PAID ANY ATTENTION TO ME WHEN I WAS A KID!
QUICK SHOW OF HANDS. WHO IN THIS JUNKYARD HAS A FATHER WHO'S PRESENT IN THEIR LIVES, EITHER PHYSICALLY OR EMOTIONALLY?
CHIRP CHIRP
THAT'S A REALLY SHITTY EXCUSE, KENNY!
WHAT AN UTTERLY PATHETIC DISPLAY.
SMASH
NO! DON'T HURT THE COMPUTER. KILL ME INSTEAD!

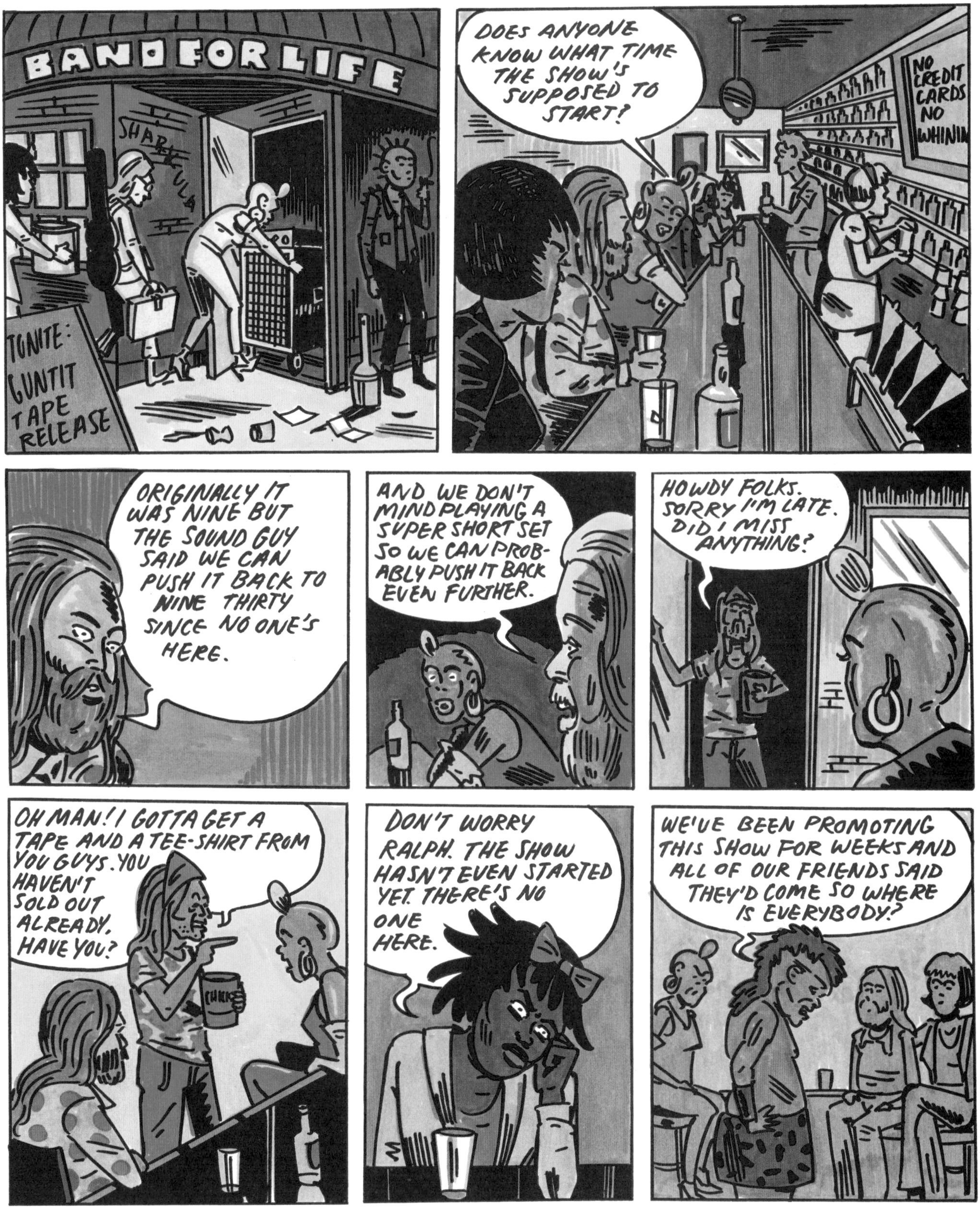
BAND FOR LIFE
SHARKULA
TONITE: GUNTIT TAPE RELEASE
DOES ANYONE KNOW WHAT TIME THE SHOW'S SUPPOSED TO START?
NO CREDIT CARDS NO WHININ
ORIGINALLY IT WAS NINE BUT THE SOUND GUY SAID WE CAN PUSH IT BACK TO NINE THIRTY SINCE NO ONE'S HERE.
AND WE DON'T MIND PLAYING A SUPER SHORT SET SO WE CAN PROBABLY PUSH IT BACK EVEN FURTHER.
HOWDY FOLKS. SORRY I'M LATE. DID I MISS ANYTHING?
OH MAN! I GOTTA GET A TAPE AND A TEE-SHIRT FROM YOU GUYS. YOU HAVEN'T SOLD OUT ALREADY, HAVE YOU?
DON'T WORRY RALPH. THE SHOW HASN'T EVEN STARTED YET. THERE'S NO ONE HERE.
WE'VE BEEN PROMOTING THIS SHOW FOR WEEKS AND ALL OF OUR FRIENDS SAID THEY'D COME SO WHERE IS EVERYBODY?

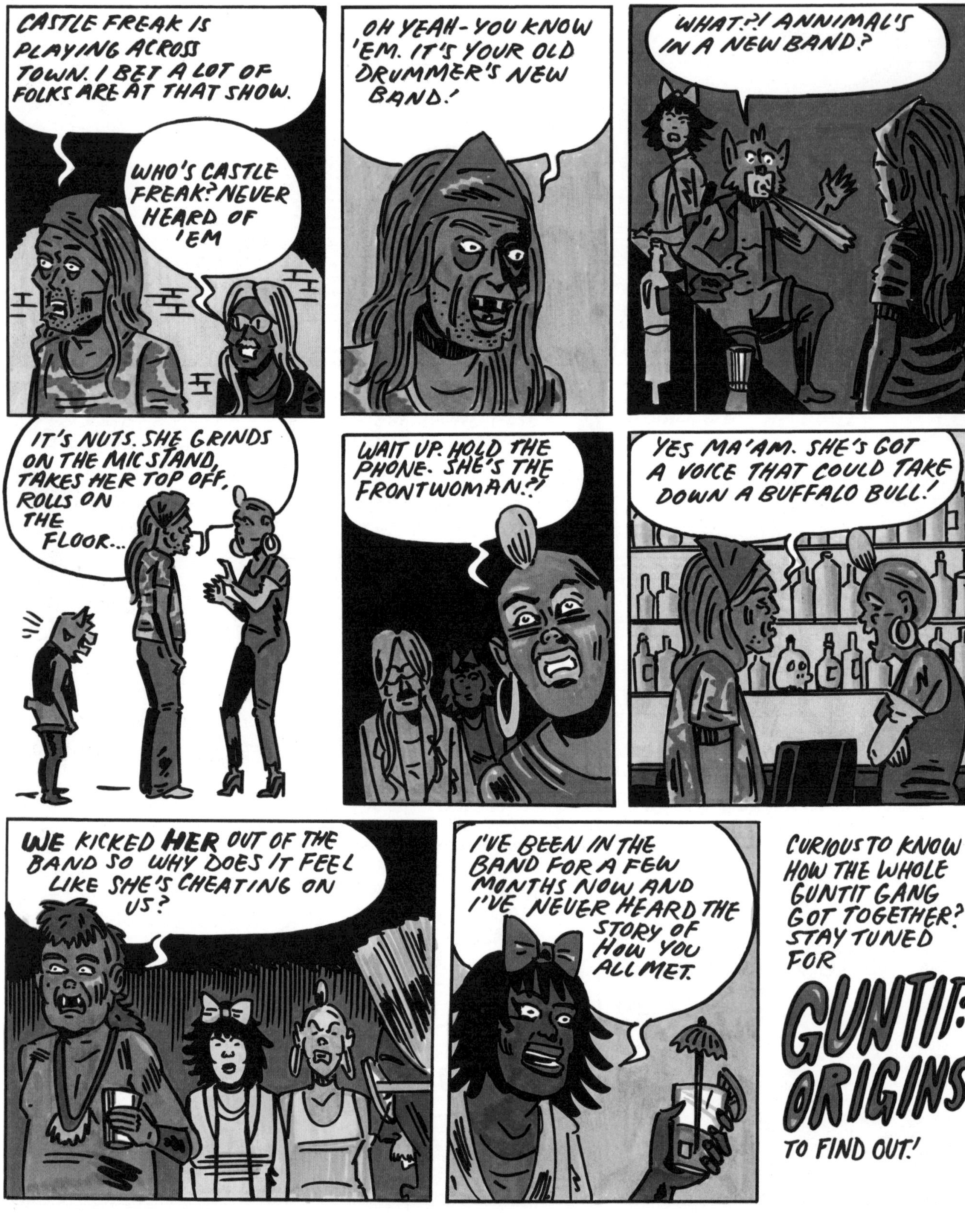
CASTLE FREAK IS PLAYING ACROSS TOWN. I BET A LOT OF FOLKS ARE AT THAT SHOW.
WHO'S CASTLE FREAK? NEVER HEARD OF 'EM
OH YEAH- YOU KNOW 'EM. IT'S YOUR OLD DRUMMER'S NEW BAND!
WHAT?! ANNIMAL'S IN A NEW BAND?
IT'S NUTS. SHE GRINDS ON THE MIC STAND, TAKES HER TOP OFF, ROLLS ON THE FLOOR...
WAIT UP. HOLD THE PHONE. SHE'S THE FRONTWOMAN?!
YES MA'AM. SHE'S GOT A VOICE THAT COULD TAKE DOWN A BUFFALO BULL!
WE KICKED HER OUT OF THE BAND SO WHY DOES IT FEEL LIKE SHE'S CHEATING ON US?
I'VE BEEN IN THE BAND FOR A FEW MONTHS NOW AND I'VE NEVER HEARD THE STORY OF HOW YOU ALL MET.
CURIOUS TO KNOW HOW THE WHOLE GUNTIT GANG GOT TOGETHER? STAY TUNED FOR
GUNTIT: ORIGINS
TO FIND OUT!

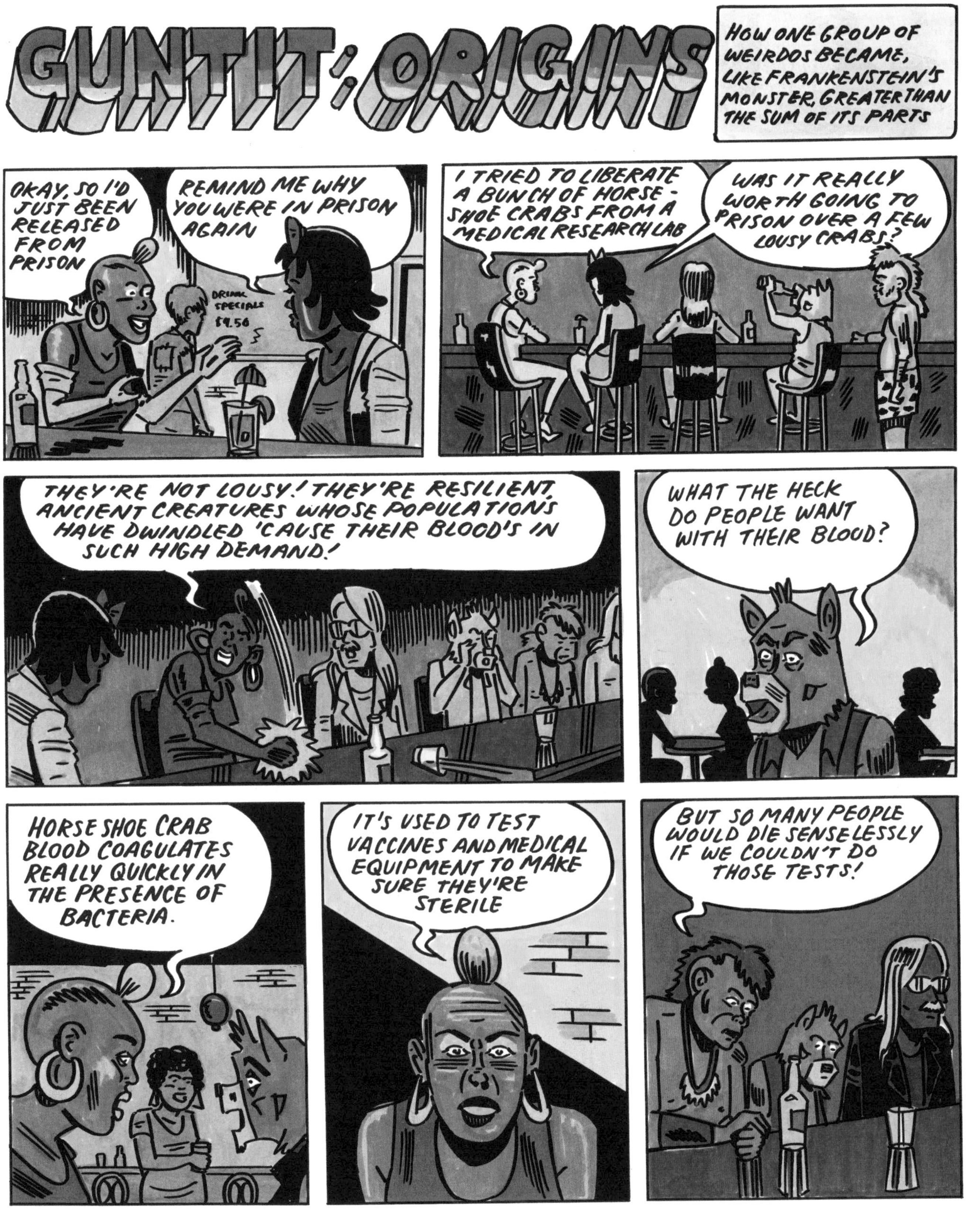
GUNTIT: ORIGINS
HOW ONE GROUP OF WEIRDOS BECAME, LIKE FRANKENSTEIN'S MONSTER, GREATER THAN THE SUM OF ITS PARTS
OKAY, SO I'D JUST BEEN RELEASED FROM PRISON
REMIND ME WHY YOU WERE IN PRISON AGAIN
DRINK SPECIALS
I TRIED TO LIBERATE A BUNCH OF HORSE-SHOE CRABS FROM A MEDICAL RESEARCH LAB
WAS IT REALLY WORTH GOING TO PRISON OVER A FEW LOUSY CRABS?
THEY'RE NOT LOUSY! THEY'RE RESILIENT, ANCIENT CREATURES WHOSE POPULATIONS HAVE DWINDLED 'CAUSE THEIR BLOOD'S IN SUCH HIGH DEMAND!
WHAT THE HECK DO PEOPLE WANT WITH THEIR BLOOD?
HORSE SHOE CRAB BLOOD COAGULATES REALLY QUICKLY IN THE PRESENCE OF BACTERIA.
IT'S USED TO TEST VACCINES AND MEDICAL EQUIPMENT TO MAKE SURE THEY'RE STERILE
BUT SO MANY PEOPLE WOULD DIE SENSELESSLY IF WE COULDN'T DO THOSE TESTS!

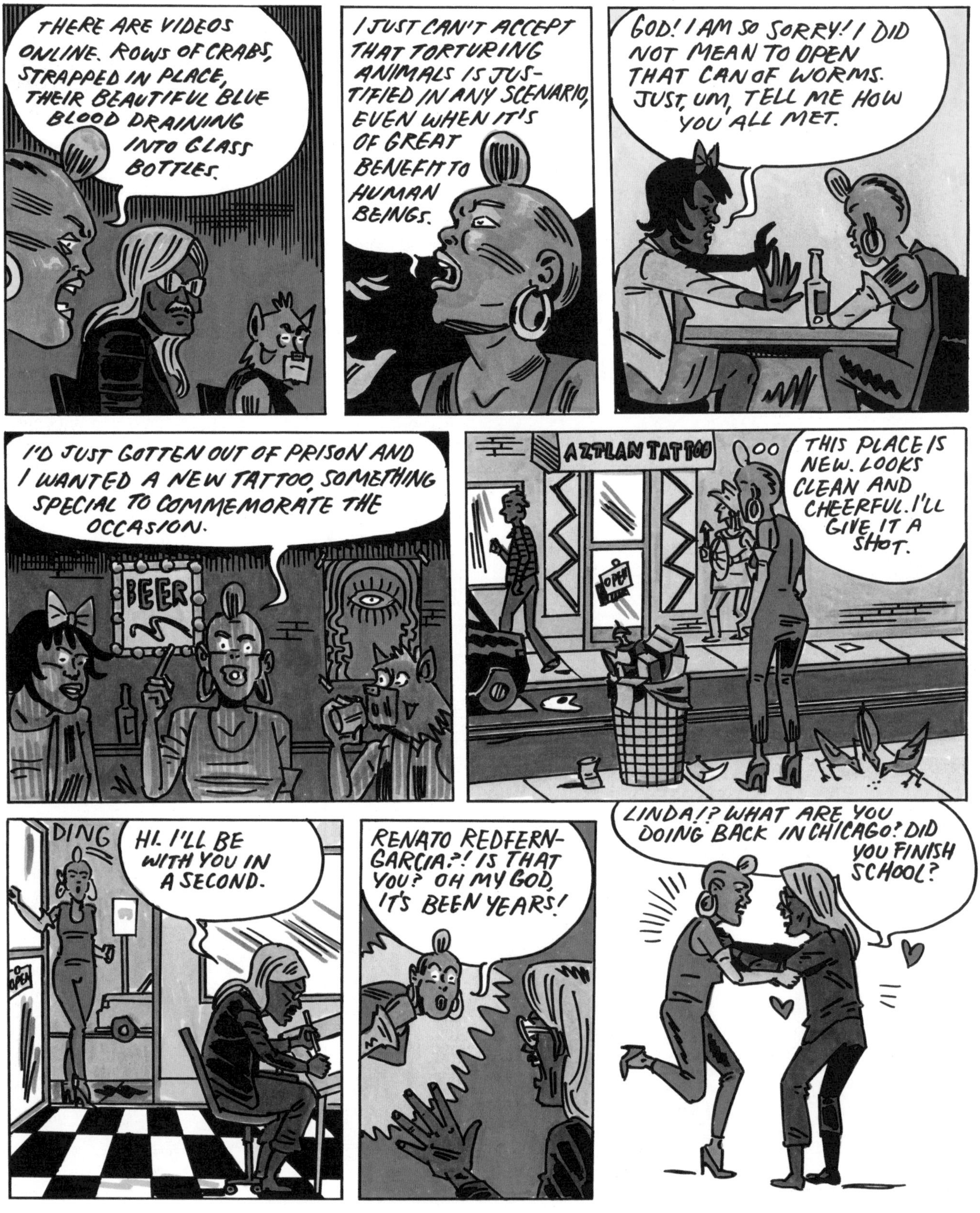
THERE ARE VIDEOS ONLINE. ROWS OF CRABS, STRAPPED IN PLACE, THEIR BEAUTIFUL BLUE BLOOD DRAINING INTO GLASS BOTTLES.
I JUST CAN'T ACCEPT THAT TORTURING ANIMALS IS JUSTIFIED IN ANY SCENARIO, EVEN WHEN IT'S OF GREAT BENEFIT TO HUMAN BEINGS.
GOD! I AM SO SORRY! I DID NOT MEAN TO OPEN THAT CAN OF WORMS. JUST, UM, TELL ME HOW YOU ALL MET.
I'D JUST GOTTEN OUT OF PRISON AND I WANTED A NEW TATTOO, SOMETHING SPECIAL TO COMMEMORATE THE OCCASION.
BEER
AZTLAN TATTOO
OPEN
THIS PLACE IS NEW. LOOKS CLEAN AND CHEERFUL. I'LL GIVE IT A SHOT.
DING
HI. I'LL BE WITH YOU IN A SECOND.
OPEN
RENATO REDFERN-GARCIA?! IS THAT YOU? OH MY GOD, IT'S BEEN YEARS!
LINDA!? WHAT ARE YOU DOING BACK IN CHICAGO? DID YOU FINISH SCHOOL?

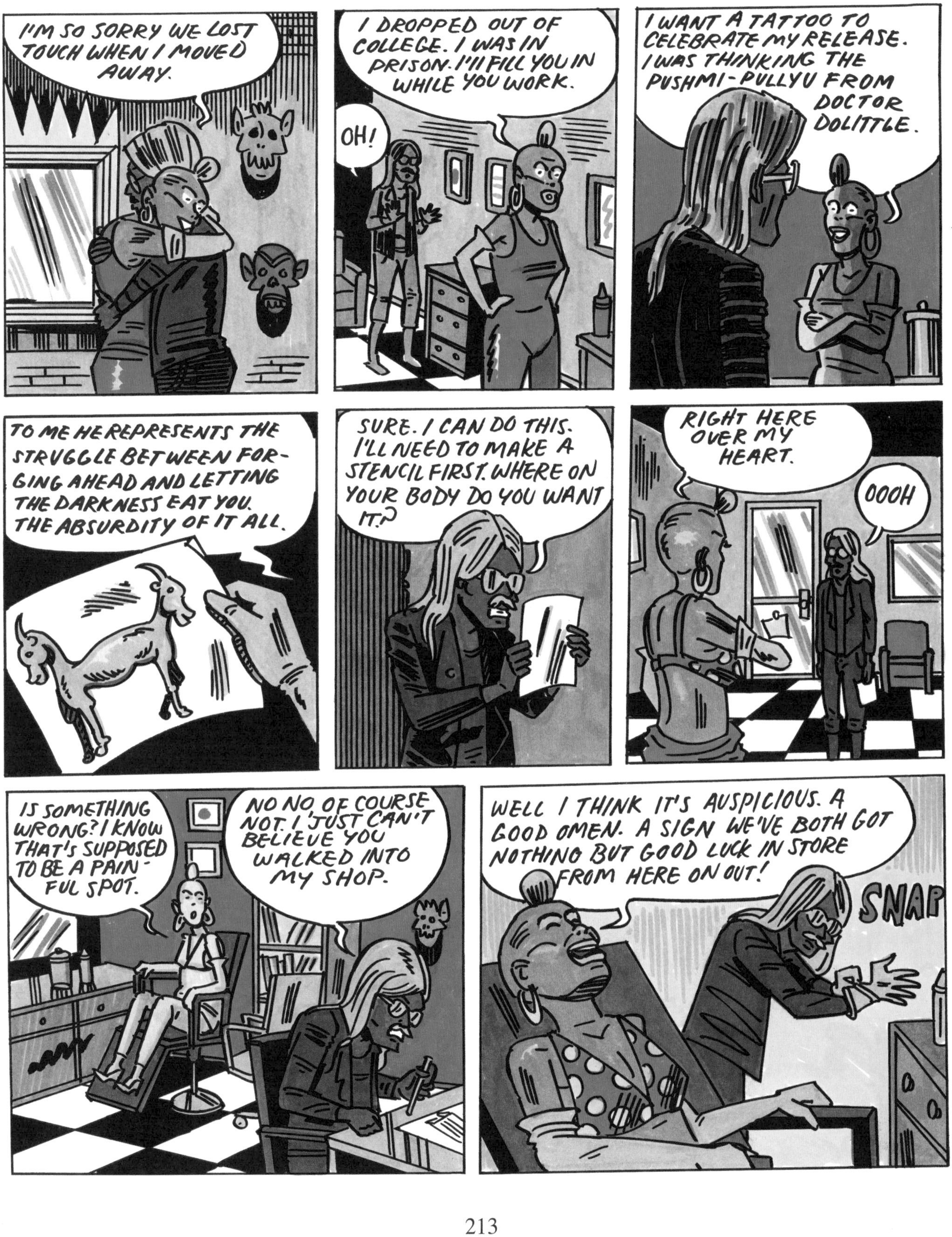
I'M SO SORRY WE LOST TOUCH WHEN I MOVED AWAY.
I DROPPED OUT OF COLLEGE. I WAS IN PRISON. I'LL FILL YOU IN WHILE YOU WORK.
OH!
I WANT A TATTOO TO CELEBRATE MY RELEASE. I WAS THINKING THE PUSHMI-PULLYU FROM DOCTOR DOLITTLE.
TO ME HE REPRESENTS THE STRUGGLE BETWEEN FORGING AHEAD AND LETTING THE DARKNESS EAT YOU. THE ABSURDITY OF IT ALL.
SURE. I CAN DO THIS. I'LL NEED TO MAKE A STENCIL FIRST. WHERE ON YOUR BODY DO YOU WANT IT?
RIGHT HERE OVER MY HEART.
OOOH
IS SOMETHING WRONG? I KNOW THAT'S SUPPOSED TO BE A PAINFUL SPOT.
NO NO OF COURSE NOT. I JUST CAN'T BELIEVE YOU WALKED INTO MY SHOP.
WELL I THINK IT'S AUSPICIOUS. A GOOD OMEN. A SIGN WE'VE BOTH GOT NOTHING BUT GOOD LUCK IN STORE FROM HERE ON OUT!
SNAP

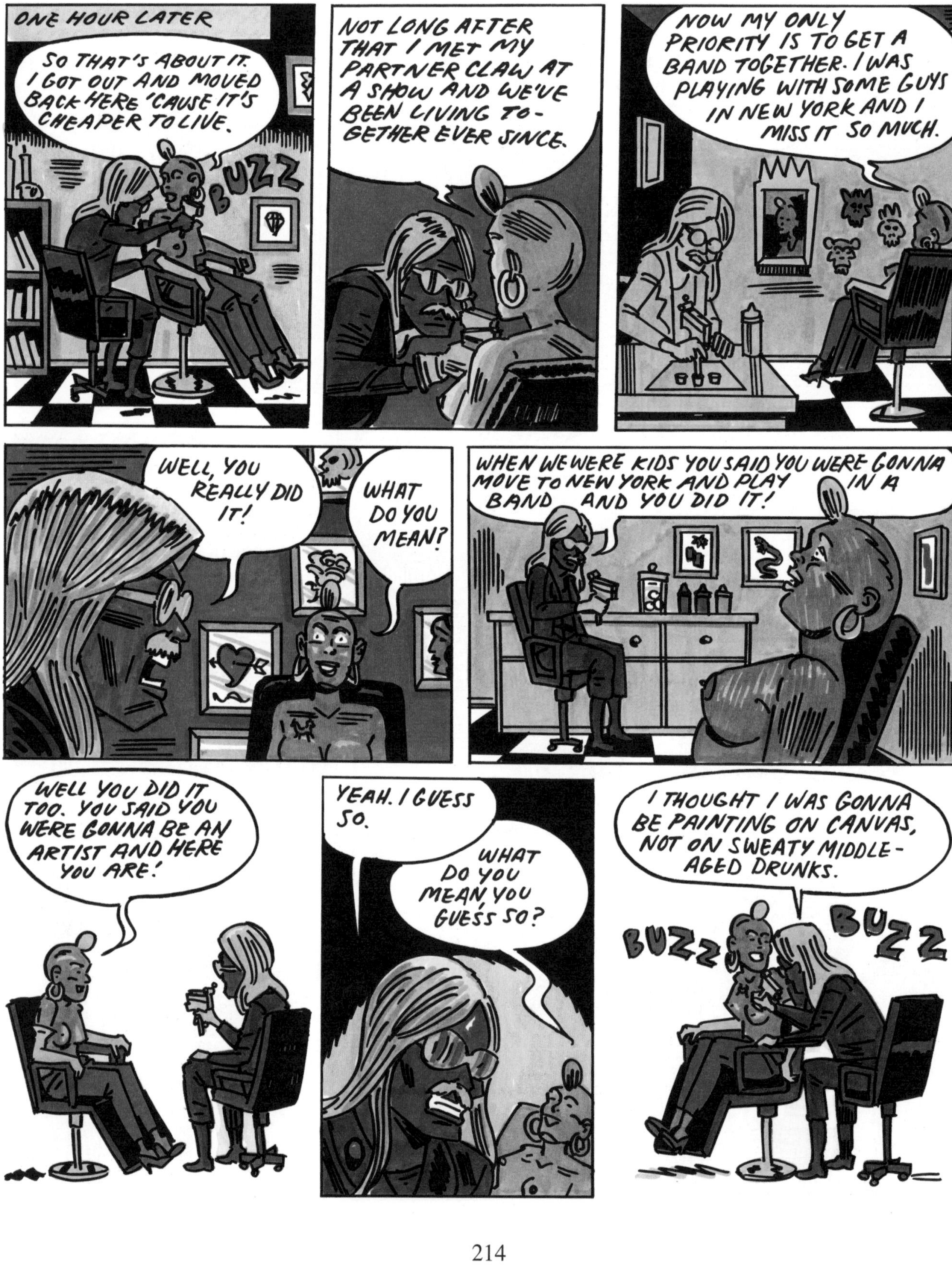

ONE HOUR LATER
SO THAT'S ABOUT IT. I GOT OUT AND MOVED BACK HERE 'CAUSE IT'S CHEAPER TO LIVE.
BUZZ
NOT LONG AFTER THAT I MET MY PARTNER CLAW AT A SHOW AND WE'VE BEEN LIVING TOGETHER EVER SINCE.
NOW MY ONLY PRIORITY IS TO GET A BAND TOGETHER. I WAS PLAYING WITH SOME GUYS IN NEW YORK AND I MISS IT SO MUCH.
WELL, YOU REALLY DID IT!
WHAT DO YOU MEAN?
WHEN WE WERE KIDS YOU SAID YOU WERE GONNA MOVE TO NEW YORK AND PLAY IN A BAND AND YOU DID IT!
WELL YOU DID IT TOO. YOU SAID YOU WERE GONNA BE AN ARTIST AND HERE YOU ARE!
YEAH. I GUESS SO.
WHAT DO YOU MEAN, YOU GUESS SO?
I THOUGHT I WAS GONNA BE PAINTING ON CANVAS, NOT ON SWEATY MIDDLE-AGED DRUNKS.
BUZZ
BUZZ

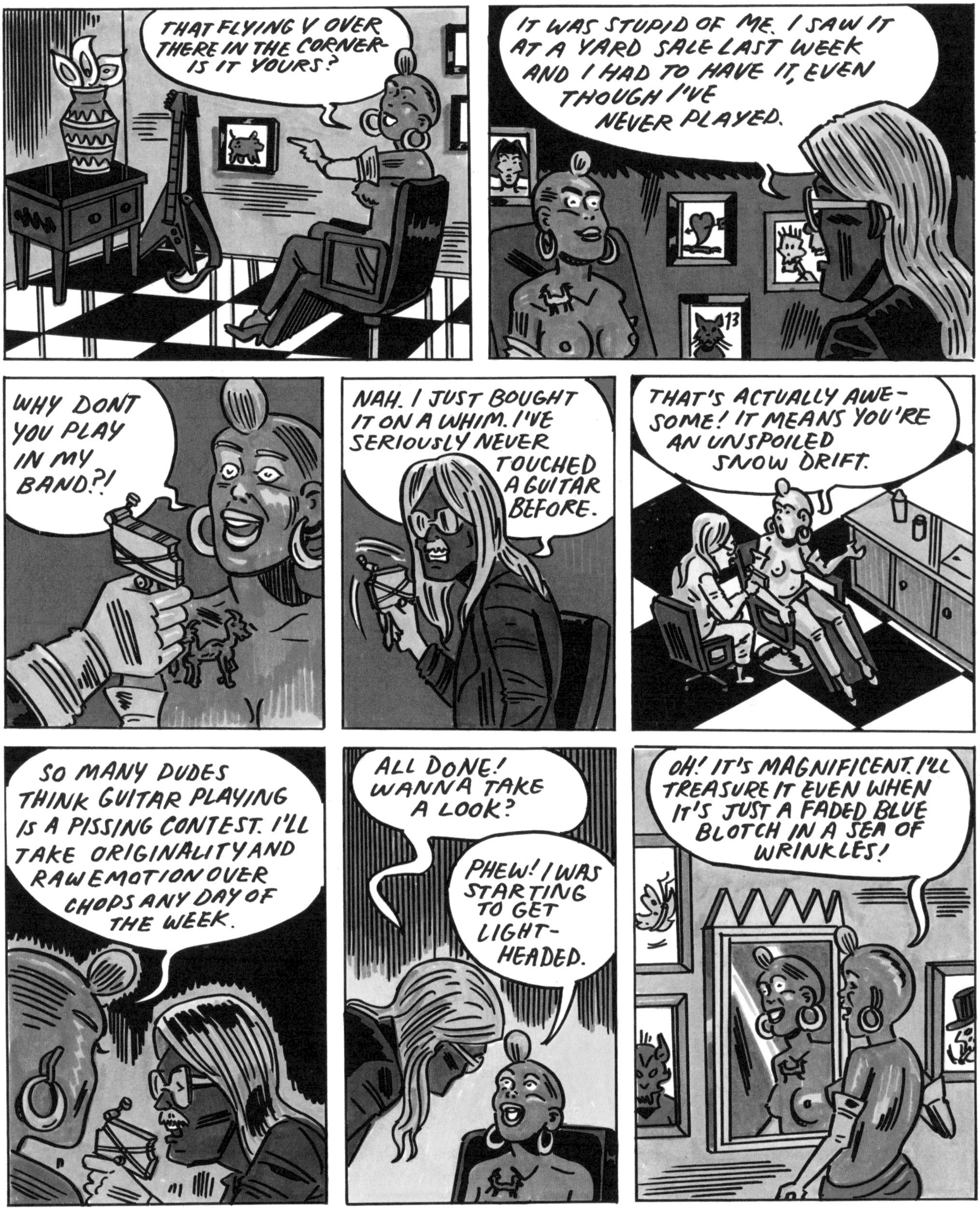
THAT FLYING V OVER THERE IN THE CORNER- IS IT YOURS?
IT WAS STUPID OF ME. I SAW IT AT A YARD SALE LAST WEEK AND I HAD TO HAVE IT, EVEN THOUGH I'VE NEVER PLAYED.
WHY DONT YOU PLAY IN MY BAND?!
NAH. I JUST BOUGHT IT ON A WHIM. I'VE SERIOUSLY NEVER TOUCHED A GUITAR BEFORE.
THAT'S ACTUALLY AWE-SOME! IT MEANS YOU'RE AN UNSPOILED SNOW DRIFT.
SO MANY DUDES THINK GUITAR PLAYING IS A PISSING CONTEST. I'LL TAKE ORIGINALITY AND RAW EMOTION OVER CHOPS ANY DAY OF THE WEEK.
ALL DONE! WANNA TAKE A LOOK?
PHEW! I WAS STARTING TO GET LIGHT-HEADED.
OH! IT'S MAGNIFICENT. I'LL TREASURE IT EVEN WHEN IT'S JUST A FADED BLUE BLOTCH IN A SEA OF WRINKLES!

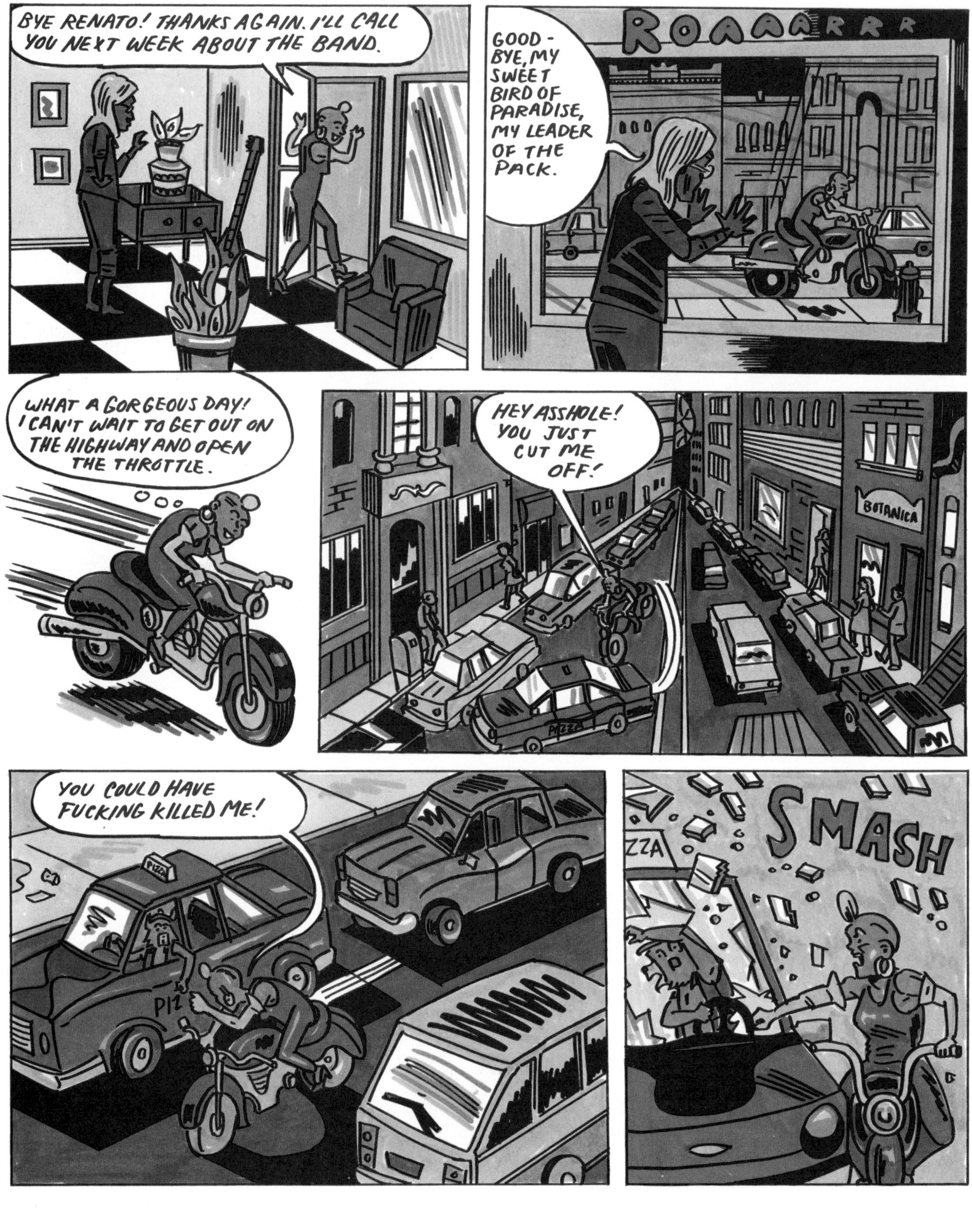
BYE RENATO! THANKS AGAIN. I'LL CALL YOU NEXT WEEK ABOUT THE BAND.
ROAAARRR
GOOD-BYE, MY SWEET BIRD OF PARADISE, MY LEADER OF THE PACK.
WHAT A GORGEOUS DAY! I CAN'T WAIT TO GET OUT ON THE HIGHWAY AND OPEN THE THROTTLE.
HEY ASSHOLE! YOU JUST CUT ME OFF!
BOTANICA
PIZZA
YOU COULD HAVE FUCKING KILLED ME!
SMASH

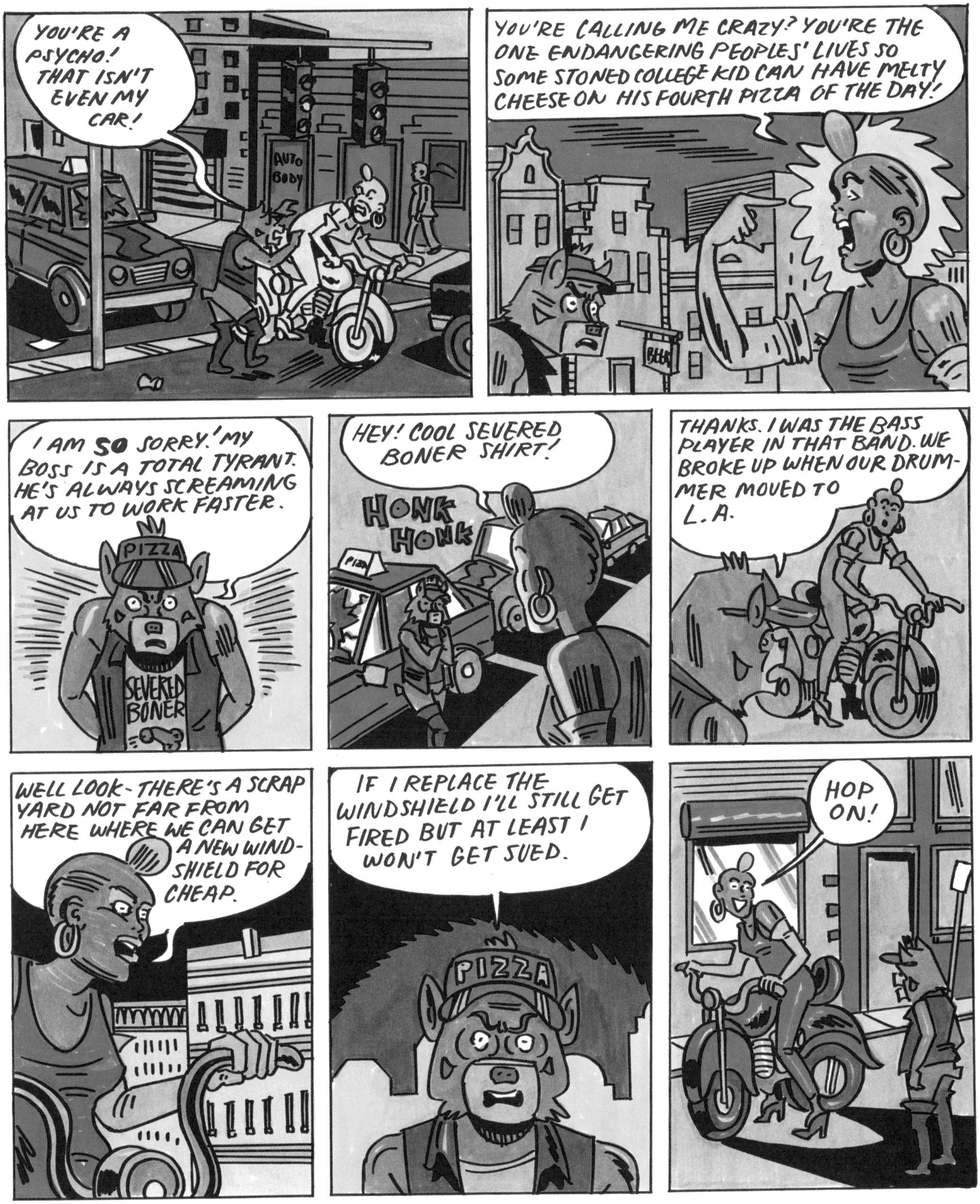
YOU'RE A PSYCHO! THAT ISN'T EVEN MY CAR!
AUTO BODY
YOU'RE CALLING ME CRAZY? YOU'RE THE ONE ENDANGERING PEOPLES' LIVES SO SOME STONED COLLEGE KID CAN HAVE MELTY CHEESE ON HIS FOURTH PIZZA OF THE DAY!
BEER
I AM SO SORRY! MY BOSS IS A TOTAL TYRANT. HE'S ALWAYS SCREAMING AT US TO WORK FASTER.
PIZZA
SEVERED BONER
HEY! COOL SEVERED BONER SHIRT!
HONK HONK
THANKS. I WAS THE BASS PLAYER IN THAT BAND. WE BROKE UP WHEN OUR DRUMMER MOVED TO L.A.
WELL LOOK- THERE'S A SCRAP YARD NOT FAR FROM HERE WHERE WE CAN GET A NEW WINDSHIELD FOR CHEAP.
IF I REPLACE THE WINDSHIELD I'LL STILL GET FIRED BUT AT LEAST I WON'T GET SUED.
PIZZA
HOP ON!

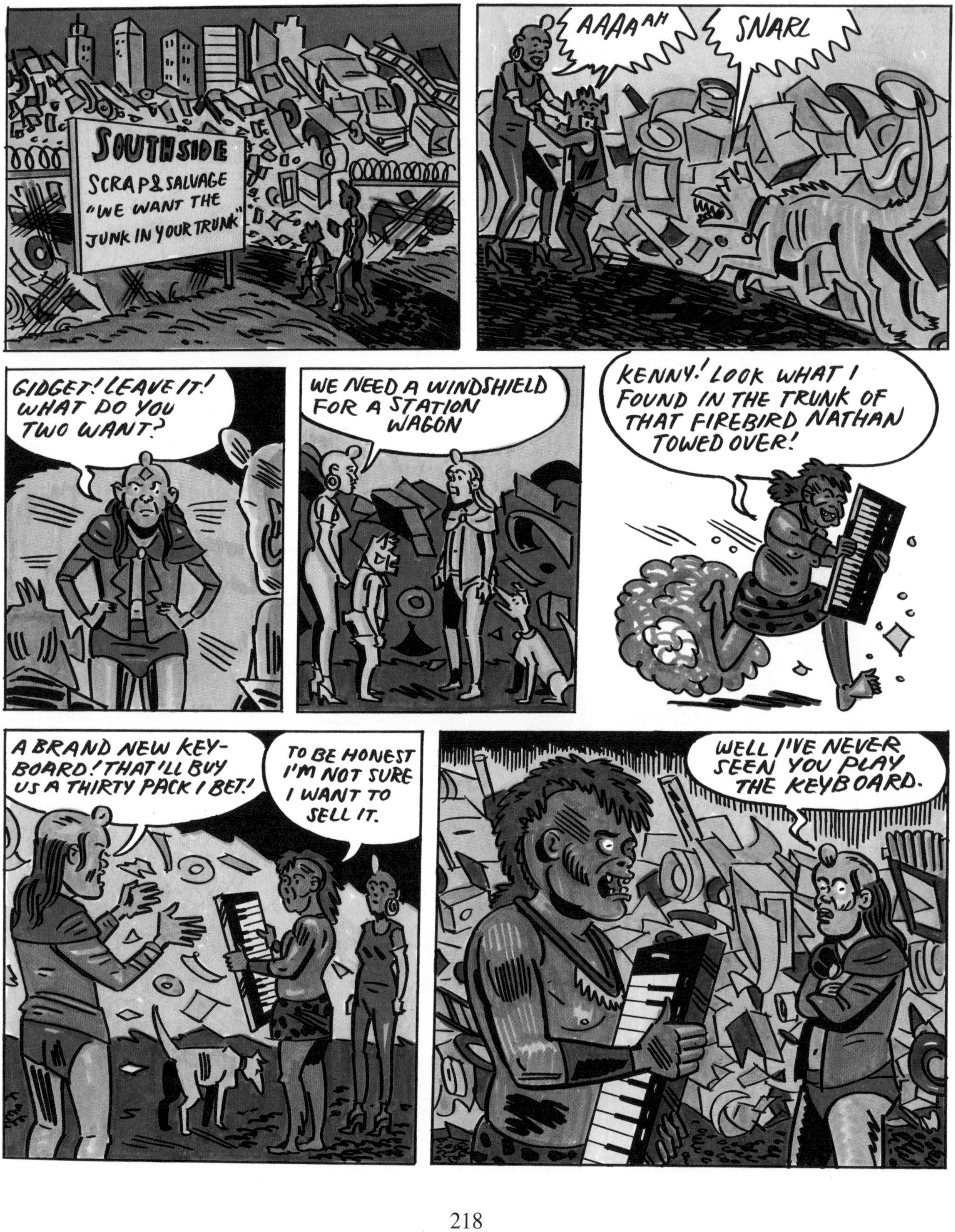
SOUTHSIDE
SCRAP & SALVAGE
"WE WANT THE JUNK IN YOUR TRUNK"
AAAAAH
SNARL
GIDGET! LEAVE IT! WHAT DO YOU TWO WANT?
WE NEED A WINDSHIELD FOR A STATION WAGON
KENNY! LOOK WHAT I FOUND IN THE TRUNK OF THAT FIREBIRD NATHAN TOWED OVER!
A BRAND NEW KEY-BOARD! THAT'LL BUY US A THIRTY PACK I BET!
TO BE HONEST I'M NOT SURE I WANT TO SELL IT.
WELL I'VE NEVER SEEN YOU PLAY THE KEYBOARD.

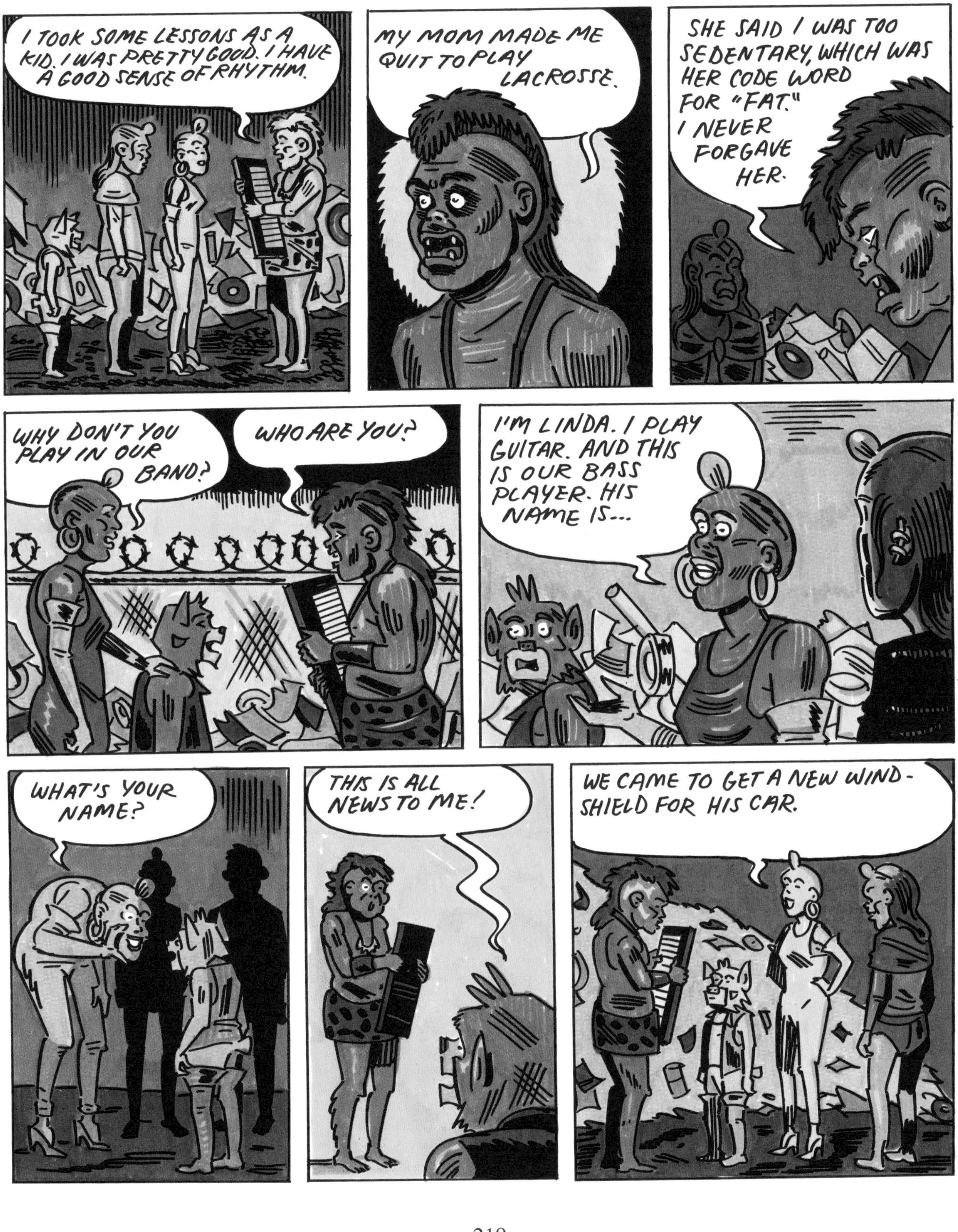
I TOOK SOME LESSONS AS A KID. I WAS PRETTY GOOD. I HAVE A GOOD SENSE OF RHYTHM.
MY MOM MADE ME QUIT TO PLAY LACROSSE.
SHE SAID I WAS TOO SEDENTARY, WHICH WAS HER CODE WORD FOR "FAT." I NEVER FORGAVE HER.
WHY DON'T YOU PLAY IN OUR BAND?
WHO ARE YOU?
I'M LINDA. I PLAY GUITAR. AND THIS IS OUR BASS PLAYER. HIS NAME IS...
WHAT'S YOUR NAME?
THIS IS ALL NEWS TO ME!
WE CAME TO GET A NEW WIND-SHIELD FOR HIS CAR.

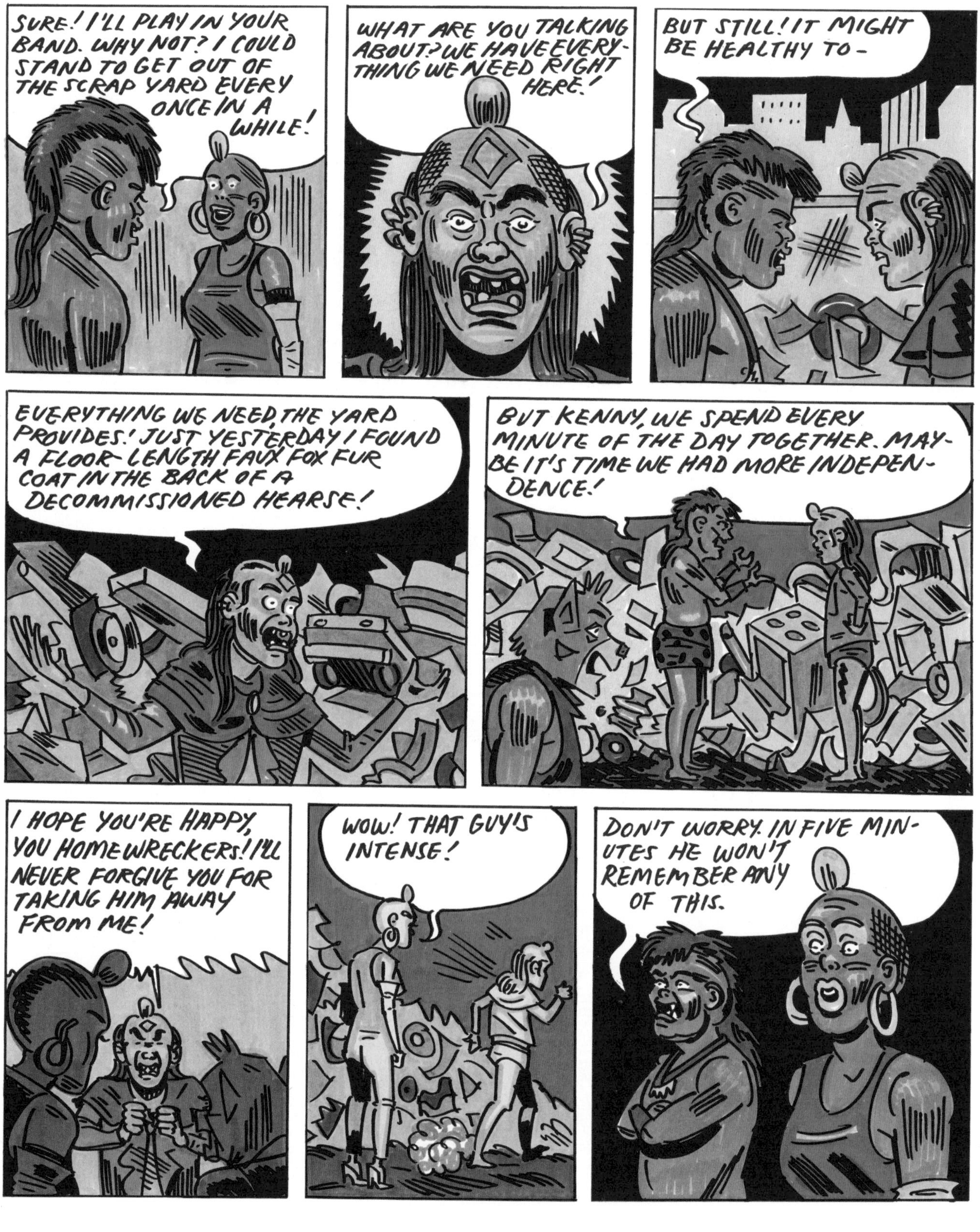
SURE! I'LL PLAY IN YOUR BAND. WHY NOT? I COULD STAND TO GET OUT OF THE SCRAP YARD EVERY ONCE IN A WHILE!
WHAT ARE YOU TALKING ABOUT? WE HAVE EVERYTHING WE NEED RIGHT HERE!
BUT STILL! IT MIGHT BE HEALTHY TO-
EVERYTHING WE NEED, THE YARD PROVIDES! JUST YESTERDAY I FOUND A FLOOR-LENGTH FAUX FOX FUR COAT IN THE BACK OF A DECOMMISSIONED HEARSE!
BUT KENNY, WE SPEND EVERY MINUTE OF THE DAY TOGETHER. MAYBE IT'S TIME WE HAD MORE INDEPENDENCE!
I HOPE YOU'RE HAPPY, YOU HOMEWRECKERS! I'LL NEVER FORGIVE YOU FOR TAKING HIM AWAY FROM ME!
WOW! THAT GUY'S INTENSE!
DON'T WORRY. IN FIVE MINUTES HE WON'T REMEMBER ANY OF THIS.

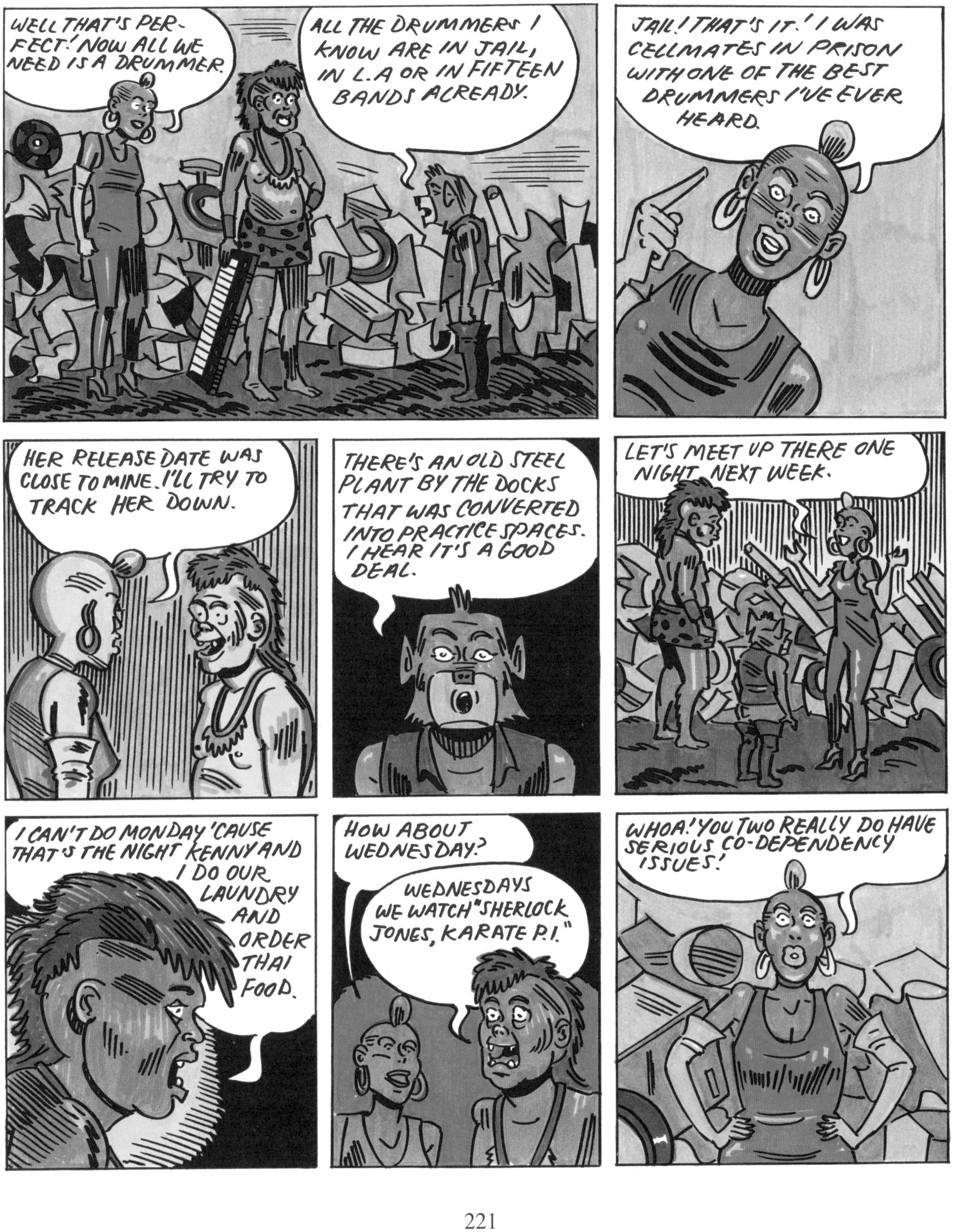
WELL THAT'S PER-FECT! NOW ALL WE NEED IS A DRUMMER.
ALL THE DRUMMERS I KNOW ARE IN JAIL, IN L.A OR IN FIFTEEN BANDS ALREADY.
JAIL! THAT'S IT! I WAS CELLMATES IN PRISON WITH ONE OF THE BEST DRUMMERS I'VE EVER HEARD.
HER RELEASE DATE WAS CLOSE TO MINE. I'LL TRY TO TRACK HER DOWN.
THERE'S AN OLD STEEL PLANT BY THE DOCKS THAT WAS CONVERTED INTO PRACTICE SPACES. I HEAR IT'S A GOOD DEAL.
LET'S MEET UP THERE ONE NIGHT NEXT WEEK.
I CAN'T DO MONDAY 'CAUSE THAT'S THE NIGHT KENNY AND I DO OUR LAUNDRY AND ORDER THAI FOOD.
HOW ABOUT WEDNESDAY?
WEDNESDAYS WE WATCH "SHERLOCK JONES, KARATE P.I."
WHOA! YOU TWO REALLY DO HAVE SERIOUS CO-DEPENDENCY ISSUES!

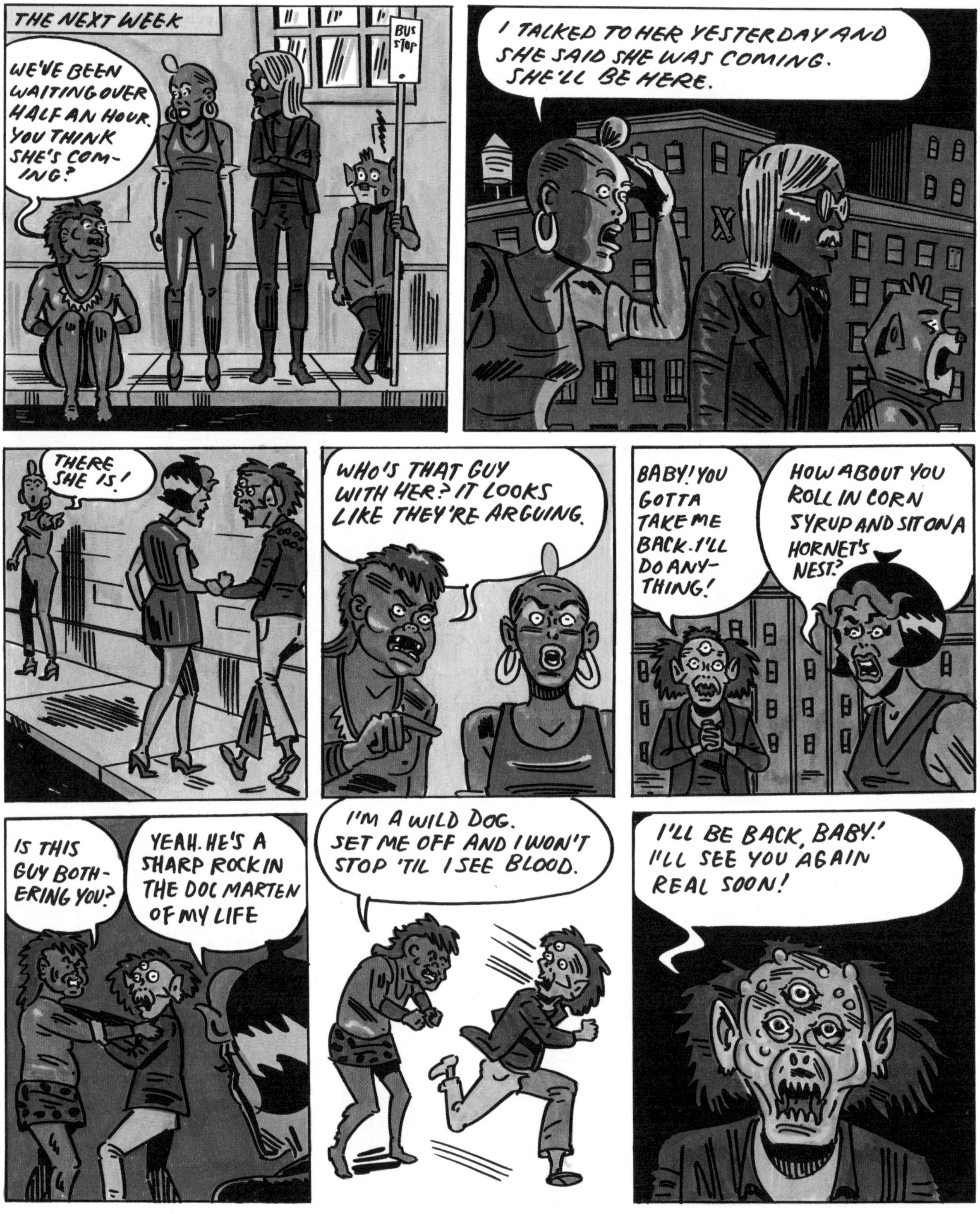
THE NEXT WEEK
WE'VE BEEN WAITING OVER HALF AN HOUR. YOU THINK SHE'S COMING?
BUS STOP
I TALKED TO HER YESTERDAY AND SHE SAID SHE WAS COMING. SHE'LL BE HERE.
THERE SHE IS!
WHO'S THAT GUY WITH HER? IT LOOKS LIKE THEY'RE ARGUING.
BABY! YOU GOTTA TAKE ME BACK. I'LL DO ANYTHING!
HOW ABOUT YOU ROLL IN CORN SYRUP AND SIT ON A HORNET'S NEST?
IS THIS GUY BOTHERING YOU?
YEAH. HE'S A SHARP ROCK IN THE DOC MARTEN OF MY LIFE
I'M A WILD DOG. SET ME OFF AND I WON'T STOP 'TIL I SEE BLOOD.
I'LL BE BACK, BABY! I'LL SEE YOU AGAIN REAL SOON!

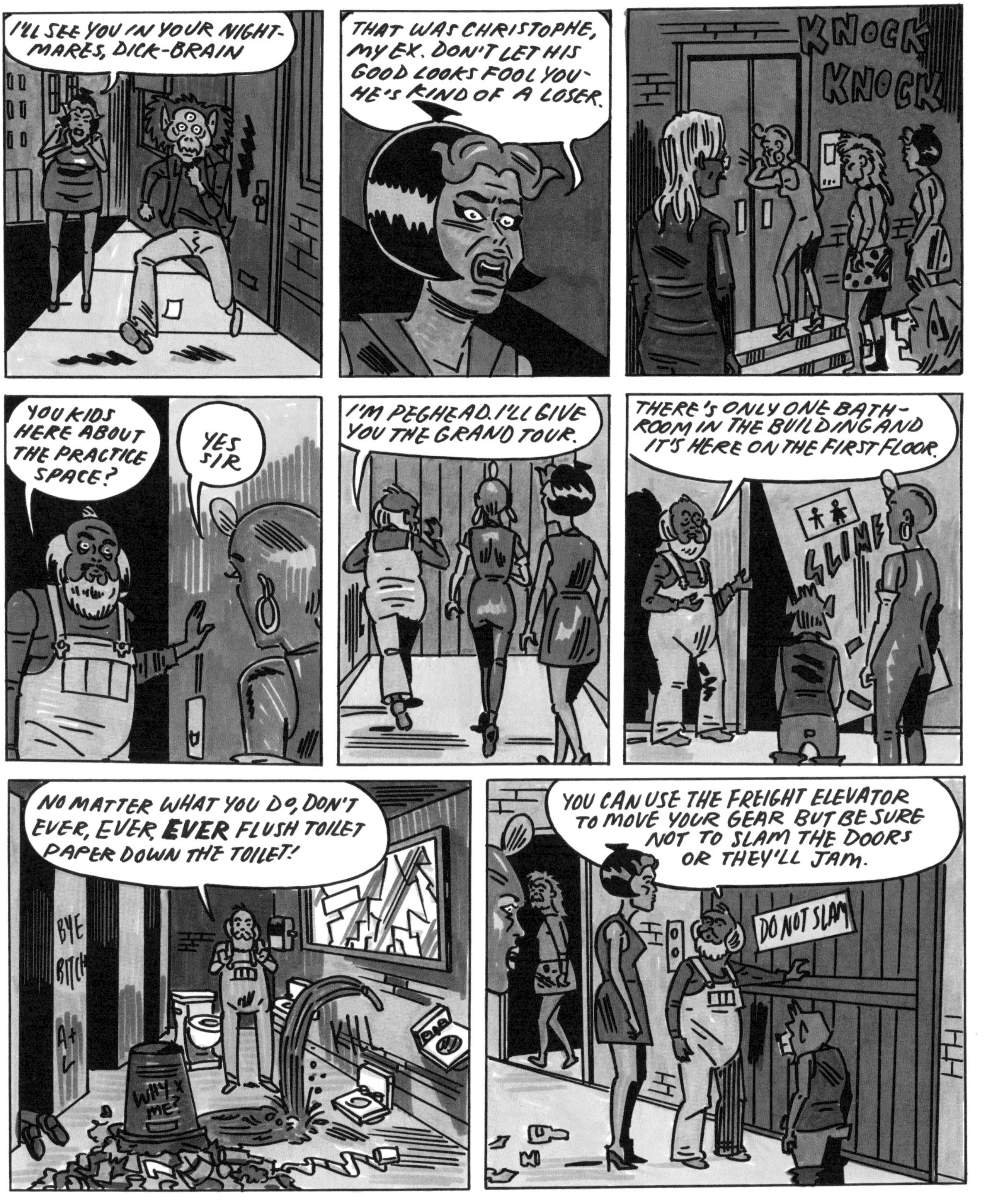
I'LL SEE YOU IN YOUR NIGHTMARES, DICK-BRAIN
THAT WAS CHRISTOPHE, MY EX. DON'T LET HIS GOOD LOOKS FOOL YOU- HE'S KIND OF A LOSER.
KNOCK KNOCK
YOU KIDS HERE ABOUT THE PRACTICE SPACE?
YES SIR
I'M PEGHEAD. I'LL GIVE YOU THE GRAND TOUR.
THERE'S ONLY ONE BATHROOM IN THE BUILDING AND IT'S HERE ON THE FIRST FLOOR.
SLIME
NO MATTER WHAT YOU DO, DON'T EVER, EVER, **EVER** FLUSH TOILET PAPER DOWN THE TOILET!
BYE BITCH
WHY ME?
YOU CAN USE THE FREIGHT ELEVATOR TO MOVE YOUR GEAR BUT BE SURE NOT TO SLAM THE DOORS OR THEY'LL JAM.
DO NOT SLAM

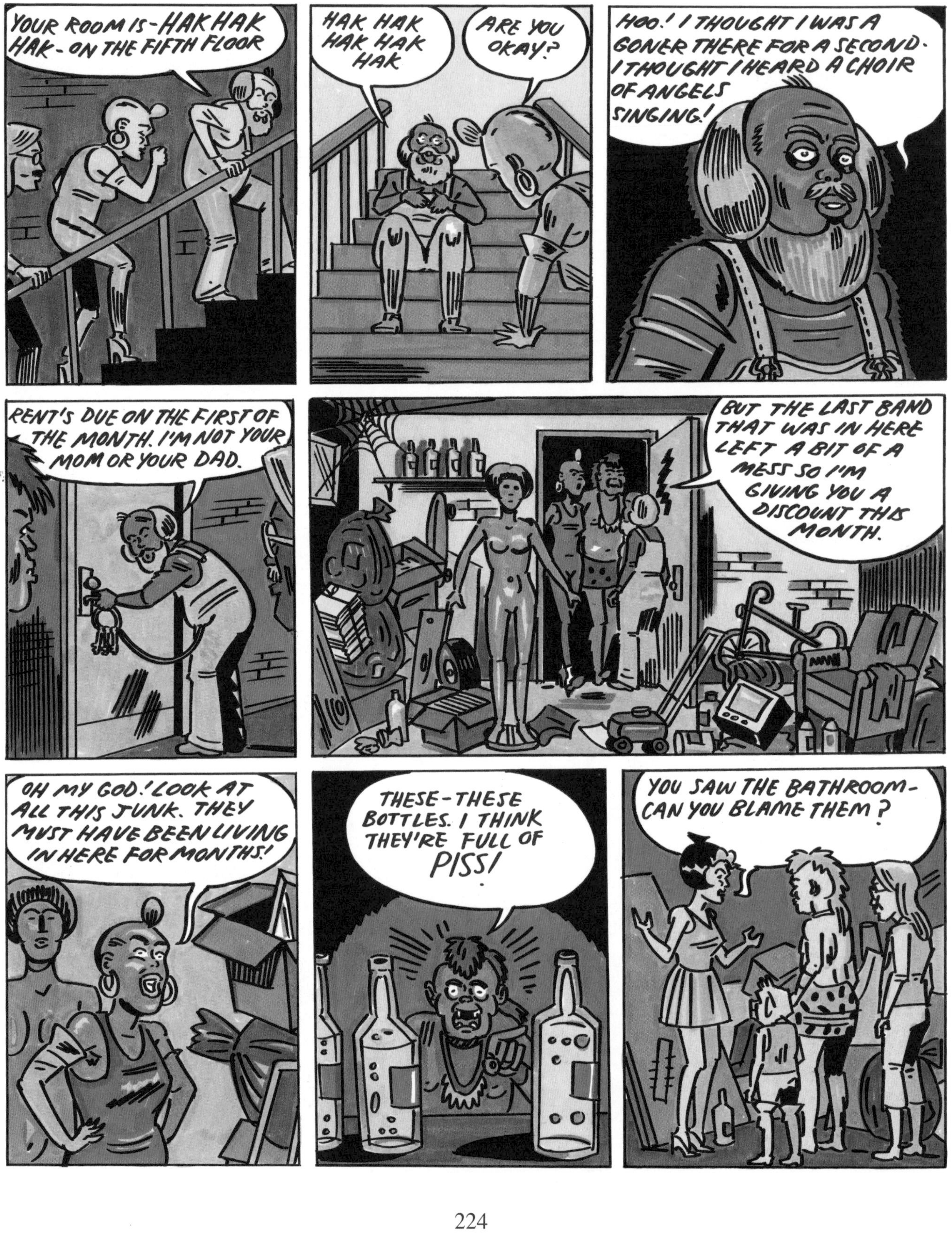
YOUR ROOM IS-HAK HAK HAK-ON THE FIFTH FLOOR
HAK HAK HAK HAK HAK
ARE YOU OKAY?
HOO! I THOUGHT I WAS A GONER THERE FOR A SECOND. I THOUGHT I HEARD A CHOIR OF ANGELS SINGING!
RENT'S DUE ON THE FIRST OF THE MONTH. I'M NOT YOUR MOM OR YOUR DAD.
BUT THE LAST BAND THAT WAS IN HERE LEFT A BIT OF A MESS SO I'M GIVING YOU A DISCOUNT THIS MONTH.
OH MY GOD! LOOK AT ALL THIS JUNK. THEY MUST HAVE BEEN LIVING IN HERE FOR MONTHS!
THESE-THESE BOTTLES. I THINK THEY'RE FULL OF PISS!
YOU SAW THE BATHROOM-CAN YOU BLAME THEM?

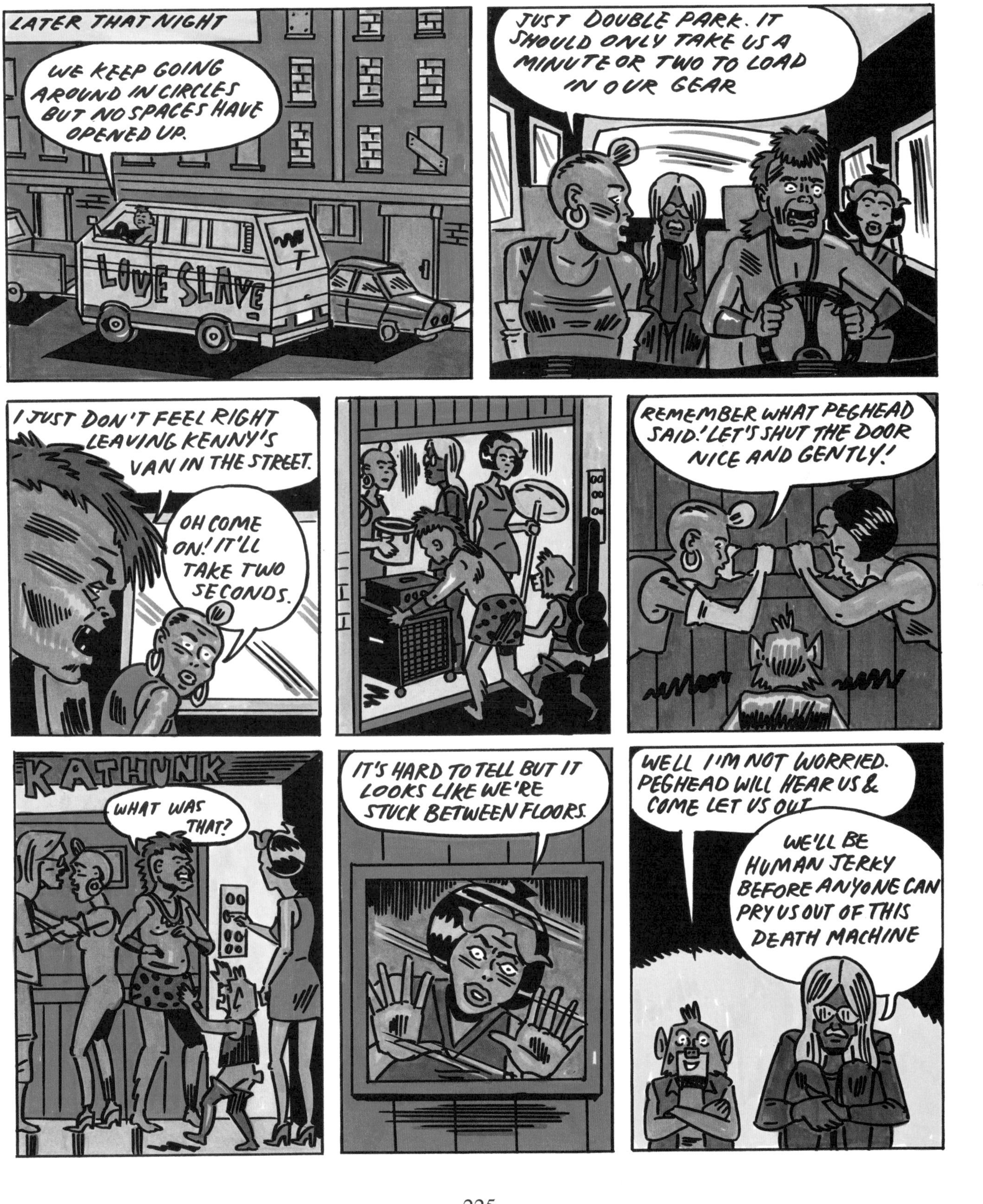

LATER THAT NIGHT
WE KEEP GOING AROUND IN CIRCLES BUT NO SPACES HAVE OPENED UP.
LOVE SLAVE
JUST DOUBLE PARK. IT SHOULD ONLY TAKE US A MINUTE OR TWO TO LOAD IN OUR GEAR
I JUST DON'T FEEL RIGHT LEAVING KENNY'S VAN IN THE STREET.
OH COME ON! IT'LL TAKE TWO SECONDS.
REMEMBER WHAT PEGHEAD SAID! LET'S SHUT THE DOOR NICE AND GENTLY!
KATHUNK
WHAT WAS THAT?
IT'S HARD TO TELL BUT IT LOOKS LIKE WE'RE STUCK BETWEEN FLOORS.
WELL I'M NOT WORRIED. PEGHEAD WILL HEAR US & COME LET US OUT
WE'LL BE HUMAN JERKY BEFORE ANYONE CAN PRY US OUT OF THIS DEATH MACHINE

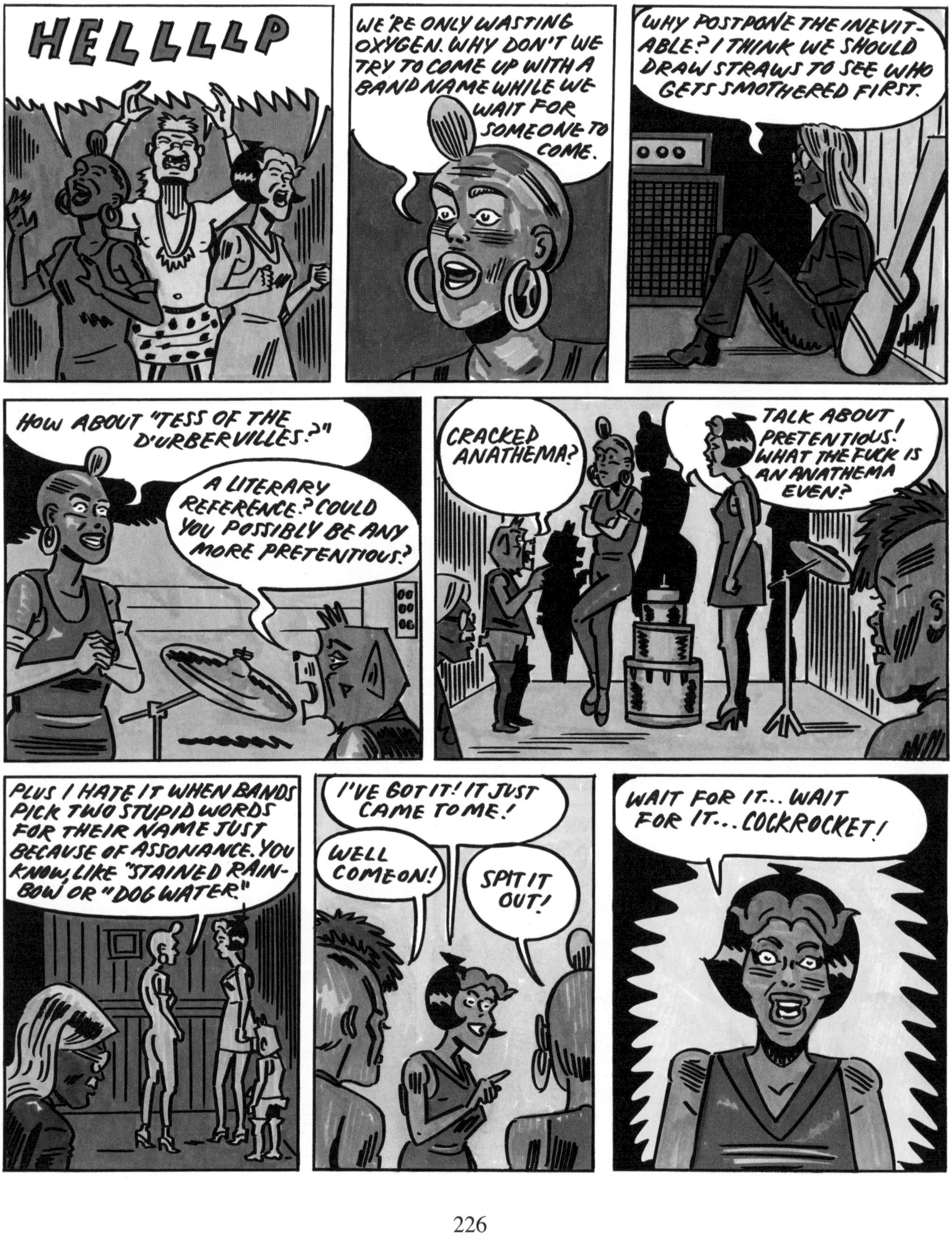

HELLLLP
WE'RE ONLY WASTING OXYGEN. WHY DON'T WE TRY TO COME UP WITH A BAND NAME WHILE WE WAIT FOR SOMEONE TO COME.
WHY POSTPONE THE INEVIT-ABLE? I THINK WE SHOULD DRAW STRAWS TO SEE WHO GETS SMOTHERED FIRST.
HOW ABOUT "TESS OF THE D'URBERVILLES?"
A LITERARY REFERENCE? COULD YOU POSSIBLY BE ANY MORE PRETENTIOUS?
CRACKED ANATHEMA?
TALK ABOUT PRETENTIOUS! WHAT THE FUCK IS AN ANATHEMA EVEN?
PLUS I HATE IT WHEN BANDS PICK TWO STUPID WORDS FOR THEIR NAME JUST BECAUSE OF ASSONANCE. YOU KNOW, LIKE "STAINED RAIN-BOW" OR "DOG WATER."
I'VE GOT IT! IT JUST CAME TO ME!
WELL COME ON!
SPIT IT OUT!
WAIT FOR IT... WAIT FOR IT... COCKROCKET!

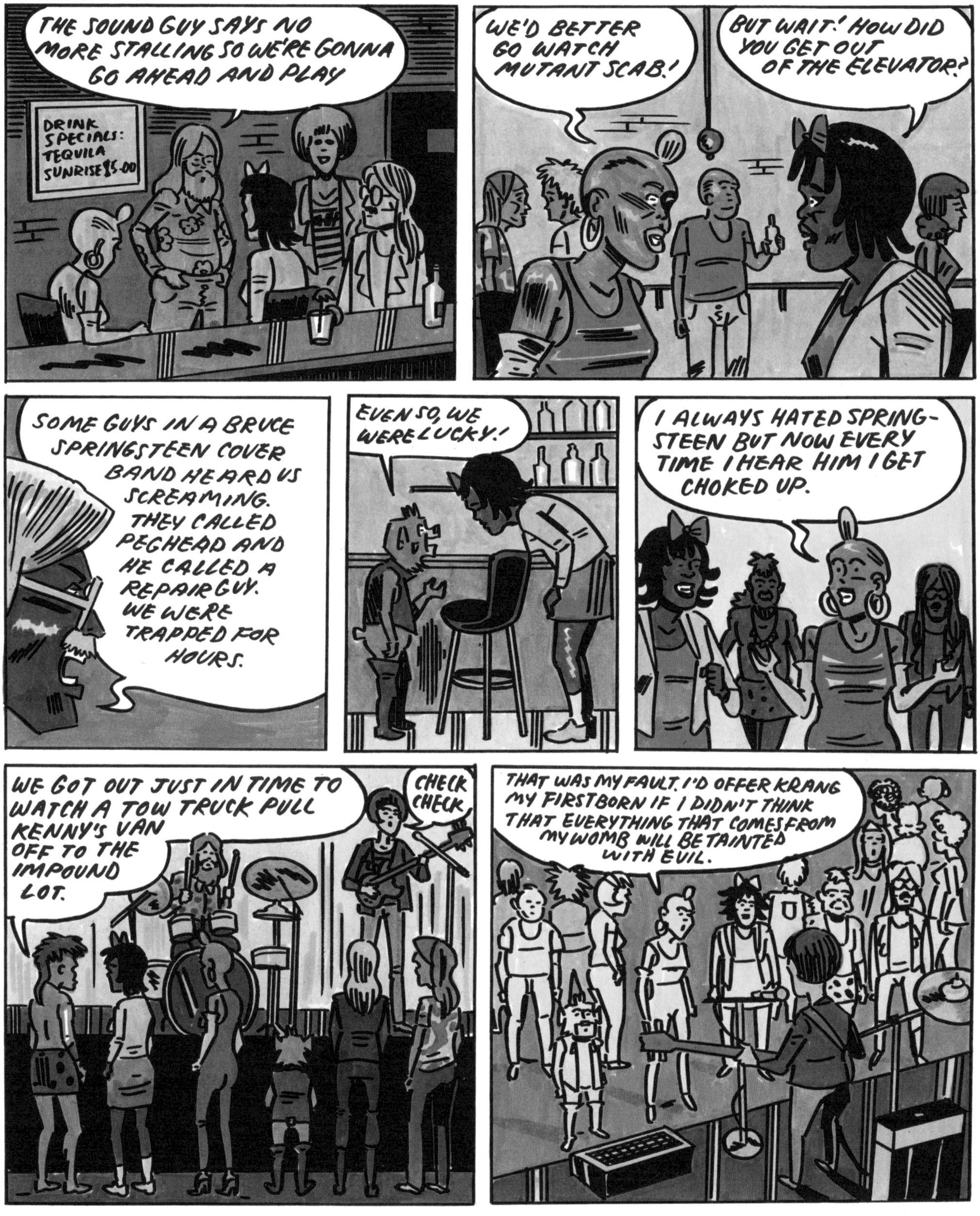
THE SOUND GUY SAYS NO MORE STALLING SO WE'RE GONNA GO AHEAD AND PLAY
DRINK SPECIALS: TEQUILA SUNRISE $5.00
WE'D BETTER GO WATCH MUTANT SCAB!
BUT WAIT! HOW DID YOU GET OUT OF THE ELEVATOR?
SOME GUYS IN A BRUCE SPRINGSTEEN COVER BAND HEARD US SCREAMING. THEY CALLED PEGHEAD AND HE CALLED A REPAIR GUY. WE WERE TRAPPED FOR HOURS.
EVEN SO, WE WERE LUCKY!
I ALWAYS HATED SPRING-STEEN BUT NOW EVERY TIME I HEAR HIM I GET CHOKED UP.
WE GOT OUT JUST IN TIME TO WATCH A TOW TRUCK PULL KENNY'S VAN OFF TO THE IMPOUND LOT.
CHECK CHECK
THAT WAS MY FAULT. I'D OFFER KRANG MY FIRSTBORN IF I DIDN'T THINK THAT EVERYTHING THAT COMES FROM MY WOMB WILL BE TAINTED WITH EVIL.

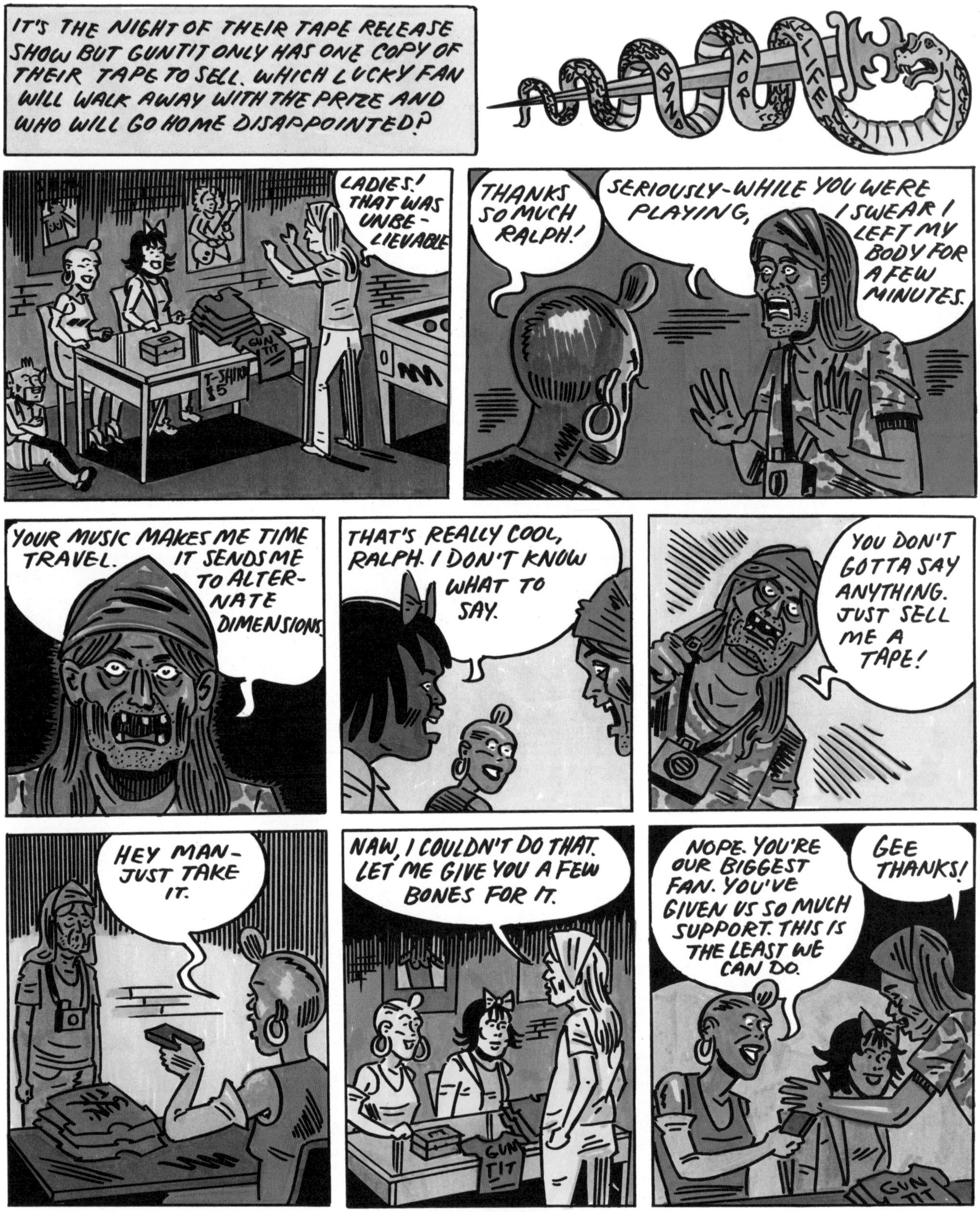
IT'S THE NIGHT OF THEIR TAPE RELEASE SHOW BUT GUNTIT ONLY HAS ONE COPY OF THEIR TAPE TO SELL. WHICH LUCKY FAN WILL WALK AWAY WITH THE PRIZE AND WHO WILL GO HOME DISAPPOINTED?
BAND FOR LIFE
LADIES! THAT WAS UNBE-LIEVABLE
GUN TIT
T-SHIRT $5
THANKS SO MUCH RALPH!
SERIOUSLY-WHILE YOU WERE PLAYING, I SWEAR I LEFT MY BODY FOR A FEW MINUTES.
YOUR MUSIC MAKES ME TIME TRAVEL. IT SENDS ME TO ALTER-NATE DIMENSIONS.
THAT'S REALLY COOL, RALPH. I DON'T KNOW WHAT TO SAY.
YOU DON'T GOTTA SAY ANYTHING. JUST SELL ME A TAPE!
HEY MAN-JUST TAKE IT.
NAW, I COULDN'T DO THAT. LET ME GIVE YOU A FEW BONES FOR IT.
GUN TIT
NOPE. YOU'RE OUR BIGGEST FAN. YOU'VE GIVEN US SO MUCH SUPPORT. THIS IS THE LEAST WE CAN DO.
GEE THANKS!
GUN TIT

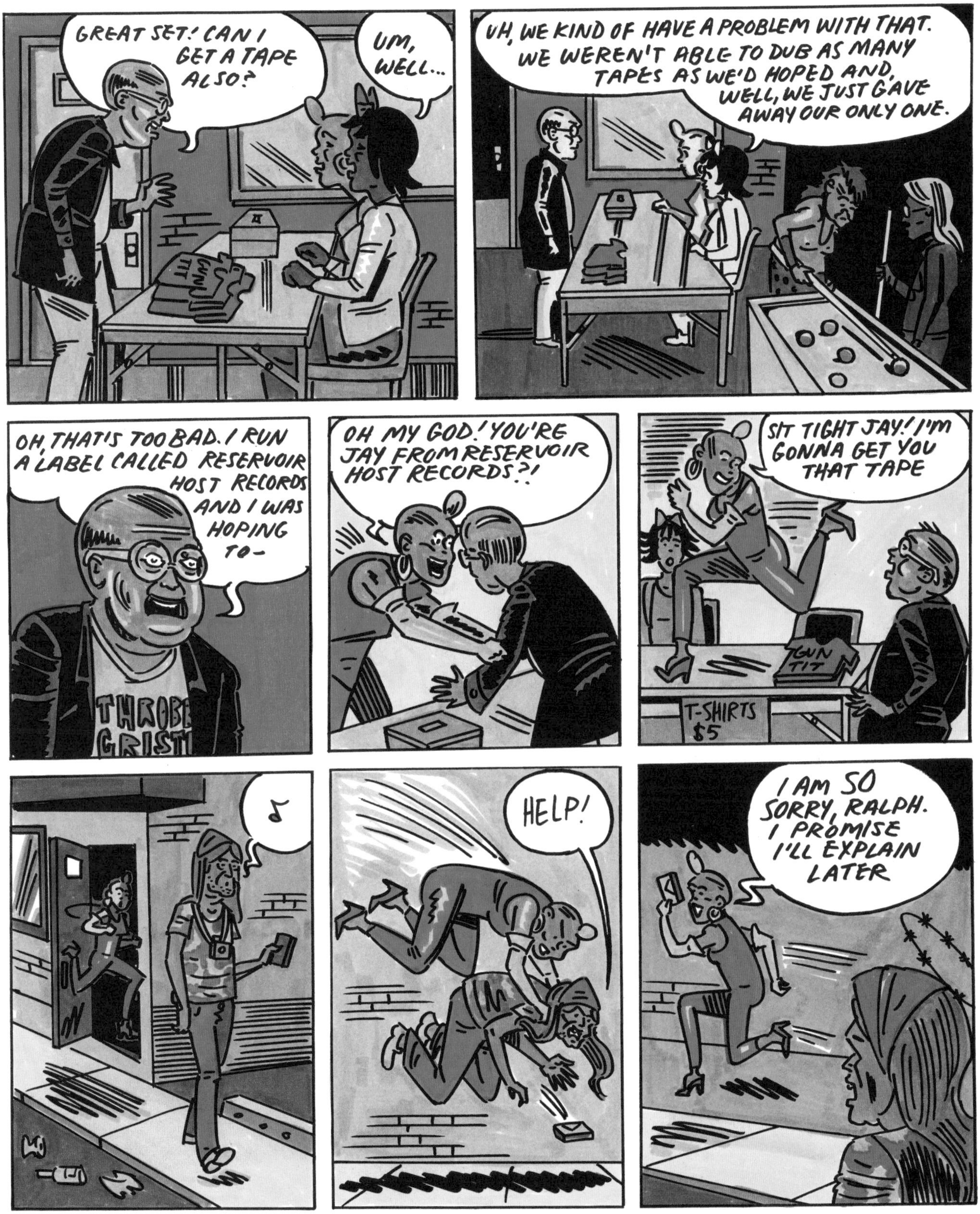
GREAT SET! CAN I GET A TAPE ALSO?
UM, WELL...
UH, WE KIND OF HAVE A PROBLEM WITH THAT. WE WEREN'T ABLE TO DUB AS MANY TAPES AS WE'D HOPED AND, WELL, WE JUST GAVE AWAY OUR ONLY ONE.
OH, THAT'S TOO BAD. I RUN A LABEL CALLED RESERVOIR HOST RECORDS AND I WAS HOPING TO-
THROBBING GRISTLE
OH MY GOD! YOU'RE JAY FROM RESERVOIR HOST RECORDS?!
SIT TIGHT JAY! I'M GONNA GET YOU THAT TAPE
GUN TIT
T-SHIRTS $5
HELP!
I AM SO SORRY, RALPH. I PROMISE I'LL EXPLAIN LATER

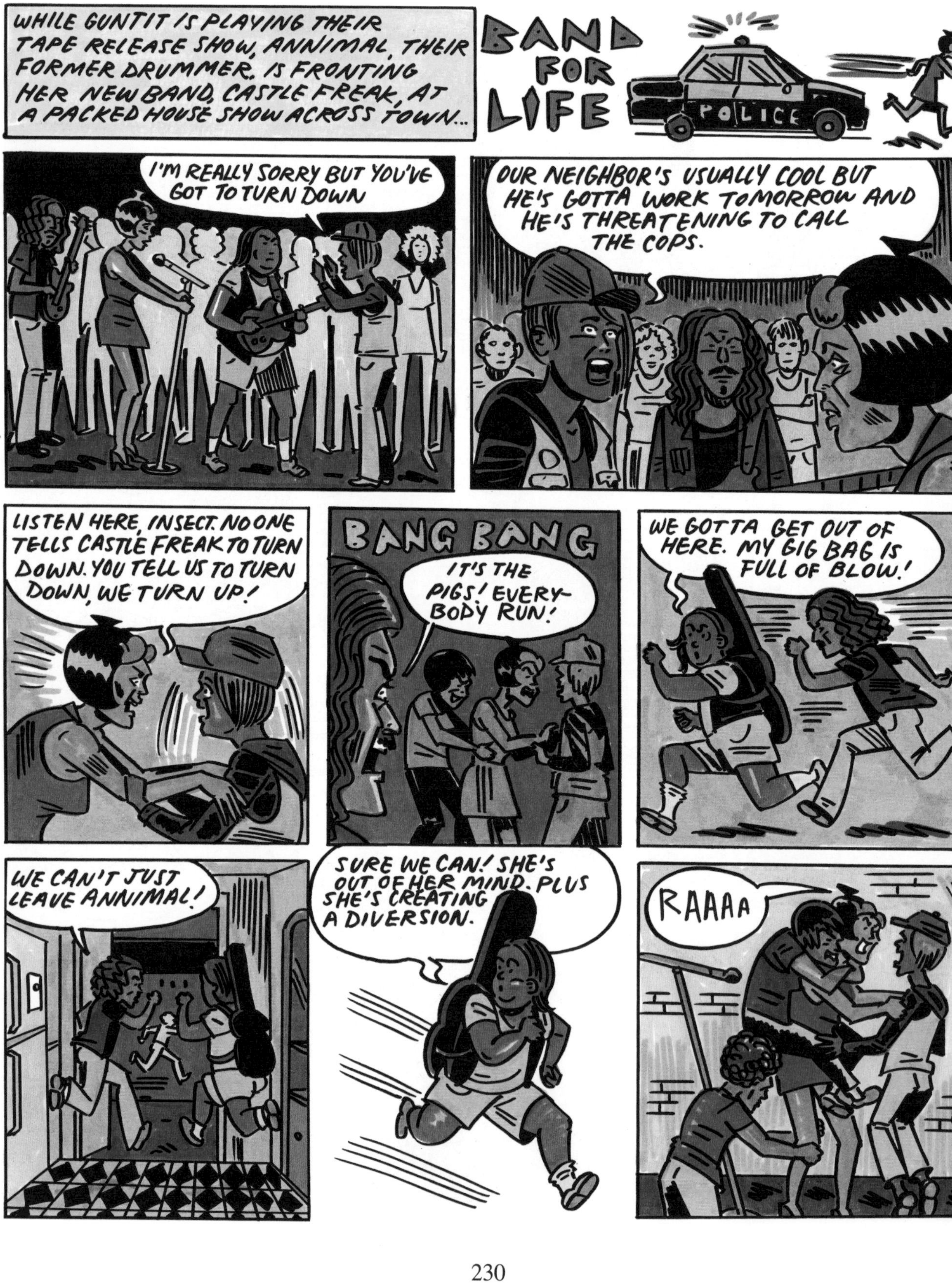
WHILE GUNTIT IS PLAYING THEIR TAPE RELEASE SHOW, ANNIMAL, THEIR FORMER DRUMMER, IS FRONTING HER NEW BAND, CASTLE FREAK, AT A PACKED HOUSE SHOW ACROSS TOWN...
BAND FOR LIFE
POLICE
I'M REALLY SORRY BUT YOU'VE GOT TO TURN DOWN
OUR NEIGHBOR'S USUALLY COOL BUT HE'S GOTTA WORK TOMORROW AND HE'S THREATENING TO CALL THE COPS.
LISTEN HERE, INSECT. NO ONE TELLS CASTLE FREAK TO TURN DOWN. YOU TELL US TO TURN DOWN, WE TURN UP!
BANG BANG
IT'S THE PIGS! EVERYBODY RUN!
WE GOTTA GET OUT OF HERE. MY GIG BAG IS FULL OF BLOW!
WE CAN'T JUST LEAVE ANNIMAL!
SURE WE CAN! SHE'S OUT OF HER MIND. PLUS SHE'S CREATING A DIVERSION.
RAAAA

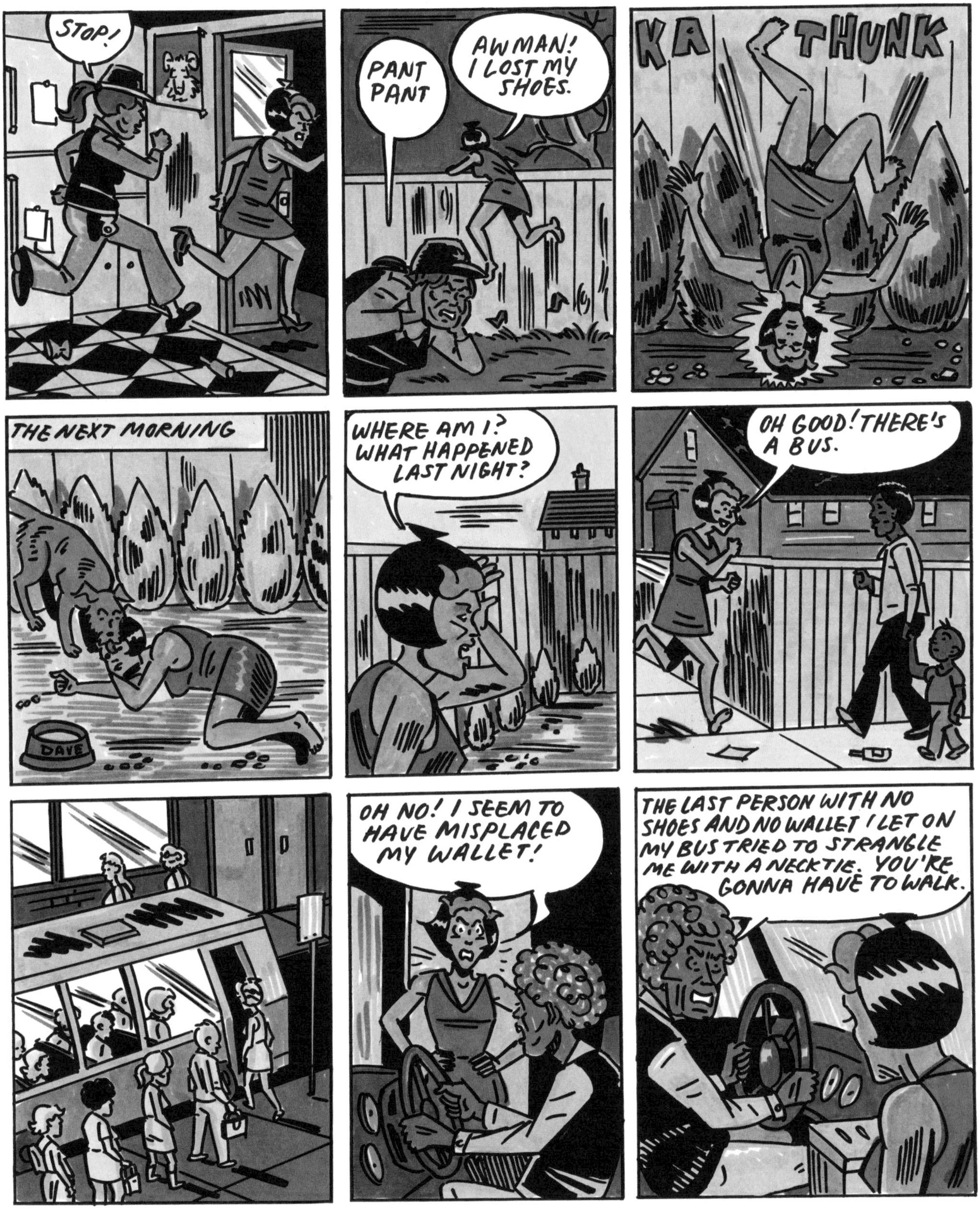
STOP!
PANT PANT
AW MAN! I LOST MY SHOES.
KA THUNK
THE NEXT MORNING
DAVE
WHERE AM I? WHAT HAPPENED LAST NIGHT?
OH GOOD! THERE'S A BUS.
OH NO! I SEEM TO HAVE MISPLACED MY WALLET!
THE LAST PERSON WITH NO SHOES AND NO WALLET I LET ON MY BUS TRIED TO STRANGLE ME WITH A NECKTIE. YOU'RE GONNA HAVE TO WALK.

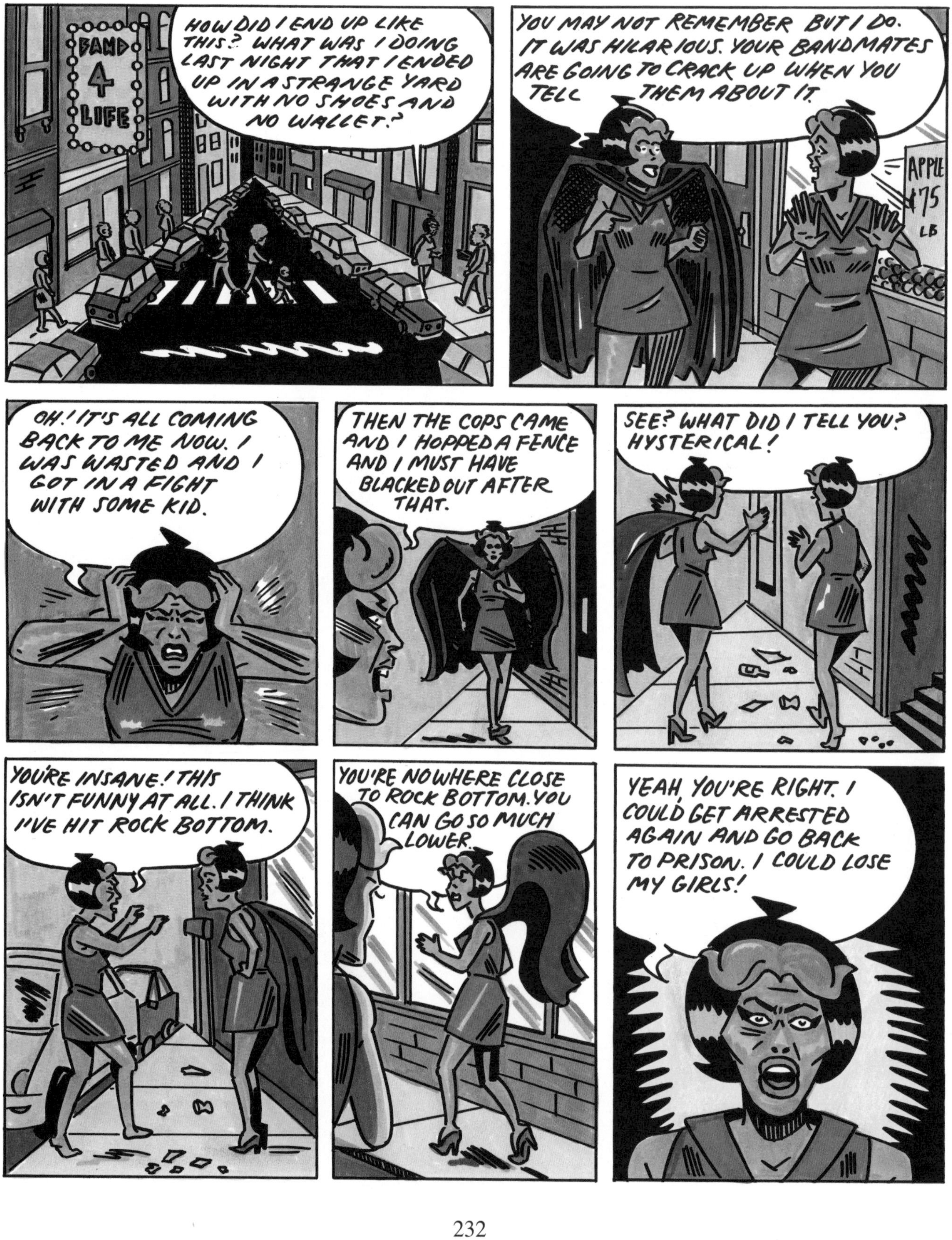
BAND 4 LIFE
HOW DID I END UP LIKE THIS? WHAT WAS I DOING LAST NIGHT THAT I ENDED UP IN A STRANGE YARD WITH NO SHOES AND NO WALLET?
YOU MAY NOT REMEMBER BUT I DO. IT WAS HILARIOUS. YOUR BANDMATES ARE GOING TO CRACK UP WHEN YOU TELL THEM ABOUT IT.
APPLE $.75 LB
OH! IT'S ALL COMING BACK TO ME NOW. I WAS WASTED AND I GOT IN A FIGHT WITH SOME KID.
THEN THE COPS CAME AND I HOPPED A FENCE AND I MUST HAVE BLACKED OUT AFTER THAT.
SEE? WHAT DID I TELL YOU? HYSTERICAL!
YOU'RE INSANE! THIS ISN'T FUNNY AT ALL. I THINK I'VE HIT ROCK BOTTOM.
YOU'RE NOWHERE CLOSE TO ROCK BOTTOM. YOU CAN GO SO MUCH LOWER.
YEAH, YOU'RE RIGHT. I COULD GET ARRESTED AGAIN AND GO BACK TO PRISON. I COULD LOSE MY GIRLS!

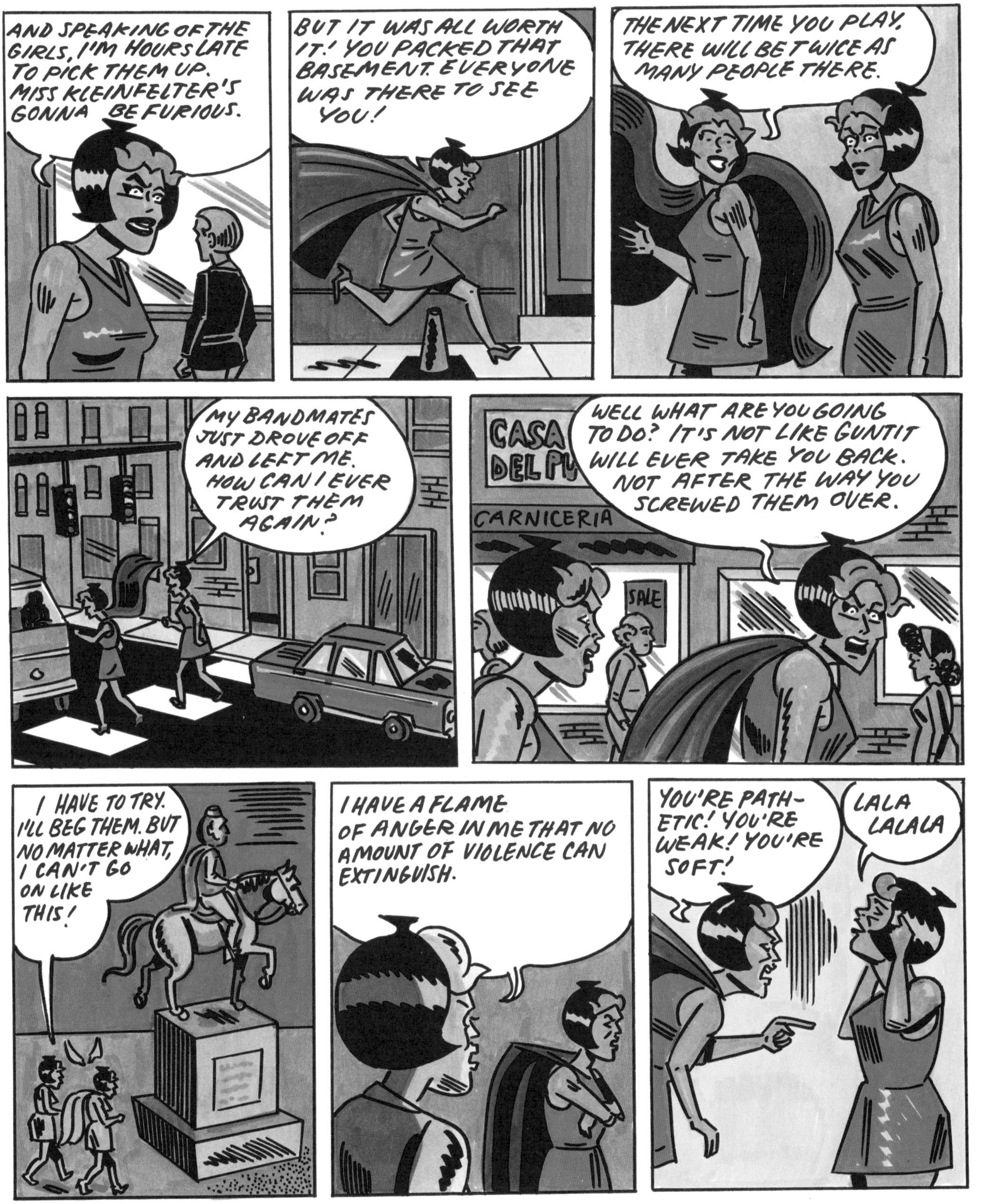
AND SPEAKING OF THE GIRLS, I'M HOURS LATE TO PICK THEM UP. MISS KLEINFELTER'S GONNA BE FURIOUS.
BUT IT WAS ALL WORTH IT! YOU PACKED THAT BASEMENT. EVERYONE WAS THERE TO SEE YOU!
THE NEXT TIME YOU PLAY, THERE WILL BE TWICE AS MANY PEOPLE THERE.
MY BANDMATES JUST DROVE OFF AND LEFT ME. HOW CAN I EVER TRUST THEM AGAIN?
CASA DEL PU
CARNICERIA
SALE
WELL WHAT ARE YOU GOING TO DO? IT'S NOT LIKE GUNTIT WILL EVER TAKE YOU BACK. NOT AFTER THE WAY YOU SCREWED THEM OVER.
I HAVE TO TRY. I'LL BEG THEM. BUT NO MATTER WHAT, I CAN'T GO ON LIKE THIS!
I HAVE A FLAME OF ANGER IN ME THAT NO AMOUNT OF VIOLENCE CAN EXTINGUISH.
YOU'RE PATHETIC! YOU'RE WEAK! YOU'RE SOFT!
LALA LALALA

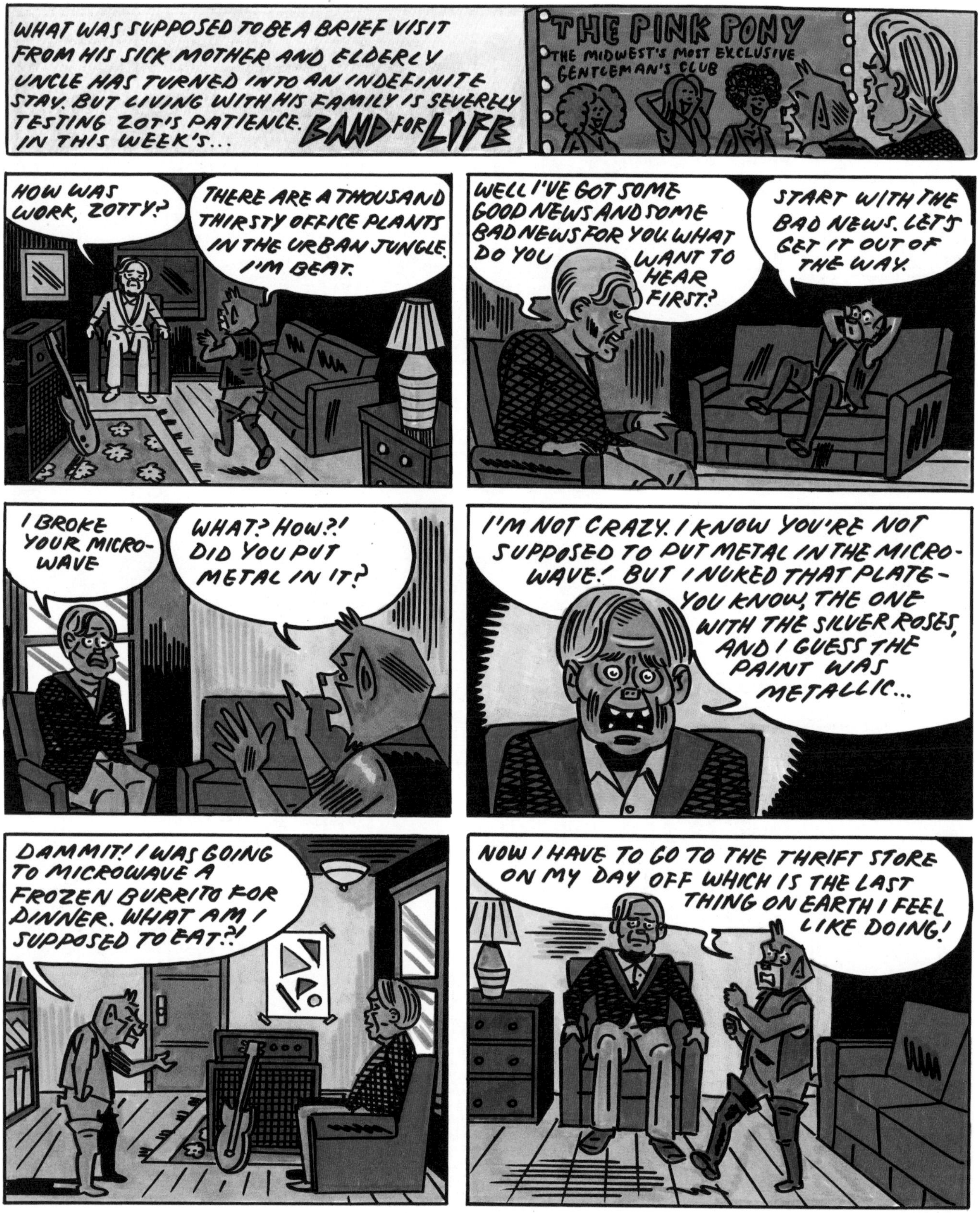
WHAT WAS SUPPOSED TO BE A BRIEF VISIT FROM HIS SICK MOTHER AND ELDERLY UNCLE HAS TURNED INTO AN INDEFINITE STAY. BUT LIVING WITH HIS FAMILY IS SEVERELY TESTING ZOT'S PATIENCE. IN THIS WEEK'S...
BAND FOR LIFE
THE PINK PONY
THE MIDWEST'S MOST EXCLUSIVE GENTLEMAN'S CLUB
HOW WAS WORK, ZOTTY?
THERE ARE A THOUSAND THIRSTY OFFICE PLANTS IN THE URBAN JUNGLE. I'M BEAT.
WELL I'VE GOT SOME GOOD NEWS AND SOME BAD NEWS FOR YOU. WHAT DO YOU WANT TO HEAR FIRST?
START WITH THE BAD NEWS. LET'S GET IT OUT OF THE WAY.
I BROKE YOUR MICRO-WAVE
WHAT? HOW?! DID YOU PUT METAL IN IT?
I'M NOT CRAZY. I KNOW YOU'RE NOT SUPPOSED TO PUT METAL IN THE MICRO-WAVE! BUT I NUKED THAT PLATE-YOU KNOW, THE ONE WITH THE SILVER ROSES, AND I GUESS THE PAINT WAS METALLIC...
DAMMIT! I WAS GOING TO MICROWAVE A FROZEN BURRITO FOR DINNER. WHAT AM I SUPPOSED TO EAT?!
NOW I HAVE TO GO TO THE THRIFT STORE ON MY DAY OFF WHICH IS THE LAST THING ON EARTH I FEEL LIKE DOING!

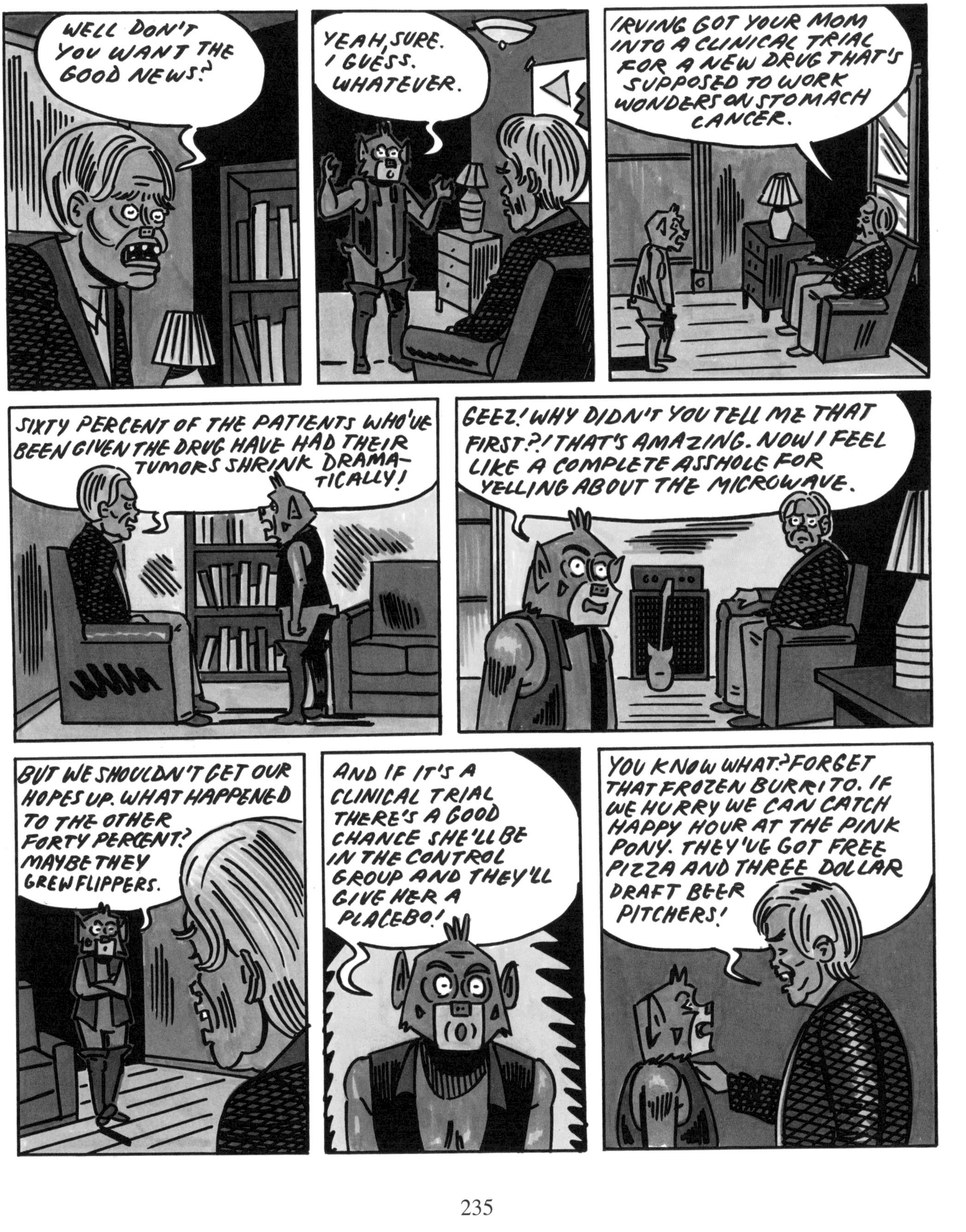
WELL DON'T YOU WANT THE GOOD NEWS?
YEAH, SURE. I GUESS. WHATEVER.
IRVING GOT YOUR MOM INTO A CLINICAL TRIAL FOR A NEW DRUG THAT'S SUPPOSED TO WORK WONDERS ON STOMACH CANCER.
SIXTY PERCENT OF THE PATIENTS WHO'VE BEEN GIVEN THE DRUG HAVE HAD THEIR TUMORS SHRINK DRAMATICALLY!
GEEZ! WHY DIDN'T YOU TELL ME THAT FIRST?! THAT'S AMAZING. NOW I FEEL LIKE A COMPLETE ASSHOLE FOR YELLING ABOUT THE MICROWAVE.
BUT WE SHOULDN'T GET OUR HOPES UP. WHAT HAPPENED TO THE OTHER FORTY PERCENT? MAYBE THEY GREW FLIPPERS.
AND IF IT'S A CLINICAL TRIAL THERE'S A GOOD CHANCE SHE'LL BE IN THE CONTROL GROUP AND THEY'LL GIVE HER A PLACEBO!
YOU KNOW WHAT? FORGET THAT FROZEN BURRITO. IF WE HURRY WE CAN CATCH HAPPY HOUR AT THE PINK PONY. THEY'VE GOT FREE PIZZA AND THREE DOLLAR DRAFT BEER PITCHERS!

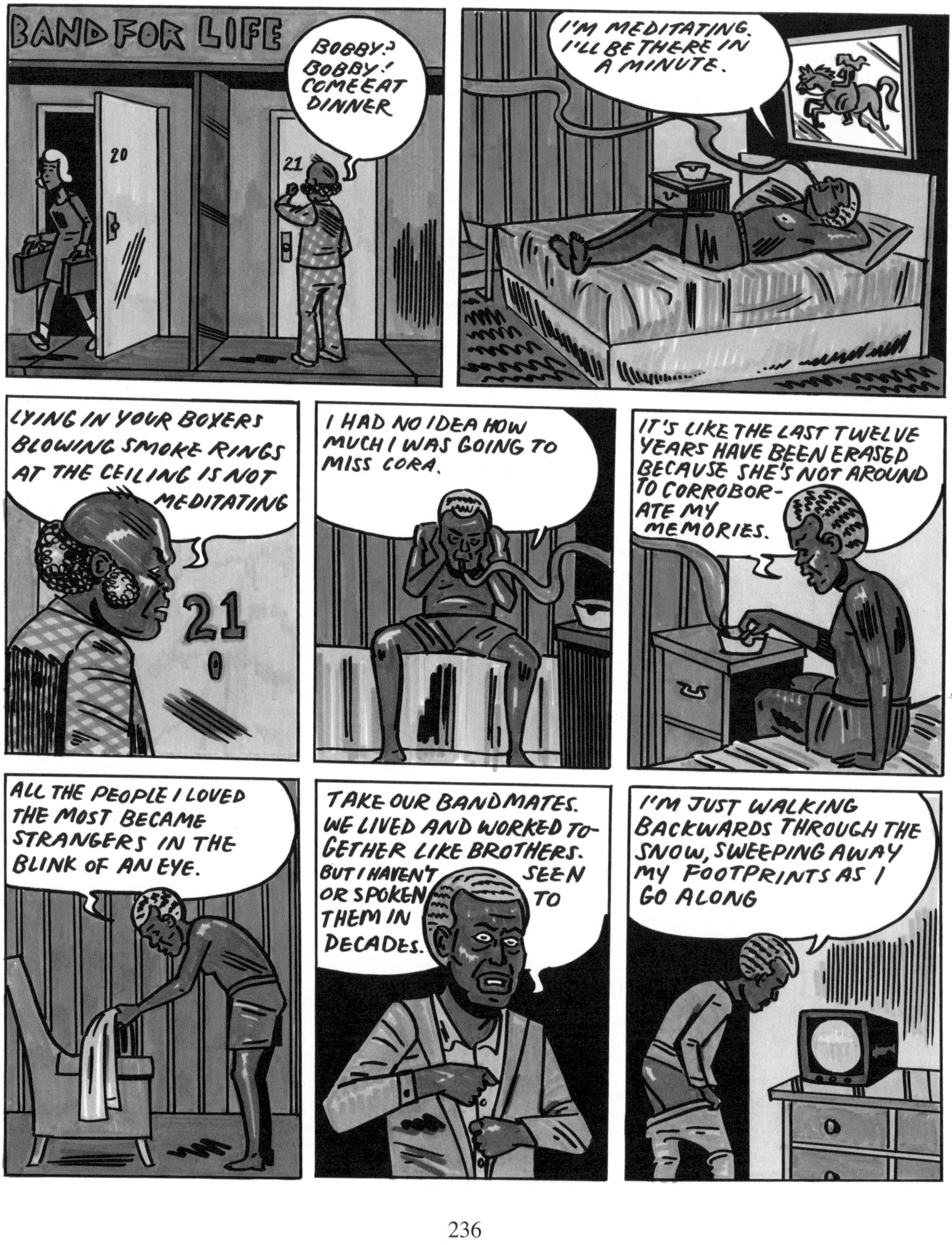
BAND FOR LIFE
BOBBY? BOBBY! COME EAT DINNER
I'M MEDITATING. I'LL BE THERE IN A MINUTE.
LYING IN YOUR BOXERS BLOWING SMOKE RINGS AT THE CEILING IS NOT MEDITATING
21
I HAD NO IDEA HOW MUCH I WAS GOING TO MISS CORA.
IT'S LIKE THE LAST TWELVE YEARS HAVE BEEN ERASED BECAUSE SHE'S NOT AROUND TO CORROBORATE MY MEMORIES.
ALL THE PEOPLE I LOVED THE MOST BECAME STRANGERS IN THE BLINK OF AN EYE.
TAKE OUR BANDMATES. WE LIVED AND WORKED TOGETHER LIKE BROTHERS. BUT I HAVEN'T SEEN OR SPOKEN TO THEM IN DECADES.
I'M JUST WALKING BACKWARDS THROUGH THE SNOW, SWEEPING AWAY MY FOOTPRINTS AS I GO ALONG

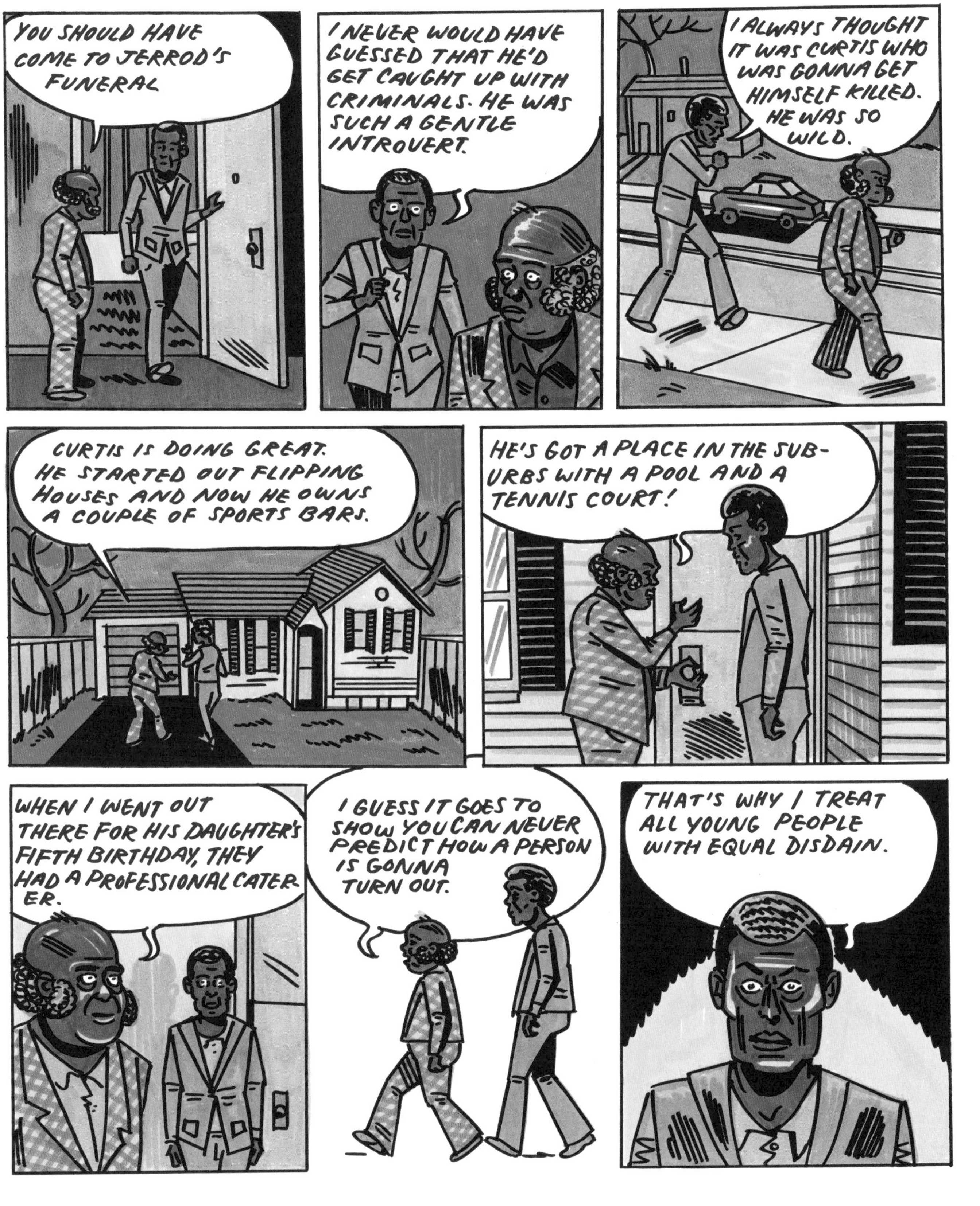
YOU SHOULD HAVE COME TO JERROD'S FUNERAL
I NEVER WOULD HAVE GUESSED THAT HE'D GET CAUGHT UP WITH CRIMINALS. HE WAS SUCH A GENTLE INTROVERT.
I ALWAYS THOUGHT IT WAS CURTIS WHO WAS GONNA GET HIMSELF KILLED. HE WAS SO WILD.
CURTIS IS DOING GREAT. HE STARTED OUT FLIPPING HOUSES AND NOW HE OWNS A COUPLE OF SPORTS BARS.
HE'S GOT A PLACE IN THE SUB-URBS WITH A POOL AND A TENNIS COURT!
WHEN I WENT OUT THERE FOR HIS DAUGHTER'S FIFTH BIRTHDAY, THEY HAD A PROFESSIONAL CATER-ER.
I GUESS IT GOES TO SHOW YOU CAN NEVER PREDICT HOW A PERSON IS GONNA TURN OUT.
THAT'S WHY I TREAT ALL YOUNG PEOPLE WITH EQUAL DISDAIN.

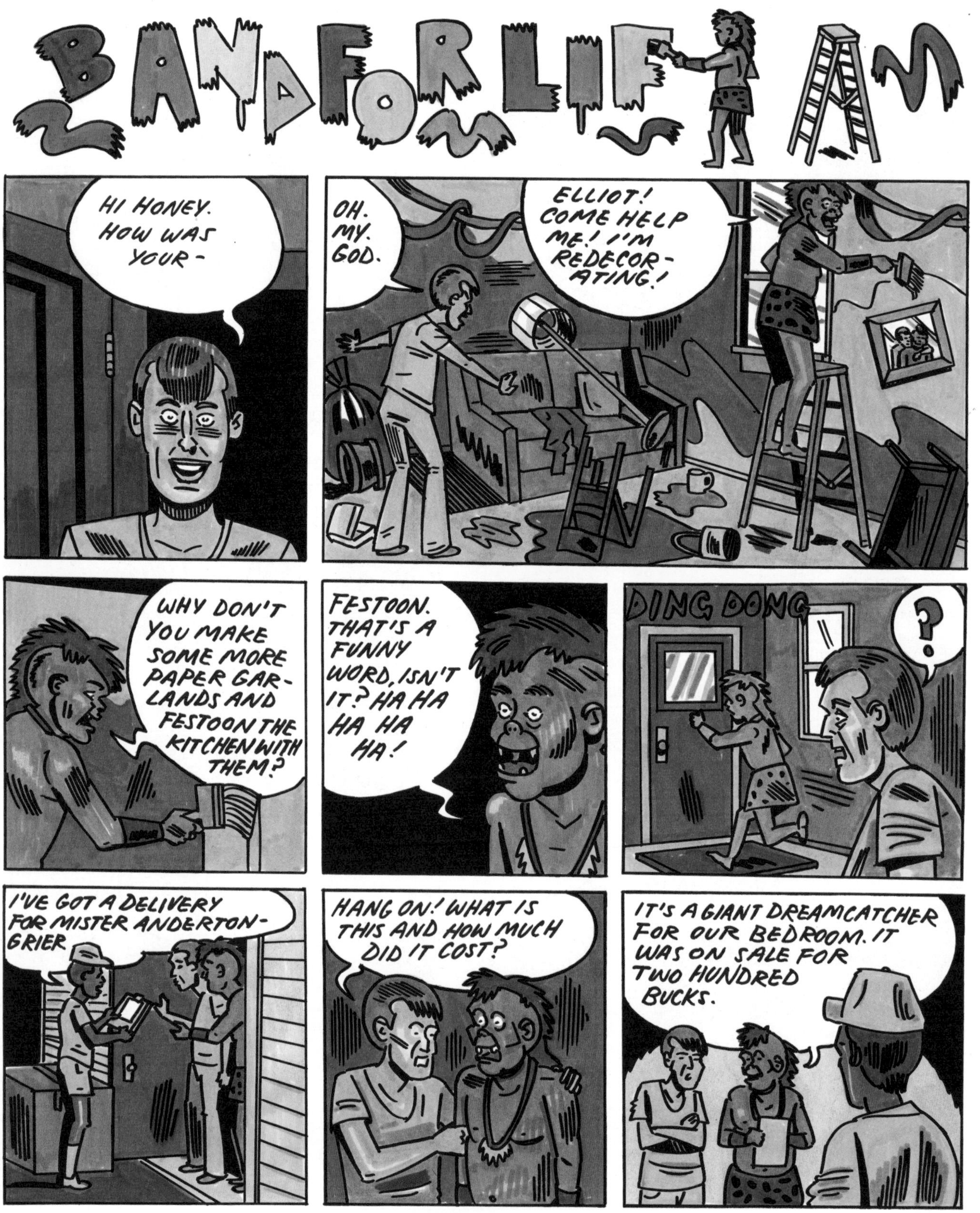
BAND FOR LIFE
HI HONEY. HOW WAS YOUR-
OH. MY. GOD.
ELLIOT! COME HELP ME! I'M REDECORATING!
WHY DON'T YOU MAKE SOME MORE PAPER GARLANDS AND FESTOON THE KITCHEN WITH THEM?
FESTOON. THAT'S A FUNNY WORD, ISN'T IT? HA HA HA HA HA!
DING DONG
?
I'VE GOT A DELIVERY FOR MISTER ANDERTON-GRIER
HANG ON! WHAT IS THIS AND HOW MUCH DID IT COST?
IT'S A GIANT DREAMCATCHER FOR OUR BEDROOM. IT WAS ON SALE FOR TWO HUNDRED BUCKS.

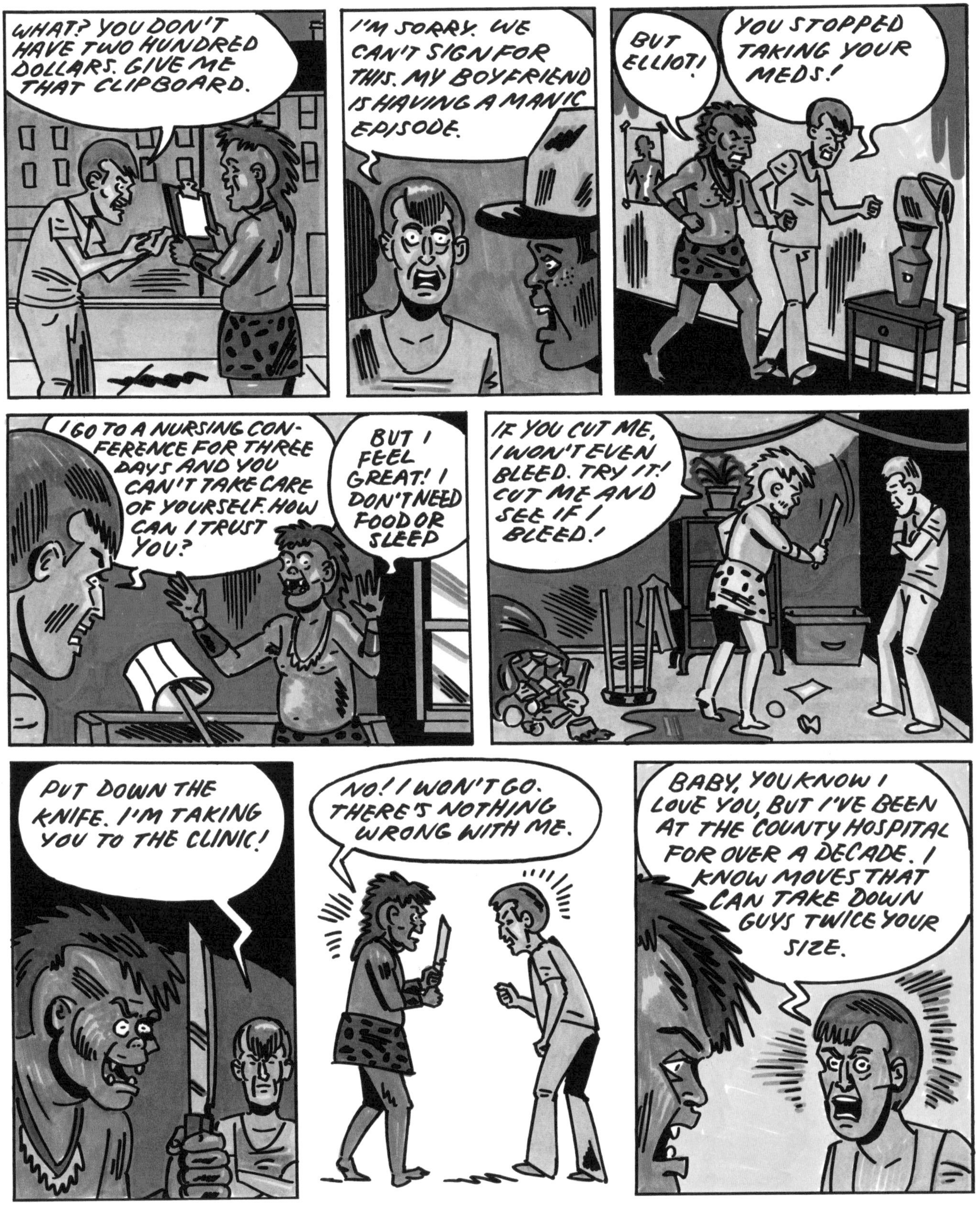
WHAT? YOU DON'T HAVE TWO HUNDRED DOLLARS. GIVE ME THAT CLIPBOARD.
I'M SORRY. WE CAN'T SIGN FOR THIS. MY BOYFRIEND IS HAVING A MANIC EPISODE.
BUT ELLIOT!
YOU STOPPED TAKING YOUR MEDS!
I GO TO A NURSING CONFERENCE FOR THREE DAYS AND YOU CAN'T TAKE CARE OF YOURSELF. HOW CAN I TRUST YOU?
BUT I FEEL GREAT! I DON'T NEED FOOD OR SLEEP
IF YOU CUT ME, I WON'T EVEN BLEED. TRY IT! CUT ME AND SEE IF I BLEED!
PUT DOWN THE KNIFE. I'M TAKING YOU TO THE CLINIC!
NO! I WON'T GO. THERE'S NOTHING WRONG WITH ME.
BABY, YOU KNOW I LOVE YOU, BUT I'VE BEEN AT THE COUNTY HOSPITAL FOR OVER A DECADE. I KNOW MOVES THAT CAN TAKE DOWN GUYS TWICE YOUR SIZE.

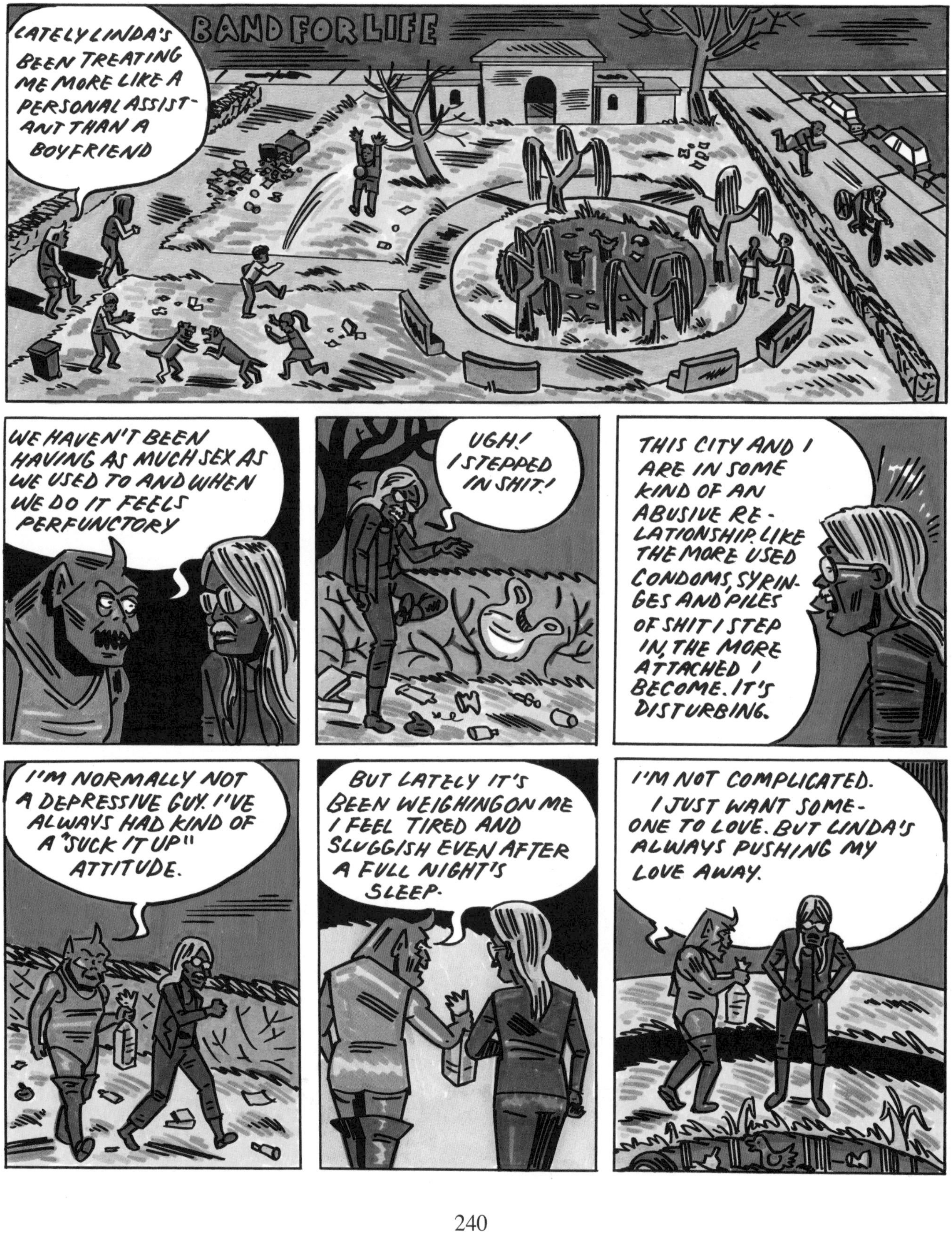
BAND FOR LIFE
LATELY LINDA'S BEEN TREATING ME MORE LIKE A PERSONAL ASSISTANT THAN A BOYFRIEND
WE HAVEN'T BEEN HAVING AS MUCH SEX AS WE USED TO AND WHEN WE DO IT FEELS PERFUNCTORY
UGH! I STEPPED IN SHIT!
THIS CITY AND I ARE IN SOME KIND OF AN ABUSIVE RELATIONSHIP. LIKE THE MORE USED CONDOMS, SYRINGES AND PILES OF SHIT I STEP IN, THE MORE ATTACHED I BECOME. IT'S DISTURBING.
I'M NORMALLY NOT A DEPRESSIVE GUY. I'VE ALWAYS HAD KIND OF A "SUCK IT UP" ATTITUDE.
BUT LATELY IT'S BEEN WEIGHING ON ME I FEEL TIRED AND SLUGGISH EVEN AFTER A FULL NIGHT'S SLEEP.
I'M NOT COMPLICATED. I JUST WANT SOMEONE TO LOVE. BUT LINDA'S ALWAYS PUSHING MY LOVE AWAY.

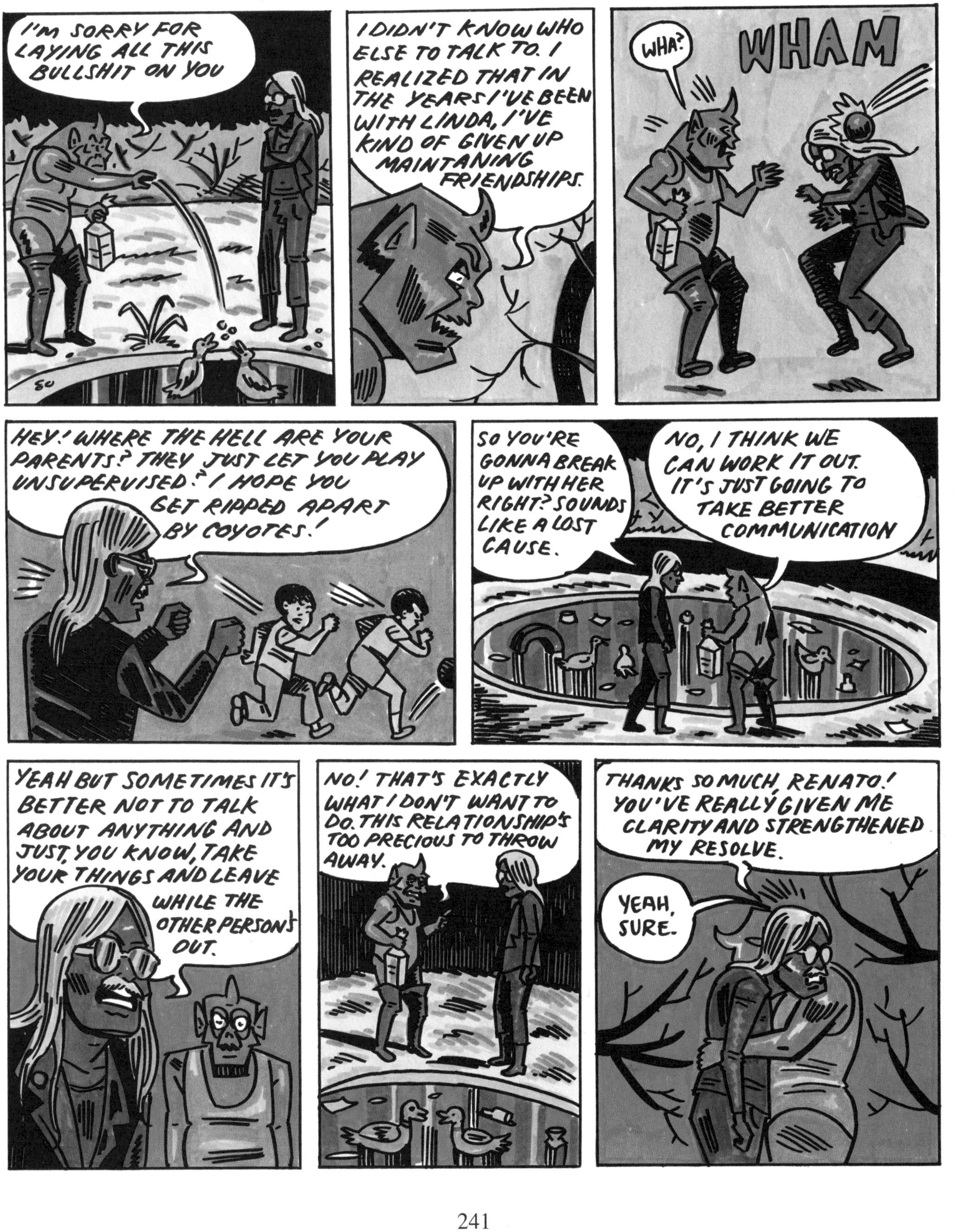

I'M SORRY FOR LAYING ALL THIS BULLSHIT ON YOU
I DIDN'T KNOW WHO ELSE TO TALK TO. I REALIZED THAT IN THE YEARS I'VE BEEN WITH LINDA, I'VE KIND OF GIVEN UP MAINTANING FRIENDSHIPS.
WHA?
WHAM
HEY! WHERE THE HELL ARE YOUR PARENTS? THEY JUST LET YOU PLAY UNSUPERVISED? I HOPE YOU GET RIPPED APART BY COYOTES!
SO YOU'RE GONNA BREAK UP WITH HER RIGHT? SOUNDS LIKE A LOST CAUSE.
NO, I THINK WE CAN WORK IT OUT. IT'S JUST GOING TO TAKE BETTER COMMUNICATION
YEAH BUT SOMETIMES IT'S BETTER NOT TO TALK ABOUT ANYTHING AND JUST, YOU KNOW, TAKE YOUR THINGS AND LEAVE WHILE THE OTHER PERSON'S OUT.
NO! THAT'S EXACTLY WHAT I DON'T WANT TO DO. THIS RELATIONSHIP'S TOO PRECIOUS TO THROW AWAY.
THANKS SO MUCH, RENATO! YOU'VE REALLY GIVEN ME CLARITY AND STRENGTHENED MY RESOLVE.
YEAH, SURE.

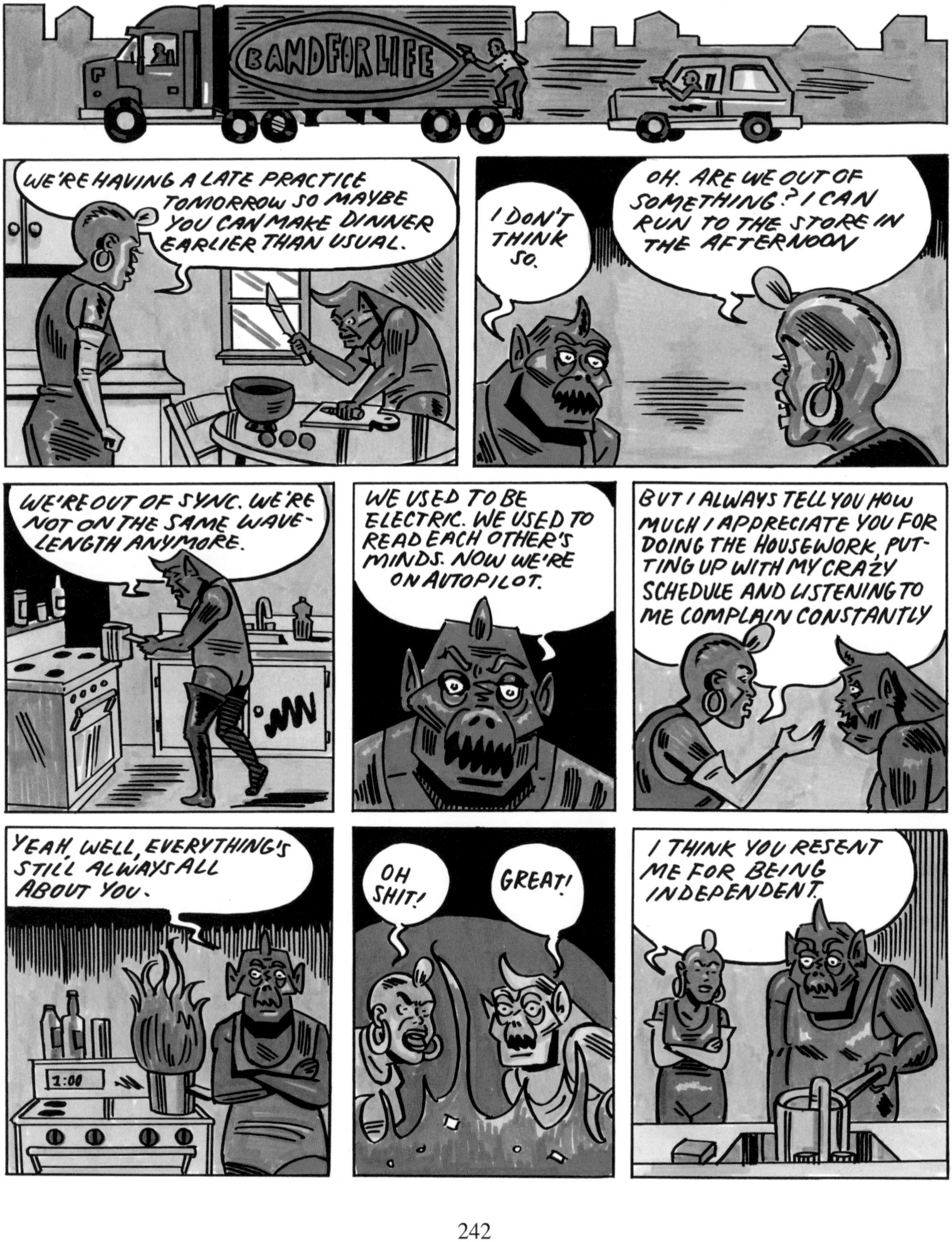
BANDFORLIFE
WE'RE HAVING A LATE PRACTICE TOMORROW SO MAYBE YOU CAN MAKE DINNER EARLIER THAN USUAL.
I DON'T THINK SO.
OH. ARE WE OUT OF SOMETHING? I CAN RUN TO THE STORE IN THE AFTERNOON
WE'RE OUT OF SYNC. WE'RE NOT ON THE SAME WAVE-LENGTH ANYMORE.
WE USED TO BE ELECTRIC. WE USED TO READ EACH OTHER'S MINDS. NOW WE'RE ON AUTOPILOT.
BUT I ALWAYS TELL YOU HOW MUCH I APPRECIATE YOU FOR DOING THE HOUSEWORK, PUTTING UP WITH MY CRAZY SCHEDULE AND LISTENING TO ME COMPLAIN CONSTANTLY
YEAH, WELL, EVERYTHING'S STILL ALWAYS ALL ABOUT YOU.
1:00
OH SHIT!
GREAT!
I THINK YOU RESENT ME FOR BEING INDEPENDENT.

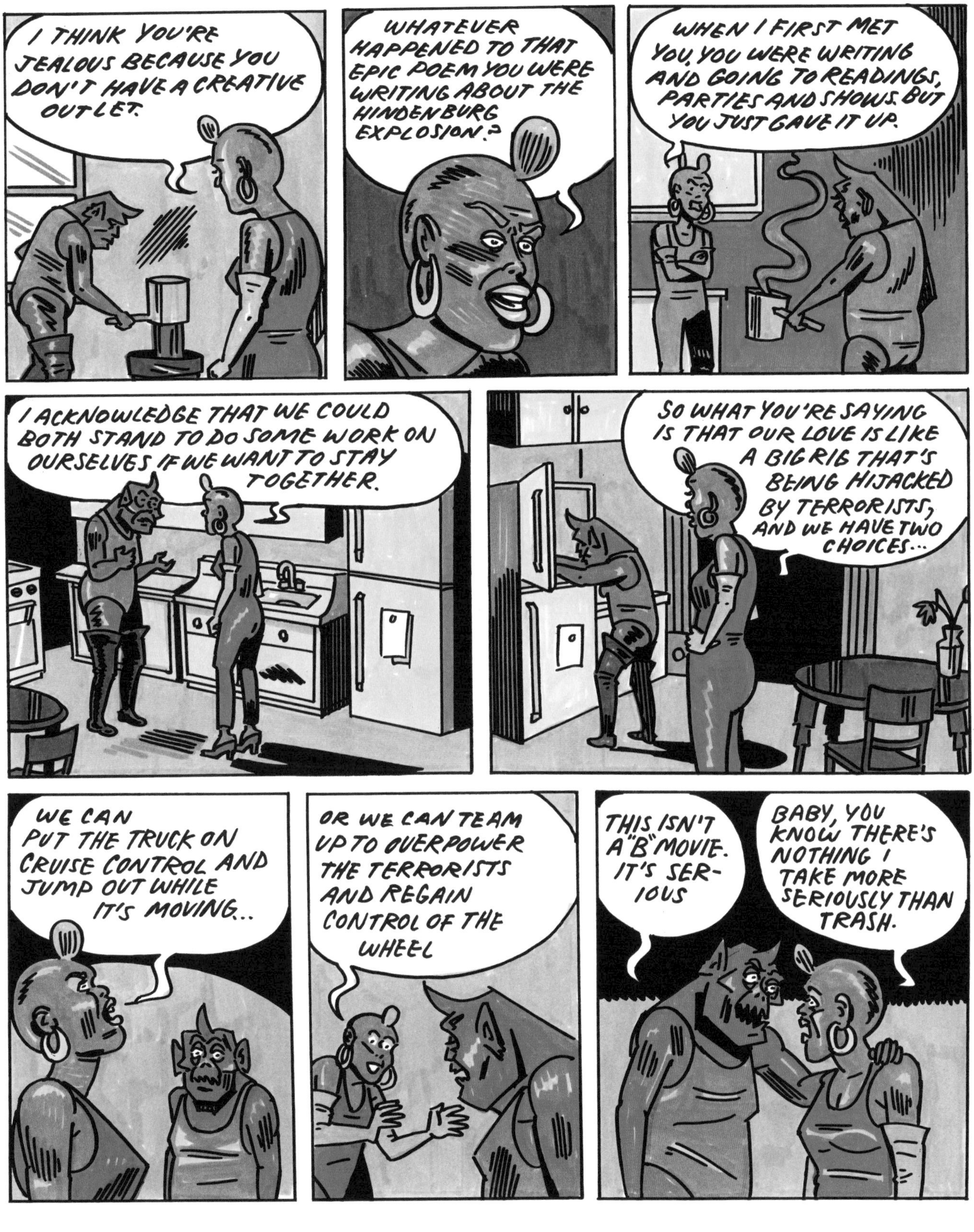
I THINK YOU'RE JEALOUS BECAUSE YOU DON'T HAVE A CREATIVE OUTLET.
WHATEVER HAPPENED TO THAT EPIC POEM YOU WERE WRITING ABOUT THE HINDENBURG EXPLOSION?
WHEN I FIRST MET YOU, YOU WERE WRITING AND GOING TO READINGS, PARTIES AND SHOWS. BUT YOU JUST GAVE IT UP.
I ACKNOWLEDGE THAT WE COULD BOTH STAND TO DO SOME WORK ON OURSELVES IF WE WANT TO STAY TOGETHER.
SO WHAT YOU'RE SAYING IS THAT OUR LOVE IS LIKE A BIG RIG THAT'S BEING HIJACKED BY TERRORISTS, AND WE HAVE TWO CHOICES...
WE CAN PUT THE TRUCK ON CRUISE CONTROL AND JUMP OUT WHILE IT'S MOVING...
OR WE CAN TEAM UP TO OVERPOWER THE TERRORISTS AND REGAIN CONTROL OF THE WHEEL
THIS ISN'T A "B" MOVIE. IT'S SERIOUS
BABY, YOU KNOW THERE'S NOTHING I TAKE MORE SERIOUSLY THAN TRASH.

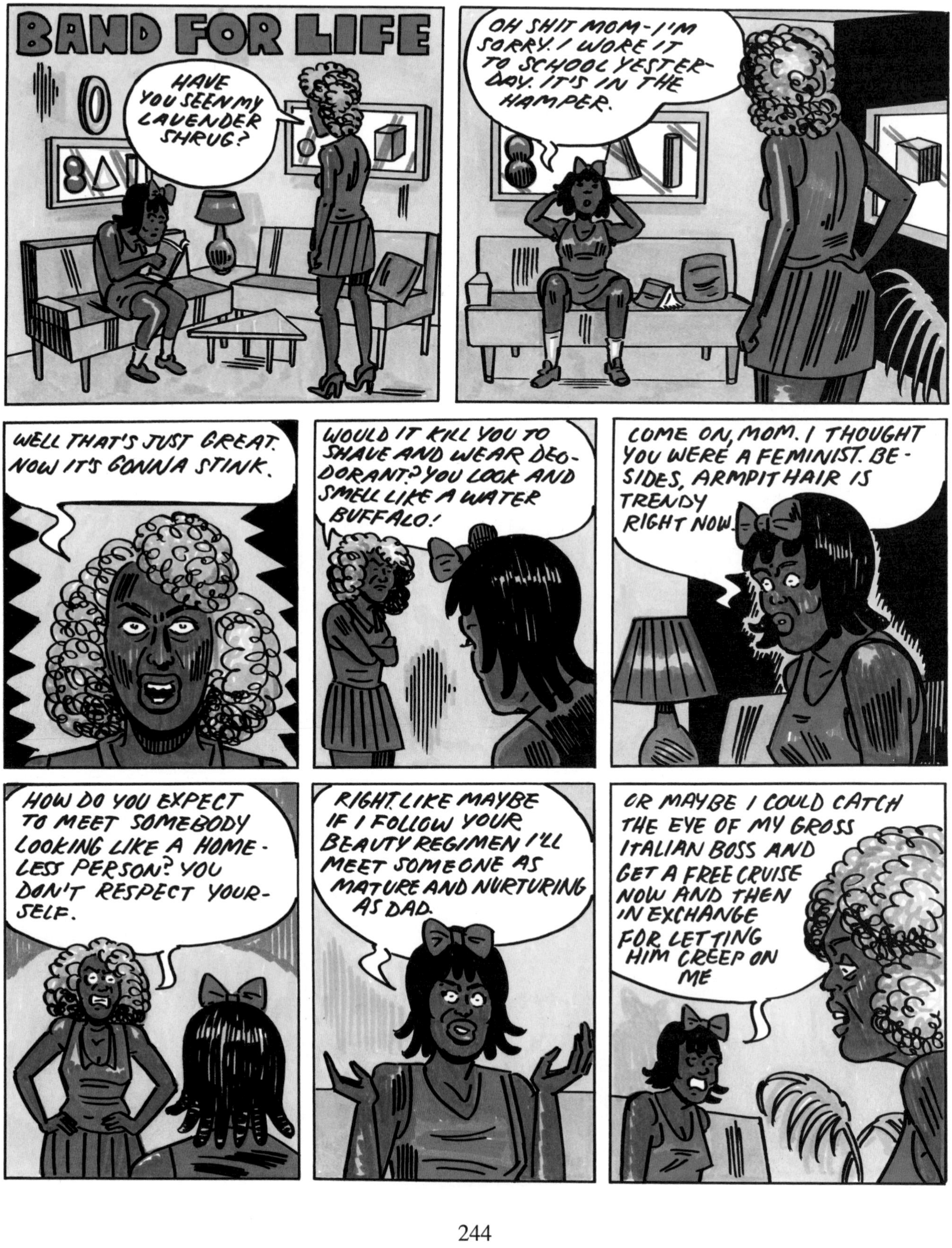
BAND FOR LIFE
HAVE YOU SEEN MY LAVENDER SHRUG?
OH SHIT MOM - I'M SORRY. I WORE IT TO SCHOOL YESTERDAY. IT'S IN THE HAMPER.
WELL THAT'S JUST GREAT. NOW IT'S GONNA STINK.
WOULD IT KILL YOU TO SHAVE AND WEAR DEODORANT? YOU LOOK AND SMELL LIKE A WATER BUFFALO!
COME ON, MOM. I THOUGHT YOU WERE A FEMINIST. BESIDES, ARMPIT HAIR IS TRENDY RIGHT NOW.
HOW DO YOU EXPECT TO MEET SOMEBODY LOOKING LIKE A HOMELESS PERSON? YOU DON'T RESPECT YOURSELF.
RIGHT. LIKE MAYBE IF I FOLLOW YOUR BEAUTY REGIMEN I'LL MEET SOMEONE AS MATURE AND NURTURING AS DAD.
OR MAYBE I COULD CATCH THE EYE OF MY GROSS ITALIAN BOSS AND GET A FREE CRUISE NOW AND THEN IN EXCHANGE FOR LETTING HIM CREEP ON ME

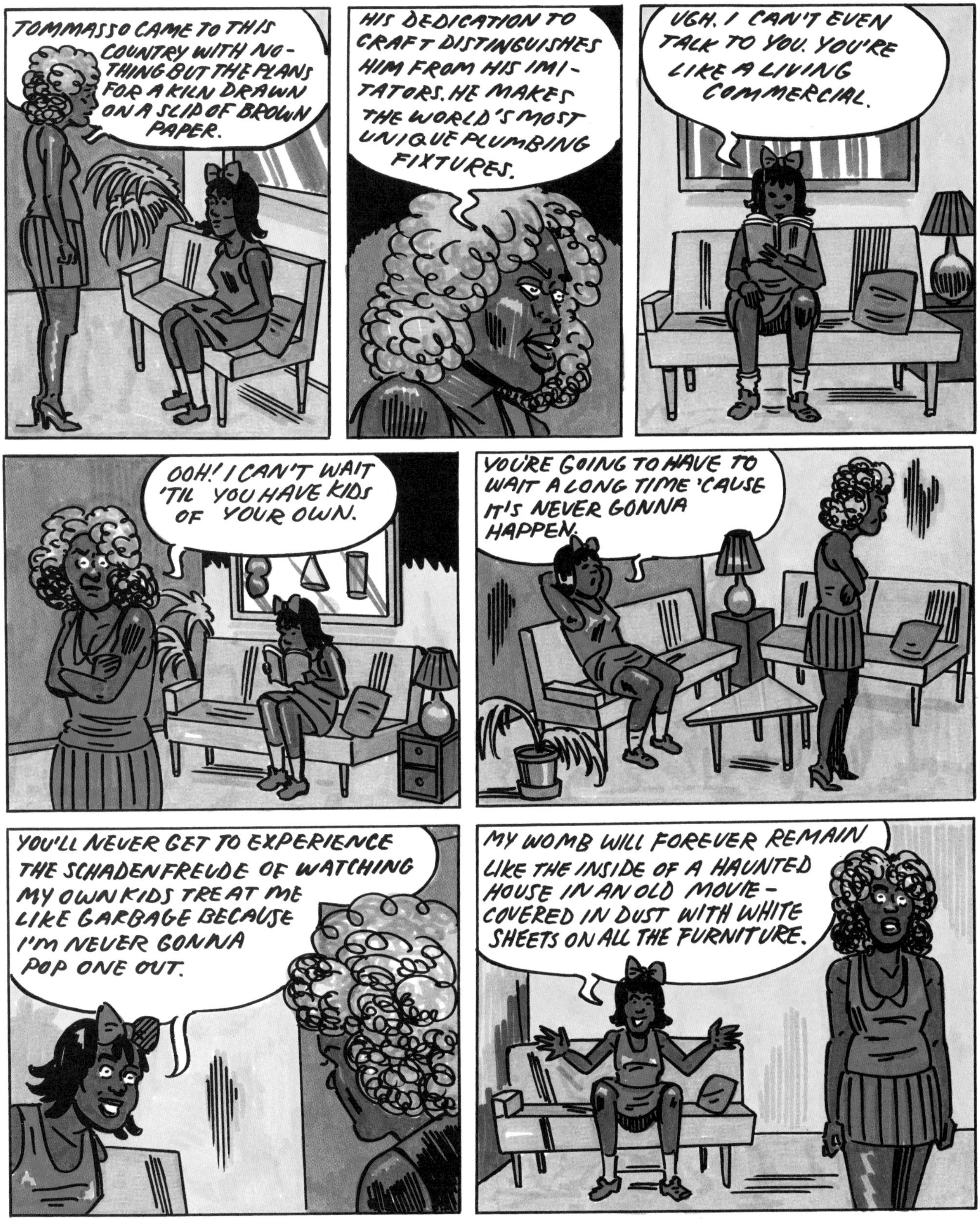
TOMMASO CAME TO THIS COUNTRY WITH NOTHING BUT THE PLANS FOR A KILN DRAWN ON A SLIP OF BROWN PAPER.
HIS DEDICATION TO CRAFT DISTINGUISHES HIM FROM HIS IMITATORS. HE MAKES THE WORLD'S MOST UNIQUE PLUMBING FIXTURES.
UGH. I CAN'T EVEN TALK TO YOU. YOU'RE LIKE A LIVING COMMERCIAL.
OOH! I CAN'T WAIT 'TIL YOU HAVE KIDS OF YOUR OWN.
YOU'RE GOING TO HAVE TO WAIT A LONG TIME 'CAUSE IT'S NEVER GONNA HAPPEN.
YOU'LL NEVER GET TO EXPERIENCE THE SCHADENFREUDE OF WATCHING MY OWN KIDS TREAT ME LIKE GARBAGE BECAUSE I'M NEVER GONNA POP ONE OUT.
MY WOMB WILL FOREVER REMAIN LIKE THE INSIDE OF A HAUNTED HOUSE IN AN OLD MOVIE - COVERED IN DUST WITH WHITE SHEETS ON ALL THE FURNITURE.

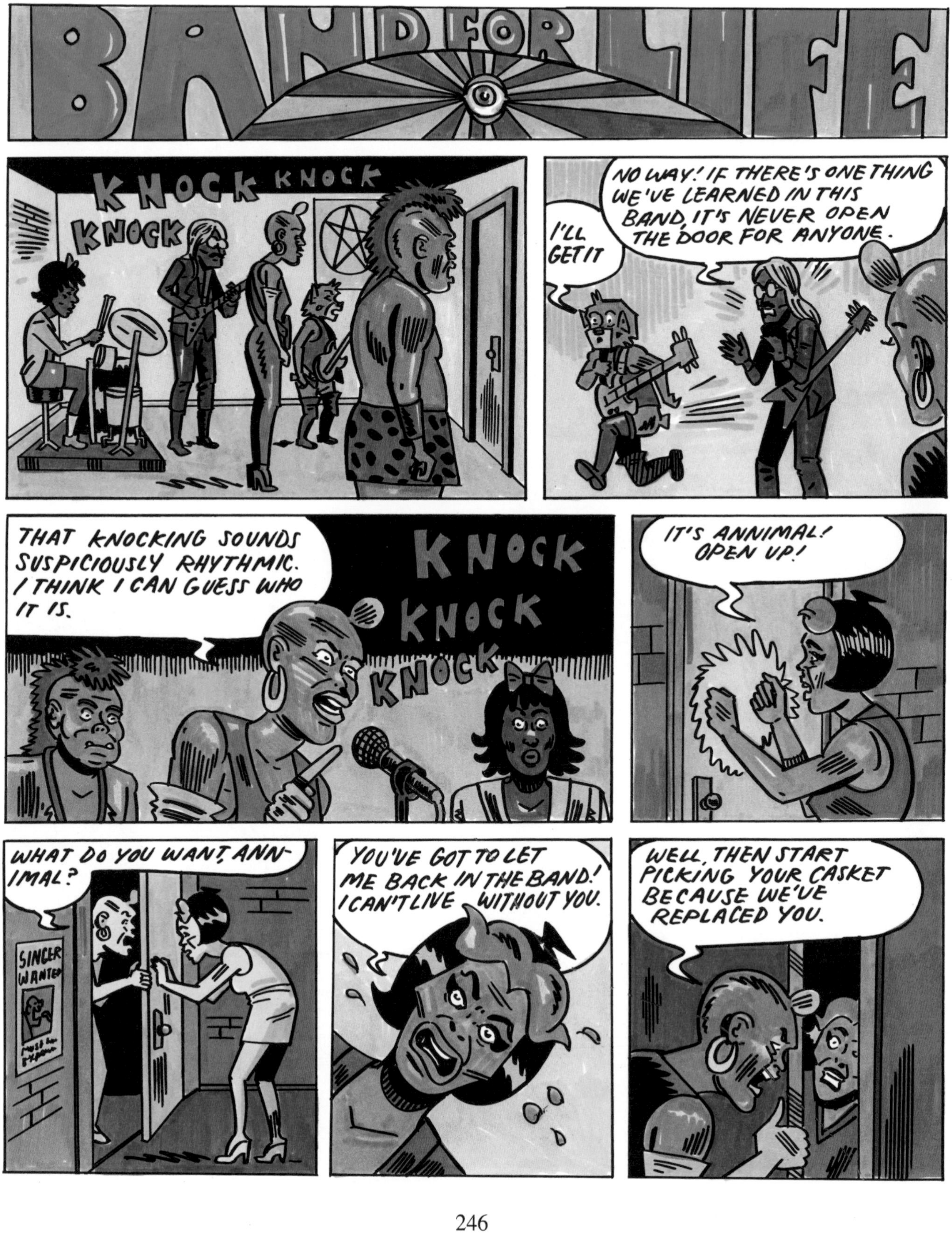
BAND FOR LIFE
KNOCK KNOCK
KNOCK
I'LL GET IT
NO WAY! IF THERE'S ONE THING WE'VE LEARNED IN THIS BAND, IT'S NEVER OPEN THE DOOR FOR ANYONE.
THAT KNOCKING SOUNDS SUSPICIOUSLY RHYTHMIC. I THINK I CAN GUESS WHO IT IS.
KNOCK KNOCK KNOCK
IT'S ANNIMAL! OPEN UP!
WHAT DO YOU WANT, ANNIMAL?
SINGER WANTED
YOU'VE GOT TO LET ME BACK IN THE BAND! I CAN'T LIVE WITHOUT YOU.
WELL, THEN START PICKING YOUR CASKET BECAUSE WE'VE REPLACED YOU.

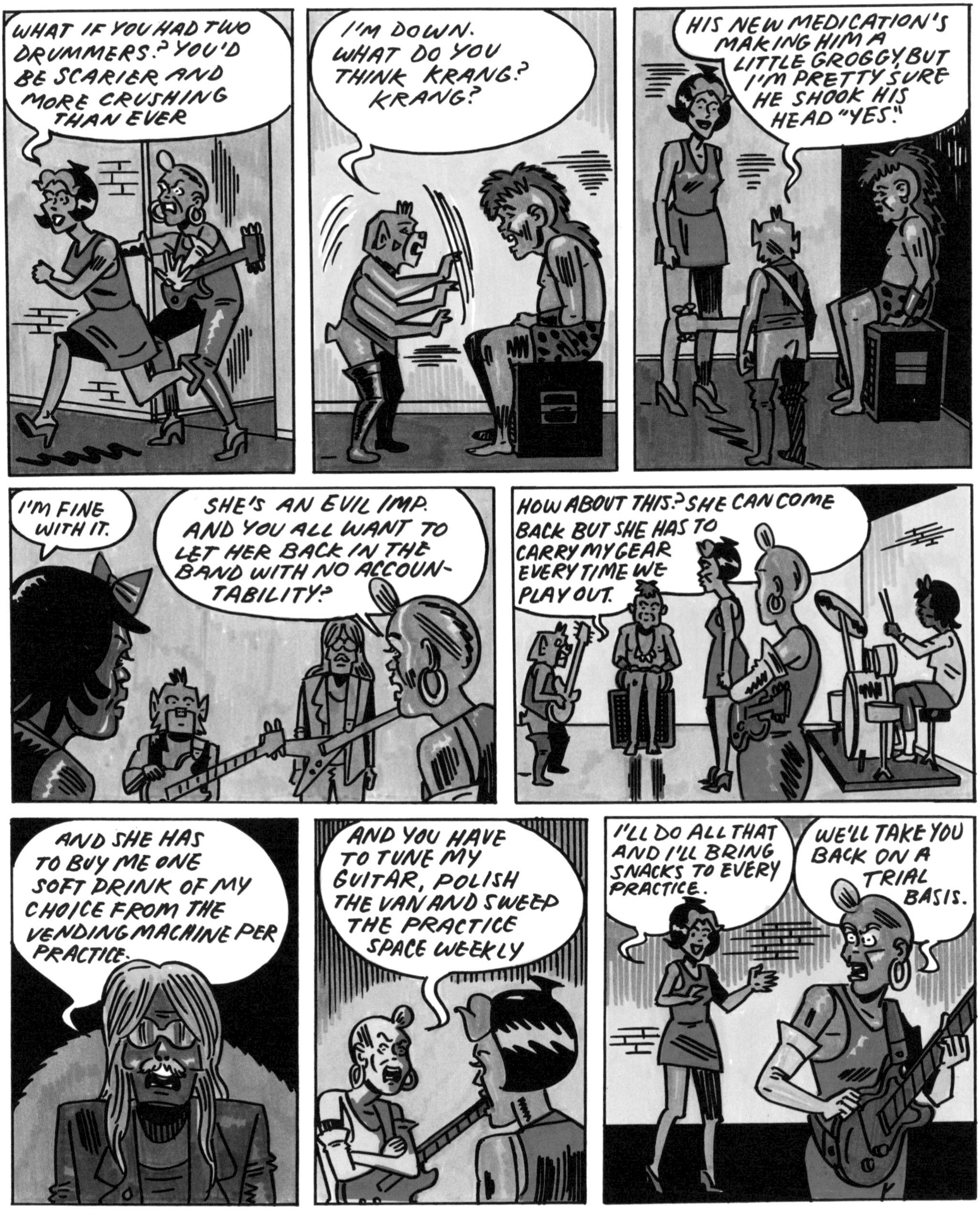
WHAT IF YOU HAD TWO DRUMMERS? YOU'D BE SCARIER AND MORE CRUSHING THAN EVER
I'M DOWN. WHAT DO YOU THINK KRANG? KRANG?
HIS NEW MEDICATION'S MAKING HIM A LITTLE GROGGY, BUT I'M PRETTY SURE HE SHOOK HIS HEAD "YES."
I'M FINE WITH IT.
SHE'S AN EVIL IMP. AND YOU ALL WANT TO LET HER BACK IN THE BAND WITH NO ACCOUNTABILITY?
HOW ABOUT THIS? SHE CAN COME BACK BUT SHE HAS TO CARRY MY GEAR EVERY TIME WE PLAY OUT.
AND SHE HAS TO BUY ME ONE SOFT DRINK OF MY CHOICE FROM THE VENDING MACHINE PER PRACTICE.
AND YOU HAVE TO TUNE MY GUITAR, POLISH THE VAN AND SWEEP THE PRACTICE SPACE WEEKLY
I'LL DO ALL THAT AND I'LL BRING SNACKS TO EVERY PRACTICE.
WE'LL TAKE YOU BACK ON A TRIAL BASIS.

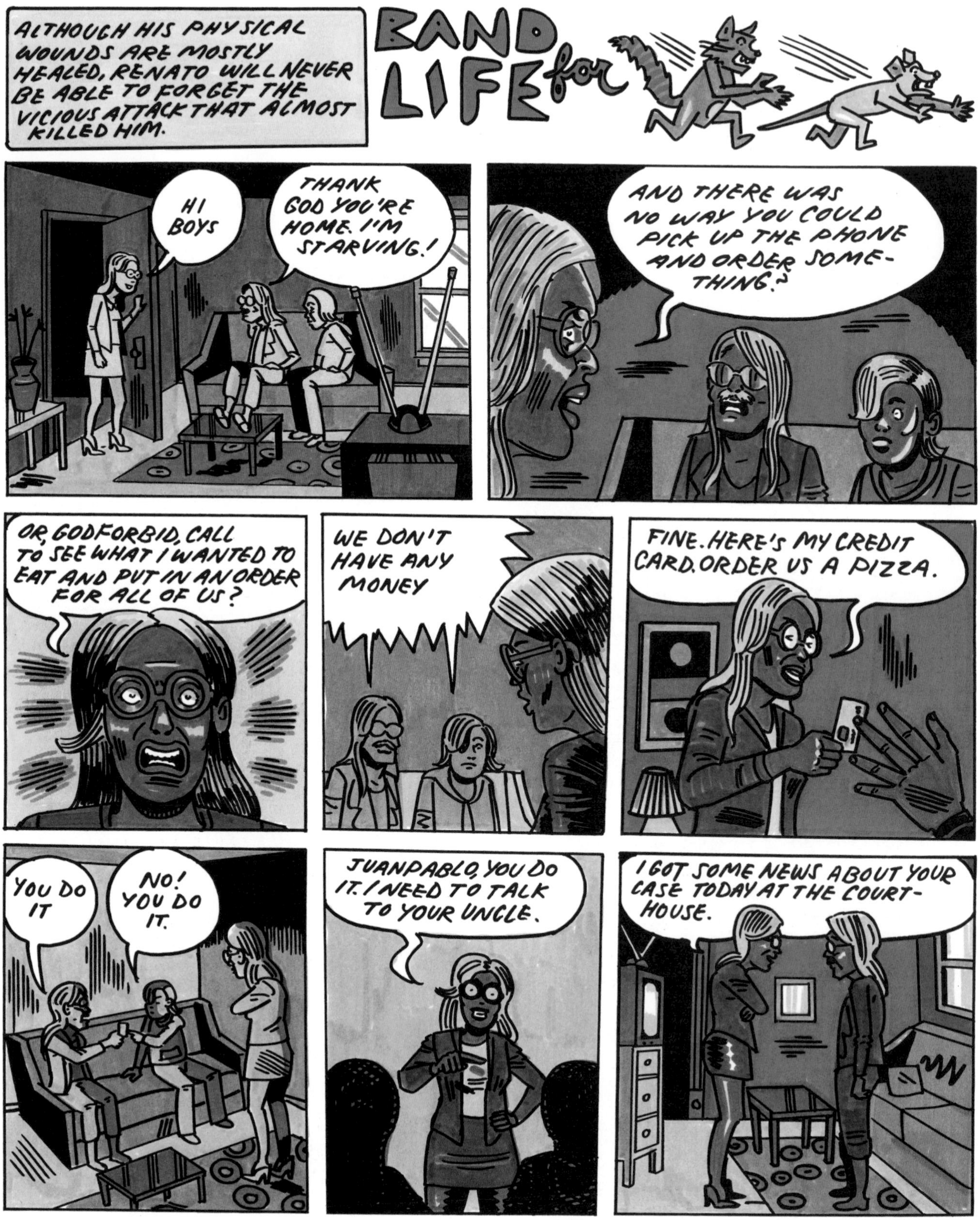
ALTHOUGH HIS PHYSICAL WOUNDS ARE MOSTLY HEALED, RENATO WILL NEVER BE ABLE TO FORGET THE VICIOUS ATTACK THAT ALMOST KILLED HIM.
BAND for LIFE
HI BOYS
THANK GOD YOU'RE HOME. I'M STARVING!
AND THERE WAS NO WAY YOU COULD PICK UP THE PHONE AND ORDER SOME-THING?
OR, GODFORBID, CALL TO SEE WHAT I WANTED TO EAT AND PUT IN AN ORDER FOR ALL OF US?
WE DON'T HAVE ANY MONEY
FINE. HERE'S MY CREDIT CARD. ORDER US A PIZZA.
YOU DO IT
NO! YOU DO IT.
JUANPABLO, YOU DO IT. I NEED TO TALK TO YOUR UNCLE.
I GOT SOME NEWS ABOUT YOUR CASE TODAY AT THE COURT-HOUSE.

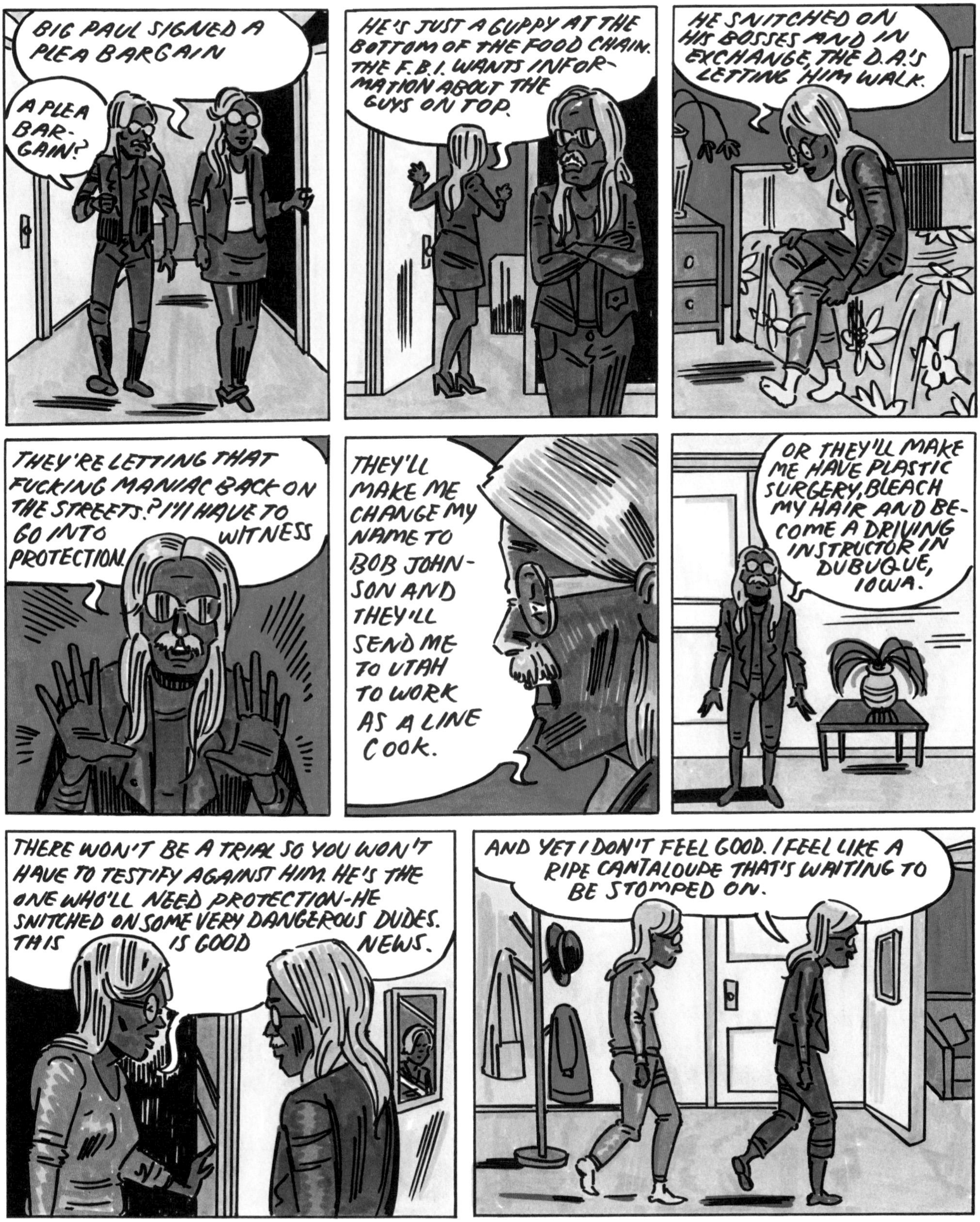
BIG PAUL SIGNED A PLEA BARGAIN
A PLEA BARGAIN?
HE'S JUST A GUPPY AT THE BOTTOM OF THE FOOD CHAIN. THE F.B.I. WANTS INFORMATION ABOUT THE GUYS ON TOP.
HE SNITCHED ON HIS BOSSES AND IN EXCHANGE, THE D.A.'S LETTING HIM WALK.
THEY'RE LETTING THAT FUCKING MANIAC BACK ON THE STREETS?I'LL HAVE TO GO INTO WITNESS PROTECTION.
THEY'LL MAKE ME CHANGE MY NAME TO BOB JOHNSON AND THEY'LL SEND ME TO UTAH TO WORK AS A LINE COOK.
OR THEY'LL MAKE ME HAVE PLASTIC SURGERY, BLEACH MY HAIR AND BECOME A DRIVING INSTRUCTOR IN DUBUQUE, IOWA.
THERE WON'T BE A TRIAL SO YOU WON'T HAVE TO TESTIFY AGAINST HIM. HE'S THE ONE WHO'LL NEED PROTECTION-HE SNITCHED ON SOME VERY DANGEROUS DUDES. THIS IS GOOD NEWS.
AND YET I DON'T FEEL GOOD. I FEEL LIKE A RIPE CANTALOUPE THAT'S WAITING TO BE STOMPED ON.

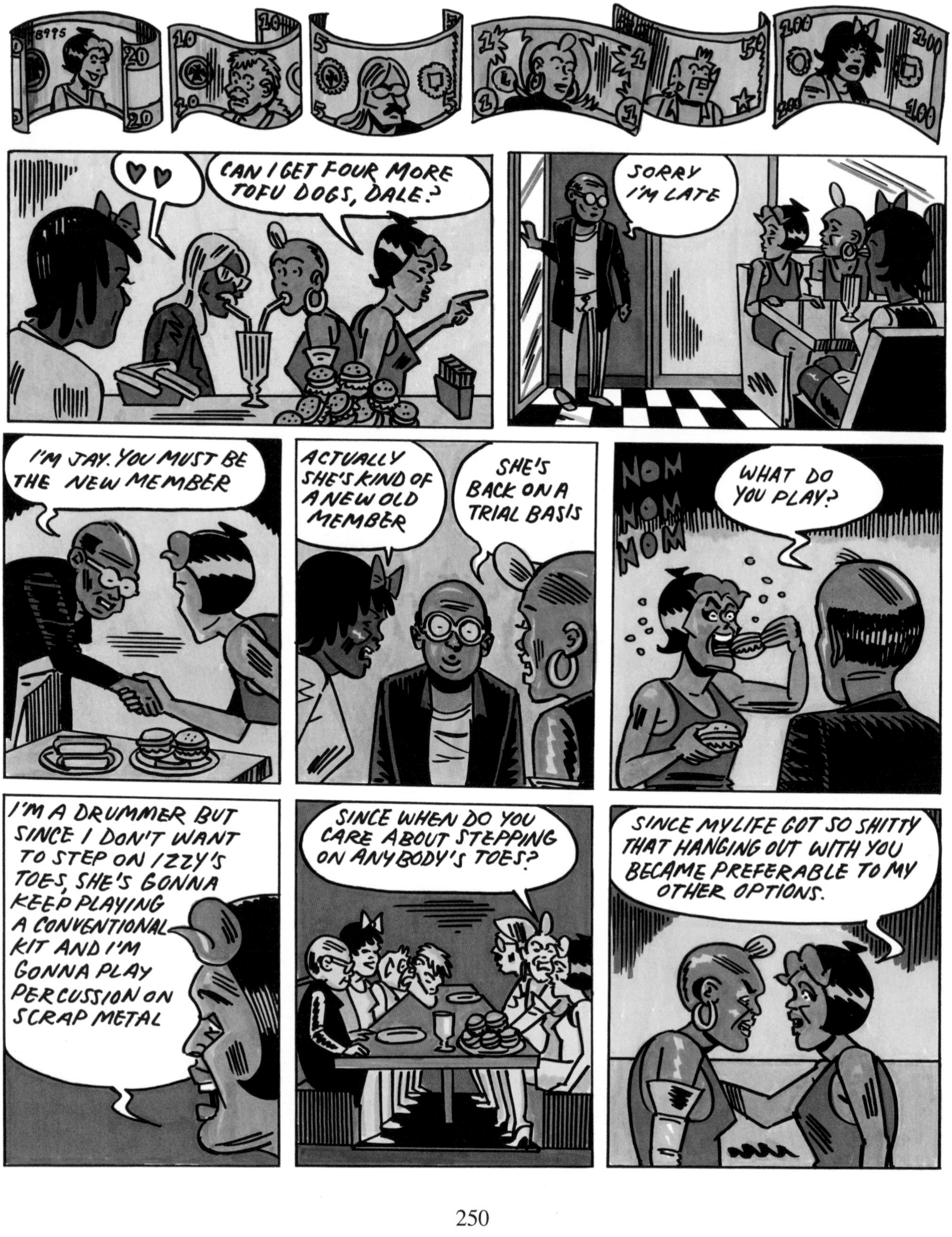
B995
CAN I GET FOUR MORE TOFU DOGS, DALE?
SORRY I'M LATE
I'M JAY. YOU MUST BE THE NEW MEMBER
ACTUALLY SHE'S KIND OF A NEW OLD MEMBER
SHE'S BACK ON A TRIAL BASIS
NOM NOM NOM
WHAT DO YOU PLAY?
I'M A DRUMMER BUT SINCE I DON'T WANT TO STEP ON IZZY'S TOES, SHE'S GONNA KEEP PLAYING A CONVENTIONAL KIT AND I'M GONNA PLAY PERCUSSION ON SCRAP METAL
SINCE WHEN DO YOU CARE ABOUT STEPPING ON ANYBODY'S TOES?
SINCE MY LIFE GOT SO SHITTY THAT HANGING OUT WITH YOU BECAME PREFERABLE TO MY OTHER OPTIONS.

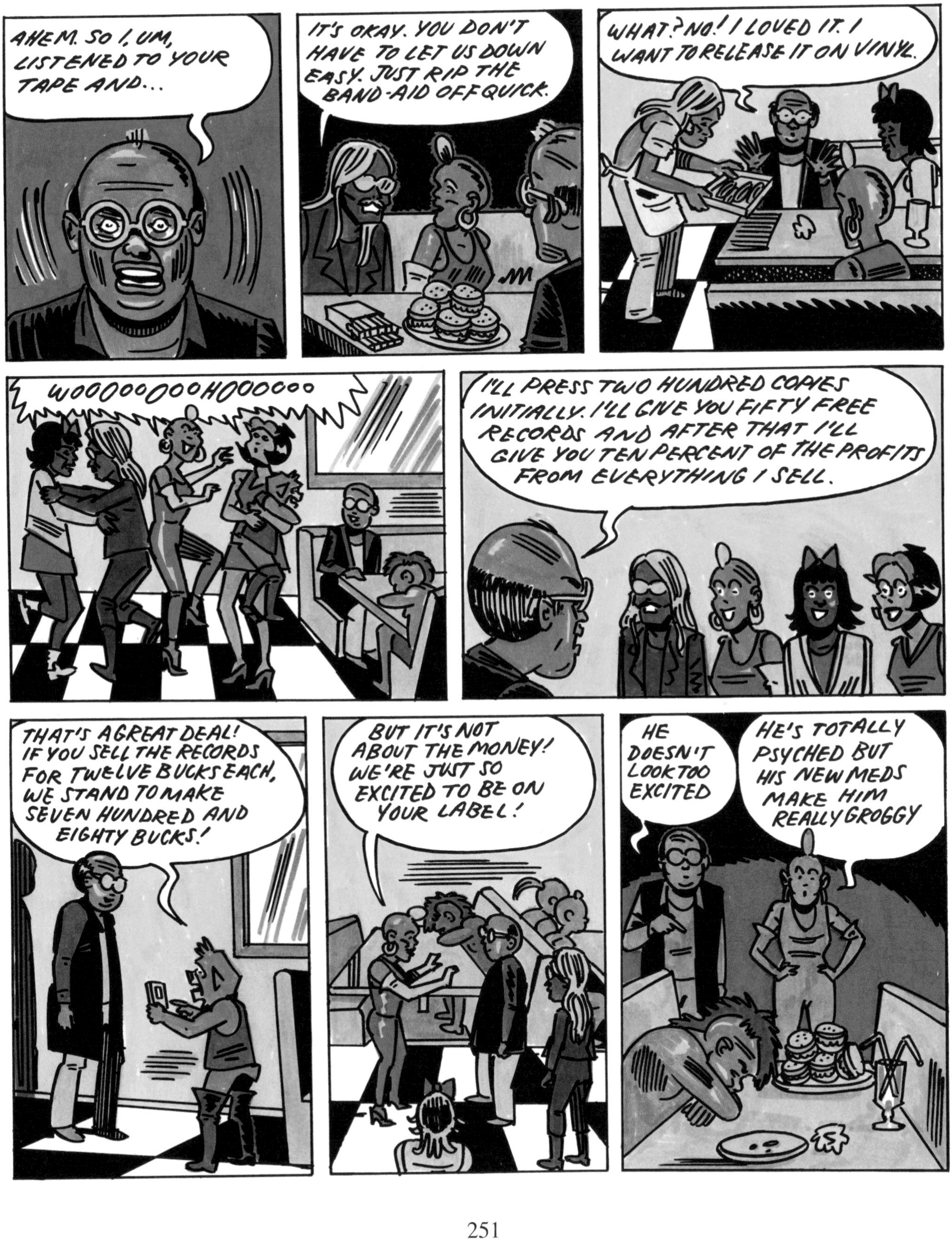
AHEM. SO I, UM, LISTENED TO YOUR TAPE AND...
IT'S OKAY. YOU DON'T HAVE TO LET US DOWN EASY. JUST RIP THE BAND-AID OFF QUICK.
WHAT? NO! I LOVED IT. I WANT TO RELEASE IT ON VINYL.
WOOOOOOOOOHOOOOOO
I'LL PRESS TWO HUNDRED COPIES INITIALLY. I'LL GIVE YOU FIFTY FREE RECORDS AND AFTER THAT I'LL GIVE YOU TEN PERCENT OF THE PROFITS FROM EVERYTHING I SELL.
THAT'S A GREAT DEAL! IF YOU SELL THE RECORDS FOR TWELVE BUCKS EACH, WE STAND TO MAKE SEVEN HUNDRED AND EIGHTY BUCKS!
BUT IT'S NOT ABOUT THE MONEY! WE'RE JUST SO EXCITED TO BE ON YOUR LABEL!
HE DOESN'T LOOK TOO EXCITED
HE'S TOTALLY PSYCHED BUT HIS NEW MEDS MAKE HIM REALLY GROGGY

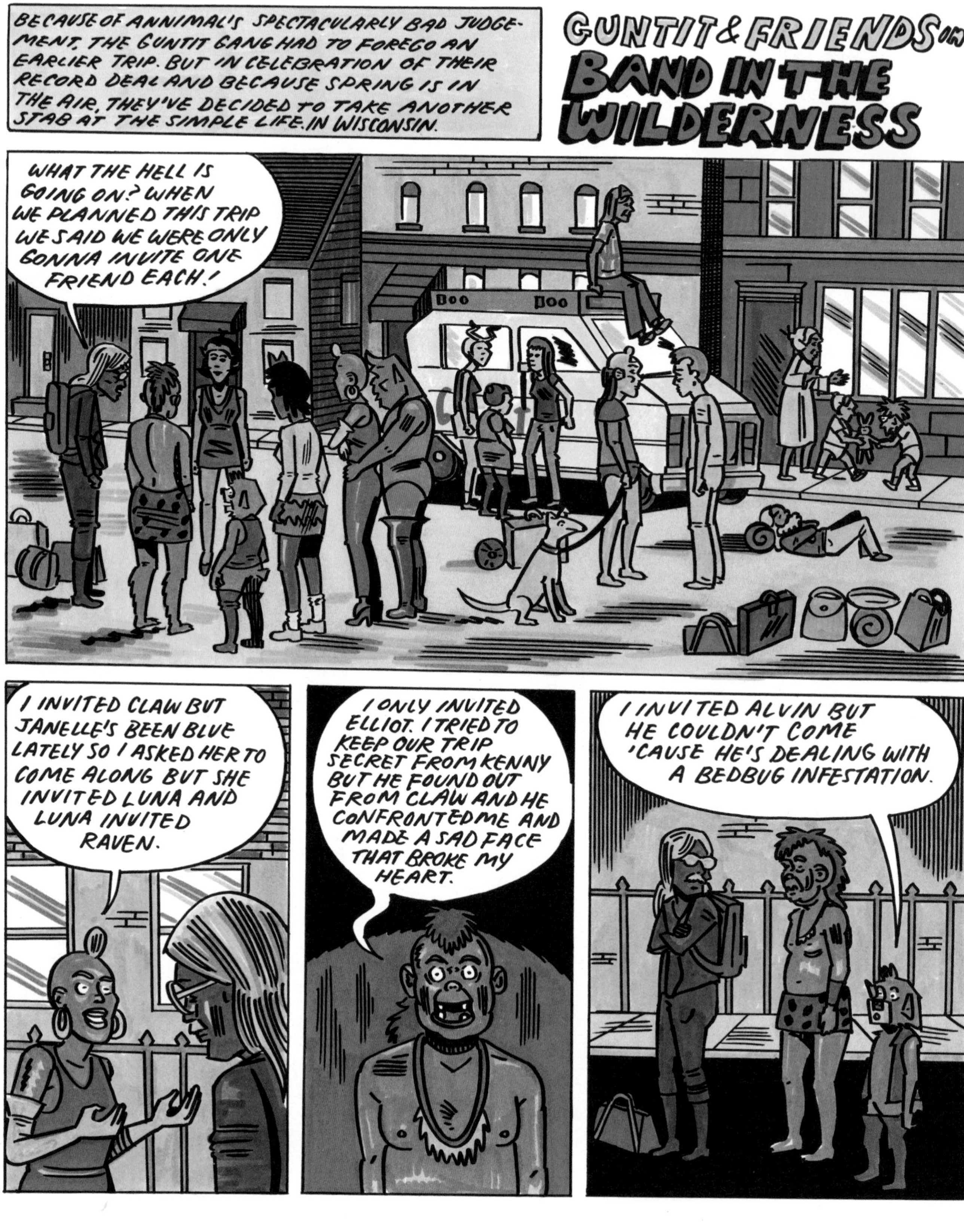
BECAUSE OF ANNIMAL'S SPECTACULARLY BAD JUDGEMENT, THE GUNTIT GANG HAD TO FOREGO AN EARLIER TRIP. BUT IN CELEBRATION OF THEIR RECORD DEAL AND BECAUSE SPRING IS IN THE AIR, THEY'VE DECIDED TO TAKE ANOTHER STAB AT THE SIMPLE LIFE. IN WISCONSIN.
GUNTIT & FRIENDS IN:
BAND IN THE WILDERNESS
WHAT THE HELL IS GOING ON? WHEN WE PLANNED THIS TRIP WE SAID WE WERE ONLY GONNA INVITE ONE FRIEND EACH!
I INVITED CLAW BUT JANELLE'S BEEN BLUE LATELY SO I ASKED HER TO COME ALONG BUT SHE INVITED LUNA AND LUNA INVITED RAVEN.
I ONLY INVITED ELLIOT. I TRIED TO KEEP OUR TRIP SECRET FROM KENNY BUT HE FOUND OUT FROM CLAW AND HE CONFRONTED ME AND MADE A SAD FACE THAT BROKE MY HEART.
I INVITED ALVIN BUT HE COULDN'T COME 'CAUSE HE'S DEALING WITH A BEDBUG INFESTATION.

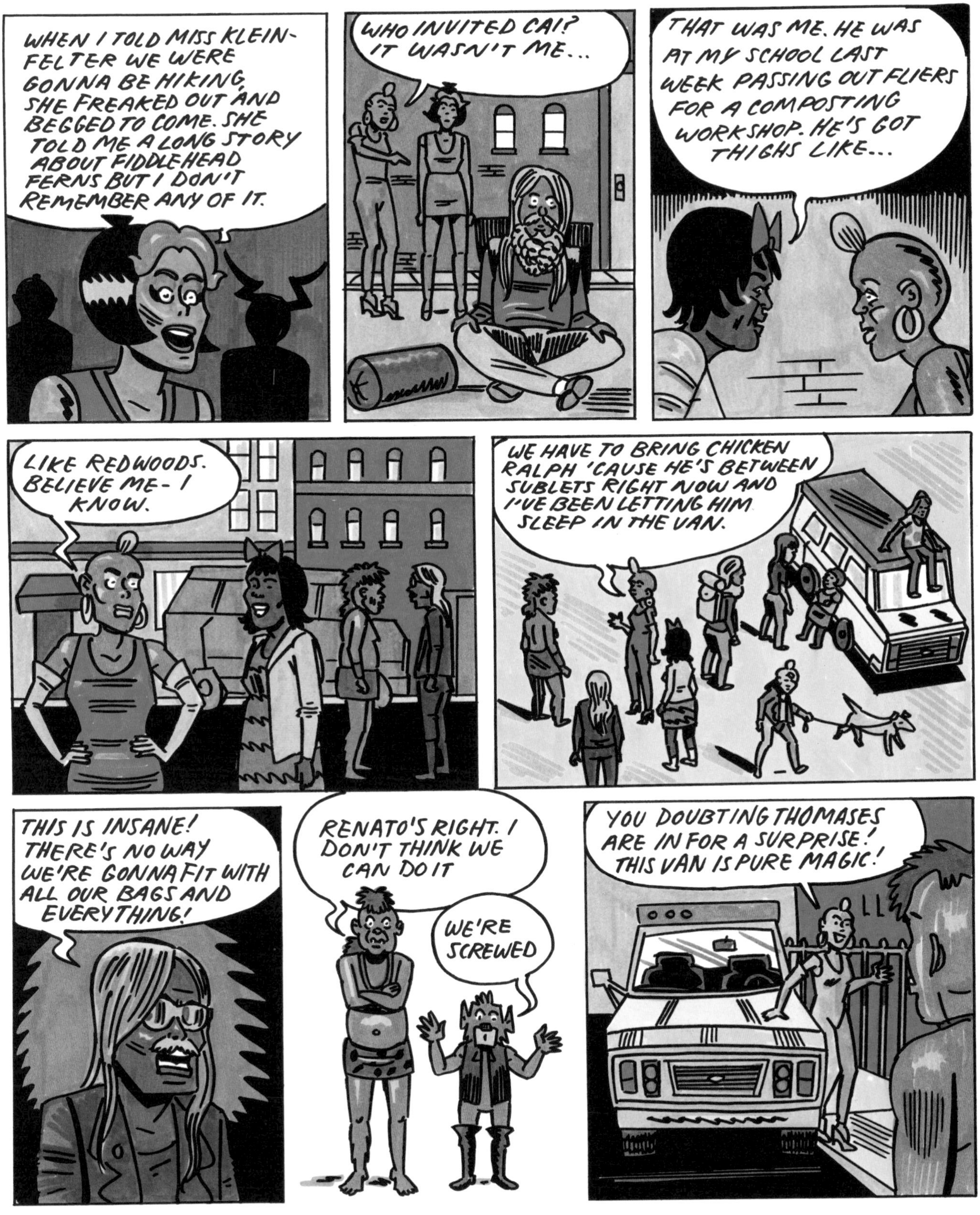
WHEN I TOLD MISS KLEIN-FELTER WE WERE GONNA BE HIKING, SHE FREAKED OUT AND BEGGED TO COME. SHE TOLD ME A LONG STORY ABOUT FIDDLEHEAD FERNS BUT I DON'T REMEMBER ANY OF IT.
WHO INVITED CAI? IT WASN'T ME...
THAT WAS ME. HE WAS AT MY SCHOOL LAST WEEK PASSING OUT FLIERS FOR A COMPOSTING WORKSHOP. HE'S GOT THIGHS LIKE...
LIKE REDWOODS. BELIEVE ME- I KNOW.
WE HAVE TO BRING CHICKEN RALPH 'CAUSE HE'S BETWEEN SUBLETS RIGHT NOW AND I'VE BEEN LETTING HIM SLEEP IN THE VAN.
THIS IS INSANE! THERE'S NO WAY WE'RE GONNA FIT WITH ALL OUR BAGS AND EVERYTHING!
RENATO'S RIGHT. I DON'T THINK WE CAN DO IT
WE'RE SCREWED
YOU DOUBTING THOMASES ARE IN FOR A SURPRISE! THIS VAN IS PURE MAGIC!

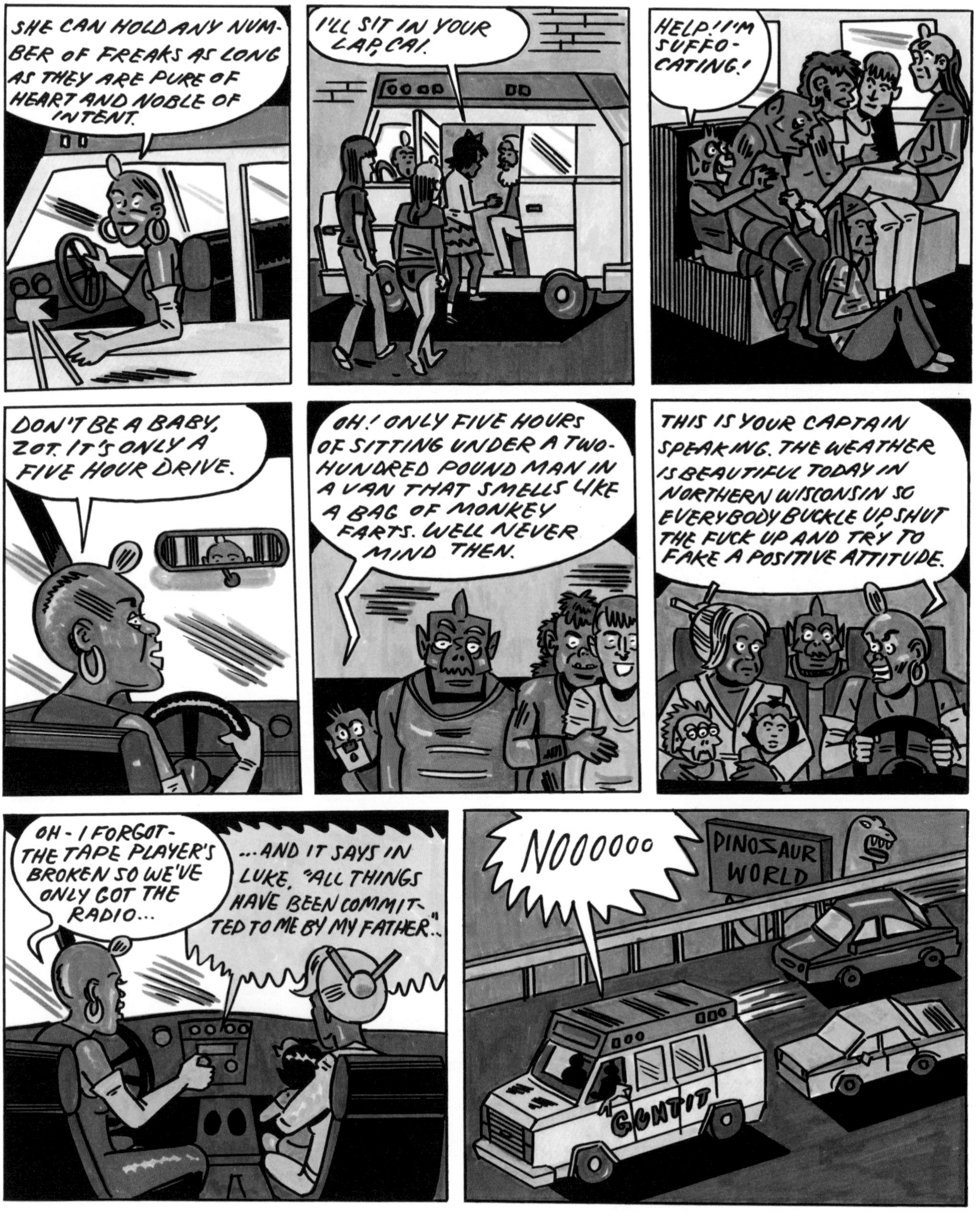
SHE CAN HOLD ANY NUMBER OF FREAKS AS LONG AS THEY ARE PURE OF HEART AND NOBLE OF INTENT.
I'LL SIT IN YOUR LAP, CAI.
HELP! I'M SUFFOCATING!
DON'T BE A BABY, ZOT. IT'S ONLY A FIVE HOUR DRIVE.
OH! ONLY FIVE HOURS OF SITTING UNDER A TWO-HUNDRED POUND MAN IN A VAN THAT SMELLS LIKE A BAG OF MONKEY FARTS. WELL NEVER MIND THEN.
THIS IS YOUR CAPTAIN SPEAKING. THE WEATHER IS BEAUTIFUL TODAY IN NORTHERN WISCONSIN SO EVERYBODY BUCKLE UP, SHUT THE FUCK UP AND TRY TO FAKE A POSITIVE ATTITUDE.
OH - I FORGOT - THE TAPE PLAYER'S BROKEN SO WE'VE ONLY GOT THE RADIO...
...AND IT SAYS IN LUKE, "ALL THINGS HAVE BEEN COMMITTED TO ME BY MY FATHER."...
NOOOOOO
DINOSAUR WORLD
GUNTIT

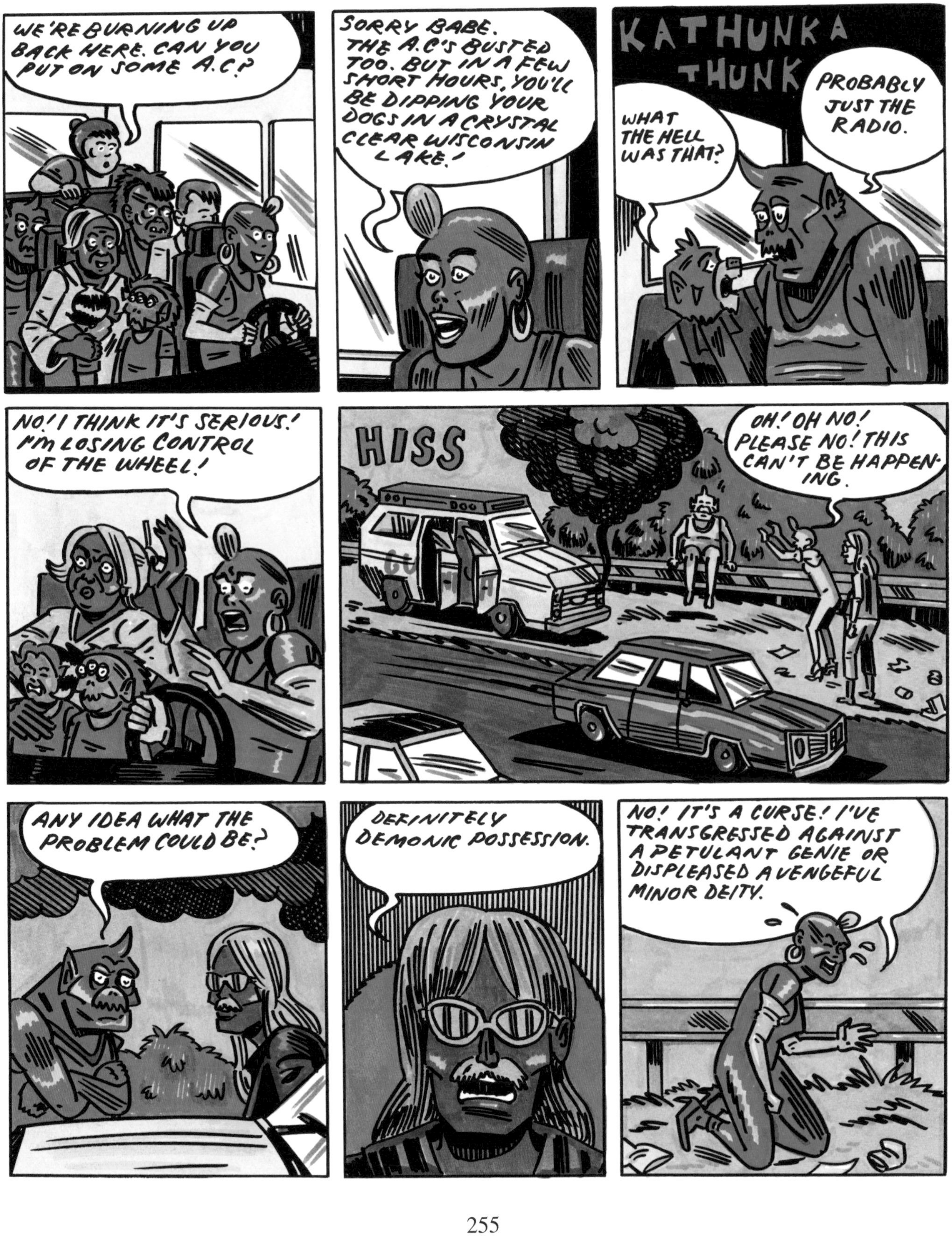

WE'RE BURNING UP BACK HERE. CAN YOU PUT ON SOME A.C.?
SORRY BABE. THE A.C.'S BUSTED TOO. BUT IN A FEW SHORT HOURS, YOU'LL BE DIPPING YOUR DOGS IN A CRYSTAL CLEAR WISCONSIN LAKE!
KATHUNKA THUNK
WHAT THE HELL WAS THAT?
PROBABLY JUST THE RADIO.
NO! I THINK IT'S SERIOUS! I'M LOSING CONTROL OF THE WHEEL!
HISS
OH! OH NO! PLEASE NO! THIS CAN'T BE HAPPENING.
ANY IDEA WHAT THE PROBLEM COULD BE?
DEFINITELY DEMONIC POSSESSION.
NO! IT'S A CURSE! I'VE TRANSGRESSED AGAINST A PETULANT GENIE OR DISPLEASED A VENGEFUL MINOR DEITY.

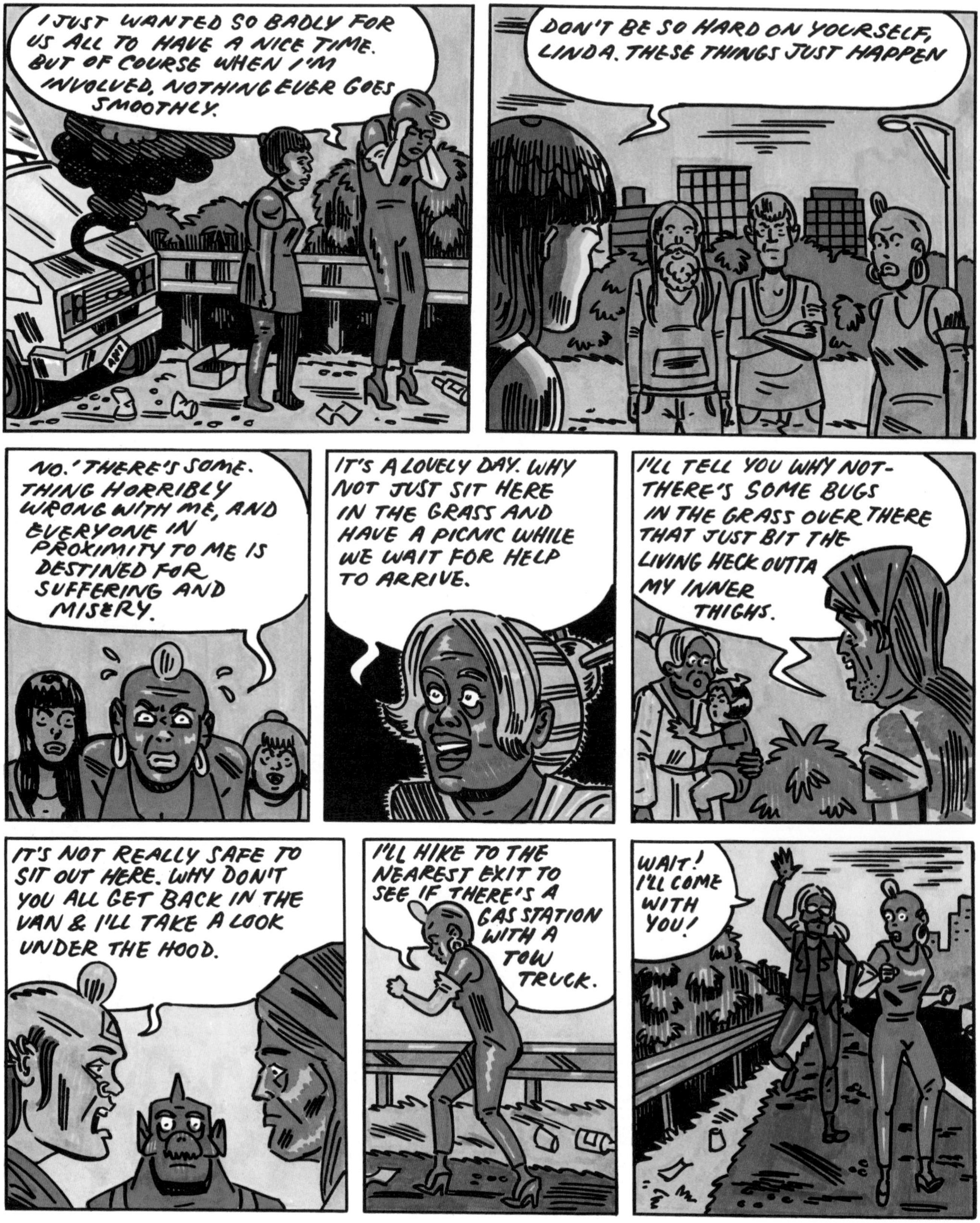
I JUST WANTED SO BADLY FOR US ALL TO HAVE A NICE TIME. BUT OF COURSE WHEN I'M INVOLVED, NOTHING EVER GOES SMOOTHLY.
DON'T BE SO HARD ON YOURSELF, LINDA. THESE THINGS JUST HAPPEN
NO! THERE'S SOMETHING HORRIBLY WRONG WITH ME, AND EVERYONE IN PROXIMITY TO ME IS DESTINED FOR SUFFERING AND MISERY.
IT'S A LOVELY DAY. WHY NOT JUST SIT HERE IN THE GRASS AND HAVE A PICNIC WHILE WE WAIT FOR HELP TO ARRIVE.
I'LL TELL YOU WHY NOT- THERE'S SOME BUGS IN THE GRASS OVER THERE THAT JUST BIT THE LIVING HECK OUTTA MY INNER THIGHS.
IT'S NOT REALLY SAFE TO SIT OUT HERE. WHY DON'T YOU ALL GET BACK IN THE VAN & I'LL TAKE A LOOK UNDER THE HOOD.
I'LL HIKE TO THE NEAREST EXIT TO SEE IF THERE'S A GAS STATION WITH A TOW TRUCK.
WAIT! I'LL COME WITH YOU!

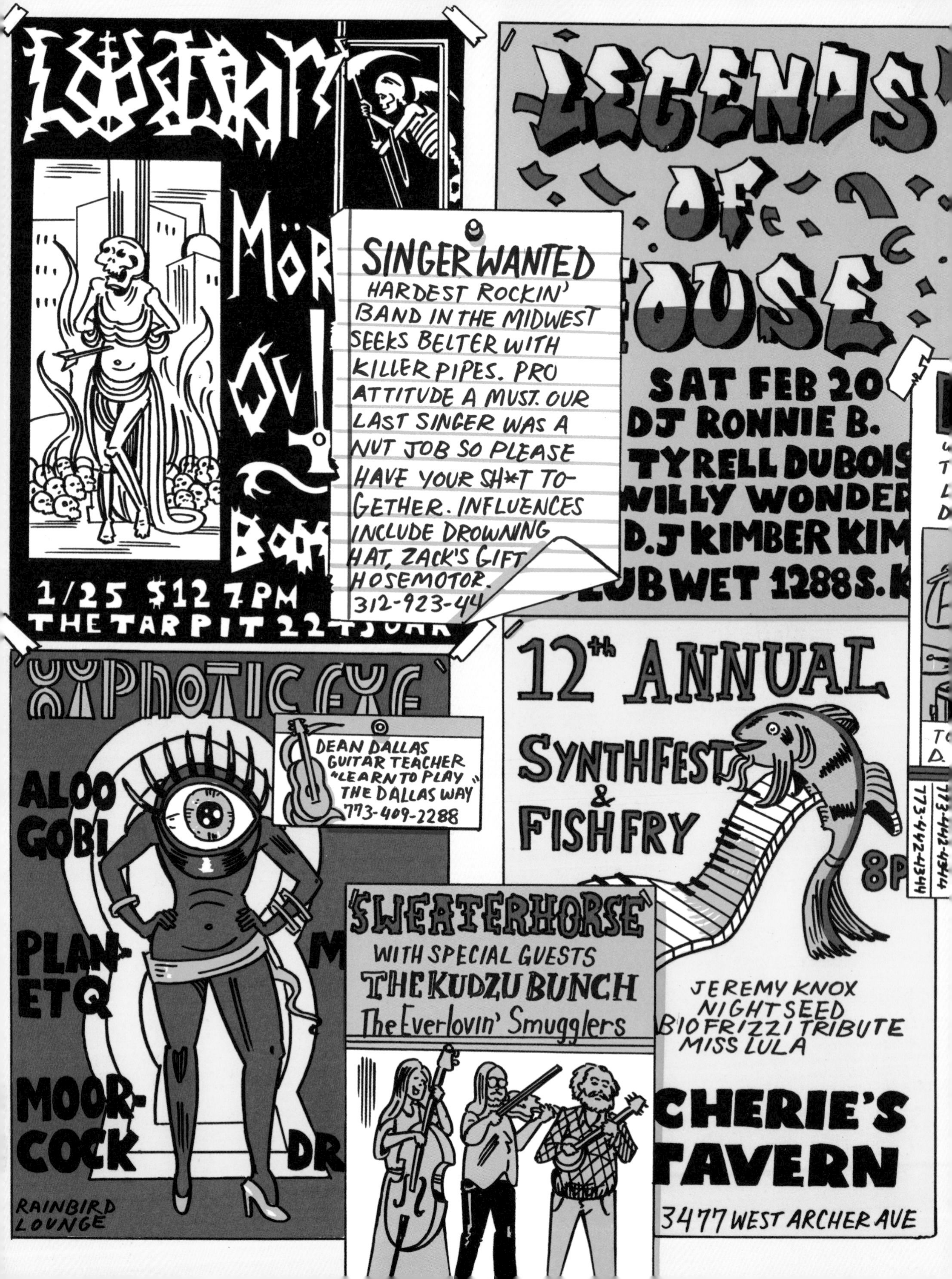
1/25 $12 7PM
LEGENDS OF
SAT FEB 20
DJ RONNIE B.
TYRELL DUBOIS
WILLY WONDER
D.J KIMBER KIM
SINGER WANTED
HARDEST ROCKIN' BAND IN THE MIDWEST SEEKS BELTER WITH KILLER PIPES. PRO ATTITUDE A MUST. OUR LAST SINGER WAS A NUT JOB SO PLEASE HAVE YOUR SH*T TOGETHER. INFLUENCES INCLUDE DROWNING HAT, ZACK'S GIFT HOSEMOTOR.
DEAN DALLAS
GUITAR TEACHER
"LEARN TO PLAY"
THE DALLAS WAY
773-409-2288
ALOO GOBI
PLAN-ETQ
MOOR-COCK
RAINBIRD LOUNGE
12th ANNUAL
SYNTHFEST & FISH FRY
773-442-4344
SWEATERHORSE
WITH SPECIAL GUESTS
THE KUDZU BUNCH
The Everlovin' Smugglers
JEREMY KNOX
NIGHT SEED
BIO FRIZZI TRIBUTE
MISS LULA
CHERIE'S TAVERN
3477 WEST ARCHER AVE